KGB

KGB
Masters of the Soviet Union

Peter Deriabin
and
T.H. Bagley

HIPPOCRENE BOOKS
New York

For information, address:
Hippocrene Books, Inc.
171 Madison Avenue
New York, NY 10016

Library of Congress Cataloging-in-Publication Data

Deriabin, Peter, 1921–
  KGB : masters of the Soviet Union / Peter Deriabin and T.H.
Bagley.
    p. cm.
  Includes bibliographical references.
  ISBN 0-87052-804-1
  1. Soviet Union. Komitet gosudarstvennoĭ bezopasnosti.   2. Soviet
Union—Politics and government—1917–   3. Internal security—Soviet
Union.   I. Bagley, T. H. (Tennent H.), 1925–   .   II. Title.
JN6529.I6D47   1990
354.470074—dc20   89-28591
                                                                          CIP

Printed in the United States of America.

. . . Every week television has showed the places where victims of mass repressions were buried . . . the burial places of tens of thousands of our citizens. . . . Undoubtedly, the members of the K.G.B. can be of essential assistance in further searches. But even today, they are shut tight. . . .

With one wing, the K.G.B. defends the people from the external enemy, and with the other, incomparably more powerful, it fulfills a particular, specific function. No, I don't mean the struggle against corruption. After the hard lessons of the past, with millions of people murdered, all of this, without exception, with the direct involvement of the Cheka and the K.G.B., the threat to democracy in our present day cannot be considered mythical.

The K.G.B. is removed from the control of the people. It's the most tightly closed, the most conspiratorial of all the Government institutions. . . . The deep secretiveness which can be explained by the specifics of its activities insures that the K.G.B. is practically uncontrollable.

When coming in conflict with the K.G.B. it is impossible to find the truth, and it is dangerous to seek it.

Even now people considered dangerous by the apparatus are threatened with seizure for supposed mental imbalance. The democratic renewal in the country has not changed the position of the K.G.B. in the political system. This agency exercises all-embracing control over society, over each individual.

We are at a critical stage of development. One hundred and fifty years ago, a friend of Pushkin's, Pyotr Chaadayev, wrote about Russia: "We are an exceptional people. We belong to that number of nations, which do not seem to be part of humanity, but which exist for the sole purpose of giving a fearful lesson to the rest of the world." There must not be any more fearful lessons.

—Excerpts from the speech of Yuri P. Vlasov, member of the Supreme Soviet, delivered on May 31, 1989, on the role of the KGB. *New York Times,* June 1, 1989. Vlasov is a former Olympic weight lifter. His father was arrested in 1953 and never returned.

Contents

Acknowledgments

This is a Foreign Policy Research Institute book, and we are grateful to that institute, of which we were Associate Scholars during its preparation, for unfailing support.

We dedicate this work to Robert Strausz-Hupé, the cofounder of the Foreign Policy Research Institute and distinguished statesman, professor, geopolitician, and sage. He early recognized the nature of the Soviet regime and more than forty years ago foresaw the crisis into which it has now fallen. He gave the first support to this work, and it is no exaggeration to say that he made it possible.

To the Smith Richardson Foundation we express our thanks for the generous support that enabled us to devote our time to this book. Our gratitude goes to those who gave us help and encouragement, especially to Owen Lock and Marc Jaffe.

Note About Terms and Abbreviations

THE INITIALS AND ACRONYMS LIKE KGB AND NKVD AND CHEKA THAT have identified the Soviet coercive authorities through the years are easy to understand even without a knowledge of Russian. The two most important initials are "GB" which stands for "state security" (*gosudarstvennoy bezopasnosti*) and "VD" for "internal affairs" (*vnutrennikh del*). They were administered by "people's commissariats" (*Narodnyy Kommissariat*, or NK) until 1946 when they were renamed ministries (*ministerstvo*, or M). Thus NKVD became MVD and NKGB became MGB and, obviously, when GB came in 1954 to be administered by a "committee" (*komitet*) one had the initials KGB.

Only in the early years of Soviet rule did State Security go under other names. At first it was ostensibly temporary and was given the form of an "extraordinary" struggle against "counterrevolution, sabotage and speculation." Since the word "extraordinary" (*chrezvychaynaya*) begins with the Russian letter "Ch" and because it was administered by a "commission" (*komissiya*), this "Extraordinary Commission" had the initials Ch.K.— pronounced in Russian "Che-ka" (with accent on the second syllable).* While local Ch.K. offices were thus becoming known as "Chekas," their center in Moscow was "All-Russian" (*Vserossiyskaya*) and was therefore called the "VCheka." In 1922 the Soviet leaders abandoned the pretense and made state security permanent with a new and euphemistic title: "State Political Administration" (*Gosudarstvennoye Politicheskoye Upravleniye,*

---

*The full title was All-Russian Extraordinary Commission for Combating Counterrevolution, Sabotage and Speculation (*Vserossiyskaya Chrezvychaynaya Komissiya po borbe s kontrrevolutsiyey, sabotazhem i spekulyatsiyey*).

Creation and Development
Organs of State Security and Internal Affairs of the USSR

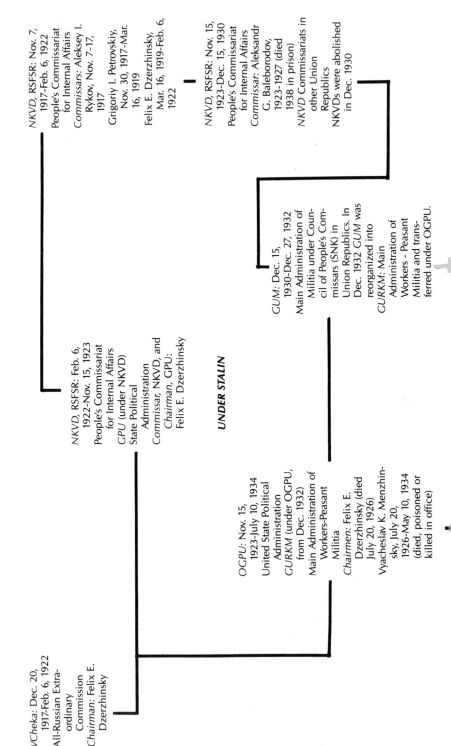

UNDER LENIN

NKVD, RSFSR: Nov. 7, 1917-Feb. 6, 1922 People's Commissariat for Internal Affairs
Commissars: Aleksey I. Rykov, Nov. 7-17, 1917
Grigoriy I. Petrovskiy, Nov. 30, 1917-Mar. 16, 1919
Felix E. Dzerzhinsky, Mar. 16, 1919-Feb. 6, 1922

NKVD, RSFSR: Nov. 15, 1923-Dec. 15, 1930 People's Commissariat for Internal Affairs
Commissar: Aleksandr G. Baleborodov, 1923-1927 (died 1938 in prison)
NKVD Commissariats in other Union Republics
NKVDs were abolished in Dec. 1930

NKVD, RSFSR: Feb. 6, 1922-Nov. 15, 1923 People's Commissariat for Internal Affairs
GPU (under NKVD) State Political Administration
Commissar, NKVD, and *Chairman, GPU:* Felix E. Dzerzhinsky

UNDER STALIN

GUM: Dec. 15, 1930-Dec. 27, 1932 Main Administration of Militia under Council of People's Commissars (SNK) in Union Republics. In Dec. 1932 *GUM* was reorganized into
GURKM: Main Administration of Workers - Peasant Militia and transferred under OGPU.

OGPU: Nov. 15, 1923-July 10, 1934 United State Political Administration
GURKM (under OGPU, from Dec. 1932) Main Administration of Workers-Peasant Militia
Chairmen: Felix E. Dzerzhinsky (died July 20, 1926)
Vyacheslav K. Menzhinsky, July 20, 1926-May 10, 1934 (died, poisoned or killed in office)

VCheka: Dec. 20, 1917-Feb. 6, 1922 All-Russian Extraordinary Commission
Chairman: Felix E. Dzerzhinsky

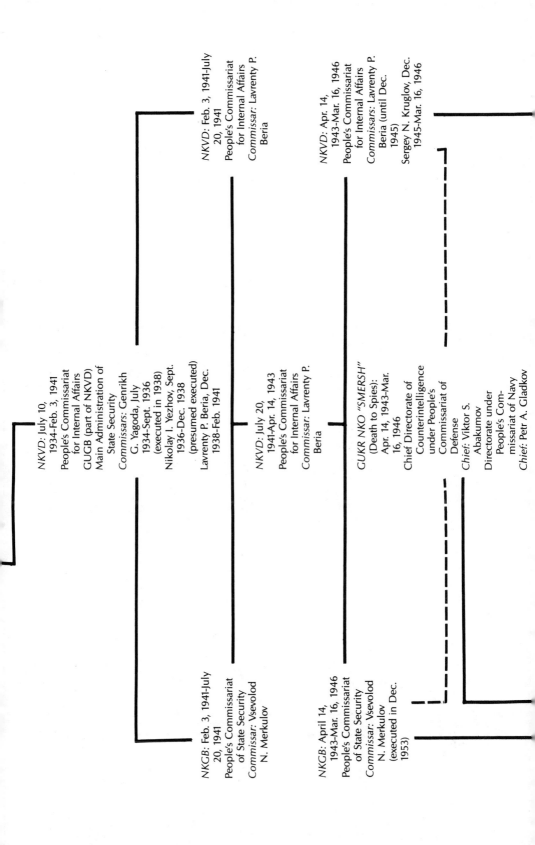

NKVD: July 10, 1934-Feb. 3, 1941
People's Commissariat for Internal Affairs
GUGB (part of NKVD) Main Administration of State Security
Commissars: Genrikh G. Yagoda, July 1934-Sept. 1936 (executed in 1938)
Nikolay I. Yezhov, Sept. 1936-Dec. 1938 (presumed executed)
Lavrenty P. Beria, Dec. 1938-Feb. 1941

NKVD: Feb. 3, 1941-July 20, 1941
People's Commissariat for Internal Affairs
Commissar: Lavrenty P. Beria

NKVD: July 20, 1941-Apr. 14, 1943
People's Commissariat for Internal Affairs
Commissar: Lavrenty P. Beria

NKVD: Apr. 14, 1943-Mar. 16, 1946
People's Commissariat for Internal Affairs
Commissars: Lavrenty P. Beria (until Dec. 1945)
Sergey N. Kruglov, Dec. 1945-Mar. 16, 1946

NKGB: Feb. 3, 1941-July 20, 1941
People's Commissariat of State Security
Commissar: Vsevolod N. Merkulov

NKGB: April 14, 1943-Mar. 16, 1946
People's Commissariat of State Security
Commissar: Vsevolod N. Merkulov (executed in Dec. 1953)

GUKR NKO "SMERSH" (Death to Spies): Apr. 14, 1943-Mar. 16, 1946
Chief Directorate of Counterintelligence under People's Commissariat of Defense
Chief: Viktor S. Abakumov
Directorate under People's Commissariat of Navy
Chief: Petr A. Gladkov

MVD: Mar. 16,
1946-Mar. 5, 1953
Ministry for Internal
Affairs
Minister: Sergey N.
Kruglov

KI: 1947–1951
Committee of Informa-
tion under Council
of Ministers of the
USSR (Combined In-
telligence Agency:
Foreign Intelligence
of State Security,
Military (GRU), and
Ministry of Foreign
Affairs)
Chairmen: Vyacheslav
M. Molotov, 1947-49
Andrey Ya. Vyshinskiy,
1949-51

MGB: Mar. 16,
1946-Mar. 5, 1953
Ministry of State
Security
Ministers: Viktor S.
Abakumov, March
1946-Aug. 1951
(executed Dec.
1954)
Acting: Sergey I.
Ogoltsov, Aug.-Dec.
1951 (fate unknown)
Semen D. Ignatyev, Dec.
1951-Mar. 5, 1953
(fired, died in 1983)

UNDER "COLLECTIVE LEADERSHIP"

MVD: Mar. 5, 1953-Mar.
13, 1954
Ministry for Internal
Affairs
Ministers: Lavrenty P.
Beria, Mar. 5-June
27, 1953 (executed
in Dec. 1953) Sergey
N. Kruglov, June
1953-Mar. 13, 1954

KGB, USSR: Mar. 13, 1954-present Committee of State Security (From Mar. 13, 1954-July 5, 1978: KGB under Council of Ministers of the USSR)

Chairmen: Ivan A. Serov, Mar. 13, 1954-Dec. 8, 1958 Aleksandr N. Shelepin, Dec. 25, 1958-Oct. 31, 1961 ("promoted")

Vladimir Ye. Semichastnyy, Nov. 13, 1961-May 18, 1967 (fired)

Yuri V. Andropov, May 18, 1967-May 26, 1982 (promoted to secretary CC CPSU, then became General Secretary; died Feb. 9, 1984).

Vitaliy V. Fedorchuk, May 26-Dec. 11, 1982 ("promoted" to minister of MVD)

Viktor M. Chebrikov, Dec. 7, 1982-Sept. 30, 1988, Politburo member, promoted to secretary CC CPSU for legal matters.

Vladimir A. Kryuchkov, Sept, 1988-present

MVD: Mar. 13, 1954-Jan. 12, 1960 Ministry for Internal Affairs

Ministers: Sergey N. Kruglov, Mar. 13, 1954-Feb. 1956 (allegedly committed suicide) Nikolay P. Dudorov, Feb. 1956-Jan. 1960 (died Mar. 9, 1977)

MVD in Union Republics: Jan. 13, 1960-Aug. 30, 1962 Ministries for Internal Affairs (No All-Union MVD) Minister of MVD, RSFSR: Vadim S. Tikunov

---

MOOP (in Union Republic): Aug. 30, 1962-July 28, 1966 Ministries for Preservation of Public Order (No All-Union MOOP)

Minister of MOOP RSFSR: Vadim S. Tikunov (transferred to ambassadorship)

MOOP, USSR: July 28, 1966-Nov. 28, 1968 Ministry for Preservation of Public Order. Minister: Nikolay A. Shchelokov

MVD, USSR: Nov. 28, 1968-present Ministry for Internal Affairs.

Ministers: Nikolay A. Shchelokov, until Dec. 19, 1982 (fired, reprimanded, and demoted; committed suicide)

Vitaliy V. Fedorchuk, Dec. 19, 1982-Jan. 25, 1986 (transferred to other unspecified work)

Aleksandr V. Vlasov, Jan. 25, 1986-October 1988 (promoted to chairman Council of Ministers of RSFSR)

Vadim V. Bakatin 1988-to present

or GPU), which in the following year took on the broader designation "united" *(obyedinennoye)* and thus became OGPU.

When State Security was merged with Internal Affairs in 1934, the OGPU functions were absorbed as the NKVD's chief directorate *(Glavnoye Upravleniye,* or GU) for State Security (GB), hence GUGB—which was later broken off as a separate people's commissariat in its own right: NKGB.

During the Second World War another name appeared: SMERSH—an acronym of the slogan "Death to Spies!" *(Smert shpionam).* There was one SMERSH for the army and another for the navy. On paper they were parts of the People's Commissariat of Defense (NKO), but in reality they were just enlarged and more powerful versions of the state security directorates that watched over the armed force. Their officers continued to work in the state security building with their state security files, without interruption. The chief of Army SMERSH, Viktor Abakumov, became deputy people's commissar not only of Defense but simultaneously also of Internal Affairs—and after the war became Minister of State Security.

These names and acronyms are encompassed in the Chekists' own expression for these institutions: "the organs" *(organy).* That "vile word" (as Solzhenitsyn called it) stems from the expression *organy gosbezopasnosti*—state security authorities. The Soviet administration has other *organy* ("organs of management" or "party organs," for example), but few Soviet citizens are likely to misunderstand when someone refers simply to "the organs."

The employees of the organs were first called "Chekists," from the letters Ch.K., and proudly kept this title throughout all the subsequent renamings. Some of their later victims prefer to nickname them from their more modern initials GB: "gebists" *(gebishniki).*

On the chart we show all the various designations of the organs through the years, with the dates of the changes and the names of the chiefs.

Because we refer occasionally to the internal subdivisions of the KGB and other agencies, a short word on Soviet organizational terms (and our translations of them) may be useful. A standard nomenclature applies throughout the Soviet administration. The largest subdivision of a ministry or state committee is a *glavnoye upravleniye,* the first word translatable as "main," "chief," or "principal," the second as "administration" or "directorate." (For the KGB's internal organization we use the translation "chief directorate" but for others sometimes "main administration".) The next echelon downward is the *upravleniye* (which we call "directorate"), although the KGB has others called *napravleniye* ("direction") or *sluzhba* ("service"). Below this level comes the *otdel,* which we translate as "department," with its subdivisions called *otdeleniye* ("section"). In any Soviet organization (KGB, government ministry, embassy, and so forth) the top leaders (chief, deputy chiefs, and sometimes the heads of the most important subdivisions) constitute its *kollegiya* ("collegium").

We sometimes refer to geographical regions and their administrations. Covering the entire Union of Soviet Socialist Republics are All-Union ministries, committees, and so forth, with "Union Republic" counterparts in each of the sixteen republics. While we have rare occasion in this book to mention such regional designations as autonomous republics or krays, we refer frequently to the largest subdivision of the republics, comparable in size to the old provinces (and to those autonomous republics and krays), namely the *oblast* (commonly translated as "region"). The subdivision of this *oblast* or of a *gorod* (city) is called *raion* (district).

Like the Communist Party of the Soviet Union, the party organization of each republic is headed by a central committee, lower geographical echelons by a committee *(komitet)*. Therefore the party leadership of an *oblast* is called, for short, the *obkom;* that of a *raion* is shortened as *raikom*.

Preface

MIKHAIL GORBACHEV HAD WORKED SUCH CHANGES BY THE END OF THE
1980s that the veteran Sovietologist George F. Kennan told the American
Congress that "we are witnessing today in Russia the breakup of much, if
not all, of the system of power by which that country has been held
together and governed since 1917."[1]

The changes did seem almost to justify Gorbachev's own description of
them as "revolutionary." Independent organizations had sprung up outside
the ruling party, the outlying republics were demanding and getting some
increased autonomy, the constitution and the penal code had been revised,
new political institutions (installed after elections involving real competition) had started to operate, some people were publicly calling for multiparty democracy and wider political rights, industries were working under
more flexible arrangements, and plans were afoot for private landholding
and a partial market economy.

Why such drastic changes? The reformers freely admitted the reason:
the system had failed. The economy was in a "disastrous" state, "in ruins."
Industry and agriculture, they confessed publicly, were badly organized
and administered by a bloated bureaucracy with lies, corruption, arrogance, and crippling waste. The soviets which had ostensibly ruled the
land were admitted to have been powerless tools of the party. Some of the
regime's proudest achievements—its low-cost housing and free medical
care, for instance—were exposed as sadly, even dangerously, inadequate.
The countryside had been so ill-treated, according to the regime's own
ecologists, that much of it might be beyond saving. From the regime's
own reports emerged a picture of a people ill fed and degraded, sunk in
apathy, idleness, and alcoholism, despising honest labor, envious, fearful,
and distrustful of their rulers.

But while admitting seventy years of failure, no leader was now
suggesting that the Communist Party should renounce its rulership. If

there was to be "new thinking" it would still come mainly from above, still inspired by Lenin. Gorbachev's reforms were a desperate response to a crisis and aimed not to dismantle the system but to stop its slide into disarray and social unrest.

Nevertheless, these changes had awakened hopes throughout the world for a final release from the constant risk of violent confrontation and war. Gorbachev emphasized "the unbreakable connection of these processes with genuinely good intentions in foreign policy,"[2] and Kennan said that "whatever reasons there may have been for regarding the Soviet Union primarily as a possible, if not probable, military opponent, the time for that sort of thing has clearly passed." Some Western governments and political parties were acting on the premise that no "Soviet threat" existed.

Was this reform process irreversible, as some Western scholars and journalists were saying? Despite the hopeful signs, it was too soon to tell.

History gave no strong reason for hope. Seldom had an entrenched dynasty voluntarily given up its power. This was not the first time that Soviet leaders had loosened their grip. With the economy collapsing around him, Lenin had introduced the New Economic Policy. When the survival of Soviet power was threatened by an invading German army, Stalin had suspended his assault on the church and reduced Communist propaganda, stressing instead the more appealing theme of Russian patriotism. Feeling too weak to maintain Stalin's oppressive terror, Khrushchev had liberalized the regime and released hundreds of thousands of political prisoners. Yet none of these earlier shifts had lessened the regime's tangible hostility to the West nor loosened the party's grip on power, and they did not last. "Reform" had moved in the other direction as well. Stalin had reformed industry (by rapid industrialization), agriculture (by eliminating private farming), and the political system (by eliminating rivalry and establishing a loyal bureaucracy); even the liberalizing Khrushchev had clamped down when he thought his liberalizing reforms were getting out of hand. So today one must wait and see.

How then is the outsider to judge whether and to what extent Gorbachev's reforms are changing the basic character of Soviet rule—and eliminating its threat to the West? Is there a way more reliable than guesswork or wishful thinking to distinguish profound changes from tactical shifts? To avoid being misled by deceptive words or promises?

I think so. The "Soviet threat" does not lie in the Kremlin leaders' policies, shifting between scowls and smiles; it does not disappear when they become more flexible in arms-control negotiations or when they withdraw troops from Afghanistan or when they promote negotiations in place of conflict in some areas of the world. The threat arises, rather—for reasons I will point out—from the imperatives of their system itself. It is only there, in the basic structures of that system, that we must look for truly significant evolution. The outsider got a glimpse of reality at the time of the elections of 1989; Gorbachev claimed the vigorous contests showed how strong was the people's support of their rulers' policy of change—but large special-troop units moved into Moscow and Leningrad in case the spirit of change were to get out of hand.

The outside observer must distinguish, as Gorbachev does, between "fundamental principles" and the things he calls "braking mechanisms." The latter are what Gorbachev attacks: the bloated bureaucracy, for example, and overlapping control bodies, exaggerated party meddling, industrial and agricultural mismanagement, corruption, and the excessive privileges of the elite. Such evils can be diminished without altering the system itself. But fundamental principles—and the structures they have begotten—are something else. These Gorbachev has repeatedly sworn not to change. Yet it is only when these basic structures have been finally dismantled or their powers irrevocably constrained that the system itself—and East-West relations—can truly change.

My purpose in this book is to focus attention on those structures. I do not mean the ones described in the Soviet constitution, of course, but the true centers of power that characterize the Leninist system and which Gorbachev and all his predecessors have preferred to hide or misrepresent. I know them well; I served in or worked with them and for many years have been watching them from the West with an experienced eye.

I do not ask the reader to draw any conclusions. I share the general hope. Real changes are afoot in the Soviet Union, and I, too, think it is too early to judge where they will lead. But I can offer benchmarks more reliable than tomorrow's headlines or speeches, benchmarks against which one can measure for oneself the real progress, or lack of it.

For instance, *glasnost*—"openness." Does it mean that the regime dismantles its remaining controls over what its people shall learn and communicate to others—the controls that I describe here? In its attempt to win the cooperation of what Gorbachev admits—and the 1989 elections showed—is an "alienated" people, will the regime not merely stage elections but also "restructure" the internal army which protected it against the electors in Moscow and Leningrad? Will Gorbachev's efforts for better international contact and understanding between peoples—those "genuinely good intentions in foreign policy"—extend far enough to break down the regime's barriers to that contact and understanding? Will the party leaders, who have manipulated laws to preserve their own power, submit to a genuine rule of law? Look at these controls, these special forces, these barriers, these laws (and answer the other questions raised in this book), watch for changes, and judge for yourself.

This is not a personal memoir; I draw on current events, on the information of recent Soviet emigrants and defectors, on Western scholarship, and even on the Soviets' own texts and statements, which can be revealing. Nevertheless it may be useful to describe the personal experience that shapes and enlightens this presentation.

After growing up in Siberia on a collective farm (of which my father and older brother were chairmen), I served in the Red Army from 1939–45 as political commissar and active soldier. During this time I was wounded four times and was awarded eleven decorations for acts of bravery and service in battles, in one of which—Stalingrad, where I commanded a mortar company—I was one of 161 survivors of a regiment of 2,800 men. For fifteen years I was a member of the Communist Party of the Soviet Union, serving as a Komsomol and party secretary and completing a university course in Marxism-Leninism.

Then, during my ten years in what is now called the KGB, I served in SMERSH; supervised investigations in a provincial unit; supported secret operations abroad from a Moscow desk; and served in the West watching over the loyalty of Soviet citizens, contacting secret sources including people within the Russian Orthodox Church hierarchy, in Western European trade unions, and in the World Peace Council, and countering the work of Western intelligence. Most instructive of all were my five years within the Kremlin rulers' own bodyguard in a central position involving personnel management and party work.

I knew and worked directly with men who were still administering Soviet power under Gorbachev, like Filipp Bobkov, who was supervising the KGB's day-to-day operations, or Vitaliy Fedorchuk, who became KGB chairman and later Minister of Internal Affairs, or Politburo candidate member Petr Demichev, or Sergey Bannikov, who moved from the deputy chairmanship of the KGB to that of the USSR Supreme Court.

Since my arrival in the West over thirty years ago, I have kept up to date on events in the USSR by talking with recent emigrants and later defectors from the KGB and by consulting with Western intelligence and security services. Enrolled for a time in the graduate school of an American university, I have talked with prominent Sovietologists and studied their writings. To my study of Soviet publications I have brought not only a native command of the Soviet Russian language but also an insider's understanding of what the specialized terms connote in their Soviet context.

My subject is Soviet rule, not the KGB as such. If the KGB occupies center stage in this book, it is because it occupies center stage in the Soviet system itself. The Leninist system is designed above all to preserve the power of its masters, and Moscow wits come close to the truth when they jocularly describe the Soviet leadership as "the Central Committee of the KGB." Curiously, however, many Western descriptions of the Soviet political and economic system largely ignore the KGB as if, like Western police, security, or intelligence services, it lay outside the mainstream of politics. Some are even inclined to wander down rabbit paths of speculation about increases or decreases in its power. In most books about the KGB itself, for every page describing its central role in the regime, five or ten pages are devoted to its spying and subversion abroad. Here, by reversing that ratio, I restore a more accurate and revealing balance.

Because Soviet rule—the system I describe here—extends far beyond Russia, I do not examine the historical roots of Russian tyranny, nor Russian character and tradition, although they surely and importantly helped the Leninists to win and hold their power base in Russia. I barely touch on the Soviet leaders' rivalries and intrigues or their luxurious life-styles. I discuss only indirectly the social and economic problems that they have imposed upon the Russian and other peoples under their sway: faltering industry, corruption, shortages of goods and (in large areas) even of food—and desperation, symptomized by the passivity and alcoholism that Gorbachev, like his predecessors, is trying to fight. I avoid, too, the scholarly debate about the labels to be applied to Soviet rule: whether or not you call these institutions "totalitarian," they are real and they define the system.

My approach to the subject differs so sharply from conventional ones, in fact, that some readers may think it the astigmatic view of "a mere secret policeman." That would be to misunderstand the contrasts between Soviet society and our own. In a Western democratic society it is quite possible that a security officer may be less closely attuned to his political system than is, say, a lawyer or a journalist or a professor. But it would be a mistake to confound two very different worlds. The Chekist—as the KGB officer is called—may be despised and feared by most of the people under Soviet rule; but from inside the internal security apparatus of a regime devoted above all to its own survival in power, he sees more directly than any lawyer or journalist or professor how that regime really works. He knows that Soviet spokesmen, when they deny Western assertions that the KGB is a "secret police," are telling a certain truth: that the KGB is no more "secret" than many another element of an essentially clandestine rule, and that it is far more than a "police" agency in the Western sense.

The KGB is, rather, an integral part of the highest leadership; it is no coincidence that, in the early 1980s, a longtime KGB chairman, Yuri Andropov, came to govern the whole system or that he was succeeded by another former Chekist, Konstantin Chernenko. Neither is it surprising that on two occasions in the 1980s more than a quarter of the voting members of the Politburo, the highest ruling body, were experienced Chekists. The Chekist—not the lawyer or journalist or professor—is the true representative and the elite of the system. He is the prototype of the New Soviet Man. As the founder, Lenin, said, "Every good Communist is at the same time a good Chekist."

Chekists in Moscow and in the provinces help make the government's most important decisions and see that they are put into action. They participate, as Soviet leaders have said, "in all the functions of the state." And all the leaders of the Soviet state have been involved with the KGB since childhood: judged (and approved) by it, serving it as officers, agents, or occasional helpers, and bound, now as always, to do its work when called upon. Soviet rule requires secrecy, which the KGB sees to; and the leaders' conspiratorial way of thinking and acting is that of the KGB. In the leaders' endless rivalries and power struggles and in their relations with the people they rule, KGB capabilities and KGB personnel are ever present. Many institutions—described in this book—unite rulership and KGB in one indissoluble entity.

The Soviet leaders' struggle to hold power—of which Gorbachev's *perestroika* is an episode—is the real driving force that some Western writers like to call a "Communist master plan for world conquest" and that others call "historical Russian expansionism." The institutions described in this book are the fingers and claws of a death grip, and their very existence reveals that the masters are waging warfare against their own subjects. In that internal war the West is inextricably involved. Will *perestroika* bring it to an end?

PART I

THE REVOLUTION DEFENDS ITSELF

CHAPTER 1

The Origins

WHEN MIKHAIL GORBACHEV PROCLAIMED THAT HIS "NEW REVOLUTION" sought to restore Lenin's purer vision of socialism, he was leaving himself plenty of room for pragmatic solutions: many of Lenin's positions, taken at various times and amassed in forty-odd volumes of writings, remain open to interpretation. But one aspect of Lenin's thought leaves Gorbachev no room for deviation: the determination to keep all the reins of power firmly in the hands of the Communist Party leadership. Upon this unshakable foundation were built the institutions that most truly characterize Lenin's version of socialism.

After his group of professional conspirators seized power in 1917 they styled their coup d'etat grandiloquently as the "Glorious October Revolution." If history owes them any glory, however, it is not for having evicted an infant and helpless democratic government or for pretending to do it on behalf of the "people": such coups and such pretensions have become commonplace in the twentieth century. Their real claim—if not to glory at least to the respect and careful attention of the West—has become clear only with the passage of time. The massive flag-waving anniversary parades on Red Square every November 7 remind the world—now after more than seventy years—of an awesome skill at holding on to power after seizing it.

Not only did these revolutionaries beat down resistance throughout the vast expanses of Russia but they then succeeded in imposing their rule on Ukrainians, Transcaucasians, Central Asians, and other surrounding peoples who, if less successfully than the Afghans sixty years later, fought long and fiercely to fend them off. Afterwards the Leninists' authority and legitimacy were challenged again and again by rebellions, riots, famine, and social chaos—but they held on. When the Nazis invaded their country, millions of their soldiers surrendered and many of their people at first welcomed the occupying Germans as liberators. Still the Kremlin masters prevailed. Exploiting the patriotism and courage of their subjects against the foreign invader, they won back the lost territories and then, as their armies moved out beyond the old borders into Central Europe, took new peoples under their domain. After the war, while the West prospered, the Moscow leaders mismanaged their economy and society—as they now admit—and are today forced to struggle against the symptoms of despair among their people: passivity, indifference, alcoholism, and corruption. No one seems to believe any longer in the secular religion of Marxism-Leninism that alone justifies their rule. But despite all this, their grip has never been broken, either in Russia or anywhere else where it has closed.

It is no coincidence; holding power was and remains their prime concern and their special genius. When Lenin (quoting Marx) said that "insurrection is an art," he had more in mind than simply grabbing power: "No revolution is worthwhile," he said, "unless it knows how to defend itself." His successors continue to treat this aphorism as a seminal principle of Soviet doctrine, citing it again and again—for today as in 1918 they are still struggling to defend their revolution.*

Although this ongoing struggle shapes Soviet foreign policy more strongly than any other factor, many in the West seem unaware of it. As conditions have improved in the USSR and decades have gone by with no weakening of Kremlin power, Westerners have found it ever easier to accept the Soviet rulers' line that only a few isolated grumblers still question their legitimacy. Some even fall into the trap of Soviet propaganda that blurs the distinction between Lenin's October coup and the Russian revolution. But that is odd: he who forgets how the Soviet leaders really won power—who may even fancy that the Bolsheviks overthrew the tsar—must find it hard to understand why for seventy years afterward such liberators still had to corral the people behind murderous border obstacles, hide outside reality from them, and use violence to quell disagreement.

The half-forgotten reality is that no revolutionary movement or party— least of all Lenin's isolated band of emigrants in faraway Switzerland or their police-saturated organization in Russia—ever seriously threatened the tsarist monarchy. The war did the job for them. Three shattering years had killed more than a million soldiers and crippled the economy, spread hunger and confusion and impatience, and so eroded the tsar's authority that finally in February 1917, to nearly everyone's surprise, a street

---

*Lenin speech of 23 October 1918: *"Vsyakaya revolyutsiya lish' togda chego-nibud' stoit, esli ona umeet zasenishchatsya."* To name but a few Politburo members who have cited it as a truism: Eduard Shevardnadze in December 1981, Viktor Chebrikov several times including June 1985, Yuri Andropov in 1977, Leonid Brezhnev in 1976, Boris Ponomarev in 1971. Articles and books have developed the theme.

demonstration was enough to blow it away. No one stood ready to pick up the pieces of the tsar's power, and those who did so, willy nilly, found themselves beset by most of the same pressures that had destroyed it. In the confused months of their democracy they could not halt the collapse of the economy or put a stop to the war; and war denied them the time needed to build democracy in a land supremely unready for it. The "masses"—meaning then the peasants-in-arms and the industrial workers—were by this time apt to rally behind anyone cynical enough to promise them the impossible, flexible enough to dodge the insoluble issues, bold enough to seize power, and disciplined and ruthless enough to restore order.

That nicely defined Lenin's group of professional revolutionaries.

Taking power was, as Lenin later admitted, "easier than lifting a feather"; it had been lying out there in the streets to be picked up. Lenin showed some art, of course, in recognizing the moment of opportunity. It arrived in early November 1917 (late October by the old calendar) when a Congress of Soviets was to meet. Lenin saw that never before or after that would the wind blow so strongly in his favor. Had he waited even a few weeks, a constituent assembly and thereafter parliamentary institutions would have displaced the workers' and soldiers' councils (soviets) wherein lay the Bolsheviks' only pretense to majority support. Within weeks, too, the army would have finally collapsed, and other parties—some enjoying far more support among the people—would have reaped the credit for bringing the peace for which everyone yearned. The peasants ripe for revolution would have scattered from the concentrated ranks of the army back to their widespread farms. Spotting this "crucial moment," Lenin urged his hesitant coconspirators to strike: "To delay the uprising means death." He prevailed, they acted, and the coup succeeded. Trotsky said later, "If we had not seized power in October, we would never have got it."

Only then began Leninism's great achievement: defending that power. First, Lenin legitimated his coup d'etat by professing to form a "soviet" government that had simply taken power out of shaky and suspect hands in order to hand it over to the people in their directly elected councils (soviets). In the early hours, after his men had won the capital city of Petrograd and not much else, he penned decrees promising everyone his heart's desire: peace to the soldier and his family, independence to the border nationalities, and land to the peasant. Lenin was buying the time and popular support he needed to extend and consolidate his grip on power; he later admitted that these famous decrees were only a "form of propaganda."[1]

Soon Lenin laid out the real objectives. As he set them out in April 1918 in a paper entitled "Immediate Tasks of the Soviet Government," these were three: first, to convince the people that they should support the Bolshevik program; second, to suppress resistance; third, to organize the administration.

To "convince," he lit a dazzling blaze of propaganda on the one hand while on the other casting a dark curtain over contrary information—a mixture of propaganda and censorship on a scale the world had never seen. His message so touched the emotions of impatient soldiers and sailors and of frustrated workers and poor and landless peasants that in the first months after "October" hundreds of thousands pitched in gladly to help the Bolsheviks wrest property from its owners, guard what had been taken, and shoot anyone the Bolshevik leaders labeled "counterrevolutionary." Indeed, Lenin kindled hopes that continued to excite and bewitch the young and poor—like myself—for many years.

To "suppress resistance"—his second task—Lenin unleashed terror and violence. He had been deceiving when he said, before taking power, that he would only suppress "former exploiters [who would number] fifty to a hundred financial magnates and bigwigs"; and he was still deceiving when he raised this estimate to "several hundred, at most several thousand, in the whole of Russia." Nor was it true, as he asserted, that this would "entail far less bloodshed than had the suppression of past uprisings of slaves, serfs, or wage-laborers."[2] His violence turned against whole categories of the population—the clergy, ethnic nationalists, farmers, his socialist rivals—and soon struck any part of society outside his direct command. In single months his men killed more people than the tsars had killed in decades. Only to the degree that resistance was quelled did Lenin relax his reign of terror, and whenever opposition arose he loosed it anew.

His third task—to "organize the administration"—was more dramatic than those bland words; he himself called it the "most important and difficult aspect of the socialist revolution." It would involve more than putting new people in old offices; he would have to create "new organizational relationships" and "introduce the strictest and universal accounting and control." To raise the workers' productivity, the government must tighten discipline, "use compulsion," apply an "iron hand."[3] This would require the strictest centralization of power and new institutions of compulsion.

It was a race against time; the Leninists, like any insurrectionists, had to fix their power firmly before counter forces could unseat them. In this race Lenin profited—as have his successors—from the history of Russia and the character of Russians. This passive and then largely illiterate peasant people had stayed cosmically distant from the decisions and doings of their rulers. Neither the parliamentary episodes of the tsarist Duma nor the confused months of the Provisional Government had engaged them in democratic politics. "Freedom" was little more than an abstraction: after centuries of dumb acceptance they needed (some say desired) to be led. Today, with the wisdom of hindsight, some Russian emigrants as well as Western scholars contend that what happened was inevitable, and one can endlessly debate exactly what degree of tyranny was really inevitable. But there is no doubt that the Russian past simplified Lenin's task. His repression, if more harsh, was not new, his breaking of promises no surprise, his attacks on "foreign conspiracies" a familiar echo of the past. The vastness of the land and the lack of cohesion among its peoples eased more than complicated his rule.

Notwithstanding their traditional passivity, however, even the Bolsheviks' supporters soon began to protest Lenin's betrayal of his promises and their hopes. Peasants were pillaged first of their produce and then of their land. Workers were underpaid, underfed, and unable to get their grievances heard. The border nations found themselves cheated of their promised self-determination. Former revolutionaries who had conspired and risked their lives to bring down the tsar—but independent of the Bolsheviks—were denied participation in the soviets, ostracized, exiled, jailed, or slain. People for or against Lenin were frightened and horrified by his massacres. So, paradoxically, resistance was growing as the civil war ended. Even his former supporters began to protest and, lacking other recourse, took up whatever arms they could find to fight the new authority.

More men now rebelled against Lenin than had carried him to power in the October coup, and theirs was to be a longer struggle. But they were doomed, and they and their battles have been forgotten. No murals or marches, no films or songs celebrate today the deeds of heroes like Petrichenko, who presided over the Kronstadt rebellion; Antonov, who with 50,000 peasants fought Lenin's rule in Tambov Province; or Cholokashvili, who for many months led gallant resistance to Soviet Russia's military takeover of Georgia. Lenin had used his time well and was ready. Power was no longer "lying in the streets," and these new rebels faced a task much harder than "lifting a feather."

When exhorting the members of his Central Committee to carry out the coup d'etat, Lenin had promised that they would be able to form "a government no one would overthrow." If they struck at the right moment, he said, "no power on earth can prevent the Bolsheviks . . . from retaining power until the triumph of the world socialist revolution."[4]

One way he fulfilled that promise was by organizing armed units of kinds unknown in tsarist days.

In early 1921 the factory workers in Petrograd—the very workers in whose name Lenin ruled—rose up against Bolshevist rule and were joined by the sailors of the nearby island garrison of Kronstadt. Only three years earlier those sailors had played a key role in Lenin's coup d'etat and Trotsky had called them the "flower and pride of the Revolution." Now they recognized and asserted that nothing the Bolsheviks had been doing in the name of the workers and peasants could be called socialism. On the contrary they viewed it as counterrevolution and demanded "all power to the soviets—and not to the parties." They called for free speech and press, secret balloting for candidates to the soviets, and other basic liberties. Specifically, they demanded the abolishment of Lenin's special armed units, of the "Communist fighting detachments in the army," and of "Communist guards in the factories."[5]

They had recognized the danger, but too late. It is an irony of history that Lenin's special armed detachments—the very forces whose existence the rebels had protested—were on hand to shoot the ringleaders as soon as the rebellion had been crushed and to march the survivors north to newly enlarged concentration camps (early parts of the Gulag Archipelago), where most of them soon died.

Through these special troops we offer a foretaste of the other extraordinary institutions by which Lenin and his followers have defended their revolution. A glimpse at their record serves, too, as a reminder of Soviet history, for the troops have played a role in every phase of it. And the very existence of these troops today—under Gorbachev's reforming regime more numerous and better armed than ever—testifies to the enduring internal war.

CHAPTER 2

Special Troops: "Beating Heart of the Party"

The Internal War

IN APRIL 1989 THE LEADERS' SPECIAL TROOPS CHARGED INTO A MASS OF unarmed and cheerfully demonstrating men and women on the streets of Tbilisi in the Georgian Republic and, according to eyewitnesses, beat and hacked many of them to death, including several women.

By this time Western television watchers had become used to seeing crowds of Soviet citizens demonstrating and being dispelled by special troops. Gorbachev had lifted the lid on long-suppressed dissatisfactions; individuals formed.groups to demand more rights, better representation, improvements in their living and working conditions, changes in government policies, and revelation of the crimes of the past. Workers struck in factories; people took to the streets; riots broke out. In a period of only ten months in 1988, by the regime's own admission, more than six hundred unauthorized meetings and street demonstrations had taken place in Moscow alone.[1] Huge crowds massed day after day in the streets of Armenia and Azerbaijan and Georgia, in Estonia and Latvia and Lithuania, calling for greater independence from Moscow. When the regime for the first time permitted contested elections in March 1989, it deployed special troops, not just riot-control police, in Moscow and Leningrad. "It was the kind of thing you do about a coup, not for riot control," said one observer.[2] Thousands of special troops were deployed in Uzbekistan in June 1989 to cope with ethnic demands that the Soviet Minister of Internal Affairs labeled "ultimatums."[3]

What was new were not the disturbances or their violent suppression by special troops but the fact that the West learned about them. Before

Gorbachev's *glasnost,* the situation was as described by Solzhenitsyn when he called the world's attention—years after it happened—to the 1962 massacre of demonstrators in Novocherkassk: "A whole town rebels, and every trace is licked clean and hidden."[4] Only in December 1986 did official Soviet sources first admit bloody rioting in the USSR, and two years later they were again trying to clamp down the old lid of secrecy; by a decree of January 1989 journalists would no longer be allowed to cover rallies, meetings, and scenes of emergencies without special passes. The word "emergency," as *Izvestiya* itself commented, could now be used to shut off any kind of event.[5]

In fact, riots and uprisings against Soviet rule have been common from the earliest days of Bolshevik rule up to the present day. Even before Gorbachev's time—in the thirty years between the death of Stalin and Gorbachev's rise—news of more than two thousand disturbances, many bloody and none publicly admitted, leaked out to the West.[6]

Like the riots and demonstrations of Gorbachev's time, these earlier ones were sparked by various causes. By food shortages and prices, for example, as in the summer of 1982 in a community south of Kiev. There the antiriot forces of the police (militia) could not or would not disperse the rioters; some even joined the demonstrators; special troop units rolled onto the scene and fired into the demonstrators' ranks; policemen fired back from the crowd, but eventually the heavily armed troops dispersed the demonstrators. Or by arguments between individuals of different ethnic groups, as in October 1981 in Ordzhonikidze in the North Caucasus. Thousands of citizens beat back the police with clubs and bricks, and not even reinforcements from the MVD Academy in the town—cadets being schooled to crush just such uprisings—could over-power them. The demonstrators occupied a government building, aired their grievances about official corruption and police brutality, and pelted arriving tanks with bricks; for two days the fighting went on as smoke rose over the city.

In the summer of 1976 it required special troops from their headquar-ters in Tashkent seventy-five miles away to quell an uprising in Chimkent. In 1964 violent rioting shook the Azerbaijan industrial city of Sumgait— quite unnoticed in the West, in contrast to the events in that same city in 1988—as it had in 1961–62 in the cities of Murom, Aleksandrov, and Novocherkassk, in 1959 in Temir Tau, and in 1956 in Tbilisi. In 1954 in Barnaul in the Altay Kray, Chechens who had been displaced from the North Caucasus rose up and took over the city for two days—taking the opportunity to execute KGB men. Special troops moved in and "drowned the city in blood."[7]

Many more of these battles remained hidden. Within the halls of the

KGB itself it was only by a chance indiscretion that I learned about one of them that took place in a suburb of Kuybyshev at the end of the 1940s. Although scores died and hundreds more were taken away to concentration camps, the affair has never come to public attention until this writing.

Although it is neither the most recent nor the biggest of its kind, this uprising illustrates the pattern that has become more visible since Gorbachev's reforms. On one side stand the workers and their families, on the other the troops specialized in fighting just such "enemies." And what started as a simple demand for better conditions quickly spread into a violent battle against the rulership itself—just as it can today.

Living conditions in overcrowded Kuybyshev after the war were miserable. The city had repeatedly sent emissaries to Moscow to plead—always in vain—for materials to build more of the rudimentary barracks in which the luckier people lived while others camped in the open or inhabited caves dug out of the surrounding hills. Tensions built up until a cold winter day when crowds of desperate workers assembled in the city to demand food and shelter. They threw rocks at party headquarters and any party functionaries they could spot; looters broke into stores and houses of officials and smashed whatever they could not carry off. The local militia could not restore order, and Soviet Army units could not be trusted to fight them. Chaos reigned. Then the rulers sent in their own special troops. They drove the workers out of town and pursued them into a housing settlement on the southern outskirts, a place called Bezymyanka ("without a name"). Not pausing to reason with their "enemy," these forces smashed the flimsy buildings with artillery, dropped mortar shells on the roofs, sprayed machine-gun fire at any sign of life, and then swept out over the hills to wipe out survivors. But people shot back from caves, using weapons seized from or handed over by the militia; and the fighting went on for at least two days. Scores of workers and members of their families were killed and wounded, and hundreds were deported to concentration camps.

One such event has become better known than the others: the battle of the first three days of June 1962 in Novocherkassk near Rostov-on-Don.[8] It gives the flavor not only of these violent outbreaks—by now all too familiar—but also of the special troops with which the regime fights them.

The twenty thousand workers of an electrical equipment factory awoke to Moscow's announcement of an increase in food prices, without pay raises. Small groups formed at the factory and moved on to a general meeting where they aired other complaints: low wages, food shortages, party manipulation of the trade unions, inhuman working conditions. In their excitement they blocked a rail line passing by the factory. The militia made a few arrests, and army troops from a nearby garrison began to take positions around the factory. The next day the workers, their numbers swollen by workers from other factories and by women and young people, gathered in the town center to talk and complain about the price increases. In the intervening hours, special troops had been moved in with armored vehicles to protect the key spots. The authorities threatened: Disperse or we will deport all of you and repopulate the city. The angry crowd shouted demands. As the tension grew, the special troops (apparently mostly Central Asians) began shooting into the air and then turned their fire directly into the masses. As the people scattered, the troops kept shooting at their fleeing backs. Scores died, and many of the wounded were never seen again. Politburo members flew into town and announced by local radio that the events were a "provocation" by the "enemy"—who would be severely punished. In the weeks that followed, the KGB arrested hundreds of participants, interrogated and tried them, shot some, and sent others to prison camps.

Such were the battles of an internal war that started more than seventy years ago and continues to this day. To fight that war Lenin formed a very special army, and his successors have never stopped committing it to action.

VV: "Beating Heart of the Party"

Only a tightly disciplined force can be counted upon to fire on unarmed workers and women and children; only a specially trained military unit can handle turbulent situations with such decisiveness; only a ready and mobile one can move so rapidly into troubled areas.

The Internal Troops (*Vnutrenniye Voyska,* or VV) that fought these battles* have these characteristics and even more unusual ones. For in-

---

*The regime's forces at Bezymyanka, for example, consisted of a reinforced regiment of Moscow-based MGB Troops. My source, MGB Lt. Col. Yuri Semyonov, was pulled away from his routine duties as an operational officer in my Guards Directorate because of his past field experience; he joined senior officers of the Directorate's Fifth Department (Search and Investigation) and others taken from refresher training courses, was attached to that MGB Troops regiment, and moved immediately to Kuybyshev.

Eyewitness designations of the troops intervening in the other incidents are, understandably, less precise. In 1988 in Sumgait they were "armored crack troops," while "green beret paratroopers" sealed the city (*London Daily Telegraph,* 12 March 1988). South of Kiev in 1982 it was "KGB special units" that rolled in and fired on the crowd. At Barnaul in 1954 they were reported as "Internal Troops from Moscow." Yelin's report on the Novocherkassk battle named them as "special troops of the KGB." In Azerbaijan and Armenia in 1988, although some Western articles erringly referred to "Red Army" units many correctly identified them as Internal Troops of the MVD, their VV insignia were

stance, although on paper they were until 1989† part of the Soviet armed forces, they are administered by the Ministry of Internal Affairs (MVD); despite this they are sent into action not by the MVD but by the central party leadership‡—and they fight under the operational command of yet another organization: the KGB.

Internal Troops are well named. Theirs is the "internal war" that Lenin said would be "more devastating than any foreign war." They were created "to face an internal counterrevolutionary enemy no less terrible than the external enemy,"[9] and they subsist to this day to fight not the external enemies of their country (although some of them did so in the Second World War) but instead the internal enemies of the party leaders. Theirs are the battles where the rulership can trust neither the army nor the police. In Poland, where a smaller version of them has been putting down serious uprisings throughout the life of the Communist regime, wags have called such troops the "beating heart of the party." (Indeed, they beat and kicked demonstrators in a Moscow city park in August 1988, and Soviet newspapers received many calls from Muscovites protesting the troops' brutality.)[10]

These are soldiers, not policemen; their task is warfare, not just public order. Contrary to some uninformed Western accounts, they are not a Soviet equivalent of the paramilitary national police, national guards, or gendarmeries of some Western democracies; that function is fulfilled in the USSR by the mobile antiriot units of the militia, a locally administered but nationally centralized police force. In fact, still more militia units, of a new type but with this same mission were reportedly formed in 1988. Soviet officials refer to the militia's "special motorized units" and "operational units," one of which, the "6th Special Unit," was identified in the brutal repression of a public gathering in Lvov on July 4, 1988.[11]

These troops are not to be confused with either the KGB's Border Guards or the KGB Troops. Although they are categorized as "special-purpose troops" *(voyska osobogo naznacheniya)*, they are unrelated to the army's similarly designated "spetsnaz" troops which are intended mainly

---

clearly visible in television shots. In Georgia in 1989 the VV were clearly identified by eyewitnesses.

†A decree of 21 March 1989 separated Border, Internal, and Railway Troops from the armed forces but confirmed that they would continue with the same procedures and conditions as the army and navy.

‡This was stressed by their overall commander in a public interview in 1988. Gen. Yuri V. Shatalin reminded *Pravda* correspondents that "the troops have never been under the jurisdiction of local authorities, as is stipulated by the USSR constitution, article 73" (on the armed forces). "Under special circumstances their involvement must be coordinated with the USSR Council of Ministers. . . . No transfer to local jurisdiction will be permitted" (*Pravda*, 18 October 1988).

for commando and other irregular service behind enemy lines. They should not be thought of as a Praetorian Guard, either, for another unit plays that role: the troops of the Kremlin Komendatura. In fact, their style is unknown outside the Soviet sphere.

The VV is an army, with its own artillery, tanks, air support, and paratroops. With more than a quarter-million men (recent estimates go as high as 350,000), it outnumbers the armies of almost any major world power.§ The VV stands independent of the nearly five million men in the Soviet Army, Navy, and Air Force (although in time of war it would be brought under unified military command).

How can such troops be justified today—unless Soviet power rests on shakier foundations than its ideologists admit? The 1960 advent of "a state of all the people" wrote finis to "class struggle" and removed even the theoretical possibility of "counterrevolution." The CPSU Party Programs of both 1986 and 1961 asserted that "in terms of internal conditions, the Soviet Union has no need of an army."

Asked in 1988 by a *Pravda* interviewer why the troops were needed in addition to the militia to enforce public order, the VV commander said with a certain truth that his forces were designed to operate during "mass" events. He cited as an example the Olympic Games of 1980 and the fencing off of Chernobyl after the 1987 nuclear disaster and also mentioned quarantine measures in disease epidemics as well as natural disasters, but he failed to mention mass uprisings. A few years earlier the existence of the troops was justified in these words: "In our country the people have no class enemies and the social roots of crime have been rooted out, but antisocial criminal elements still exist, sometimes connected with agents of imperialist intelligence services." The VV "vigilantly struggles with such elements."[12]

If these are the best public explanations that can be offered for maintaining a special army of a quarter-million men with tanks and air support, one can understand why the masters are sensitive about the whole subject.

The people under Soviet rule recognize the VV as their enemy. In the frankness of *glasnost* the Soviet press has admitted that the troops suffer an "inferiority complex" about their "poor image." "We would like to meet a girl, but as soon as they see our insignia, they turn away from us," said one VV trooper. Their own commander admitted with "pain" in 1988 that his soldiers "are sometimes described as cruel and lacking compassion." The

§If one adds to their numbers certain other special-purpose and paramilitary forces of the KGB and MVD, they outnumber the U.S. Army—and this without counting the militarized units of the police and such guard units as the Railway and Waterway Militias and convoy and guard troops.

media are reluctant to write about them (despite regime exhortations) because they are regarded as "secret forces."[13]

Only their work and their numbers are really secret, however. The VV's recruits are selected openly from among regular draftees. The men of one of its divisions, wearing the well-cut uniforms of elites, mount ceremonial guard at prominent places in Moscow and march through Red Square among the leading elements of the big annual parades as loudspeakers hail their division's Chekist name—Dzerzhinsky. As part of the campaign begun in the mid-1960s to brighten the image of the agencies of repression, the leaders award money prizes for writings and films exalting the VV's romantic revolutionary origins, its civil war harshness against "former exploiters," its fights against "bandits," and its wartime service.[14]

But these blurbs give no accurate idea of the VV's work, neither today nor in the past. They belittle its extended campaigns as "skirmishes" and defame its adversaries as bandits, kulaks, religious fanatics, bourgeois nationalists, and fascist collaborators. The large-scale guerrilla struggle of the Ukrainians to be free of Soviet rule (most recently quelled only in the early 1950s) is dismissed as "subversive activities of bourgeois nationalists not yet completely destroyed." The VV's deportation of hundreds of thousands of Balts in 1940–41 and 1945–51 and its violent forcing of Baltic farmers into collectives from 1948–51 are presented as a "fight against bourgeois and kulak elements in the Baltic republics." And the patriots who fought them there for years afterward are derided as an "underground directed by foreign intelligence services."[15]

Not even a Soviet student of administrative law can get any real notion of the troops' work; his textbooks barely mention their name.[16] Western researchers may find, buried in the pages of a military newspaper, a rare item telling that Internal Troops have captured some hoodlums, but it will not tell where. Their commander in 1988 cited a couple of recent examples of work against terrorist extortionists in Volgograd and the freeing of hostages and the arrest of criminals in Kaluga Oblast. But when they go into action to quell riots and uprisings—their real prime task and raison d'etre—the party leaders will still, if they can, do as they have in the past: cut off travel to, and communications with, troubled areas, ban publicity, and punish anyone who leaks the news.

Thus deprived of hard facts, Western writers on the USSR have left a gap. On one side, political analyses rarely mention these unusual troops while, on the other side, writings that describe the KGB and other security services do not usually point up the troops' political significance.[17] The gap is serious, because to the extent that the West remains ignorant of Internal Troops—their history, their mission, their size, and the uprisings that still make them necessary seventy years after the

Bolsheviks took power—it is deprived of a precious insight into the very nature of the Soviet regime and its problems and priorities today.

A Short History of Internal Troops

The Internal Troops came into being soon after the coup d'etat. Within days after Lenin formed the VCheka (today called the KGB) in December 1917, its local branches (called Chekas) began arming groups of men to help them round up "counterrevolutionaries," dispose of "former exploiters," seize food from the peasants, and stand guard over the places and things and captives they had taken. These units were formally incorporated in June 1918 under the name "Corps of VCheka Troops" with the mission "to secure Soviet power inside the country." However, they still celebrate February 24, 1918, as their birthday**—by no coincidence, following by only one day the formal birthday of the Red Army.

These troops absorbed many of the early Bolshevik Party rank-and-file. The whole party had been called to arms early in the civil war; every able-bodied member not otherwise occupied was made into a "Communist with a rifle" in so-called "Units of Special Purpose" (*Chasti Osobogo Naznacheniya,* or ChON) which were put under the orders of the local Chekas. Thus did the regime apply on a grand scale Lenin's principle that "every good Communist is at the same time a good Chekist." The ChON helped the Chekas to "liquidate White Guards and kulak bands. . . . Together with the Kiev Cheka, ChON arrested about a thousand suspects during the counterrevolutionary uprising . . . fought against the Tambov uprising . . . suppressed uprisings in 1921–22 in the Kuban, Siberia including the Altay Kray, the Far East and helped the Chekas fight against sixty bandit organizations in the Ukraine. . . . After the end of the civil war the ChON's intelligence service worked closely with . . . the VCheka."[18]

VCheka Troops were soon to get the help of other auxiliaries, too. Various administrations of the new regime were hastily arming groups of men to guard their factories, railways, bridges, and stocks of sugar, oil, and textiles. By the middle of 1918 at least sixteen such armed organizations, distinct from the Red Army and Navy and from VCheka Troops, had come into existence. All worked under local Cheka supervision; "everything was done along with VCheka and Army units," wrote a Soviet historian.[19] These auxiliaries provided local Chekas with the sheer num-

---

**On that date a small motorized group formed and put itself at the disposition of the VCheka. In March it escorted the government from Petrograd to Moscow and helped guard the Kremlin.

bers they needed to carry out mass registrations, arrests, deportations, and slaughters. But they were little better than rabbles, and in March 1919, when VCheka chief Dzerzhinsky took command of Internal Affairs (NKVD) as well, his VCheka began to take these auxiliary armies away from their parent organizations. Dzerzhinsky's men reorganized them and, for the nearly two years which remained of the civil war, managed them through complex and shifting staff organizations bearing clumsy acronyms like "VOKhR" and "VNUS." All were subordinated to Dzerzhinsky under one or another of his hats, as VCheka chief or as NKVD commissar. Eventually most of them were fully incorporated into VCheka/GPU Troops. When the ChON was disbanded in 1924–26, most of its remaining units were transferred to the Red Army—but only after many of their individual members had already joined GPU and OGPU Troops in 1922–23.

To feed the cities, his power base, Lenin chose to confiscate grain and farm produce by force: "The peasant will have to go hungry for a while in order to save the towns and factories from famine. . . . We shall not be able to do without coercion."†† The Chekas, charged with such a massive task, depended on VCheka Troops. In turn, they and the troops used armed toughs enlisted in a huge "Food Supply Army" (*Prodovolstvennaya armiya*) to force the farmers to reveal their hidden stocks, carry away this food and grain, and protect it from hungry marauders while it was stored and moved to the cities. This "army" lost thousands of lives to irate farmers.

Most of the massacres for which the Russian civil war of 1918–21 became infamous were committed by VCheka Troops and their auxiliaries. When they captured former White-held areas they unleashed murderous wrath. In Kiev the Chekas arrested a thousand and, with the troops' help, slaughtered most of them. Later, when White forces retook Kiev and other cities like Kharkov, Odessa, and Tsaritsyn (later Stalingrad and still later Volgograd), they found the grisly evidence: parts of bodies, torture instruments, graves, and other evidence of mass killings (five thousand in Tsaritsyn alone, thousands in Odessa). Faced (like the Nazis in their "final solution" twenty years later) with the technical problem of how to kill so many people so fast, the Chekas found it convenient to load many onto barges and sink them in the sea. Estimates of killings in the Crimea alone at this time run from 50,000 to 150,000.[20]

---

††Later Lenin also wrote, "We actually took from the peasant all his surpluses and sometimes even a part of his necessities to meet the army's requirements and to sustain the workers" (cited by Gerson, p. 182).

The end of the civil war did not reduce the winners' need for VCheka Troops. On the contrary, in the six months between late 1920 and mid-1921 their numbers were doubled, from 68,000 to 137,000 men, to fight peasants and workers who kept rising up in arms—in the single month of February 1921, by official count, 118 times.[21] More than 50,000 joined the year-long uprising in Tambov province under Antonov in 1921–22. When the Kuban Cossacks rose in arms that same year it took large army forces accompanied by VCheka Troops to crush them. Sympathizing soldiers deserted and joined these uprisings and sometimes mutinied in whole units. In Smolensk, for instance, VCheka Troops and army units shot 1,200 mutineers; in Bryansk, hundreds. Armed rebels, defamed then as now by the regime's appellation of "bandits," fought on. In the single year 1924 the regime killed and captured 500 "bandit leaders" and 14,000 of their followers.[22]

VCheka Troops faced industrial workers as enemies, too. The harsh discipline, low wages, and worsening conditions brought strikes, riots, and rebellions, of which the most dangerous to the regime was the already mentioned Kronstadt uprising in February and March 1921.

Internal Troops marched along when the Red Army at the end of the civil war moved out against the border nations who had naively accepted Lenin's promise of self-determination. They helped "normalize" the Ukraine and Byelorussia, Transcaucasia and Central Asia, shooting, jailing, and deporting people who opposed or might be likely to oppose the Sovietization of their country. Then they stayed on to fight rebellions and guerrilla resistance, which in the Ukraine and Cental Asia lasted for two decades.

In 1928 Stalin set out to drive the farmers into collectives and thereby to eliminate that permanent threat to Soviet power, the independent farmer on his own land. This violent task could not be entrusted to a peasant-based conscript army, so Stalin vastly expanded the Internal Troops (by then called OGPU Troops), set up schools to train new officers for them in a hurry, equipped them with more trucks than equivalent Red Army units possessed (so that after quelling one outbreak they could move quickly to the next one), and sent them out in a pattern of activity that was already familiar. First they helped arrest and deport as "enemies of the people" the potential resisters who had been identified by the OGPU in each community, and then they helped remove the most successful and competent farmers (condemned on various pretexts such as "tax evasion"). Just as they were to do when they deported whole nations late in the Second World War, the troops separated families and packed the victims tightly into cattle cars from which, after weeks of travel with little or no food, the survivors were dropped out in the empty wastes of Siberia or Kazakhstan without equipment, shelter, or other means of survival.

When farmers resisted with whatever weapons they could find—sometimes pitchforks—Internal Troops cut them down with machine guns, rifles, and sabers. When whole villages joined to fight together, the troops crushed them with artillery fire and cavalry charges, shot the ringleaders (and often their families), burned the villages, and led the survivors off to the camps.

In those same years of the late 1920s and early 1930s this agrarian society was being industrialized by force—often the force of Internal Troops. Among their tasks was blocking the escape route of workers fleeing oppressive factory conditions. Checking papers at key points, they marched off the offenders to imprisonment or to places where their labor was needed.

Beyond the frontiers their role continued even after they had pacified Central Asia. In 1933 a Moslem uprising in Sinkiang raised in the Kremlin the specter of Moslem influences leaking into areas of Central Asia where anti-Soviet resistance still flickered. So—as later in Afghanistan—Stalin's agents helped organize a coup d'etat which brought to power in 1933 a new warlord (Sheng Shi-Tsai) to whom they then sent military aid in the form of two brigades of NKVD Troops (as the VV were then known). They marched in at the beginning of 1934 and were ostensibly withdrawn the following year, but one regiment stayed for six years, in Chinese uniforms, to help Sheng put down revolts and to prepare the area for eventual Soviet takeover. They recruited their own secret agents and murdered anti-Soviets. The Chinese governor of Yarkand, for example, was an NKVD agent; when Moscow sent word that he was "working for the British," the local NKVD assassinated him. Soviet officers interrogated prisoners, charged them with being spies, and (using their own Kirgiz troops) shot and secretly buried them in groups of fifty to seventy at a time. All this work of Internal Troops remained hidden from the public, then and now. "It was a standing order that any strangers who might discover the secret of what was going on should be executed along with the prisoners."[23]

For the great purges of the mid-1930s—which permanently cowed Soviet society—the Internal Troops were augmented yet again. Huge numbers were needed, for they were to bear a major share of the work of arresting, transporting, and guarding the victims. By reasonable estimates, some eight million people were arrested—and all found guilty and punished—in little more than two years. In every town of any size, Internal Troops stood by with armored cars, horse cavalry, and machine guns to handle the prisoners and to prevent or put down resistance. Orders (documentary copies of which have been obtained from captured Soviet files) went out from NKVD headquarters ordering 10,000 arrests here, 1,000 shootings there. The obedient tribunals issued death sentences so fast that the NKVD could hardly keep up. Several times a day Internal Troops took groups of twenty or more from their crowded cells* out into prison yards or fields (some close to heavily populated areas), shot them, and buried them on the spot. The German invaders later found some of these mass graves; 95 of them in Vinnitsa held 9,439 bodies shot in 1937 or 1938, as determined by pathology tests conducted by an international commission.[24] Other mass graves—and the Internal Troops' role not only in the massacres but in helping the KGB to cover up the evidence as recently as 1987 and 1988—have come to light. The burial pit of victims murdered by Internal Troops in 1937 near the Kiev-area village of Bykovniya was covered up by the VV in 1988 with a monument attributing the "6,329" killings to "the fascist occupiers in 1941–43" (local citizens estimated the number at more than 100,000). In the Kuropaty forest near Minsk in Byelorussia, an estimated 200,000 bodies were found in five hundred communal graves.[25]

In 1939 and 1940, by Stalin's arrangement with Hitler, new nations were opened to Soviet invasion and occupation: Estonia, Latvia, Lithuania, Bessarabia, Bukovina, and much of Poland. The familiar routine of "Sovietization" now began again: Internal Troops arrested, brutally interrogated, and shot community leaders, and deported to concentration camps masses of people fitting into "dangerous" categories. In the twenty months up to the German invasion of the USSR in June 1941, Internal Troops took from the Soviet-occupied half of Poland about one in every five men, women, and children, whom they had labeled as "class enemies" and "nationalists," including nearly a quarter-million troops of the Polish Army.[26]

Then the Germans invaded the Soviet Union, on June 22, 1941. Stalin was aware that many of his subjects welcomed the arrival of foreign armies as a deliverance from Soviet rule; between two and three million Soviet soldiers had surrendered by October, and the front was giving way. Border and Internal Troops reportedly stood up to the German assault better than most. There was a reason: caught between a German invader who would execute them as Communist activists and a population of Byelorussians or Ukrainians or Balts who hated them as oppressors, the troops had little

---

*In Vinnitsa, a town with a population of fewer than 100,000, the jails held 15,000 prisoners in town, 12,000 more in a nearby quarry. Cells designed for 5 commonly held 60 or more; in Vinnitsa 370 were confined in a cell designed for 18. These statistics come from reports of the Germans who captured the town in 1941.

alternative. When the German advance overwhelmed their front, they would doff the insignia of their "special purpose" and try to blend in with retreating soldiers; when recognized by local populations they were massacred or handed over to the Germans.

To save Soviet rule from the people's wrath, Stalin drafted new laws against "spreading rumors and panic" (i.e., telling about the retreat or complaining of short rations), arrested several generals, loosed the Chekists to make mass arrests, and—while issuing appeals to the people to fight for Mother Russia—gathered his loyal Internal Troops around him. The task of defending the capital he assigned to the former Internal Troops Maj. Gen. Artemyev, with trusted NKVD generals in key posts. They brought an end to the panic and looting, mobilized the population to dig trenches and build fortifications, and called up a volunteer "people's militia" to supplement the depleted troops at the front.

Even as the Germans advanced toward Moscow and Leningrad the Internal Troops concentrated as much on defending the regime from its internal opponents as on defending the country. They herded populations eastward to keep them under Kremlin control. Using railway cars desperately needed for supplying the battle front, they moved thousands of political prisoners eastward to prevent their liberation by the Germans. When they lacked time or means of transport, they would simply kill them with grenades or machine-gun fire. The Germans found the bodies in prison cells along their route of advance.

Although the Germans were approaching Moscow, Stalin decided defiantly to hold the traditional parade on the anniversary of the October Revolution. But, unknown to the population or the outside world, the troops that Stalin caused to pass briefly through Red Square on that now-famous day contained not a single unit from the army defending Moscow. All were special-purpose troops—whose special purpose was to protect the leaders against their own people. (Stalin took the same precautions for the historic victory parade in Moscow on June 24, 1945: no frontline fighting unit was invited to march, but only some of their individual heroes—carefully frisked for weapons by State Security—were compelled to march with units from the Internal Troops' Dzerzhinsky Division.)

Nine divisions of Internal Troops were formed for frontline combat to meet the desperate needs of 1941–43. By 1942, one Internal Troops division was assigned to each front to guard its rear, some in so-called blocking detachments (*zagraditelnyye otryady*) to enforce Stalin's order against retreat. Caught retreating by these NKVD units, soldiers were shot or assigned to punishment battalions with suicidal missions.

At the same time, they continued to fight armed uprisings in the interior. In 1942, for example, it took two Internal Troops divisions from

Tashkent to put down an insurrection in the Kara-Kalpak region of Central Asia, while others in the Penza region fought rebels who had been joined by thousands of armed men, including a mutinous brigade of the Red Army. In the Urals, "green partisans" fought off Internal Troops artillery and air strikes.

When the tide turned and the Soviet armies advanced over lands the Germans had held, Internal Troops faced new tasks in support of frontline units of SMERSH (the State Security's military security and counterintelligence service then nominally subordinated to the supreme military command). SMERSH not only set out to find and deal with those who had helped the German occupiers but went further to strike down anyone who, during his brief "liberation," may have revealed anti-Soviet feelings—and used this pretext to rid the regime of other potential opponents such as priests and intellectuals. SMERSH used Internal Troops to conduct the executions—public hangings, individual or mass shootings—and to carry off hundreds of thousands of people to prison and death elsewhere. Regime historians put it this way: Internal Troops "were responsible for keeping order near the fronts, fighting enemy intelligence and subversive groups, guarding important communications, constructing defensive installations, convoying and guarding prisoners of war as well as persons sentenced by the Soviet courts for major crimes. [They] did garrison duty in towns liberated from fascist occupation, acting as an aid to local organs of the NKVD [from 1943, primarily SMERSH and, when the front moved on, NKGB] to render harmless enemy agents left behind on Soviet territory, unmasking traitors and enemy collaborators."[27]

When Stalin ordered the deportation of whole nations whom he considered disloyal to Soviet rule—Volga Germans, Karachai, Kalmyks, Chechen-Ingush, Balkar, Crimean Tatars, Greeks from the Black Sea coast, Kurds, and others—it was mostly Internal Troops who executed the commands of the top-level State Security leaders who ran the operations. Chekists and Internal Troops were assembled from all over the USSR so that widespread tasks could be performed in one quick stroke to prevent the victims from sensing and evading the terrible thing that was about to happen to them. Internal Troops shot resisters and indiscriminately herded old men, pregnant women, and children into rail cars for shipment to deserted areas of Kazakhstan where they were thrown out to fend for themselves.[28]

As Soviet forces in 1944 and 1945 rolled back into the western parts of the country and beyond, Internal Troops began fighting on a new front: whole divisions went into action against the armed resistance which sprang up. The longest of these campaigns—against guerrillas in the Ukraine, Byelorussia, and Lithuania—stretched into the 1950s.

In Poland and other parts of Eastern Europe, Internal Troops got help from local forces that the Soviets had created in their own image: Internal Troops, Border Troops, and, of course, State Security. Manned by trusted Communists, some of whom had spent the war in the Soviet Union and fought in Soviet units, these new forces were commanded by veteran Soviet officers wearing local uniforms and sometimes assuming native-sounding names even when they had not mastered the local language.††

Internal Troops carried much of the burden of processing the emaciated Soviet soldiers who were returning home from their mistreatment and starvation in German prisoner-of-war camps: on Stalin's orders they arrested most of them as "traitors"—for Stalin had ordered Soviet soldiers not to surrender—and led them off to Soviet prison camps with ten-year sentences.

Stalin's postwar repression denied the increased freedom the people had expected to follow the victory. Their disappointment, combined with strains of poverty, harsh conditions of life, and the soldiers' problems in adjusting to civilian life, produced a dangerous mix. Again and again it exploded. By the spring of 1947 hungry Leningraders had rioted so often that the political leaders, judging the situation too volatile for the unreliable police to handle, replaced the Leningrad Militia with a division of Internal Troops. In Odessa that same spring, disabled war veterans put on their medals and gathered near government offices to demand improvements in their living conditions. Sailors and marines from ships in the harbor joined them, and the militia (with many demobilized men in its ranks) refused to intervene. It took a division of Internal Troops to restore

††In Bulgaria, Hungary, and Czechoslovakia, where for a while democracy survived, these new Soviet-style internal and border troops played a role in the final Communist takeover of power.

In Czechoslovakia the Soviets were so impatient that they jumped the gun: in 1945 through the Czech Communists they created a semiofficial "Special Readiness Battalion" (*pohotovostniplik*) of some 1,700 reliable young Communists. The still-democratic government and the public reacted so strongly that they had to disband it in the fall of 1946. Not to be denied this essential power factor, the Communist-run Interior Ministry simply moved the newly created and highly mobile Border Guards, four times as numerous, into the interior to take over the same role—and they were outside Prague to support the Communist coup in February 1948. After the coup, with no more resistance, the new regime—under Soviet control—set up its own Internal Troops, or "Guard of the Interior."

In Hungary, too, the new Soviet-style, Soviet-controlled Border Guards became the party's private army—and a force accelerating the takeover—even before the 1948 coup. Set up in 1946, they soon numbered 15 battalions, two-thirds as large as Hungary's armed forces. After the coup the Soviet-led Hungarian State Security (*Allamvedelmi Hatosag,* or AVH) set up its own internal troops in the form of "special battalions" with artillery and armor.

order.§§ Similar hardships, facing the same governmental indifference or paralysis, triggered the winter events in Bezymyanka near Kuybyshev, already described.

Neither the end of the war nor Stalin's death in 1953 did much to ease this unrest; it has kept Internal Troops busy and alert to the present day.

The Permanent Guard

Resentments have always smoldered under the seeming passivity of Soviet society. Today they feed on shortages of food and goods and housing, restrictions on private life, unequal opportunity, stupid mismanagement and corruption, cruel and illegal punishments, ethnic tensions, and more. It takes only a small spark to light a flame: an ethnic taunt or an argument over a taxi fare, a dance-hall brawl or a tussle between football fans, or the excitement of people gathering for a historical anniversary, a folk festival, or religious observance. Violence can break out when anything changes, for better or for worse, in the tightly stretched conditions of life.

So widely are these grievances shared throughout the country, moreover, that a spark in one place can ignite a general conflagration and threaten Soviet rule. The Kremlin leaders are sharply aware of this; Gorbachev noted in March 1988 that the violence in parts of Armenia and Azerbaijan threatened "to undo the work of seventy years."

Gorbachev's reforms sought to alleviate these tensions, but in the short term they were increasing the danger. By bringing problems out into the open and inviting people to face them; *glasnost* and *perestroika* were stirring the ashes. Hardly had Gorbachev promised to reexamine the Stalinist past, for instance, than his forces had to break up a demonstration in Moscow (in March 1988) demanding just that.

So the party leaders need their own military force. Neither the Soviet Army nor militia can be relied upon in such situations. The army's soldiers, although assigned far from their home areas and ceaselessly indoctrinated, are likely to sympathize with the local population. An army tank officer was seen to commit suicide when ordered to fire upon the demonstrators in Novocherkassk in 1962 before the Internal Troops moved in. The police too have proved unsteady in the face of mass unrest; they or their weapons went over to the side of those demonstrators near Kiev in 1982 just as they had done a generation earlier in Bezymyanka.

Thus the VV—more numerous and better armed today than ever

§§The Ocessa events were reported by a Soviet marine who witnessed the events and later escaped to the West, where I had access to his reports.

before—stands as witness to the permanent insecurity of Soviet power. During the turbulent revolutionary and civil war period when the regime was most at risk, it had about 137,000 VCheka Troops plus some 94,000 Border Guard Troops and 281,000 auxiliary troops (including ChON). In the late 1980s, claiming the wholehearted support of its people, it maintained twice as many: more than 250,000 Internal Troops, 75,000 KGB Troops, 300,000 Border Troops, and approximately 400,000 in organizations equivalent to those earlier auxiliaries.

The troops' mission remains unchanged. As in June 1918 they "secure Soviet power inside the country." To this end, they perform "urgent military tasks" that are designed to "preserve public order."[29] This requires them "often to meet face to face with enemy elements and decisively put a stop to their criminal activities."[30]

Atop their basic training along the lines of standard Soviet Army regulations and doctrine, these troops are taught how to handle uprisings and riots, raid and search city buildings and rural settlements, subdue their inhabitants, inspect documents, investigate, make individual and mass arrests, and cut off whole regions from the outside.

Wherever the threat to the regime seems sharpest—where outbreaks have most often broken out or where the KGB's latest information points to imminent trouble—the VV stands ready. The most sensitive areas are always the key cities, Moscow, Leningrad, and Kiev, and the nations where Russian rule is resented: the Baltic republics, Western Ukraine and Western Byelorussia, the Caucasian republics, and Central Asia.

In the latter areas the VV assumes the character of colonial troops: they assure Moscow's grip on the outlying republics. The leaders do not let the troops serve in their own republics but instead exploit racial hostilities to defend their own power. They post Kazakhs, Uzbeks, and Kirgiz, for instance, in the Russian and other republics.

At least one VV division is garrisoned as a full division: the First Dzerzhinsky Motorized Division in Moscow. At least until the 1950s, to my personal knowledge, there was a "Second Motorized Division" outside the capital. The rest of the troops are managed by divisional headquarters responsible for broad areas but garrisoned as independent regiments, battalions, and companies.

While the troops wait for emergencies they play the passive role of "guarding state installations."[31] A new decree in mid-1988 defined their functions as "protecting public order, state installations, special cargoes, corrective-labor facilities, and education and labor clinics." Their commander noted the troops' role in mass events. He added, significantly, "They have a number of other tasks, too."[32] Garrisoned near major cities, they stand guard over important party and scientific installations, strategic industries, bridges, and rail centers, sharing the task with other elements including special troops of the KGB, which are discussed in a later chapter.

They also help patrol the dangerous streets of some crime-ridden cities and help the militia capture groups of armed criminals. They help control crowds and cordon off the areas of earthquakes, floods, fires, river shipwrecks, or manmade disasters like the nuclear leaks at Chernobyl.

Even the regime's own manifestations bring Internal Troops to the alert: on May Day, for example, and for celebrations of the October Revolution anniversary, and when leaders die. Three times during the early 1980s Westerners could see in press photos and on television the eerie emptiness of central Moscow, ringed by the VV after the deaths in quick succession of Brezhnev, Andropov, and Chernenko. The leaders evidently fear that any mass gathering, however carefully organized or solemn, may turn against them.

Thus it was that in March 1989, at the height of the first contested election since 1917 and one that they described as an expression of popular support for their programs, the worried leaders moved the VV's Dzerzhinsky Division into Moscow and other units—with no previous ties to the military commanders on normal duty there—into Leningrad.[33]

Although a powerful force in its own right, the VV is but an auxiliary to more commanding institutions of Soviet coercion, which we will examine in detail. But to fully sense these troops' role in the system—and the reason for their survival throughout Soviet history—we must first step back and recall the roots from which they spring.

CHAPTER 3

The Roots of Coercion

Lenin's Institutions

LENIN VIEWED POLITICS AND GOVERNMENT AS WARFARE. HIS FAMOUS question, "*Kto kogo?*"—Who will beat (or dominate) whom?—set the tone. His was a world of struggle, his program a march, society an armory of weapons (schools and the press, for example, he called "sharp weapons" and the law "a mailed fist"), and those who disagreed were "enemies." After he had taken power Lenin admitted that "a socialist revolution is inconceivable without internal war even more devastating than external war."[1] The most characteristic institutions of the system that he created and his successors built up—and that today's leaders continue to promote—are, essentially, institutions of internal warfare.

They *concentrate all power* in the hands of a single party subjected, under military-style *discipline*, to the *centralized* command of a *narrow* and *exclusive* leadership legitimized by an all-knowing *ideology*. Each of these six characteristics demands the use or threat of violent coercion and draws the instrument of that coercion (today called KGB) into the innermost core and topmost echelons of the rulership. To the extent that any of these underlying principles is eroded, so too is the KGB, and with it the power monopoly of the Communist leaders.

But their system has led the country into economic and social catastrophe and today the Kremlin masters face the difficult—and perhaps impossible—task of changing it without undermining the principles that uphold their power.

They are keenly aware of the danger. When they saw some of these principles crumbling under their satellite rulers in Poland in 1981, Czechoslovakia in 1968, and Hungary in 1956, they expressed their fears openly and reacted with violent force. Now those principles are eroding again, this time also in the USSR itself. How far can they let this continue before their power crumbles? Neither they nor anyone else, inside or outside the Soviet Union, knows the precise answer.

Let's look, then, at each of these foundations of Leninism—these roots of coercion—with an eye to signs of erosion.

All Power to the Party!

When the party leaders changed the Soviet constitution in late 1988, they were indirectly admitting what had long been obvious: that the constitution had been deceptive. The highest authority in the land was not, as Soviet constitutions had always maintained, those councils of people's deputies (soviets) for which Lenin had seized "all power" but instead the meddlesome, manipulative, self-sustaining bureaucracy of a single party. Now, Gorbachev's men claimed, they wanted to turn over some real independence and authority to the soviets.

Gorbachev pretended that this would return things to Lenin's ways. In the good old days under Lenin, he said, the soviets had "made decisions and implemented them on their own . . . under open control of all those whom their moves might concern." According to his disingenuous version the soviets were "somehow pushed back" only by the advent of the "command-economy system of management"—meaning Stalin's reforms of 1928.[2] But Gorbachev knew perfectly well that the subservience of the soviets to the Communist Party is Lenin's own legacy. It was Lenin who "pushed back" the soviets, and he did it soon after he took power. He destroyed all other parties (and the possibility of creating other parties), built a centralized hierarchy within the system of soviets (assigning the soviets' powers to their leaderships—called "executive committees"—and subordinating these to higher executive committees),[*] and simultaneously took power away from all levels. Already by the spring of 1919, Trotsky wrote later, "the Central Executive Committee had lost all its actual power to the Central Committee of the Party. . . . Locally the soviet committees were entirely subservient to the corresponding party committees."[3]

That was and is the reality—but the Communist Party leaders have had to pay lip service to a myth (embodied in the country's deceptive name, "Soviet Union") that power lies where Lenin's slogan—"All power to the soviets!"—promised to deliver it when his Bolsheviks overthrew a nascent parliamentary democracy. In 1989 when Moscow television announced the

---

[*]A hierarchy topped by what was first called the All-Union Central Executive Committee (VTsIK) and renamed by Stalin's 1936 constitution as Presidium of the Supreme Soviet. Some local officials quickly recognized, and expressed by March 1919, this "tendency to liquidate the soviets in favor of a government of executive committees."

results of the first contested election in Soviet history—still dominated and controlled by the single party—the announcer sat in front of a red poster bearing that simple slogan, offering mute proof of the embattled party's continued reliance on the myth. As Gorbachev wrote, "If there had been no soviets we [meaning the Bolsheviks] would not have won the Civil War. If there had been no soviets, we would not have succeeded in rallying millions of people, notably workers and peasants, in so vast a country."[4]

The lip service has been embodied in constitutions. When drafting the first ones in 1918 and 1924, in a time when their power was still shaky, the rulers dared not even mention the existence of their party. Only after they had finally closed their grip—by collectivizing the peasants and assuring the servility of the bureaucracy by purge and terror—did they feel confident enough to do that. Stalin admitted this when he introduced in 1936 the first constitution that mentioned the party.[†] Even then the party's first constitutional appearance was a modest one, far down in the 126th article and presented only briefly and vaguely as the "leading core" of all Soviet institutions. Forty years after that the party rulers felt confident enough, if not to dispel the myth, at least to raise this article to a more prominent place.

That one article, now Article 6 of the USSR Constitution of 1977, admitted a glimpse of reality. The Communist Party of the Soviet Union (CPSU), it says, is "the leading and guiding force of Soviet society and the nucleus of its political system, of all state and public and social organizations." The party "determines the general perspectives of the development of society and the course of the home and foreign policy of the USSR, directs the great constructive work of the Soviet people, and imparts a planned, systematic, and theoretically sound character to their struggle for the victory of communism."

Party documents and Soviet textbooks have been more explicit. The 1986 Party Program said that "all other components of [Soviet society's political] system—the Soviet state, the trade unions, the Komsomol, and the cooperatives and other social organizations . . . function under [the party's] leadership." A Soviet dictionary in 1984 put it this way: "The policy of the Communist Party determines the entire life of society under socialism." "Not one important decision concerning the general problems of state activity," wrote an academic, "is taken without the directives of

---

[†]Stalin wrote in 1936 that at the time of the previous constitution (1924), "the old question 'Who will win?' [*Kto kogo?*] had not yet been settled. . . . The state farms and collective farms were mere islands in a boundless ocean of individual peasant farms. . . . Entirely different was the picture in 1936."—*History of the CPSU (Bolshevik)* (Moscow: 1939), p. 342.

the party." "Every act of the Soviet state—a statute, an edict of the Presidium of the Supreme Soviet, the decrees and decisions of the government, the orders and instructions and decisions of a minister, the decisions of the local soviet—all of them express the policy of the Communist Party."[5]

Under this guiding hand the rest of the institutions of the Soviet system were reduced to the role of advisory bodies or transmission belts for the party bosses. This is the meaning of the phrase "the leading role of the party."

Gorbachev's constitutional reforms of 1988 were designed, he said, to draw a more distinct line between party and state and to grant the soviets more independence and authority. In order to judge how much more, it is useful to recall the institutions he supplanted.

Earlier, the members of the soviets were routinely picked by the party bosses—one candidate for each seat. These they drew from three general categories. To holders of key jobs in party, state, trade union, and public organizations, "election" came automatically. To other individuals, who had demonstrated lifetime fidelity to the party line, it came as a reward: brief glory and a few days' paid holiday in the faraway, better-fed capital. Still others were tokens—cosmonauts, dairymaids, "shock workers of socialist labor," and tribesmen from exotic regions, for instance—chosen to create an outward show of national cohesion, progress, and democracy. Numbering about fifteen hundred (of whom about three-quarters were party members), the deputies to the Supreme Soviet met only twice a year for three or four days, during which time they managed to "consider" dozens of decrees, decisions, and resolutions which, while ostensibly prepared by their own Presidium, had really been worked out by the Secretariat of the Central Committee of the CPSU and rubber-stamped by a plenary meeting of the Central Committee in preparation for the added rubber stamp of the Supreme Soviet. In its half-century of existence the Supreme Soviet never rejected any measure submitted to it; and although they went through the motions of voting, not one of the thousands of deputies over the decades ever voted against anything. The first few daring "no" votes were cast in October 1988.

When the Supreme Soviet was not in session its powers were exercised by a Presidium of thirty-nine leading or obedient party members who left their day-to-day work not to standing committees (which were few and inactive) but to a permanent staff—each of whose departments was guided and controlled by a parallel department of the party apparatus. Similarly at lower levels the work of soviets was left to executive committees and, further, to their leaderships (buros and secretariats). And all these executives were subject to party discipline and responsive to parallel departments of the local party organization.

These soviet deputies were called "servants of the people"; and as long as one avoids confusing the "people" with the "population" or the "citizenry," the term was apt. In Communist doctrine the will of the people is embodied in, and their interests expressed by, the Communist Party, which calls itself the people's "brain" and "heart" and "vanguard." Because the decisive power within the party is reserved to a narrow leadership, the "people" means a small group of Communist Party bosses. In this light the bold opening words of the USSR Constitution—"All power belongs to the people"—become understandable, and one sees the truth underlying the constitution's claim that the "people" exercise their total power through the soviets—their "servants."

This constitutional fraud was widely recognized, of course, but seldom expressed openly until Gorbachev prepared to change its format. In May 1988 a political philosopher admitted that constitutional rights had become meaningless because "real power remains behind the scenes." Referring to the 1977 USSR Constitution he noted how terms like the "sovereignty of the people" and the "sovereignty of the laws" really meant the "sovereignty of the party." What exactly does it mean, he asked, to describe the party as the "leading and guiding force"? In what laws, acts, or instructions is it embodied and how in practice is the leading and guiding accomplished? He called for "a new law on the party" to establish publicly "the forms and methods of party leadership at all levels, the party's relations with other bodies" including the state and judiciary and the new, informal groups that have sprung up under Gorbachev's liberalizing regime.[6]

In the fall of 1988 Gorbachev and his followers changed some aspects of the system. For one thing, they offered the prospect of a more democratic vote. Instead of a single candidate imposed upon them by the party, voters might have a choice between two or even more. "Public organizations" (party approved and dominated) could select candidates of their own for seats reserved for them (eventually some such seats might be allocated to organizations independent of the party). Such candidates, and others, are voted into a huge new body called the "Congress of People's Deputies" (50 percent bigger even than the former Supreme Soviet and meeting just as rarely) where among other responsibilities they pick between 400 and 450 of their members to serve in a smaller body that took over the old name of Supreme Soviet. The latter stays in more or less permanent session and (according to the theory) makes laws with a minimum of party supervision.

At the same time the party itself shook up its own internal structure that supervises state and society. Until 1989 it was a huge secretariat of the Central Committee (CC) (and at lower levels, the secretariat of party committees) that had handled the party's day-to-day oversight of government, the economy, and society. With about twenty departments permanently at work, the CC CPSU Secretariat had effectively replaced the CC which met only infrequently and briefly. Now, with the stated aim of shifting power back to the Central Committee, the reformers set up six permanent commissions of CC members, each headed by a Politburo member or CC CPSU secretary, to oversee a broad area of state and society (including the work of one or two departments of the secretariat). That secretariat was slashed by about half its functionaries and lost a number of departments that had been overseeing industry. Henceforth, the reformers promised, the party would limit itself to political and ideological guidance and leave the oversight of the economy to the soviets without party interference.

But would these new structures really transfer executive power from the party? Would they really free the soviets from party manipulation, as Gorbachev promised? Neither history nor the details of Gorbachev's rearrangements offered grounds for optimism.

For example, Gorbachev seemed simply to be repeating old themes. Lenin had also insisted that the party stay apart from the workings of the soviets (indeed, he called it "impermissible" to confound party and soviet work)—yet while so saying, he was busily taking real authority away from them. He ostensibly limited the party's role to "political leadership, without any substitution in the activity of" the soviets—precisely what Gorbachev was saying seventy years later. Lenin worked out formulas like this: "Party leadership may be compared with the art of the conductor, who strives for harmony but, of course, does not try to play for every musician." His successors Stalin and Khrushchev and Brezhnev played the same theme, usually citing Lenin's words.[7] But in sharp contrast to these pious words, the party has never relinquished even a fraction of its tight control. Every twist and turn of Soviet history has been interpreted as increasing, never diminishing, the party's responsibilities—and in this respect Gorbachev's *perestroika* is no exception.

The end of the civil war, for example, and the crushing of the last significant uprisings and foreign interventions in the early 1920s seemed to remove the need for leadership by these militant cadres. They had, after all, ostensibly seized power for the people and now might be time to hand it over. So in 1923 some delegates confronted a party congress (the last under Lenin's rule) with the proposition that the "soviet apparatus should be allowed to manage things independently, so the party should not have so much influence." Lenin evidently disagreed, and his Politburo lieuten-ant Grigoriy Zinoviev warned, "No one but a clever enemy would so much as suggest moving the Communist Party even a little to one side from the soviet apparatus [or] demand any division of function between them. The party must hold the state apparatus completely in its hands." That congress laid the matter to rest: "At the present moment," it resolved, "the Communist Party directs and must direct all the political and cultural work of the organs of state power; directs and must direct the activity of all economic organs of the republic."[8]

That "present moment" never ended. The last remnants of the pre-revolutionary society died out, Stalin passed away, the people became better educated, and the system failed, eroding the rulers' credence and the ideology that upheld them. Then in 1960 the party leaders proclaimed the end of the "dictatorship of the proletariat" and the advent of a "state of all the people." Might that not have been the logical moment for it finally to step aside? Quite the contrary, replied its ideologues: its role must grow. Now the party ("the brain of the Soviet people") "extended its guiding influence to all spheres of social life." "The period of full-scale Communist construction is characterized by a further enhancement of the role and importance of the Communist Party as the leading and guiding force of Soviet society," said the Party Program of 1961. What party leaders meant was that the party's rule would never end, and they were openly teaching this to would-be revolutionaries in foreign countries. "After the revolution the role of the Marxist party as leader of the working class and all the working people not only does not decrease but, on the contrary, becomes immeasurably greater. It now becomes responsible for everything that goes on in society, for the policy of the state . . . , for the development of productive forces and culture, for the improvement of the people's welfare."[9]

Amid the people's flush of enthusiasm for the democracy they were allowed to glimpse in the 1989 elections to the Congress of People's Deputies, voices (some of them within the party itself) called for a multiparty system. Still the leaders stayed determined. The party's chief ideologue declared it "obvious that the party's leading role cannot be diminished . . . On the contrary, we intend to intensify its influence on social processes."[10] The "new historical conditions" marked by Gor-bachev's reforms "naturally" expand the party's responsibilities.[11] Making no distinction between Gorbachev's reforms and earlier "sharp turns," Politburo member Viktor Chebrikov pointed out that "the role of the party is especially great at sharp turns in social development."[12]

Why? Answering this question its spokesmen, under Gorbachev as under Khrushchev, got mired in specious pleading. Like its 1961 predecessor the 1986 Party Program listed the "basic factors" conditioning the "natural" growth of the party's leading role. They included "the increased dimensions and complexity of the tasks of improving socialism and accelerating the country's socioeconomic development," "the intensification of democracy," "the people's involvement in the management of production and state and social affairs," "the search for scientifically substantiated and timely answers to the questions set by life," the interests of "strengthening the unity of the international Communist, workers', and national liberation movement," "the complication of foreign policy conditions connected with the growth of imperialist aggressiveness,"—and, of course, "the need to ensure the country's security."

But justifications and rationalizations aside, it had long since become "difficult"—as Konstantin Chernenko admitted with a bit of understatement in 1980—"to examine the activity of the party apparatus in isolation, apart from its ties with the work of state and economic administration. Their close interaction is today an inalienable trait of the leadership style of the party organs."[13] It certainly is. Even before Gorbachev openly unified the overall leadership of party and state, members of the party's Politburo and republic buros simultaneously commanded government ministries as well as the soviet executive committees. All key positions in the state and social organizations were reserved for selected party members who, as individuals, remained under strict party discipline. Before any functionary of a ministry or executive committee—no matter that he himself was a party member—decided on policy or personnel matters, he referred to his "guide" within the party bureaucracy. At the working level in each state institution or factory, the party members are grouped in a primary party organization that sees to the execution of the party leaders' will. "Control organizations," run by the party and heavily staffed by party members, check from within "on the fulfillment of state plans . . . and help improve the working of the state machinery."[14] These are but a few of the mechanisms through which the party is inextricably mixed with all the organizations of the state.

The party meant to keep its monopoly of power, as Gorbachev demonstrated in late 1988 by formally merging in one person the command of party and government—and by calling the idea of more than one party "rubbish."[16] At each regional level from top to bottom the party chief was to become head of the soviet. Until that time the local party chief had been compelled to manage the state indirectly, the chairman of the local soviet executive committee being subjected to his party discipline within the party buro. Now even the facade of separation tumbled, and many Soviet citizens, some prominent, objected to this concentration of power. Andrey Sakharov called it "insane." Although past general secretaries of the CC CPSU had sometimes assumed the added role of chairman of the Presidium of the Supreme Soviet, that had been a powerless, largely ceremonial office. Now with Gorbachev's constitutional changes, the "state president" was given real executive powers over domestic and foreign policy. Like Lenin before him, Gorbachev had promised power to the state—and at the same time had taken it away. ‡

Moreover, the party kept its hold over the selection of deputies to these new bodies by insisting on its right to screen and approve candidates and reserving to itself the right to judge whether election results are valid. (In the preliminaries to the first Congress election in 1989 the party found various ways to block the candidacies it disliked.) And the formula allocating candidacies to the Congress insured a permanent and overwhelming majority for party members and other party-selected and party-approved candidates. Even more important is how these new constitutional provisions were to be interpreted and applied.

The 1989 elections gave the people an opportunity to show how deeply they resented the party's monopoly of power. They struck out the names of uncontested party candidates on ballot sheets, voted for party members who were themselves calling this monopoly into question, and overwhelmingly supported nonparty candidates.

When the party leadership kept these new, popular Congress electees from getting into the smaller and more powerful new Supreme Soviet, tens of thousands of people massed in Moscow on 28 May 1989 to protest— and one worker won "tumultuous cheers" when he shouted the truth known to all: "The party bosses are holding onto their seats only because the KGB is the guardian of the party."*

The system had also brought under party control and direction all the other organizations of society, industry, and agriculture: indirectly through the party-dominated state and directly through party oversight. Professional associations of, say, jurists, engineers, or doctors and societies with such innocuous aims as preserving cultural monuments or promoting sports were categorized as public or social (*obshchestvennyye*) organizations and drawn into a single centralized system. Theater groups and writers' clubs, for example, were subordinated to the cultural section of the district soviet executive committee. By 1930 any organization not under the party/state aegis was illegal.

‡Through this arrangement Gorbachev also anchored his personal power more firmly. Now, while the Central Committee might vote him out as party chief, the constitution would make it difficult for the CC to remove the "popularly elected"—and powerful—executive boss of the state.

*Daily Telegraph, London 29 May 1989.

The regime formed its own mass organizations to ensure a grip over everyone. Workers, for example, were grouped in associations (*profsoyuzy,* misleadingly translated as "trade unions"), today numbering more than 140 million members, capped by an All-Union Central Council of Trade Unions. Young people between 14 and 28 years old were assembled in units of a Communist Youth league (Komsomol), today about 40 million strong. Even children from age 8 to 15 were brought together for indoctrination and service and called "Pioneers." The regime enrolled more millions in "people's control" organizations and police auxiliaries.

The leaders never hid their purpose: to harness every organized element of society to their goals. They endowed each of these organizations with a formal charter that proclaimed its purpose to "carry out the policy of the CPSU within the sphere of its activity." "Voluntary societies and unions must take part in the construction of socialism by organizing activities of the working masses to fulfill current industrial, political, and cultural tasks." Each of them was expressly "set up to act under the guidance of the Communist Party."[17] Article 51 of the USSR Constitution of 1977 specified that it is "with the aim of building communism" that people are granted the right to associate in public and social organizations.

In practice over the decades this rigid monolithic system, far from building enthusiasm for communism, spread boredom, cynicism, and passivity—and helped create the economic crisis that forced the Kremlin leadership toward *perestroika.* Gorbachev discovered—and so stated—that without genuine "grass-roots support" and participation from the people, his restructuring was doomed. The people must be encouraged to feel a part of the functioning of the system, and for this they must be allowed to know more (through *glasnost*) and communicate more freely.

Undoubtedly Gorbachev hoped that this increased popular initiative would work through the institutions that the party has created and controlled—"the work collective . . . the management system . . . party and state bodies."[18] But grass roots pushed up more grass than Gorbachev had counted on. Thousands of unauthorized clubs, organizations, or groups, dozens of them putting out journals, sprang up throughout the country: research and discussion groups (some of which conducted their own public opinion polls), activists for human rights, youth and rock music performers, sports teams breaking out from under trade union sponsorship, gatherings of would-be emigrants, historians trying to save monuments that city officials had planned to demolish, ecologists demanding the abandonment of industrial projects.

These unofficial groups—which became known as the "informals" (*nyeformalnyye*)—became bolder in 1987 and began to coordinate their activities. Hundreds of representatives held a conference in Moscow in

August; in late October editors of about two dozen independent publications from several cities gathered to inform one another (and the official press) of their work and met again in May 1988 to unite, with a charter, in order to increase their influence. In March 1988 "informal" activists gathered in Moscow to discuss human rights and the future of the USSR (although the police prevented some from participating). In early 1988 some political activists in Estonia formed a political party. In May 1988 people from twenty cities met in Moscow and joined in an all-union political organization—a party in all but name—that they called the "Democratic Union" in order to challenge not the Communist Party but (as they expressed it in a 34-page statement of principles) "the system of party autocracy" which "has become the main source of the people's trouble in the past seventy years." They called for free elections, a multiparty parliamentary system, a separation of powers between party and government, a mixed market economy, and independent trade unions.[19] In 1989 a writer in a Leningrad magazine suggested that the party should not exercise unrestrained control over anything but its own internal party affairs. He called the constitution a "sham" and pointed out that to prohibit other parties is to prohibit democracy.[20] Such demands had often been made before in *samizdat* (self-publishing by private retyping and distribution); now they were backed by organizations or published in the regime-approved press.

At first the party leaders professed to approve of these informals, and Gorbachev even promoted a notion of "socialist pluralism." But at the same time they were trying to bring some of these groupings under the official wing of the Komsomol by offering the carrot of official legitimacy and were thwarting others—for instance, outlawing private book-publishing cooperatives by denying them paper and presses.

As the movement grew bolder the leaders' alarm grew and they began to utter dark warnings, "Playing with democracy may result in catastrophe," they warned in *Pravda* in mid-November 1987 and a few weeks later complained that some informals were sponsoring illegal demonstrations, "printing and distributing anti-Soviet literature," agitating for a "surrogate culture," and "calling for the creation of opposition political parties and free trade unions." "Extremist-minded leaders" of informal associations, according to KGB Chairman Chebrikov, were trying "to lead the masses on the road to anarchy and lawlessness, towards destabilizing the situation and creating legal and illegal structures opposing the Communist Party." It was necessary to "deal a rebuff" to them.

Ominously they began to link this agitation to foreigners. Demonstrations by Crimean Tatars in Moscow in July 1987 were blamed on American Embassy instigation. In September KGB Chairman Viktor Chebrikov (while praising these groups "as a concrete manifestation of socialist democracy") said that "foreign subversive centers" were seeking to divert them "into antisocial positions and hostile activity." In April 1988 publishers of independent papers like Sergey Grigoryants of the journal *Glasnost* were accused of having participated with Western radio stations in stirring up the mass demonstrations in Armenia and riots in Azerbaijan. Chebrikov linked these demonstrations to the work of "secret services of imperialist powers and foreign anti-Soviet centers" which "actively join extremist nationalist actions."[21]

But the people's fear was dissipating and "socialist democracy" found itself confronted with demands for Western-style democracy. In the republics, independent patriotic unions that were promoting greater autonomy from Moscow—even sovereignty—put up candidates who overwhelmed the party's in the 1989 elections.

To keep a sharp eye on this menace—and to prepare to stamp it out wherever it grew too dangerous—the Kremlin leaders relied upon their KGB. In many if not all of these groupings the KGB undoubtedly recruited or inserted secret informants, not only to inform but to manipulate some of the groups for the regime's purposes. To this provocative task, as we shall see, the KGB brought tremendous experience—but it was facing a fast-growing mass movement toward democracy and away from party rule.

The Narrow Leadership

It is not really the party that leads, nor even its Central Committee. The ultimate power of decision on key questions still lies where Lenin put it: in the hands of a small group at the very top.

As early as 1902 Lenin had worked out his idea that power could be won only under the direction of a small band of full-time "professional revolutionaries." Neither the workers in their sodden masses nor the peasants in their dark ignorance could perceive their own advantage, much less fight effectively for it. They must be led and taught by a core of experts able to avoid traps, make quick decisions, and seize opportunities. These leaders would guide the overt propaganda and organize the masses through a revolutionary newspaper while themselves hiding in conspiratorial secrecy. Lenin set out this proposition in the famous pamphlet "What Is to Be Done?" which he distributed in time for the 1903 congress of the Russian Social Democratic Party. His program split the party and became the essence of Bolshevism, today called Leninism.

Although this formula had been designed for seizing rather than administering power, Lenin's conspiratorial group had no intention of letting power, once won, slip from their own hands. So they adjusted the principle to the new circumstances. As his party—that so-called "nucleus"—ballooned in size, with tens of thousands of enthusiasts and opportunists joining the winning side (by the 1980s they numbered nearly twenty million), Lenin had the formula ready: the nucleus needs its own nucleus. Working-class parties "can operate successfully only if they have stable groups of experienced, authoritative, and influential leaders. Such people constitute the leading nucleus of a party, its cadres, its elected leadership, which organizes in practice the execution of adopted decisions and ensures continuity of experience and traditions."[22]

And that nucleus of the nucleus has, in turn, its own nucleus: an inner core within the party leadership. Hardly had Lenin's men seized power than a "directing group" (or "clandestine directing circle," as Stalin called it) took the key powers—including state security and defense—into its own hands and, disregarding the other Central Committee members, made all the crucial decisions that shaped the system in its early days.[23]

As early as March 1919, at the 8th Party Congress, some party leaders argued against the formation of a Politburo. They feared that an inner circle of four or five people would make all the decisions and merely announce them to the Central Committee (which then numbered fewer than twenty members). Their foresight was quickly confirmed: only two years later, at its 10th Congress, the party agreed that the Politburo would do the day-to-day work while the Central Committee need hold only bimonthly meetings and quarterly or semiannual conferences.

Over the years the Central Committee grew to an unwieldy size; today it counts more than three hundred full members and half as many candidate members. The Politburo too has swollen. Counting its voting and nonvoting members, it now compares in size to the entire Central Committee during the early years of Soviet power—evidently beyond the narrow limits of Leninist leadership. So today as always, the highest priority decisions—"defending the revolution"—are reserved for an inner group, today's equivalent of Lenin's "clandestine directing circle," which is described in chapter 5.

The old Bolsheviks recognized that any narrow leadership can rule only by the use or threat of coercion. A scant ten days after Lenin's coup d'etat some leaders even insisted on allowing other socialists into a coalition government. When the "directing circle" categorically rejected the proposal, eleven of the fifteen members of the first Central Committee in power submitted their resignations (albeit temporarily). They recognized that without a coalition "there is only one other course: the maintenance of a purely Bolshevik government by means of political terrorism." They accused the inner group of wanting that exclusive power no matter what, "without counting the number of worker and soldier victims it may cost."[24]

They saw clearly. The narrowness of the top leadership not only gave monstrous power to the instrument of coercion, today called KGB, but also assured it a place in the highest echelon and endowed it with extraordinary missions.

The Exclusive Leadership

The party bosses have a way to ensure that none but their own kind and of their own choosing shall get his hands on the levers of power or influence—and they consider it "the most important element" in their guidance of state and society.

They call it the "cadres system" and it began with Lenin. "You will not allow important state appointments to be made by anyone but the ruling party," he commanded. "If the Central Committee is deprived of the right to distribute forces it will be unable to direct policy."[25]

In each region the party leadership has listed every job whose incumbent might make real decisions or have the power to appoint others, whether in party, state, industry, or public/social organizations: factory or trade union, radio state or newspaper, technical institute or university. Only the party leaders have the right to make appointments to this list, which they call their *nomenklatura*. Party rules define it as "the list of the most important functions, for which candidates are examined in advance, recommended, and approved by the competent Party Committee (of district, city, region, etc.)."[26]

The *nomenklatura* lists not only functions but also individuals. "Included in the *nomenklatura* are workers occupying key positions" whose functions "can be terminated only with the agreement of the Party Committee."[27] Once a member of the *nomenklatura*, an individual remains one; if he is not occupying one of its positions, he is on "reserve."§

---

§A member of the *nomenklatura* may be moved up or down or sideways at the party's whim, but with rare exceptions he will get some other job on the same or perhaps another *nomenklatura*. When Georgiy Malenkov was ousted by Khrushchev in the 1957 power fight, he moved from head of government to head of an electric-power station. Of that smaller sphere, however, he remained boss, not laborer. Vladimir Semichastniy, who disappeared from Western view after losing a similar power fight, surfaced years later as deputy chairman of the relatively unimportant Znaniye society, an organization promoting antireligious and other regime propaganda. Boris Yeltsin, Politburo and Moscow party chief, was ousted by Gorbachev in early 1988, only to become a deputy minister and rise again with the congress election of March 1989.

Whenever a *nomenklatura* position becomes available, the party may fill it with someone from outside the institution, even from outside the district.

Inevitably this system has promoted political conformity at the expense of professional competence. The route to administrative and industrial command passes exclusively through the party.

Some Western observers have discerned in official Soviet biographies the rise to power of increasing numbers of "technocrats." They call Mikhail Gorbachev a "trained lawyer" and point to other Politburo members and government ministers whose biographies show service as engineers or lawyers or factory managers. It is true that younger party leaders are better educated than their elders and have better technical qualifications and experience, but official biographies are misleading. In practice, the cadres system blocks the route to power against the genuine technocrat.

He who aspires to power must put party work ahead of anything else. In his student days he must sacrifice his studies, and later his work time, to party lecturing or helping administer trade union, Komsomol, or "people's control" bodies. Having thus demonstrated his devotion he drifts even farther from the substance of his profession. The party may arrange his formal release from some or all of his professional tasks and give him salaried work, full- or part-time, perhaps as secretary of a trade union or party primary organization. From here he becomes a candidate for higher, full-time service in the district party apparatus or in the headquarters of a public organization. And there he may come to supervise the professional field he had abandoned.

A party member who focuses on his studies and earnestly pursues his professional career is relegating party work and the party's interests to a lower priority. With talent and luck he may get ahead anyway; the party will help him rise in his profession but not in the party hierarchy where real power resides and where "industrial" or "legal" experience is largely irrelevant.

The cadres system has thus helped drag Soviet administration and industry into its present crisis. "Leninist principles for the selection of cadres are not working," admitted one regional party committee in 1987, "because of the great influence of subjective factors."[28] Inevitably it became a target for reform. In the second half of the 1980s the party leadership tried new approaches in factories, offices, and farms. In some it permitted employees to nominate their own supervisors (keeping its right of veto, of course), and in others it allowed its own nominees to be overruled by work collectives. Some reports suggested that the *nomen-klatura* for industrial positions had been reduced in size, leaving more posts available for candidates not proposed by the party organization.

But demands grew for more drastic measures, including the complete removal of party supervision from industry and agriculture. When putting into effect his constitutional reforms and inner-party restructuring in late 1988, Gorbachev promised to lighten the party's hand.

But can the reformers really take the party's hand off the controllers of industry? They are striking here against the Leninist system itself. "Party organs cannot under any circumstances be separated from economic matters," says party doctrine, "because these matters are directly and closely connected with the fundamental, vital interests of the people, with the economic and military power of the state, and with the creation of the material and technical basis of communism."[29]

There is room, of course, for some relaxation of formal party controls over all kinds of organizations, for many such controls are redundant. As we shall see, through its KGB the party leadership has many less ostentatious ways to control people and organizations. Local party bosses can reduce their interference in technical operations of factories and can cut back the number of *nomenklatura* positions. (As party doctrine puts it, "the *nomenklatura* is not fixed once and for all. The list of functions included in the *nomenklatura* is established in relation to tasks imposed by the party at a designated time."[30]) But one way or another, it can and will continue to keep its grip on controlling positions. As *Pravda* warned in late 1987, "The Communist Party is a ruling party. Its leading role is fixed by the constitution. That is why the party committees have the right to express their opinion *(sic)* on the people recommended to this or that post."[31]

And that "opinion" is formed, as always in the past, with the help of the KGB's dossiers. No one rises to any position of power without KGB approval. The cadres system has brought the KGB into the very heart of Soviet rule.

Centralism

As Gorbachev promoted new ideas like "socialist pluralism," as he encouraged factories to organize (and be responsible for) their own production, as he granted more autonomy to the republics, as he encouraged grass-roots movements to form and conflicting voices to rise, he was striking against another pillar of Leninism—and another root of violent coercion.

Lenin made it an "inviolable rule" that a "single will" must prevail. "Only a centralized leadership is capable of uniting all forces, directing them towards a single goal, and imparting unity to the uncoordinated actions of individual workers and groups of workers."[32] Within the party the guiding rule is "absolute centralization and the strictest discipline" with "subordination of the minority to the majority and unconditional obedience by lower organs to the decisions of higher-echelon organs."[33] Stalin, who inaugurated the five-year plans for Soviet industry, said that "our plans are neither predictions nor conjectures—they are directives."

This is euphemistically called "democratic centralism." The "democratic" part of this famous formula would have it that lower echelons participate in formulating the decisions that they later must obey and that higher authorities are accountable to them. This is just as meaningful as saying that a military commander consults with, and accounts to, the troops he commands; and indeed the Soviet Army's command structure is officially described as "a refraction of the principle of democratic centralism applied to conditions of the military organization."[34] The "democratic" part of the formula is thus meaningless, but the other half—"centralism"—is very real indeed.

Not only the party but all the organizations of Soviet life have been centralized. The state, for instance: "The principle of democratic centralism welds the system of soviets into a single whole [. . . with] centralized, planned guidance . . . decisions taken by higher soviets are binding on all lower ones."[35] And industry: most factories were subordinated not to the local soviet executive committee but to higher industrial organizations. Others reported to industrial departments within local soviet executive committees but these departments were primarily subordinated not to regional authorities but through a vertical chain of command to a central branch of that industry in Moscow.** A careerist heading an industrial section in a local soviet would seek his approval from higher echelons of his own industrial branch rather than from the local chairman.

This left little authority at local levels. Even a small-town youth organization, for instance, that staffed the police auxiliaries or helped the local soviet executive committee to organize unpaid "volunteer" work on the farms reported not only to the executive committee but also upward through all-union Komsomol channels. This robbed the territorial administrations, the so-called "federated" and "autonomous" regions, of any real authority. As long as their own component parts responded (and reported) directly to management echelons in Moscow, the republics remained impotent—and this was one source of the nationalist upsurge against the Soviet system when Gorbachev began allowing open expression in the late 1980s. Lenin had seen that his centralism would not really permit local

**This vertical subordination is, in theory, accompanied by responsibility to their own soviets. Under the euphemistic tag of "dual subordination," this principle is enshrined in Article 150 of the USSR Constitution: "Executive committees of local Soviets of people's deputies shall be directly accountable both to the soviet that elected them and to the higher executive and administrative body."

autonomy and—before he won power—admitted that federalism was "an unfit form for our state." It was only after his armies had encountered fierce resistance invading the lands of outlying nationalities that Lenin saw its advantages. The semblance of autonomy might not really win support from those non-Russian peoples, but it would at least give them—and the outside world—a way to rationalize their defeat and subordination to Russian rule. Federalism would also provide a useful framework for absorbing new nations in the future, as it later did when the Kremlin took over and made union republics of Estonia, Latvia, Lithuania, and Moldavia.

Gorbachev has admitted that such centralization has created a deadening bureaucracy and that, when applied to industry and agriculture, has driven the country into crisis. Administrators had to wait passively for instructions from above, the regime now admitted; factories could not get needed supplies, machinery was badly designed, products quickly wore out, trucks and trains were diverted or broke down and failed to make scheduled deliveries, buildings were shoddily constructed, machinery lay idle and rusting, harvests rotted, food shortages plagued most areas—and the workers had become indifferent and undisciplined, drank on the job, and habitually stole state property.

So central control and planning became a prime target of *perestroika.* Local soviets were to be given funds to use as they saw fit, and all but a few of the enterprises in their area would be subordinated primarily to them rather than to centralized structures. In an effort to lift the heavy hand of the state planners (Gosplan) off the myriad details of industrial and agricultural production, the leaders abolished many regulations and made tens of thousands of state planners redundant. Only a few strategic industries would be planned in detail while the rest would get only general guidance and long-term plans and development programs. Most factories would become "self-financing" and do their own planning within these central guidelines. They would be informed of the government's needs and allowed to bid competitively for contracts. (And they would be expected to make a profit or fall into bankruptcy.) And in their main press outlet, *Pravda,* the leaders claimed even to have discussed the possibility of eliminating state economic planning altogether.[36]

But central planning cannot be done away with; it is too firmly embedded in the system. "The [socialist] form of property creates its own objective laws," pointed out a primer of Leninist principle. "The most important of these is the law of planned, proportional development of the national economy. . . . In socialist society the national economy is an integral organism, directed by a single will. . . . The fact that . . . production is planned and directed from a single center has created unprecedented opportunities . . . for a high productivity of social labor. . . . When the state functions as the representative of society as a whole, it is natural that the state and its central organs must, in the name of society, define the direction, the proportions, and the pace of development of the national economy."[37]

Thus even as the Gorbachev-era reformers were trying to mitigate the disastrous effects of centralization, they clung to the principle. Gorbachev made it clear that "we do not want to weaken the role of the center" and called simply for "a new concept of centralism." All his changes, he wrote, "will take place within the mainstream of socialist goals and principles of management." He extolled "the enormous advantages of a centrally planned economy" and warned that "we will even have to strengthen the principle of centralization where necessary." In late 1988, when dealing with the demands of republics for more independence, the leaders formally noted, in a Supreme Soviet resolution, that the central government "must retain its powers so that it will be able . . . to manage the country's economy as a single national economic complex." The party's top ideologist, discussing in 1988 the new methods being introducing into the economy such as leasing contracts and cooperatives, said that "in all this we proceed from the premise that it is impossible to have a socialist economy without a strong role played by the center."[38]

Such a tightly centralized system depends on coercion—and endows the forces of repression with extraordinary powers.

Since the beginning of industrial plans, the KGB has acted as watchdog and whip. Managers lived in constant danger. Because no blame could fall on the planners (who were, ultimately, the infallible leaders themselves), production failures had to be attributed to someone else's laxness, ineptitude, or criminal sabotage. Unless he were foolhardy or suicidal, the manager would not dare admit failure. Instead he lied and cooked his production statistics and cheated in a hundred other ways: keeping false books, passing off goods stored in a warehouse (or bought from another producer) as his own current production, bribing inspectors and political protectors, paying off customers to falsely certify the receipt of deliveries, stealing or diverting supplies, or buying them on the black market. All of these things violate the law—and deliver supervisors and workers alike into the hands of the KGB.

Even by its failure, central planning boosted the KGB. A huge "second economy" of fraud, barter, and illicit private enterprise sprang up to compensate for the failures of planning and for some of its shortcomings (offering some real incentives for workers, for example). It has provided a vital safety valve, but it remains illegal and many of its functions punishable by death. Almost all who are involved in this illicit trade are known to the law-enforcement organs, especially the KGB—which can pressure them into clandestine cooperation.

Centralism exalts the KGB too. The more centralized an institution—i.e., the more direct its channels from bottom to top of the system—the more important and powerful it is. As we shall see, no institution of Soviet life is so vertically structured as the KGB.

Thus to the extent that Gorbachev's efforts diminish centralism they diminish the role of centralized coercion—embodied in the KGB—and loosen the party leaders' grip on power.

Discipline and "Like-mindedness"

Whatever the effects of *glasnost,* the reformers hoped that the press would use its new freedom to encourage "stronger discipline at work" and "observance of socialist law and order," while opposing "violations of social principles and ethical standards of the Soviet way of life."[39] While approving "the deepening and widening of democracy," they noted that *glasnost* also involves "the imposition of order everywhere and in everything, the heightening of discipline, organization, and responsibility."[40]

Thus an old tenet of Leninism survives into Gorbachev's new revolution. The system demands soldierlike discipline and conformity—and thus grants tremendous power to the institutions of coercion.

The leaders of the party (where internal discipline is well known) have always tried to grip all people with the same firm hand they hold over party members. The CPSU calls duty the "cornerstone" of its principles. According to its rules the member must give "unconditional obedience to decisions adopted" and is expected to agree wholeheartedly with the decisions his superiors have taken, for he is a "like-minded person" (*yedinomyshlennik*). Lenin defined the party (and its statutes still use his words) as "a voluntary and militant union of like-minded persons united to carry out the historic mission of the working class." This means, in theory, that the party member obeys joyously, yearning to carry out the party's historic mission and happily subordinating his free time and personal interests to those of the party.

No matter that this is, usually, a fiction. No matter that the party member may be lazy or cynical, or bored with party meetings and using his ingenuity to avoid party tasks. (Indeed, he may have joined only to get ahead in his career, and the party recognizes this.)[41] But "like-mindedness" catches him in a web of complicity. He must conform or seem to conform. If he dares differ from the party position he risks being labeled "antiparty" or even treasonous. Lenin's dictum, "Anyone who even in the slightest degree weakens the iron discipline of the party . . . in effect helps the bourgeoisie against the proletariat,"[42] is still repeated today when the only "bourgeoisie" is outside the country. Unless he quickly recants he must be purged like a medieval heretic; otherwise the party would "break up." Should he go further and join others in opposing the official ("majority") view, they become what the party calls a "faction" and "to tolerate factions is equivalent to renouncing ideological unity and the leadership of the struggle."[43]

So the party member stays in line, for fear of expulsion. To be expelled from the party is worse than never to have been a member at all. Along with his party card the expellee may lose his job (the stain of such "treason" might rub off on his boss) and the apartment that may go with it. That is not the worst. Forever afterward the expellee must admit his disgrace whenever he fills out a questionnaire applying for a job, for membership in a society, or for travel abroad. If, as sometimes happens, he cannot find a job in his town he faces jail as a "parasite." And his children must admit their father's shame in their own questionnaires, which will deny them higher education, responsible jobs, and travel abroad.

So the party member remains alert—if not to do his all for the party, at least to avoid accusations by rivals (or scorned or jealous lovers) that he has violated the party's norms or moral code. To the degree that his job is desirable, he lives in a jungle where the ambitious lurk in the shadows ready to promote themselves at his expense, the frustrated to vent their spite, the fearful to denounce him to save themselves. The last thing he wants is to get in the bad books of the party—and the KGB.††

This kind of discipline, and these kinds of problems, shape the life not only of the party but of the whole society. "Absolute discipline of the proletariat [is a] basic condition for victory over the bourgeoisie," decreed Lenin, calling for "the most decisive, draconian measures" to tighten it up.[44] It might be thought that by the 1930s "victory over the bourgeoisie" had been won, but the state prosecutor Andrey Vishinsky left no doubt that those "draconian measures" were still in force and would remain so. "From its first days the soviet state, having abrogated bourgeois legality and created a new (socialist) legality, required that all citizens, institutions and officials observe soviet laws precisely and without any

---

††Similar discipline is demanded of members of the Komsomol, all 42 million of them, in its charter and rules. Because it takes in practically anyone between the ages of 14 and 28, the penalties cannot, of course, be as drastic as for party members. But the threat of punishment—and the pressure—is there: "Strict sanctions must be imposed on those [Komsomol members] who take no part in social work. . . . There cannot be any leniency toward those who violate the norms of our morality" (B. N. Paustukhov, speech on 18 May 1982 to 19th Komsomol Congress, in *Komsomolskaya Pravda,* 19 May 1982).

protest."[45] Party leaders ever since have demanded it; Andropov made it a central theme of his short regime, and today Gorbachev equates it with *glasnost* and *perestroika*.

Of course, no one really expects such obedience. With the lack of incentives in today's USSR, people work less, steal more, get drunk more often, and show up less often on the job than before the arrival of Communist rule. But reality is not important: what matters is that the principle of discipline serves as a basis for law and jurisprudence.

Whenever necessary the leaders have created harsh laws and inflicted long imprisonment—in the worst times, even death—for minor infringements of labor discipline. The ideology, by likening shiftlessness to treason, justifies whip-cracking by the KGB.

By decreeing in 1960 that class differences have been eliminated, the masters permit themselves to treat the whole population as "like-minded" and to demand "implacability toward everything that is contrary to socialist standards and morals and which impedes our building of communism."[46] High among such impediments are shiftlessness and disobedience. "Any violation of labor discipline," said Andropov, "affects the interests of all society [. . . which therefore] has the right to make the negligent worker strictly accountable and if necessary to punish him fittingly."[47] The ideology identifies lazy and indifferent workers as antisocial or "politically immature" (needing reeducation in the form of forced labor), and repeat offenders can be seen as enemy-influenced "ideological saboteurs," madmen, or even traitors.

With the constitution of 1977 the regime openly tied the citizen's human rights to his obedience. In what might be called a "bill of duties" it specifies that the citizen must perform (implied: to the satisfaction of the authorities) a whole set of duties before he can enjoy rights that elsewhere would belong to him merely for being alive. The underlying idea is expressed in two articles: Article 39 says: "Citizens' exercise of their rights and freedoms must not harm the interests of society or of the state." Article 59: "Citizens' exercise of their rights and freedoms is inseparable from the performance of their duties and obligations."

The duties are spelled out in eleven others. Articles 59 through 69 demand that citizens "comply with the code of socialist conduct." That code is spelled out in these vague and flexible terms: devotion to the Communist cause, conscientious labor, a high sense of public duty, intolerance of actions harmful to the public interest, and an uncompromising attitude toward the enemies of communism. These articles also compel citizens "to strictly observe labor discipline," "to preserve and protect socialist property," "to safeguard the interest of the Soviet state and to enhance its power and prestige," "to be uncompromising toward antisocial behavior and to help in every way to maintain public order," and "to raise their children as worthy members of socialist society."

It is the responsibility of the coercive agencies to see that they do.

Ideology

Upon their ideology rests the party leaders' right to rule the country. Marxism, they claim, "educates the vanguard [i.e., the party], making it capable of assuming power and of leading the whole people to socialism, of directing and organizing the new order, of being the teacher, the guide, the leader of all the toilers in the task of building their social life."[48] And Lenin has been exalted as an infallible god.

Therefore when Gorbachev's reformers admitted major flaws in their system, they took pains to avoid blaming the ideology. Gorbachev claimed that his reforms "draw inspiration from Lenin" and were "reviving the living spirit of Leninism."[49] But this requires artful dodging, for he was attacking practices that had themselves been justified by Lenin's wisdom. To make the economy work, for example, the leaders had to decentralize and thus violate Lenin's precepts on centralism.

By the end of 1980s the reforms were beginning to shake the ideology. Leaders spoke of changing the "entire view of socialism." "It is time to understand," wrote a colleague of Gorbachev's (evidently with his approval), "why our country with its colossal riches in land, timber, oil, gas and minerals, with its energetic and fully educated people, still cannot provide quality or quantity of food, clothing, housing, books or films." Take another look at "socialism," he suggested. It need not mean state socialism, which he called Stalinist—in fact, "the chief Stalinist idea still unshaken in the Soviet Union." He argued for "self-managed socialism" in which the state is subordinated to society and for a "planned market economy" with "socialist competition" and "a division of power, authority and function between party, state, and social organizations."[50] Others pointed to Marxist-Leninist doctrine as the source of Stalin's regime of terror. One close to the Politburo dared suggest that Marxist doctrine "has little relevance to the Soviet Union's present problems."[51] This cut too close to the nerve, so the leadership rebutted his thesis in *Pravda;* but the problem would not go away.

Indeed, as the party's chief ideologist Vadim Medvedev admitted, the party faced "great tasks on the theoretical front." "Irresponsible attempts are being made," he said, "to cast suspicions on Lenin's legacy and on the basic tenets and values of socialism." The party must somehow find ideological justifications for the new changes: "We need the closest possible link between [Marxist-Leninist] social science and the practice of *perestroika.* The new trends demand deep scientific generalization"—meaning, of course, ideological rationalization.[52]

Happily for Gorbachev, the ideology is adaptable; in the KGB we used to call it "a cork to plug any hole." From the storehouse of political, moral, economic, and historical philosophy that goes under the name of Marxism-Leninism one can pull out the opposing sides of almost any argument. From it the leaders, self-proclaimed priests of the ideology, pluck the formulations they need to justify their pragmatic decisions of the moment. Thus Gorbachev felt free to read Lenin's works "each time in a new way," to adopt "a new way of thinking," and to call his reforms a "new revolution"—no matter the old doctrine that Lenin's was the final revolution in a long historical process.[53]

Such drastic ideological turnabouts are not new. When Lenin was confronted with imminent economic breakdown and spreading rebellion, he was flexible enough to promote private enterprise where only weeks before it had been anathema. Stalin, having long said he was against it, abruptly ordained the collectivization of agriculture. In August 1939 he transformed Hitler overnight from archenemy into brotherly ally. With a single speech Khrushchev wrenched the party from adoration to open rejection of Stalin. In a dramatic "thaw" Khrushchev relaxed social controls and tried economic reforms, only to reverse his policies afterwards. Each shift simply required a new dig among the words of Lenin or Marx.

Gorbachev seemed to seek a way around the pitfalls by claiming to restore a purer version of Lenin's thinking—while blaming past ideologists for "deviations" from it. He criticized "dogmatic" interpretations and stressed that Lenin himself had changed his own ideas under changing circumstances.

But some contradictions in the doctrine defy even the wiliest ideologist and plague the leaders in an era of more open debate. How can they explain, for example, if class struggle has ended, why they prohibit their people from doing things that in most societies are considered normal, like traveling freely, talking to foreigners, or changing jobs at will? Why if "all the people" support their rule do they need vast (and growing) internal security forces like Internal Troops? Why should the party, seventy years after winning its revolution for the people, still hold exclusive power? The ideological answers are neither consistent nor logical, but—*buttressed by coercive power*—they have sufficed to keep ideology alive, if tattered.

The leaders cannot do without it. Ideology not only legitimates them but it also helps them rule. For one thing, it cushions the people's reactions to the drab conditions of life that Communist rule has created. "The fundamental feature of Soviet social democracy," the leaders admit, "is its orientation towards the future." Unless the people can be made to accept the idea that they are, as Gorbachev put it, "building a shining temple on a green hill,"[54] they are likely to recognize—as many intellectuals have long recognized—that their sufferings and deprivations have not been a necessary sacrifice but an unnecessary price to pay for the cruel and often stupid policies of their rulers.

With their ideology the party bosses can explain the harshness and intolerance of their rule. With it they can pretend that they know better than anyone else the direction and correct pace of the march to the radiant future—and they can insist, with force if necessary, that everyone march to their drumbeat and that misguided souls come back onto the one true path. The ideology authorizes them to root out and isolate the incorrigibles who hamper "progress." It permits them to suppress other opinions and information because it could only distract or mislead the marchers.

And for their failures, ideology provides a scapegoat: the foreign menace. Marxism-Leninism teaches that the forces of the past ("capitalism" and "imperialism"), in their death throes, are preparing aggression against "socialism" and blocking the road to its inevitable victory. "The Soviet people's entire vast creative activity has been applied in an atmosphere of incessant struggle against forces standing in the way of our socialist development, impeding in every possible way our building of the new life," said party chief Yuri Andropov.[55] "Ever since the October Revolution we have been under permanent threat of potential aggression," said Gorbachev explaining the USSR's huge military budget.[56] If housing is scarce, merchandise shoddy, food in short supply, the reason is clear: Gorbachev (following the lead of his predecessors) ascribes to the United States the "immoral intention to bleed the Soviet Union white economically, to prevent us from carrying out our plans of construction by dragging us ever deeper into the quagmire of the arms race."[57]

The very shape of the Soviet system—such characteristics as centralism and collectivization—have been attributed to the foreign bogy. Only a tightly centralized system, the leaders have alleged, "could withstand the pressure of internal and external predators."[58] In the USSR's forced industrialization and collectivization of agriculture, according to Gorbachev, "external conditions played a primary role—the country felt a continuous military threat against it."[59]

And with a desperate enemy at the gate the KGB appears to be indispensable. Under every Soviet leader since Lenin—including Gorbachev—leading spokesmen have quoted Lenin's statement of December 1921: "Without [these security organs] the workers' power cannot exist, as long as there are exploiters in the world."[60] That is why the Soviet people must reject "alien influences" and help the security authorities by vigilantly spotting their fellow citizens who may be seduced by Western "ideological sabotage."

Even without that outside threat, this narrow ideology can survive only with iron-fisted protection. One can sense this union of ideology and violence on occasions such as the anniversaries of Lenin's birth, when a top leader is selected to deliver the ideological message of the year. Repeatedly the honor falls upon Chekists: KGB Chairman Yuri Andropov in 1977 and 1982 and KGB veteran Geidar Aliyev in 1985. Evidently the Soviet rulers think it appropriate that the state of Leninist ideology should be explained to the party and people by leaders of their organs of violent coercion.

And ideology supplies the euphemisms that justify aggressive policies abroad. Wherever the Kremlin leaders send military forces or aid, they are simply "consolidating the positions of world socialism" or "supporting the struggle of peoples for national liberation"—as they are committed to do by Article 28 of their constitution.

So, when outsiders toll the knell of Soviet ideology they mark the passing not of ideology but of faith in it, which is not the same thing. Few, even in the party apparatus, truly believe the claims or arguments made in the name of Marxism-Leninism, and many are contemptuous of its specious and transparently distorted messages. Everyone resents the ceaseless pounding he gets from boring books and newspapers, lectures, posters, films and radio, everywhere he goes, from kindergarten on up. Many ignore ideology as best they can. A few joke about it—but carefully. The managers of industry have long been aware that they are receiving from "doomed" capitalism not only technology and materials that their own system cannot produce but also, and especially, the new ideas and initiatives that their system suppresses. Even the party's top ideologist admitted this at the end of the 1980s. "We cannot overlook the experience of mankind as a whole," he said, "including that of the nonsocialist world."[61]

Never mind this decline of faith, however, and never mind whether the doctrine has any objective validity. The practical reality is that the rulers protect it humorlessly. Whoever has anything to lose, whether he is party leader or schoolchild, must treat ideology with the semblance of respect, no matter that as a result he lives a lie and knows that everyone else is doing the same.

Far from dying, this root of Kremlin power has taken on a life of its own and has grown stronger than those who nourished it. Not even a self-styled "revolutionary" like Gorbachev dares challenge it openly. Proposing reforms, turning in new directions, he exposes his back to a rival's dagger that could pin on him the label of "deviationist" or "revisionist" that has started so many Soviet party leaders on their way toward jail cells and the executioner's bullet. Whatever *glasnost* did mean, it surely was not meant to open the doctrine to question.

So the play of words goes on. The reformers must somehow find a way to introduce capitalist economic ideas and "bourgeois-democratic" political and social forms without eroding the Leninism that supports them. It is a narrow and dangerous path, if it exists at all. They will have difficulty in detecting the exact moment when their foundation threatens finally to crumble. But should they find, at some point, that they must abandon either the ideology or the reforms, their choice is likely to be easy. Without the reforms they can muddle on for a while, sustained in power by their organs of repression, principally the KGB. Without the ideology, those organs of repression are crippled and their power is doomed.

CHAPTER 4

Socialist Legality

The Role of Law Under Leninism

"THE PERFECTION OF SOCIALIST LEGALITY" IS A GOAL OF *PERESTROIKA,*
wrote Mikhail Gorbachev, for "democracy cannot exist without the rule of
law."[1] His reformers dubbed their version of Soviet society the *"sot-
sialisticheskoye pravovoye gosudarstvo,"* variously translated as the socialist
"rule-of-law" or "legal" or "law-governed" or "law-based" state.

The controlling word in this formulation is "socialist." Contrary to the
Western conception of the rule of law, socialist legality does not subordinate political interests—specifically, those of the Communist Party—to an
independent law. It cannot, for that would put an end to Leninist rule,
and Gorbachev has made it clear that this is not his intention. In fact, at
the same time as his men were resolving to establish this socialist rule of
law, they were also reaffirming the leading role of the party—that euphemism for the monopoly of power.[2] They have never clarified the relationship between these mutually contradictory principles.

The term "socialist legality," in fact, is used to express several different
ideas. In one usage it masquerades as a synonym for the Western idea of
rule of law. In another it conveys the impression that today, in contrast to
the past, Soviet laws apply with as much firmness to the authorities as to
the people, punishing brutal policemen and corrupt officials. It also serves
as a sort of antonym for the term "cult of personality," representing the
good that was "distorted" by Stalin (never mind that Stalin used the same
term to describe his own justice); and used this way it carries a sense of
nostalgia for a more perfect justice that supposedly existed under Lenin.
"From the very beginning of Soviet rule," Gorbachev wrote, "Lenin
attached paramount importance to the maintenance and consolidation of
law."[3] To illustrate this, Gorbachev and countless others since Stalin's
death have cited Lenin's 1918 resolution "On the Strict Observance of

Laws." It is a telling example, for it highlights the gap between Western and Soviet thinking about law. Lenin issued that edict just when he was unleashing his Chekists in an orgy of lawlessness known as the "Red Terror"—and his main purpose was to warn any who might be tempted to resist the tightening grip of his power. The bloody activity of the VCheka (today called KGB) was always based, as *Pravda* reminded the public as recently as late 1987, on "strict adherence to socialist legality."[4]

Lenin's essential use for law was, as Gorbachev explained, to avoid chaos and "to consolidate our acquisitions, ensure the normal functioning of the Soviet system of government, and establish new principles in public life."[5] To Lenin the law was a weapon, a "mailed fist," and that view survives. As recently as November 1988 Viktor Chebrikov, KGB chief, described the current USSR Constitution in Lenin's words as "a powerful weapon in the struggle to implement socialism."[6] The law's role is not to create some abstract justice and certainly not to overrule politics but to "reinforce and protect the social and political system and its economic basis."[7] To strengthen socialist legality, Gorbachev's legal experts set the priority on these tasks: "to combat mismanagement and wastefulness, the loss of labor and material resources, the misreporting of output, and other deviations from socialist principles of management" and "to make better use of the whole power of the law to combat crime, drunkenness, drug addiction, parasitism, and unearned income." At the bottom of the list came the task of "eradicating unfounded accusations against citizens."[8]

Stripped of pretensions and deceptions, socialist legality means nothing more or less than the Soviet form of law and jurisprudence. It is "socialist" as against "bourgeois" legality, just as the term "socialist democracy" contrasts the Soviet political system to the pejorative term "bourgeois democracy." Lenin was indeed its true father, not because he attached importance to law as such, but because he declared his rule to be "unrestricted by any law." That is precisely what socialist legality has been: a system of laws and jurisprudence designed not to restrict Communist rule but to protect and facilitate it.

From the first days of Bolshevik power the rule of justice was to execute the political leaders' will. As a result the courts tended to specialize (and their sentences to vary) in tune with the leaders' secret instructions or decrees or public exhortations.

Each new propaganda campaign presented the courts with a "burning issue." One day the focus would be on corruption—and the courts' dockets would bulge with corrupt farm officials or factory managers. Then it might be absenteeism or hooliganism or alcoholism. In 1982, for example, the burning issues were waste in industry (and specifically the worrisome increase in workers' theft of tools and materials) and in agriculture. Thereupon, the party bosses warned judges that their performance would be weighed not by their fairness but by their contribution to this political need. "In present conditions the effectiveness of the work of the courts, like other legal institutions, is judged largely by their influence on . . . saving raw materials, other materials, fuel, and labor resources. The decisions of the CPSU Congress mobilize the courts to do this. Legal levers and jurisprudence must actively promote, too, the implementation of the country's food program adopted at the CC CPSU Plenum."[9]

This sort of thing was thus no Stalinist excess; moreover, it began with Lenin. A peak was reached in 1922, as Solzhenitsyn has reminded us, when "many famous political decrees supplied abundant human material for the insatiable Archipelago." "One was the Decree of Absenteeism. One was the Decree on Production of Bad Quality Goods. Another was on *samogon* [moonshine] distilling. . . . This steady pulse of decrees led to a curious national pattern of violations and crimes. One could easily recognize that neither burglary, nor murder, nor *samogon* distilling, nor rape ever seemed to occur at random intervals or in random places throughout the country as a result of human weakness, lust, or failure to control one's passions. By no means! One detected, instead, a surprising unanimity and monotony in the crimes committed. The entire Soviet Union would be in a turmoil of rape alone, or murder alone, or *samogon* distilling alone, each in its turn—in sensitive reaction to the latest government decree. . . . At [the] precise moment, the particular crime which had just been foreseen, and for which wise new legislation had just provided stricter punishment, would explode simultaneously everywhere."[10]

The burning issue having been identified by the party bosses, each part of the system had its role to play. The organs of public order chose and arrested the appropriate victims, the judges issued appropriate sentences, and the press propagated the news as cautionary tales for the people. A former member of a procurator's office cited the example—from the Brezhnev era—of Yu. Volkov, who was sentenced to five years for "malicious hooliganism." "This unusually severe sentence resulted from the recently passed law called 'Strengthening responsibility for violation of public order.' One year later, for the same crime, one V. Smirnov was sentenced to only one year. Why was Smirnov so lucky? Because by that time this issue was no longer 'burning.'" He told, too, of a metal worker who had removed from his workplace an old, unusable, and written-off typewriter—probably no crime at all and the first offense of a man supporting a wife and two children. Yet this man was sentenced to a year in prison—because the Moscow party chief had just warned that "a judge who sentences a criminal for less than a year is going to have to face me personally!"[11]

The practice survives. In 1987 a man—caught by the party's campaign against crime and the judges' habit of dealing out maximum sentences— got a year and a half for taking two jars of pickled cucumbers from his mother-in-law's cellar. [12]

How then can judges be independent? Gorbachev wrote that "it is especially important to guarantee the independence of judges"[13] and the special Party Conference of 1988 affirmed the courts' "absolute independence" of political authority. Article 155 of the 1977 USSR Constitution says that "judges and peoples' assessors are independent and subordinate only to the law." It was a familiar old theme in Soviet rhetoric* but it has always failed to address the contradictory theme of the leading role of the party. The constitution contradicts itself on this point; Article 155 butts against Article 6. As we have seen, "the policy of the Communist Party determines the entire life of society under socialism" (as a Soviet dictionary put it). Therefore it is only natural that, as a jurist wrote, judges "cannot carry out any other policy than the policy of the Communist Party and the Soviet government."[14]

Judges are members of the party and obedient to its orders, and so are more than half of the "people's judges" and about half of the "people's assessors." Some judges have been KGB officers or controlled informants, and they and anyone else allowed to work in the court system must have clean KGB records, which means they can be counted on to do the leaders' will. The defense lawyers are mostly party members and must be specially licenced to plead serious cases including those KGB-prepared cases of "serious state crimes." (That license is granted or denied by the party's Administrative Organs Department, which, as we shall see, works in close collaboration with the KGB.) All of these party members—investigators, judges, prosecutors, defense lawyers, and court personnel—are grouped into primary party organizations where their party supervisors see to it that their chamber does the leaders' bidding.

A Soviet legal expert noted in 1987 that "the biggest cause of abuse from the level of police through the courts is the overwhelming tendency . . . to bow to the demands of party officials, thus undercutting the principle of an independent legal and judicial system."[15] The chairman of the USSR Supreme Court admitted that leaders often interfered in legal

---

*Back in the Khrushchev era the same theme was being played. In 1962, for example, a plenary meeting of the CC CPSU "criticized party officials for shielding violations by exerting pressures on investigative organs and the courts" (Mironov, 1964, p. 17; this former head of the KGB was at this time head of the CC CPSU Administrative Organs Department).

processes and that judges lacked the courage to oppose their pressure.[16] The practice became known as "telephone justice."

The courts are, in fact, but one element of a broader subsystem of government, taking guidance from the same party organ as the police and other agencies of coercion. Within it they have a specific role to play and they play it in close collaboration with the KGB. The career of my personal friend and colleague in SMERSH, Sergey Bannikov, illustrates the unity of this subsystem and the easy transition from Stalin's "distortions" to today's "socialist legality." It was as an investigator for Stalin's infamous OSOs that Bannikov got his legal experience. Those drumhead courts within State Security and SMERSH, with scant attention to legal niceties and no acquittals, sentenced tens of thousands to be shot or to slower death in the camps. Bannikov was able to put this experience to work under socialist legality, first directing KGB counterintelligence,[17] then moving to Sofia as "chief adviser" (in reality, supreme authority) of the Bulgarian state security service that later became infamous for its assassinations in the West, and finally shifting directly from the deputy chairmanship of the KGB to become first deputy chairman of the Supreme Court of the USSR. A Western reader may think this a strange background for the deputy chief justice of a nation's highest court, but it is perfectly logical in the Soviet system. Bannikov's various jobs, administering summary judgment, detecting subversives, guiding Bulgarian assassins, administering the KGB, and delivering justice from the highest bench, are all functions of a single unified and structured system, the "administrative-political organs," that has one overriding mission: to preserve the rulers' power. (We discuss it in Chapter 5.)

Codifying New Laws

When after Stalin's death the leaders set out to codify more laws (and thus, as they proudly claimed, to enhance socialist legality and correct Stalin's "distortions"), their aim was to make the law clearer, not more permissive. Then when their economy neared collapse, they were forced to take measures to win popular support and create a will to work. Thus Gorbachev set out to revise the more oppressive laws and soften practices that the regime admitted had been overly harsh. Out came a whole series of new laws granting more economic rights (authorizing some forms of private enterprise and cooperatives, among other things), social rights (for example, liberalizing some controls over the press, association, religion, and personal movement), and political rights (with new institutions and electoral methods). Moreover, the authorities began to restrain their application of some laws,* imposing shorter terms of imprisonment and releasing some political prisoners. In mid-1988 a Party Conference even proposed to put individual rights above the construction of "socialism": "It is necessary to give paramount attention to the legal protection of the individual and to consolidate guarantees of the Soviet people's political, economic, and social rights and freedoms."[18] In 1989 the regime even tolerated the formation of a sort of bar association by advocates who until then could only accept passively the "guilty" judgments that the regime's courts delivered almost automatically; they aimed to change procedures so they could truly defend their clients.

The lasting impact of Gorbachev's reforms can be assessed by watching this conflict of two trends: on one hand the party's traditional use of the law to protect itself and, on the other, the regime's concessions to individual rights. When and if the leaders pass irrevocable laws that truly constrain the powers of the party and government (and particularly of their repressive institutions), they will approach a rule of law—and the collapse of Leninism.

Toward the end of 1989 that had not happened. The population still owed its expanded freedoms less to new laws than to the regime's lenient interpretation of existing ones. The battle between the leading role of the party and a true rule of law had hardly been joined. And the Politburo member overseeing changes in the law until September 1989 was none other than Viktor Chebrikov, former chairman of the KGB.

Gorbachev's reforming acts and promises of future ones seemed to lighten the oppressive hand. They offered protection from arbitrary arrest and, among other things, promised freedom to receive and transmit information (with guarantees of the privacy of the mails and other communications) and for parents to give religious instruction to their children. But the cautious observer will remember how tenacious are the laws the party deems essential to its monopoly of power.

He will recall, for example, how Stalin's infamous "Article 58"† survived its own "elimination." Covering what are called "especially dangerous state crimes," that article was vital to our work in the KGB; it permitted Chekists to say, "Give us a man and we'll find a charge for him." Solzhenitsyn called it the "great, powerful, abundant, highly ramified, multiform, wide-sweeping 58, which summed up the world not so much

*For years they did not invoke Article 70, covering "agitation and propaganda" against the system, before finally modifying and dispersing it in a revised Criminal Code in 1989.

†Each union republic has its own criminal code, but all get their precise texts from a USSR Code of Law. We refer here, as is customary, to the numbers in the Criminal Code of the RSFSR.

through the exact terms of its sections as in their extended dialectical interpretation. . . . In all truth, there is no step, thought, action, or lack of action under the heavens which could not be punished by the heavy hand of Article 58."[19] It earned such notoriety as an expression of Stalinism that Stalin's successors felt obliged to draw up a whole new criminal code. But they found it easier to eliminate the number "58" (and its most egregious and unnecessary injustices like "guilt by analogy" and "indirect intent") than to dispense with its essential provisions. Those provisions were simply spread among various new articles, of which the most important was Article 70, covering "anti-Soviet agitation and propaganda." It delimited this crime in almost the same words as had Article 58,‡ and like its parent was worded in a way that allowed broad interpretation.§ By the end of the 1980s Article 70, which had in its turn become infamous, disappeared—but not its essential protections for the Kremlin rulership. "New" laws would cover "agitation and propaganda." "Like any other law-governed state," remarked a Soviet jurist at the end of 1988, the USSR needed to defend itself.[20] Article 70's essential elements were subsumed in a special section of the revised Criminal Code devoted to "crimes against the state," with reduced punishments and relaxed terms. The new Article 7, decreed on 8 April 1989, provides up to three years imprisonment for "public calls for the overthrow of the Soviet state and social system or for its change by methods contrary to the USSR Constitution, or for obstructing the execution of Soviet laws for the purpose of undermining the USSR political and economic system." The new Article 11 prohibits, among other things "deliberate actions aimed at inciting

‡Article 58's Section 10, for example, covered "propaganda or agitation containing an appeal for the overthrow, subversion, or weakening of the Soviet power . . . and equally the dissemination or preparation or possession of literary materials of similar content." The "new" Article 70 covered "agitation or propaganda conducted with the aim of undermining or weakening the Soviet regime or of committing individual specially dangerous state crimes; the propagation, with this aim, of slanderous distortions calumniating the Soviet state and public regime; the distribution, preparation, or possession for these aims of literature of such content."

§For instance, in the 1970s Soviet jurists confirmed that opinions expressed in private conversations and letters or phone calls, even between a husband and his wife, might be punishable as "agitation and propaganda." (The KGB may learn of such views by way of a secret informant or microphone or telephone tap or mail opening—all legal under its charter.) In 1973 the regime amended the USSR Regulations on Communications to authorize its men to disconnect telephones that are being used for "antisocial conversations damaging to the interests of the USSR." (Article 74, as amended, but not published. Report by I. Poltinnikov to the International Telecommunications Union in Geneva, cited by Shindler, p. 89.) However in 1989 the wording of Article 70 was being revised so that, among other things, individuals should no longer be prosecuted for statements made in private.

national or racial enmity or dissension, degrading national honor and dignity," and "the public insulting or discrediting" of the government, officials, or public organizations." Now it remains to be seen how the regime chose to apply its terms and those of other laws and regulations.

When the outsider hears the regime priding itself on codifying ever more laws—enshrining in the law administrative rules and practices that had been applied "lawlessly"—he may recall that in the past this offered little relief to the population. Many new laws simply plugged loopholes to assure that the law covered everything. Far from "consolidating the guarantees of the rights and freedoms of the Soviet people," they simply clarified the law and reduced the need for "extended dialectical interpretation."

One loophole, the result of progress in electronics, appeared soon after the "new" Article 70 replaced Stalin's Article 58. Article 70 forbade objectionable uses of "literature" but did not foresee the advent of tape recorders, video, and modern reproduction techniques. So in 1984 the regime amended it to cover "materials in written, printed, or other form." Another loophole, equally unforeseen, opened when inmates of the labor camps began to beat up the secret informants of the KGB and MVD who had been planted among them. Thereupon the ruler's amended the law on discipline in corrective labor camps to punish by fifteen added years of imprisonment—and death in some cases—any beating up of "inmates who have started on the path of rehabilitation." Then, too, the massive influx of foreign tourists, businessmen, and journalists raised the risks that the Soviet people would be contaminated with alien ideas. So in the 1980s no fewer than four new laws erected barriers against contacts with them. Other unexpected situations arose. What law could have anticipated, for example, that Aleksandr Solzhenitsyn from his Western exile would make available funds to help the families of writers imprisoned or made jobless by Soviet persecution or that brave men and women inside the USSR would dare to administer those funds? Then Jewish organizations and individuals abroad started sending in packages to alleviate the misery of Soviet Jews who had not only been refused permission to emigrate but had then been lawlessly deprived of their livelihoods. Soviet lawmakers—with the KGB leading—got to work on these two problems and in 1984 added "aggravating circumstances" to Article 70 which raised its maximum sentence from seven to ten years for "actions carried out with the use of funds or other means of material value received from foreign organizations or from persons acting in the interest of such organizations."

Loopholes had been spotted and filled in the late 1950s and early 1960s, too. The criminal code did not mention strikes—they were then unthinkable under "developed socialism"—but workers in some Soviet factories were stopping work and blocking transport. When a few bold men and women began to hold small demonstrations in favor of human rights, the authorities discovered that the criminal code (which covered "mass demonstrations") said nothing against tiny groups of people unfurling a banner or two. Then, too, *samizdat*—self-publishing by private retyping and distribution—threatened to slip through the mesh of the law. In the infamous 1966 trial of Andrey Sinyavskiy and Yuli Daniel the KGB had embarrassing difficulty in proving, as Article 70 required, that the "aim" of *samizdat* writers was to "weaken the Soviet system."

To plug all these loopholes the party leaders slipped a new Article 190 into the criminal code in the fall of 1966. Its first section threatened three years in jail for "the systematic dissemination by word of mouth of deliberately false fabrications bringing the Soviet state and social system into disrepute, and especially the preparation or dissemination of such fabrications in written, printed, or other form." Its third section covered "the organization of, or active participation in, group activities involving a flagrant breach of public order, or explicit refusal to submit to the lawful demands of representatives of authority, or the interruption of transport, or of the work of state or social institutions or enterprises." Already in its early days this law scandalized some. A group of distinguished intellectuals (including the composer Dmitry Shostakovich, some well-known writers, the physicist Igor Tamm, and, for the first time in public dissent, the physicist Andrey Sakharov) audaciously protested to the Supreme Soviet that Article 190 was "contrary to Leninist principles of socialist democracy." The authorities ignored their letter and began without delay to arrest and try the dissidents who had eluded them.**

After forcibly expelling Aleksandr Solzhenitsyn and other independent-minded writers in the 1970s, the rulers—faced with Western protests that no law provided for this punishment—got around to passing such a law. A decree of the USSR Supreme Soviet of July 15, 1979, made it legal to deport people who had been deprived of USSR citizenship—for "acts defamatory to the lofty title 'citizen of the USSR' and detrimental to the prestige or state security of the USSR." In the 1980s scores were thrown out.[21]

As long as they preserve their "leading role," the party leaders can shape laws quickly to fit their needs of the moment. When for instance in 1987 public protest demonstrations became so frequent as to seem threatening, the leaders quickly passed a decree banning any in central Moscow.

**In 1989 amid Gorbachev's reforms, the party leaders, after disagreements, decided that they could do without this article, no doubt confident other laws or administrative regulations, such as the new Articles 7 and 11, as mentioned above, could punish the offenses it had covered.

In January 1989, when press coverage of public demonstrations became embarrassing to the leadership, they passed a law forbidding journalists to cover such events without special permission. When ethnic turbulence in Armenia became menacing in December 1988, the Supreme Court issued directives that made it legal to punish anyone spreading "ill-intentioned rumors" through the press, leaflets, or public statements and to consider offenses committed in extreme situations (such as natural disasters) as aggravated crimes punishable by three years in prison. And in April 1989, faced with huge crowds in the Baltic and Transcaucasia demanding independence from Moscow and denouncing local leaders, a new decree reaffirmed heavy penalties for "kindling inter-ethnic or racial hostility" and for "public insults or discrediting" of state bodies or officials, and for calling for changes in the Soviet system.

Even more important than the wording of their laws is the leaders' ability to interpret and apply them as they choose—and to punish outside the law.

Punishing Outside the Law

One of the proud claims of post-Stalin socialist legality was to have done away with extralegal punishments. No longer, it was claimed, could Soviet courts rely only upon their "revolutionary sense of justice" to assess a person's guilt, as Lenin had enjoined the early tribunals to do,[22] and no longer could the KGB take people out and (legally) shoot them without trial, as did Lenin's Chekas and Stalin's NKVD. Now, in theory, a citizen could only be punished in ways specified by the law and after being sentenced by an established tribunal for a crime specified by law.

The reality was different: the regime has consistently punished outside the law. Without any legal justification it moves people out of their homes and even their cities whenever it deems them "threats to security." Like many others, Andrey Sakharov was deprived of his freedom, harrassed, robbed, and beaten on the authorities' orders, exiled and cut off from the outside world (in Sakharov's case, for seven years) without being accused of violating any particular law and without formal arrest or trial. No law authorized deportation of Soviet citizens—so the authorities simply deprived unwanted dissidents of their citizenship and threw them out. Without any law, the regime persecutes applicants for emigration by having them fired from their jobs, harassing their families, and keeping them from lawful means of livelihood. It holds farmers like serfs on their collective farms by simple administrative regulations. Its functionaries frighten citizens with dark threats against their lives and the safety of their children. Behind the walls of its KGB, the regime sharpens the skills to carry out such threats in the guise of muggings, accidents, or illnesses.

Prison terms are likely to stretch long beyond the limits set by law: new sentences are frequently tacked on just before a prisoner is released. In October 1983 the authorities made it even easier to extend sentences by authorizing prison and camp directors themselves to do it.†† This new decree was soon put to use against the mathematician Valeriy Senderov, the philologist Vladimir Poresh, and the psychiatrist Dr. Anatoliy Koryagin. The latter had protested the violation of prisoners' rights and had two years added to his sentence for "insubordination and inciting indiscipline."[23] The Ukrainian poet Yuriy Lytvyn, in bad health after spending a total of twenty-one years in prisons and labor camps for his struggle in favor of human rights and Ukrainian national autonomy, found himself in 1984 facing his fifth term—another ten years. Instead, he committed suicide.[24] By 1987 prisoners serving second or third terms far outnumbered first offenders.[25]

And the regime has been killing in secret and illegal ways—not only people who are legally free (see chap. 15) but its own prisoners who have never been given a formal death sentence.‡‡ The KGB unit in camps and prisons, directed from the KGB center in Moscow, uses special procedures to break or destroy prisoners. The KGB introduced these procedures into its satellite states, as former Romanian intelligence chief Ion Mihai Pacepa reported in 1987. "Created by the Soviets in 1950, the Romanian Service K does the dirtiest work against jailed prisoners. . . . In some cases it secretly liquidates them, staging alleged suicides or using poison that causes what looks like a natural death. In the spring of 1970, Service K added radioactive substances supplied by the KGB to its deadly arse-

---

††Now the camp directors and prison staff, as the former Soviet lawyer Dina Kaminskaya has commented, "can fabricate a criminal charge against any prisoner on the basis of a single deposition compiled by themselves" and no longer need to use false witnesses. She noted that the "trend towards the employment of terror methods against prisoners who stand up for their rights" is directed, as a rule, against political prisoners (Radio Liberty Research, RL 283/85, 29 August 1985). The law of 1983, providing three years more imprisonment for "malicious disobedience" of camp orders, is described in RL 430/83, 14 November 1983.

‡‡The death penalty was extended in the 1970s and 1980s to cover embezzlement and other economic crimes. The regime admitted carrying out about thirty executions a year, but the true figure, according to Konstantin Simis, was closer to nine hundred—and those were only a third of the total death sentences doled out, the rest having been commuted. The maximum prison term for persons with commuted death sentences is, since 1986, twenty years.

nal. . . . The radiation dosage was said to generate lethal forms of cancer."[26] Confirmations of this KGB work have come from Soviet prisoners. Sergey Soldatov, sentenced to six years for proposing reforms in the system ("anti-Soviet agitation and propaganda") learned in 1979 that his camp management in Mordovia had been secretly instructed to insure that he would never get out alive. In a letter to the United Nations, published in *samizdat,* he told how the regime eliminates imprisoned dissidents by controlling their food and medicine, by administering drugs, bacteria, and radiation, by using incarcerated criminals to beat and murder them, and by arranging work accidents. Just from his personal observations Soldatov was able to describe the strangely fatal illnesses of no fewer than three fellow prisoners.[27]

These KGB "special measures" combine with prison conditions to destroy opponents of the regime. "As a Soviet political prisoner and a doctor," reported Anatoliy Koryagin, "I state that the condition in which prisoners are held in political camps are designed to break their physical and mental health. The conditions directly threaten and shorten their lives. This derives in no small degree from the physical torturing of them through starvation, cold, and deprivation of sleep."[28] The medical director of Vladimir prison admitted to the political prisoner A. Sergeyenko that doctors were empowered only to treat existing ailments, not to alleviate conditions. "Not one of the prisoners in our camp is healthy," reported one dissident in 1987. As a result, even "short" sentences can be as fatal as the executioner's bullet. In December 1987, 23-year-old Sarkis Ogadzhanyan, jailed as a member of the Hare Krishna sect, died in the Orenburg labor camp in the Urals shortly after being condemned.[29] In December 1986 the heroic Anatoliy Marchenko died in the Christopol prison (where many dissenters were imprisoned) as a result of mistreatment, medical neglect, and a hunger strike.[30] Camp conditions caused the deaths of several Ukrainian campaigners for civil rights in 1984–85, including (in addition to the above-named Yuriy Lytvyn) Vasily Stus, Oleksii Tykhy (who was denied proper medical attention), and the 36-year-old journalist

§§The terrible conditions have been confirmed by scores of victims, many of whom have since come to the West like Koryagin, Yuri Orlov, and Vladimir Bukovsky. The USSR Social Group for the Respect of the Helsinki Agreements has reported on these cases and conditions in numerous reports reaching the West through *samizdat.* See, for example, *Cahiers du Samizdat,* No. 42 (February–March 1977). "Prisoners are confined in narrow humid cells, nearly without air or light of day, subjected to inadequate and low-quality diet and forced to do dangerous and unhealthy work in places ill-equipped for safety, and punished by hunger, cold, lack of sleep, and isolation." These sources gave long lists of political prisoners suffering from spinal and pulmonary tuberculosis, atrophy of nerves and neuritis, liver, kidney, gastric, cardiovascular, and other disorders—intentionally imposed by the political leadership.

Valeriy Marchenko.*** With medical neglect it took little more than two years of a seven-year sentence to cause the death of the 33-year-old writer, poet, and dissident Yuri Galanskov in 1972 and only half of his three-year sentence to end, in a prison hospital at the beginning of 1971, the life of Boris Talantov, who had "defamed the Soviet state" by writing about its persecution of religion.

Convicts, some of them reprieved from death sentences, are sent to work in uranium mines and chemical factories where their life expectancy is less than a year because safety standards are low and they are given no protective clothing. Instead of dying by a firing squad they succumb to tuberculosis and to leukemia and other cancers induced by radioactive gases and other causes.[31]

No laws, either, permitted the regime to confine dissidents in psychiatric hospitals. In the late 1980s there were still about sixteen "special psychiatric hospitals" under the controlling hand of the KGB and MVD although formally administered since the end of 1987 by the Ministry of Health. Any militia or KGB office could send an opponent to them for indeterminate periods, and order injections of drugs designed to destroy his or her will, concentration, and health. Some were committed for as small an offense as not working for ten days or not carrying identity papers or refusing to work on a "volunteer" Saturday,[32] or for trying to enter foreign consulates (and there is no law against this),[33] or for criticizing the regime. In November 1987 the regime's own press described the case of Marina Pristavka, whose factory boss in Leningrad forced her into a psychiatric hospital because, although she was a hard worker, she criticized working conditions and "was always searching for the truth." A similar case was that of Vladimir F. Lokhmachev of Kiev, committed in the summer of 1986 for making critical suggestions about production methods at his workplace. This was a standard way of punishing human rights activists; Irina Pankratova, a 17-year-old girl member of an unofficial "Group for Trust," was committed to one of these institutions at the end of 1985 after taking part in two demonstrations to mark Human Rights Day. Another member of the group, Nina Kovalenko (now in emigration), was similarly punished.[34] There were no time limits, and a chief in one of the psychiatric hospitals revealed how little the medical diagnosis matters when he told the dissident Aleksandr Shatravka in the 1980s, "You're coming to us this time for a long time. . . . Your

***Valery Marchenko was already suffering from nephritis when sentenced for "anti-Soviet agitation and propaganda" and in the camp his condition worsened and he was transferred to September 1984 to Leningrad. There the authorities refused to permit his transfer to a nearby hospital which alone had the kidney dialysis machine he needed—and so a few days later he died.

departure from the hospital does not depend on us at all."[35] Aleksey Nikitin, who had dared organize an independent trade union organization and expose to foreign correspondents the reality of Soviet workmen's lives,[36] died at the age of 47 in April 1984, just weeks after his release from unjustified confinement in a mental hospital. Lyubov Shteyn was still being held in 1987, sixteen years after she was convicted of trying to leave the country illegally. In December 1987 the dissident Lev Ubozhko, who had already spent fifteen years in "special" hospitals, was arrested and locked up in one of them again. The Ukrainian political activist Viktor Rafalski was released in 1987 after twenty years of such confinement.[37]

At the end of 1987 a new law, evidently born of Western pressures, supposedly corrected such abuses of psychiatry. It prohibited committing an "obviously healthy person" and gave a patient's relatives a right of appeal. But it failed to provide any independent controls and left the ultimate decision where it had always been: in KGB hands. It is enough that a workmate or neighbor or police or investigator (all of whom are susceptible to KGB pressure) judge that a person is acting contrary to "the norms of Soviet life" to send him or her for psychiatric examination. There, the bizarre Soviet definitions of schizophrenia and other mental illnesses leave no reliable way to tell who is "obviously" healthy. Relatives, in order to protest, would have to be on the scene, and even then their voices could not override the decision of the psychiatric authorities. The new law transferred the management of the "special" psychiatric hospitals from the MVD to the Ministry of Health, but that, too, changes little; when in the past KGB functions have been transferred to other ministries, the Chekists have always kept operational control of them.

And at the end of the 1980s, with or without a new law, independent-minded and perfectly sane individuals were still being committed routinely for periods of weeks or months, to intimidate and bring them to heel.††† In March 1989, for example, Yuri Sobolev was committed for

---

†††In a gesture of *glasnost* in early 1989, Gorbachev's regime permitted a group of American specialists to vist any Soviet psychiatric institutions and to interview any patients they chose. They visited seven hospitals, including three of the "special" ones run by the MVD, and talked to twenty-seven inmates from a list supplied by human rights groups. Other patients refused to meet them, and in some cases the authorities tried to prevent interviews. They found patients confined for political reasons and treated with heavy doses of pain-causing drugs that Western doctors regard as medically useless—and they recommended that the Soviet Union not be readmitted to the World Psychiatric Association until it acknowledged past abuses and made more reforms. A group of Soviet mental health specialists on their own formed an independent association to fight the regime's abuses (*International Herald Tribune,* 13 March and 14 July 1989).

As late as the end of February 1988 Anatoliy Koryagin knew the names and details of ninety detainees and was sure that many more were unknown to him or to anyone in the

harboring "extremist ideas" and heckling his party boss at a pre-election meeting. His boss had called the militia chief and told him "to get Sobolev out of the way."[38]

West (Conference on *Glasnost*, Brussels, 20 February 1988). The old leadership of Soviet psychiatry remained in place and unrepentant, still refusing to admit that dissidents had ever been locked up to punish or intimidate them. See for example *Daily Telegraph*, London, 13 February 1988.

PART II

HIGH COMMAND OF THE INTERNAL WAR

CHAPTER 5

The Summit of Power

The Subsystem

ONE OF GORBACHEV'S PROMISES WAS TO OPEN A WINDOW ONTO THE inner workings of high state and party bodies. Already in 1982 *Pravda* had begun publishing decisions and resolutions it said had been approved by the Politburo at a weekly meeting held the day before. Now high spokesmen hinted at opening the sessions themselves to television coverage. In 1986 Gorbachev revealed that "in the meetings of the Politburo there are sometimes clashes, conflicts."[1] In March 1988 Politburo member Lev Zaikov said that because these weekly meetings were dealing with reforms, they sometimes went on for five to ten hours as against only one hour "in former times" and that at "practically all" such meeetings "nearly all members express their opinions." "But," he added (contradicting Gorbachev's statement), "there is virtually no disagreement in the Politburo. We never vote, because after we have all worked together to arrive at an opinion, there are no objectors left. And if there is still someone with his own opinion, we discuss it and work out some kind of convergence so that there will be unity."[2]

From such fragmentary revelations emerges the impression that the Politburo still does its most important work as it always did in the past— that is, outside its formal meetings. This point is more important than it may seem at first glance. Any other image—for example, of the whole Politburo gathering to decide matters by voting (perhaps by a majority of raised hands)—would misrepresent not only the reality of Soviet governance but, especially, the special place and powers of the KGB.

A vote in a Politburo meeting—for anything other than an internal power struggle—would be meaningless. By the time a resolution is ready for the Politburo's formal stamp of approval it will already have passed through the offices of every member directly concerned, usually including the General Secretary, and other high party and government leaders will have taken positions on it. Along this path it may indeed have occasioned "clashes and conflicts" but, as Zaikov confirmed, these are resolved before it could reach a full gathering of the Politburo. If at that late moment a member would raise his voice or hand in disagreement, he would be opposing the collective, challenging the authority of the General Secretary, and opening up a destructive conflict.*

The party rulers do not need this kind of confrontation. They have well-grooved channels for making workaday decisions. Politburo members have secure telephones on their desks, couriers standing ready, office staffs knowing whom to write, phone, or see in the offices of their colleagues, and many opportunities to see one another. *Pravda*'s Friday reports are probably little more than a weekly press release of decisions taken in the traditional manner—and not necessarily during the preceding week.

Not all Politburo members deal with all Politburo matters. They have their own domains. Those who really work closely together at the Politburo level are the members, candidate members, and CC CPSU secretaries who supervise related and overlapping fields of responsibility. Soviet administrative law recognizes related fields as "subsystems of government," and one can find references to some of them. One is "social-cultural activities"[3] (including education, culture, science and health, physical training, sports, and social security). Another is industrial planning and transportation. In a clarification of this principle, the CPSU Central Committee itself was reorganized in late 1988 into six major fields of responsibility: (1) party matters (including personnel), (2) ideology, (3) social and economic policy, (4) agrarian policy, (5) foreign policy, and (6) legal affairs. Each of them was overseen by a CC commission headed by a Politburo member (supervising one or two departments of the reorganized CC secretariat).

Some of those subsystems being more important than others, their supervisors naturally have greater influence. Because the rulers' dominant concern is holding on to their power ("defending the revolution"), a subsystem responsible for that would surely be the true summit of Soviet power. Such a subsystem exists.

The agencies making up this subsystem are called "administrative-political organs" (*administrativno-politicheskiye organy*). They are the ones that manage "national defense, protection of state security, internal affairs,

---

*Such happenings are not unknown, of course. In the 1970s Dmitriy Polyanskiy had the temerity merely to abstain when a shift within the leadership was proposed to the full Politburo; Brezhnev expelled him from the Politburo and sent him into political exile as ambassador to Japan. (Polyanskiy told this to one of his KGB officers in the embassy in Japan, Maj. Stanislav Levchenko, who recounted it to me.)

justice, and foreign relations" and that "ensure social order inside the country."[4]

These are the agencies of coercion. "A characteristic of the administrative-political field, in comparison with other fields, is the application of measures of coercion, including direct and material force and other state coercive measures, as well as the use of all sorts of prohibitions and the system of permits."[5] And their writ is broad: "the administrative-political organs participate actively, in practice, in implementing all the functions of our state."[6]

Clearly, then, these words "administrative" and "political," so bland in translation, carry special meaning in the Soviet-Russian language.† Since they characterize the hard inner core of the Soviet system, they deserve a brief explanation.

When a Soviet official says that "the party should start to work by administrative methods," a Westerner might think he means to bypass judicial formalities or, alternatively, to work more strictly in accordance with regulations. The Soviet word "administrative" could carry such meanings, too, but a Soviet functionary hearing the same words would first understand them to mean that the leadership should crack down with force against those who obstruct the execution of its will. Above all, the word connotes application: as administering a medicine or applying pressure or punishment.

Throughout Soviet history the word "administrative" has served as a euphemism for violent coercion. The Chekas, who perpetrated massacres, burned villages, and tortured prisoners to fix Soviet rule upon the country, were called "organs of administrative power."[7] Later Stalin unabashedly called them "punitive" (*karatelnyye*) organs, and the CC CPSU department responsible for them (known today as the Administrative Organs Department) was called Punitive Organs Department.[8] However, Stalin's successors were anxious to cleanse themselves of the stain of Stalinism and reverted to the word "administrative," reserving "punitive," with all its ugly connotations, for the law-enforcement and security authorities of capitalism and tsardom.‡

---

†While clarifying some legal terms during their "return to socialist legality," the Soviet leaders avoided this one. Significantly, there is no entry for "administrative organs" or "administrative-political organs" in the current edition of the *Politicheskiy Slovar* (Political Dictionary).

‡Apparently even the bland word "administrative" was not bland enough, for since the mid-1970s the leaders have been using an even more equivocal word to describe the agencies directly concerned with law enforcement: *"pravookhranitelnyye."* (Early examples include *Kommunist,* no. 18, 1977, and Kozlov, 1979, pp. 158–59. Brezhnev's Minister of Internal Affairs, Shchelokov, used the term in his articles and speeches.) Its meaning is

The word "political" holds surprises, too. Its Soviet version connotes none of the Western conception of parties and campaigns, competition and confrontation, and is better translated as "executive," as in the name of the CC CPSU ruling executive, the "political bureau" or Politburo. To those who have lived through Soviet history, the word "political" conveys the sense of violent coercion. The VCheka from its beginnings was described as "an administrative and political organ in the fight against counterrevolution."[9] When district (*uyezd*) Chekas were abolished in January 1919 in favor of higher, provincial command echelons, their local work was carried on by "political bureaus" in the militia headquarters.[10] The central administration that Lenin created in 1919 to control publishing (Gosizdat) concentrated its censorship functions in a "Political Department" overseen or directly administered by the VCheka. Indeed, the VCheka itself, when made permanent in early 1922, was renamed State Political Administration (GPU), and its orders were executed at local levels by "Political Departments" (*Politotdely*). Within the KGB the department that has always suppressed religious, nationalist, or cultural opposition—and even intraparty opposition to Stalin—was long called the Secret Political Directorate (SPU). "Political" defines the KGB itself: "the activities of the organs of state security have a strongly pronounced political character. They are political organs which implement the line of the CC CPSU."[11] As Andropov expressed it, "The Chekists are the political fighters of our party."[12]

Center of the Subsystem

This subsystem amalgamates the KGB with the armed forces, the direction of foreign affairs, the police and courts—and this is no mere legalistic abstraction. Under Soviet administrative law these agencies compose a "unified system" that appears from the outside as a "single mechanism of management," with a "center that gives it internal organization and independence of other subsystems."[13] So unified is it, in fact, that its party oversight is concentrated in a single department of the Central Committee secretariat: the Department for Administrative Organs.§

But when one looks for that "center"—which must be the seat of ultimate power on the matters of deepest concern—one comes up against a

---

intentionally elusive; it is variously translated as "rights-protecting," "law-protective," or "legal-protective"—three quite different meanings.

§The terms "administrative" and "administrative-political" are used practically interchangeably.

blank wall. No Soviet publication names, locates, or describes it, and Western studies of the Soviet system ignore it entirely. The only place where such power could reside, of course, is at the top of the party hierarchy, among those who supervise these coercive agencies. But the subsystem is explicitly described as a "state mechanism," so these party chiefs must operate as a state body. In fact, such a body is available to them (and was even before Gorbachev united party and state command in one person). That body is the USSR Defense Council.

The outside world learned of the existence of the Defense Council only in 1976 and even then only from a casual note in the Soviet press that announced the promotion of CPSU General Secretary Brezhnev to the military rank of Marshal of the Soviet Union. It added that he was "chairman of the USSR Defense Council," thus mentioning that body for the first time in public. And it was just such a passing notice in the press that let the public glean the fact—two years late—that Mikhail Gorbachev had become its chairman.

In 1977 the Defense Council was mentioned in the new constitution and since then routinely in Soviet reference works. Gorbachev in his 1987 book said that he could tell accurately why the USSR modernizes its weapons, "because I am chairman of the Soviet Union's Defense Council."[14] The West has learned that its general mission is to prepare the country politically, economically, and militarily for the eventuality of war, but never have the Soviet authorities told when or why it was activated,[15] what it does, or how it works. Of its members only the chairman and his deputy have been publicly identified. Thus do the Kremlin rulers succeed, even in the era of *glastnost,* in hiding their most important power structures.

But they leave no doubt about the Defense Council's supreme powers, for they have equated it to Stalin's wartime State Defense Committee (*Gosudarstvennyy Komitet Oborony,* or GKO).[16] The GKO, let us recall, "unified the military, political, and economic leadership of the country [and was] the highest agency of command for the country and armed forces . . . possessing complete state and military power."[17] Today the Defense Council is similarly defined as the "highest organ for directing the defense of the country." That, in the Soviet concept, stretches far; it means "defending the revolution" not only against foreign armies but also against the incessant efforts of imperialism to destroy Soviet power from inside and outside the USSR.

The Defense Council thus commands, even in what the West calls peacetime, authority over not only military forces and matters of internal security, public order, and justice but also industrial planning and Soviet relations with the outside world. It is the successor to that "clandestine directing circle" of Lenin's time, and one can readily accept as true the reports of high Soviet sources in 1988 and 1989 that the decision to invade Afghanistan in December 1978 was taken by a small inner group of about five Politburo members and against the advice of the General Staff. [18]

In a Leninist regime such extraordinary powers could be placed in no hands other than those of the Communist Party chief. In 1981 a high regime spokesman confirmed that the post goes automatically to the General Secretary. [19]

The Defense Council's membership, too, must resemble that of its predecessor GKO and thus include, under the General Secretary, the top party figures commanding directly or overseeing the government (Council of Ministers), state security, defense, foreign affairs, cadres, and questions of ideology and military-related industry. In late 1988 Gorbachev reorganized the Central Committee apparatus, as we have seen, and created six powerful commissions headed by top Politburo members. Those responsible for legal and foreign affairs are surely members of the Defense Council and presumably so too are those responsible for ideology and cadres.

The KGB is represented on the Defense Council by its chairman, if he is a Politburo member, or his Politburo supervisor if not. In the postwar years when Viktor Abakumov was Minister of State Security—and not even a CC CPSU member—no one, least of all Abakumov himself, was left in any doubt that Stalin himself was running State Security. For some months after Politburo member Yuri Andropov moved from the chairmanship to become CC Secretary and later General Secretary, he surely kept his directing hand on the KGB, whose chairman, Vitaliy Fedorchuk, was not a CC CPSU member. In 1989 Politburo member Viktor Cherbrikov—as chairman of the CC's Commission on Legal Affairs—unquestionably continued to supervise the KGB, of which he was long the chairman, while KGB Chairman Vladimir Kryuchkov was only a CC CPSU member.**

Supporting the permanent members of the Defense Council is an advisory council composed of the operative heads of the state institutions that compose this "administrative-political" subsystem, who presumably participate in Defense Council decisions affecting their fields. Among them would be ministers who are not full or candidate members of the Politburo (including Internal Affairs) and several first deputy ministers (and first deputy KGB chairmen). The Main Military Council of the Armed Forces (of which the first deputy KGB chairmen are also members) surely has similar advisory status.

**During Lenin's time Dzerzhinsky was not a Politburo member but was a member of the inner circle that ran all the vital affairs of the country.

Formally, the Defense Council is a state authority: according to Article 121.14 of the 1977 USSR Constitution, it is established and its composition determined by the Presidium of the Supreme Soviet, just as was Stalin's "State" Defense Committee. In this lies its special value to the party leadership: it nicely resolved—before Gorbachev in 1988 combined in one person the top leadership of both party and government—the constitutional question of how a party chief shall command the government. In the Defense Council the chairman of the Council of Ministers is subordinate to him.

The Defense Council probably does not meet regularly as such. It is more likely that its permanent members exercise their supreme power in the traditional ways of the Politburo and issue orders through a secretariat in the name and authority of the Defense Council whenever they find it convenient or necessary.

Why did the Soviet leaders activate this body in peacetime? Perhaps, at a time when a new constitution was being adopted, to assure party command over the state. But just as importantly, the leaders were preparing for peacetime threats to their rule. If an internal emergency arises—of the kind, for instance, that confronted the Polish Communist leadership in 1981—this inner circle of party leaders can by a mere stroke of the pen transform themselves into the national military leadership. They have presumably established local equivalents throughout the country. With a word from the center this structure would be activated, making each regional party boss the military commander with the KGB chief, the military district commander, and the chairman of the local soviet executive committee (or republic council of ministers) as his military deputies.††

This is what happened in Poland, where the arrangements were surely inspired, guided, and triggered from Moscow. While the Solidarity movement gained strength in 1980–81 the Polish leaders, under Kremlin guidance, prepared this kind of structure and in December 1981 activated it. The "military" had taken power—but it was still the same old party.

The Place and Powers of the KGB

Here is the true place of the KGB: as the driving element of this dominant subsystem. Upon its shoulders lies prime responsibility for

††Shortly after the activation of the Defense Council was revealed, KGB chiefs were promoted to unprecedented military ranks. Chairman Andropov, his successor Chairman Chebrikov, and three of their first deputies became army generals; republic and important oblast KGB chiefs were promoted to lesser general officer rank.

preserving the leaders' power. It assures them of the loyalty of the military, it performs their highest-priority missions abroad, it works closely with the judicial system to achieve their political aims, and it employs, practically as auxiliaries, the law-enforcement agencies administered by the Ministry of Internal Affairs.

It was but a short step, therefore, for KGB Chairman Yuri Andropov in 1982 to move up to become General Secretary of the CC CPSU. As Brezhnev weakened and the succession struggle began, some foreign observers—perhaps influenced by the myth that Khrushchev had diminished the KGB—wrongly predicted that the "stigma" of Yuri Andropov's KGB service might block his rise. But command of the party's "combat detachment" carries no stigma, and no party leaders have ever diminished the KGB's power, for that would be tantamount to loosening their own grip.

Such misconceptions can be avoided by recognizing, as does Soviet administrative law, that the KGB has two distinct aspects. In one of these, it is true, the notion of diminished power is plausible. As a bureaucratic entity embodied today in a "committee" and earlier in a "ministry," "people's commissariat," "administration," or "extraordinary commission," the KGB's range of authority has indeed fluctuated. At times in the past it has been empowered to act simultaneously as policeman and investigator, prosecutor and judge, jailer and executioner, information gatherer, feeder and healer and watchdog of the leaders, commander of armies, and guardian of borders. From time to time it has lost one or more of these responsibilities, had them restored, or seen them divided or reassigned. The formal institution that is today called KGB administers fewer special troops than it did when it was called MVD or MGB or NKVD, and it no longer has under its roof the Politburo's farms and hospitals or—as it had sporadically in the past—the regular police (militia). Nor does it any longer possess courts of its own, those OSOs or "troikas." In this sense it is indeed diminished from its days as Stalin's NKVD.

But the KGB's more important aspect is as core of that subsystem. Here it commands all the functions ostensibly removed from KGB management. Soviet administrative law notes the difference between the KGB's responsibilities on the one hand for running "the KGB system itself" and on the other for "protecting state security" by (among other things) issuing "orders to other agencies."‡‡ In this second aspect the KGB acts

---

‡‡"The law governing the KGB's task includes, on the one hand, guarantees of the correct structure and performance of the KGB system itself . . . and, on the other hand, the rights it is directly granted to accomplish its tasks of protecting state security. Of

not as a mere agency of government but as the executive arm of the party leadership.

Underneath the fig leaf of subordination to the state the KGB has always functioned as a party organ and has never taken operational direction from the Council of Ministers as such. In July 1978 the leaders even removed most of the fig leaf by changing its name from "KGB under the Council of Ministers" to "USSR KGB." They state unequivocally that "state security" is the party's business and that they attend to it through a KGB that is peculiarly their own: "The organizing and directing role in the protection of state security in our country belongs to the Communist Party of the Soviet Union. . . . All activities of the Soviet organs of state security are conducted in terms of the current requirements of the party. . . . These are political organs executing the line of the Central Committee. . . . Their direction and methods in dealing with the enemies of the Soviet state respond to current requirements and political aims of the Communist Party. . . . Their organization and activities are carried out under the leadership and unremitting control of the Communist Party. . . . Clear party instructions orient Soviet Chekists in the present situation."[20] Andropov called Chekists the "political fighters of our party," and Gorbachev rightly pointed out that the "party wields the highest authority and has a decisive voice politically" in the KGB.[21]

The Leninist system itself, as we saw in a previous chapter, demands that the party operate just such an all-powerful coercive institution. Because it subjugates all organizations of society to the purposes of the party bosses, any grouping which claims independence becomes a challenge or a potential threat. The cadres system, screening and promoting on the basis of loyalty, requires that the Kremlin rulers put their hands into every Personnel Department in the country. Because they direct everything from the center and demand discipline, they must apply, as Lenin put it, an "iron hand" on the economy and administrative hierarchies. By equating misbehavior with potential treason and by hanging the people's constitutional rights on their good behavior, the party bosses have cast the KGB's shadow over all of society. By politicizing the law, the Leninist system assigns to the KGB a dominant position in the legal system and sole right to investigate the most serious crimes. By operating everywhere in secrecy (even in an era of so-called "openness") the economic and political system throws a protective shield (the KGB) over all the structures of state and industry and authorizes the KGB to decide,

---

primary importance in the latter group are rights to conduct criminal-law procedures and external administrative activities (especially the right to apply measures of administrative coercion), and to issue orders [to other agencies]" (Yu. M. Kozlov, 1979, p. 85).

ultimately, who shall be appointed or promoted or travel abroad. Because the ideology must be defended against contrary information and viewpoints, a system of censorship has extended the KGB's power over the printed or broadcast word or image.

Ranging thus over all of society, the KGB draws unique power from its formal status as a "state committee".[22] One commonly reads in the West that State Security was "demoted" in 1954 when its status changed from ministry to state committee. Just how wrong this is becomes clear with a look at Soviet administrative law.

The KGB works at the same level as a ministry§§ but has broader scope and special powers. It is empowered to "coordinate the direction (*rukovodstvo*) of special questions that are interagency in character,"[23] supervising the work of "all organizations—ministries, institutions, enterprises—in its field of specialization." It can inspect them whenever it wishes to see how they are performing and obeying orders, laws, and regulations.[24] If it finds flaws, the state committee can "give compulsory orders [*davat' obyazatelnyye ukazaniya*] for their elimination" and "see to it that these orders are executed."[25] This gives the KGB power over any organization "independent of its official subordination," whenever or wherever the KGB construes that an organization has touched its (enormous) area of responsibility.

To KGB workers is given the status of "representatives of authority." Like policemen on duty or procurators, judges, deputies of soviets, and government inspectors, KGB operatives have the legal right "to give obligatory instructions to people who are not officially subordinated to them."[26]

The KGB gets both "general" and "specific" powers from formal statutes—and gets any other powers it needs informally from the party leadership.

Its general powers are, for the most part, openly listed in Soviet administrative law texts. Some are obvious: the power to investigate crimes and to arrest or detain suspects, for instance. Others are well known: the KGB is given responsibility for guarding the USSR borders, for example, and for safeguarding state secrets. (To fulfill the latter mission, the KGB is empowered, among other things, to decide how

§§"While in name the KGB and similar organs in the republics as well as the Central Statistical Administration are agencies [*vedomstvo*], in law they are different. They were created not by the Council of Ministers but by the Supreme Soviet of the USSR, and their chiefs (*rukovoditel*) are members of the USSR government (Council of Ministers)" (Yu. M. Kozlov, 1968, p. 108).

secret material shall be handled everywhere and who shall be granted access to it.) Less well known in the West is the fact that the KGB decides whether or when to allow any foreigner or Soviet citizen to enter or leave USSR territory. It is the KGB, too, that makes the "recommendation" to the Presidium of the Supreme Soviet on questions of USSR citizenship.

Some of its general powers are even more extensive: "first, to prevent or suppress anti-Soviet behavior which could grow into state crime and, second, to eliminate those conditions which imperialist intelligence services can exploit for subversive activities against the Soviet state."[27] In theory, the KGB is supposed to apply such comprehensive powers only in a "strictly delimited" field and "only in the framework of probable subversive activities." But in a Leninist system the "enemy" may be anywhere.

In 1986 the regime published plans to issue new statutes for various state and public organizations, most to be completed by 1987.[28] Those of most of the administrative organs (KGB, Justice, Defense, Procurator, MVD) were to be the last, and a "USSR Law on State Security" would not appear before 1990 or 1991. Designed to "refine the status of the KGB within the socialist rule-of-law state," this public law could only define "general" powers.

Specific powers of the KGB are listed in a statute that is classified top secret. I knew and worked under such a statute, and a more recent version was brought to the West and published by former KGB Maj. Aleksey Myagkov.[29] It formally authorizes the KGB to work with secret agents and to maintain the facilities it needs to meet and communicate with them. It lets the KGB put a clandestine watch on "anyone the KGB considers it necessary to keep under observation in the interests of the security of the state"*** and to use for this purpose secret informants, surveillance, photography, listening devices, phone taps, and mail openings. With these special powers the KGB may intercept telegraph, telephone, and radio communications, search private residences or offices, and confiscate material. It is given control of the service that creates and uses codes and ciphers and control over the handling of all classified communications. The KGB is authorized to check documents, luggage, and printed matter at the USSR borders and to check foreigners operating or

***This specifically includes people who have been released after serving time for "slander on the Soviet social and state system" or "anti-Soviet propaganda and agitation," or former agents or officials or capitalist states of possible interest to the enemy, former leaders of nationalist underground movements, of postwar anti-Soviet organizations, prominent members of church organizations, foreigners, "criminals proved to be guilty but not yet arrested," relatives and friends of state criminals sought by the KGB, people being checked by the KGB, etc. (Myagkov, p. 31).

using trains, trucks, buses, airplanes, ships, or any other means of transport into or across Soviet territory.

However sweeping these formal powers may be, they cannot cover everything entailed in protecting Soviet rule. The KGB simply goes ahead with the rest and does without formal authority. Without benefit of law, the KGB harasses its victims, burns or pillages their property, beats up people on the street or at home, threatens murder and physical harm, moves people away from their homes, and supervises the often deadly treatment of prisoners. Whatever cosmetic restraints may be imposed, they cannot alter the ultimate reality that Soviet law exists to defend the regime and to promote its interests, not to hamper or restrain its defenders. KGB chiefs know that the party leaders will support them if they have to work outside the letter of the law, for whatever they may have to do to "defend the revolution" is surely within the spirit of that law.†††

How then, can such an organization be controlled?

†††In February 1987 the Soviet press reported the punishment of an oblast KGB chief for gross violations of the law." The keys to this unusual event can be found first in the fact that the oblast party chief (a member of the CC CPSU) was held responsible and sacked and, second, that the events occurred in the Ukraine. The Ukrainian Republic party chief Vladimir Shcherbitskiy was counted as a potential opponent of Gorbachev. It is likely that this was only coincidentally a show of *glasnost* and primarily a political move against Shcherbitskiy.

CHAPTER 6

The KGB: Controlled or Controlling?

The Myth of Party Control

A MYTH HAS BEEN REPEATED SO OFTEN IN SOVIET WRITINGS THAT MANY in the West have come to accept its broad outlines as historical fact. It is a tale of "political adventurists" gaining the leadership of the security organs* and "moving them out from under party supervision" and "isolating them from the people." Those villains continued to misuse what is today called the KGB until Stalin's "cult of personality" came to an end. Then the party leaders got together and ousted the evil adventurers, cleaned up the mess, and restored things to the goodness that prevailed under Lenin. The story has a happy end: "In recent years, day-to-day party and government supervision over their activities has been established" and "the Soviet security service is under the continuous scrutiny of the people, their party, and government."[1]

The truth is entirely different. The KGB is no more controlled by the party today than during Stalin's time. At no time from Lenin to Gorbachev (with one ironic exception, noted below) have its operations been controlled by the government. And the only "continuous scrutiny" that the people—if the word refers to the population—have ever given the KGB is the looks of fear they have cast over their shoulders.

The whole idea of party control over the KGB is in fact little more than

---

*The "adventurists"—as Soviet texts occasionally specify—were Stalin, Beria, Beria's protege and NKGB chief Vsevolod Merkulov, others in Beria's coterie, and Viktor Abakumov. Not mentioned by name are the infamous NKVD chiefs of the purge years, Yagoda and Yezhov.

85

a cliche of Soviet propaganda and, moreover, an old one. A Soviet spokesman told a news correspondent that "stronger legal safeguards" were being developed and that State Security itself has fallen victim to them. "It used to be a completely independent, sovereign, secret police force. Now it is a normal department of state bound by law, an agency that can no longer interfere at any rate in the existence and rights of other officials." Familiar—but here the tale was being told in 1936 on the very eve of the bloodiest period of Stalin's great purges.[2] From then until Stalin's death those "stronger legal safeguards" did not prevent that "normal department of state" from officiating over the killings of tens of millions of citizens.

What, indeed, can party control mean if State Security is, as the doctrine makes clear, the instrument of the party, its "leading edge" and "combat detachment"?[3] All KGB members are party members, except for a few still in the Komsomol. Its leaders occupy commanding positions in party leaderships throughout the country. The very word "control" is misplaced; it is more accurate to say that this portion of the party interacts with other portions in complex ways.

If Stalin's heirs had really imposed constraints on the KGB, Lenin would have turned in his tomb. If ever the security organs truly ran amok, it was at Lenin's urging. He personally wrote the key phrases of orders freeing the then-new VCheka from any effective state control.[4] In its first year its wild excesses appalled even government leaders. Provincial soviets complained that "Cheka operations were totally independent of local control [and] had been wreaking havoc upon local administration."[5] The People's Commissar of Justice, Izaak Steinberg, tried to curb the VCheka's powers of arrest and sentencing and to force it to get the government's approval in advance for its repressive actions. But Lenin opposed any controls that might hamper the VCheka, because it "applied the direct dictatorship of the proletariat." He consistently backed VCheka chief Dzerzhinsky, who decreed that the Chekas were "unquestionably autonomous" and "completely independent in carrying out searches, arrests, and executions" and had only to tell the government afterwards what they had done.[6] As Steinberg later wrote from emigration, "Anything the Cheka felt necessary to defend the dictatorship would be approved by the party leadership, notwithstanding any formal or legal limitations on its powers."[7] In the last months of 1918 several party and government commissions looked into these criticisms; one recommended that only experienced party men should command local Chekas—and indeed, this has been the practice ever since. The final one concluded that the VCheka was doing its work correctly.[8]

Ironically, State Security has never been more tightly controlled than during the Stalin's time. Stalin had—by Soviet standards, legally—made himself head of both party and government. So complete was his (i.e., the party's and government's) control over the security organs that when he ordered the massacre of their own top officials in 1937 and 1938, those organs never raised a finger to protect themselves and even did the massacring for him. Stalin never relaxed his "party" and "government" control: over a decade later, Minister of State Security Abakumov was widely quoted within MGB ranks as saying that when he was called in to Stalin's office, he never knew whether he would sleep that night in his bed, in prison, or in his grave. Anyone, from Abakumov down, who would set out on a course independent of party chief Stalin's would be not an "adventurist" but a suicidal madman.†

Of what then does party control consist? How many more Politburo or Central Committee members—in addition to one like Stalin—would have to oversee the KGB's work in order to insure proper "party" control? Would it be two? Five? Fifteen? Three hundred? While lamenting the "loss of party control" under Stalin, today's leaders never address this question.

What they mean, in fact, by "party control of the KGB" has little to do with preventing a maverick KGB from victimizing the populace. When Khrushchev expressed outrage at Stalin's cruel mistreatment of party comrades he had no word of pity for the millions of nonparty lives that Stalin had terminated or ruined. Nor was he really concerned with the party either, if by that one means the rank-and-file. If he introduced changes in procedures that complicated the KGB's work against party members, he did not offer them any shelter from it. If today the KGB finds it necessary to act against a party member, in the provinces or at the center, the KGB chief will usually have no difficulty getting his fellow party leaders to approve.‡ If the party organization wishes to avoid the embarrassment of KGB arrest of a party member, it expels him in time for the KGB to arrest him as a common citizen.

In the leaders' eyes, Stalin's most dangerous "distortion" consisted of

†In fact Abakumov's downfall can be traced to a lack of adventurism; he backed off the investigation Stalin had ordered into the death of Zhdanov (because he had discerned Stalin's hand in that death). His treacherous subordinate Ryumin denounced this reticence to Stalin—who failed to appreciate it.

‡The experience of party member Vladimir Korzh is not unusual—except that he recounted it to the Western press. The KGB had used him to report on fellow party members in a Ministry of Foreign Affairs in Moscow and apparently took drastic action against a colleague whom Korzh had reported for critizing members of the CC CPSU. When in February 1975 Korzh complained to the Politburo and Party Control Committee about this "misuse" of his reporting, he was expelled from the party and fired from his job (*Agence France Presse,* 7 December 1977).

bringing the KGB under his personal control and using its powers to destroy his rivals for power. This and nothing else was Beria's "crime," too—a crime that other leaders yearned to commit but could not.

The masters' immediate concern is that one of them might use the KGB's powers against the others, so they have imposed procedures to ward off each other. But since their joint and permanent concern is to ward off the people, they would not allow these procedures to weaken the KGB. They still cite Lenin's admission, dating from 1921–22, that their power "could not exist without this kind of organization, as long as exploiters survive in the world."[9]

In looking at the ways the KGB might be controlled, it is useful to bear in mind two characteristics of the Leninist system that we discussed in chapter 3, for they put insurmountable obstacles in the way of any real control.

First is the concentration of power. All jobs depend on people higher up and ultimately on a handful of individuals at the top of the party. Anyone who might exercise "control"—auditor or investigator, even one fiercely zealous to eliminate corruption or inefficiency—knows that this applies to himself. By setting out to check on the KGB he implies suspicion or blame of someone "up there," ultimately in the Politburo where the KGB chairman (or overseer) works closely with the General Secretary. Would he dare imply that the Politburo cannot adequately control its own activities?§

The second obstacle is centralism. The party leaders have given their KGB unassailably vertical lines of communications and command. No outsider—not even the regional party boss (unless the General Secretary so orders, which he does not), not even the head of the soviet executive committee, not even the procurator—is permitted access to KGB records or communications. Each of the hundreds of thousands of KGB men and women, from the remotest corner and most insignificant post—the skulker in the dark doorway of a provincial town, the security officer of a factory or scientific institution, the district KGB representative taking part in the deliberations of a draft board, the "special section" (00) officer counseling the commander of a tank division, or the typist or "diplomat" in an embassy in Africa—reports directly to his or her KGB superior and

§To investigate corruption, despite Gorbachev's exhortations, can be dangerous. We have described the cases of high officials fired, jailed, or executed for corruption since the mid-1970s. But they were not caught by some stable-cleaner who set out earnestly to suppress corruption. Those caught and punished are probably people who were caught so flagrantly that their crime could not be papered over, or who had lost their protection by higher-ups, or who were needed as scapegoats for someone with greater authority.

he to his, straight up to the KGB chairman and Politburo. At any level, the local KGB chief might consult or confer or inform or cooperate or take advice, but his command lines remain impenetrable.**

If no one has the right to break into the KGB's line of command and communications to the top in the Politburo, how can anyone "control" it below the top? Where shall a controller get the evidence to prove a misdeed?

Against this background, let's look closer at each point where the party might control the KGB. These are realities I know intimately from my own experience as a party secretary within the KGB.

Party Control: Over KGB Personnel

Party organizations within the KGB function much like any others: they hold regular meetings during which, among other things, members deliver prescribed lectures and try to stimulate discussion—and may criticize each other's conduct. (All party organizations watch over the "Communist morality" of their members.) These primary party organizations are subordinated to the party organization of the region in which they are located. That of the all-Union KGB is subordinated, for instance, to the city Party Committee *(gorkom)* of Moscow, that of the KGB Guards

---

**On this point Soviet administrative law is unequivocal: "In the field of protection of state security, there is one centralized line keeping local conditions in mind. The KGB's management is generally structured along lines of a State Committee, but this leaves out significant characteristics of centralization. Central planning and regulating, overall direction of the struggle with subversive activities of the enemy, the study of experience, the control of all measures taken, the selection and distribution of senior cadres—all these functions are held in the hands of the USSR KGB. Also, the Border Troops and the training institutions of the KGB are held directly under the USSR KGB without attachment to the republics. The high degree of centralization is also manifested by the fact that the local organs of the KGB are not part of the local city soviets. They are responsible only vertically to the KGB of the union republics and in the RSFSR to the USSR KGB. Strict subordination of the whole chain of command to the USSR KGB gives it the possibility of conducting operations on an all-Union scale" (Yu. M. Kozlov, 1979, p. 86).

It has always been thus. In the VCheka's first year, Dzerzhinsky made clear to other soviet agencies that "the Chekas are indisputably autonomous as regards their work, and must carry out implicitly all instructions issuing from the VCheka as being the highest organ to which they are subordinate. The Chekas are merely accountable to the soviets, but neither the soviets nor any of their departments may under any circumstances countermand or suspend the VCheka's instruction" (cited by Leggett, pp. 124 and 126). Local departments of justice and internal affairs were specifically forbidden to interfere in the Chekas' work.

Directorate to the district Party Committee (*raikom*) of Moscow's Dzerzhinsky District, and that of the Uzbek Republic KGB to the Tashkent *gorkom*.

But this subordination differs from that of other party organizations.

For one thing, in their party meetings and in their criticisms, KGB members avoid referring, even indirectly, to the substance of their work, which they must keep secret from everyone, even colleagues.

Also, the regional Party Committee is not allowed to know how many members there are in its KGB component, much less their names. These secrets are kept in the Party Committee's "special sector," locked in a safe accessible only to the regional first secretary and usually the second secretary. Even these two will not find much there: these records consist only of a card on each employee containing dates of his party membership, the party organization from which he transferred, and notes on how he has performed party (not KGB operational) tasks. Except for the first and second secretaries, no *gorkom* functionaries are likely ever to encounter anyone from the KGB party organization in an official capacity, except its secretary, who comes to party headquarters to get central party directives or to report on their fulfillment. These directives prescribe the number of party meetings to be held, the prescribed topics of lectures (such as vigilance or drunkenness or other party campaigns of the moment), and the hours of study that are to be devoted to the decisions of the latest Party Congress or to recent speeches by Politburo members.

The right to reprimand a party member is reserved by CPSU statute to *raikoms* and *gorkoms*. One might therefore expect that the local Party Committee would penetrate the walls of KGB exclusivity when a member of a KGB primary organization is reprimanded for personal misconduct or infringements of party discipline. But no: four KGB party organizations, all in the KGB center in Moscow, have been given *raikom* status because of the sheer numbers of party members in the KGB,†† and it is they who handle all reprimands. The KGB Party Committee at the Moscow center reports periodically to the Moscow *gorkom* only on the number of reprimands, not on details.

As a byproduct of this arrangement, KGB men often get lighter party punishment than other members. Their party superiors (who are also their

††The party organization of the Guards Directorate, with about 16,000, had three times more members than the average *raikom* and massively more than small *raikoms*, which may have as few as 200 members. The four such organizations are the KGB Party Committee and the party committees of the KGB's Guards Directorate, First Chief Directorate (foreign operations), and Directorate for Administration and Supply. The party secretary of the KGB handles hundreds of thousands of members and enjoys prestige equivalent to that of the first secretary of an important oblast.

KGB colleagues) recognize the pressures under which they operate and the importance of their work. Those superiors, moreover, work closely with the highest party leaders, which puts them in a position to arrange informally for the easing of subordinates' punishments. As a party secretary, I dealt with many cases where a member who might elsewhere have been expelled from the party was simply transferred to a less sensitive KGB component (or to the MVD) or, instead of a strong reprimand that could ruin him, got only a light and temporary sanction.

Since the party must approve promotions and appointments—KGB included—might not the party exercise some control here? Again the answer is no. Such matters remain within KGB walls, up to the rank of department chief. It is the party organization of the man's KGB unit that supplies the required party certification (*kharakteristika*) and no party organization outside the KGB is consulted or even informed about a promotion, except to the position of local KGB chief.

The CC CPSU does get into these procedures at a certain level. There is a CC CPSU department responsible: the Department for Administrative Organs that we have already mentioned.‡‡ The KGB routinely sends to the Administrative Organs Department of the CC CPSU its planned promotions or reassignments at the level of department chief (*nachalnik otdela*) and above. The department initials the paper and sends it back; no one is likely to question assignments made by the Politburo member who is KGB chairman. Then the KGB chairman or one of his deputies makes the appointment. When the chairman nominates residents (chiefs of posts abroad), the KGB merely informs the Administrative Organs Department. When KGB department chiefs are up for party reprimand, their cases go through the Moscow *gorkom* to the Party Control Committee; the Administrative Organs Department is again simply informed.

At this upper level of KGB personnel matters, one feels the intimacy of the KGB and the party. When a senior KGB position is to be filled, a KGB deputy chairman or the chief or deputy chief of the KGB's Personnel Directorate picks up the phone or drops in to talk informally with leaders of the party apparatus—the chief or deputy chief of the Administrative Organs Department, a CC CPSU secretary, or even a Politburo member

‡‡The Administrative Organs Department is divided into sectors, one each for defense, KGB, foreign affairs, and MVD, and one or two sectors for justice (one may handle the Ministry of Justice and the courts, another the Procurator's Office). This structure is replicated in the secretariats of republic and other regional party organizations, and the subsectors there report directly to their parent sector in Moscow. Its principal job is to help channel Politburo guidance to these agencies and to keep the hand of the party apparatus on the assignments of their key personnel, as well as their party discipline.

other than the KGB chairman. If they find that a certain party functionary is better qualified than any available KGB professional candidate, his appointment will usually be welcomed by the KGB chairman. If he opposes it, it will not be forced through. Party and KGB leaders generally have the informal relationship of colleagues, not the adversary relationship between overseers and overseen.

KGB chairmen in the union republics are also replaced this way—in Moscow. The republic first secretary will, as a courtesy, be consulted, and his own preferences may prevail; but he does not have the right of veto.

When a KGB man is being sent abroad under the cover of one or another Soviet institutions, the central party apparatus again has a role to play. The Administrative Organs Department, working with the KGB office that specializes in this task (currently called the 12th Department of the First Chief Directorate), may help arrange the cover with the other Soviet agency concerned. Such KGB candidates for assignment abroad were interviewed by the CC CPSU's Department for Cadres Abroad (until its disbanding in 1989) and the unit screening all exits from the USSR, but they seldom know that the candidate is actually being sent by the KGB rather than by his cover institution.

Such arrangements—in use for decades under Stalin and Beria—are about as far as the party goes, today as in the past, in controlling KGB personnel.

Party Control: Over KGB Administration

When the KGB needs to raise the number of its staff or to reorganize or create new departments or directorates or needs added funds, it turns to the Politburo. (I helped prepare such requests.) The KGB gets whatever it needs. The people who make the final decisions in economic planning and allocation of resources put the KGB's work at the top of their priorities. Whatever competition there is between agencies for the available moneys—in the Soviet budget as in any other—the KGB and the other "administrative-political organs," and at least until recently the military and military industry, have generally been exempt.

Because much of the KGB's budget is hidden among other state expenditures, it has to be worked out at the highest party level—where the KGB chairman bears great weight. It is no exaggeration to say, under these conditions, that no independent "control" exists over the KGB budget. Neither Gosplan nor any other economic agency knows fully what goes to the KGB, nor are they in a position to question it. After the money is allocated, there is no chance whatever for outsiders to pierce KGB centralization and secrecy to control how the KGB manages it.

Party Control: Over KGB Operations

Propaganda to the contrary, the party as such has no control over active KGB operations.

Regional party first secretaries are expressly forbidden to ask for details of secret KGB operations, while for their part regional KGB chiefs are forbidden to allow the party secretaries to see their secret communications. This situation appears never to have changed since the earliest VCheka days. I witnessed it in the Barnaul District MGB in the late 1940s, and the Smolensk party archives disgorged documents from the 1920s and 1930s that forbade party officials "to interfere in NKVD operational work."[10]

The same situation applies at the center in Moscow. No party organization inside or outside the KGB has any authority to control KGB secret operations except the General Secretary and the head of the Legal Affairs Committee of the CC CPSU—until September 1989 Politburo member Viktor Chebrikov, who moved to that job from the chairmanship of the KGB itself.§§ At that level the word "control" is inappropriate: the KGB's operations are the Politburo's own operations. These top party leaders— along with those of the Ministry of Defense, scientific institutions, the Central Committee's International Department (ID), or other party or state institutions—use the KGB's capabilities to solve their common problems.

In principle the KGB keeps no secrets from the Politburo. It sends reports or proposals, typed separately for each recipient, to Politburo members, perhaps asking them to approve a particularly sensitive operation—like overthrowing a Third World government, abetting a strike in a NATO country, or assassinating a foreign political figure—or informing them of some especially interesting development. I personally prepared such a report, for example, when the KGB kidnapped a prominent West Berlin lawyer. (No Politburo member objected.) But the KGB does not have to report automatically to every Politburo member. The General

§§As long as Chebrikov's successor, Kryuchkov, was not a Poliburo member, Chebrikov is surely remained the top supervisor of the KGB. In 1989 there was a suggestion that another committee (for party affairs and personnel control) might also be given some measure of oversight (*Krasnaya Zvezda*, reported in *London Daily Telegraph*, 13 March 1989).

Secretary, the Legal Affairs overseer, and the KGB chairman together may decide not to inform certain of their colleagues.

KGB operations are the secret operations of the Politburo's inner circle. Thus there is and can be no independent control, as understood in the West. This is as true today under socialist legality, when there are four or five members of the inner circle, as in Stalin's time when there was only one.

The CC CPSU's Administrative Organs Department is often said to "oversee" the KGB. As we have seen, it exercises only limited controls over KGB personnel matters and over secret operations none at all unless and until they reach the stage of arrest and prosecution. Many KGB operations that, to a Western eye, might seem most to need outside restraint never reach that stage. When and if they do, they are taken over inside the KGB by its Directorate for the Investigation of Specially Important Cases, whose job is to prepare and turn over to the procurator and party leadership (local or central) an investigative dossier that tells as little as possible about the operations that contributed to the case. The KGB is calling the tune: on the orders and under the supervision of the highest party leaders it is bringing some "especially important state criminal" to his just punishment. The party is not, at this stage, going to oppose itself; the Administrative Organs Department (and the procurator) do no more than see that the KGB's prosecution conforms to the laws and prescribed procedures.

The department's small size, if nothing else, reveals that it is not there to control KGB operational activity. Perhaps no more than ten party functionaries ("instructors") are in the CC CPSU sector for the KGB, and as few as one or two are in each provincial party apparatus. So few could not follow, even if they were allowed to, the activity of hundreds of case officers seeking information, recruiting and manipulating thousands of helpers, and strong-arming and harassing countless victims. These party functionaries are kept busy enough with "investigative" dossiers and with the assigning and disciplining of higher-level party members within the KGB.

They get no closer to secret operations than reading the KGB's annual report and those of some of its chief directorates. Such reports are phrased in generalities, focus on administrative matters and statistics, and reveal no details about ongoing operations, much less the names of secret collaborators or targets. (They do sometimes discuss cases that have been brought to a successful conclusion.) If he wishes, the department chief may call in a member of the KGB leadership to discuss matters in these reports. He may then criticize or make recommendations to the Politburo or a responsible CC secretary. But he never forgets that the KGB chairman is in or close to the Politburo and as such not compelled to report to him, a mere member of the Central Committee. The department chief will not make criticisms of the chairman, nor will he be too harsh on the perform- ance of the chairman's men.

Not even the KGB's internal party organization, staffed mainly by professionals, is allowed to learn about operations. At a party meeting a member may be criticized not for operational but only for personal misconduct. As party secretary I personally dealt with accusations against operational officers for sleeping or getting drunk on duty, firing a rifle accidentally (and hitting a friendly embassy), and committing adultery with a party official. But if such misdeeds are connected with operations— sex with an operational contact, going to the movies instead of staking out a surveillance target, mishandling a secret assignment—the guilty Chekist's unit commander deals with them and any reprimand goes into the officer's personnel file, not his party record.

In the provinces the usual relationship between the chiefs of KGB and party apparatus is similarly one of collusion, cooperation, and common cause. (It should be remembered, too, that they are both members of the buro of the local party committee.) The KGB chief keeps the party first (and sometimes second) secretary informed of his activities that have political importance and tells them things that might concern them directly. If, for example, the KGB is about to arrest someone with family connections to the local party first secretary, the KGB chief will normally warn this secretary and perhaps even change the plans, depending on his reaction. The party chiefs, for their part, suggest things the KGB might do. If a disagreement arises that they cannot resolve, their KGB and party superiors in Moscow will get together and settle it. But this cannot be called control.

KGB Control of the Party

While taking public pride in the party's control over the KGB, Soviet sources never mention the other side of the coin. Who, in fact, controls whom?

Whereas the party's Administrative Organs Department does not really oversee much of what the KGB is doing, the KGB chief stands higher in the party hierarchy than the head of the Administrative Organs Depart- ment and can probably have him replaced.

All internal party matters are secret, according to the party's own rules, so party officials (including those of the Administrative Organs Department) need security clearances that are granted (or not) by the KGB.***

A department of the KGB not only administers these clearances but, in the process, can check a party hierarch's contacts and neighbors and follow him secretly with specially cleared surveillance teams, (of which there were twelve in the mid-1970s). It can go further than this and with the approval of the General Secretary, can tap his phone or plant microphones in his office or apartment and accumulate a compromising dossier (augmented by agents and other sources). This, as KGB Chairman Andropov rightly told a Romanian spy chief in the 1970s, "is the KGB's most delicate task."[11] The party can never be rid of this KGB oversight, for its secrets must be protected, and that is the responsibility of its "combat detachment," the KGB.

The KGB is likely to hold a dossier on any party member, for it accumulates information from school days onward—from secret informants, denunciations, investigations of crime and corruption, etc.—and will have taken note whenever the party member got into trouble. When such information comes into his hands, the local KGB chief has a choice: if their relations are good or it serves his purposes, he can pass on to the local party first secretary things he has learned about him or his underlings, or he may keep it to himself or pass it up the line to the KGB chairman. Such knowledge may add to someone's power.

Party officials sometimes fall chance victim to the KGB's omnipresent eyes and ears, as did Rumyantsev, the second secretary of the Moscow *Gorkom,* in my time. He was enjoying an illicit affair with an attractive Moscow woman when Nikita Khrushchev, then *gorkom* first secretary, bluntly asked him, "So you've having a love affair?" No, Rumyantsev answered. Khrushchev mocked him and said, "I even know who the lady is. For your own good, drop it immediately." For two weeks Rumyantsev abstained but then fell again into temptation. Immediately Khrushchev called him in, showed that he knew where and when he had secretly met the woman, and this time warned him officially. But he strayed again, whereupon Khrushchev threw him out of the *gorkom.* (Rumyantsev was offered a first secretaryship in a remote oblast but turned it down; I do not know where he ended up.) Although Rumyantsev couldn't know it, his mistress had been meeting socially with American diplomats and was

***In my time in the KGB this practice was already long established. In the party archives of Smolensk Oblast, too, were found OGPU orders from 1927 that no worker in the party apparatus would be allowed to handle secret party correspondence unless he or she had been checked and cleared by the OGPU (Fainsod, *Smolensk,* pp. 73, 79, 163–65, 459 n.35).

under KGB surveillance; Guards Directorate chief Vlasik was informally keeping Khrushchev informed.

When the party verifies the dossier of one of its members, whether for a routine purpose or for a purge, a Central Committee department will check with the KGB. And if, say, a wife complains about the sexual adventures of an official of the Ministry of Heavy Industry, the KGB officer responsible for that ministry will accompany the CC CPSU instructor who looks into the matter.

In conversations with the CC CPSU Administrative Organs Department in Moscow, top KGB leaders discuss not only the assignments of KGB department chiefs but also the forthcoming transfers and appointments in other administrative organs. They can thus influence key appointments throughout the subsystem.

Locally, in their capacity as members of the Buro of the Party Committee, KGB chiefs have a voice in approving assignments to party positions and to jobs on the committee's *nomenklatura*. Their voice is particularly strong: the other buro members know the KGB chief has secret knowledge and a direct line to the top. A shake of his head or a lift of his eyebrow can undo a candidacy.

Top party leaders are surrounded by KGB bodyguards responsible to their KGB superiors. As soon as Mikhail Gorbachev, for example, was appointed to the Politburo, the KGB Guards Directorate in Moscow immediately began providing not only services—chauffeurs, cars, servants—but also instructions, such as not to buy food in outside stores and not to invite people to his house or dacha without advance warning to the bodyguards.

To get permission to travel abroad, party officials must, like others, pass through procedures dominated by the KGB.

Chekists play a role, too, in the disciplining of high-level party members. The Committee of Party Control is the party's supreme disciplinary organ. In its earlier incarnation as the Central Control Commission, Stalin used it as a weapon in his fight to win power, and Trotsky called it "a special OGPU for Communist Party members."[12] It is no coincidence that from the time in 1966 when party and state control functions were separated (as they had been before 1962) Arvid Pelshe, a veteran of the Moscow Cheka (and one of Stalin's and Suslov's men) was made chairman of the Committee of Party Control, a post he was to hold until his death in 1983. Pelshe was a fitting man to control party cadres under Brezhnev and Andropov, thanks to his varied Chekist experience as supervisor of Stalin's sovietization of Latvia in 1944–45, commander of NKVD forced-labor construction projects, and lecturer at state security schools.

KGB personnel protect the premises of the highest party organizations and all places where classified correspondence is kept. They tell the party how to store its secrets, and they approve (or assign) the people who will do it. The party uses KGB couriers and KGB-controlled telephone systems and radios to handle its secret communications.††† When I was in the Kremlin Guards Directorate, I myself helped manage those KGB personnel who were handling the highest-level Politburo correspondence.

Thus, party control of the KGB is far more complex than the slogans of Soviet propaganda. Party and KGB are mutually interacting parts of the same body, and the word "control" is inappropriate to describe their relationship.

Government Control?

So well hidden are the true workings of the Soviet system that in the late 1970s Yuri Andropov could permit himself to assert publicly that "day-to-day government supervision over the activities of the security organs has been established. . . . The KGB is under the continuous scrutiny of the government." This was nonsense, and later KGB chiefs made no such claim. When asked in 1988 what guarantees exist against misuse of the KGB's powers, they cited only the supervision of the party and the procurator—"and the very atmosphere of expanded democracy and *glasnost.*"[13] "Government" control over the KGB is nonexistent. As we have seen, the KGB does not take direction from any element of the Council of Ministers, and it is unlikely that the Committee for Constitutional Oversight of the new Supreme Soviet will assert control over this, the party's own "combat detachment."

The function called "state control," established by Lenin, cannot touch the KGB. Article 92 of the Soviet Constitution of 1977 said that "the soviets of people's deputies will form people's control bodies combining state control with control by the working people at enterprises, collective farms, institutions, and organizations." In the 1980s these bodies counted nearly ten million members.‡‡‡ At their crown is the USSR Committee

---

†††Since the Smolensk Oblast Party Committee's correspondence to other towns was to be sent through OGPU channels, "the typist or copyist of secret correspondence, and the courier who delivers it, is placed on the rolls of the OGPU."—1927 regulation, cited in Fainsod, *Smolensk*, p. 165.

‡‡‡First established in 1918 as a "People's Commissariat of State Control," it was renamed in 1919 the "Workers' and Peasants' Inspection" (RKI, or Rabkrin) and put under Stalin. Later it was again made a People's Commissariat and then Ministry and was finally embodied in a public organization called the Committee of People's Control. As of 1982 its ten million adherents were organized in 762,000 groups and 504,000 posts, subordinated to 890 committees of people's control, of which 57 are in ministries and state committees.

of People's Control, established by the Supreme Soviet, its chairman a member of the government. What they do is spelled out in Article 92: ". . . check on the fulfillment of state plans and assignments, combat breaches of state discipline, . . . and help improve the working of the state machinery." Their own statutes (Article 3) say that they are to "systematically verify the execution of party directives, Soviet laws, and government decrees, to take a firm stand on anything that prejudices the interests of the state, and to develop the citizen's feelings of responsibility for the course of soceity."

This was never conceived as a means of controlling or inspecting the KGB. Subordinated to local soviets, these organizations have the stated purpose of "controlling the work of authorities accountable to the soviets." Not even in theory could these organizations inspect or control an agency that is specifically excluded from any such subordination—and whose files are exempt from their examination.

Moreover, these state or people's controllers are themselves controlled—first of all by the party. This is spelled out explicitly: "Party control is the nucleus of all social control . . . and in particular of . . . people's control."[14] "The activity of the organs of people's control is carried out . . . in conformity with the decisions of the CPSU."[15] The controllers—40 percent of whom are members of the party, the rest of the Komsomol—get their guidance through their own party organizations. It would be unthinkable for party-disciplined people to conduct an inspection that could harm those top-priority party interests that are embodied in the KGB.

But the reality goes deeper than this: the KGB is itself the "state controller." These mechanisms have always been weapons of state security, commanded or overseen by Chekists, Lenin appointed as the first People's Commissar of State Control the Chekist K. I. Lander.§§§ Stalin used the oversight powers of the Workers' and Peasants' Inspection (RKI) and those of the party's Central Control Commission and of Dzerzhinsky's VCheka/GPU/OGPU to discredit and eliminate those who opposed or rivaled him.[16] RKI's connection with state security was not hidden: Stalin's first deputy there was Varlaam A. Avanesov, who from 1920–24 was simultaneously a member of the governing board (Collegium) of the VCheka. There followed a series of Chekist "state controllers,"**** but this was no

§§§This Latvian later went out to terrorize the North Caucasus, carrying out his threats to shoot opponents of Soviet power, raze their settlements to the ground, and take their relatives hostage. "For every Soviet worker killed," this people's controller threatened, "hundreds of inhabitants of such localities will pay with their lives" (Leggett, pp. 156, 335).

****Lev Mekhlis worked under Stalin in RKI and later became People's Commissar (and first Minister) of State Control in 1940–41 and 1945–50—after having purged for

Stalinist phenomenon. In November 1962, when Khrushchev unified party and state control, he put at the head of the new Party-State Control Commission the former chairman of the KGB, Aleksandr Shelepin. To this day "State Control" remains under Chekist control. In the 1980s the first deputy chairman of the Committee of People's Control was none other than KGB Maj. Gen. Aleksandr Ivanovich Shitov.††††

Once again, control of the KGB turns out to be quite different from the Soviet fairy tale.

Procurator's Control?

KGB spokesmen assert that their work is supervised by the Procurator's Office, the prime investigative organ of the Soviet state and ombudsman for the complaints of the people.[17] Indeed, Article 164 of the USSR Constitution of 1977 gives the USSR Procurator General "supreme power of supervision over the exact uniform execution of laws by all . . . state committees."

It was counted an accomplishment of the reforms following Beria's downfall that the Procurator's Office established departments to watch over the KGB and MVD.[18] But that was mere propaganda; in reality this was nothing new. The Procurator's Office has performed this function since its creation in 1924, before which the People's Commissariat of Justice handled it. The powers given to the Procurator General of the USSR and his subordinates since Stalin's time differ in no essential way from those granted him in the constitutions of 1924 and 1936.

The procurator's control function consists of making sure that in-

---

Stalin the command of the Red Army. In 1950 Mekhlis was replaced by Vsevolod Merkulov, who had been head of State Security (NKGB) under the aegis of Beria. Under Merkulov was Mikhail Ryumin, MGB investigator who played a sinister role in postwar intrigues like the Leningrad Affair and the Doctor's Plot. In the period of my direct knowledge, every inspection or review group under Mekhlis or Merkulov included at least one State Security officer.

††††Shitov was also a candidate member of the Central Committee of the CPSU. His KGB career began in 1940, but he is better known to the Western world as "Aleksandr Ivanovich Alekseyev," the alias he adopted for his service as Soviet ambassador to Castro's Cuba from 1962–68. During those critical years he brought under tight KGB control the Cuban state security service (DGI) and thus the Cuban state, helping Castro build the coercive institutions to hold power. After Western newspapers exposed him as a KGB official, he shifted his attention to Allende's Chile, traveling there under cover as a *Pravda* journalist in the early 1970s. Later Shitov became deputy chairman of the Committee for Cultural Relations with Foreign Countries, a KGB tool, and moved from there to the Committee of People's Control. In August 1987 he contributed an article to the magazine *Latin America*.

vestigations and prosecutions follow established procedures. It was Lenin's idea, expressed in 1922, that this highly centralized office (its district representatives responsible only upward, to the Procurator General's Office in Moscow) would assure uniform applicaiton of the law and be "able to resist local influences." But its scope has always been limited: the procurator's work does not extend to party organs, nor is he empowered to judge the legality of decrees of the supreme soviets or councils of ministers of the republics.

And he is certainly not able to resist the influence of the local Party Committee. On the contrary, he follows its guidance to the letter, as delivered to him through its Administrative Organs Department—or he loses his job. The Procuracy is staffed by party members, under party discipline. They have their own party organization, which, like all others, is formally dedicated to carrying out the will of the party leadership.

The procurator oversees a specific, narrow part of the KGB's activity: the cases the KGB has turned over to its own "investigations" unit for arrest and prosecution. Soviet administrative law distinguishes operational from investigative information, the latter usable as evidence in formal prosecution.‡‡‡‡

No procurator has the right to know about, or ask for information on, the operational activity of any KGB unit. He has nothing to say about how the KGB pursues its aims or meets its objectives.[19] If he were foolhardy enough to request sensitive or potentially incriminating material from the KGB (which is headed or closely supervised by a top Politburo member) he would get only what the KGB chose to release to him. Before he would do any such thing, a local procurator would have to have the support of the party first secretary and the party buro (on which the KGB chief sits and, since 1970, the procurator does not). The Procurator General of the USSR would similarly have to have the support of the Politburo.

Far from restraining or obstructing the KGB, the procurator's oversight provides it the cover of legality. KGB officers usually welcome the procurator's help; it is not always easy to prepare a case properly. In the Altay Kray MGB, I used to meet routinely with the local procurator to ensure that my investigative procedures conformed with the law. Our relations were friendly and cooperative: both of us pursued the same ends.

---

‡‡‡‡"Operational activity is a system of intelligence measures aiming to uncover and suppress crimes and to search for criminals and missing persons. These are designed to get information about crimes being prepared or already committed. Their conduct is governed by existing laws and corresponding regulations issued by the organs of state administration. Information obtained by such preliminary investigative methods cannot be used as evidence and cannot be a base for a judgment by the court" (Yu. M. Kozlov, 1979, p. 112).

The complaining letter—proud institution of "socialist legality"—
illustrates the collusion between the Procurator's Office and the KGB.
Every Soviet citizen has the legal right to complain, by letter or in person,
to the Procurator's Office (or to any other state or public organization,
many of whom pass the complaints on to the procurator).§§§§ The
procurator is compelled by law to look into such matters (often simple
denunciations) and, if legal action appears justified, to start the process.*****

Among the quarter-million such complaints received each year, some
tell of KGB abuses. If the procurator could or would pursue these, there
might be a degree of plausibility in his supposed control of the KGB. But
he cannot and does not: there is no known case of the procurator's ever
quashing, revising, or differing publicly with any KGB action. In fact,
the Procurator's Office passes such complaints to the KGB, which files
them for appropriate action at the appropriate time—action not by the
procurator, but by the KGB.

Vladimir Bukovsky tells of a typical workingman whose complaints
have gone too far. Called into his factory's (KGB-controlled) personnel
office, he is met by a man unknown to him—but from the KGB—who
leads him to an office outside where he explains how such complaints can
lead to treason. Then he "takes a bulky file from his desk and opens it, and
to his horror, the workingman catches sight of all his complaints, declarations, and protests, including his letter to the UN, lying there with blue-
pencilled comments in the margins."[20]

Thus at each of the points where control might be exercised over the
KGB, there is none. The leaders of party and state are one with the KGB,
the procurator subservient to it, and the people at large under its thumb.
Blurring the distinctions still more, the leading personnel of the party and
the KGB shift back and forth between each other's organizations.

---

§§§§Many such letters are addressed to the KGB—but to help, not criticize. Chairman
Chebrikov said the letter-writers "warmly support the KGB's measures to suppress anti-
Soviet manifestations on the part of renegades," and pledged the KGB to "react promptly
and correctly to them" (*Kommunist*, no. 9 [1985], p. 51).

*****In practice, at least until the 1980s, a large percentage of these complaints went
without answer and others got only a form reply that "the matter has been looked into and
found to be without substance" or that "it has been dealt with appropriately" (Neznanskiy;
also Bukovsky, pp. 36, 40, 44, etc.).

CHAPTER 7

The Two-Way Flow of "Good Communists"

Communists and Chekists

WHEN VLADIMIR KRYUCHKOV BECAME KGB CHAIRMAN IN 1988, HE moved up from within the organization where he had been commanding all KGB operations abroad—sabotage, terrorism, theft of secrets, and other unsavory activities—so one might consider him a professional Chekist. Yet in reality Kryuchkov was a career party official, like Mikhail Gorbachev, and had come directly from the CC CPSU apparatus into the active management of KGB operations. His move was not unusual; and at his side in the KGB leadership sat other party careerists like his fellow deputy chairmen, Vladimir Pirozhkov and Geniy Ageyev, under Chairman Viktor Chebrikov, who had himself been second secretary of an oblast Party Committee and moved on to become a CC CPSU secretary. "The most important units in the KGB system are filled with workers who have passed through the school of party and Komsomol work," Chebrikov said.[1] Therefore a Westerner, thinking in terms of his own society, might take comfort from the thought (encouraged by Soviet propaganda) that the once-dangerous secret police is now safely in the hands of "politicians" (or, as Soviet speechmakers call them, "staunch party cadres") rather than irresponsible professionals.

But look, then, at the Central Committee's own headquarters nearby on Staraya Ploshchad. There, while Kryuchkov was directing KGB spies, a high party functionary named Ivan Kovalenko, as deputy to the head of the CC's International Department, was supervising the party's relations with Japan. But this Kovalenko was really a Chekist: he had come to this party position directly from overseeing in Moscow the KGB's secret operations in Japan.*

Now the Westerner observer might wonder, are these men Chekists or are they politicans? In the Soviet framework, his question would be meaningless. No such clear distinction exists. Kryuchkov and Kovalenko are, necessarily, both. The KGB has always been made up of party cadres while the party has always been doing Chekist work. Since the first days of Soviet power, party functionaries have taken over key positions in State Security while Chekists were moving into key positions in the party apparatus. And some serve simultaneously in the leaderships of both party and KGB.†

Lenin distilled this reality in a simple sentence: "Every good Communist is at the same time a good Chekist."[2]

Party Men into the KGB

The first to command "the organs" were the very founders of the party regime. Having taken power, the "general staff" of the coup d'etat (the Military-Revolutionary Committee of the Petrograd Soviet, or VRK) immediately took up the fight to hold it. Some of its members ran the VCheka while at the same time sitting on the party's Central Committee and directing local administration, industry, and transport.‡ Inside the Chekas, Bolshevik party members took over the leading positions and, to the extent possible with their limited numbers, staffed the ranks. They called to arms all able-bodied party members not otherwise engaged, grouped them in "units of special purpose" (ChON), and put them under the orders of VCheka Troops. In 1920 Dzerzhinsky boasted that no Soviet

---

*According to his official biography Kovalenko was a career party functionary and had risen to this eminence after twelve years' service in that same department. But his biography, like so many others, was hiding the truth, as I learned from former KGB Maj. Stanislav Levchenko, who served in Japan.

†I refer not only to the full-time party secretaries within the KGB but also to those members of the highest party offices throughout the USSR who command the regional KGB. In the Soviet framework it was quite natural that a Politburo member (Yuri Andropov, soon to be political head of the whole country) should be called "the model Chekist of our time." (It was his Chekist colleague A. N. Inauri who thus honored him in December 1980.) Even a CC CPSU secretary could function as a KGB operational supervisor. I officiated at an MVD party meeting in 1953 welcoming CC CPSU Secretary Shatalin to his new job as deputy minister of what is now called KGB. (At that time the MVD united both State Security and Internal Affairs.) One of the Chekists asked, before the assembled party members, "Are you still CC CPSU secretary as well as being deputy minister?" Shatalin answered firmly, "Yes."

‡The Chekist CC members were Felix Dzerzhinsky, Iosif Unshlikht, and Yakov Peters, with Moisey Uritsky until his assassination in August 1918.

organization had a higher proportion of party members than his VCheka,[3] and this remains true today of the KGB.

These party men, moreover, have been doing State Security's bloodiest work. The NKVD's orgy of killings in the mid-1930s, now recalled with horror as the *Yezhovshchina,* took its name from one of those "staunch party cadres." In fact, to judge by the length of his service, that infamous Nikolay Yezhov deserved the title of Chekist less than today's Chebrikov or Pirozhkov or thousands of others: he served only two years in "the organs." When other party men moved into the KGB later, supposedly to correct Stalin's "distortions," they carried on Chekist work without interruption. One high Central Committee functionary came in to take command of the KGB's foreign operations (just as Kryuchkov did thirty years afterward), whereupon the KGB's assassination specialist Colonel Okun gloated to his subordinates that "the new boss [is . . .] a man of colossal experience. . . . an expert in all our work." He was quite right: Aleksandr Panyushkin quickly took over the supervision of a delicate murder operation.[4] So, too, did Aleksandr Shelepin; only a year after leaving the post of chairman of the nation's youth organization, there was Shelepin as KGB chairman personally rewarding a successful assassin (Bogdan Stashinsky) before moving smoothly back to full-time party activity and becoming a member of the Politburo. The fact that party functionary Yuri Andropov had supervised the brutal suppression of dissidence as well as assassinations and terrorism for fifteen years atop the KGB in no way disqualified him from moving on to become the political leader of the whole country.

This flow from party to KGB has never ceased; where else would the party's "combat organization" get its people? As a KGB personnel officer and party secretary, I helped administer it. A glance at the procedures (which cannot have changed since that Stalinist time)[5] gives an idea of the essential unity of the ruling party and the KGB.

Periodically (usually once a year) the Central Committee in Moscow instructs republic and oblast party committees to designate specified numbers of party members for service in the KGB. Republic and oblast party leaders pass these central demands on to the *raions,* adding their own needs for staffing the local KGB departments. Five hundred people a year were thus sent from the Moscow party organizations alone to the central apparatus of state security.§ These were not only young men starting careers but also mathematicians (for cipher-breaking and other technical specialties), automobile mechanics and radio operators, historians and

---

§Moscow is always a preferred source for the central KGB apparatus, because people coming in from outside would have the problem of finding accommodations. Similarly, in the republics and oblasts throughout the country, local party men were shifted into local KGB organs, with only the best being siphoned off to the center in Moscow.

librarians, linguists, and people with the special backgrounds needed to manipulate informants persuasively in diverse milieus. Military men are also brought in from, and with the help of, the Political Administration of the Army and Navy.

Only after the *raion* party organization has let the KGB review its candidates informally in advance, to make sure they are satisfactory, does it formally submit their names to the KGB. Then a KGB personnel officer comes to the *raikom* offices (as I often did in Moscow) first to screen their files and later to interview the most promising candidates—to whom he introduces himself, truthfully, as "a party official." We would select the best—hardly more than one in twenty—and would then start checking their private lives and contacts through surveillance and secret informers.

Any highly regarded party secretary in a district or regional Party Committee—in Lenin's and Stalin's time as well as more recently—might be tapped for a leadership position in the KGB.** Within the armed forces, political officers shift easily into the KGB's military counterintelligence.†† Men from the party departments overseeing "the organs"

**To name but a few, Serafim N. Lyalin, a secretary of the Tula *Obkom* from 1944–51, moved then to State Security as chief of the KGB's cipher-making and cipher-breaking Eighth Directorate and later headed the Moscow City and Oblast KGB until his retirement in 1973. Vasily Ryasnoy, secretary of a district party committee, was transferred to the NKVD where he organized concentration-camp laborers for Soviet industry (later Beria put him atop the foreign operations directorate where I worked for him). Vasily Ye. Makarov, *apparatchik* of the CC CPSU and of Moscow party committees from 1938–51, spent the remaining 24 years of his career in "responsible positions in the MGB and Ministry of Defense" (obituary in *Krasnaya Zvezda,* 3 September 1975). Eduard Shevardnadze, much in the news today as foreign minister, moved from long party work in Georgia to the post of deputy minister and then minister of internal affairs there, before moving up to the position of first secretary of the Georgian CC and candidate member of the Politburo.

††In 1985, shortly before he died, Aleksey Yepishev finally retired after twenty years in the rank of CC CPSU department chief, as head of the Political Administration of the Army and Navy and member of the Central Committee; he had been personnel chief of the KGB in 1951, when I briefed him several times on MGB personnel procedures. Nikolay R. Mironov was a party official, became KGB head in Leningrad, and then returned to CC CPSU as head of the Administrative Organs Department. Georgiy Tsinev, a prewar party functionary and an army wartime political officer, moved in 1953 into a leading position in the KGB's Third Chief Directorate (military security and counterintelligence) and finally left the KGB only in 1986, as first deputy chairman. Dmitry S. Leonov moved from his post as member of the Military Council of the Leningrad Military District to the top of the KGB's Third Chief Directorate. N. A. Loyko was chief of the Political Department of the Panfilov Division when he was assigned to head a department of the Third Chief Directorate. Sergey Semenovich Shornikov, an artilleryman in the war and a prominent party member, served for fifteen years in the KGB's military counterintelligence before becoming in 1967 Commandant of the Kremlin, a post he held until at least 1983. Georgiy M.

easily shift into them, and KGB men move into those departments; the overseers become "overseen" and vice versa.‡‡

At critical times the flow of party cadres to state security swells, sometimes dramatically, as during the years of Red Terror and civil war, for example, and in 1921–22 when new recruits were needed for operations in Transcaucasia and Central Asia and then to watch over the people during the dangerous economic liberalizations of the New Economic Policy (NEP). For the collectivization of agriculture in 1929–30 the leadership practically doubled the size of the OGPU and assembled tens of thousands of party and Komsomol members into agitation groups to work with it. In 1934–36 the party again assigned more, this time to cope with the vast and bloody tasks of the purges.§§ After the NKVD was itself purged in 1937–38, hordes of party men—mostly young—came to refill NKVD ranks. And in the immediate postwar years large numbers of military-political officers shifted into state security.

The turbulent months from mid-1951 to late 1953 saw various "families" of party and state security officials being shifted, sometimes violently. Four times the upper and middle levels of state security were shaken out. MGB Minister Abakumov was arrested in mid-1951, along with nine of his deputies and about a dozen other officials. In early 1952 a commission headed by Beria, Malenkov, and Bulganin, supported by the CC CPSU Inspector Semyon D. Ignatyev, reorganized and slimmed down

---

Bespalov, prewar party secretary in the Ukraine, moved through his wartime service to head MGB intelligence operations in postwar Berlin (Ostryakov, pp. 272–3 and, for Leonov, *Sovetskaya voyennaya entsiklopediya*, vol. 4, p. 622).

‡‡Vladimir Ilyich Stepakov came from party work in Moscow to be deputy head of the Moscow City and Oblast MGB in 1952. In the turmoil of 1953 he returned to the Moscow City Party Committee, where he became second secretary—the party official responsible for contact with the Moscow KGB—and later became a member of the Central Committee of the CC CPSU. (Afterward he became a chief of a department of the CC CPSU and chief editor of *Izvestiya* and, following the path of Aleksey Yepishev, ambassador to Yugoslavia. Nikolay R. Mironov, secretary of the Dnepropetrovsk *Obkom*, transferred to high KGB position and then back to command the CC CPSU Administrative Organs Department. A. N. Malygin moved to the KGB from his post as secretary of the important Kaluga *Obkom*; A. V. Alekseyev came to the KGB from the Fergana *Obkom*. Viktor S. Paputin, second secretary of the Moscow *Obkom*, was appointed in 1974 first deputy MVD Minister, in which position he was killed in Afghanistan during the first hours of the Soviet invasion while on a secret mission.

§§Several such instructions were found in the party archives of Smolensk. For example, the Oblast Party Committee on 19 November 1934 ordered a *raion* party committee, "upon receipt of this letter, to strengthen the organs of the NKVD [in this instance, its corrective-labor and fire-prevention institutions], guiding yourselves by the principle of choosing people who would be completely worthy of the lofty title of workers in the militant organs of the proletarian dictatorship—the NKVD" (Fainsod, *Smolensk*, p. 159).

the inflated security organization. (Ignatyev became chief of the MGB.) Then Stalin died. Beria took over state security and moved his own cronies into the top positions; they in turn got rid of lower officials they didn't trust. Practically all the republic and oblast state security chiefs and their key officers were being shifted when Beria's rivals finally overcame him and ousted his appointees (arresting the more important ones) and others they thought sympathetic to him.

As a result of this political infighting—not of the restoration of socialist legality—many KGB positions became vacant, and each time "the party" (whoever chanced to be leading it) sent in "staunch cadres." After Beria's fall, some six hundred party executives were installed as chiefs and deputy chiefs of sections, departments, and directorates.***

When Khrushchev in 1958 appointed his Komsomol chief Aleksandr Shelepin to head the KGB, the latter brought many party and Komsomol leaders with him into the organs. Three years later that scenario was repeated when another party executive and Komsomol chief, Vladimir Semichastniy, replaced Shelepin. Among those who now moved in from the Komsomol leadership was Vadim Tikunov, who became deputy chairman of the KGB and later Minister of Internal Affairs (then called MOOP). Soon thereafter, as Brezhnev consolidated his power (1966–67) and put party functionary Yuri Andropov in charge of the KGB, these two moved their own favored party officials into top positions in the organs— men like Chebrikov and Pirozhkov, who remained there under Gorbachev.

But never did the influx of party men change the KGB. Look at the man who, at the time of this writing, supervises all its operations, at home and abroad, responsible only to the general Chairman and the Politburo. First Deputy Chairman Filipp Denisovich Bobkov (whom I knew personally) is a longtime professional who learned his trade under such infamous Stalinists as Beria, Merkulov, and (especially) Abakumov, as well as under Yevgeniy P. Pitovranov and Oleg M. Gribanov. The continuity of Chekism remains undisturbed.

***

***They are too numerous to name here, but a few examples give the flavor. We have already mentioned CC CPSU Secretary Nikolay N. Shatalin, inserted by Malenkov in the summer of 1953, into a top position. (Shatalin was exiled the following year to a post in the Far East by Khrushchev as part of his power struggle with Malenkov; after two years, nothing more was heard of him.) Konstantin F. Lunev, a CC CPSU *apparatchik*, became first deputy chairman of the KGB and was transferred later to head the KGB in the Kazakh Republic. Khrushchev put his trusted associate from the CC CPSU apparatus, Aleksandr M. Lenev, into the critical command of the Ninth Directorate (bodyguards), replacing an old colleague of Beria's. (Lenev was soon replaced there by yet another Khrushchev man from the Moscow party organization, Vladimir I. Ustinov.) Later in 1956, Khrushchev brought in Nikolay P. Dudorov from the CC CPSU apparatus to be MVD minister.

Chekists into the Party Leadership

All that is only one side of the coin. When the regime boasts about those staunch party cadres strengthening the KGB, it neglects to publicize the equally significant flow in the other direction. Chekists have been moving into leading party positions from Lenin's time through Stalin's to Gorbachev's.

Gorbachev's two immediate predecessors as General Secretary were former Chekists. Konstantin Chernenko moved to party work in the 1930s after four years with the Border Guard Troops, fighting resistance to the Soviet occupation of central Asia. Yuri Andropov became General Secretary after fifteen years at the head of the KGB. In Gorbachev's Politburo at this writing are KGB Chairman Kryuchkov, former Checkist Boris Pugo and former MVD Minister of Georgia Eduard Shevardnadze (who reportedly promoted the torture of prisoners there).[6] Until late 1987 there was also the 28-year KGB veteran Geidar Aliyev and until September 1989 KGB Chairman (and later overseer) Viktor Chebrikov. Together they represented about a quarter of the Politburo's voting membership, which is not unprecedented: for a time in the 1970s, Aliyev, Andropov, and Pelshe were among only eleven voting members.

Lavrenty Beria shifted back and forth between party and State Security and later was one of the four principal Politburo leaders to inherit Stalin's power—while simultaneously heading State Security. His predecessor at the head of State Security, Yezhov, was also a Politburo member at the time he was conducting the purge of 1937–38. Felix Dzerzhinsky was elevated by Stalin to the Politburo (as a candidate member) in 1924. While remaining chief Chekist, Dzerzhinsky simultaneously headed two People's Commissariats (Internal Affairs and Railways) and later all industry, commerce, and transport as chairman of the Supreme Council of the Economy. Forty years later Aleksandr Shelepin headed, in succession, the Komsomol, the KGB, and the trade unions.

So prominent did many Chekists become in the party hierarchy that outsiders may forget their earlier State Security work. Nikolay Bulganin, later chairman of the Council of Ministers, served four years in the Cheka during the Red Terror, first in the province of Nizhniy Novgorod††† and then in Turkestan. Anastas Mikoyan is better remembered as deputy prime minister and Minister of Foreign Trade than as an operative of the

---

†††According to some sources which I cannot confirm, Bulganin and others were forced to leave Nizhniy Novgorod because their savagery was so extreme that it was criticized even by their own party leaders.

Baku Cheka—or as the man who, in an address on the VCheka's 20th anniversary, said that "every worker of the soviet must be an assistant of the NKVD." Nikolay Ignatov, Politburo member from 1957 until after Khrushchev's fall in 1964, had been a VCheka and OGPU official from 1918–32, helping (like Chernenko) to suppress the resistance of Central Asians. At the provincial level, careers like that of a regional OGPU chief named Yevdokimov were routine: after using fabrication and provocation to set up an infamous show trial in 1928, he was raised to the top of the North Caucasus party organization.

Active and former Chekists occupy top levels of the party hierarchy. Every State Security chairman except Abakumov and Fedorchuk has been a Central Committee member,‡‡‡ as have some deputy chairmen starting in Lenin's time and most recently under Gorbachev with the appointment of Filipp Bobkov—head of the KGB directorate charged with repressing internal dissent—at the 27th Party Congress in 1986. Ex-Chekists sit in high Central Committee positions too, like Pavel P. Laptev, who in 1988 was first deputy chairman of the General Department which coordinates the secretariat's activities. The KGB chief of a union republic routinely becomes a member not only of its Central Committee but also of its ruling buro, and the same applies in regional party committees. It is thus a short and logical step for the top Chekist, like Givi Gumbaridze in Georgia in 1989 and Boris Pugo in Latvia in 1984, to become the overall party chief.

An unusual window onto such moves was opened in the 1970s in Azerbaijan. From this land where the Chekist Geidar Aliyev had risen (like Beria before him) to the top levels of the CPSU, a party functionary named Ilyz Zemtsov brought detailed information to the West. He showed that during the three years between August 1969 and August 1972, Aliyev moved nearly two thousand KGB-connected people into high party and state positions. In the party they became, for instance, CC secretary, first secretaries of Baku and Kirovabad City party committees, chiefs of two departments of the CC apparatus, 12 *raion* first secretaries, and one second secretary. In the state, Chekists became chairman and first deputy chairman of the Republic's Council of Ministers, chairman of the presidium of the republic's Supreme Soviet, and chairman of a regional soviet. "In all, 37 district Party Committee secretaries and chairmen of the Executive Committee, 7 ministers, 14 vice-ministers, 29 directors of administrations of the republic, and directors of the university, of the Institute of National Economy, and of a theater."[7]

---

‡‡‡Vitaliy Fedorchuk, who replaced Andropov as KGB chairman in 1982, did not become a CC CPSU member in that post because no CPSU Congress was held during his eight months there.

Such transfers of KGB men into leading positions in the state hierarchy are by no means uncommon. An old Chekist, Aleksandr F. Gorkin, was for twenty years secretary of the Presidium of the USSR Supreme Soviet.§§§ At the top of the USSR Council of Ministers until 1987, as first deputy chairman, was the longtime Chekist Geidar Aliyev, while some of his old Chekist comrades headed the governments of union republics, including those of Estonia**** and Byelorussia.†††† Chekists head ministries of those union-republic governments, too, and not only those of State Security or Internal Affairs. So well did one KGB colonel do his cover job as deputy trade representative in Tokyo procuring secret electronic products that on his return to Moscow he was appointed all-Union Minister of the Electronics Industry.[8] And as we describe in a later chapter, many agencies of government that serve KGB purposes are led by active and reserve KGB officers; among them are the censorship organization Glavlit, the International Copyright Agency, Intourist, and foreign trade organizations including the Chamber of Commerce. Also, of course, Chekists serve in the closely related institutions of justice. The above-mentioned Aleksandr F. Gorkin was for two years chairman (chief justice) of the Soviet Supreme Court, whose deputy chairman was my old KGB friend Sergey Bannikov.

Chekism is an aspect of party work, and it can safely be assumed that anyone who reaches high party position has long cooperated with the KGB.‡‡‡‡ Lenin's dictum is true: every good Communist is at the same

§§§Election as a deputy to the USSR or union-republic supreme soviets is, of course, more of an honor than a position of power, but it is worth mentioning that of those elected to the USSR Supreme Soviet in March 1984 eighteen were active KGB officers and three were former ones. (Among them are the USSR KGB chairman and his principal deputies plus practically all the union-republic KGB chairmen and the ex-Chekist who headed the GRU.) Chekists can similarly be found in union-republic supreme soviets and in the executive committees of major city soviets.

****Valter Ivanovich Klauson, who retired in 1983, had been a lieutenant general of State Security and participated in the ruthless NKVD-MGB elimination and deportation of loyal Estonians and "class enemies" in 1941 and again from 1945–51.

††††Aleksandr N. Aksenov had earlier been deputy KGB chairman, then Minister of Internal Affairs of the republic, before rising to its top governmental post. He moved in 1983 to nearby Poland as ambassador and in 1985 was appointed head of the USSR State Committee for Radio and Television Broadcasting.

‡‡‡‡Naturally this is omitted from official biographies, but it is nevertheless surprising that such records—and even obituaries—often conceal even the fact of staff service in the organs. To cite only a few individuals already mentioned: Aksenov's biography in the list of deputies of the Supreme Soviet omits his KGB service. When Aleksandr Panyushkin died,

time a good Chekist. And this also helps to understand the role of the KGB within the armed forces.

---

his obituary (signed by Brezhnev, Andropov, and other Politburo members) simply omitted all of his work from 1947–56 as a top KGB officer. In 1984 Semen D. Ignatyev's obituary did not mention that he had been MGB Minister. In 1977 Nikolay Dudorov's omitted his work as MVD Minister. Vadim Tikunov's two most prominent positions, deputy chairman of the KGB and Minister of MOOP (MVD) of the RSFSR, simply disappeared from his life story. Celebrating in 1978 the 90th anniversary of the birth of Ivan Alekseyevich Akulov, *Pravda* told of his high office in the Workers' and Peasants Inspection, office of the USSR Procurator, and Supreme Soviet—but omitted his service as first deputy chief of the OGPU in 1931–32.

CHAPTER 8

Controlling the Armed Forces

Solution to a Problem

"THE ATTITUDE TOWARD THE ARMY POSES ONE OF THE MOST COMPLI-cated problems facing the ruling party," warned a party theorist in the 1980s, addressing himself to Marxist revolutionaries in Asia and Africa.[1] How indeed can a narrow and intolerant one-party leadership defend itself against the people to whom it must entrust deadly weapons? The Soviet rulers have found the solution. Military men may overthrow political leaders in other countries but not in the USSR.

When they formed their own "Worker-Peasant Red Army" to take over from the disintegrating, war-weary Russian Army and to fight their civil war, the Bolsheviks were creating dangers for themselves. Because they never had enough volunteers, they were compelled to conscript their soldiers; that meant, in this agrarian society, taking them from the peasantry, a class that had quickly come to resent Bolshevik rule. To train and lead them in battle, moreover, the Bolsheviks had to rely on officers and noncoms who had served the tsar.* To prevent such "class enemies" (to

---

*By the end of the civil war nearly 50,000 ex-tsarist officers formed three-quarters of their officer corps, supported by nearly a quarter-million ex-tsarist noncommissioned officers. Such officers commanded the whole Red Army and field armies and held key positions on the general staff. Among them were tsarist Col. Sergey Kamenev, who became commander of the Red Army; tsarist Maj. Gen. Aleksandr Svechin, who became head of the Red Army general staff, and tsarist Col. Boris Shaposhnikov, who occupied high staff positions; in command of field armies were tsarist Col. Aleksandr Yegorov, Maj. Avgust Kork, and Lt. Mikhail Tukhachevsky. Some former tsarist officers and noncoms joined the Communist Party and gained high rank and great renown, but their numbers were gradually reduced until by 1930 they composed only a tenth of the officer corps.

whom they temporarily granted the more acceptable label of "military specialists") from turning their weapons in the wrong direction posed a complicated problem indeed. Lenin and his men solved it by creating unique institutions of self-defense.

Those institutions remain active to this day.

They subordinated the armed forces at the center and at fronts and regions to joint party-military staffs (called "revolutionary-military councils," "workers and peasants council of defense." "military councils," etc.) that assured party chiefs of ultimate command authority.

They appointed "military commissars"—trusted Bolsheviks—as the "immediate political organ of Soviet power in the army." Independent of military command channels and reporting directly to the party leadership, the commissars were positioned at the shoulder of every military commander, were given power equal to his, and cosigned all orders and reports. They made sure that the army did as the party ordered, but above all they were there (as the then rulers put it) "to prevent army institutions from becoming nests of conspiracy or using weapons against workers and peasants."[2]

Third, they spread the available Communists (party and Komsomol members) throughout the army. During the civil war they rarely amounted to more than ten percent of any troop unit and sometimes much less than five percent. They were organized into party cells subordinated to the commissar and were given a mission of propaganda, recruitment, and surveillance. They were to indoctrinate the soldiers and sailors with "Lenin's ideas of socialist power and its preservation, devotion to the socialist revolution, and other high moral and political principles."[3] They recruited military men into the party (bringing them under party discipline) and watched over the morale and obedience of the other soldiers while helping the commissars to "control the military and administrative activities of the commanders."

Fourth, they formed Chekas at the military fronts in mid-1918 and by the beginning of 1919 had inserted Cheka units (designated as "special departments"—*Osobyy Otdely,* or OO) into all major army commands. Like the political commissars, these Chekists remained independent of the army commanders, reporting only to their VCheka superiors through their own channels.

As a final safeguard, the families of the "military specialists" were made hostage to their good conduct. If any of the ex-tsarists should go over to the enemy or get involved in plotting, their wives and children would be arrested and sent off to concentration camps.

Much has changed since that early, revolutionary time. By the 1970s all officers and 70 percent of the enlisted ranks (in elite units 100 percent) were members of the party or Komsomol; no officer advances higher than captain unless he has made the step from Komsomol to party. Today the armed forces represent the party, the vanguard of what propaganda calls a unanimous people.

What has not changed, however, are the leaders' precautions. All of those original elements of control remain active. Military councils that include the local party first secretaries oversee military districts and other commands, and the USSR Defense Council holds supreme authority at the center and uses the Main Military Council of the Armed Forces as a subordinate body. The party still runs its own parallel organization of political commissars, today called the Political Administration of the Army and Navy. Party and Komsomol maintain primary organizations within the armed forces to recruit military men into the party and ensure that their units subscribe to the party line. Party organizations still have tasks that in other armies would be command responsibilities: promoting military discipline and professional efficiency, and dealing with morale problems. Security remains in the independent hand of the OOs, part of the KGB. And just as in that earlier period, families are kept hostage to the soldiers' good behavior. Officers are not allowed to take their wives with them on postings abroad (even within the Soviet Bloc) unless they are leaving close family members behind in the USSR; every soldier abroad is made to understand that if he defects, his family will suffer punishment.

One justification for such precautions is the conditions under which the Soviet soldier is made to serve. His restricted and Spartan life may simplify the job of political control and indoctrination, but it also creates problems of morale and discipline. He is given only a few hours' free time each week and no vacation during his two-year service. If stationed abroad, even in Communist-ruled countries like Poland or East Germany, he is kept in compounds that he and his fellow soldiers liken to concentration camps. He is not allowed out of his barracks except during rare outings (in a supervised group) nor is he allowed to talk to any natives of the country. His food is bad: sometimes for weeks on end he is served half-spoiled frozen fish, few (and sometimes near-rotten) vegetables, and nearly inedible gruel. His noncoms are often drunk and beat up young draftees. Hostility between Russians and Central Asians or other nationalities create tensions and fear. Alcoholism is common; drugs a growing problem. The soldier does not have the comfort of serving with friends from the same neighborhod or village: the leaders separate them, fearing this *zemlyachestvo* as a bond of loyalty that they did not form and cannot fully control.

The leaders remain wary. When they spot a security threat within a military unit and cannot precisely determine who is responsible, they not only punish the commanding officer and his deputies but may also disband the entire unit.[4] Punishment for infractions may extend up to the commander of the regiment or division. An army unit in training must turn in every emptied cartridge case it has fired, to be checked against the remaining ammunition. If a single round is unaccounted for, the area is searched carefully. If it is not found, the matter is turned over to the OO/KGB for investigation. If the mystery is not solved, the commanding officer, security officer, and others will be reprimanded or punished.

Party Control

Two days after Trotsky's April 6, 1918, decree formally recognized the rights and duties of political commissars, their organization was established. It was first called the All-Russian Bureau of Political Commissars, later (May 26, 1919) the Political Directorate of the Military Revolutionary Council (*Politicheskoye Upravleniye Revvoyensoveta,* or PUR). At this time it also became the equivalent of a department of the Central Committee of the CPSU. On January 26, 1920, it established political departments for fronts, armies, and divisions, and political-educational directorates in military districts. Since April 1958 it has been called (as it was previously, during the Second World War) the Main Political Administration of the Army and Navy (Glavpu; the acronym Glavpur is seen in historical texts, referring to the PUR period).

The meddling by these "politicals" irritated the military commanders and hampered operations from the very beginning, but it was not until 1925–28 that the principle of unitary command (*yedinonachalstvo*) was established, reducing the commissar from coequal of the commander to the status of his political deputy *(zampolit).* In 1942 the political commissars dropped their special "commissar" titles and assumed regular military ranks. Today an ever-increasing proportion of them come to their political tasks with military training and qualifications appropriate to their military units—as sailors, paratroopers, or pilots. Some even shift to military command or staff positions; but their organization remains separate, reporting, as always, through party channels to Glavpu. And their power is immense, for no officer or noncom gets a promotion without his party organization's *Kharakteristika*—certification of a good party record.

The political officer was earlier called a "political instructor" (*kommissar,* or *politruk*) and is today called a "political worker" (*politrabotnik*). Despite his apparently reduced authority, he still exercises a measure of independent, parallel command by controlling his military unit's party and

Komsomal organization—of which the commanders and other officers are members—which watches over professional efficiency and questions of discipline and morale.

Like any party secretary throughout the Soviet government and society, the *politrabotnik* works according to a plan which specifies the number of hours his unit must devote to meetings and lectures and to studying the latest policy speech of the General Secretary or recommendations of the latest Party Congress or CC CPSU Plenum. He commands a captive audience. Here in the armed forces men live and work in groups, their whole lives submitted to tight discipline and constant oversight; they can practically be marched to party meetings. As the early *politruks* discovered and Soviet leaders still repeat, the armed forces are "a splendid school" for indoctrinating the entire population. It is a school in which the masters can equate conformity with patriotism and patriotism with hatred of "enemies," a school which prepares its graduates to return to civilian life imbued with discipline and infused with zeal.

Gorbachev's *perestroika,* with its promise of separating party and state functions, shook these military structures as well as political ones and offered new opportunities for the military to shake off some of the political burden. By 1988 reformers were debating the elimination of conscription and the formation of a "professional army," and some went so far as to propose that the union republics have their own armies. In early 1989 the head of the Glavpu himself called for clearer distinctions between political and command functions in the armed services and criticized the practice by which *politrabotniki* approve military decisions.[5]

Some Western observers had already come to consider party-political work in the Soviet armed services as little more than a pro forma exercise affording no real control over the armed forces.[6] It is no doubt true, as they point out, that the troops are bored with, and indifferent to, these party harangues, but this is not the heart of the matter. More important is the party's role in selecting those who will advance in rank. Primary party and Komsomol organizations have an impact, too: their meetings and tasks bring young people together in a common, militant cause, carrying on the indoctrination begun in schools.

The party leaders will not lightly dispense with this political indoc- trination and control upon which they think their own safety depends. Their two experiences of slackening their grip on the military—during the Second World War (when Stalin found it expedient to soft-pedal ideology in favor of national patriotism) and briefly under Marshal Zhukov after the death of Stalin—gave them a sense of danger to their own power and they quickly backtracked. In 1956, while the post-Stalin "thaw" loosened controls over the arts and prison conditions improved, Minister of Defense and war hero Marshal Georgiy Zhukov reduced the amount of party indoctrination for soldiers and noncommissioned officers to one hour per week. At the same time, he took positions independent of his Politburo colleagues, raising in their minds the specter of Bonapartism. Frightened, Khrushchev and others threw Zhukov out and reversed the trend. Marshal Malinovskiy, who succeeded him, criticized Zhukov's relaxation of party indoctrination in the army, condemning "the break in Leninist principle in the armed forces and the attempt to undermine the work of party organizations, party authorities, and military councils. You remember, comrades, how the work of our party organization and authorities was reduced and how little their influence was felt in the training and education of military personnel."[7] He reintroduced the morning political-information sessions (that Zhukov had stopped because they cut too deeply into military training and leisure time) and increased the hours devoted to political education and Marxist-Leninist theory.

This party work plays another indispensable role: it complements KGB controls to inhibit or prevent any military action against the rulers.

The Blend of Party and KGB Supervision

The party's work in the armed forces stretches beyond ideological exhortation while the KGB's stretches beyond intimidation, so that the two overlap enough to confuse even the victims themselves. In his memoirs of service with the Soviet fishing and merchant fleets (where the political and security organizations resemble those of the navy), Vladil Lysenko repeatedly refers to the political assistant to the ship's captain (*pompolit*) as if he were a KGB officer. The mistake is natural, so closely do they work closely together.

Imagine a sergeant, call him Skladin, serving in an artillery battery, who is told one day to come get a message from his parents at the division's Political Department (every division has one). There he is led into an unmarked office where, as he expected, it is not a political but a KGB officer who is waiting. Skladin is a secret informant (*seksot*), and the message was simply a ruse to cover his absence. He tells the OO/KGB officer, Arkadiyev, about things his comrades are doing or saying, how they are reacting to various pressures, and especifically what he has been able to learn about Private Kuznetsov, whom Arkadiyev is investigating for having listened to foreign radio broadcasts (either here in the army or earlier at home). This is a common situation, and in it party and KGB work blend: Skladin is also a member of the primary organization of the Komsomol of his unit. Here he is telling the OO/KGB, via Arkadiyev, how the men are reacting to the party's campaign for stricter discipline and higher morale.

Political and state security officers work closely together today as they did during the Second World War. Among the many CPSU bosses who served as military political officers was Leonid Brezhnev, chief political officer of the 18th Army. He is reported to have encouraged the OO's to "react with lightning speed" in "uncovering spies in the army and the front line area." He stressed that the "OO must maintain close contact with the officers of the Political Department", and he lived according to his own teachings: he "often participated in operational meetings with OO officers, teaching them the art of combining counterintelligence and general military work." Brezhnev "reacted swiftly to information from the OOs about disorders within the ranks."

The Chekist Arkadiyev of our example does indeed "maintain close contact" with the *politrabotnik* of that artillery division and advises him of the situation as seen through the eyes of his *seksots* such as Skladin. Together they review the records of new arrivals in the unit and share their information and suspicions. Of course there is bound to be some misunderstanding between officers whose responsibilities overlap, especially since the political officers know that they, like everyone else, are under the KGB's watchful eye. At times (notably in the early years and in the Second World War) military authorities have debated their respective rights and responsibilities, but the OOs always emerged free of any real constraints. There is much less friction between them, however, than between regular troops and the political officers or between regular troops and the KGB/OO officers. Often they keep company with each other apart from the regular military officers. *Politrabotniki* often shift, as did I myself, to the OO/KGB. They bear the common burden of protecting the party leadership against military forces and weapons.

The Special Sections: OO/KGB

Within the army the KGB enjoys the same independence as throughout the rest of society. Its military OOs report directly up to the KGB headquarters, where they are supervised by the Third Directorate, formerly known as the Directorate of Special Departments and, during the Second World War, as SMERSH.

For obvious reasons, this has always been one of the most important

elements of Soviet State Security. Of the sixteen State Security chairmen
since Lenin took power, five rose from the OOs and some commanded the
OOs at the same time as the whole KGB.†

Sometimes the Third Directorate's function is referred to as "military
counterintelligence" or "military security" but these terms are misleadingly restrictive. The OOs do, of course, combat foreign spying (and
wartime sabotage) aimed at Soviet armed forces and military-industrial
installations and they do guard secrets and keep a wary eye on military
personnel—but they have done and still do much more than that.

At the beginning, for example, the OOs defended the nation's borders;
and even after the creation of Border Troops, they continued, from 1918–
26, to supervise them. They helped pacify the country—through terror,
burnings, and massacres—during and after the civil war. They fought
peasant uprisings in the 1920s and helped uproot the peasants during the
collectivization. They battled against nationalist freedom fighters in
Transcaucasia, the Ukraine, and Central Asia in the 1920s and 1930s. In
the Second World War they were given a vast range of tasks as SMERSH.

In 1942–43, as the Soviet armies began to roll forward over lands that
had been occupied by the Germans, Stalin separated the OOs from the
NKVD and subordinated them directly to himself as head of the State
Defense Committee, giving them the now-infamous name of SMERSH.
He himself selected this acronym from a slogan that originated with Lenin
and Trotsky in 1919: *"Smert Shpionam!"* (Death to spies!) To SMERSH he
gave powers seldom equaled during the KGB's powerful history. SMERSH
was to eliminate, by whatever means, the threats to Soviet rule stemming
from the alien contamination of war. SMERSH identified, arrested, interrogated, and imprisoned or executed people who had helped the Germans
administer the occupied lands or who had used the opportunity to try to
escape Soviet rule or who had given vent to their disaffection with that
rule. In its more strictly military work, SMERSH countered German
spies, shot deserting (and sometimes even retreating) soldiers, shot re-
covered Soviet soldiers who had surrendered to the Germans (I witnessed
such executions), and punished the slightest breach of military discipline
or the vaguest suggestion of disloyalty to Stalin.

---

†Dzerzhinsky did so while heading the whole VCheka; Menzhinsky and Yagoda rose
from command of the OOs to deputy chairman and then chairman. Viktor Abakumov was
head of SMERSH and Deputy People's Commissar of Internal Affairs when Stalin appointed him Minister of State Security. Vitaliy Fedorchuk had spent more than thirty years
in OO work before becoming KGB chairman in the Ukraine, and while he was USSR
KGB chairman in 1982 his first deputy, Georgiy Tsinev, was also a former head of OO.
Longtime OO officer Gen. Pyotr Ivashutin had been first deputy chairman of the KGB
when in 1963 he took over Soviet Military Intelligence (GRU)

Operating with the Soviet armies taking over Eastern Europe in 1944–47, ‡ SMERSH set up in these countries' military-security organs in its own image, such as the Polish *Informacja*. For years it commanded them directly, via SMERSH officers wearing local uniforms. Today its successor, the KGB's Third Directorate, still coordinates and manipulates the work of these satellite military-security services, partly through liaison and advisory staffs, partly through secretly recruited agents among their key personnel. The OO directorate for the Soviet Group of Forces in Germany still manipulates the East German military counterintelligence service.

The OOs in postwar years have murdered, kidnapped, and spied on emigres abroad. Under the rubric of protecting Soviet forces, they continue to send spies across borders from Soviet military districts and groups of forces into Sweden, West Germany, Iran, Turkey, China, Pakistan, and other countries.

There are OOs in all the armed forces (ground, navy, air, rocket, and antiaircraft), in the Ministry of Defense, in all military district headquarters and groups of forces abroad, and in every military academy and training center. The KGB's Third Directorate also supervises OOs in the KGB's own Border Guard Troops and in KGB Troops. It has its hand in similar units within MVD Internal Troops and specialized militias.

The OOs can punish anyone, of any rank. Since the mid-1950s they have needed only the permission of the commander of the army before arresting officers to the rank of captain; for higher ranks they must get authorization from the Minister or Deputy Minister of Defense. This may seem to reduce the OO's powers (in Stalin's time they needed only the authority of division or corps commanders), but in practice it does not. If the KGB proposes to an army commander to arrest one of his officers, how can he say no? The KGB always has its reasons, and the army commander himself—a party member—would be responsible for defending someone the KGB had reason to suspect as a criminal. The Minister of Defense would be even less likely to prevent the KGB chairman, his Politburo colleague, from arresting a person who might endanger their common security. And it can be done even more simply, as in the case of Gen. Pyotr Grigorenko, a prominent army officer who had become a dissident: he was simply removed from the army before being arrested as a civilian.

The OOs' methods are those of KGB operatives everywhere: collecting information and denunciations and conducting provocations via secret

‡Although SMERSH was officially disbanded in 1946 and its military-security components became the Chief Directorate of Counterintelligence (GUKR) of the MGB (under its old chief, Viktor Abakumov, now Minister), that directorate continued until 1948 to use the name GUKR/SMERSH.

informants throughout every platoon, squadron, and patrol boat. They handle these informants directly or through "residents"—trusted agents who maintain contact with individual informants. Of a company's five or six officers, one or two are usually *seksots;* the chief NCO *(starshina)* in a company is often a *seksot* or resident. By serving the KGB these helpers boost their military careers and get desirable postings.

The OOs' work is eased, as we have noted, by military conditions. It takes fewer secret informants to keep an eye on individuals living and working so closely together, and it is easy to control their mail and to quarantine them from outside influences—contact with foreigners, unauthorized books, foreign news broadcasts. Nevertheless, the OO officer is compelled by his annual plan to add *seksots* to his network. He inherits others, too, who join his unit from the outside after being recruited elsewhere, perhaps in the Komsomol (where secretaries help the KGB spot likely candidates) and perhaps in high school. In each high school a "military leader" *(voyenny rukovoditel,* commonly called *voyenruk)* introduces the children to military equipment and weapons, marching and camping, physical education and discipline—and most if not all *voyenruks* are KGB *seksots* alert to pick up promising secret collaborators.

When a young *seksot* is drafted into the army he is instructed to check in secretly with the OO officer as soon as he can identify him. Even if he fails to check in, he will quickly be found: his operational file or a summary will have been forwarded to his new address by his previous controllers. The OO officer responsible for a regiment reviews with the political officer the records of all new arrivals and will check them against KGB central records. (He must: if any member of the regiment defects, or commits some grave delinquency, the OO officer will be the first to be asked, "Didn't you check him?")

Using these residents and *seksots,* the OO officer tries to spot the nonconformists. He works on an annual plan that requires him to detect potentially dissident soldiers or sailors to be saved by prophylactic "chats"or disloyal ones to be eliminated from the healthy social body. The political leaders seem convinced that traitors exist, so if he can't find them he will stir them up—or create them—by the use of provocation. His and his boss's careers depend on it.

In this military environment, punishment can be swift, severe, and exemplary without the complications of civilian jurisprudence. The OO can simply transfer a military man from a desirable foreign post (where he cherishes the hope of acquiring things that he can sell at home) to a remote spot in the Kurile Islands or to a construction battalion. (The OO unit gets the same credit for "vigilance" as if it had sent him to a concentration camp.)

Hence where a cohesive group might form—the thing the leaders fear—the invisible but palpable presence of secret informants and provocateurs and clandestine mail-openings sow fear and wariness. Thus do the KGB OOs avert a permanent danger for the leaders.

Other Means of Control

The KGB dominates the armed forces in other ways, too.

It influences the appointments of higher military commanders through the CC CPSU Administrative Organs Department. Not only has the KGB chairman at most times been a Politburo member, but his organization maintains lifelong dossiers on all military personnel.

The KGB controls security clearances within the armed forces. Whoever aspires to high command or to elite units or special weapons must have the KGB's approval.

At a lower level, too, the KGB's hand is felt. Its representative sits on the district military commissariat (which serves as draft board) along with the representatives of the local Party Committee, Soviet Executive Committee, and militia. Because of his access to secret files and secret sources, his voice, above all others, will determine whether a draftee is assigned to one of the more sensitive branches—air force, navy, rocket, border, internal, and other elite troops—or (at the other extreme) to a construction battalion.

When a soldier has violated the code of military justice, his unit's OO officer and *politrabotnik* confer with the military procurator to find a way to cope with his (or the unit's) problem.[9] They discuss the whole range of options available to them all, including KGB investigation (through secret agents and provocations), propaganda by the party representative, or demonstrative punishments by the procurator.

The armed forces' most potent weapons—atomic warheads, missiles, chemical and bacteriological weapons—are subject to KGB controls that we discuss later in the context of the little-known KGB Troops.

Through Glavlit the KGB controls the censorship of all armed forces publications, including newspapers such as *Krasnaya Zvezda* and publications of the Military Publishing House (*Voyenizdat*).

We have already mentioned, and will note again later, the special troops that the KGB and MVD possess as an eventual counterweight to army divisions.

And above all, the KGB chairman on the Defense Council and his local subordinates on local military councils, exercise command responsibility in military affairs.

Control of the GRU

Many sources have spoken about a rivalry (some call it bitter) between the KGB and the military intelligence service, GRU (*Glavnoye Razvedyvatelnoye Upravleniye,* Chief Intelligence Directorate of the General Staff of the Soviet Armed Forces). In fact, the rivalry is superficial. Never since the late 1920s has there been any question of which was dominant.

For one thing, the GRU has been under Chekist command. Pyotr Ivashutin, who retired in 1987 after heading the GRU for a quarter of a century, had been the KGB's top OO specialist. He went to the GRU in 1963 from the deputy chairmanship of the KGB, taking the place of the famous Chekist Ivan Serov, who had commanded the GRU for five years after a lifetime of Chekism and a decade as KGB chairman. During the period 1936–38 NKVD chief Nikolay Yezhov simultaneously commanded the GRU. The GRU's famous chief during the 1920s and 1930s, Jan Berzin, moved there from the OOs. Before that, military intelligence had been commanded by A.K. Artuzov, former head of the OOs who simultaneously held the State Security (then OGPU) position of chief of counterintelligence.

A large OO department not only controls GRU personnel, but occupies offices within the GRU's headquarters and reviews the security of GRU secret operations.[10] No secrets can be kept from its eyes.

The OO/KGB watches over the GRU as it does other parts of the military command by manipulating secret informants among GRU personnel. And KGB officers abroad oversee them, too; in Vienna during the Soviet occupation I was personally responsible for the files of no fewer than five GRU officers, under various diplomatic and commercial covers, who were KGB *seksots.*

The KGB has other controls. Any GRU officer going abroad must go through KGB-controlled exit procedures. Furthermore, the GRU's Department for Foreign Relations is staffed largely by KGB officers. Much of the intelligence (especially scientific and technological secrets from the West) that the GRU collects abroad is processed in an interagency system in which the KGB occupies the key positions.

Whether or not its field officers are aware of it, the GRU operates in effect as a military arm of the KGB. Though there may be frictions (as between any competing components, even within the KGB itself), the GRU cannot constitute a separate force in internal power rivalries or in some putative military attempt to take over the rulership.

The Military as a Political Power Factor

Against this background it is difficult to imagine the military establishment constituting a separate factor in Soviet power struggles. Surely military commanders exercise great influence over budgets and even policy decisions, but their influence is derived not from the threat of using their forces against the party's rule but from their specialized knowledge of a field essential to the regime's survival.

A military coup would be difficult to mount. Imagine, for example, an infantry captain or artillery colonel or the commander of an army who would start such a conspiracy. Anyone he would try to draw into the conspiracy would probably suspect OO/KGB provocation and to save his own skin would report him immediately. For these two to enlist others would increase the danger geometrically. Then if these conspirators took unusual steps, others would notice; army ranks are riddled not only with secret informants but also with young people who have the party line ceaselessly drilled into them without any contrary information. An army unit could not start moving toward critical areas, least of all the key places in the city of Moscow, without the knowledge of its political or OO/KGB officers.

It would, moreover, find itself faced by the strong—and separately administered—forces of the Moscow Military District. The personnel of its Taman (infantry) and Kantemirov (tank) divisions are screened with particular care by the CC CPSU Administrative Organs Department (with KGB participation) while the KGB, invisible but palpably present, operates throughout their ranks. They and the VV's Dzerzhinsky Division are not adversaries: Soviet writings stress their cooperation, joint exercises, military and sports competitions, and use of common facilities such as rifle ranges.[11] The Politburo keeps operational control over these forces through the Minister of Defense, who is a Politburo member (full or candidate) and through the Defense Council chaired by the General Secretary with the active, permanent participation of the KGB chairman.

In an acute economic or other crisis the Soviet Communist Party might conceivably become so discredited that it would have to defend itself by drastic military measures throughout the country, as it has done so often in the face of purely local uprisings. For this contingency the necessary structures are ready: the Defense Council can impose martial law while the party holds on to its rule.

The armed forces can thus be said to control the Soviet regime as much as the regime controls the armed forces. Like the KGB and with the KGB, they compose with the party a single entity.

CHAPTER 9

Power Struggles and the KGB

A THEORY POPULAR IN THE WEST HAS IT THAT THE COMMUNIST PARTY apparatus, the KGB, and the armed forces compose the three legs of a triangular balance of power, applying mutual restraint almost akin to a separation of powers. Adherents of this theory watch for signs that this balance is shifting: in 1982, for example, they saw Andropov's rise from the KGB to the top of the party as a sign that KGB power and influence were growing and similarly assessed the 1986 appointment of ex-Chekist Aleksandr Aksenov to head the State Committee for Radio and Television Broadcasting. When in 1987 the misconduct of a KGB officer was castigated in the press and KGB Chairman Chebrikov publicly apologized, some Western observers saw the KGB being "challenged" or "brought to heel." To some it seemed in the late 1970s and 1980s that the military establishment was gaining ascendancy over the party; but in 1986 when the Party Congress failed to promote the Defense Minister to full Politburo membership, they saw the power of the military being restrained.

Despite its superficial appeal, this formula is misleading. As we have seen in the previous three chapters; both army and KGB are so tightly intertwined with the party that neither can act as an independent entity in power struggles. They are parts of a whole over which the top party leadership—of which they are part—exercises unchallenged command.

But the Soviet system does invite and even demand power rivalry and intrigue. The only way an ambitious careerist can get his hands on the levers of power is by appointment from above—by party hierarchs and with the KGB's clearance. To make his way upward in the party structure he needs help. If at the beginning he lacks a patron (a relative, say, of himself or his wife) he must attract one by doing zealous party work for him and by toadying. At the same time he must conform to party

standards and humorlessly mouth party propaganda and must avoid
showing too much skill, ambition, or zeal, which might be construed as
threatening to patron or rival alike. He must be ready to undercut rivals
and remain alert to their intrigues, keeping his nose to the political winds
to detect shifts that warn him when to drop one patron and adopt another
with better prospects. This requires deftness and luck, but if he succeeds,
and rises, the party careerist attracts toadies of his own, who tie themselves to his coattails just as he did to his patron's. However, this system
offers no safety: the careerist may lose this support by a misstep or a rival's
intrigue. Such intrigues are not unknown in open societies, of course, but
they are wonderfully nourished by a system where all power to hire and fire
is concentrated in a single narrow leadership, where the true political
processes remain unwritten, and where so much is done under the cover of
secrecy. At the level where rivals compete for the top leadership, they are
likely to try to use—or to forestall others' use of—some of the KGB's
powers.

No longer can a single hierarch manipulate all the KGB's powers: this
is the legacy of the Beria case. Stalin did indeed use the KGB as a personal
instrument, and upon his sudden death Beria inherited that essential part
of Stalin's power and seems to have set out to use it against his rivals. That
was Beria's real "crime" that causes Soviet leaders so much pretended
outrage. They had to eliminate Beria or be eliminated themselves, and
after they succeeded they made arrangements to keep each other's hands off
what they had taken from Beria's.

Some of the KGB's powers, of course, are at the disposition of its
chairman (or one or another of his top deputies); and, perhaps more
important, he can prevent others from using them. When in 1957 a group
of Politburo members combined in an effort to oust Khrushchev, a loyal
KGB chief helped fend them off; in 1964 when other opponents made
their move, a different KGB chairman brought KGB facilities into play to
help topple Khrushchev. His successor, Brezhnev, was able finally to
anchor his own power only when, after three years, he had become strong
enough to replace successively the heads of the MVD and KGB with
people on whom he could rely.

A word of warning: accounts of high-level Soviet power plays—even
such as those surrounding the rise and fall of Khrushchev and Brezhnev,
which may be accepted by many Western historians—may not be true;
and a scholar takes a risk when he relies on them, for such matters rarely
become known. Even people inside the party hierarchy are unlikely to get
more than fragmentary glimpses, echoes of hearsay, and clouds of rumor

confounded by purposeful misinformation and sheer invention. All this is likely to get further distorted by Western guesswork and analysis.

Nothing more dramatically illustrates the need for skepticism than the mystery that has shrouded the death of Stalin. For a third of a century after this momentous event, historians in the West had to rely upon the versions put about by Khrushchev and others. I personally learned enough, from a position with Stalin's bodyguard organization, to certify that those versions are false. [1]

In the story as I know it, Beria, over an eighteen-month period beginning August 1951, gradually increased his influence over State Security at the expense of Stalin's. While Stalin prepared to purge Beria and other rivals, Beria was managing to dismantle Stalin's inner ring of defenses. By February 1953 he had deprived Stalin of the ability to control CPSU cadres through the intimidation that he had long exercised via State Security. Stalin's death on March 5 came as a logical step in a sequence of events and occurred in circumstances indicating that it was not due to natural causes. Certainly those circumstances, with which I became acquainted thanks to my friends in Stalin's bodyguards, are different from the ones described by Khrushchev (in conversations and in his so-called memoirs) or other Soviet sources in the late 1980s.

The powers that were redistributed in the course of this struggle surely survive in some form in today's KGB and MVD. The KGB must still investigate party leaders as it did earlier; and it is known that, with the huge Surveillance Directorate of today's KGB, at least one unit is reserved for "especially sensitive operations such as surveillance of a hierarch." [2] The KGB must still keep secret files on the private lives of party leaders. Even if the KGB and MVD were no longer actively seeking compromising information on party leaders, it would continue to spring to their eyes as they observe the rest of the community.

The KGB has facilities to fabricate and surreptitiously leak information that could weaken or destroy a hierarch's power. Stalin was able to document his accusations of Trotsky during the Moscow trials with forged letters, false agent reports, and obedient witnesses. Whenever this evidence could be tested in the West it was exposed as false and often ridiculous, but it served its purpose. In recent decades the West has witnessed the growing sophistication of KGB forgeries made to embarrass or discredit Western governments and leaders; the same capability can be turned against Soviet hierarchs.

Through its power over the press and its control of censorship, the KGB can not only suppress information but also let it pass—or insert it. (Some high Soviet leader seems to have done both in 1981 to discredit and ridicule Brezhnev as his health declined.) With its network of agents the KGB is deft at planting rumors.

The KGB has ways, too, to exercise direct control over the person of hierarchs. One is via the bodyguards. When Stalin in the late 1940s began to regard the wartime hero Marshal Zhukov as a potential rival, he passed orders to Zhukov's bodyguards to restrain him in his provincial headquarters to keep him away from Moscow and make it more difficult for him to keep contacts with other high officials. When Nikita Khrushchev was flying from his vacation back to Moscow in 1964 (according to the recent report of a party insider),[3] he noticed that his personal bodyguards had been switched without his knowledge. Recognizing the danger, he ordered the pilot to divert to Kiev, but the pilot—inevitably an employee of the KGB Guards Directorate—refused. Upon landing Khrushchev was met by KGB Chairman Semichastniy (who, to accommodate the plotters, had had the guards switched), who escorted him to the Central Committee meeting where he was ousted from power.

The bodyguard organization also controls the Kremlin clinic, although it was formally transferred to the Ministry of Health, and the Politburo canteen that serves hot meals to the leaders. The Kremlin Komendatura controls the physical premises where the top leaders work. A KGB department develops poisons without antidote, illnesses without cure. And the KGB controls the leaders' communications, as well as special troops in Moscow and key areas of the country.

Of its many potential weapons of political infighting, perhaps the most permanently threatening to the hierarchs is the information on them that the KGB collects. Stalin quickly recognized the possibilities inherent in secret dossiers. In the first years of Bolshevik power, as head of the Orgburo, he controlled files on the party cadres; as head of the Party Control Commission he supervised disciplinary action against high officials; as overseer of the inspectorate (RKI) he got more information. He cultivated a special relationship with state security chiefs Dzerzhinsky and Yagoda through whom he got access to secret information, including old tsarist files. All this was ammunition against his rivals to destroy them or force them to his own side. They all had things to hide: crimes, arrests, early collaboration with the tsarist police or with "bourgeois" or foreign elements*; and these files exposed to Stalin what had been concealed from

---

*Stalin may have been inspired by the presence of skeletons in his own closet: compelling circumstantial evidence suggests that from 1906–12 he secretly served the tsarist police—and his own ambition. (See E. E. Smith, *The Young Stalin*. (New York: Farrar, Strauss and Giroux, 1967.) Since Stalin's death, Khrushchev and his successors have shown great interest in the tsarist files that slipped out to the West during the civil war and which may compromise Stalin or others.

official party records. When he later purged his rivals in the mid-1930s and late 1940s and when he prepared to do it again in 1953, Stalin's accusations against them were mainly invented, but some of his fabrications grew from germs of truth culled from the secret files of the NKVD/MVD.

This capability, which inevitably remains intact (see chapters. 6 and 12), has surely contributed to the rise of recent General Secretaries as it did to Stalin's. Konstantin Chernenko, after many years spent handling all of Brezhnev's correspondence and files, and Yuri Andropov, after fifteen years atop the KGB, both commanded secret and compromising information on their rivals. Politburo member Mikhail Suslov, close to State Security since Stalin's day, not only survived through all the leadership changes until his death but sponsored the fast-rising career of Mikhail Gorbachev. In the late 1980s quite believable rumors were circulating in Moscow to the effect that, as one press report put it, "the present KGB boss, Mr. Chebrikov, clinched Mr. Gorbachev's selection as party leader by threatening to unveil secret compromising dossiers on the two other Politburo members vying for the job."[4]

Today's circumstances invite blackmail. "Corruption even in the highest stratum of the Soviet ruling elite has become a fact, and not even a rare fact," wrote Konstantin Simis, a former Soviet lawyer. "After years of working on the lower levels of the party-state apparatus and clambering up the official ladder, bribes and gifts [have become] a daily routine" for Soviet officials. In Georgia, he reported, a "reckless orgy of corruption was raging almost openly."[5] Ilya Zemtsov has revealed the same, or worse, about Azerbaijan. In Central Asia, leaders of republic, oblast, and district party and government organizations have been exposed in the Soviet press; 200,000 government officials (a few at high level like Deputy Foreign Trade Minister Vladimir Sushkov arrested for smuggling) were prosecuted in 1986 for such misdeeds as corruption and manufacture of substandard goods.[6] These are only the tip of the iceberg, exposed because of lack of high protection. In Politburo member Frol Kozlov's safe "were found packages of precious stones and huge bundles of money," Simis reports.[7] The punishment for corruption can be drastic—hundreds have been executed—but no one seriously suggests that the regime, however dramatically it publicizes its cleansing campaign, could or would ever put an end to it. Corruption is built into the system, and the KGB knows about much of it.† You can sense the KGB's power in the question that hovers

†Other agencies that investigate corruption share this power with the KGB. The MVD's Chief Directorate for the Protection of Socialist Property has secret informants inside these circles, and the Criminal Investigation Directorate as well as the Chief Directorate of the Militia collect information. The Customs Service detects illegal importations from abroad. The Party Control Commission reviews party accusations against high-level members.

over this whole scene: among all these corrupt leaders, which ones will be exposed, and who will select them?

You can glimpse in a Polish case of the early 1980s the way a high KGB or MVD official might use this secret knowledge. Mieczyslav Moczar, a former head of the Polish version of the KGB and member of the Polish Politburo in the 1970s, was apparently maneuvering to rise to the top of the party hierarchy when instead he was shunted aside. He was appointed head of a control commission, a sort of general accounting office, and—as an old Chekist—recognized that this apparent backwater offered opportunities. Knowing what to look for, he dug out receipts, sales contracts, bank documents, denunciations, and police reports which proved corrupt dealings. He built up compromising dossiers on about 350 Polish party and military leaders including the then party leader Kania and two of his predecessors, the chief of the government and some of his predecessors, about sixty ministers, scores of Central Committee members, and prominent civilian and military personalities. Moczar seems to have been planning to use these materials either for revenge or to blackmail his way back into a top power position, but he was thwarted when General Jaruszelski's regime imposed martial law in 1981. (Jaruszelski himself was reported to have been implicated by the files but managed to use some of the information to put down and make scapegoats of his own rivals.)[8]

Such maneuverings—like the elimination of Stalin—tell much about the Soviet system and are worth trying to spot. But no outsider is likely to get more than tenuous wisps of information that leak out like smoke from underground fires. It would be wrong to draw conclusions from them, but equally wrong to dismiss or forget them, because these may be all the West will ever learn of turning points in Soviet politics.

Was there, for example, a shoot-out between military forces and KGB while Brezhnev was solidifying his power? Not a word of such an event ever leaked to the West, but twenty-four hours after Brezhnev fired KGB Chairman Semichastniy in the spring of 1967 the Soviet military press began to announce the deaths of high military and KGB figures in such number as to defy coincidence. The first, moreover, was a top commander of OO/KGB, Maj. Gen. Vasily A. Lukshin, and the announcement used the word *konchina* that usually connotes sudden or unexpected death. In quick succession followed notice of the deaths of some fifteen other high military and KGB officers. Then a month later came a commendation of the Kantemirov Guards Tank Division, an elite army unit that has been used to support the leaders during political crises. Oddly, this commendation was dated precisely on the fourteenth anniversary of the day its tanks had moved into Moscow to protect the hierarchs when they arrested State Security chief Beria.

Another series of events during the last months of Brezhnev's life suggest intrigue and perhaps murder in the struggle for his succession. In December 1981 the KGB "chanced" to uncover a ring of corruption involving Brezhnev's daughter, and at just that moment a strange lapse of censorship allowed a satire against Brezhnev to appear in a Leningrad magazine. Then in January within the space of a week came two sudden deaths: that of KGB First Deputy Chairman (and head of its day-to-day operations) Semen Tsvigun and that of the powerful Politburo leader and reputed kingmaker Mikhail Suslov. Shortly afterward the top leadership of the KGB was changed, and for the first time in history two military-security specialists found themselves in its two top positions.

Soviet history is full of mysterious deaths of leaders such as Menzhinsky, Kuybyshev, Gorky, Ordzhonkidze, and Zhdanov and of bloody purges such as those in Leningrad in 1949–50 and in Georgia in 1951–52. They affected the course of Soviet history, they involved State Security, and they remain to this day only dimly known or understood.

Even such inconclusive fragments tell something about the Soviet system (beyond demonstrating how well the regime can hide its secrets). They suggest that, in the absence of legitimate procedure for turning over power at the top, violence continues to play a central role. This puts at the forefront of Soviet "politics" the decisive instruments of violence controlled by the KGB.

PART III

A LOOK INTO THE KGB

CHAPTER 10

What the KGB Does

WHAT THE KGB DOES INSIDE AND OUTSIDE THE COUNTRY IS HIDDEN, and the full picture is available only to a few top Kremlin leaders. To the extent that the outsider can observe the KGB's functioning, he will find it the surest gauge of whether and to what extent *perestroika* is transforming the Soviet system. Has the KGB's power been restrained—not only by law but also in practice? Have any of its key functions been dissolved? Its numbers and capabilities reduced? Its past crime truly exposed and its criminals punished? Have its activities been subjected to nonparty scrutiny?

A starting point is to review what the KGB really does and to discard some common illusions. To call the KGB, for example, a "secret police" and thus to liken it to the Shah of Iran's SAVAK, Chile's DINA, or even Hitler's Gestapo, is to miss its essence. It is wrong, too, to think of it as a Soviet-style combination of the American FBI and CIA. Nor are its responsibilities correctly delimited as "guarding Soviet borders, conducting foreign intelligence and counterintelligence, and investigating serious crime, including political offenses."[1]

It is not that such descriptions, all common in the Western press, are false. They are simply misleading. Parts of the KGB do perform missions like those assigned to the American FBI and CIA—not to mention the National Security Agency, military counterintelligence, State Department communications division, the Customs Service, Immigration and Naturalization Service, the Coast Guard, the Secret Service, parts of city and state police departments, governors' and mayors' offices and draft boards, and security and personnel staffs of industrial corporations. It is also true that the KGB does everything that the secret police of Nazi Germany or the Shah's SAVAK did. But such comparisons, in their effort to help Western readers understand the KGB, wrench it from the Soviet context that alone makes it understandable.

No Western security or intelligence agency—and not even the secret police organization of an authoritarian regime—is likely to occupy the highest seats of political power as the KGB does. Nor do Western security services "participate in all the functions of the state." None of them would pretend to be "educating the people," "improving society" or "perfecting democracy," much less "guaranteeing moral health." The Soviet leaders make precisely these claims for their KGB—and back them up with laws and regulations.

Even a KGB insider would have trouble delimiting the KGB's missions, for Soviet doctrine gives them almost unlimited scope. They "ensue from the program of further developing the political system, improving Soviet statehood, and developing socialist democracy," said a recent chairman. He added that "this is a modern formulation of Lenin's own description of the role of the VCheka: it 'directly implements the dictatorship of the proletariat.'" Put another way, "The Chekists' main mission is to help translate into action the socioeconomic program of the party."[2]

It is the muscle of a party whose monopoly of power demands violent coercion. "Without this organization," Lenin admitted (and KGB leaders still repeat on every anniversary), "the power of the working people cannot exist, as long as there are exploiters in the world."[3] (For "working people" read the "party leadership.") Thus the State Security organs' tasks shift with the masters' changing needs[4]—such as, today, the needs of *glosnost* and *perestroika*. "Under conditions where the country has embarked on a qualitatively new stage of its development," said Chairman Chebrikov in 1986, the KGB's responsibilities "increase substantially." Its principal task now, he said in 1987, is "to promote to the maximum the successful process of *perestroika*."[5]

With such a broad mission the KGB might do almost anything, but in practice most of its activities fall into one or more of the following categories.

(1) Helping Govern the Country

KGB leaders help make and execute domestic and foreign policy. Its voice counts heavily, as we have seen, in the Politburo and in the party leadership of republics, regions, and towns throughout the country. It dominates the fields of law and public order but is by no means restricted to them. As the KGB chairman pointed out, the KGB is "actively involved" in reforming the political system and its role in the economy is considerable.

The KGB helps select and assess the people who will be given any important post by granting or denying security clearances in the party apparatus, the armed forces, government, research institutes, or factories.

Such are the regime's priorities abroad that its most important foreign tasks are assigned to the KGB rather than to its diplomats, and KGB men occupy key positions in all agencies involved in foreign affairs. In addition the KGB keeps an eye on personal contacts with foreign governments or citizens and determines who will be allowed to go abroad. It also has some powers to propose, negotiate, sign, ratify, and abrogate international treaties. [6]

(2) Eliminating or Neutralizing Internal Resistance

Although the regime long ago destroyed what it termed "counter-revolution"* it has never stopped watching—and where necessary harassing or destroying—any groups outside direct party control. This function took on new urgency as independent groups grew in number and stridency under *glasnost*.

(3) Shielding the Leaders from the People

The KGB protects the leaders' persons (with oversight of their food and health care), makes sure that the armed forces' weapons cannot be used against them, handles their communications with each other and the outside world, and insures that outsiders will not get a close-up look at their luxurious life-styles. Being ultimately responsible for the secrecy upon which the system depends, the KGB sits atop the vast system of information control. Through its role in the cadres system, the KGB keeps undesirables out of jobs that would allow them close to the leadership.

---

*The very word "counterrevolution" disappeared from Soviet administrative-law textbooks by the mid-1960. (For example, Yu. M. Kozlov's 1964 edition still mentioned it on page 251 while that of 1968 and subsequent editions did not.) The criminal code deals instead with crimes like antistate agitation and propaganda, which can be very broadly interpreted.

(4) Helping to Make the Economy Run

In an ideological system where every worker is considered "a warrior in the building of communism," the KGB has always been responsible for rooting out that "negative phenomenon" called indiscipline. Dzerzhinsky's VCheka worked hand in hand with Dzerzhinsky's NKVD in "assuring at local levels the execution of orders of the central power." In February 1920, with the civil war won, Dzerzhinsky urged that the Chekas "turn their attention to fighting the enemies represented by economic disorganization, by speculation, and by abuse of office, so that when they are overcome the Chekas can devote their entire effort to reconstructing our economic life and surmounting the obstacles born of sabotage, lack of discipline, and ill-will."[7] This mission never ended. With its authority over hiring and firing, promoting, demoting, and punishing in every Soviet factory and enterprise, the KGB puts the teeth in the Five-Year Plan. And today, instead of fighting what used to be called "economic counterrevolution," the KGB is "putting a stop to attempts to inflict economic, political, or moral damage on our society."[8]

Using Internal Troops, the KGB puts down strikes (in Dzerzhinsky's words, "malicious sabotage" and "economic counterrevolution"). Indeed, the KGB's first task, when founded in December 1917 as the VCheka, was to break a strike.

To find laborers for unappealing "shock projects" and for dangerous mines and chemical works, "corrective labor" still serves the regime as it has in the past. The administrative organs spot delinquents, arrest and sentence them, supervise the corrective labor camps, and extend prisoners' sentences and periods of exile.

(5) Enforcing Public Order and Investigating Crime

The leaders, in their fear of the people, have given crime a political flavor. A KGB leader explained: "The successful struggle against crime, apart from generally improving the situation, also helps to ensure state security and restricts the potential of our class enemies for operations in a medium that suits them."[9] Not only does the KGB "actively participate in the preventive work of Soviet state authorities aimed at liquidating crime in the country,"[10] but it dominates the police and other institutions administered by the MVD.

Throughout most of Soviet history only two organizations—the KGB and the Procurator's Office—had the right to investigate and prepare criminal cases for prosecution. The MVD, despite an increase in its investigative function, is still excluded from the more serious cases. To the KGB is reserved the right to investigate crimes—labeled "especially important crimes against the state"—that might even indirectly affect the leader's grip on power. The KGB may take over from the Procurator's Office any investigation it deems to fit into that category. Such crimes today include not only the obvious ones of treason, espionage, terrorist acts, sabotage, "wrecking," anti-Soviet agitation and propaganda, and disclosures of state secrets, but also things seemingly removed from state security concern: smuggling, preparing or instigating or participating in mass disorders, illegal exit abroad, violations of currency regulations, and thefts involving groups of criminals.

All such crimes are defined more broadly than in Western law. "Terrorism," for instance, extends to any physical assault on any "representative of authority"—from the cop on the beat to the KGB officer or party official. In 1984 treason was extended to include "acts threatening state security," a term so broad in the Soviet context that it could cover almost anything.

The KGB investigates all crimes involving foreigners. It shares with the Procurator's Office responsibility for cases of theft of large amounts of money or state property.

The system of permits—for weapons and their repair, explosives, duplicating machines, dies and stamps, and so forth—is managed by the militia but has such implications for state security that Soviet administrative law recognizes the KGB's oversight responsibility.[11]

(6) Enforcing Morals

"Moral education of the working people is a crucial area of the party's ideological activity."[12] The leaders have imposed moral duties in their constitution and insist that personality weaknesses of the individual threaten the security of the state. The external enemy is the connecting link:

> The enemies of socialism . . . are trying to deflect and distract Soviet citizens from the principles of our ideology . . . from the moral, ethical standards of our socialist community life . . . using the poisoned weapon of disinformation, slander, falsification, and lies . . . to arouse in man feelings of egotism, distrust, and uncertainty, to sow apoliticism, to confuse and poison his mind with nationalist prejudices, and to shake his Communist convictions. . . . Imperialist special services are trying to exploit problems

that at first glance seem unrelated to politics, in the sphere of morals, tastes, and daily habits. . . . The instigators of ideological sabotage are abroad but their subversive actions are directed inside our country, and their target is our Soviet man.[13]

The leaders have therefore sent out their KGB to grapple with the imperfection of mankind. "Of great importance among the responsibilities of the KGB is, first, to prevent or suppress anti-Soviet behavior which could grow into state crime and, secondly, to eliminate those conditions which imperialist intelligence services can exploit for subversive activities against the Soviet state."[14] This engages the KGB in "an aggressive struggle against all negative phenomena."[15] When a Soviet individual has deviated, "Chekists are called on to help him get on the right track."[16] The KGB "plays a tremendous role" in the party's "struggle against enemies of socialist morality and petty-bourgeois manifestations of a philistine mentality." It "takes the most decisive steps against people who try to bring into our environment ideas and views that are alien to us and incompatible with the principles of our socialist way of life." The KGB is, in fact, "an increasingly important instrument in guaranteeing the high morals of our society."[17]

It is in this "prophylactic" context that the KGB calls in dissidents, like problem children, for warning "chats." Later, if they have persisted in "other-thinking" and have been "isolated" in prisons, camps, or psychiatric institutions, the KGB tries to extract from them, before releasing them, an admission of their weakness and a promise not to repeat their "crime."

(7) Punishing

Prisons and labor camps are formally administered by components of the MVD, but the KGB maintains "special sections" throughout the prison system (in addition to the investigative cells in its own provincial headquarters) that control the treatment of political prisoners. (Prisoners may, in fact, be "political" even if the courts have sentenced them for other crimes trumped up by the KGB.) And in these prisons, as already mentioned, the KGB often seeks to destroy its victims.

The KGB punishes outside the law, too. It intimidates its victims with threats and assaults, induces illnesses, and kills. Freely using all the agencies of the state and social organizations, it gets people fired and refused employment, interferes with careers, sends people into exile, and harasses and victimizes whole families. It oversees, in special psychiatric clinics, the administration of debilitating and disorienting drugs, isolation, and painful and frightening treatment, in an effort to break the will to resist.

(8) Keeping the Leaders Informed

Through the KGB's secret informants and interception of communications, the masters of the Soviet system keep their eyes on the mood and reactions of their subjects and detect spots where trouble may break out. As early as June 1918 the VCheka had assumed the task of "providing information to the authorities about disorders, abuses."[18] Similar reports made during the 1920s and 1930s were among the NKVD archives captured in Smolensk by the advancing German army in 1941. I myself submitted many such reports. Today as in the past, KGB case officers are supposed to probe and report quickly and frankly about popular reception of the leaders' new directives—whether muttering, cursing, or cheers.[19]

And, of course, the KGB supplies information from abroad—secrets from within foreign governments, scientific and technical data—upon which the leadership builds its policies and programs.

(9) Reducing the Foreign Menace

To weaken and eventually eliminate foreign opposition to the Soviet regime, while blocking the people from the infection of foreign contacts and information, the KGB performs scores of tasks that are discussed in later chapters.

(10) Carrying Out Tasks of Special Secrecy

If the General Secretary and his Politburo colleagues want to do things in special secrecy, they work through the KGB. They use it, for example, to keep an eye and ear on party and government colleagues. To eliminate or discredit opponents within the USSR and abroad they depend on KGB specialists.

For decades they have constructed a labyrinth hundreds of meters deep under the surface of Moscow to protect themselves in case of war—or against their own people, who have been told nothing of this construction or its gigantic expense. Thus the KGB, in what may seem a strange role for a "secret police," has a "Directorate of Tunnel Diggers."[20]

(11) Creating and Preserving the Climate for Soviet Rule

The KGB acts as publicist and propagandist, abetting the regime's other efforts to excite fear and hatred of outside "enemies." The KGB writes and sponsors books, articles, and television and radio programs inside the USSR. As its chairman reported in 1988, "We are engaged in joint work with journalists, writers, and filmmakers. . . . We collaborate actively with the editorial offices of . . . a number of newspapers." He also reported that "to increase the political vigilance of the Soviet people, KGB men systematically lecture workers at enterprises and institutions."[21]

Through its agent networks and provocations (and threatening "chats"), the KGB has played an important part in the Soviet power system by creating a climate of wariness and distrust, preventing people from comparing their true feelings and making common cause against the regime. Despite its apparent conflict with Gorbachev's policy of "openness," this work cannot be stopped; it prevents a complete loss of control by the party leaders. (This atomization of society can also be seen in the armed forces, where they prevent what they call *zemlyachestvo*—local ties—by sending recruits far from their homes and separating them from people from the same village.)

Merely by existing—and having done what it did in the past—the KGB plays a tremendous role. As a constant reminder of its potential for arbitrary terror, standing in fact today with its spies everywhere and its files burgeoning, with huge forces armed and equipped as never before, the KGB keeps fear alive and makes the old form of mass terror unnecessary. No matter how often it changes its initials, they quickly take on the same aura of terror and arrogant overlordship.† "Every time I pass by the solemn facade of the building that houses the KGB," wrote one citizen, "I feel a vague anxiety, uncertainty, and even fear."[22]

By standing at the very top of the pyramid of power, the Chekists send a message. Every time an Andropov, an Aliyev, a Chebrikov or a Kryuchkov is appointed to the Politburo or a local KGB chief to the local party leadership, the message is clear to even the humblest worker, farmer, or functionary: there is no real hope of change.

When Solzhenitsyn suddenly learned that the leaders, after seeming to consent, would not after all permit publication of his book *Cancer Ward,*

---

†This is probably why Brezhnev, in 1968, gave back to the Ministry for the Preservation of Public Order (MOOP) its older name of Ministry of Internal Affairs with the initials "MVD" and their dread-filled memory.

he wrote: "So that what we thought was an untroubled sky overhead was the enormous observation dome of the KGB, and now it had winked at us, like the severed head in Ruslan. 'It's my turn now! You're finished.' . . . They can see it all—all our antlike scurryings—and we are in their hands."[23]

CHAPTER 11

Inside the House on Dzerzhinsky Square

Dom Dva—From the Outside

ALL THIS WORK OF THE KGB IS SUPERVISED FROM THE BIG BUILDING that dominates the square in central Moscow that is named for the first Chekist leader, Felix Dzerzhinsky. The building's nickname "Lyubyanka" (derived from the old name of the street on which it stands) gained infamy from the KGB's prison that occupied part of the building until the late 1960s. Chekists, however, call it *dom dva* (House Number Two), the street number of its first entry along Dzerzhinsky Street, which distinguishes it from other KGB buildings on a street filled with them.

Seen even from the outside, *dom dva* has much to tell about the Soviet system. It conveys, for one thing, a sense of historical continuity that is particularly useful in a time when the West is dazzled by Gorbachev's "new era." Behind those same fourth floor windows where KGB Chairman Kruychkov sits in 1990, so, too, did Viktor Abakumov when his MGB was dispatching hundreds of thousands to the camps after Stalin reversed his wartime relaxation of repression. Before him, the infamous Beria looked out from the same line of windows, as did Yezhov while commanding the mad, nationwide terror that is remembered by his name: the *Yezhovshchina*. From there Dzerzhinsky unleashed the VCheka's wild killings that became known as the "Red Terror." (The Chekists leaders have always occupied the old section of the building, preferring its more solid construction, larger offices, and higher ceilings.)

The building gives concrete evidence of the expansion of "the organs," proof that the leaders' fear of their own people has never diminished. The Chekists who seized it from the All-Russia Insurance Company in 1917 were supposedly members of a temporary ("extraordinary") commission, but the leaders could never do without them, not even after they had secured their revolution and won their civil war and relaxed the harshness of their rule to give their economy a chance to recover: during that NEP period, ever more Chekists moved into the buildings around *dom dva,* expanded into others down the side streets, cut up large offices into smaller ones to make room for the growing staff, and began about 1926 to add four floors to the original building. The end of the Second World War did not clear any space, either; on the contrary, in 1945 and 1946 prisoners of war were put to work doubling the building's size along Dzerzhinsky Square. Not even after 1960–61, when the leaders proclaimed the end of class warfare and the unanimity of their people: new offices were crammed into the space vacated by the closing of the building's infamous prison in the late 1960s. Not even when the Foreign Operations Directorate moved out of *dom dva* in 1970 to a huge new building at the southern edge of Moscow: in 1981 and 1984 construction cranes were raising yet other annexes nearby. Not even under *glasnost* was there room to house everyone: in 1987 yet more construction was underway.

Inside the Walls: The Internal War Exposed

Along the corridors behind that huge facade, the doors give access to directorates, departments, and other bureaucratic subdivisions that in any other office building would be a matter of bored disinterest for the outsider. But in the KGB they hold a unique interest, for they expose beyond any debate an internal war that the leaders seek to hide.

This internal organization is top secret, and the leaders have a vested interest in keeping it so: the very existence of certain KGB departments reveals the leaders' fear of whole categories of their supposedly unanimous population.

One directorate, for instance, is designed to fight the regime's own intelligentsia: writers and artists, scientists and philosophers. It contains a department fighting full time against the worship of God, and another that prevents people from taking too active a pride and interest in their own ethnic heritage. Subdivisions of another directorate ensure that every kind of foreigner in the USSR—tourist, diplomat, businessman, journalist—gets individual and hostile attention. It also keeps a wary eye on citizens known to have met or corresponded with Westerners. Other directorates and departments reveal that no one is exempt from the leaders' apprehensions and scrutiny: some keep watch over industrial managers and workers, others over Soviet soldiers, sailors, and airmen. Each such element on this table of organization must prove its vigilance by exposing its quota of enemies or bringing its quota of strays back into the herd; it reports its results quarterly and annually like an army reporting progress across enemy terrain.

In that table of organization are also reflected the warlike techniques that the leaders use against their own people. Surveillance departments send out at least five thousand men and women like military scouts onto the streets of Moscow alone. A "PK" department surreptitiously opens mail, while others intercept telegrams and tap telephones. One staff spends all its time identifying writers of anonymous letters and graffiti. Another coordinates KGB-party decisions about what the people must be kept from knowing and then passes suitable instructions to the huge censorship offices. A specialized unit researches the latest techniques of social control, while another develops weapons and poisons to administer secret death.

This internal structure also reveals, through the cloud of contrary propaganda, that the leaders' fears of their own people were no transitory phenomena of a "revolutionary" situation, nor the paranoid excesses of a Stalin, for that table of organization has changed remarkably little in seventy years. The main differences are reflections of victories in the internal war. The leaders no longer need departments to combat "monarchists" or remnants of the short-lived democratic political parties, or successful private farmers (Kulaks).* And sometimes old structures are reborn.

The Work of SPU

One of the KGB's units has earned such infamy that the leaders have repeatedly changed its designation for cosmetic reasons. The "Secret Political Directorate" (*Sekretno-politicheskoye Upravleniye,* or SPU),† but it enjoyed a

---

*The few survivors of such categories—after the Red Terror and the purges of the 1930s—long ago became "former people *(byvshiye lyudi),* and all but a handful have since died of old age. Even their memory, however, seems potentially dangerous to these fear-ridden hierarchs: they still make sure, through passive defenses like the omnipresent questionnaire *(anketa)* and the KGB's control over personnel offices, that the children and grandchildren of these old "class enemies" are kept away from sensitive positions.

†It bore the designation SPU in the NKVD and MGB; earlier it was known as the "secret operations department" of VCheka and OGPU.

particularly sinister reputation when Stalin was using it to keep his secret eye on his party followers (preparing blood purges), to crush a whole generation of intellectuals, to neutralize nationalist movements, and to decimate the churches. So satisfactorily did it accomplish its bloody work that Stalin felt able to distribute its functions among other directorates. But paradoxically it was during "de-Stalinization" that SPU was reborn, and it is amid *glasnost* today that it faces its most trying tasks: trying to hold in check the flood of nationalist, religious, and intellectual activity loosed by Gorbachev's reforms.

The Kremlin, as after Stalin's death, now faces the consequences of its failure to convert writers and artists into "engineers of the soul," to tame the human spirit. It is useful today—when that failure is more obvious than ever—to see how the SPU faced the issue a generation ago.

In the mid-1960s *samizdat* was spreading and exposing the regime's violations of human rights (a few brave souls even unfurled banners protesting regime actions), authors were publishing works abroad to avoid the regime's censorship, Jews were asking to emigrate, nationalities were venting their resentment of Russian domination in street demonstrations and in brawls inside the armed forces. The leaders took fright. With the KGB's participation they devised new laws to sharpen the KGB's teeth; enlarged its sections watching over religion, bourgeois nationalism, intellectuals and their *samizdat,* Jews, and people with contacts abroad‡; gathered them into one large Fifth Chief Directorate—the SPU reassembled—and loosed it upon those they feared.

This new-old unit unleashed a new wave of arrests, committed hundreds of dissidents to mental institutions (finally attracting world outrage), and added to their spy networks. " 'They are infiltrating their men everywhere," said Bishop Benjamin Novitskiy in 1973 of his Catholic church hierarchy.[1] Against the Jews the responsible department cut back the number of exit visas and harrassed the "refuseniks" and their children. By the mid-1980s, the Fifth Chief Directorate seemed to have succeeded. *Samizdat* had been reduced, the Helsinki Watch Groups disbanded and their members jailed or exiled, and most of the talented and prominent Soviet writers forced out of the country.

But with the invigorating rain of Gorbachev's *glasnost,* all these manifestations of independence sprang up anew, swelled, and overflowed the dams set up against them by the Fifth Chief Directorate. In June 1988,

---

‡Most of these sections were taken from the Second Chief Directorate, an overblown body that had encompassed everything from work against foreigners and foreign espionage in the USSR to the security of industry and (according to some sources) rail and air transportation. The Jewish problem had been handled in subsections of other departments.

10,000 believers turned out in Moscow to celebrate the milennium of the Russian Orthodox Church, and in early 1989 about 30,000 Catholics in Lithuania marked the reopening of the Vilnius cathedral, and perhaps 20,000 in Kiev participated in a ceremony of their still-illegal church in the Ukraine. Here was a double menace to the regime: religious faith reawakened along with church organizations strengthened and made more independent, becoming focal points of resistance.

What can the Kremlin, with its KGB, do about this? If there is any answer to that question it lies in the record of the past. The KGB remains hard at work preparing an eventual crackdown, under the leadership of an old Chekist who gained his experience under Beria, Merkulov, and Abakumov through periods of the most severe repression, who commanded and then supervised the Fifth Chief Directorate, and who is today first deputy chairman of the KGB—and, I am sure, the real manager of its operational activity: Filipp Denisovich Bobkov. I personally knew and worked with Bobkov and know his reputation after my departure as a skilled and hard specialist in internal repression and work against foreigners in the USSR.

The work of the Fifth Chief Directorate illustrates that of the KGB as a whole, and its ways can be seen in the activity of just one of its departments; I single out the one that fights organized religion.

Even before the recent upsurge of church activity, religious faith posed a constant threat to Communist rule. It offers a perpetual challenge to the leaders' legitimacy: if Marx's atheism is not "truth," by what right do they rule? Then, too, the church can never be integrated into collectivist society and stands as an independent center of influence. Besides, an individual's faith, sustained by an active church, offers him a defense and refuge against the regime's claims upon him. Ever since Lenin's days the KGB has been guided by the view that the church's teaching is "an attempt to prepare a mood preliminary to preparing a revolt in the future."[2]

Therefore, the leaders have sought not only to destroy religious belief but also to fence in those who continue to practice their faith. They assigned the bulk of this work to the KGB. A department specifically designated to work against the Christian church was established in 1920 and has fought its unending war through all of the renamings of its parent organization, from VCheka to KGB. §

§It originated as the Third Section of the VCheka's "Secret Department," which in turn was subordinated to a "Secret Operational Directorate," forerunner of SPU. It became the Third Department of the Directorate of Secret Operations of the OGPU, which in 1934

This department controls counterparts in provincial offices, such as the departments formed in the Georgian and Armenian republics to fight the autocephalous Orthodox churches in each of those areas. When I was working in the Altay Kray, a Captain Gavrilov worked full time with two case officers against the local churches and sects.

Such Chekists are not chosen for their sensitivity. E. A. Tuchkov, the department's chief during the OGPU's persecutions of 1929–32, became infamous for his cruelty to churchmen and churchgoers. The brutality of a KGB interrogator named Volkopyalov became so scandalous in Yaroslavl that the KGB felt compelled to transfer him to faraway Moldavia—where he was made responsible for KGB operations against the church.[3]

Just as Lenin had exhorted his Chekists to shoot and jail priests not as such but as "counterrevolutionaries," later leaders treated religious tracts as anti-Soviet propaganda and those who distributed them as anti-Soviet agitators. By 1920 the Russian Orthodox Church estimated that more than 322 bishops and priests had been executed; by 1923, more than a thousand, and finally tens of thousands of priests were sent off to death in concentration camps like Solovki or driven out of the country. To discredit the organized church hierarchy, the Chekists launched provocations— supporting, for example, "reforming" churches to compete with the powerful Orthodox churches in Russia, Armenia, and Georgia.** The party and Komsomol deluged society with antireligious propaganda, turning children against their "superstitious" parents, and had believers fired from jobs and exiled on various pretexts. The attack grew especially violent in 1922, when the regime confiscated church properties to pay for grain imports during the famines it had created. Though the assault slackened in the mid-1920s, it resumed in 1929–33, the era of the collectivization of agriculture. It was then that I saw a gang of young Communists, to the wails of the women and elders of my village, cutting down and smashing the bell from the tower of its only church. Only during the Second World War did Stalin relax the oppression—to induce believers to fight—but his successors criticized his leniency and in 1960,

---

became the Secret Political Directorate of NKVD. The department stayed with SPU under the separate NKGB and in 1946 was enlarged, separated from SPU, and designated Department O of the MGB.

**The same pattern can be seen today in client states of the USSR. The Marxist government of Nicaragua is promoting a loyal "people's church" to compete against the established one; in Grenada before the 1983 invasion, the Marxist government planned one, too. See *Grenada Documents: an Overview and Selection* (Released by Department of State and the Department of Defense, Washington DC, September 1984.), p. 4, and document nos. 2, 5, 6, 7, 8, and 9.

under Khrushchev, renewed the attack. In the next four years the number of parishes was reduced by more than half, most candidates for the priesthood were rejected, and almost all remaining monasteries were closed.

Where before the First World War there had been nearly 5,000 Orthodox churches, some 25,000 mosques, and tens of thousands of synagogues, Protestant churches, and Buddhist temples, there remained in the early 1980s probably fewer than 4,000 churches or temples of all religions and sects together.††

Despite this apparent victory, the regime never stopped treating religion as an active menace and never disbanded the KGB's religion departments. The Central Committee apparatus, along with groups like the Znaniye ("Knowledge") Society, and the directors of all schools and youth and children's organizations continue to propagate hatred against religion.

The KGB leadership at *dom dva* has done the enforcing in four principal ways.

First, it manipulates the Council on Religious Affairs (CRA). This extraordinary institution, which because it is formally subordinated to the Council of Ministers can only be staffed by atheists, was first established during Stalin's wartime truce with the churches and took its present form in 1966. Its stated aim is to "restrict the activity of the church to the limit of the law."‡‡ The CRA has routinely transferred bishops, broken contracts between priest and parish, decided which candidates will be allowed to study for the priesthood, and controlled the church's academies and seminaries.

Seen from *dom dva,* the CRA is little more than a subsection of State Security. KGB Col. (later Maj. Gen.) G. G. Karpov, who headed the CRA from its formation in 1943 until 1960, was also head of State Security's department to combat religion. The CRA's deputy chief for many years thereafter was KGB Maj. Gen. V. N. Titov; and when he was removed in

---

††For the last thirty years or more, the regime has made claims that anywhere from 20,000–30,000 still exist, but their figures are hugely exaggerated; regime spokesmen have boasted that some 10,000 of these were closed in the 1960s. See, for a summary of regime claims, Donald A. Lowrie and William C. Fletcher, "Khrushchev's Religious Policy," in Marshall, pp. 151–3, n. 133.

‡‡The Kremlin leaders can impose restrictions as they wish, and until Gorbachev's time their laws—while allowing "freedom of conscience"—forbade any religious instruction even by parents or attempts to convert people, and treated possession of Bibles as punishable subversive activity. A new Gorbachev-era law on freedom of conscience promised in 1989 to lift such extreme restrictions and to restore certain rights and properties to the churches.

the mid-1970s, Vladimir V. Fitsev, chief of that KGB department, shifted over to take his place (and died in the job, in March 1985). It is the KGB, ultimately, that selects, approves, and assigns bishops, priests, and seminarians, writes the laws for conduct and administration of church organizations, and sees that these are obeyed.§§

Second, the KGB infiltrates secret agents and even KGB staff officers into the seminaries and moves them into top positions in church hierarchies. Every key position in the Orthodox Patriarchy has been occupied by someone whom the KGB considers reliable and willing to collaborate—because the KGB had awarded itself the deciding voice in appointments.

During a conspiratorial contact in 1953 in which I was passing him KGB money, Metropolitan Nikolay said to me, "Well, these have been difficult times. In order to serve God I have to serve others." Thus, surely, did the Patriarch Sergey reason when, in 1927, he became the first head of the Orthodox church to accommodate to the regime. A churchman thus explained the problem to Solzhenitsyn, "Should we become involved in a clandestine movement, which is unthinkable, or should we join the system and exploit those possibilities available to us? The Russian ecclesiastical hierarchy has adopted the second decision—and from this flows all the evil you have truthfully described, Aleksandr Isayevich, and more. But there was no other choice. . . ."[4]

While many churchmen remain in their hearts more loyal to God than to the Politburo, there are some who do not. Before cracking down ferociously on the church in 1960, the regime first took the precaution of replacing the aging Metropolitan Nikolay, who retained scruples, with a real Chekist who carried the title of Metropolitan Nikodim. Official records name him as Boris Georgiyevich Rotov, but former KGB officer Anatoly Golitsyn believed that he was none other than a KGB officer named Viryukin, former deputy chief of the KGB's Emigre Department, who had been working against churchmen abroad before being inserted into the church hierarchy and sent to Jerusalem.***

§§A typical scene was reported from a synod of bishops in Zagorsk in 1961. Three outsiders in civilian clothes sat silently behind the line of leading bishops at the head table. These members of the CRA (undoubtedly officers or agents of the KGB) were there to make sure that the bishops approved the motion that had been put before them: a new statute denying priests the right to manage the financial and other affairs of their own parish churches (Radio Liberty Dispatch, 3 September 1973, "The Council for Religious Affairs Under the USSR Council of Ministers").

***Golitsyn, p. 292. Nikodim/Rotov was in Jerusalem from 1956–59 as representative of the patriarchy. Subsequently he headed its foreign relations department (replacing Nikolay) in 1960 and became exarch for Western Europe in 1974. From 1961–75 he was a member of the presidium of the Ecumenical Council. In the summer of 1978 he died in Rome (some think by divine intervention) at the feet of the new Pope John Paul I.

By controlling such hierarchs the KGB ensures that church activity will not undermine Soviet rule. The position that Nikolay and Nikodim held, for instance, is important to the political leadership not only because its incumbent ranks second only to the patriarch but especially because he supervises the patriarchy's foreign relations.

The KGB pulls the strings on these church hierarchs in other directions, too. It lent Metropolitan Nikolay's authority, for instance, to the Soviet regime's fraudulent 1944 "inquiry"—which cleared itself of guilt—into the massacre of the Polish officers whose mass grave had been discovered by the Germans in the Katyn Forest near Smolensk.††† With Nikolay's visit to Vienna in 1953 the KGB gave the church's blessing to the World Peace Council, a political-action operation of the CC CPSU. (Nikolay's specific KGB task in Vienna was to help bring back under KGB control an emigre Catholic priest, Father Arseniy Shidlovskiy.)

Third, the KGB keeps track of believers and persecutes activists. In every town and village the KGB makes lists of all who go to church, readying action against them whenever the regime feels especially threatened by this category of potential enemy. The KGB puts secret informants among religious activists, surveillants on their heels, and microphones in their homes. It harrasses and intimidates them and sends vicious thugs to break up their meetings and to beat them up, sometimes killing them. For this low task it is willing to expend high resources, as illustrated by an operation in 1974 when the KGB became aware of Baptist literature beginning to circulate in Latvia. The Religion Department of the Latvian Republic KGB arranged surveillance of known Baptist activists and noticed that they were buying large quantities of paper from a certain store. Enlisting the help of the paper store, KGB operatives put radioactive traces on the paper being sold to the Baptists. Then they sent out helicopters with sensors, tracked the shipment to a rural house, surrounded it with hundreds of operatives—and succeeded in nabbing a few young Baptists printing New Testaments.[5] I remember how State Security finally disposed of the "menace to the regime" posed by the Dukhobor sect of Old Believers in the Altay Kray. Using the excuse that one of them had helped his son evade military service, Captain Gavrilov organized a dragnet in the town of Kamen-on-Ob where the sect was most active. In the night thirty Chekists swept down and rounded up all they could find: thirteen shabby believers.

†††As noted later, the NKVD, acting on SMERSH orders, carried out the massacre of some 12,000 officers whom they had interned when Soviet troops occupied eastern Poland. In September 1939 some 4,500 bodies were found at Katyn, although the Soviet report— significantly—estimated the number at 11,000. In the late 1980s the Polish press openly accused the Soviets of this crime.

Fourth, the KGB prosecutes. Using trumped-up charges, intimidation, provocateurs and false witnesses, it has played the central role in all the trials staged to discredit and isolate those who persist in their religious faith. On one charge or another—the laws being vague enough to permit arrest of any churchman or activist—it has imprisoned thousands of believers. Until reforms in 1989 a Bible on the shelf could constitute "possession of anti-Soviet propaganda" under Article 70 and a parent who told his child about God could be found guilty of "anti-Soviet agitation and propaganda."

The Watch over Factory, Office, and Farm:
EKU and the First Departments

In the early 1980s, to face another of their growing concerns, the Soviet leaders reassembled another old Chekist structure.

Soviet industry has always operated in the grip of State Security. By force the Bolsheviks took over the factories, and by what Lenin called "an iron hand" they compelled people to work, and the iron hand was the VCheka's. Its very name confirmed its mission to fight "speculation" and "sabotage" (the latter broadly interpreted as anything that opposed the leaders' will or their production plans) as it set out to punish bribery, profiteering, misappropriation of state property, and currency dealings by bank employees. Its first task, in fact, was to put down a strike of bureaucrats.

By 1919 the VCheka had concentrated such activities in an Economic Directorate (EKU) which in the 1920s had the task of ensuring that the relative freedoms of the New Economic Policy did not get out of hand. (From 1923 on, as we have seen, VCheka chief Dzerzhinsky was simultaneously head of the Supreme Council on the Economy.) In the 1930s EKU played an important role in Stalin's forced industrialization: finding workers for the projects in bleak or frigid outlands (administered by the closely related Chief Administration of Camps, or GULag), imposing discipline within factories, and finding scapegoats for the inevitable failures of unrealistic plans. EKU succeeded so well that the leaders could scatter its functions among other directorates.

As the regime aged, new threats arose—or more precisely, old threats grew newly acute: absenteeism, drunkenness, indiscipline, theft, and mismangement. Illicit private enterprise, supported by corrupt officials, spread throughout the country. By the late 1970s the leaders had evidently decided that their survival in power depended on getting the factories and farms to produce more efficiently. In 1982 within the CC CPSU itself, where KGB chief Andropov had just become a secretary, they formed a new "Economic Department" to concentrate the work that several other CPSU departments had already been doing and at the same time formed a new Economic Directorate within the KGB to put teeth in its work. Thus was the old EKU back in business—and again, as in the 1920s, the top Chekist was wielding the leaders' whip over the economy.

As Mikhail Gorbachev offers new incentives to workers and relaxes some of the oppressive restrictions on their work and movements, it falls again to the EKU to see that things do not get out of hand.

One of EKU's means to do this is the so-called "First Department," the "security" department in each factory, scientific, or educational institution, enterprise, or other organization. Ostensibly an integral part of the institution and often listed on its overt table of organization,‡‡‡ it is really an outpost of the KGB, staffed by KGB officers or retirees or, in smaller organizations with fewer secrets to protect, by KGB resident-agents or trusted collaborators. It responds more directly to the KGB district office than to factory management.§§§ For instance, the chief of the First Department of a chemical plant in Novosibirsk reports to the KGB officer responsible for chemicals within the industrial department of the city KGB. (He may, in fact, have worked in that very office before he retired from the KGB and took his post in the plant.)

Ostensibly its task is to protect the enterprise's secrets, but the Soviet system interprets that task very broadly and the first departments do most of the things that the military OOs do.

Even in protecting secrets, in the strict sense of the word, the First Department has extensive powers. Following KGB policy guidance and the local KGB's instructions, the department chief tells the management, in precise detail, how its employees will handle and store secret material. The department grants or withholds clearances for access to it, decides which positions require such clearance, and approves promotions to such positions. The First Department also registers all incoming and outgoing

---

‡‡‡This unit is not invariably designated as a "department" (*otdel*); a small one may be "section" (*chast* or *sektor* or *otdeleniye*). Nor is its adjective invariably "first"; it might be "special" (*obsoby* or *spets*); the word "secret" (*sekretnyy*) is also used to denote certain of the activities of such units (usually files and registry of documents). In the first years of Soviet power, some of this work was done by so-called political sections (*politotdely*), whose deputy chiefs were invariably State Security officers.

§§§Indeed, in some fields such as atomic energy, the First Department bypasses local KGB offices and reports directly to a higher KGB echelon.

classified materials and stores them in its own locked area, into which not even the director of the institution may enter without KGB approval and under conditions which the department sets.

The First Department supervises the plant's—and its party organization's—classified communications with the outside, prescribing how packages will be wrapped and envelopes sealed and who will carry them (usually designating its own employees to act as couriers). In important ministries, too, the people who carry classified documents (the diplomatic couriers of the Ministry of Foreign Affairs, for example) are controlled by the KGB, which also enciphers and deciphers classified radio messages. In government ministries the KGB controls the communications departments; in plants or enterprises that send or receive relatively few enciphered messages, the work is done by a subdivision of the plant's First Department.

The department is also responsible for the enterprise's copying machines (there is often only one), which it keeps in a locked office of its own, operated by a person whom the department clears and appoints. When an employee wants copies made, he must get his immediate supervisor's signature, that of the supervisor's boss, and—no matter how innocuous the material to be copied—that of a First Department officer.**** The department keeps samples of the typescript of all typewriters in the plant or ministry, against which to compare anonymous letters or *samizdat*.

But like the rest of the KGB, the First Department's primary concern is people. It oversees the Personnel Department and keeps its own cards on the managers and workers. It notes any hint of dissent or misbehavior such as listening to foreign radio broadcasts or having a child baptized, as well as any undesirable relatives or contacts. The department handles secret informers among the personnel, closely collaborating with the local KGB office.††††

Then, too, this department oversees the physical protection of the installation by departmental militia (hired by the MVD) or, in the case of military-industrial or research institutes, by Internal Troops. Where atomic and special weapons are produced, KGB Troops do the guarding.

For all this work a First Department may have four or more subsections:

****Although these rules are sometimes violated and copying machines misused, it is usually by the operator. The employees rarely have the opportunity.

††††As former Politburo member Boris Yeltsin said on 14 July 1989 during the Supreme Soviet's discussion on the reappointment of Vladimir A. Kryuchkov as KGB Chairman, the KGB "is an army of many thousands who inform on people in their work places." In a lie of colossal proportions, Kryuchkov denied that the KGB keeps files on private citizens "unless they pose a danger to the state." (*International Herald Tribune*, 15 July 1989.)

one maintaining files, archives, and registry (the so-called "secret section"), at least one for communications, one for operations (issuing security regulations and investigating personnel, for example), and another supervising the physical security of the installation (guards, fences, and other precautions). In larger plants it may have as many as twenty employees; in smaller ones perhaps only two or three. In small factories and those making innocuous objects like shoes or toilet seats, the security representation may merge with the Personnel Department.

First departments gained importance in the late 1920s and 1930s, as Stalin set out to find scapegoats ("wreckers") for the failure of his industrial projects. Lev Kopelev, who helped them, gives the flavor:

> After I became a full-fledged member [in 1930] of the Komsomol, they put me in charge of a paper at a tank shop. Leaving my lathe, I worked at my new job virtually around the clock, sleeping on piles of newsprint. The GPU representative at the factory, a stern but good-natured veteran of the Cheka, would often visit us in the evenings, asking us to take note of the workers' attitudes, keep an eye out for Kulak propaganda, and expose any remnants of Trotskyist and Bukharinist thoughts. I wrote several reports. . . . My editorial colleagues did the same. . . . The GPU man would chide us for our frankness in public. "Don't you see, now they'll hide things from you—they'll give you a wide berth. No, fellows, you've got to learn Chekist tactics."[6]

During the great purge of the 1930s, the security department of every factory became the real seat of power, sending directors—ostensibly their bosses—off to be shot to death or to die slowly in the concentration camps. The punishments today are milder, but the relationship is the same.

Aleksandr Solzhenitsyn tells that Andrey Sakharov in 1968 arranged the typing for *samizdat* of his famous memorandum "On Progress, Peaceful Coexistence and Intellectual Freedom" by giving it to different typists of his institute, to each a few pages at a time, thinking they would not understand its import or piece together the parts. Solzhenitsyn comments, "They were, however, clever enough for each to take her own batch of copies to the Special Section, which was reading the memorandum before he had the pages laid out on his table to sort them for *samizdat*."[7]

Yuri Andropov surely had first departments in mind when he said confidently that "people who take the path of anti-Soviet activity [and] spread false rumors . . . would not dare speak out at any plant, on a *kolkhoz,* or in an establishment. They would be forced there to take to their heels."[8]

Other Departments and Methods

In other chapters I describe some of the work of other KGB directorates. We have already seen the Third Directorate, which manages the OOs, in the armed forces. In the next chapter we describe the directorate (Ninth) that provides the innermost ring of protection of the Soviet regime, the bodyguarding of the leaders themselves. When describing the foreign dimension of the leaders' internal warfare we tell of the work of two large organizations: the chief directorate responsible for operations abroad (First) and the one that operates against foreigners in the USSR (Second). The Border Guards Directorate is discussed in the context of the leaders' controls over exit from the USSR. There is also a huge Surveillance (Seventh) Directorate. Others are less pertinent to our subject and need no mention here.

From their first days in power, the Bolsheviks considered the network of rail, road, and waterway communications as critical to their survival. VCheka Chairman Dzerzhinsky himself took over as People's Commissar of Railways in 1919 and established a large VCheka directorate for transportation. It has presumably persisted to the present day, although its precise designation and areas of authority have varied according to changing needs. Today, the failures of transportation are contributing to the crisis in industry; because of mismanagement and corruption, supplies fail to arrive at factories and harvests rot while awaiting transport. Problems were also delaying the construction of the Baikal-Amur railway (which was using forced labor and military construction units as did the NKVD-run projects of the 1930s). In a step reminiscent of Dzerzhinsky's time, General Secretary Andropov put in an experienced Chekist, Politburo member Geidar Aliyev, to solve them. To shake up the railway system, Aliyev must have relied on a KGB transportation directorate. Within the local KGB offices throughout the country, officers watch over the personnel of the railway and maritime administrations with ultimate power over their careers. They also command the cooperation of the special police forces (transportation militias) that guard trains, stations, and other key points; airports; and seaports.***** Whenever his own repressive operations require, the KGB case officer can manipulate transportation facilities at will—donning a militia uniform himself or giving orders to the guards—to place the people he is watching, for example, into whatever

---

****In the past these railway and maritime militias (air militias later added) have been under direct State Security command but are today administered by the MVD. At the beginning of the 1920s the Railway Militia alone numbered 70,000.

train compartment, ship's cabin, or airplane seat he chooses, where his agents can watch or make contact with them.

The KGB's Technical Operations Directorate runs secret laboratories, applying the latest scientific advances to the task of repression. In 1987 the newly constructed American Embassy in Moscow was found so riddled with high-technology listening equipment that nothing short of destroying it and building a new one from scratch could make it secure. Perhaps even that would not help: with such new technologies as lasers, pin-sized transmitters, and spread-spectrum transmission, there seemed no escape from the KGB's ears. These labs have always been ready to apply the latest scientific principles, at whatever cost, to KGB purposes. As early as 1952, when Soviet technology was far behind the West's, American technicians were amazed to find on their ambassador's wall a device using a scientific principle the West had not even dreamed of applying to such an apparently trivial purpose.††††† In my time there was a laboratory called Kamera ("the Chamber") which tested the efficacy of poisons, drugs, and mind-control techniques upon living people under sentence of death. Its medical director, KGB Maj. Gen. Blokhin, was nominated for a Stalin Prize for his research. Although this laboratory was closed after Beria's fall, the style of KGB assassinations since then, using poisons without known antidotes, leaves no doubt that its work continues.

Thus the KGB's internal table of organization exposes the central concern of the leadership: its own survival. Just how concerned they are begins to emerge, too, in the numbers of people they commit to this mission.

The Size of the KGB

To count the Chekists you must look far beyond *dom dva*. The thousands who occupy that building and its annexes make up only what they call the "Center." Even in Moscow itself there is a separate, huge KGB for the city and oblast, and elsewhere throughout the country hundreds of thousands more are conducting the leaders' internal war. You can find them in republic and oblast and city headquarters (where they are known as "State Security directorates"), and in research laboratories, in small

†††††This was a so-called resonant cavity, a small metal cylinder without power of its own, tooled to reflect sound waves beamed from outside. It was found imbedded in a plaster model of the Great Seal of the United States, which had been the gift of the "Soviet people" to the "American people."

operational groups, in harbors and border outposts, in ships at sea, in prisons and labor camps, and in Soviet embassies and other representations abroad. You will find them in each institution of government or industry, where Chekists dominate at least three departments: those responsible for security, communications, and foreign relations. Other KGB personnel occupy leading positions in the censorship organization Glavlit, in the MVD, and in all organizations offering services to foreign diplomats, businessmen, and tourists.

In each of the approximately two thousand cities there is a KGB office. Its size depends on local conditions (such as the number of factories) and local problems (in Riga, nationalism; in Odessa, shipping; in Brest, border control). According to an emigrant, one town inland from the Black Sea whose population in 1970 was about 70,000 had a KGB office numbering about a dozen, including its secretary and driver. In the KGB of my own Altay Kray—remote, with little industry, and a population of hardly over two million—more than a thousand Chekists were working along with me in the second half of the 1940s.

Whole towns that you cannot find on even the most detailed maps of the USSR, identified only by post-box numbers, are administered by the KGB. These are the locations where the most secret research is done and the most secret weapons made, stored, tested, and deployed. In these settlements live hundreds of thousands of Soviet citizens: the personnel, their families, and those who service them. All are cleared by the KGB, and all forbidden to disclose their location even to relatives back home. The KGB controls their courts and prosecutors and the police on their streets and protects them with a secret army of its own, the so-called KGB Troops.

Today in the era of *perestroika* Chekists are more numerous than at any time except during two periods: the time of terror in the 1930s when more were needed to arrest and process eight million victims, and during the Second World War when special troops alone numbered many hundreds of thousands. Today Gorbachev needs more Chekists than Lenin did during the civil war and pacification, more than Stalin did to root out the alien contamination and restore discipline after the Second World War.

Of course this is a secret; the true size of State Security has always been hidden. The early Chekists occasionally gave out some figures but they varied wildly: for one and the same year 1920, one of their leaders said there were 4,500, another said 31,000. Thus the Western world has had to rely on estimates, and even these vary, perhaps inevitably. For one thing, there are units that have been alternately administered by Internal Affairs and by State Security and by merger of the two. Not all counts are clear about what kinds of people they include and exclude. State Security has, of course, fluctuated in size. Stalin himself began some cutbacks. In the mid- and late 1950s, Khrushchev eliminated offices in many less-populated *raions* and reduced the concentration camp staffs as hundreds of thousands of prisoners were released. By 1974, however, Brezhnev and Andropov had restored the *raion* offices and by the 1970s had practically doubled the minimum numbers reached by Khrushchev. Under Gorbachev's *glasnost* there have been public calls for cutbacks in the KGB's size, and cuts could be made without seriously diminishing its powers.

On the basis of my own service in various types of KGB units (including five years as a personnel officer) and talks with more recent defectors, I can make a reasonably accurate estimate. For this purpose I divide Chekists into two categories. The first (category A) includes active staff officers: operational, analytical, and administrative specialists, as well as support personnel—technicians, clerks, secretaries, and drivers. Also included, although their numbers are relatively small, are the party leaders' household staffs, all of whom are hired by the KGB Guards Directorate. In what I call category B are Chekists who are sometimes overlooked: KGB reservists actively at work doing KGB-related work in other agencies. Such people may be formally separated from the KGB—retired or dropped from active service because of age, physical disability, disciplinary problems, or bad records—but they continue to do the KGB's work and to put its mission above other priorities. Along with officers of category A they manipulate certain agencies—like Glavlit, the MVD, the Chamber of Commerce, the Copyright Agency, Intourist, UPDK servicing foreign embassies, and others—for KGB purposes, and they staff certain departments in factories, research institutions, and ministries, especially the personnel, first (security), and foreign relations departments.‡‡‡‡‡ They often handle informants and agents and are trained, experienced, and fully cleared Chekists but must be counted in this separate category.

On the other hand, I do not count the following kinds of KGB-related personnel:

- Employees of the former Guards Directorate units that since 1952 have been administered by other ministries (Health, Agriculture,

‡‡‡‡‡One writer on scientific affairs in the Soviet Union tried to estimate the numbers in just the first security departments in just the scientific field. "Such departments exist in every university, research institute, and independent laboratory. Most of them are amply staffed, and the three hundred research institutes in Moscow account for a whole division of warriors protecting the nation's secrecy" at a rough estimate, about 100,000 (Popovsky, p. 71). Since there are about 3,000 institutes devoted only to defense-related research and development, his estimate is by no means excessive, and first departments are not limited to scientific institutions. Many of these are not professional Chekists, active or retired, and so I have not included them all in my count.

Internal Affairs) even though they are all cleared and still closely supervised by the KGB. In this category there may be about 20,000.

- So-called "residents": often highly trained, experienced operatives who, under secret KGB contract, do much the same work as KGB operations officers. They handle informants and pass in reports to a KGB office; they direct surveillance teams, listening and observation posts, and so on.
- Co-opted workers: Soviet officials abroad who have signed contracts with the KGB, have received training in clandestine procedures, and work out of embassies, trade missions, news representations, etc., in much the same way as KGB officers. There must be more than 3,000 of them abroad at any given time; those transferred back to the USSR by their parent agencies remain, of course, secret collaborators of the KGB.
- The many experts in specialized fields of science, medicine, psychiatry, and high-tech development who have signed secrecy agreements with the KGB and often do the same work as KGB officers.
- Those performing municipal services in the "secret cities," although they are likely to be on the KGB payroll.
- Clandestine agents and informants of the KGB or those of MVD-administered organizations whose reporting benefits the KGB.

With these criteria, I estimate the size of the KGB staff as follows:

- All-Union KGB center, Moscow: Category A: 71,000; Category B: 8,000
- Moscow City and Oblast KGB: A: 8,500; B: 3,500
- KGB in other republics, oblasts, cities, and *raions:* A: 96,000; B: 40,000
- KGB abroad (on permanent assignment): A: 6,000
- Prisons and camps (KGB staff only): A: 2,500; B: 5,500
- KGB Troops (not to be confused with Internal Troops): 75,000
- Border Guard Troops: 325,000

The total in category A is 184,000; in category B, 57,000; in troops directly commanded by the KGB, 400,000 for an overall total of about 640,000.

But for a more accurate picture one must add the Internal Troops of the MVD which perform KGB missions, go into action on KGB orders, and have been an integral part of State Security through most of Soviet history. By adding their strength of more than 250,000 the total rises to more than 900,000.

While the regular police (militia) and the criminal and economic investigation offices of the MVD are attacking common crime rather than political offenses, many of them act as auxiliaries for the KGB—and many "crimes" under Soviet law are essentially political or caused by political conditions. The MVD's strength is not published but totals roughly 2.75 million plus about ten million "volunteer" auxiliaries.

Thus the regime employs for its fight against internal enemies and criminals between 3.5 and 4 million (almost as many as in the Soviet armed forces) plus 10 million part-time helpers and more millions of secret collaborators.

The Status of "The Organs"

The KGB enjoys high status and honor. It was upgraded on July 5, 1978, and removed from its nominal subordination to the Council of Ministers and renamed "USSR KGB." In 1981 at the 26th Party Congress, General Secretary Brezhnev—as Stalin had done once in a speech in 1937—paid homage to State Security before even mentioning the armed forces. Unusual awards have been heaped on Chekist leaders. No fewer than three were made Heroes of Socialist Labor (Andropov and two deputies), a distinction no KGB chairman except Beria had ever received while in office.

Until Andropov in 1969, no active State Security chief had previously been a full member of the Politburo, with exceptions too brief to be meaningful. Andropov's rise in Moscow was echoed in the provinces; all republic and oblast KGB chiefs have been appointed to their Politburo or buro as quickly as possible. Soon after Viktor Chebrikov was appointed KGB chairman in 1983, he too was appointed to the Politburo, first as a candidate member and a year later as full member. And in September 1989 KGB chairman Kryuchkov was vaulted into full membership without an interim period as candidate—while the defense minister (Yazov) remained only a candidate member.

In 1976 for the first time in history, KGB first deputy chairmen were made full members of the CPSU Central Committee; others were similarly appointed in 1981 and 1986. The number of KGB men selected to be deputies to the Supreme Soviets of the USSR and the union republics and Moscow and Leningrad City Soviets has risen from 14 in Khrushchev's time to 60 in 1984—approaching the maximum of Stalin's time of 79.

KGB leaders are being given prominence in the field of ideology as never before. Andropov, the first KGB chairman in office ever to make the important ideological speech on the anniversary of Lenin's birth, did it twice: in 1976 and 1982. The leading party theoretical journal, *Kom-*

munist, which had never printed an article by a KGB deputy chairman, published three by Tsvigun between 1979 and 1982. KGB Chairman Chebrikov had an article in its June 1985 issue, and then in November 1985 delivered the prestigious speech on the anniversary of the October Revolution.

The early automatic appointments of KGB chiefs to the highest party organizations (Politburo, republic buros, and regional committees) may be a reflection of the activation of the USSR Defense Council with its regional counterparts. This speculation gains support from the unprecedented military promotions of KGB leaders at about the same time. Andropov and Chebrikov, their deputies, and republic KGB chiefs were given higher military ranks than ever in peacetime history. Three first deputies (like Chairman Chebrikov and Chairman Andropov before him) were promoted to the rank of army general,§§§§§ and all chiefs of republic KGBs (and many oblast KGB chiefs) got ranks of between major general and colonel general.

While the leaders shower honor upon the KGB—the prime support of their power—the attitude of the people has been more accurately expressed by stones hurled against KGB headquarters during outbreaks of violence. The leaders, entirely aware of this, loudly pretend that it is not so. Yuri Andropov said, characteristically, "The State Security organs are the flesh and blood of our people."[9] In 1963 a dictionary of abbreviations included, in addition to abbreviations in current use, "those that live and will live in the history books of our motherland and in our literature, such as VKP(b) [the former designation of the party itself], Comintern, NEP, and Cheka."[10]

The regime has done what it could in the last twenty-five years to polish the KGB's image. Viktor Chebrikov reported in 1988 that just in the previous year, with the KGB's "active collaboration," 235 books and 7,500 articles on Chekist subjects had been published, plus 50 full-length or short movies for cinema and television.[11] The people are reminded that the KGB was Lenin's own creation: "Lenin personally met often with Chekists [. . . and] instructed them in the fight against class enemies. He personally drafted most of the key directives and resolutions on the VCheka."[12] Money, gifts, and prize certificates have been offered since the early 1970s for the best films, telefilms, and books glorifying KGB operatives and their gallant deeds.[13] To inspire adolescents "who want to understand the meaning of life, to develop strong character, to learn what it means to be a citizen," a booklet offered them in 1967 the thoughts of

§§§§§Beria and Merkulov during the Second World War held that rank, and Beria was later promoted to marshal.

six selected heroes of the nation in its opening section entitled "What Is Most Important in Life." Of the six, Karl Marx was first, Dzerzhinsky second, and the Chekist operative "Rudolf Abel" fourth. [14]

The Chekist: Power, Privilege, and Personality

The leaders bestow great privilege upon their Chekists.

KGB officers have always been better paid than officials of other agencies, including the military. The military-style ranks they adopted for the first time in 1940 reflected their privileged status: a "captain of State Security," for example, was officially equivalent to (but much better paid than) a colonel in the armed forces. "Major of State Security" equated with army major general and "senior major of State Security" with lieutenant general; the top Chekist during the Sovietization of Lithuania was "Senior Major of State Security" Pyotr Gladkov. Although these ranks were restructured in 1944 to equate with regular military ranks, the pay for functional positions such as case officer, chief of section, and chief of department is higher than that of similar positions in other agencies. The operational Chekist gets an added 10–20 percent for doing secret work, plus 10–15 percent for language knowledge, plus 5–15 percent for length of service. As if that were not enough, in the mid-1970s KGB Chairman and Politburo member Andropov raised KGB salaries by 20 percent across the board. [15]

The KGB controls some of the best apartment buildings in Moscow and the provinces, and a KGB man will always get preference for the best apartments available elsewhere. KGB stores provide Chekists with food not available to the common citizen. The KGB has a sumptuous club next door to House Number Two (House Number Twelve); it has its own well-endowed sports club that is world famous not for its KGB affiliation but for its championship soccer teams: its name is Dynamo.

Wherever he goes the Chekist walks in an aura of personal power and a certain sort of respect. Aleksey Myagkov, as a young KGB lieutenant, arrived at his army unit wearing a normal military uniform and dropped in unexpectedly at the office of the regimental commander.

He stared at me angrily and barked, "What do you want, Comrade Lieutenant? Can't you see I'm busy? Report to me later." When I said I was an officer of the KGB and was to work with his regiment in the coming year, the expression on [Colonel] Nikishin's face was at once transformed; it became friendly and somehow obsequious. "Please come in, Comrade

Lieutenant, for you I have always got time." . . . He fawned on me . . . inquiring if my quarters were well equipped, if there was anything at all that I needed. He expressed a readiness to assist me in any possible way. . . . Other officers behaved in precisely the same way. . . . This gave one a pleasant consciousness of one's own authority and power. After working for approximately 18 months in the KGB, I accepted all this as being quite commonplace and my rightful due.[16]

The regime depicts the Chekist as a man (in Dzerzhinsky's words) of "clean hands, cool head, and warm heart" and depicts Dzerzhinsky, the founder, as a man of great compassion and such purity that he is usually called the "shining knight of the revolution." His love for children is emphasized, and it is a fact that he and Stalin ordered the Chekists to round up the stray children orphaned and turned loose on the countryside by the Bolshevik terror and civil war—and raised them, in special state institutions, into faithful Chekist cadres.

It is impossible to generalize accurately about the Chekist as a personality, of course. The KGB hires people of many different types, from different stations, and for different missions. One Chekist may be stealing scientific secrets from foreign governments and companies to bolster his country's defenses; another may be threatening a writer in his town or beating up a dissident; yet another may be adding a new sentence to the punishment of a prisoner in a faraway concentration camp or shooting down unarmed people trying to cross the border. The quality of people, and the level of their education, has varied over the years. The old Chekist who survived and advanced by zealous and merciless participation in mass deportations, tortures, and killings may well be different from a younger man who has not yet faced such tests.

Certain pressures, however, do shape any Chekist's personality. By the act of joining this organization, even its less objectionable portions, he has taken sides in a war; he has opted for the regime against the people. He quickly senses the barriers that now separate him from them. When I was a young man fresh from wartime service in SMERSH and a posting in Moscow, I returned to my native village in Siberia with the idea of staying there and teaching school. Quickly I found that I had become a man from another planet; some villagers called me "Mr. Minister" and treated me with embarrassing deference, while others seemed wary and distant. I came to realize that I could never "descend" from the heights of State Security into normal village life. Throughout my career, whenever I came into social contact with outsiders who knew or guessed my line of work, I could sense an aversion, a shrinking away, and sometimes, when drink overpowered prudence, even outspoken hostility. (Policemen in the West sometimes experience a degree of this, of course, but far deeper fears and more horrible memories pervade Soviet society.) Because once inside the KGB he can only be thrown or carried out, the Chekist is likely to rationalize his position.

KGB veterans who have come over to the West naturally stress the good qualities of Chekists. One, for example, tells (quite correctly) that the KGB seeks as employees people with "a good general education, intelligence, . . . self-reliance, self-control, a capacity for establishing connections, resolution and courage."[17] I mentioned in an earlier work that "as individuals, State Security officers are often extremely intelligent, thinking people," and pointed out that the KGB's foreign-intelligence specialists have among them "some of the most intelligent, technically accomplished and sophisticated members of Soviet society. Their level of education is the highest in the country, generally including years of graduate as well as normal Soviet university study."[18] But there is another side of the coin more evident to the KGB's victims.

In isolating himself from the people and rationalizing the choice he has made, the Chekist is ever more vulnerable to pressures to become what he appears to outsiders. He develops a callousness to protect his self-esteem. Enjoying the support of rulers with unlimited powers, getting more pay and perquisites even than other Soviet officials, taking for granted his immense privileges, feeling everyone's cringing servility, this "representative of authority" with his *passe-partout* red booklet is likely to become arrogant and to despise the common man at his mercy. My uneducated and brutal colleague Colonel Kirilin almost went mad with this power; off duty, he sometimes wandered about the streets confronting people, demanding their papers, reviling and spitting on them, challenging them to oppose him—and go to jail. In the most secret place of a secret system, the Chekist may be tempted to deceive and betray, to slander and intrigue. Knowing the truth and defending the lie, he can only be cynical.

Having chosen his side, he commits himself to its goals and subjects himself to its disciplines. An obedient party worker eager to get ahead—and having sacrificed his own independence and integrity—he finds it increasingly easy to toady to his bosses. His efforts to seek their favor and avoid their displeasure require that he conform to their norms. At best this would make him gray and drab, but usually the KGB demands more: it prides itself on being the "merciless sword of the revolution." He does the party's bidding as well as he can, and he is always under pressure to produce, because his own career and, indeed, survival depend on it. Therefore he is unbending and humorless about anything touching his job. Chekists may be thinking and intelligent, but as servants and products of their system they can seldom afford to let their personal reasoning processes interfere with the basic premises of their job.

Procedures and the Pressures They Create

The Chekist is a slave to a demanding master; the prime characteristic of his work is personal responsibility.

That responsibility is clearly set out. To root out opponents from every corner of society, the Soviet leaders have identified such corners and assigned a KGB department to cover it. That department is further divided and subdivided until finally a single officer will have a sphere of authority of his own. As Chairman Andropov put it:

> The invariable norm for Chekist activity as a whole is to delineate specific work sectors and to make each worker strictly and personally responsible for the sector entrusted to him by the party. That sector where the duties have been imprecisely set out or the tasks imprecisely executed can prove to be just the vulnerable spot, just the flaw, that the adversary will take advantage of. You understand, comrades, that this pertains equally to the workers in every subdivision of the organs of State Security. [19]

Whether his sector is a restaurant or a railway station, a ministry or part of a town, a religious cult or a group of Estonian nationalists, the KGB officer is responsible. His very title says so; the Russian term for his status is *operativnyy upolnomochennyy*, the literal meaning of which is "bearer of full powers for operations" or "authorized operative." (The KGB jargon is "operativnik." The usual English translation, "case officer," is too bland.)

He studies his target area (a theater, restaurant, religious sect, factory, or ministerial office, for instance) and reviews the files of its employees. There he draws up a plan to make his area watertight against "enemies." He must always assume that existing procedures are too lax. Again and again he must propose steps to improve the secrecy of his agent network, to recheck the loyalty of its existing members, and to add new ones to it. Within his sphere he not only deals with the regime's permanent targets, such as churchgoers or bourgeois nationalists or people with foreign contacts, but must also bear in mind the leaders' latest preoccupations. If at the moment they are exhorting the nation against the evils of Zionism, the case officer will have to uncover some machinations by Jews within his sphere. If the leaders need fodder for a campaign against ideological subversion, he might for instance try to identify people who affect Western manners or dress or listen to foreign radio stations and bring them in for a "chat"—and thereby chalk up statistics proving his and his KGB sector's vigilance and permitting the KGB its boast that it is "educating" and "influencing" and "preventing."

The KGB case officer's search for the maverick who might pose a threat to the regime is simplified by the collective nature of Soviet society. Every working person is a member of several collectives. The athlete can train and compete only in a regime-sponsored club; the scientist can do his research only in state-controlled institutions on state-approved projects; the farmer can plant or harvest only in a collective; the office or factory worker, the writer, and painter are all organized in unions. Enthusiasts of the local customs and dances of, say, Estonia or the Altay Kray pursue their interests through regime-sponsored societies. Even apartment houses are organized in collectives, with permanent secretaries and "comrades' courts" to settle disputes. And the members of these collectives watch over each other and criticize the nonconformist. The KGB case officer, responsible for a sector of society, uses them as a military commander uses scouts.

In the town KGB offices of the Altay Kray, to take an example I know personally, the officers responsible for industry invariably enlist the informal help of secretaries of the party, Komsomol, and trade unions in the factories; those working against religion use the local representative of the CRA; those coping with the intelligentsia call on the help of the secretariat of the local writers union. They need only ask for any information they want; the secretaries (all loyal party or Komsomol members and sometimes registered KGB collaborators) cannot refuse them. The town of Barnaul was typically divided up geographically into sectors, too, each of which was supervised by a KGB case officer. Whenever he has a problem to look into or a suspect to watch, he can draw upon the militia's neighborhood coverage for help in collecting information, finding likely agents, or inserting his own. When he chooses to harass or intimidate, he can call on the *druzhinniki*, the volunteer police auxiliary.

The case officer will be inclined to see potential conspiracy in every group of people—even friends who meet regularly. He will make it his job to find out what they are up to (by recruiting one of their number, or inserting one of his own agents) or to throw up obstacles (warnings or harassment) to their meetings.***** Should a fire or an accident occur in a factory for which the case officer is responsible—or should such a factory fail to fulfill its production plan—he may be under pressure to find an "enemy" at the root of the trouble.

But his ultimate aim is to prosecute his victims. I described in another

*****The examples in the literature of dissidence are endless. In October 1980 about a thousand Jews held a large picnic in a forest on the outskirts of Moscow. This bothered the authorites, since forest meetings are hard to listen in on. When the Jews arrived for another picnic in early May 1981 they found signs saying, "The forest is closed for cleaning. Entry strictly forbidden." KGB men (some dressed as police) barred paths leading to the picnic ground. (Nigel Wade, Moscow correspondent of *London Daily Telegraph*, 4 May 1981.)

book the course of the case officer's preparation of a "case" for eventual turnover to the procurator.[20] Briefly, the case officer will put secret agents into contact with a suspect to discover more or perhaps to tarnish his image or exacerbate his "criminality"—and ultimately to testify at his trial. The case officer will put surveillance teams on the suspect's trail to uncover his accomplices and put microphones in his home and office. By the time the "case" reaches the procurator, the file may be fat. That of the writer Andrey Amalrik amounted to nine volumes totaling some 5,000 pages.[21] The administrative organs will see to it that the victim's punishment sets an example to the rest of the population.

In all this work, there is no room for slackness or lenience. The case officer's plan has become part of the larger plan of his department and, ultimately, of the whole KGB; and he must report periodically on its fulfillment. This creates pressure: he and his boss must meet their quotas if they are to advance in their careers.

The victim of this deadly bureaucratic procedure, that stems from the leaders' fears, is the common citizen.

As a motorcade of Politburo leaders sped over the Borodinskiy Bridge in Moscow, driven by Chekists and accompanied by State Security protective cars, a jaywalker imprudently tried to cross the street. The cars made no effort to avoid him and killed him outright. From State Security's viewpoint he was of no interest; State Security men sent his body to the morgue without even trying to identify it. What did matter was that someone had failed his duty. Each step of the leaders' route was in some Chekist's area of responsibility, and no one was to be allowed on the street when the leaders passed. Orders are orders. During the ensuing hours while higher-ups discussed his case, the responsible officer committed suicide.

This incident happened during my time in a particular KGB unit, the Guards Directorate; and like so much of that directorate's work, it epitomizes the KGB's attitudes and ways. Perhaps more vividly than any other part of the KGB, the Guards Directorate exposes the nature of the Soviet system. This "KGB-within-a-KGB" has always been among the most secret elements of a secret organization and deserves a chapter of its own.

CHAPTER 12

The Innermost Ring: The Bodyguards

A Secret System

AMBITIOUS PLOTTERS HAVE FOUND IT HARD TO GRAB POWER FROM Soviet leaders. Nikita Khrushchev stands as the only party chief overthrown by anyone other than death itself.*

But at the end of the 1980s Gorbachev was vulnerable. On one hand he was building up people's hopes and letting them organize and air their discontent, while on the other hand he was failing to improve their welfare—and the harsh light of his own *glasnost* was exposing just how dim were the prospects for improvement. His restructuring was casting confusion among industrial managers and disquiet among bureaucrats. Like Khrushchev, he was exposing his flanks to his rivals' attack.

So Gorbachev might come finally to rely, like many of his predecessors, on his innermost ring of protection.

When Westerners think of bodyguarding, they are likely to picture the sort of precautions that are visible throughout the Western world (in the present era of terrorism more so than ever): armed functionaries checking the premises of important meetings, surrounding the dignitaries, keeping watch from rooftops, verifying entry passes. Soviet bodyguards do this work, of course, and more rigorously than their Western counterparts. Soviet leaders are likely to be seen only from afar, atop the Lenin Mausoleum at Red Square parades or as dim shapes in cars speeding on

---

*I do not count Malenkov. He held the party leadership for only a few days as part of the sequence of events surrounding the sudden death of Stalin.

reserved lanes of Moscow streets. Here, for instance, was a midnight appearance of Mikhail Gorbachev in 1983 in Leningrad:

> A black KGB Volga car raced into the [great square in front of the Winter Palace] and drove round and round the 90-ft. high Alexander's Column. Its loudhailer barked non-stop: "Clear the square. Get off the square and onto the pavement. Move yourself! Faster . . . faster . . . faster!" Dozens of tourists and Soviet citizens out for a stroll began rushing from the square, some seized by panic. The car kept up its sinister noise as though in a scene from Kafka, driving people before it like sheep.
>
> There was an eerie minute's silence. Then the caravan [of Politburo member and Leningrad party chief Grigoriy Romanov] arrived, comprising two Mercedes police cars with flashing red and blue lights, two huge Zil limousines for the top people, and two other big cars. They raced across the square to the column and screeched to a stop. Security police leaped from the cars and fanned out around Mr. Romanov, 60, and his new young wife, a former light opera singer, and Mr. Mikhail Gorbachev, another member of the ruling Politburo and also a party secretary.
>
> The group stood for a few minutes [then . . .] got back into the Zil and the cars drove off, lights flashing, sirens wailing. [1]

Leaving aside for the moment Gorbachev's walkabout in that same city less than two years later (when he seemed to stroll confidently through the streets chatting with passers-by), that surrealistic night scene offers a good idea of the relations between rulers and ruled; but it exposes only the most superficial part of the Soviet bodyguard system.

What those KGB men were doing with their bullhorns and flashing lights and submachine guns that night was simply—in the less inhibited Soviet way—what political leaders' bodyguards do anywhere in the world: protecting bodies. But underneath these visible elements, concealed as one of the tightest-held secrets of Soviet rule, lies a vast mechanism that has no Western parallel. It is fully known only to a few top party and Chekist chiefs; most KGB officers know little about it. That I can here recount details is due to a bureaucratic oversight during the turbulent period following Beria's arrest. An officer of the Guards Directorate— worse, a personnel and security officer who knew its internal structure as few others and who as a party secretary also knew its internal scandals— was afterward allowed, contrary to unwritten rules, to serve abroad. I seized that unique opportunity to come over to the West.

The Soviet leaders live and work behind the protection of an elaborate defensive screen. It has a long tradition, rooted in the Oprichnina, the guards of Ivan the Terrible, but enjoys capabilities that Ivan would have envied. Spurred by the Soviet leaders' fears, fortified by their almost unlimited powers, and equipped with modern technology, the KGB Guards Directorate must be the most perfect and sophisticated body ever organized for the personal safety and comfort of a political leadership.†

It supervises soldiers with heavy-duty weapons and armored vehicles, microbiologists, traffic policemen, doctors and nurses, plumbers and electricians and cleaning personnel, farmers and butchers, chauffeurs and truckers, footpads and hit men and interrogators, cooks and communications specialists, railway engineers, and field operatives handling secret informants. In my time all of these, fifty thousand strong, were on the payroll of a single directorate under the barely educated drunkard Nikolay Vlasik, to whom Stalin had given the rank of lieutenant general. Today Stalin and Vlasik are gone and many of the fifty thousand are administered by other agencies, but the bodyguards unquestionably retain control over them. Their importance and stature survived Stalin, too: Brezhnev gave to his personal protector, Ryabenko, even higher rank than Stalin had given to Vlasik.

There is a reason for this fantastic scope, this prestige, this mystery. This is the innermost ring of defense and protects the party bosses not only against outside intruders but also, in the absence of procedures to turn over power, against their rivals in the hierarchy. For this they need their own, autonomous resources. The General Secretary and his inner circle cannot allow just anyone in the party hierarchy or even in the KGB to know where they are infiltrating agents or planting microphones, whose telephones they are tapping and mail they are reading, and whom they are having followed on the streets. The inner ruling circle must have its own facilities to mount provocations, to gain control over individuals by blackmail, to put down dangerous rivals by slander or even by murder. That requires them not only to preserve the Guards Directorate and to hold it closely under their direct command but also to assure it of capabilities similar to those of Stalin.

Stalin created this mechanism. Although his rivals weakened it even before his death,‡ enough of it survived that when it fell into Beria's hands it posed a deadly menace to Stalin's other heirs. No doubt, after shooting Beria, the Kremlin leaders took steps to keep one another's hands off such

---

†This bodyguard component has had, within State Security, a series of different designations, in this chronological order: First Department, Sixth Directorate, Guards Directorate (reviving the tsarist word *Okhrana* for guards), Main (or Chief) Guards Directorate, and Ninth Directorate, which it has held since the renaming of State Security as the KGB. For the sake of clarity, I use the previous and generally descriptive term "Guards Directorate."

‡The details of how Stalin's rivals dismantled his inner defenses are to be found in my book *Crime Without Punishment*.

dangerous capabilities. But they cannot have done away with bodyguards, for they are essential to the survival of Soviet rule. Therefore it is to understand the present, not to resurrect the past, that we briefly review that bodyguarding system in which I served.

First of all, Stalin controlled his protective apparatus personally and almost independently of the MGB as such—the heads of its various components reporting either to him or to his personal secretary, Poskrebyshev, or to State Security Minister Viktor Abakumov. In these matters Abakumov acted less as chief of an agency than as agent of Stalin.

The principal elements of his system consisted of:

(1) That vast bodyguard organization that I have already sketched, those fifty thousand people divided into departments according to their specialties: food, health, physical protection, etc. Its most important element, Operod, deserves separate mention.

(2) The central investigative apparatus that was called the Operational Department (*Operativnyy Otdel,* in short "Operod"). In its sixteen departments were concentrated the capabilities—independent of the rest of State Security, which had its own parallel departments—for surveilling, spying, liaising with other agencies, and eliminating people. It was a KGB-within-a-KGB.

(3) A special technical section, formally subordinated to the MGB's Technical Operations Department. It was headed by that department's deputy chief, Lt. Col. Karasev, who reported outside normal channels.

(4) The military units under the Kremlin Komendatura. This Praetorian Guard, if largely ceremonial, counted some 3,000 elite troops with powerful weapons, high discipline, and loyalty to Stalin. During my time there were proposals to separate it from the MGB altogether and subordinate it directly to the Central Committee of the CPSU, but this was not technically feasible and was never adopted. The troops of the Kremlin Komendatura are today as powerful as ever.

(5) The part of the MGB's Secret Political Directorate (SPU) that was responsible for security cases involving Communist Party members. Although nominally part of the MGB it was closely supervised by Stalin and Poskrebyshev. At least part of it survives within the KGB.

Under Stalin's command, Operod had informants—including bodyguards recruited to work against their own masters—reporting on the private doings of Politburo members. Privately ordered to plant microphones in the homes and offices of Politburo members and taps on their phones, Karasev would pass the transcripts directly to Abakumov, who handed them to Poskrebyshev or (if particularly important) directly to Stalin.

With this information, with these means of control and watching, with all the key positions held by loyalists reporting directly to him, Stalin was safe against any plot and able to compile dossiers thick with details of the indiscretions and collusions of his colleagues—rich material for a future blood purge.

Today, Operod probably has a different name and shape. It may still be administered outside of the Guards Directorate (Beria and Malenkov shifted it out to SPU in 1952 as part of the plot to weaken Stalin's power), and it has surely been reduced in size since the days when some of its individual departments employed thousands. But we do not know these things. § The only sure thing is that an operations center of the bodyguards system survived. I myself found evidence of its survival through Khrushchev's time and well into the era of Brezhnev.** And it was Operod's work that Andropov was describing in 1972 as "the KGB's most delicate task"—from which "only Comrade Brezhnev is tabu."[2]

Bodyguarding, Soviet Style

Even if one disregards the intrigues of Operod, Soviet bodyguarding takes surprising forms.

They begin with the sort of bodyguarding familiar in the West but done on a scale hardly thinkable here. The Guards Directorate assigns 700 to 1,000 men as personal guards for the General Secretary and other top

§It is not surprising that we do not know its current status. The very existence of Operod itself nearly passed unnoticed in the West. As far as I know, only one other person ever told that such an organization existed. This was Aleksandr Orlov, a senior NKVD officer who went over to the West in 1938; if he knew any details, he did not publish them.

**That evidence includes the travels and residence of Leonid Nalepin and Vasily Shatalov. Nalepin was Operod's chief and participated in some of Stalin's bloodiest intrigues, such as the "Leningrad Affair" in which Stalin in 1949 wiped out the Leningrad party organization that had been built up by Andrey Zhdanov. In that affair Nalepin personally accompanied MGB Minister Abakumov and the latter's deputy, General Selivanovskiy, in arresting Nikolay Voznesenskiy, who had been a Politburo member, and Aleksey Kuznetsov, who had been a CC CPSU secretary. He sent them on their separate paths toward Operod's executioner, a drunken brute named Okunev (who held the rank of lieutenant colonel), who shot them in the back of the head. (I have seen Okunev drooling and reeling along the corridors of house number two.) When later condemning Stalin's crimes, Khrushchev chose to single out the scything of the Leningrad organization as one of the worst. Yet, ironically, he kept Nalepin at the old stand. Nalepin was surely still on secret bodyguarding business when he traveled to the West at the end of 1963, because he was accompanied by Shatalov. Shatalov was a Guards Directorate colonel with whom Nalepin and I had worked closely as party secretaries. Those two veterans must have continued working under Brezhnev, because as late as 1970 the Moscow telephone directory still listed them both at an address I know to be an apartment house of the Guards Directorate on Sadovaya Kudrinskaya.

leaders of party and government, in addition to whole sections assuring their safety on the streets, in trains or planes, at home, or in vacation dachas. To serve their households the directorate assigns between 30 and 200 men and women to each Politburo member and candidate, CC CPSU secretary, and first secretary of republic and oblast. About 500 of its men oversee the guarding of top-level party and state offices by KGB Troops and MVD Internal Troops. Other large units watch over the areas in and around Moscow where the leaders commonly move. Still others protect (and watch) visiting foreign Communist Party leaders, whether they are in power or not.

Food tasting—a profession as old as poison and ambition—has its place here, too. The tyrant or rich man would give a courtier the dubious privilege of the first helping of his delicacies and might choose with care his cooks and food carriers, but there his defenses usually stopped. Not so the Soviet leaders. Their protectors actually grow the food on their own fields and pastures and ponds and vineyards, with their own cleared farmers. The department that manages all this was transferred in the early 1950s to the Ministry of Agriculture but is still under the control of the Guards Directorate of which, until then, it was an integral part. The department supervises the slaughtering of animals and the transport of the produce in its own trucks along protected routes to its own storehouses.

Before it reaches the special commissaries provided by the Guards Directorate, it is tested in a biological laboratory equipped with batteries of mice, guinea pigs, and other test animals, sometimes undergoing culture tests lasting three days. This laboratory and these commissaries probably remain under Guards Directorate command—and for more reasons than mere precautions against poison. Ludicrous as it may sound in the West, only the KGB with its rigid discipline could be entrusted with the key to this sumptuous larder (with delicacies in and out of season, some imported from abroad), and only the KGB with its tight security could keep the secrets of this opulence from the deprived populace. Finally the food gets its final check in the leaders' households, where all servants are cleared and employed by the KGB.††

The West caught a glimpse of this elaborate system when Brezhnev visited Bonn in late November 1981. His personal chef, Ivan Biryukov

††When Stalin dined at home, no matter how few guests sat at his table, he drank from his own wine bottle, freshly opened by his personal guard; then (sometimes after serving others) the guard would take the bottle away with most of the wine remaining, for fear that someone might slip something into it. A similar process was observed with cigarettes: Stalin would smoke only the first cigarette in each pack, although the pack had been prechecked and its seal opened by his own servant; once it was laid aside, someone might substitute a poisoned one. His pens and pencils were carefully checked and new ones provided every day, in case a pencil bomb had been slipped in.

(unquestionably a KGB Guards Directorate employee), took over the kitchen of the West German guest mansion and prepared meals of food flown in from Moscow, under the supervision of Brezhnev's KGB-cleared physician. When Biryukov was not in the kitchen it was kept locked and watched by the bodyguards.[3]

Another aspect of Soviet bodyguarding is the administration of medical care to the leaders. The KGB, responsible for their safety, faces the problem: who shall be allowed to choose their medicines, stick needles into their bloodstreams, put pills into their mouths? Their answer is: the KGB itself.

The uniquely well-equipped hospital on Kalinin Prospekt and polyclinic on Granovsky Street, reserved for the use of the Kremlin leaders, are administered and policed by the Guards Directorate. Everyone who works there, from top medical professor to lowest floor mopper, is fully cleared; in my time, all were staff members of State Security.‡‡ They were organized as a section of the Guards Directorate called the Medical-Sanitary Directorate of the Kremlin (LSUK). In 1952 it was formally transferred to the Ministry of Health where it became the Fourth Chief Directorate; but it remains under Guards Directorate control, and its chief today holds the rank of major general of KGB Medical Services.

Transportation of the leaders poses more problems. Of course, any government, democratic or autocratic, would protect its leaders when they move about. But here again the Soviet system resembles no other. Consider, for example, the precautions Stalin would take for train travel. (Because of his fear of flying, he flew only once or twice.) Two spare trains were prepared to depart for other destinations, simply to hide the real plans. A third train rolled ahead of the leader's for safety's sake, filled with heavily armed troops ready for any trouble along the way; the fourth carried the dictator, with a separate compartment for Vlasik; the fifth, guarding the rear, carried the bodyguards who would be staying in the Caucasian resort as long as Stalin did. Along the whole two-thousand-kilometer roadbed, State Security men stood, each within eyesight of the next, watching every foot of the way to keep saboteurs from approaching the rails over which the leader's train would come. The same precautions were also taken when Stalin went to the Potsdam Conference in 1945. As he rolled across reconquered but still turbulent Byelorussia, across a

---

‡‡Not even that degree of security was enough to calm Stalin; he at least pretended to believe that these Kremlin doctors had purposely caused the death of Andrey Zhdanov. To promote a new purge of lieutenants, he unleashed KGB interrogators upon some of the most prominent of these KGB medical functionaries. Killing two of them in the process, the KGB compelled the survivors to confess murderous plotting against other Kremlin leaders.

Poland being "normalized" by Soviet special troops, and across chaotic eastern Germany, every foot of the rail lines was under the eye of NKVD and Border Guard Troops, SMERSH, and NKGB men.

The neighborhoods of political leaders' offices and residences and their planned routes of travel get protection in the West as in the East. The precautions in the Soviet Union, however, have no parallel. The entire "official" part of Moscow is a special security domain—a "secret city" which the hierarchs occupy and the Guards Directorate watches over. Centered on the Kremlin, the Central Committee building, and the KGB headquarters, it spreads out over the streets containing the guards' living quarters, MVD headquarters, and other key installations, out to the neighborhoods where the leaders live and to the barracks of the Dzerzhinsky Division of Internal Troops on the Garden Ring.

This secret city has its own power plant, its own communications system, its own cleaning and maintenance personnel, electricians, plumbers, and door guards—all controlled by the Guards Directorate. Plainclothesmen of a 2,000-strong department under the close supervision of the Guards Directorate mingle amid the throngs—alert to any unusual intruder or happening. If someone loiters more than half an hour on Arbat Street, for example, these men are instructed to follow and identify him, often getting a regular policeman to check his papers. Another section (once under Operod but presumably now part of the Second Chief Directorate) handles about 3,000 secret informants living or working on the streets of the secret city, checking people who have windows onto these streets and, if it finds derogatory information, having them moved away. As an additional precaution, neighborhood busybodies, house superintendents, militia, militia auxiliaries, and party and Komsomol members who live in these sensitive areas are pushed, more actively than elsewhere, to report visitors and unusual events. A Western tourist returning to his hotel thinking he had not been followed in this area might be right—but watchful eyes were upon him.

All the traffic policemen of Moscow were, for a time, part of the Guards Directorate. In 1947–52, when the MGB had taken over the militia from the MVD, the entire 2,000-man traffic-control militia of Moscow (*Otdel regulirovaniya ulichnogo dvizheniya,* or ORUD) was subordinated intact to the Guards Directorate. It no longer is, but it still cooperates closely to protect the leaders under Guards Directorate supervision.

The guards' control of this territory does not stop at the street level. To search out potential dangers, their "Section for Below-and-Above-Ground Maintenance" (*Podzemnogo i nadzemnogo Khozyaystva*) regularly inspects every attic, basement, water main, sewer line, and telephone wire in areas of interest. In my day this section was under Operod and included about a hundred staff members.

If central Moscow is the principal focus of the guards' territorial coverage, Red Square is its center, and the parades on May 1 and November 7 the high points of its year. On these days everyone knows that the leaders (whose itineraries are normally kept secret) will be assembled on the terrace of the Lenin Mausoleum. Now the Internal Troops are alerted and the guards multiply their already meticulous precautions.§§ The "Below-and-Above-Ground Maintenance Section" makes a fresh check; the watch is sharpened along every road to or from Red Square. In the Square itself, as the leaders look down at the marching ranks and across to the huge banners celebrating their power—the "people's" victory—one out of every ten people in the reviewing stands nearby is an armed officer of State Security, his hidden pistol loaded. The "loyal troops" marching past, on the contrary, have been carefully inspected to be sure that they have no ammunition; the penalty for failure to enforce this rule was in Stalin's time twenty-five years' hard labor for the soldier, his officers, and all State Security personnel involved in his clearance. Still that is not enough protection: the right-hand files of every marching column—the men and women closest to the rostrum—are specially cleared and selected by the party organization (and, if they are in a military unit, by the KGB's special department within the unit).

More: machine guns nestle in the crenellations of the Kremlin walls above. In the windows of the GUM department store, the slits in the quaint towers of St. Basil's cathedral, and the windows and roof of the Historical Museum opposite, armed State Security men stand on the alert.

Still more: down in the basement tunnel connecting the inside of the Kremlin with the Lenin Mausoleum stand guard troops ready to pour out and turn their automatic weapons against any of the marching masses who might be tempted to abuse the privilege of temporary proximity to their leaders.

This Praetorian Guard, known as the troops of the Kremlin Komendatura, contains an "Independent Officers' Battalion" of 900 men (responsible for the pass system and patrols) and a "Regiment of Special Purpose" of 2,000 men formed into companies with light antitank artillery with shrapnel shells suitable for crowds. It also includes a communications

§§In 1988, as the Moscow Militia chief reported, the militia augmented its patrolling forces by 25 percent to insure "that nothing would spoil the people's celebration" on November 7 (Tass, 2 November 1988).

company to maintain the underground telephone installations—buried so deep under the Kremlin that only a nuclear bomb could destroy them.

Who Shall Be Allowed Near the Masters?

Men and women of the Guards Directorate are selected and screened with meticulous care, for of all the Soviet population it is they who will be allowed closest to the leaders—and bearing arms, at that. If the procedures seem excessive to a Westerner, they do not seem so to the Soviet leaders who know that many a citizen would happily wreak revenge for a tortured or heartbroken relative, a broken life. The flavor of this screening process[4] will emerge here from a few examples.

All candidates for employment by the Guards Directorate must be party or Komsomol members recommended by the secretaries of those organizations. They are Russians—never Jews, and, unless they are guarding leaders of those other nationalities, not Central Asians or other border nationalities. Ironically, there are no Lithuanians or Latvians, the nationals who composed Lenin's first bodyguard.

Once a candidate has passed this first screening, every period of his life is checked, not only his early childhood but also his family backward for generations past and extending through cousins and in-laws and cousins' in-laws. If any one of those relatives had been abroad, had relatives or correspondents abroad or in prisons or labor camps, or was of Jewish background, or even of the intelligentsia, the candidate would be excluded. If a candidate has a large family, the personnel department will reject him categorically; the chances are too high that in any large family there is some such shadow.

To recruit about 500 new people each year, the KGB would screen thousands of party and Komsomol members. Such party members, it is worth remembering, would already have been screened and guaranteed by three members before being admitted into the party—but still the KGB screening officers rejected about 50 for every one they finally accepted into the overall KGB and more than 100 for every one accepted for the Guards Directorate. I personally screened the files of more than 1,000 each year and interviewed about 700. Of these, only 80 or 90 seemed suitable to be passed on to the next phase, the medical examination. About 50 of them would be found healthy enough to qualify, and they were then subjected to detailed personal investigation—which would disqualify about 40 of them, leaving ten for KGB employment. The Guards Directorate would select about 5 or 6 of these.

Even after he is cleared, the candidate must pass more barriers before being given close access to a leader. A friend of mine, Lieutenant Losev of the Guards Directorate's plainclothes surveillance group for Arbat Street, was selected (without his knowledge) for more sensitive work. The personnel security section of the directorate tailed him secretly for weeks, as it does routinely in such cases. The footpads noticed that Losev would regularly stop off on the way home from work at the bar of the Kursk railroad station for a single vodka and would talk idly with the transients there. That was enough. He was dropped from consideration and, although allowed to remain at his Arbat Street post, warned to stop going to the bar.

A waitress named Zina in a state-operated restaurant in Moscow seemed suitable by virtue of her appearance, her ability, and especially her lack of relatives, except a widowed mother, for service in Stalin's household. After being enticed into State Security by the offer of triple pay, she worked for two years in a Guards Directorate restaurant under close watch before she was offered "a job outside of town." Her reluctance to leave her mother was overcome by double pay and the offer of a chauffeured car to bring her back and forth. So she became a domestic servant in one of Stalin's dachas. There she met and married another guard and fell afoul of a security precaution: the rules forbade close relatives to work in the same unit or area. State Security moved her husband away but, because she could not immediately be replaced, forced her to stay.

The bodyguards' already proven and tested loyalty is reinforced with extraordinary privileges. Their pay is high and their ranks beyond any reasonable relationship to their tasks. Brezhnev's personal bodyguard was a three-star general; a minor watchman over an outbuilding might be a major. They enjoy special food supplies and housing privileges, too, avoiding the frustrations of city life in the USSR.

The risks, however, are as high as Mt. Olympus itself. The ground is slippery and the fall long and steep. The discipline is rigid and unforgiving and the slightest error can bring dismissal not only from the directorate but from the KGB and party as well; in the process the culprit would lose his apartment and privileges and become unemployable. Guard slang for such dismissal is a "wolf's ticket," and it does indeed mean being thrown to the wolves. I knew of more than one bodyguard officer who committed suicide in preference to disgrace and slow death by starvation. When a picture book was found in a guards recreation room with an "X" penciled over the face of Stalin and a painstaking investigation failed to identify the culprit, the unit was disbanded, its officers dismissed and dropped from the party, and its men sent off to distant camps as guards.

Even if he works well, the guard's service may come to an abrupt end. The Soviet system does not permit a bodyguard of one leader to be transferred to another's personal retinue; if the guard's master dies or falls from grace, the guard goes too. This applies not just to the head bodyguard but to the entire staff—cooks, gardeners, drivers, housemaids. If the situation of a common bodyguard is precarious, that of high Guards Directorate leaders is downright perilous. Their glory and perquisites can be short lived and dearly bought.

Parts of the Guards Directorate have been transferred to other administrations, mostly in 1952: the farms to the Ministry of Agriculture, food and clothing supply to the Ministry of Trade, hospitals to the Ministry of Health, traffic regulation to the Moscow Militia, management of the leaders' Caucasian resorts to the Council of Ministers. This did not, however, diminish the KGB's power; these changes simply reduced the huge budget and administrative burdens of State Security and specifically of its Guards Directorate. Each of these units kept its organizational integrity, no matter who paid its bills; and the Guards Directorate kept control over them, putting its own officers wherever it considered necessary to assure the leaders' safety, whether as heads of state farms, for example, or in command of the Fourth Chief Directorate of the Ministry of Health.

What, then, is the observer to make of Gorbachev's walkabouts? From 1985 onward one could see press photographs and television scenes of this party chieftain talking informally with groups of factory workers or with passers-by on the streets of Soviet cities—apparently with no fear of rubbing shoulders with the people. Yet, up to that moment the leaders (including Gorbachev himself—remember that midnight scene in Leningrad) had had to be protected against these people by forces unprecedented in world history. Now less than two years later here was that same Gorbachev strolling about that same Leningrad, apparently having shaken off decades of dread in little more time than it would take a dog to shake off water. Had relations between ruler and ruled really changed so drastically? Had the Communist Party bosses suddenly won acceptance and gained the people's confidence?

Surely not. Any veteran of the Guards Directorate could certify that Gorbachev's "informal" meetings with workers and passers-by were carefully staged. No local party or KGB chief would assume the personal responsibility of allowing anyone this close to the leaders without assurance that he is loyal—and unarmed. Those "passers-by" talking with Gorbachev on the street or in the factory hall were undoubtedly screened and selected, arranged in their proper places, and briefed on what to do or say (even when what they said sounded contentious). Some of this deception became obvious, as in a press photograph taken during his visit to Krasnodar in September 1986; the photo was doctored to erase Gorbachev's burly KGB bodyguards and to make him appear closer to "the people."[5]

Moreover, it is only Gorbachev among the top leaders who may be seen this way among the populace. It is only Gorbachev's family who is exposed in public; he and his wife tell Westerners about themselves, and old schoolmates and workmates reveal to Western journalists vignettes of his personal life and character—while other Soviet leaders remain as aloof as ever, known to the people only from touched-up pictures and incomplete and often deceptive official biographies.

Perhaps for economy reasons some excess numbers of bodyguards have been reduced and, to meet public complaints, some of the middle-level party leaders' perquisites reduced as well (a "special store" on Granovskiy Street, for example, has been closed).[6] But the precautions surrounding Gorbachev's visit to the Ukraine in February 1989 showed how little had been changed. Areas of the cities were sealed off, leading nationalists were detained during his stay, and selected workers were taken by bus to meet him during his walkabout.[7]

The capabilities of the Soviet bodyguarding system cannot really be dismantled as long as the Leninist leaders continue their internal war against their people. In this extraordinary system lies their ultimate defense.

CHAPTER 13

The KGB's Use of the MVD

Auxiliary of the KGB

THE AGENCIES COLLECTED TOGETHER UNDER THE ROOF ORGANIZATION known as the All-Union Ministry of Internal Affairs (MVD) help the KGB to control the Soviet population. Whereas the KGB and MVD appear to be separate and parallel agencies of the Soviet government, ever since 1919, when Lenin gave to the Chekist chief Dzerzhinsky the simultaneous command of the NKVD, Internal Affairs has been in practice a subordinate or auxiliary of State Security.

Parts of the MVD's work are an extension of the KGB's, and some of its units have in the past been organic parts of the KGB. If they are no longer, it is for the administrative convenience of the KGB and not (as Soviet propaganda hints) to reduce the KGB's powers after Stalin's time. The unification of State Security and Internal Affairs in 1934 had proved unwieldy, and it was Stalin himself who broke it up, in 1943. (Beria's formal recoupling of the two after Stalin's death never got further than a paper exercise.) The KGB simply continued the work of the former Ministry of State Security (MGB), with one exception. But whenever the functions have been assembled within a single organization, the Chekists have been in command.

For years at a time, in fact, the Soviet regime has done without its All-Union MVD. Most of the latter's agencies have no day-to-day need for national headquarters; what could be more natural a function of local authority than, for instance, its police or fire department or offices that inspect automobiles, register inhabitants, and issue permits? Even this highly centralized Leninist regime has repeatedly abolished it. *

Moreover, the MVD's employees—for the most part policemen and detectives, prison guards, soldiers, and file clerks—are less educated and less well paid than the KGB's. From the earliest days they have been plagued by inefficiency and corruption. †

Here, briefly, is what the MVD does, especially its functions that most directly complement and support the work of the KGB:

(1) Routine police work, done by the so-called militia and supervised from Moscow by the MVD's Chief Directorate of Militia.

(2) Investigations. Until recent years all investigative work (collecting evidence and preparing it for prosecution) was limited to the Procurator's Office and the KGB, but with the intensification of the fight against crime in 1975 the local offices of the MVD's Chief Directorate of Criminal Investigations (*ugolovny rosysk*) have been authorized to investigate petty crime. ‡

(3) Preservation of public order. In addition to the Chief Directorate of Militia, the MVD has a Chief Directorate for the Preservation of Public Order supervising mobile police units designed to quell minor distur-

---

*It was first abolished in 1923 when the USSR was formally established as a federation. After reestablishment it was again disbanded in 1930, to be resuscitated once again in 1934 as part of Stalin's Chekist-run NKVD. It was suppressed for a third time in 1960, when Khrushchev transferred its oversight to its union-republic components. Two years later he changed the name from MVD to the milder-sounding "Ministry for the Preservation of Public Order" (MOOP). But the alarming rise of crime and corruption brought the need to reestablish central police control.

†The regime made strenuous efforts in the 1960s and 1970s to improve working conditions. It increased the MVD's investigative powers in 1963 and still further between 1965 and 1968, gave its employees higher pay and more benefits, reestablished the All-Union ministry to increase central control, and restored its old name MVD (of more fearsome memory). In the 1970s new academies were formed to train its men, new measures were taken to raise their morale, and their numbers were augmented. The proportion of university graduates has risen, but the level of education, professional skill, and pay lags far behind that of the KGB.

‡MVD units are not allowed to investigate serious cases such as murder, crimes against public order, crimes against the state, or crimes involving groups or foreigners. Until the 1960s, functionaries of the Criminal Investigation Directorate could only do inquiries: finding clues and questioning witnesses on the scene of a crime. Then they were authorized to do preliminary investigations—determining whether the circumstances warrant a court proceeding and if so, what must be proved—but only for minor offenses such as petty theft, assault causing minor injury, defamation of character, small-scale currency trading and smuggling, moonshining, hooliganism, and vagrancy. Since the 1970s, with the growing problem of theft and corruption, the MVD has been allowed to investigate (prepare court cases) but still only involving smaller amounts of money and isolated individual criminals.

bances. They patrol streets at night and, in the more sensitive areas, work closely with the local command of Internal Troops.

(4) Combating economic crime. This function is centered in the MVD's Chief Directorate for Combating the Embezzlement of Socialist Property and Speculation (*Glavnoye Upravleniye Borby s raskrishcheniyem Sotsialisticheskoi soobstvennosti i spekulyatsiyey,* or GUBKhSS). It handles the less important cases of corruption, embezzlement, and theft of "state property"—the major cases being reserved for the KGB. As these crimes grew in the 1960s and 1970s, this unit grew in size and was successively upgraded from the rank of department to directorate to chief directorate. It works closely with the KGB.

(5) Organizing and exploiting people's auxiliaries—the *"druzhinniki"* and the "strong points."

(6) Managing the prisons and labor camps and the convoy of prisoners to and from them.

(7) Registering the population and controlling residence, movements, typewriters, and printing presses, as well as weapons, poisons, and explosives. Issuing internal passports and permissions to go abroad. Inspecting and registering motor vehicles and other matters.

(8) Guarding offices, installations, strategic points, and means of transport. For this purpose the MVD administers Internal Troops, the militia, the Railway, Waterway, and Airways militias, and the so-called industrial guards (*vedomstvennaya militsiya*), watchmen recruited by the militia but paid by the institutions whose factories and depots they protect.

(9) Firefighting.

The KGB controls these functions to the degree that they complement KGB work. So direct is its control that it freely transfers its personnel to the MVD, either as punishment for incompetence or wrongdoing or to increase control when the MVD's performance slips.

Some ostensible MVD activity is simply KGB work in disguise. The KGB puts its men in militia uniforms, for example, to "guard" foreign embassies. It puts active and retired Chekists into controlling positions in the MVD office that issues exit visas, the OVIR. It takes over command of Internal Troops when they go into action against riots and uprisings. As part of its task of protecting the leadership, the KGB assigns its personnel to the traffic militia in neighborhoods where the leaders live and move regularly. Other MVD units are similarly used, as and when needed; the KGB uses the firefighters, for example, when it investigates the origin of a fire in an important plant or when it causes a fire with the purpose of gaining access to foreign embassies and consulates.

Sometimes the KGB takes over parts of the MVD in toto to straighten out problems. In 1946, for example, the police (militia) was found to be ridden with corruption, indiscipline, and poor security practices. The KGB (then MGB) simply absorbed the entire militia (first of Moscow, then of the rest of the country),§ moved hundreds of MGB officers into key militia positions, fired about 1,200 militiamen (700 in Moscow alone), reorganized the work, improved discipline, raised some salaries, and returned them to the MVD in 1952. Again in 1982 elements of the MVD had become so ridden by inefficiency and corruption that they were failing to cope with crime and corruption. Soon after Andropov became General Secretary he dismissed the corrupt MVD Minister Nikolay Shchelokov and his deputy, Yuri Churbanov** and moved the KGB Chairman Vitaliy Fedorchuk over to his place, along with a dozen or more KGB officials who took key positions in the MVD leadership.††

When in the second half of the 1980s the Soviet press began to publish articles criticizing police abuses, it was the MVD—and specifically the militia—that was singled out, not the KGB, for its brutal and corrupt practices. (The well-publicized chastisement of a KGB oblast chief in the Ukraine in early 1987 was an exception probably related to the internal struggle for the Ukrainian Republic party leadership.)

The Police and Its Auxiliaries

The regular police are called "militia" because Soviet doctrine vilifies "police" as an instrument of class oppression. Lenin initially planned to have the proletariat maintain its own public order, everyone taking his turn (without pay) in a "Workers' Militia." This idea quickly went aground on the rocks of reality: giving police powers to uneducated, untrained, and undisciplined people produced more chaos and violence than order. The leaders quickly came up with an ideological formula to define a professional police service—"a class instrument of Soviet democracy"—and in 1918 formed the Chief Directorate of Militia of the NKVD RSFSR (called off and on until 1934 "Chief Directorate of Workers and Peasants Militia").

---

§This was not the first time: from late 1932 until 1934, too, the militia was formally subordinated to State Security.

**Both were charged with corruption. Shchelokov committed suicide and Churbanov, after a trial in December 1988, was sentenced to twelve years in prison.

††Fedorchuk's two successors were functionaries of the central apparatus of the party: Aleksandr Vlasov, who in the fall of 1988 became prime minister of the Russian Republic, succeeded by Vadim Bakatin, an *obkom* first secretary and member of the CPSU Central Committee.

Today this land without "police" employs 3 million policemen‡‡ and 10 million volunteer police auxiliaries.

In addition to routine police work the militia handles the registration and documentation of citizens: residence, movement, and other controls discussed in a later chapter. In any district the militia is subordinated locally to the Internal Affairs Department of the Executive Committee, but it also reports upwards to higher echelons of the militia. It recruits and manages the *druzhinniki*, often for KGB purposes.

In 1959 the Soviet authorities established a system of young "volunteers" to help the militia keep order. They gave it the name of an old Russian organization of paramilitary volunteers called the *druzhina*, roughly meaning friendly association (individual members are called *druzhinniki*), which has been translated into English fifteen or twenty different ways as "people's volunteer militia," for instance, and "volunteer people's patrols" (or "detachments"), "militia assistance squads," "citizens' auxiliary police," military group leaders, "people's squad militia." When the *druzhiny* (plural of *druzhina*) were activated, Khrushchev's regime emitted a cloud of ideological explanations about "the withering away of the state" in favor of "spontaneous, volunteer" self-administration by the people. Their volunteer status is a farce: the party and Komsomol organizations in factories, offices, and farms simply assign members to the *druzhiny* as a party/Komsomol task, under the implied threat of losing vacation and housing privileges. A farce, too, is their independence of the state: they are in fact extensions of the state (specifically, of the militia), as became clear when, with time, they were granted formal rights and legal protection and subordinated to the local soviets. As a decree stated in the mid-1970s, "the entire activity of the *druzhiny* is meant to strengthen public order and the struggle against law breakers."[1]

The *druzhinniki* are mostly in their teens and twenties, although many older people participate as well. Each squad is supervised by a militia officer who is a party or Komsomol member, responsive to the district party committee and the KGB; some units whose tasks are directly linked to KGB work—those harrassing religious groups, for example—may actually get their directions directly from a KGB officer. Members work about once a week, though between times they stay alert for any "violations of socialist conduct" or for "negative phenomena" like drunkenness, idleness, or rowdyism.

‡‡The figure comes from Deputy Minister of Internal Affairs Nikitin. Addressing a meeting of procurators in the mid-1970s, he lamented that such numbers (which do not include firefighters or other specialized units administered by the same umbrella organization but not directly fighting crime) were still unable to master the problem of crime in the country (source: Fridrikh Neznansky).

Their work is facilitated by *opornye punkty* ("strong points," also translated as "social law enforcement stations" and "public order bases"). These are informal mini-police stations consisting of a small room with a telephone, conveniently set up in neighborhoods or apartment house complexes, where volunteers stand by to receive complaints, denunciations, and calls for help. Each installation is overseen by a party member.

The *druzhiny* help the KGB, remaining on call to fill a courtroom or carry out strong-arm attacks, (posing as street hooligans) against individuals or groups the KGB wants to intimidate. In these cases the KGB officer instructs the militia officer controlling the squad or gives orders directly to the squad leader.

The *druzhiny* also help the militia carry out tedious or time-consuming and low-priority aspects of its work. They work everywhere: on construction sites and on trains and buses, in schools and on collective farms, in border areas or in apartment building complexes, at sporting events or parades. Each squad covers a certain area, such as a city sector (*mikroraion*) or group of apartment houses, and has its own specialty. Some check documents on the street or go around to house superintendents to make sure that no one is beating a child or living without registering. They may break in on apartments where the presence of strangers has been denounced to check documents. Some, in the guise of preserving peace and quiet, break up parties of young people, especially those playing Western music and given to wearing Western clothes—anathema to the regime—and sometimes smash audio equipment and records. Others fight alcoholism, roaming the town to find drunks whom they can report to the police. Some help in the regime's campaign against absenteeism by going into public places, parks, and steam baths to find working-age people who might be shirking their duty—and to help the police drag them to work or to the militia post. Other *druzhinniki* look out for strangers in border zones and escort them to the police. Some specialize in attacking groups of religious believers.

They have been given the legal right to demand documents, to hold a suspect until a policeman can arrive to arrest him, and to take people to the militia post. Generally despised, they were so often beaten up by outraged citizens in their early years of work that the authorities were compelled to rule that an assault on a *druzhinnik* would be equivalent to an assault on a regular militiaman or some other "representative of authority"—which, by Soviet law, can be considered "terrorism" and punished by years of imprisonment.

Within a decade they had expanded all over the country and had enlisted millions. By 1982, according to regime figures, there were more than a million *druzhinniki* in the city of Moscow alone (population 8 million) and more than 10 million throughout the USSR, supported by more than 250,000 strong points. These figures may give an exaggerated impression of the impact of these vigilantes; regime spokesmen sometimes complain that these "volunteers" fail to show up for work or that they lack the training and discipline to do much good. Nonetheless they hugely expand the capabilities of local police—and of the KGB.

Points of KGB Control

The KGB dominates the MVD from the very top down onto the street level.

Chiefs of the two services in each region meet frequently and usually cooperate smoothly despite occasional friction. (KGB officers generally have a low opinion of the militia, and the latter sometimes react with resentment.) Both are keenly aware that the KGB chief, being the senior in party rank and power, will prevail in any confrontation; he has only to refer the issue to higher echelons, where the KGB will arrange that higher MVD authorities command their subordinate to cooperate. The local KGB chief, wanting someone he can trust atop the local MVD, can usually persuade the party boss to replace the MVD chief if he disapproves of him.

Several staffs within the MVD assure KGB control. The MVD's Department for Coordination of Relations with KGB Organs is staffed by active and retired KGB officers and KGB collaborators who screen MVD correspondence and reports for items of interest to various KGB departments. The Counterintelligence Department of the USSR MVD is responsible for the loyalty and internal security of all MVD personnel, operating much like the Special Departments (OOs) within the armed forces although not directly subordinated to the KGB's Third Directorate. Since 1970, too, the MVD USSR has a Main Staff *(Glavnyy Shtab)*, mirrored by the "Staff of the MVD" of each union republic, oblast, large city, and district, to coordinate and tighten central control of the MVD's diffuse functions, analyze the MVD's performance and problems, shape new laws as needed, and study new ways to improve public order.[2]

The MVD and its chief directorates also have departments of foreign relations which (as in other ministries) are KGB outposts. The department chief, either a KGB officer or collaborator, has under him active and retired KGB officers and agents. They handle contacts with Interpol and foreign police services, procure police technology and equipment from abroad, and allow the KGB to develop personal contacts with foreign police officials in its continuing efforts to recruit them as agents.

In each camp and jail of the MVD's Chief Directorate for Corrective

Labor Camps and Jails, the KGB has its own special sections, with their own networks of secret informants among the prison staff as well as among the prisoners.

The local units of the Rail, Waterways, and Air militias, administered by the MVD's Chief Directorate for Transportation, work closely with the KGB, and contain many officers detached (or demoted) from the KGB.

While formally part of the MVD, the office that issues, or refuses, visas for travel abroad (called OVIR) is staffed and run by KGB officers, reservists, and agents.

The guards outside every foreign embassy and office or residence occupied by foreigners, although in militia uniform, are in fact KGB officers reporting directly to a department of the KGB's Second Chief Directorate.

At the working level, the KGB uses MVD facilities routinely. In the warehouses of its Surveillance Directorate it holds, and uses whenever it chooses, thousands of uniforms of militia, Internal Troops, firefighters, and other MVD services, supplied by the MVD along with the false identity cards to go with them. By flashing his red identification booklet to a street policeman, a KGB surveillant can get him to identify, on some routine pretext, people he has seen (for example, talking with a foreigner). To harass a dissident, a KGB officer can command *druzhinniki*, acting as "hooligans," to beat and rob him. The MVD's doors are open to KGB operatives: if an MVD man makes difficulties, he knows he will get into trouble from his bosses. A KGB case officer frequently checks people's residences or other data in police files, or, in work against dissidents and *samizdat*, refers to MVD records on typewriters.

And the KGB continues to direct the important operations of Internal Troops.

The KGB and Internal Troops

The KGB when established in 1954 was deprived of one element that State Security had commanded since its outset. The Internal Troops (*Vnutrenniye Voiska*, or VV) were given over to the separate MVD. On the surface this appeared to reduce the KGB's size and powers but actually little really changed; the KGB got rid of the administrative headaches while retaining operational control.

You can see this relationship in the guarding of state installations. The KGB is formally responsible for preserving state secrets and hence, directly or indirectly, for the security of all installations where secrets are kept. The VV, with the mission of "guarding state installations," is there to help. As a general rule, the closer one moves in toward the core of power the more guarding is done directly by KGB personnel. At the very center, Politburo leaders are protected only by the KGB's Guards Directorate whether in their homes or offices or moving around. The inside of the Kremlin and the Lenin Mausoleum are guarded by the KGB's Kremlin Komendatura, the outside by a company of the VV's Dzerzhinsky Division especially cleared by the KGB. KGB headquarters, outside or inside, is solely under KGB watch. At other key headquarters, such as the CC CPSU, Council of Ministers, and Academy of Sciences, the inside is guarded by the KGB's Guards Directorate, the periphery (and sometimes the entrances) by Internal Troops (Dzerzhinsky Division) under KGB supervision. Lesser party headquarters in Moscow and in the republics and oblasts are guarded by Internal Troops alone, although they respond to the orders of the KGB's security supervisors on the spot. The Internal Troops also guard the most strategic bridges in areas where they are stationed. The ordinary installations of the armed forces—but not their most sensitive ones—are guarded by their own troops. Nonsensitive administrative centers, factories, transport, and communications are guarded by the already mentioned departmental *(vedomstvennaya)* militia.

But guarding is only one of the two missions of Internal Troops and far less important than the other which is vaguely defined as "urgent military tasks assigned to the USSR MVD." The passive voice nicely skirts the question of who assigns these tasks. It is, of course, the party leadership—including the KGB chief.

In areas of nationalist unrest—the Baltic, the Western Ukraine, Transcaucasia, Central Asia—party and KGB chiefs together make plans for contingencies. When trouble actually breaks out, it is they (together with emissaries from Moscow and the Internal Troops commanders) who plan and direct operations. The troops go into battle under KGB direction.

This has not changed since earlier years when all Internal Troops were organic parts of State Security. This command relationship emerges from the memoirs of a senior officer. When arriving for duty as chief of staff of an Internal Troops division fighting Ukrainian guerrillas in the late 1940s, he first reported to the division commander and the chief of its political department—then immediately afterwards to the first secretary of the district Party Committee *(raikom)*. With the latter he discussed plans for a forthcoming battle. Later, "the first secretary of the raikom, the chief of the Executive Committee of the *raion* soviet, the secretary of the *raion* Komsomol, and the chief of the *raion* MGB came to our regimental staff. . . . Together we planned in detail the operation"—to destroy a guerrilla unit in a nearby marshy woodland.[3] Today the local MVD chief may also participate in these planning sessions, but command rests with the party and KGB chiefs.

When Internal Troops celebrated their 50th birthday in 1968 in Moscow, the guest of honor was not an MVD leader but the first deputy chairman of the KGB. Even if formally administered by the MVD, they are still "Chekists" and proud of it. They were VCheka Troops, GPU Troops, OGPU Troops, and MGB Troops, and under the combined NKVD and Beria's MVD, were commanded by Chekists.§§ The very term "internal troops" first came into use in 1921 to distinguish these VCheka troops of the interior from the VCheka troops on the borders*** which are still administered by the KGB today.

Some Internal Troops, in fact, were never separated from the KGB at all.

KGB Troops

When in 1954 most of the Internal Troops were transferred to the MVD for administration, some remained under State Security and were renamed "State Security Troops" (*Voyska gosudarstvennoy bezopasnosty*). They are sometimes referred to as "Special Troops of State Security" or just "KGB Troops."

The regime seems reluctant to reveal even the existence of these troops. Only by carefully scrutinizing Soviet administrative-law textbooks can one even find a mention of them. One, for example, delineates the responsibilities of the KGB thus: "The KGB conducts the practical management of the whole system of organs and of State Security Troops."[4] Another

---

§§"They continue the glorious traditions of Soviet Chekists," wrote Kalachnikov in his book. In his article on Internal Troops in the *Sovetskaya voyennaya entsiklopediya* (vol. 2, 1976, p. 165), Kalachnikov puts it this way: Internal Troops "continue the great tradition of the troops of VCheka, OGPU, and NKVD." The same cannot be said of the MVD in general or of its militia, convoy, or guard troops.

Internal Troops were a part of the MGB from the late 1940s until 1953, although the Soviet authorities apparently want to hide this fact. The authoritative Military Encyclopedia implies that they were subordinated to Internal Affairs from 1934 onward, without a break. In fact, Soviet texts even hide the MGB's postwar control of the militia; Sorokin's 1966 textbook for university law students, summarizing the history of the MVD and KGB, skips over the whole period.

***With the civil war ended, the borders had begun to require specialized guards, but these now-separated border and internal troops were administered by a single chief directorate. When borders again vanished in the Second World War, the Border Guard Troops joined Internal Troops and composed a high percentage of their divisions at or behind the front.

refers to the ". . . system of organs and of special troops (state security troops, border troops) performing functions for the protection of the state security of the USSR."[5] (Both books clearly distinguish these from Internal Troops, which are listed separately among the components of the MVD.) Several garrison regulations from the mid-1970s refer to "military units [also, troops] of the Committee of State Security," similarly distinguishing them from MVD Internal Troops.[6] But nowhere are their duties mentioned.

There are grounds for such reticence. For one thing, those troops are doing the most sensitive jobs. Moreover, their very existence exposes a fact of Soviet life: that the party bosses dare not relax their private control, through the KGB, over the most deadly military weapons and the most sensitive communications of the state.

The separation of this elite force from the VV was one side effect of the Beria affair. In their effort to keep one another's hands off the concentrated power that Beria had held, Stalin's heirs undid his brief reunion of State Security with Internal Affairs and for the first time in Soviet history broke off the Internal Troops from State Security. Never, however, could they let out of their own hands the incalculable powers that lay in the special weapons that some Internal Troops were guarding. Not to the armed forces and not to the MVD would they dare disperse those powers; only the KGB—"the combat arm of the party"—could assure them of control. Hence some Internal Troops had to remain with the KGB.

Today, in the form of KGB Troops, the party bosses retain a specially screened elite that for many decades has guarded the most dangerous weapons, the factories producing the most advanced military equipment, and the institutions doing the most secret military-oriented scientific research and development. This elite had always stood somewhat apart from the rest of the Internal Troops and even before the Second World War guarded certain chemical and aviation facilities. After the war they gradually took over, from my own Guards Directorate, the guarding of the supersecret development of atomic weapons.††† Large KGB Troops units

†††In the first eighteen months to two years of the bomb's research and development—under the supervision of Lavrentiy Beria, whom Stalin had moved out of State Security work in early 1946—the MGB's Kremlin guards (where at the time I was administering personnel) protected Beria's offices in Moscow and the travels of the top officials to and from the sites where the bomb was being developed (especially in the Chelyabinsk-Kyshtym area of the southern Urals) and cleared and supervised the Internal Troops (then MGB Troops) who, in increasing numbers, protected the site. As the project moved closer to the actual assembling and explosion of atomic weapons (the first large military reactor for plutonium production was begun in 1947 and started functioning in 1948; the first bomb was tested in September 1949), the MGB clearly needed a new, separate department to handle its

guard, and even perform the municipal services of, the scores of secret townships where the most sensitive research and production is done— including "Star Wars" and chemical and biological weapons.

The KGB controls ballistic-missile sites, setting and enforcing the security procedures. KGB Troops not only guard the premises but stand duty in the launch silos. It is they—not the rocket troops—who arm the nuclear warheads.[7] And the orders to do so would come from the Defense Council, as they would have come, in my time, from its predecessor the State Defense Committee (GKO). It is KGB Troops, not the armed forces, who escort these special weapons—missiles and chemical and biological weapons—whenever they are moved from factory to deployment sites, between sites, or to be dismantled.

Today as in the past the KGB's Chief Directorate of Communications operates the government's most sensitive communications facilities. In Moscow KGB Troops guard those facilities, working closely with the KGB Guards Directorate.

They may do more than passively stand guard. According to former KGB Maj. Stanislav Levchenko, KGB Troops were organized into five divisions and not only for administrative purposes. Shock units may have been formed, ready to intervene against uprisings or disturbances near the secret centers they guard—a front-line unit of the regime's unending internal war.

---

growing involvement. It was formed in 1948 and given the bland designation "Department K." It was a separate department of the MGB, unrelated to the Guards Directorate or to MGB Troops. Directly controlled by Minister of State Security Viktor Abakumov, it also reported to the Supreme Military Council (i.e., for all practical purposes, Stalin alone; Beria was not then a member and never got his hands on Department K during Stalin's lifetime).

Department K's officers used traditional Chekist methods: clearing all personnel, imposing draconian measures of security (including tight restrictions on the movements of the scientists and administrators), infiltrating secret informants into their ranks, staging provocations to test their discretion and loyalty, and humorlessly investigating even the most trivial problems. Since Department K was responsible for overall security, the Internal Troops guarding the atomic installations, which by 1953 numbered several regiments, were put under its direction.

PART IV

METHODS OF INTERNAL WARFARE

CHAPTER 14

Identifying the Enemy: The Deadly Labels of "Social Prophylaxis"

A War Against Categories

IN 1918 DZERZHINSKY'S DEPUTY, MARTIN LATSIS, DEFINED THE ESSENCE of the new regime's Red Terror. "We are not waging war against individual persons," he said. "We are exterminating the bourgeoisie as a class. During the investigation, do not look for evidence that the accused acted in deed or word against Soviet power. The first questions that you ought to put are: To what class does he belong? What is his origin? What is his education or profession? And it is these questions that ought to determine the fate of the accused."[1]

Latsis was expressing a first principle of Soviet political control and a key to the leaders' survival in power. Not waiting to beat down opposition after it arises, the leaders prevent it from arising in the first place. They identify categories of potential opponents—and then treat as an enemy anyone who fits into them. Labels like "bourgeois" and "Kulak," "bourgeois nationalist," and "religious fanatic" sound as absurd as the regime's caricatures of greedy landowners, fat capitalists, conniving priests, and arrogant officers. But as we saw in the history of Internal Troops, they have been applied with a deadly lack of humor to justify massacres, dispersals of ethnic nationalities, the starvation of millions, incarcerations, and executions in the Gulag camps.

This is preventive security at its highest pitch of development; the Soviets call it "social prophylaxis." A KGB order of 1964 defined prophylaxis as "a system to forestall the occurrence of particularly dangerous crimes against the state as well as politically harmful antisocial acts of Soviet citizens."[2]

In 1960 the regime declared the end of class warfare and the advent of "mature socialism" with a "unanimous" people." "Counterrevolution" was no longer conceivable. Now, however, "the enemies of socialism are still struggling in the sphere of politics and economics,"[3] and the Kremlin leaders have shifted their labels onto individuals:

> It is well known that in the Soviet Union there are no social or class bases engendering anti-Soviet activity. But this by no means signifies that individual persons whose views and conduct are contrary to our morals and our laws may not appear under socialism. Such views and conduct may be engendered by various factors: insufficient ideological tempering and political confusion, religious fanaticism and nationalist survivals, life's difficulties, moral degradation, and sometimes simply a reluctance to work.[4]

So the labeling continues. The individuals who fight back against party-police violence are labeled "terrorists." For a variety of sins people earn such labels as "parasites," "hooligans," and "antisocial elements." By showing undue interest in other countries, listening to forbidden radio news or donning alien clothing, a citizen emerges as a "tool of ideological subversion." Various human frailties ("money-grubbing," "self-seeking," and "reluctance to work," for example) are linked to "alien influences" and thence to "ideological subversion" and treason. "Renegades who slander Soviet reality are sometimes in direct complicity with imperialist intelligence services. . . . Dissidence has become a sort of profession, generously paid in foreign currency and handouts, little different from the payment of spies."[5] Sixty years after Lenin had pledged to rid the land of all "harmful insects," Yuri Andropov said, "We have not yet got completely rid of those who violate the norms of socialist communal life but they will die out, because the fight against them is being waged by all honest Soviet citizens."[6]

Name-calling is the key. Usurping a genuine revolution, Lenin's group arrogated to itself alone the word "revolutionary" and called its rivals "counterrevolutionary" (including longtime revolutionaries), just as today's Leninist rulers of Nicaragua disparage their opponents as "contras." Many different kinds of people, and for different reasons, opposed Lenin's seizure of power: Constitutional Democrats and Socialist Revolutionaries and Mensheviks, monarchists, bourgeois, farmers, workmen, and local nationalists, but Lenin lumped them together as "White Guardists" to identify them with the tsar and the pre-February "oppressors"—and to identify himself with the February overthrow of the tsar, in which he had played no role.

By naming itself "soviet," Lenin's government made any rivals "anti-soviet." By claiming to have found the ultimate Truth, it could deride any disagreement as false, benighted, or mad. By calling itself the vanguard of the march of history, it took possession of the word "progress" and branded opposition as "reactionary." The early Bolshevik leaders dubbed themselves the "proletariat's" vanguard (although there was not a worker among them) and proceeded to discredit opponents—even the Socialist Revolutionaries whose bomb-throwing terrorists had gained worldwide infamy—as "petty bourgeois."

Taking power in the name, first, of the "working people" and, later, of "all the people," the Leninists took it upon themselves to define these people's interest and enemies. By ordaining that "he who is not with us is against us," they exposed anyone outside their iron discipline to the danger of being labeled an enemy of the people, however passive or neutral he might be.

Time and changing conditions created new categories. Whereas Lenin originally said he would suppress only the "former exploiters," his VCheka soon "discovered" that others—the "clergy," the "kulaks," and supporters of rival socialists—had "joined the enemy camp."[7] Having dispossessed the "bourgeoisie" and the "kulaks," Lenin's men made further discoveries: under the conditions of New Economic Policy a "new bourgeoisie" and a "new upper layer of the peasantry" had materialized.[8] With collectivization the term "kulak" stretched to cover any farmer who stuck to his own ideas; if he resisted the seizure of his land or animals, he became an "agricultural counterrevolutionary"; if he took up arms with others to defend himself, he was labeled a "bandit." When even such flexible terminology could not be stretched to cover all rural opposition, the regime invented new terms like "supporter of the kulaks" (podkulachnik). Collectivized farmers who took a bit of grain or an ear of corn to feed their own families became "ear croppers" and "famine organizers," and laws were passed to send them, too, off to the camps.

"Economic counterrevolutionaries" were targeted by the founding charter of the GPU in early 1922. Later, after mismanaging raw materials and factories to the point of chaos, the Soviet leaders found scapegoats whom they called "wreckers," "limiters," and "economic saboteurs." "Engineers" became a category of enemy: "This caste must be destroyed. . . . There is not and there cannot be loyalty among engineers."[9]

When Soviet forces invaded border nations like Armenia and Turkestan to force them under central Communist rule, those who fought back were labeled "bourgeois-nationalist bandits." In the 1980s the resisters in Afghanistan were called that and also *Basmachi,* likening them—correctly—to the "bandits" who resisted the Soviet invasion of Central Asia in the 1920s and 1930s.

No one under Soviet rule can be confident that he or she can stay out of one or another of the regime's flexible categories of "enemy."* So, when the leaders grow desperate over the failures of industry—where laziness, absenteeism, and drunkenness play their parts—the worker is almost as vulnerable to labels as his predecessors who were condemned as "wreckers" or "saboteurs" during the early years of Bolshevik rule. † In the face of the Politburo's growing disquiet about erupting nationalism at the end of the 1980s—and of its dark warnings about the "provocative demands" of "extremists" who are "perpetrating actions objectively aimed against the interests of our society," "flirting with reactionary cricles," and even "cooperating with capitalist 'special services' to betray the motherland"[10]—what Ukrainian or Estonian or Armenian could be sure that he would not, if the Kremlin should lose patience and take fright from his demonstrations and demands, find himself tagged as a "bourgeois nationalist"—and traitor? What young person fond of punk rock, who has become a nuisance to the authorities, may not be labeled a "tool of ideological sabotage"? He who becomes too active in a church—even under new laws of religious tolerance—risks earning the title of "religious fanatic." A troublesome citizen seeking respite from a thankless job may become a "parasite." Even without a law that specifically punishes such vague categories, the Kremlin has proven its ability to find one that fits.

Labels await the party leaders, too, should they lose out in power rivalries. Zinoviev, Trotsky, Bukharin, Beria, Malenkov, and thousands of others lost their positions and went to the executioner or into limbo as "criminals," "traitors," saboteurs," "enemies of the people," or perhaps as

---

*Labels can be pasted on or ripped off according to the regime's needs. When it no longer needed the skills of the old-regime engineers and scientists and military officers, however devotedly they had served the new regime, the leadership removed their protective label of "specialist" and made them scapegoats for failures.

†The British ambassador wrote to Lord Curzon on March 5, 1919, "Industrial workers who oppose the Bolsheviks are treated precisely similarly to peasants who do so. Last December a hundred laborers belonging to [a factory] near Perm were shot merely for having protested against the Bolshevists' doings in the locality." The Soviets' own statistics confirm that 40 percent of those who died in prison were industrial workers and peasants (British White Book, p. 54, cited in Melgounov, p. 126). Responding to "false rumors" that the Cheka had shot workers and peasants, "The Presidium herewith announces that in no instance has such a worker, nor yet a peasant, been shot, but merely a few proven bandits and murders" (ibid., p. 138). Yet 80 percent of the prisoners were illiterate, by the regime's own figures (Gerson, p. 176).

"factionalists," "deviationists," "right (or left) opportunists," or "anti-party." Not even servility and conformity can guarantee immunity: the most zealous party functionary may suddenly find himself caught in shifting tides: today's orthodoxy is tomorrow's heresy.‡

Lenin pledged that his regime would "show no mercy or vacillation to enemies of the October Revolution, regardless of what flag they take refuge under." Those strangely named categories are not mere insults but the "flags" of the regime's enemies. Its war against them—as merciless as Lenin had promised—has created the atmosphere of Soviet history: "The Soviet people's entire vast creative effort has been exercised in an atmosphere of incessant struggle against forces impeding the building of the new life."[11]

Making Lists

By honing these general categories down to specific categories and fitting real people into them, the Soviet regime has directed the fire of its internal war.

As soon as it was founded, the VCheka began compiling lists. The task of "publishing lists of enemies of the people" was assigned to it in its founding decree. In 1919, Dzerzhinsky's NKVD was registering "former landlords, capitalists, and persons who occupied responsible positions in the tsarist and bourgeois system."[12] By the following year, a Cheka department was fighting organized religion; it was busy listing church leaders and activists throughout the country. The VCheka's "Secret Operational Department" (the forerunner of the KGB's Fifth Chief Directorate) was doing the same for members of former political parties, including socialists. Even before the Soviet armies—with VCheka units—moved into Azerbaijan and Armenia, Georgia, and Turkestan, Chekist agents were preparing the ground by compiling lists of those most likely to resist the process of Sovietization.

That task never ended but became routine KGB practice. From the captured files of the Smolensk office of State Security came lists dated from the early 1920s to the second half of the 1930s of various kinds of "socially alien elements." One such list contained 21 names, for the most part former kulaks and children of kulaks, merchants, and priests.[13] District

---

‡One of Stalin's flunkies warned (after Stalin had abruptly decreed the collectivization of agriculture, which he had earlier opposed): "Whoever doubts the correctness of the general line of the Leninist Central Committee follows only one path—a path that leads into the camp of the counterrevolutionaries. And with such persons the party speaks in the language of the Cheka" (Avtorkhanov, *Stalin and the Soviet Communist Party,* p. 41).

officers were keeping "careful account" of all former members of political parties who at one time or another had opposed the Bolsheviks; one Cheka commander knew precisely that his district contained, in 1922, "17 Socialist Revolutionaries, 16 Mensheviks, 7 anarchists and 4 Kadets."[14]

Stalin was an avid list-maker; his former secretary Boris Bazhanov has reported that Ivan Tovstukha, head of Stalin's secretariat even before Stalin won sole power, "composed long lists of people who were naively taking positions against Stalin. . . . In a few years these lists would permit the shooting of people by the bunches, by hundreds, by thousands."[15]

Accompanying Soviet armies in their invasion of eastern Poland in 1939 and the Baltic states and Bessarabia in 1940, State Security units carried orders specifying the categories of people to be listed. These documents fell into Western hands after they were left behind by fleeing Soviet authorities when the Germans invaded Lithuania in 1941. Here are samples.[16]

An order of November 28, 1940, of the NKVD of the newly incorporated "Lithuanian SSR" called for registration of all "anti-Soviet" and "socially alien" elements, including: former members of anti-Soviet political parties, organizations, and groups [these would include all organizations not sponsored by the Communists]; former members of nationalistic parties, organizations, and groups; former police, gendarmes, and army officers; persons expelled in the past from the local Communist Party for antiparty offenses; political emigrants and repatriates; citizens of foreign countries and those who work for foreign firms or diplomatic or consular representations or the Red Cross; people with relatives or personal contacts abroad; former noblemen and estate owners; merchants, bankers, and employers of hired help.

Order No. 0023 of April 25, 1941, of the NKGB of the Lithuanian SSR instructed each district NKGB to fill out every five days a "Five-Day Summary" of persons it had registered over the preceding five days. Each of the NKGB departments, according to its specialization, had its own categories. The NKGB's Special Political Department (SPO) was required to report on former leading officials of the state apparatus under each of several rubrics, such as department directors, principal referents, district chiefs and military commandants, policemen, gendarmes, prison administrators, prosecutors, judges, and security and intelligence personnel. Also to be listed were: persons who had been members of the armed bands that had fought the early (1920) Soviet invasion; Trotskyists, Social Revolutionaries, and Social Democrats; large landowners, manufacturers, merchants, and houseowners. For each of six nationality groups—Lithuanians, Poles, Jews, Russian White-Emigres, Ukrainians, and Byelorussians—the State Security authorities were to identify "national counterrevolutionaries." This meant (as the instructions specified) leaders and activists of nationalist organizations (and regular contributors to their newspapers), labor unions, associations of merchants and industrialists, and committees of teacher's unions, as well as all members of emigre organizations.

The NKGB's Counterintelligence Department (KRO) was to list employees of foreign legations and firms, Germans who had applied for repatriation, frontier residents with relatives in Germany, "people who have tried to flee the country," and "families and relatives of persons who have fled abroad (traitors to their country)."

In the 1970s, a KGB officer brought to the West current lists, testifying to the permanence of this classic Soviet practice.[17] The KGB chairman's Order No. 00117 of 1964, for example, lists the following "actions which call for prophylaxis" (as contrasted to criminal prosecution): links with foreigners for speculative and general purposes which could be exploited by espionage agencies; membership of immoral groups; membership of sects and religious followings whose activities are forbidden by law; incorrect interpretation of questions relative to policies of the Soviet government and CPSU, in cases where the interpretation is not hostile in intent; links with nationalists, where the links have no criminal intent; and worship of bourgeois influence.

The KGB chairman's Order No. 0080 of 1965 lists people who, because of their past activities, shall be followed secretly "until death itself": active participants of anti-Soviet nationalist organizations during the Second World War, of nationalist underground movements, and of postwar anti-Soviet organizations; persons who occupied positions of command in the "Russian Liberation Army" (the Vlasov army that fought against Soviet rule in German uniforms); former members of bourgeois governments; prominent members of church organizations and sects whose ideology is anti-Soviet; and former members of foreign anti-Soviet organizations, Trotskyists, and Zionists.

Every regional unit of the KGB is continually adding to its lists from information culled from school records, questionnaires, and other official records, from things said in party, Komsomol, and trade union meetings or gleaned from the personnel and security officers of factories and offices, from secret mail coverage, phone taps, surveillance, informants, and interrogations. Each case officer keeps his own lists of the most likely suspects in the sector for which he is responsible: army regiment, factory, or part of town.

For areas not yet conquered, the lists are prepared in advance. As I know personally, SMERSH and the NKGB had already started by 1943 to prepare lists of leaders and potential leaders in Eastern Europe, Finland, the three Baltic countries, Poland, Germany, Czechoslovakia, Hungary, Romania, Yugoslavia, Bulgaria, Albania, Austria and Trieste, as well as Manchuria and Sakhalin.

When I worked in the KGB's residency in Vienna, its Austrian operations section was systematically compiling lists of known and probable anti-Soviet and anti-Communist individuals, with a view to removing them when we eventually took power. This work evidently continued: in the 1960s Marshal Yakubovsky, commander-in-chief of the Warsaw Pact forces, told Jan Sejna that "the Russians had more than 4,000 collaborators in Austria who would help us round up undesirable civilians once the country was occupied. The KGB would take over executive power under the protection of the Warsaw Pact armies."[18]

In Britain, too, lists are being compiled. Jan Sejna reported that the KGB under Shelepin had in the 1960s passed to the Czechoslovakians—to get their assistance in action against the targets—

> a list of British leaders in politics, industry, the army, and police who were considered potentially hostile to a progressive government, as well as influential in the community. . . . The list ran to several hundred names. [It] was compiled by the KGB with the help of agents in the British Communist Party. Beside each name was a short biographical note, together with the action contemplated. The latter ranged from temporary detention to execution without trial. Prominent figures such as Edward Heath, Sir Alex Douglas-Home, and Harold Wilson were to undergo show trials before execution. . . . The Kremlin incorporated this list into the Strategic Plan and vigorously kept it up to date.[19]

Wherever the Soviet system is applied, this practice applies. On October 12, 1981, the following was reported in the Western press: "Humberto Ortega Saavedra, commander of Nicaragua's army, called for members of the country's militias to draw up lists of government enemies whom he vowed to 'hang along the highway'."[20]

Putting the Lists to Work

These lists help the leaders to aim the weapons of their internal warfare. Those they registered during their early months in power—"persons who had employed hired labor with the aim of making profit," for example, and "private merchants and their middlemen" and "clergymen,"[21]—were denied jobs, civic rights, and rations; and many were imprisoned or shot. Today, listed citizens are watched, discriminated against in their jobs, denied opportunities for higher education or foreign travel, harassed, provoked, and made to fear even worse. Like an ax poised ready to chop, these lists await their time.

Abroad, this ax falls wherever Soviet troops arrive, even temporarily. The first lists may, in the turmoil of revolution or invasion, be compiled instantly: a person's category—and his fate—may be decided by a mere glance at the house he lives in, the softness of his hands, or his officer's uniform. In September 1939 the officers of the Polish Army meekly obeyed orders and surrendered without a fight to the self-proclaimed "friends" rolling in from the East. They had the misfortune to fit into a category the Soviets considered inherently and incurably anti-Soviet and, what is worse, capable of leading an eventual Polish national resistance to Sovietization. For them, the listing was a formality; State Security massacred them almost to the last man. Of the 12,000 bodies, 4,500 were later found in a mass grave in the Katyn Forest, the others never; some, according to hearsay reports, were loaded onto barges and sunk in the Baltic Sea.

Against the civilian population, that September 1939 in Poland, the Soviet occupiers moved almost as fast. Using preliminary lists already drawn up with the help of Polish Communists, they added on the spot other names given them by secret informants or extracted from local citizens in conversations and interrogations. Within only twenty-one months after moving in, they had listed, located, arrested, loaded into trains and trucks, and shipped off to far destinations in Siberia more than a million and a half Poles, one-fifth of the entire population of their occupation zone (now known as the "Western Ukraine" and "Western Byelorussia"). All had been fitted into one or another of those familiar categories: politicians, officials, civic leaders, landowners, merchants, anti-Communists—and not one in ten ever returned.

Soviet authorities completed the job at more leisure when they returned in 1944 and took over all of Poland. SMERSH and the NKGB/MGB created and managed an ostensibly Polish state security service through which they prepared the usual list: "a card file on the entire adult population," a former officer of that service has reported, "classified according to categories." "The new regime could maintain itself only thanks to the Soviet military presence and by massive terror directed against selected social and political groups which were considered especially dangerous . . . faithfully imitating Soviet practices."[22]

During the purges of the early 1950s in Czechoslovakia, such lists served deadly purposes. A Politburo-approved "List of Enemies of the Party Who Are to Be Isolated," for instance, carried several hundred names, Jan Sejna reported. "Later the party officially admitted that 1,600 Czechs had been executed in the purge trials. This certainly is an understatement, even taking into account that his figure did not include the large number who were murdered without trial."[23]

During the great purges of the 1930s the KGB learned how important it is to keep such lists complete and up to date. At that time every local State Security chief was under pressure to "unmask the enemy" and failure to meet his huge quota of arrests meant that he would join the condemned. So his men squeezed every list, milked every file, beat every prisoner to extract names of people whose backgrounds or connections (however remote or even potential) might qualify them for arrest as "bourgeois" or "nationalist" or "foreign-connected." Still the State Security officers could not meet the demand and were forced to invent such connections or to label common criminals—or whoever happened into their offices—as traitors and subversives.

Ten years later, my KGB office in Barnaul was better prepared for such demands—and today, no doubt, its lists are more complete than ever.

The lists serve preventive purposes, too. They help the KGB clean out potential dangers from areas that foreigners visit, for example. And they are put to work outside the USSR, too. When Leonid Brezhnev visited West Germany in late 1981, for example, the Soviet Embassy in Bonn was quickly able to supply to the West German government a list of names of Afghan, Turkish, and East European exiles living in West Germany, insisting that they be closely controlled by the West German police.[24]

Sometimes the lists may serve mundane purposes. A prominent Soviet government leader turned to my MGB unit for help in finding a reliable woman with whom his wife could practice her English. For the MGB the task was simple: just refer to the lists (normally kept in the form of card files). The MGB officers went to the category of fluent English speakers and selected the name of a woman on whom there was no derogatory notice. They called her, found her willing to give conversation lessons, and then, to their embarrassment, discovered that they had inadvertently picked, under her maiden name, the wife of Nikolay Bulganin. Mrs Bulganin went ahead with the task, apparently to occupy her leisure hours.

These categories and lists have little in common with the "black lists" that have been drawn up in other times and places by governments or companies or social groups. They are aimed at whole categories of society, are endlessly refreshed, have annihilation as their long-range aim, and are used as a permanent method of governing. They serve as a threat and a reminder—perpetuating the fear that has made a people docile.

CHAPTER 15

Violence and Fear

OF ALL THE WORKS OF *glasnost*, NONE CARRIES GREATER RISK FOR Communist power than its lifting of fear. Already by early 1987 Gorbachev noted that people were more forthcoming with him, whereas in the past "you would put a question to someone but he would remain silent, perhaps out of fear or mistrust."[1] By the end of the 1980s some had become bold enough to say in public things they would hardly have dared whisper to trusted friends a year or two earlier: criticizing party leaders, assembling to demand separation of their republics from the Soviet Union, raising monuments to past victims of the regime's brutality, grouping into informal unions and strike committees to oppose managers, demanding ever more freedom. Dizzying as was *glasnost's* spread of news and information, even more heady was the growing confidence of the people in using it. If this trend continued they might even lose their fear of the KGB's threats and might even join forces against its intimidation—and the strongest pillar of Soviet power would have begun to crumble.

If fear was eroding, enough yet remained. Soviet man was lifting his head warily. His job and welfare still depended on the state, and the new freedoms were too new and strange for him to feel confident of them or to know what to do with them. His position remained precarious, his mood uneasy. He knew that nothing yet prevented a quick return of the old ways. He was still living in the world of fear that Lenin had created and his followers had built.

In April 1986 the power plant in Chernobyl spewed out nuclear contamination over a huge area of Europe. The outside world learned of its danger from detectors in Scandinavia, not from any warning from the USSR. On the contrary, Soviet authorities denied the accident for days. "Even when a pillar of radioactive fumes was soaring into the sky over the city, when people trod on radioactive debris emitting hundreds of roent-gens," a Soviet journalist revealed, local party bosses were trying to cover up the disaster even from their own people. For hours they refused to sanction even the most elementary precautions and for a day and a half delayed the evacuation of nearly 50,000 people. Fearing to displease higher authorities and to lose their comfortable jobs, they allowed the traditional May Day parade in Kiev, with thousands of young children, to go ahead five days later—and only afterwards evacuated the children from the city.[2]

In February 1982 the Soviet cargo ship *Mekhanik Tarasov* (4,262 tons, Captain Bilkin commanding) began to sink 230 miles off the coast of Newfoundland. Bilkin refused to send an SOS and refused the offer of a Dutch trawler to take off his crew. The ship went down; 32 died and only 5 were saved.[3] Captain Bilkin had merely followed the precedent of the captains of the trawlers *Artek* and *Suzdal* in the Atlantic in 1967, the trawler *Toucan* off Denmark in 1968, and uncounted others. All refused to send SOS signals in time; all (except the *Artek*) went down, losing most of their crews; all could have been saved as the men of the *Artek* were. The captain of the Soviet ship that, at the last moment, pulled the *Artek* back as it drifted onto the rocky Norwegian coast, explained that these ships' officers were afraid. They had been warned—by the all-powerful party, backed by the KGB—that they must not abandon a ship that can be saved, that they must not incur the hard-currency costs of rescue by foreign ships. They had been "so terrorized by the authorities that they preferred death to an inquiry." The prime cause of Soviet shipping acci-dents and sinkings has been the "psychological condition of many cap-tains, who under the pressures imposed upon them by the authorities dared not take the rational, humane decision to save their crew and themselves."[4]

Scientists suffered the same malady. "What all scientists have in com-mon is their terror of the authorities," wrote a former Soviet science writer of the 1970s. "This applies alike to internal emigres, to those who would lay down their lives for the workers' and peasants' state, and to the academicians, professors, and directors who run the system. Fear is the key to the mentality of a Soviet scientist." He continued:

There are so many open and secret prohibitions that it is impossible to foresee or remember them all. I am not speaking now of the constant fears that beset the life of an overtalented scientist whose work attracts the attention of foreign colleagues, or the tribulations of one who is a Jew, or the panic of a laboratory head who finds that he has a dissident on his staff. People in these categories live in a state of unremitting terror. But even those who are not Jews or dissidents and have nothing on their conscience cannot feel at ease, for one can never know what the authorities will choose, at a given moment, to regard as criminal and subversive.

A mathematician from Donetsk was copying out by hand rare editions of poetical works. . . . One summer he had copied into notebooks no less than 800 pages of print. When I asked him why he did not hire a typist to copy these out-of-print books, he raised his hands in horror. Apparently the party authorities at Donetsk were extremely strict about any form of copying, and if literary works were copied onto standard size sheets it counted as *samizdat*. . . . It would be dangerous to keep on one's shelves a typed copy of Anna Akhmatova's poems; the professor's students and assistants came to his house, and any of them might denounce him. . . . I asked him if he did not think the prohibition strange. "Yes . . . I suppose so. . . . But the law is the law and I can't risk losing my job."[5]

A Russian proverb says that "the beaten dog need only see the stick"; the Soviet rulers, having done the beating, hold the stick—the KGB—menacingly over the head of the dog—the population. As an early Chekist said, "The successes of the Red Army would not have had their present significance, and the revolution itself would have been shaken to its roots, if the Cheka had not preserved its aspect of righteous scourge."[6]

This dog was truly beaten; that "righteous scourge" did its work well. In the late 1980s one could debate whether the Soviet prison camps held 200 or 2,000 "political prisoners," but the people still remembered the 1940s when they held more than 15 million at a time. The people were subjected to terror of a sort that a younger generation is more likely to associate with the killing fields of Cambodia or the Soviet attempt to subjugate Afghanistan.

In fact, the more recent tribulations of Afghans serve as a useful reminder of what many peoples called today "Soviet" endured at the hands of Soviet forces. During the ten-year Soviet occupation, a million Afghans were killed, more than 5 million were driven out of their country (one Afghan in three or four), and more than half the population was dislodged. In November 1982 (to take a date for which statistics are available) nearly 50,000 political prisoners were being held in Kabul alone and perhaps twice as many elsewhere. Groups of ten at a time were being carried out and shot, their bodies dumped in mass graves; in that one month, "12,000 were executed in Kabul alone," reported a defecting Afghan state security colonel.[7] The slaughter and destruction, shootings, torture, mining of farmlands, bombing of villages, ruin of crops, killing of animals, and wrecking of irrigation systems were not a side effect of battle nor even a punishment for resistance, but were a method of establishing rule.

It was a method the Soviets had used before and quite nearby in what is now called Soviet Central Asia. The difference is that only dry statistics remain and the cries of terror and despair are largely forgotten. Yet the statistics deserve attention; if each victim is multiplied by the number of relatives, friends, and coworkers, one can sense how widely the Soviet forces spread fear and how enduring is their power of intimidation.

Because the Soviet regime initially justified its own killings as a response to earlier tsarist oppression, we can use the latter as a measuring stick. In the 88 years from 1826 to the First World War, including times of revolution and terrorist murders of tsarist officials (and one tsar), a grand total of just over 3,000 were executed—and of those nearly 1,000 in a single six-month period during and after the full-scale revolution against the tsar in 1905–06. The prison population never reached 200,000. Now compare what the Soviets have done.*

During the Bolsheviks' takeover and the Red Terror of 1918–20, nearly 2 million "oppositionists" were executed; millions more were killed in the civil war and later uprisings. While no one knows the exact numbers, their scale can be grasped through the estimate that between 1914 and 1920 some 20 million perished—of whom "only" 1.7 million were Russian war dead.

Numbers unknown, but surely in the millions, died in the famine of 1921–22 which was mainly due to the policies of the new regime.

In the collectivization of agriculture, from 1928–33, between 10 and 25 million died, including at least 7 million in the purposely induced famine of 1933 in the Ukraine.[8]

In the purges and terror of 1935–39 about a million and a half were executed.

Tens of millions were sent to the camps between 1935 and 1953; the camp population, by various estimates, totaled in any given year between 5 and 15 million prisoners, of whom at least 10 percent died each year. More than 15 million (some Soviet sources under *glasnost* estimated about 20 million) were killed or died there, including more than 90 percent of the 1.6 million deported from the Western Ukraine and Western Byelorussia. Of the survivors, millions were kept in exile.

*The figures we use are the best estimates of Western and ex-Soviet (and some Soviet official) observers and analysts and may be underestimated. Some statistics coming from the Soviet Union itself in 1988 attributed at least 17 million (and perhaps 25 million) deaths to Stalin's purges, state-induced famine, and farm collectivization (Roy Medvedev in *Moscow News*, November 1988, and *Argumenty i Fakty*, January 1989). Other good sources of such estimates include Dyadkin; Conquest (*The Great Terror*, Appendix A, and his article, "The Forgotten Holocaust," *London Daily Telegraph*, 5 November 1983); Kuganov in *Novoye Russkogo Slovo*, 14 April 1964; and Antonov-Ovseyenko, pp. 210–13, 307, citing Soviet officials.

In the winter war against Finland of 1939–1940 about 1.8 million died.[9]

Deaths in battle during the Second World War probably totaled about 20 million—while another 10 to 12 million died during those same years 1941–45 in the regime's other war, against its own people.

The numbers that have died in the camps and in the harsh conditions of exile in the post-Stalin period, 1953 to the present, cannot be estimated, but some think they may total 3 million.

Up to the era of *perestroika,* therefore, more than 50 million Soviet citizens died—*independent of battle casualties*—as a result of their own regime's repression. Soviet citizens are not allowed to know these statistics, but they are aware of the magnitude of their own losses—and they have inherited the fear.

Soviet doctrine describes the Red Terror of 1918–20 as retaliation against White Terror; some Western apologists have dismissed it as the egg-breaking of any revolutionary omelette. Neither explains the persistence of terror as a principle of government.

Permanent fear and the threat of violence is Lenin's legacy, not Stalin's. It was only after the Red Terror ended, after the "bourgeoisie" and the "former exploiters" had been uprooted, and after the White armies had been crushed and their remnants chased from the country that Lenin decreed the continuation and institutionalizing of terror. In 1922 he wrote to his Commissar of Justice, who was in the process of drafting the first Soviet criminal code, "The court must not exclude terror. It would be self-deception or deceit to promise this, and in order to provide it with a foundation and to legalize it in a principled way, clearly and without hypocrisy and without embellishment, it is necessary to formulate it as broadly as possible, for only revolutionary righteousness and a revolutionary conscience will provide the conditions for applying it more or less broadly in practice." To this end—"to supply the motivation for the essence and the justification of terror, its necessity, its limits"—Lenin personally drafted an article for the criminal code providing that terror should strike anyone guilty of "propaganda or agitation, or participation in an organization, or helping (objectively helping or being able to help) . . . organizations or persons whose activity has the character" of opposition to Soviet power.[10] Lenin made the instruments of terror permanent, too. Though ostensibly "dissolving" the "extraordinary" VCheka, he established it in lasting form as the State Political Administration (GPU). He explained at the time, "We have no other way besides coercion. . . . Without this agency the workers' power could not exist."[11] In the same year Trotsky, too, said that until that happy day when the world holds no more class enemies, "the question as to who is to rule the country . . . will be decided . . . by the employment of all forms of violence."[12] More than a half-century later, KGB chiefs were still citing Lenin's words to remind citizens of the abiding need for Chekists.[13]

The process of administering Soviet terror is cold-blooded and systematic, not passionate with revenge for enemy outrages. Even as Chekists were crushing skulls and machine-gunning groups of victims, the deputy head of the VCheka said—correctly—that his organization was waging the terror "in a planned and deliberate manner."[14] Because successful farmers ("capitalists in agriculture") are, as Lenin put it, "the resolute enemy of the revolutionary proletariat [and] will oppose it by all means from sabotage to open armed counterrevolutionary resistance," *ipso facto* "they must be dealt a relentless, crushing blow."[15] By 1920, after millions had been killed, incarcerated, or exiled, Lenin could report that "this class has been at last taught the price of the slightest attempt at resistance."[16] Stalin, too, saw his violence as a deliberate plan: "The problem of repression may be reduced to that of finding the minimum necessary from the point of view of the forward movement."[17] (As we have seen, that "minimum necessary" was high—at least 10 million.) Then after causing the deaths of millions more of his countrymen in the five years 1934–39, Stalin could report the results ("that the remnants of the exploiting classes have been completely eliminated") under the heading of "social and political development of the country."[18] The same cold logic appears in a Chekist chief's note on a list of death sentences in Latvia: "In view of the danger to the socialist system, all must be shot."[19]

Khrushchev, even when criticizing Stalin in the famous 1956 "secret speech," did not renounce the process of terror. He reproached Stalin only for turning it against party members—and for poor timing. Stalin had launched his campaign during a period when, according to Khrushchev, there had been "no serious reasons for the use of extraordinary mass terror."[20] Wherever and whenever those serious reasons appear (as they did in Khrushchev's own time, in Soviet towns and in Hungary), the institutions of terror are loosed.

In the 1970s and 1980s the killings continued, if only on an individual scale. The unorthodox writer Vladimir Voinovich said that the KGB tried to kill him with poison in the Hotel Metropol in Moscow.[21] A distinguished translator of Rilke, Konstantin Bogatyerev, was found dead near his home, in a pool of blood, his skull broken by a heavy object (but none of his possessions taken) a few days after a book appeared in the West that had exposed (with his help) the way Soviet translators tamper with Western writings.[22] An acquaintance of Aleksandr Dimov pointed out a privileged young man in Moscow whose father "directs training in 'auto accidents'—you know, where they teach how to make auto accidents and send certain people to the next world.' "[23] The car-accident death of Politburo candidate member Petr Masherov in October 1980 was widely suspected of being no accident but an episode in a political power struggle. Some such "accidents" are less well staged than others. In November 1981, for example, a few days after being accused by the party press of pernicious influence on youth, Father Bronius Laurinavicius, a Lithuanian Catholic priest and outspoken advocate of human rights, was run over and killed by a truck. He had earlier told close friends that trucks had twice tried to hit him.[24] "Suicides," too, are staged. At the end of April 1979 Vladimir Ivasyuk, a 25-year-old Ukrainian song writer and nationalist dissident, was made to follow an unknown man out of the conservatory in Lvov—and was never seen alive again. The authorities claimed to be looking for him, and three weeks later said they had found his body hanging on a tree in a remote spot in the forest. A relative who attended the autopsy told the parents, however, that Ivasyuk did not appear to have died by hanging.[25] And we have seen the KGB secretly shortening the lives of prisoners in jails and camps.

The rulers could not kill everyone who differs with them, but they could paralyze the will to oppose. "Shootings had to be employed to intimidate the population," said a Chekist leader, "to kill any leanings toward sabotage and conspiracy."[26] The terrible repressions of the 1930s and 1940s did just that, and ever since then the regime has been able to enforce obedience with less visible terror: "prophylactic" warnings, a few trials, and much extralegal harrassment—and beatings and other forms of violence when needed.

The KGB's prophylactic "chats" (besedy) with potential dissidents carry open or veiled threats of death or injury to themselves or their children, or other, unspecified, "trouble"—and Soviet citizens know that these threats are carried out if the victim persists in displeasing his masters. The KGB's thugs still beat people up although today, unlike Stalin's time, they are more likely to pose as thieves, hooligans, or drunks. Not a single member of dissident doctor Anatoliy Koryagin's family escaped beatings in the 1980s, including young children. In the seventeen months ending October 1970, as part of a nationwide KGB program, a single squad of druzhinniki in Petropavlovsk—as testified by its own leader, Sergey Kourdakov—raided more than 150 quiet meetings of religious believers, brutally beating old men and women and young girls, killing and crippling several of them.[27] In 1989 a hired gang attacked and beat to death a young reporter from the radical magazine Ogonyok. He had been investigating organized crime, but the question arose, especially after the recent death of another reporter, "Is someone trying to frighten the press, to cut its throat?" (*Literaturnaya Gazeta*, 2 August 1989, quoted in *Daily Telegraph*, London, 3 August 1989.) Houses are broken into, possessions stolen. Poisons are secretly administered—to sicken, weaken, and warn. Andrey Sakharov's experiences are simply better known than similar cases of violence perpetrated daily throughout the country; he was held by force for years in a town not of his choosing, cut off from communications with relatives or friends, stoned in the street, showered with obscenities and insults, drugged, and robbed of manuscripts, personal documents, radio, and camera.

The leaders, through their KGB, wage chemical warfare against their own citizens, too. Several dissidents in Leningrad, including Ilya Levin, Boris Rubenshtein, Yuri Kharkev, Valery Panov, and Lev Zhvigun, reported having been poisoned by the KGB in the 1970s. They were all victims of the same enhanced liquid mustard gas that produces pain, third-degree burns, and potentially serious internal effects, but is apparently not intended to be fatal. It had been surreptitiously applied to the socks of one of them while he was sleeping in a train, sprayed onto the trousers of another, to be felt only when he sat down, and was coated on a chair in a cafe where another had been induced to wait for twenty minutes.[28] (This substance is the same or similar to that sprayed on the West German technician Schwirkmann, who was finding KGB microphones in his country's embassy in Moscow in 1963.)

The purpose of these actions has always been the same as that expressed by the Chekist leader sixty years earlier: to intimidate, to kill any tendency to oppose. It still works. This violence lurks beneath the sunny surface of *glasnost* and, while not obvious to the outsider, is not hidden from the Soviet population. The people are acutely aware, too, that it could break out anew at any time, as long as the KGB remains secure in its power, watching, taking notes, and updating its lists of "enemies."

Gorbachev faces, then, this dilemma: his system is based on and requires fear—his regime cannot afford to let the people become self-confident or self-reliant—but to get the people to work and save the country from economic disaster, he must promote their self-confidence and self-reliance. Somehow he and they must tread a narrow middle path between too much violence and too much liberty.

Should the Soviet citizen need a reminder of the limits on his freedoms, he carries one with him at all times—in the form of personal documents.

CHAPTER 16

Controlling the Population

THE SOVIET CITIZEN IS TRAPPED IN AN INTERLOCKING, CENTRALIZED system of controls that brands him and inhibits his movements while giving others great power over him. It consists of four elements, each alien to Western democratic practices: first, personal documents more numerous and revealing than Western ones; second, strict regulations governing their use; third, criminal punishment for violating what, in most other countries, are mere administrative rules; and finally, unique institutions that enforce the system at home, on the streets, in the workplace, and in public transport.

The Documents

The citizen's documents constitute a sort of portable dossier. The three most important ones—standardized throughout the country and centrally numbered—are the internal passport, the work booklet, and (for males) the military reserve booklet. To these are added a permanent collection of character references and certificates. There are membership booklets, too, that open the door to certain privileges—or, if he does not have them, deprive him of benefits that, in the West, are considered everyone's due. And in his personnel file lies the questionnaire—tool of the KGB and permanent, nagging source of fear.

The Soviet internal passport (*pasport grazhdanina SSSR*) has this in common with the national identity documents of many Western democracies: it is put to the same workaday purposes of enabling its bearer to collect parcels or money transfers at a post office, register a child in school, vote, or get married or divorced. But little else. Its appearance alone announces the difference: this is no card but a little book, fat as an international passport, that tells much about its bearer. It reveals, for example, his ethnic origin; and by labeling him a Jew (or Crimean Tatar or ethnic German) it marks him for discrimination in employment, housing, and education. Whereas Western identity cards usually show the bearer's marital status, the Soviet internal passport goes on to give the details of all his marriages and children—and every divorce, noting any court decisions for failure to make alimony payments. Marks will reveal, too, whether and when the bearer has been in jail or exile. This book carries the regime's permission for him to reside or to move. In it, too, can be read his military status.*

This internal passport can thus be a heavy burden, and that is how the rulers want it. "There are," as an MVD official said, "some citizens who lose their passports on purpose hoping that in the new passports there will be no unfavorable entries about them . . . but they face disappointment, because all the entries are completely renewed."[1] And the passport is issued for life: pages are provided for new pictures as the bearer grows older and grayer.

The work booklet *(trudovaya knizhka)* is a companion and supplement to the internal passport and resembles it in size and shape.† Everyone must have one, from his sixteenth birthday throughout life. It certifies that he has a job—as the law requires. It becomes, eventually, proof of his right to a pension, too; by official definition it is "the basic document for recording the duration of his uninterrupted labor service," and so he has an interest in not losing it.

The present version, the first to be printed on watermarked paper with numbering keyed to an all-union system, came into effect at the beginning of 1975 as a step toward more efficient control from the center. This document can be used against the bearer in ways that his passport cannot. It is, for example, "the basic document for establishing the cause of a worker's departure."[2] It tells—by means of a number keyed to articles of the Labor Code—why he left every one of his past jobs. For some,

---

*Until the early 1980s his whole job history was included on its pages; to simplify the paper work, that is now carried only in the labor booklet.

†In the early years of Bolshevik rule, in fact, it served as the internal passport. The work booklet was temporarily replaced during the New Economic Policy by a questionnaire *(anketa)* that the worker himself filled out with his own work history. In 1926 a new system of "labor lists" was introduced: the employer kept records on the worker's employment and performance, which he sent to the worker's next employer, who continued to make entries, and so on throughout the individual's working life. The present work booklet was introduced at the end of 1938, effective in 1939. For a good summary of these developments see Vsevolod Skorodumov, "Labor Documentation in the USSR," Radio Liberty Research, RL 20/75, 24 January 1975.

therefore, it can bear permanent witness to "inability to cope with the job," "systematic failure to do duties," "absence from work without adequate reason or coming to work drunk," or an "immoral act." In addition to such marks come more explicit notices, good and bad. To offer the worker an incentive, the booklet has room for notations of awards and commendations—for exceeding his quotas or making useful suggestions, for example. To deter him from indiscipline, the booklet has a place for notes such as "sentenced by a people's court to one year of corrective labor with loss of 25 percent of salary" or "severely reprimanded for being absent from work for five days." The Soviet Labor Code spells out what should and should not be entered in the workbook but leaves much room for error and for damaging entries by spiteful bosses or KGB operatives in the Personnel Department.‡

The military reserve document (*voyennyy bilet*), about the same size and shape as the internal passport and work booklet, reveals yet more about the bearer: his level of education, his civilian profession, results of physical examinations, and his membership (or lack of membership) in the Communist Party or Komsomol. In this booklet the military authorities enter the dates and military district of his active service (and any reserve call-up), the functions he performed (rifleman, tank driver, construction work, etc.), and his specialized training and qualifications. If he never served in the armed forces the booklet shows why he was (and is) considered unfit. From age 18 to age 55 every Soviet male must carry this booklet. Women who have served in the armed forces or who, for various reasons, have reserve status are issued these books too.

Specialized booklets identify members of the party, Komsomol, and trade union (*profsoyuz*) and show whether they have paid their dues and remain in good standing. Every student in higher education must carry a student's booklet (*studencheskiy bilet*), accompanied by certificates attesting to his status, his institution, the nature of his studies, and the results of his examinations.

Almost everyone carries a trade union booklet (*profsoyuznyy bilet*) because on one's membership may depend one's housing and vacations. The trade union at the enterprise controls its housing, and often there are not enough rooms for all (and some spaces are better than others). It controls the vacation facilities, too, and assigns schedules—and not everyone will find a desirable place or time. So the *profsoyuz* offers carrot and stick: the carrot to him who works well, the stick to him who causes trouble to the authorities.

‡The worker can appeal such an entry to his trade union; if that does not help (as it usually does not, for it works closely with the director) he must carry his case to a people's court, with relatively little hope of success.

The character reference *(kharakteristika)* is defined in Soviet encyclopedias and dictionaries as "an official document containing an evaluation or conclusion about a person's work or social activity."[3] One evaluation is written periodically for his personnel file and every time he changes jobs or is promoted or applies for membership in an organization, travel abroad, or other things. If it serves some of the same purposes as a Westerner's letter of recommendation or efficiency report, there are fundamental differences. The Westerner gets his letter of recommendation for a temporary and local purpose and can use it or throw it away as he pleases; Soviet *kharakteristiki* are official documents and a permanent part of his record, forever available to investigators. And there is, after all, only one employer in the USSR, which gives immense power to the person who writes the *kharakteristika*. That person may be a school authority or a party or trade union secretary, but most are written by personnel officers and they are controlled by the KGB.

For hundreds of specific purposes, the citizen also needs *spravki*—official authorizations and certifications. An employee must have one or more to make a business trip; the farmer needs one to travel away from a *kolkhoz*. A *spravka* tells the authorities that an apartment house has room to house the bearer or confirms that he is duly registered there. It certifies that he has a reservation in a vacation spot or is authorized to travel to or within a border zone. It proves that a military officer has permission to live outside the base, and so on ad infinitum.

And then there is the questionnaire *(anketa)*, that central institution of Soviet life. Again and again, to get a job or register in a school or to join an organization, to be baptized, or to travel abroad, the citizen fills out this form that lays bare his life: family background, residences and travels, education, jobs, punishments, contacts abroad. The *anketa* goes as deeply as the situation requires. For manual labor, it asks the job applicant only the barest information. If, however, he is to be baptized (by definition, opposing the government's policy), it asks details about his parents and grandparents. To get a job with access to secrets or foreign contacts or to travel abroad, the applicant must answer questions that might astonish a Western reader; we have translated in full, in a later chapter, an *anketa* for travel abroad.

The System of Regulations

These are no mere identity documents but are part of what the authorities define as a "system" designed to strengthen state security and law and order. "The new passport system in the USSR is a whole complex of legal norms [laws and regulations] designed to keep track of and regulate the movements of citizens by standardized documents that certify a person's identity, by registration and deregistration, and also by the address-information service *(adresno-spravochnaya rabota)*. It is a dependable means of strengthening law and order, legality and the state security of the USSR."[4]

The system is vital to the controlled economy, all the more so at a time when long-term population trends are depleting the labor force. The regime must grapple with contradictory needs: on the one hand, to promote labor migrations in desired directions (for which they have revitalized migration programs and institutions) and, on the other, to hold people at their workplaces (offering incentives to stay).§ "The passport system plays an important role in regulating the distribution of the population."[5]

A more down-to-earth explanation was given by Aleksandr Zinoviev through the words of one of his fictional characters in Moscow:

> Our country is large. All kinds of industrial enterprises are scattered over it. And people are needed to operate them. How can they be persuaded to stay? For Marxist theorists there is no problem: the high level of consciousness of the workers, eager to overfulfill production quotas; good food supplies; television; cinemas; theaters; libraries; public transport and so on. We are, after all, moving towards communism! . . . But there is also the question of specific reality. Food supplies? In Moscow there's nothing to eat, and when you go into the surrounding country, what do you find? Who has ever counted the number of people who flood into Moscow daily looking for food and consumer goods? . . . What about our roads? What about public services? And what do we see on the television? Just try and get tickets for a decent play in Moscow! And that's to say nothing about the rest of the country! Art clubs? Folk dance clubs? Singing groups? Just go out into the country and have a look at what's going on. Drink. Boredom. Punch-ups. Crime. Do you think it's by chance that young people prefer low salaries and bad living conditions here, nearer to the center of real culture? . . . In reality—give people freedom of movement and a chance of settling wherever they like (for example, by abolishing compulsory registration with the police), and then you'll get enormous migrations. Certain places will be totally deserted.[6]

The leaders put the best light on it. Not only do they take pains to justify the system, but they also paint the documents in rosy colors, as badges of honor. "Henceforth," as one put it in the mid-1970s, "the main

§This was the purpose of, for instance, the 1979 decree "On the Further Strenghtening of Labor Discipline and the Reduction of Labor Turnover in the National Economy."

document attesting to the identity of a citizen will bear the proud and majestic title of 'Passport of a Citizen of the USSR.' "[7] Another writer quoted a poem of Vladimir Mayakovsky, "And I, I pull out of my pocket a document worth its weight in gold. Read it and envy me: I am a citizen of the Soviet Union."[8] The authorities arrange ceremonies to solemnize the first issuance of the passport and work booklet, orating to the sixteen-year-olds and their parents about patriotism—and about duties and discipline.

Those duties, that discipline—as every Soviet citizen knows—are the heart of the matter. After lauding the passport's "proud and majestic title," Soviet spokesmen invariably add a "but": "but its owner is responsible before the law and must strictly observe the regulations of the passport system."[9] They do not let people forget this. In the internal passport is a page of instructions (extracts from the passport regulations)[10] that tell nothing about rights the passport confers but spell out the duties it imposes. In 1983 the MVD was inspecting the working of the passport system in residences and workplaces—and, of course, catching many people who were living without registering or avoiding work or debts. Such inspections, wrote an MVD official, would "strengthen discipline and socialist legality and promote a respectful attitude toward the passport."[11] Another warned that the citizen "faces a criminal charge for taking a casual attitude towards this, the citizen's principal document."[12]

These documents are instruments of repression. Internal passports had been introduced in Russia more than two hundred years earlier by Peter the Great, and Lenin (while he was still trying to overthrow the regime) demanded that they be abolished. The same Lenin in 1918–19 (in power, and anxious to stay there) introduced his own version.

Lenin made them weapons in his internal war. The first personal document issued throughout Soviet Russia was a "Temporary Labor Certificate for the Bourgeoisie" in 1918, which stigmatized "former exploiters." Without it no one could get food rations or move outside of town. With it the bearer invited discrimination, was given smaller food rations, was forced to get monthly entries about his job performance, and still found it hard to get permission to travel. The new regime thus doomed many scholars, scientists, and creative artists of the old regime to mistreatment and sometimes to death of hunger and cold.

It was Stalin who first introduced the Soviet "internal passport" by that name—and as a weapon in a violent struggle. His men were seizing private farms, jailing and exiling the well-to-do farmers, and corraling the rest in collective farms which they stripped of produce in an effort to feed the city populations building heavy industry. Millions of farmers and their families were starving, and some were roving about searching for food. Many workers—forced into new industries and harsh conditions—were also moving about, in search of more promising jobs and less dismal places. It was into this setting that the Soviet internal passport was born, on December 27, 1932, in one of a series of decrees designed to tie the farmers to their fields and workers to their factories and to punish anyone who tried to thwart the new policies.

In similar circumstances arrived the new version of the internal passport in the early 1970s. The country was suffering an economic crisis; and, as Stalin had, his successors introduced their new passport in one of a linked succession of decrees that limited work and personal freedom.** The purposes today are also the same as Stalin's. In 1938 the regime (via *Pravda*) commented that the newly announced work booklet would "help us to strengthen labor discipline . . . will make many 'rolling stones' stop flitting from job to job . . . will be one of the serious measures to combat labor turnover."[13] In 1973–74 the regime introduced the new version (and all the laws and regulations surrounding it) to help "strengthen labor discipline"[14] and to tie the worker to his workplace.

The peasants have always been special targets of the passport system. It has tied them like serfs to collective and state farms where life is poor and boring and where they have little incentive to till the fields or keep up the farm machinery. Many of the young look for any opportunity to escape. Coming home at the end of his military service—legally obliged to return within days to the farm from which he was called up—the young man is likely to stop over in a city and try to get a job or marry a city resident so

**It is worth recalling the parallels between the decrees of the early 1930s and those of the early 1970s. September 1930: decree forbidding free movement of labor, removing social benefits and food cards from anyone who left his job. December 1930: decree forbidding factories to employ workers who had left their previous employment without permission; also banning employment for six months of "flitters" and "disorganizers of production." January 1931: jail sentences for violations of labor discipline. January 1931: compulsory wage-books (at first limited to transport and industry and to individual plants, not as a national system). July 1932: elimination of a 1922 requirement that workers consent to any transfer to other jobs. August 1932: death penalty for theft of state property. December 1932: internal passport. The series of the 1970s included, in the spring of 1972, a decree on "Procedures in Implementing the Labor Code of the RSFSR" that made it harder for workers to shorten their work contracts. On 29 September 1972, "Model Regulations of Internal Labor Order" made one's freedom to choose his work dependent upon "the interests of society." On 8 June 1973 the police were given the right "to enter living accommodations to check on the observance of passport regulations when they have information about infringements." Eleven days later a law prevented farmers from leaving collective farms even for seasonal work elsewhere, unless they had official permission. On 6 September 1973 the new work booklet was announced, followed on 20 July and 28 August 1974 by regulations for the use of the work booklet and passport, respectively. On 25 December 1974 the new internal passport was announced; in April 1975, work booklets for farm workers.

he can stay there. Failing that he may sign up for two years' work in the *khimiki*—dangerous and arduous construction or mining projects where, by risking his life and health, he can at least be documented as a worker and not have to return to the *Kolkhoz*.

For nearly half a century the peasants were issued no internal passports at all. At the end of 1974 the regime announced that this would change. The "main, fundamental feature" of the new passport system was the "establishment of a standardized procedure for use of passports by all citizens, whether they live in the city or country and whatever their work."[15] Finally, thought some in the West, the serf had been liberated.

They were wrong: the new rules tied the peasant down more firmly than ever. Before this he could leave a collective farm with a mere *spravka* from the rural soviet. In theory he had to prove that he had a job elsewhere, but in practice he could sometimes get the *spravka* by bribing the chairman of his collective farm. (One bottle of vodka might be enough.) Now, under the "uniform nationwide passport system," he cannot leave unless the militia stamps his passport, which the militia will do only if the work collective votes approval—and party leaders dominate both militia and work collective. The peasant has little prospect for escape by this route: his fellow-workers, themselves unable to leave (and perhaps jealous or resentful) are being asked—under the eye of all-powerful bosses whom they know are anxious to keep them on the farm—to release one of their number and to increase their own workload.

The new regulations were, in fact, equivocal: passports were to be issued to farmers only for "departures for another area for a prolonged period of time";[16] for vacation or official trips outside the collective farm a *spravka* would still do. Within a few months, however, the leaders stressed their determination "to strengthen collective farm-labor discipline." This meant, in plain language, that they would do their utmost to keep the peasant on the farm and to make him work harder—as they made clear when they revealed, in the same announcement, that they would now, for the first time, issue work booklets to farmers.[17] The collective-farm office will, of course, keep the work booklets, just as factories hold those of their workers. To get permission to leave (and thus to get hold of his work booklet) the farmer must prove that he has another job elsewhere, but to get that job, he now needs his work booklet. The coils have tightened around him.

Propiska and *vypiska* are powerful weapons in the rulers' hands. No one is allowed to leave his residence for more than forty-five days without the MVD's permission (*vypiska*). To stay somewhere else he must get the

MVD's permission there *(propiska)*. The MVD will not give him the *propiska* unless he already has a *vypiska*.††

Many cities are "closed" to any new residents. Thus do the leaders prevent Moscow from becoming overcrowded like Cairo or Mexico City—but thus, also, do they keep their opponents out of centers where their influence might be pernicious. In mid-1974 it was decreed that "persons regarded by courts as especially dangerous recidivists, and persons who have been punished by deprivation of freedom or exile for especially dangerous state crimes . . . are not to be granted residence permits in cities, districts, and regions listed in decisions of the USSR government."[18] Four months later they published the new passport system; and a few weeks after that the authorities of Moscow City—premier among those "listed" cities—distributed to officials a list of categories of citizens to be denied residence permits in Moscow and, if they already possessed such permits, to have them revoked. This measure was concealed from the people.[19] Presumably other major cities issued similar lists and will reject anyone whom the leaders have categorized as a problem, which may be revealed by his passport.

Thus Nikolay Kots, on returning to his home in Novovolynsk in September 1979 after imprisonment for dissidence, could find neither work nor lodging. Although the MVD would not register him, a kind woman finally agreed to give him a room—and she was fined for breaking the law.[20] (Any subsequent offense could send her to prison as well.) Thus the KGB could exile Andrey Sakharov from Moscow without making any legal charge against him: the MVD had only to rescind his *propiska* for Moscow, issue him a *vypiska,* and then register him in Gorkiy, making a notation in his passport that confined him within the town's limits.

Even if he does not qualify for such a list, the transient faces a Catch-22 problem. To get the *propiska* he must prove to the MVD that he already has a job in the town; but an employer may legally hire him only if he has a *propiska*—and certification that he has a place to live, which one cannot obtain without proof that one has a job.‡‡ To his new employer he must

††A third element is *registratsiya,* which applies to stays of fewer than forty-five days. It requires the same basic procedures of registration and deregistration with the militia but does not require entries in the passport and is usually arranged through the house manager, hotel clerk, or administrator of vacation camps or construction sites, where the individual need only show his passport. (To get a *propiska* the citizen must submit his passport and military reserve booklet; to get the *vypiska* he must first submit an "application" telling the militia why he wants to leave and where he wants to go.) All these requirements are spelled out in the decrees of 28 August 1974.

‡‡To get around this problem, in cities willing to take him (which Moscow and

also prove that his previous employer has formally released him. But to do that he must show his work booklet, with its revelation of why he left his previous employment (and all others before it); to have quit on his own initiative brands him as unreliable. He may therefore not be able to get the work he wants.

In their attempts to enforce labor discipline, the rulers (apparently floating a trial balloon) proposed in 1983 that the city worker, like the collective farmer, should be held on his job "unless his workmates agree" to let him go. The rulers did not follow through on the proposal, but they did tighten their grip on the worker: for example, he would have to give two months' notice of intention to leave, instead of one, and was prohibited from quitting during a punishment period of three months.

The military reserve document *(voyennyy bilet)* has its own requirements, its own laws and punishments, bringing the military command into the document-control system. When the bearer of the document arrives at a new place of residence he must report with it (and his internal passport, with its *propiska*) to the local military district office. They inscribe him on their reserve rolls and make entries in both his passport and his *voyennyy bilet*. The bearer must also turn over the *voyennyy bilet*, along with his passport, to the housing superintendent *(upravdom)* wherever he resides, for registration with the local militia.

Underneath the document system lies another: that of personal records, a system I became familiar with when I was a personnel officer in the Soviet system. In the 1920s and 1930s managers kept their own secret records on each worker, often containing derogatory and sometimes false information. When he moved to another job they would send these records to his new employers. This practice persists today in the form of the personal cards kept by every personnel office, which contain secret notations on the worker's conduct and misconduct and a summary of evaluations by his supervisor. As recently as 1973 the USSR Minister of Social Security recommended that the employer, after hiring a worker (and collecting his work booklet), should request the personal card from the previous employer.[21]

Leningrad and Kiev are not), he gets a paper from the apartment house certifying that there is space for him once he gets a job. But that is not so simple either: the minimum living space allowed by law (nine square meters per person) is generally not available for those already living in Soviet cities. Thus housing shortages help the leaders control their subjects.

Criminal Punishment

The regime sharpens this system of controls by punishing violators not merely for infractions of administrative rules but for crimes. "Citizens guilty of malicious violation of the rules of the passport system are held criminally responsible," say the passport regulations.[22] "Malicious violation" is defined as "repeated infraction of the established rules for residence registration [and] continuation of residence without a passport by those who have already been investigated for this infraction." A "repeated infraction" is usually interpreted as one committed for the third time.

The penalty is whatever the criminal code imposes at any given time; it can be adjusted quickly as the rulers see fit. Under Lenin, a person could easily be shot for not having the right documents. In April 1920 (during the civil war) a party congress called for listing as "deserters" those who were "leaving their jobs" and "moving from place to place," and for forming them into punitive work squads and then putting them in concentration camps.[23] In January 1931 Stalin imposed prison sentences on violators of labor discipline: six months' correctional labor for being twenty minutes late to work, prison for repeated infractions. If a transport worker caused economic loss or disarranged the timetables by being late to work, he could get ten years in prison; if he was motivated by "malicious intent," he could be shot. In 1932, after the new internal passport regulations had come into effect, the OGPU swept up many of the huge numbers living illegally and sentenced them to one year in the Gulag (where time was often added to their sentences).[24] The infamous decree of June 26, 1940, ordered that people who left their workplaces without authority were to be jailed for two to four months; those guilty of unjustified absenteeism were to get six months' corrective labor and forfeit 25 percent of their wages.[25]

Even in the era of *glasnost,* the penalty for a "repeated infraction" is up to one year deprivation of freedom in jail, corrective labor, or concentration camp. Yuriy Bacherov, for example, was living unregistered in Riga, evading work and neglecting his daughter. Official reports were made on him twice; then, on July 15, 1981, he was sentenced by a people's court to one year's deprivation of freedom (and treatment for alcoholism). Mikhail Kavalkov got six months for living without registering in Riga.[26] A Moldavian MVD chief criticized several district soviets for putting only 30–40 percent of the offenders into jail.[27]

The leaders use these rules to jail those who bother them. They have arranged to have dissidents and would-be emigrants fired (the bosses, of course, comply) and then, by blocking their further employment, set them up for sentencing not as "political" offenders but as "parasites." Hundreds, perhaps thousands, of such cases were documented in the 1970s and 1980s. On December 19, 1984, for example, a Leningrad city court sentenced the linguist and mathematician Nadezhda Tredkova to two years in a labor camp for "parasitism"; she had applied six years earlier for emigration to Israel and had in the meantime spent months in a mental institution.[28] Iosif Begun, a teacher of Hebrew, got two years' internal exile as a "parasite" and, upon his release, was not allowed to return to Moscow.[29] More than a hundred Crimean Tatars were sentenced for violation of internal passport regulations between 1975 and 1979.[30]

Men and women returning from the camps in the 1950s and 1960s found that having been in jail is grounds for further persecution. Many could not go home: they had been deregistered from their places of residence. Although by law they must be reregistered anew on returning to the living area they occupied with their families before conviction,[31] in practice they often lose their right to return.

The punishment stretches far beyond the sentences, resting like a brand in the victim's passport and work booklet. Many employers are afraid to hire returnees from the camps or from exile; apartment-house administrators may refuse to house them. And, of course, no one who has been sentenced will normally be allowed to go abroad. (The release of Jews and prominent dissidents are exceptions.)

Thus what appear to be minor punishments serve the regime as powerful deterrents to indiscipline and dissent.

Enforcers, Soviet Style

The fourth element of this control system—its enforcement—involves huge numbers of people.

It is the militia that is formally responsible for overseeing and operating the passport system and checking on its functioning. Passports, *propiskas,* and *vypiskas* are issued by a Passport Directorate in the All-Union MVD headquarters and passport departments (operated by the militia) of regional MVD offices. But that is just the beginning. In addition, the militia monitors itself: district inspectors check at workplaces and residences to make sure the passport departments are doing their job.

Everyone who may house or hire others—the dwelling manager, the tourist-camp operator, the owner of a house, the boss on the job—is brought into the control system by laws that make him legally responsible, under threat of punishment, to see that his tenants or employees register their presence.

The *druzhiny,* the volunteer police auxiliaries, have organized squads throughout the country to enforce the rules. To these brash and arrogant youths the rulers have given the task of examining the documents of people on the street (or even in their own homes, when groups have gathered in apartments). If they find an irregularity, the *druzhinniki* can escort their victim to the militia station.

Any so-called representative of authority—policeman, MVD or KGB, or party or Komsomol member, or government functionary—can legally stop a citizen on the street, demand to see his papers, and under certain circumstances confiscate them. (Since this has caused popular outrage— the victim can hardly carry on normal life without his passport—article 35 of the passport law of 1974 threatened fines for "officials who unlawfully confiscate passports.")

Related to these institutions is the "address information service" *(adresno-spravochnaya rabota),* which the militia administers. This public directory service functions the way a telephone book does in most developed countries. In the USSR so many people live in multifamily dwellings, so few have private telephones, and telephone books (treated almost as secrets) are so hard to come by that a special service is needed. Kiosks on streets and squares dispense addresses upon request. Of course, in this land of secrecy, the service is limited. The clerks often demand to see the inquirer's passport; they are instructed to try to identify any foreigner who seeks a Soviet citizen. "Sensitive" names (those of government officials, for example, or scientists in military-related research) are available, if at all, only by special request. Anyone who would have contact with such people is presumed to know where to find them.

In the workplace the KGB-controlled Personnel Department and First (security) Department control the documentation of every employee.

Prominent among the watchers is the dwelling manager *(upravlyayushchyy domom,* or *upravdom* for short). No mere janitor or apartment office administrator, the *upravdom* is the leaders' permanent watchman over the smallest geographic segment of their realm. His domain may extend no farther than part of an apartment building, and he may be a drunken lout; but he carries the authority of the omnipotent rulers. Named or approved by the MVD, he is a cog in the national machine; he is required by law to keep official records according to a prescribed format and is in regular touch with the militia and often the KGB.

The *upravdom* may knock at the door and force his way in uninvited (he needs no warrant), sometimes alone and sometimes accompanied by a militiaman or a *druzhinnik,* to look around and check everyone's papers. Some spiteful neighbor, perhaps, has denounced a tenant's life-style or the presence of unregistered guests.

He keeps a "house book" *(domovaya kniga),* an official register according to a form established by the MVD,§§ of people moving in or out or staying temporarily. He also keeps a card file on his tenants with notations about their jobs (as proven by work certificates) and, depending on his own zeal, about their behavior and contacts.

The *upravdom* gets this information not only by keeping his own eyes open but also from an informal network of caretakers, cleaners, and busybodies about the premises—and from *druzhinniki* assigned by the MVD to help him. Does a tenant spend too much time at home—perhaps shirking or without a job? Does he have unidentified visitors—perhaps even foreigners—or do groups assemble in his apartment? Noisy parties or brawling? Do he and his wife fight—or leave their children alone, or beat them? Does he come home suspiciously late or have his lights on at odd hours? These things spice up the *upravdom*'s reports when he routinely meets his militia contact to show his house book and turn over the personal documents submitted to him by tenants checking in or out. If the KGB has shown interest in goings-on in this apartment house, the *upravdom* will pass tidbits directly to his KGB contact. The *upravdom* may suspect that the police or the KGB have their own secret informants in the place, so he is likely to report zealously in order to avoid criticism for lack of vigilance.

A competent *upravdom* can help his tenants, too, by locating a plumber or repairman or getting a ticket or a reservation or an urgently needed bottle of vodka. He is not always a stern instrument of the regime; he may even connive to help people get around the rules. In 1958, however, a decree on the passport system warned that "severe penalties before the criminal courts" would hit the *upravdom* who allowed infringements of the regulations.

Of course, the armed forces also help enforce the system by administering the military reserve booklet—required in order to get housing—and by marking the internal passport as well.

Thus the rulers know, by and large, where to find all their citizens. Each registration and deregistration is reported through militia channels

§§The Great Soviet Encyclopedia *(Bolshaya Sovetskaya Entsiklopediya)* describes the house book as a "legal form, maintained by every city housing authority that has lodgings, in which are registered the tenants in a house." (The owner of a house who takes in tenants— even friends—also must keep a house book.)

and is available to central MVD and statistical authorities. This control has tightened—not relaxed—since Stalin's time, although the punishment for infringements is less severe. In the postwar period, as soldiers returned and displaced millions moved about, millions of people were improperly documented or registered. "Search" (*rozysk*) was the full-time task of a large MGB directorate set up in headquarters and field offices in the summer of 1946. Since then, document controls have been tightened and standardized, and from the 1960s on, the computer has been put to work. Whereas in certain large cities in my time more than a million citizens were unaccounted for, those cities' search lists had been reduced by the late 1970s to a few dozen.[32]

The rulers can not keep a thumb on everyone. Citizens still find ways to get around the rules to avoid responsibility and, in fact, devote much ingenuity to this pursuit. However, what the rulers have done is to reduce to a harmless minimum the number of people able to escape their control.

CHAPTER 17

Denunciation

A SOVIET PHILOSOPHER DESCRIBED LIFE IN THE 1970S THUSLY:

> Just try and look at our life from outside. Look at our newspapers, our films, our magazines, our novels, our meetings, our symposia, our assemblies, our conversations, our reports and so on. What are they all? Nothing but denunciations, denunciations, denunciations. Denunications of ourselves, our neighbors, our colleagues, our superiors, our subordinates. What is referred to as a system of control and accountability is in fact an official system of denunciation as the normal pattern of life in society. [1]

Then in the 1980s the Soviet leaders made it even easier for people to betray or harass one another anonymously: they handed out preprinted postcards.

With these so-called "signal cards" a spiteful busybody no longer had to ponder his phrasing: all he had to do was fill in the name and address of his victim—enemy or rival, envied neighbor or former lover—and mark the selected misdeed. Twelve were listed. One of these was satisfyingly broad: "committing crimes." Another let the police know that someone had been "previously tried by the courts" (no space is provided to mark whether he was found innocent or guilty). By a stroke of the pencil the denouncer could accuse his victim of failing to register earnings, hiding from the police, having no full-time job, drinking too much, using narcotics, abusing children, failing to pay alimony, or incurring other court judgments. If this list didn't cover it, he could underline a catch-all category—"Other violations of social order and of the rules of socialist society"*—and leave it to the police to find out which one. The accuser

---

*When a Western journalist asked Muscovites what the latter point might mean, they suggested loitering, living in the city without registering with the police, or inviting foreigners to one's apartment (Robert Gillette, "Soviets Introduce System of Denunciation

would then put the card in an envelope and mail it to the police. The reverse side of the card was conveniently reserved for them to note "measures taken." Meanwhile, the denouncer was led to believe he would not be identified: "The signature of the sender is not required." However, the police and KGB have well-developed techniques to identify the writer of anonymous notes, graffiti, or other messages; the sender could usually be identified if the authorities so wished.

The hand of my old colleague Vitaliy Fedorchuk showed beneath this advance in Soviet social control. Shortly before the signal card was distributed, he had become USSR Minister of Internal Affairs and had done this sort of thing before. In September 1981, while he was KGB chairman of the Ukrainian Republic (and a member of its ruling Party Buro), the authorities passed out cards in Kiev asking the people to denounce one another:

> Dear Comrades! The support station for public order and the organs of internal affairs are trying hard to establish exemplary public order in our district. Timely reaction to each breach of the law and punishment of the guilty will help in many ways to accomplish this task. For this the widest support and participation of the population is needed. The sooner a transgression or crime becomes known, the quicker measures will be taken. We ask you to report, without mentioning your name, on all violations of public order and the rules of socialist communal life known to you, on people leading an antisocial way of life, not working, or abusing alcoholic beverages, on problem families and adolescents who have given up their studies, to the Council of the Support Station for Public Order of Zhdanov Microdistrict, telephone 274101 between 1900 and 2300 hours, or at other hours to the Department of Internal Affairs of the Zaliznichnyy District, telephone 767021 or 773100. Signed: Support Station for Public Order, Zhdanov Microdistrict.[2]

One recognizes Fedorchuk's progress: two years later he made it easier, and with a wider menu.

The cards were new; the central role of denunciation under Soviet rule was not. Just after taking power the Bolsheviks asked people to denounce others,[3] and soon they went further and insisted on it. The USSR constitution, as we have seen, requires the citizen "to be intolerant of actions harmful to the public interest, to take an uncompromising attitude toward the enemies of communism [and toward] antisocial behavior," and "to help in every way to maintain public order."[4] The

---

by Mail," in *Los Angeles Times*, 3 July 1983). These cards were reported from Krasnodar, Tallinn, Vilnius, and Riga and were evidently distributed in other cities (*London Daily Telegraph*, 21 March 1984).

criminal code makes it a crime to fail to denounce violations of the law; and such failure, depending on the gravity of the violation, can earn one a ticket to the prison camps. All the while, KGB and MVD provocateurs prowl about, testing loyalty.

In fact, the regime ennobles the act. Under the name of "criticism and self-criticism," denunciation is one of the tenets of Leninism and a pillar of *glasnost*. The party member (or Young Communist) is expected to expose in meetings his party brethren's imperfections and, if his comrade has struck first, to admit to his own. In 1982 the party leadership called for more of this. "It is necessary to continue and intensify this positive trend by every means and to assert a spirit of intolerance toward shortcomings," wrote *Pravda*. Its editorial singled out for praise Engineer A. Minayev of the Cheboksary automobile repair plant in Mordovia, who "has frequently raised the question of wastefulness, of instances of embezzlement of socialist property and the production of poor-quality output." (Such *cirmes*, let it be noted in passing, may be punishable by death.) *Pravda* noted with approval that the Oblast Party Committee had backed Minayev and "removed the suppressors of criticism from their leading posts."[5]

The party and Komsomol have no monopoly on this sort of denunciation. It is a standard feature of the meetings of social and work groups—anywhere people do things together. It is taught and practiced in the schoolroom. Vladimir Sakharov gives his own recollections of first grade (i.e., age seven):

> The class was divided into three "links" consisting of ten children apiece. Each link had a leader, who was elected by his group on a rotating basis. . . . Every morning the link leader would go before the class and denounce failings he or she had observed by link members. "Sasha didn't finish his homework. Nina has dirty fingernails. Boris picked his nose. Sakharov, again you are wearing non-uniform trousers." Everyone had a chance at being a snitch. It put each of us into a bind. The children didn't like snitching, on the whole, although some took a perverse pleasure in it. At the same time, the teacher and the class leader expected the link leaders to be critical. One learned to play the game.[6]

Soviet society is a giant collective composed of countless smaller collectives. The system tries to cut off any route of individual escape. Kindergarten and school, workplace and army, apartment house and neighborhood are all organized. Fundamental laws regulate family life. The regime identifies religion with "the aspiration to withdraw into a narrow little philistine world and to evade broad public interests."[7] Everyone, of no matter what age or position, is expected to give and take denunciation as a form of "building communism." Eyes are constantly watching for departures from "norms of socialist life." Careerists knock off their rivals, retired people fill their idle hours, the spiteful wreak revenge for real or imagined hurts.

The impact is inestimable. "People were not only destroyed in camps and prisons" in the Soviet past, wrote a Soviet historian and novelist in 1988. "There was another form of destruction—a deep, psychological, moral deformation whose spirit is still alive today."[8]

The most famous little snitch of history—fourteen-year-old Pavlik Morozov who denounced his own father and mother for trying to help banished farmers in 1932 and was "martyred" by angry uncles—was eternalized in bronze; his proud name graced schools, youth centers, ships, and collective farms, and schoolchildren have been taught to revere him and his act. Under *glasnost,* however, there were signs that this icon might be shattered. Pavlik Morozov, wrote a Soviet historian, "is not a symbol of revolution and class consciousness but a symbol of legalized and romanticized treachery."[9]

But with or without the role model of little Pavlik, Soviet young people are called on to adopt his mode. For example, Viktor Chebrikov, Politburo member, wrote: "A young person who encounters acts of ideological sabotage and other subversive actions must be able to evaluate them correctly and emphatically rebuff them . . . political vigilance demands the daily unremitting attention of the Komsomol organizations, labor collectives, and study groups, and their informal, concerned participation in the fate of each young person."[10]

This has its drawbacks for the party bosses too. For one thing, they might seem openly to be sowing distrust. After inciting young people, KGB Chairman Chebrikov piously added that "implacability toward any manifestations of hostile ideology and high political vigilance have nothing in common with suspiciousness and distrust." Just before Brezhnev's MVD issued the signal cards to facilitate denunciation, he proclaimed that "there is no room in our life for anonymous vilifications."[11] For another thing, the party bosses themselves become targets of anonymous complaints. By 1985 they felt compelled to pass a law making the sending of "slanderous, unsigned letters" a crime punishable by three years' imprisonment.[12]

But denunciation is an integral part of the Leninist system and will not disappear until the system does. In late 1988 the KGB again stressed its reliance on "the support of the broad masses" and was having its staffers "widen and strengthen their ties with the working people" to "improve the forms of public participation in the cause of safeguarding state security." To this end the KGB keeps a reception service open twenty-four hours a day in its central and provincial offices where people "come to report a planned or committed state crime. . . . Many of these reports have helped prevent serious crimes and expose dangerous criminals," said Politburo member (and KGB Chairman) Viktor Chebrikov.[13]

One long-standing channel for denunciation has become less comfortable for the party chiefs since the advent of *glasnost:* their "letter campaign." From the mid-1960s onward they encouraged the public to take advantage of the long-standing right to address letters of complaint to public and state institutions and insisted that each and every one of them would be answered. This "enhancement of socialist democracy" was written into the USSR Constitution of 1977 (Article 49), and a unit of the CC CPSU apparatus was created to cope with the letters.† Gorbachev described such letters as "the major feedback linking the Soviet leadership with the masses" and—quite rightly—as a measure of the people's increasing self-confidence and diminishing fears.[14]

As a constitutional guarantee, the letter campaign offered about as much "democracy" as the medieval king's justice, the arbitration of tribal chiefs, or the factory suggestion box. But that was not its purpose; what the leaders most wanted was to dramatize and personalize their propaganda campaigns for this or that new effort: to bring in a bigger harvest, take better care of tools, or fight theft or absenteeism, for instance. The letters also served to convey the idea that far from cracking the whip, the authorities' harsh policies were responding to popular demands. In 1984, for example, "thousands" of workers wrote in to ask for a longer work week;[15] others pleaded with the authorities to help make industries more efficient or to apply a firm hand against drunkenness, indiscipline, and other "negative phenomena." Such "popular demands" recall the one put forward in Stalin's time by "trade unions, peasant organizations and cultural representatives"—asking that the death penalty be written into law.[16] In fact, such of those letters as were genuine were written by party workers (sometimes as part of a plan formulated in their collective, sometimes fired by agitators' exhortations) and by KGB agents acting on secret instructions.

Letters to the editors of publications had offered the regime similar support; before *glasnost* the only ones likely to be published were the "constructive" ones. When *glasnost* gave editors a freer choice of what to print, several newspapers and magazines began printing letters making comments and proposals stretching far beyond Gorbachev's initial conception of "restructuring" and striking close to the foundations of the

†Konstanin Chernenko said that from 1976–81 the CC CPSU had received more than three million letters and the local party organizations fifteen million more—and public organizations presumably get as many, and newspapers yet more. Chernenko, chap. 10.

system. The more such letters a periodical published, the more popular it became—and the more letters came flowing in. By 1989 the lively magazine *Argumenty i Fakty* was receiving a thousand letters every day and *Ogonek* almost as many.

It was still too early to know how the regime would ultimately deal with the letter-writers and the editors who print them, for underneath the "letter campaign" lurks the KGB.

Every serious letter addressed to a state or public organization (and those addressed to some newspapers) reaches the Chekists. If the letter shows the right spirit, the KGB has a lead to a new informant. If it accuses people, the KGB handles it like any other denunciation. If it says or implies that the system or the government is at fault—which the regime can regard as the crime of "anti-Soviet slander"—the KGB will identify and investigate the author. The authorities ask that the letters be signed, and complain that more than half of them are not.[17] Today as during my time in the KGB, those letters are being used to locate not only problems but also the people who, by daring to complain, may pose a threat to the regime. With surprising candor the regime itself admitted this in 1987: "those who are criticized, instead of setting about . . . finding ways to eliminate the shortcomings, start digging into the histories of those doing the criticizing, looking for any murky areas or transgressions in their work and life. And when they find something, or sometimes unscrupulously make up something, then they punish the critic. The range of punishments is quite broad—from a warning to prison bars."[18]

The pre-*glasnost* case of citizen Treskunov offers a glimpse into this reality. Soviet journalist V. Viktorov inadvertently revealed how the authorities view these letter-complaints by deriding the "lampoonist" Treskunov, who had written a hundred anonymous letters "casting dirt on the Soviet government, using dirty language, criticizing everything in our country as if only he knew how to do things right, blaming everything on the government." Clearly, the regime does not want criticism: "We know better than anyone else our shortcomings and difficulties, we speak of them openly . . . Renegades like Treskunov will be thrown overboard from our mighty ship, the Soviet Land." Of course, the article dared not tell what Treskunov was complaining about—but he was an enemy, and he was caught.[19]

"No matter how trickily he tried to hide his identity, Treskunov was identified," Viktorov reported—and hinted at how. Treskunov, he said, had "used any paper that came to hand." There is a special unit within the KGB, which in my day had twenty members and the rank of a department, dedicated to the task of identifying authors of anonymous messages.

Able to call on all the facilities of the vast Soviet control system, the department developed extraordinary skills in its specialized business over the years. One citizen, for example, carefully used block letters so his handwriting would not be identified—but wrote on paper with widely spaced lines, which is used only by first graders. State Security investigated all the schools of the district and found the child whose notebook had the page torn out. Her father was condemned to prison camp.

Soviet citizens may not fully recognize the sophistication and determination with which the KGB opposes them, but they sense the danger of complaining. They have heard what happened to people like the party member Vassiliy Lisoviy. Placing his faith in the regime's protestations of socialist legality, he mailed a letter in January 1972 to the Central Committee of the Communist Party of the Ukraine calling their attention to the illegality of several recent arrests—and two days later was himself arrested. For this "slander" and "anti-Soviet agitation" he got ten years in camp and exile.[20] A Western correspondent in Moscow reported several such cases on the eve of Gorbachev's reforms. Nadezhda Kurakina, a waitress for twenty-five years in a Volgograd restaurant run by the local party organization, complained first in letters (no reply) and then at her work collective that restaurant administrators were stealing crockery, accusing the waitresses of breaking it, and then docking their salaries for it. She was dismissed, and her husband also lost his job. The party secretary of the Volgograd region, whom she had served for twenty years, would not even see her, and she lost her pension. Because her dismissal was noted in her work booklet, no one else would employ her. Valentin Poplavsky was ordered by his factory at Klimovsk, near Moscow, to write a false criticism of a woman employee who had complained that officials used factory funds to finance drunken parties. When he refused, he was warned by the factory's party organization and then by the public prosecutor and finally dismissed. The dismissal was marked in his work booklet, and he could not get another job. Shagen Oganesyan, an engineer in Yerevan who was appointed to a People's Control Commission, checked and found that his agency had done only about half the work it claimed— and that the money had disappeared. When he insisted on reporting the irregularity, he was first denied a pending job assignment in Poland and then demoted. He quit in protest.[21]

Gorbachev's reforms may have somewhat tarnished the image of Pavlik Morozov, but anonymous denunciation still thrives as a technique of Soviet control. And it seems almost benign when compared with its more aggressive and focused manifestation, the secret informer.

CHAPTER 18

Secret Collaborators: The *Agentura*

THE CENTRAL PEG OF THE SOVIET SYSTEM OF REPRESSION IS THE SECRET collaborator (*sekretnyy sotrudnik,* or *"seksot"*).

Denunciation was never enough; not even a blizzard of anonymous letters or signal cards would have satisfied these wary rulers, nor would they feel safe from their people even if their microphones were picking up conversations from every office, living room, bedroom, and kitchen in the land. These experts in holding power have gone further and tried to possess their subjects. One way is through the obedience demanded from party members (and less effectively from Komsomol members). Then there is the agent work of the KGB, through which they fasten a permanent grip on millions of others and spread fear and mistrust.

The KGB's agent network—the *agentura*—seeks to cover every corner of society. Each is assigned to a case officer who must keep bringing more people under control—making them, as KGB doctrine demands, firmly "ours" (*nash*). The KGB officer is trained how to spot and manipulate the individual's desires and fears and vulnerabilities. While it may be better to have an agent who cooperates out of genuine ideological or patriotic conviction, the essential thing is that he does as he is told. Whatever the recruit's openly expressed motive, the case officer must reinforce his ties to the KGB by compromise, threat, and blackmail, always implied and often explicit—and never let him go.[1]

The *agentura* is vital to the survival of the regime. Through its eyes and ears the leaders sense the first stirrings of unrest or disaffection or other threats to their power. *Seksots* search out potential opponents of the regime and also the mood of the populace, its reactions to shortages of food or consumer goods or to new government measures (things that the KGB reports regularly and systematically to the leadership). As *glasnost* gradu-

ally lifted the shadow of fear the leaders—confronted by mass demonstrations and an increasingly outspoken press and then by the dramatic
election of March 1989—found it all too easy to detect this mood and to
identify it as general dissatisfaction. The *agentura* became more vital to
them than ever. *Glasnost* would not dismantle this bastion of Kremlin
power. As a KGB officer wrote in March 1989, responding to a newspaper
reader's letter asking how *glasnost* could be reconciled with the presence
everywhere of KGB informants, "The KGB still regards the organization
of work with citizens' written and oral communications as a way for
citizens to participate in ensuring state security."[2]

Simply by existing, the *agentura* applies powerful pressure. The KGB
case officer takes pains to hide the identity of his secret sources, but
everyone knows they are there and fears them; and that is what matters.
Some may be recognizable* but even one's best friend can be pressured
into reporting—because in this country everyone is vulnerable. So the
citizen has become wary of his coworkers, acquaintances, and even of his
friends.† Thus does the regime deter people from concerting their dissatisfactions and grouping together outside its control.

While thus contemptuously manipulating their people's weaknesses
and encouraging them to betray one another, the rulers were, paradoxically, creating genuine support for themselves. Every time a citizen signs
on as a KGB informer, he not only compromises himself but also alienates
himself from his countrymen and enters into unbreakable complicity with
the rulers. He can thenceforth be counted as their supporter and might
have to defend them on the final barricades.

Having fragmented society with the agent network, the Soviet leaders
use that same network to bind the fragments together in a new pattern—
making people responsive to an authority they cannot refuse. Even tighter
than does the party itself, the *agentura* links the people to the rulers.

To grasp the role of the *agentura* in preserving Soviet rule, one must

---

*People have ways of recognizing the *"stukach"* ("knocker"). In this land where everyone
knows its danger, curiosity or inquisitiveness is quickly sensed. It is easy to notice a man's
career outstripping his talent and hard not to notice someone getting "lucky" breaks with
suspicious regularity (like a journalist granted "scoops" by the authorities while other
journalists are neglected). And there are people doing things with impunity that condemn
others to the camps.

†Many react like Vladimir Bukovsky: "Once upon a time I had been a very sociable
fellow, got on easily with people, and after a few days' acquaintance regarded them as
friends. But as time went on . . . I gradually came to avoid new acquaintances. I could no
longer face the pain and turmoil when a person you had relied on and loved suddenly
turned coward and betrayed you, and you had to excise him from your mind forever" (*To
Build a Castle,* p. 52).

appreciate the length of its reach and the density of its ranks. In the early 1980s, a former KGB man told a Western journalist that every third citizen in the USSR cooperates regularly with the KGB. At first glance this looks absurd; one-third of the adult population would exceed 50 million people, an impossible work load for the KGB case officers if they had to meet them all regularly. Moreover the regime finds it useful to exaggerate the size of the *agentura*. But this claim deserves a closer look.

If you focus on specific portions of the population rather than the entirety, you must come to some comparable estimate, as have I and many other veterans of Soviet State Security. Depending on the population group in question, we have estimated that one person in two is a *seksot,* or one in four or seven or ten or twelve. And these estimates cover long ago as well as recent times; Georgiy Agabekov, for example, wrote in 1930 that one in four residents of cities in the early 1920s was an informant. In the secretarial apparatus of unions of Moscow writers and journalists or in the lay organizations of churches, one in three could have been assumed to be working systematically as a secret informant for the KGB; the situation is comparable among adult residents of certain border zones. In the staff of organizations like Intourist that cater to foreigners there are even more. On the staff of Moscow hotels and restaurants serving foreigners, everyone is required to report to the KGB; and so numerous are the registered secret informants among them that to manage them (and the technicians handling the microphones) the KGB usually inserts one of its officers as manager or deputy manager. In every delegation traveling abroad, everyone must sign a commitment to report to the accompanying security officer; moreover many of them are on the delegation in the first place because they have the KGB's favor or KGB business to do. In Soviet embassies abroad everyone reports not only about his foreign contacts but, on demand, about his colleagues too. On collective farms, however, or in remote regions peopled by seminomads,the KGB needs fewer informants—perhaps one in twelve or even twenty. In the armed forces it is hard to generalize because in larger, compact units, such as the ground forces, fewer *seksots* (probably not more than one in eight) can do the job, whereas in units whose people are scattered in isolated posts, such as radar stations, the proportion is likely to be higher.

But the numbers do not matter to the KGB: what counts is whether each and every part of the population is covered to the regime's satisfaction. It rarely is; the leaders are insatiable and the KGB case officer's plan forces him to keep adding to his network. As former NKGB Minister Vsevolod Merkulov used to tell State Security workers, "The finer the net, the more fish are caught."

In addition to the KGB's *seksots* one must bear in mind that other Soviet agencies also have confidential informants: the MVD's militia and Chief Directorate for the Fight Against Theft of State Property, for example. The KGB, through channels already described, gets the information from those informants when it is of any interest, and can establish direct contact with them if it seems necessary.

In any case, estimates become meaningless in light of the reality that the whole party, the Komsomol, and finally the common citizenry stands available to serve the KGB.

Party and Komsomol members offer the KGB a pool of 19 million and 42 million, respectively—most of them not, of course, regularly cooperating with the KGB but all of them expected to be ready to do so. This is hard reality, not theory. Soon after I arrived as a nineteen-year old soldier at my first military unit, an officer of its OO proposed that I inform for State Security. Before I could be signed up, however, I became Komsomol secretary of his unit. Then the OO officer said, "No need to sign up—now you'll be cooperating openly with us." Much later, in occupied Austria, my KGB group called on another party man to do his duty. Aleksandr Kralov was director of a Soviet-run factory where Ivan Bedniy, one of his subordinates, was denounced for being friendly with his Austrian employees and put under KGB watch. An officer of the KGB residency went to Kralov for help—and so Kralov immediately began reporting on Bedniy. He had no choice: by joining the CPSU and becoming a *yedinomyshlennik,* a "like-minded co-conspirator," he had in effect joined the KGB reserve and could be presumed to burn with desire to help the KGB achieve the historic mission of his party. Now he was simply being called to active service.

Even if they are not tapped directly by a KGB recruiter, party members are useful eyes and ears and hands. In their meetings they are exhorted to vigilance against the regime's opponents and reminded of their duty to report any potential threat or crime they perceive. They also perform extra duties as a routine aspect of their party work, which may involve service in People's Control or in auxiliary police work, manning "strong points" or border-zone support brigades.

How, for that matter, can any Soviet citizen refuse to cooperate if the KGB asks him to? He has his constitutional obligations; as Yuri Andropov put it, "The constitution has insured that the security of the state is regarded as the sacred duty of each individual."[3] The fiction of "like-mindedness" exerts irresistible pressure when coupled with the regime's overwhelming power over his life.‡

‡Vladimir Bukovsky has pointed out the relationship to the regime's pretension to

Fear is therefore the first and most important reason to consent to work with the KGB against one's fellow citizens. On one side in this confrontation looms a force able and willing to take away a man's job and apartment, prevent his promotion or higher education, or send him off to jail and death and ruin his family. Facing this juggernaut, fully aware of its powers and its ruthlessness, his own sins and weaknesses known, cowers an individual with only the most precarious hold on his own livelihood. Just to survive he has had to cut corners in his past, and it is the KGB who decides whether he has merely bent or actually broken the law. Offered by this giant the chance to assert his loyalty and high civic spirit simply by doing what the bosses call his "sacred duty," he is ill-placed to say no.

One who did was Igor Guberman, the editor of the underground journal *Jews in the USSR,* art expert, and collector of icons. A KGB case officer asked him to write character profiles of his associates in the Jewish national movement, warning him that they knew he possessed icons and that he could be prosecuted if he refused. He did refuse, and so was arrested on August 13, 1979, charged with buying stolen icons.[4]

Another reason for a citizen to say yes is advantage. The KGB does not only take away but also can grant. It can get an informant that coverted apartment, that new job, that degree, that promotion, that much-desired place for a child in summer camp or university—if he plays along.

A third incentive is psychological: being a secret collaborator brings a chance finally to talk freely, if only to the hated and feared authorities. There may also be a feeling of secret power over one's fellows, of finding an outlet for spite, frustration, and jealousy, that has motivated spies in the West as well.

And last of all is the tattered remnant of the "high civic spirit" that Soviet leaders vaunt. It surely existed in an earlier day. I had it when I joined the army and became a Komsomol secretary there. Lev Kopelev had it when he willingly assisted the GPU man in his factory:

> We were taught, when we were young, that it was our duty as citizens and members of the Komsomol to denounce friends and relatives, if need be, and to keep nothing from the party. I wrote several reports on conditions at the plant. . . . They had some full-fledged undercover agents

---

change human nature. "This concept of 'Soviet man' was really the starting point for all the illegality in the country. . . . Any interpretation differing from [the leaders'] was in itself a crime. 'You are a Soviet man,' says the KGB detective, 'and therefore obligated to help us.' And what can you say in reply? If you're not Soviet, what are you? Anti-Soviet? That alone is worth seven years in a labor camp and five in exile. And Soviet man is obliged to collaborate with our glorious security organs—that's clear as daylight. What was I kicked out of the university for? For not conforming to 'the ethos of a Soviet student' " (*To Build a Castle,* pp. 237–8).

working for them at the factory, whom they saw only at special meeting places, but they were also dependent on more or less open cooperation with party and Komsomol activists like us. . . . To be a Chekist in those days seemed worthy of the highest respect, and to cooperate secretly with the Cheka was only doing what had to be done in the struggle against a crafty foe.[5]

The same emotion has inspired many people, some for many years. Even today some people are sincerely stirred by the leaders' incessant calls to hatred and fear and vigilance against ever-present enemies. (They have no contrary information to counteract such calls.)

The agent network also provides the leaders with the hands to do the hidden work of their essentially secret government. The KGB can give its agents any sort of jobs; it has all kinds of agents.

Some may pose as thugs to beat up a daring dissident or a nosy journalist. Some may throw rocks at embassies to demonstrate the "Soviet people's" wrath at foreign governments' policies. Others may be placed, along with KGB case officers and *druzhinniki,* in courtrooms to pose as "the public" when dissidents are tried.

Some protect the regime's secrets from the eyes of curious foreigners— by misinforming them or even, as one did while escorting a prominent foreigner, by physically preventing them from making a discovery. The former vice-president of the United States, Henry A. Wallace, while traveling through the USSR during the Second World War, expressed curiosity about what lay over the brow of a hill. Nothing, said his hosts— but he started to walk up toward the crest. His KGB escort was appalled: just over that hill lay one of the concentration camps they were trying to persuade Wallace were figments of Western propaganda. KGB officer Grigoriy Dolbin raced up after Wallace and brought him down by a diving tackle, just in time. Apologizing for having to do this to save him from "the danger of falling," Dolbin escorted him back down the hill—his own career saved.[6]

Many a KGB agent has been called upon to thrust a "secret document" into the hand of an innocent foreigner or one of his own countrymen so that the other can be arrested and "proven" to be a spy. Or he may be enlisted in a more sophisticated provocation: instead of spying on or provoking a potential opponent of the regime, he may himself become that opponent—on KGB orders.

CHAPTER 19

Provokatsiya

The Real World

FREE AT LAST! PERVUKHIN JOYFULLY EMBRACED THE GUIDE WHO HAD led him out of the Soviet Union by a secret forest path and knelt to kiss the Finnish soil. Soon they ran into patrolmen, who escorted them to the nearby border post, where the staff gave them a friendly welcome, warm food, and Finnish liquor. There for four days uniformed authorities questioned Pervukhin (in Finnish through an interpreter) about his life, why and how he had fled from Soviet tyranny, and the people he knew who felt the same way.

It had been a stroke of luck; Pervukhin had never dared plan to escape by himself. He had been confiding his misgivings about the Soviet system to an office colleague named Malysheva, who shared his views (her husband was in a prison camp). A few months later, while Pervukhin was visiting her in her Leningrad apartment, a certain Guryshev came by. He had, he said, just been released from her husband's camp and brought her a pack of cigarettes from him. It was a strange gift, clearly some sort of message. After Guryshev left, Malysheva and Pervukhin drew the blinds and carefully took the cigarettes apart. Cunningly hidden in each of the filters they found, piece by piece, a message: her husband had made arrangements to escape and get across the border. He would send someone to guide her across to join him. Malysheva rejoiced, Pervukhin was thrilled, and in the emotion of the moment Malysheva agreed to let him join the escape. But weeks later when the guide arrived and gave the password, Malysheva was too ill to leave Leningrad. Though the guide could not wait, he agreed to take Pervukhin alone back to Finland with him. So here was Pervukhin, safe in Finland and ready to start a life in freedom.

But no—his interviewers brought him bad news. Bound by its treaty arrangements with the USSR, the Finnish government, after days of deliberation, felt compelled to deny him asylum and to turn him back to the Soviet authorities. After being blindfolded and driven for hours in a car, he stepped out into the arms of Soviet State Security and was tried and sentenced to twelve years' imprisonment for leaving the USSR without permission.

Bad luck? Finnish perfidy? Not at all. Pervukhin was a victim of Soviet provocation.

What had really happened was far from this fairyland of shared confidences, loyal couriers, secret messages, prison escapes, and border crossings. It had happened in the real Soviet world. A frightened office employee had secretly denounced Pervukhin for criticizing the regime. State Security had then picked his colleague Malysheva to report on him because she was easy to recruit and control. (Her husband really was in prison camp, and State Security could promise to make life easier for him there if she faithfully cooperated—or destroy him if she didn't.) Of course her husband had never had a chance to escape. Guryshev was a State Security agent, the hidden message in the cigarettes a trick to build Pervukhin's trust, Malysheva's illness a sham. The "border crossing guide" was from State Security, and they had never crossed the border at all: the "Finnish border post" and Finnish-speaking guards and interrogators were all a hoax.

The false border was not built solely for Pervukhin: it stood there as a permanent trap into which State Security provocateurs lured malcontents and was surely not the only one along the periphery of the USSR.* The "Finns" who debriefed Pervukhin (like "American officials" in false border posts on the East German frontier with American-occupied West Germany, and perhaps "Turkish" ones in the south) sought evidence of antiregime actions the escaper had committed and the names of dissident contacts inside the USSR who might be willing to help Western intelligence. (Then they, in their turn, would be approached by State Security operatives posing as spies from the West, inducing them to "escape" or to reveal their own friends who oppose the regime.) It was an old practice: in 1918 Dzerzhinsky's deputy Latsis had pseudo-Chilean and pseudo-Bra-

---

*The KGB evidently passed the technique on to its Eastern European satellite services, for a false border post (manned by pseudo-Americans) sprang up at the edge of Czechoslovakia, too. There the denouement was staged even more dramatically: after "preliminary debriefing" the escapees would be loaded (with the reports of their "American" interrogation) into a "U.S. Army" truck which, before it could get out of the area, would be intercepted by a daring Czechoslovakian police raid into "Western" territory and hustled "back" to Czechoslovakia (testimony of former Czech state security officer, Josef Frolik, before the Internal Security Subcommittee, Committee of the Judiciary, U.S. Senate, 18 November 1975, pp. 42–3). I learned of the Pervukhin operation inside the KGB.

zilian consuls—actually Cheka employees—offer citizens the chance to escape abroad, and then "caught" them. [1]

Pervukhin was never told. He probably died without ever learning that he had never been a free man, not even for those four short days.

The Soviet Meaning of Provocation

Provokatsiya is an aggressive technique, or more precisely, a whole bag of techniques, designed to cause an opponent—even a potential opponent—to expose himself or take action to his own disadvantage or disaster. The Soviet regime denies using it, and the word ranks in their vocabulary with "gendarme" and "police" as a symbol of tsarist oppression. Yet every security agency of the Soviet Union uses it as a standard operating procedure. †

Not content to let an informant like Malysheva simply keep an eye on a suspect like Pervukhin, the Soviet rulers prefer to provoke him into crime and isolate him from the community. Sensing a threat when people gather regularly out of their sight and hearing, they are not content merely to insert or recruit a spy in every sort of group but prefer to take over its leadership (arresting, discrediting, or intimidating its genuine leadership in order to clear the way to the top for their own inside agents), for, as the Chekists know from long experience, a "hostile" group that is secretly responsive to their orders is a tool with many uses.

Far from suppressing this insidious practice, *glasnost* has undoubtedly pumped new life into it. By tolerating those already mentioned independent *(nyeformalnyy)* organizations, Gorbachev may in fact have launched a new golden era of provocation. Whatever lip service the party pays them as "manifestations of socialist democracy," it recognizes these "informals" as a threat to its monopoly of power. On the surface the KGB merely complains that some are going too far or that foreign conspirators are trying to divert them into anti-Soviet activity, but below this surface the Chekists are undoubtedly acting to neutralize their danger—using their well-tested weapon of provocation.

Glasnost fosters provocation in another way, too. While opening up public debate about how to make the system work better, *glasnost* by its

---

†Soviet security authorities have since the 1960s admitted some of their earlier provocations but refer to them by other words—like "dangerous operations" to infiltrate enemy organizations and "to frustrate anti-Soviet activity, and to subvert it internally"(Ostryakov). They accuse internal enemies of using "provocation," however, as when describing the Georgian Republic leaders' "provocative" creation of a "nationalist group" (*Zarya Vostoka*, 16 and 21 April 1953, cited by Conquest, *Power and Policy in the USSR*, pp. 144–45). Harper and Row, N.Y. 1967

very permissiveness stirs up questions about the system itself: why the huge security forces? why the restraints on travel? why the remaining controls over information? why the repression of "other-thinking"? Gorbachev cannot admit that these restraints serve mainly to preserve the party's power, so he must answer as his predecessors did: by showing that "enemies" are threatening "socialism." His Chekists must produce ever-fresh examples of Zionist and German revanchist plots, more CIA dirty deeds, new cautionary tales of weak or "politically immature" citizens lured into the coils of "ideological subversion." And when someone steps beyond the limit and calls into question the party's exclusive right to rule, that person must be discredited as foolish, despicable, criminal, or treasonous. For such tasks the preferred tool is provocation.

Although Soviet provocation has done as much as massacre and torture, as much as the *agentura* or the special troops, to crush or paralyze opposition within the USSR, it remains little understood in the West. People safe in a democratic system may find it difficult to conceive that rulers would systematically use such hostile techniques against their own subjects. The very word "provocation" may divert Western attention, so different are its Western connotations from its Soviet ones. A typical Western dictionary, defining it as "summoning, challenging, stirring up," runs through three definitions of the verb "to provoke" before reaching the idea of incitement and then only in these domestic-sounding terms: "4. To incite (emotion, action, activity, etc.); to stir up (as to provoke a scene, a controversy, or anger)."[2] Here, by way of contrast, is the *first* definition in a Soviet dictionary:

> *Provokatsiya* (from the Latin provocatio—to call forth). 1. In capitalist countries—a system of struggle used by the ruling classes against the revolutionary movement, whereby the political police send into the ranks of the revolutionary organizations (or recruit from among the unstable members of these organizations) their own secret agents, who inform the police about the activities of the revolutionaries and the revolutionary organizations, betray the revolutionaries to the police, and also provoke the revolutionary organizations to take actions which could lead to their destruction.[3]

And this barely scratches the surface of the technique as the KGB has evolved it over seventy years.

Western rulers, too, have infiltrated and manipulated opponents. The practice of ancient Greek and Roman tyrants was recalled and refined by Machiavelli in Renaissance Italy and has been widely applied in the modern era. In republican France in 1880, for instance, the editor of an anarchist journal publishing instructions for making bombs turned out to be a police spy funded by the prefect of the Paris police. Indeed the universally used term *agent provocateur* comes from there and not from Russia. But provocation is a weapon of revolutionary struggle that tapered off as democratic societies offered legal outlets for opposition.‡ In Russia, however, tsarist absolutism stood rigid, and the only form that party politics could take was revolutionary plotting. It was in that dark and exotic environment that the seeds of Soviet provocation were sown and germinated—to grow, after the Bolsheviks took power, into new and monstrous forms that would have been unthinkable to the tsarist police.

The Seeding and Flowering of Soviet Provocation

It was to cope with the growing illegal party activity toward the end of the nineteenth century that the tsarist government formed a new police organization, Okhrana, "protector" of the tsar. By trial and error its operatives learned that "the only efficient way to be informed of the enemy's intentions" was to work inside the enemy's own organizations, and so they adopted this means as "the main part of the Okhrana's activity."[4] And it worked. As late as January 1917 Lenin in Zurich thought that he would probably never live to see revolution in Russia, and had the war not finally exhausted the country he would probably have been right. Certainly no revolution could be expected from the actions of the revolutionary parties, for all of them had been paralyzed by Okhrana provocation.

Lenin's organizations were no exception. When the Social Democrats tried to hold an organizing conference in Bialystok in 1902, a tsarist police spy in their midst betrayed them and the entire committee was arrested. When they met the next year in Brussels, the police spy Jakob Zhitomirsky was among the important delegates. At their congress in London in 1907 at least three of the delegates were tsarist agents—and Stalin perhaps made a fourth.[5] In 1908 Lenin started up his newspaper *Proletary* in conjunction with the Kommissarov couple, who had already helped him to smuggle arms into Russia—and both were police spies. To smuggle his secret revolutionary literature, Lenin used his man Brendinsky—a tsarist plant. From his exile Lenin issued guidance and support to his organizations inside the country—in Moscow headed by four Okhrana spies, in St. Petersburg by a committee of seven of whom three were tsarist agents. His chief representative in Russia, sometimes called "Lenin's deputy," the man who headed the Bolshevik fraction in the

‡In areas where terrorists conspire today against established order, similar techniques are undoubtedly used by both sides—but episodically and not as a matter of established government practice.

Fourth Duma in 1912, was Roman Malinovsky—later uncovered as a police spy. To evade the attention of Okhrana agents, Lenin called his 1912 conference in an unusual site, Prague—but of the fourteen delegates who came, two were tsarist spies. When in that same year he founded in St. Petersburg the first legal Bolshevik daily newspaper, *Pravda,* to campaign for the election to the Fourth Duma, one editor (Miron Chernomazov) was secretly collaborating with the Okhrana while another (that same Malinovsky) was a contributing editor. While the Okhrana was thus effectively "editing" *Pravda,* they chose to close down another Bolshevik paper, *Nash Put,* and arrest its editors—who had been betrayed to them by its editor, Malinovsky. As the Bolshevik historian Grigory Zinoviev (himself later to fall victim to provocation) wrote in his history of the party, "At that time there was not a single local organization into which some provocateur had not crept. Every man regarded his comrade with suspicion, was on his guard against those nearest to him, did not trust his neighbor."[6]

This was more than mere penetration—and this is the significance of "provocation": the Okhrana was, effectively, in charge. It could and did decide which of Lenin's men would remain free and which would go to jail. A famous incident, a bank robbery in 1907, caused an intraparty scandal and might have cost Lenin the party leadership if the tsarist police had wanted him out. As it happened they did not, because his policy of splitting the Marxist movement chanced to coincide with their own. The Okhrana decided whether to allow Lenin's propaganda to circulate and what to let his party do inside the country. The Okhrana was in a position to propose actions that (succeeding or failing, as the Okhrana decided) could discredit one man or promote the fortunes of another or divide the party against itself. (Malinovsky and others, for example, provoked splits in the party's fraction in the Duma.) Thus the Okhrana effectively decided the fate and direction of the whole Socialist Democratic party inside Russia. If Lenin succeeded in anything in Russia before the tsar fell— which is doubtful—it was because the Okhrana permitted it, for its own purposes.

Lenin and Dzerzhinsky learned the extent of this disaster when the tsar fell. The Provisional Government set up an Extraordinary Commission to investigate tsarist repression (Lenin was one of the 59 witnesses who testified) and published lists of about 140 police spies who had penetrated the various political parties. After seizing power the Bolsheviks enjoyed the rare experience of publishing documents that portrayed for posterity their own revolutionary movement—as seen through the reports of police spies within it.

But Dzerzhinsky's Chekists learned more than that; they also learned the Okhrana's methods and could begin their own provocations from the point of high technical expertise that the Okhrana had reached.§ They did not come to these techniques as wide-eyed innocents, of course; they had long worked under conspiratorial conditions and had run their own spies within other revolutionary parties (including the Mensheviks and Socialist Revolutionaries), the tsarist-sponsored workingmen's societies, and the tsarist armed forces. Only weeks after seizing power they began turning these spies, and new ones, to provocation. A year later the first People's Commissar of Internal Affairs, Grigoriy Petrovskiy, was complaining that the Chekas were seeing what they wanted to see—conspiracies and threats everywhere—and when they couldn't, they would manufacture them.[7]

Lenin's world outlook inclined him naturally to these techniques. His philosophy of provocation can be traced in his later, famous pamphlet "Left-Wing Communism—An Infantile Disorder." In this, he exhorted Communists abroad to show flexibility in dealing with their enemies and not to engage them in open battle before victory was prepared. They were not to shun the governments, parties, parliaments, labor organizations, or other institutions of the hated and hostile bourgeoisie but, rather, should join and destroy them from within. This work had to be systematic: "resorting to all sorts of stratagems, manoeuvers and illegal methods, to evasions and subterfuges, in order to penetrate [them], to remain in them." By working within, "accelerating the inevitable friction, quarrels, conflicts," they could put the "class forces hostile to us . . . at loggerheads with each other" and weaken them on the way toward their "complete disintegration."

When they took power and began systematic provocation against their opponents, the Leninists enjoyed two great advantages over their tsarist forerunners: their Communist morality and a solid foundation of mass terror. Supported by an ideology ordaining that good is what helps the cause and evil is what opposes it, they would not be hampered by the moral compunctions that beset the "bourgeois" Okhrana. Now provocation could make cruel sacrifices of men and women and secrets, spend sums of money, involve numbers of people, and draw on facilities on a scale never before imagined.

Terror was a help, too. Lenin had taken careful note of the one overwhelming flaw in the Okhrana's work: the leniency of tsarist punishments. The revolutionary Vera Zasulich, for example, had shot the police

§The principles of provocation laboriously worked out over years of trial and error by the Okhrana chiefs were contained in secret Okhrana instructions, dated 1907 and updated in 1916, entitled "Instructions for the Organization of Internal Observation." The latter term still persists in Soviet usage, distinguishing "external" work like street surveillance from "internal" penetration.

chief—yet a tsarist court acquitted her. The revolutionary Vera Figner, implicated in the assassination of Tsar Alexander II, was arrested but not severely punished and survived to incite, the very next year, the assassination of a police chief in Odessa. Then, after being betrayed by a police provocateur, she was condemned to death; but the tsarist authorities commuted her sentence, and she continued from her prison cell to offer important encouragement to revolutionaries. Though all of the future leaders of the Communist state were betrayed and arrested (some several times) every one of them was released or so lightly held that he could escape and carry on the preparations for revolution. This leniency was a mistake that Lenin would not make. As soon as he took power he set out systematically to destroy not only actual opponents but also whole categories of people he thought likely to oppose him—and many innocents for good measure. After that his provocations, directed against cowed survivors, were immeasurably more effective.

Lenin and his men expanded the dimensions of provocation, too. Whereas the Okhrana had simply manipulated existing organizations of real revolutionaries, the Bolsheviks invented their own organizations to enwrap and entrap people who had never taken (or perhaps even contemplated taking) a hostile step. Their Marxist-Leninist doctrine opened whole new horizons for creative provocation. The ideology of "class struggle" and "historical forces" spawned potential, hypothetical, hidden, even "subjective" enemies. The ideology endowed them with the spectral form of conspiracies, movements, fronts, forces, blocs, centers, and groups, manipulated by such vaporous sponsors as "imperialism," "capitalism," "colonialism," "reaction," and "counterrevolution." To these abstractions were attributed scheming brains, lying tongues, hairy paws with sharp claws wielding weapons and handing out filthy money to tools and minions and lackeys and dupes. "Foreign interests" and "monopolies" probe with slimy tentacles the chaste and defiant body of "socialism." The "forces of hate" send out their wreckers, diversionists, saboteurs, propagandists, warmongers, and spies to turn the naif, the parasite, the hooligan, and the weakling against the "people," the "toiling masses," the "builders of communism." Now the rulers could weave "enemy centers" from threads of pure fantasy.

And no longer would provocation be limited to police and security work. The Communists would apply its techniques—penetration, fabrication, misdirecting, dividing opponents against themselves—to their political aims at home and to their foreign policies as well.

From the 1920s onward the Western public saw the Soviet leaders condemn, in successive show trials, members of socialist parties, industrial managers, founding fathers of their own party, and leading members of foreign Communist parties. Westerners saw these people accused of treason, sabotage, and murder on behalf of conspiratorial "centers" sponsored by an unlikely parade of "imperialist" states. Even when they did not take all this at face value, many Westerners preferred to shrug off the whole spectacle as an obscure and passing phenomenon—refusing, or unable, to recognize that underlying these affairs lay a frame of mind and a permanent method of government.

The Individual as Target

Provocations aimed against individuals like Pervukhin may superficially resemble the "sting"-type entrapments of Western police. But when endowed with the unlimited resources of all-powerful rulers, when guided ruthlessly, and when used day to day to silence or destroy anyone who opposes the rulers' will, they become a different—and devastating—thing.

So commonly is provocation used that every KGB officer in internal security work can supply examples like mine of Pervukhin. Former KGB Maj. Aleksey Myagkov, who worked in the 1970s in the OO/KGB of the Soviet Army in East Germany, wrote that a KGB general had exhorted his department "if you can't find any [anti-Soviets], then create them." This was not difficult, Myagkov noted, because "every Soviet citizen who was even slightly dissatisfied could, given the desire, be transformed into a violent enemy of communism and the Soviet regime." The majority of his unit's counterintelligence successes were, in fact, invented. KGB operations transformed into "enemies" and "socially dangerous elements" officers who had merely been put on report for listening to Radio Free Europe, for example, or for criticizing some aspect of the regime.[8] When the Kremlin for its own campaigns wanted evidence of Zionist conspiracies, the KGB was ordered to step up its work against Jews; and down the line, Myagkov, like all KGB security officers, had to show results—despite the fact that the division for which he was responsible was an elite one which admitted no Jews. Myagkov did what he could: he looked for Jewish wives. He could find only one, and she had no blemish on her record. But Myagkov's KGB boss—his career at stake—was categorical: "You must find something. We must remove her from the German Democratic Republic within a month." Happily for the KGB, the woman was friendly with an East German shop assistant. This could be construed as a breach of the rules of conduct and, because a store was involved, could be made to look like "speculation." The KGB called the wife in for a "chat" and, using threats and false promises, got her to "admit" something along these lines, enough to get her and her husband transferred to the Soviet Far East. Myagkov's unit could mark up another success.

In an incident that occurred in 1977, provocation can be perceived on several levels. A Soviet parapsychologist named Valery Petukhov asked an American newspaper correspondent in Moscow, Robert Toth of *The Los Angeles Times,* to carry out to the West a paper on his specialty. On the street after Petukhov had handed it over, plainclothesmen jumped from a car, grabbed Toth, and took him to a police station where an official from the Soviet Academy of Sciences "happened" to be on hand to certify that the Petukhov manuscript contained secret scientific information.[9] After being interrogated and held for a time—and publicly branded as a spy— Toth was permitted to leave the USSR without formal charges. So far this appears to be just another blatant provocation of the kind that the KGB routinely uses to get rid of overly observant Westerners, to inhibit other journalists, and to discourage anyone tempted to smuggle manuscripts out of the country. But this particular provocation had deeper aims; its real target was the dissident Anatoly Shcharansky, for whom Toth had translated innocent material, and a whole group of Jews trying to leave the country. The regime was preparing a show trial to discredit Shcharansky (and by association the others) by making him out to be a traitor. No fewer than seven KGB provocateurs had been inserted into this milieu.[10] One of them, Dr. Sanya Lipavsky, gave them medical advice and joined them in signing letters and protests—while, on the side and unbeknown to the group, he was getting into secret contact with CIA in Moscow and offering secret information on Soviet science. It took the CIA only a few months to recognize Lipavsky's game and draw away from him, but that was enough for the KGB to have manufactured a link between Shcharansky and the CIA. Under "socialist legality" it made no difference that Shcharansky had had no contact whatever, direct or indirect, with Western intelligence or that Toth had translated nothing more "secret" than reports on the regime's refusal to let Jews emigrate. Shcharansky was convicted in 1978 of espionage and sentenced to fifteen years' loss of liberty. He served nine years before being allowed to emigrate to Israel in 1986.**

** Petukhov was undoubtedly a trusted man of the regime and had been allowed to serve in the Soviet delegation to the World Health Organization in Geneva. (It was alleged, in fact, that he had been called back from there because the KGB needed him to infiltrate a group of people meeting regularly to discuss parapsychology.) Petukhov's credentials as a provocateur were subsequently confirmed. His boss at the Academy of Sciences had suspended him and promised punishment for trying to pass material to the West—but a high official called to tell him that, far from being a traitor, Petukhov was a hero and must be kept at his job. Two days after Toth left the USSR, Petukhov was awarded the coveted

To prevent escape from Soviet rule the KGB supplements its border obstacles with provocations as elaborate as that employed against Pervukhin. It started early. Soon after the Bolsheviks seized power, its agents were offering illicit documents and escape routes to would-be emigrants and leading them not to freedom but to jail cells. And so it continues. In August 1982 Ruslan Ketenichev wanted to emigrate to America; because he lived in Nalchik in the Caucasus, far from any American consulate, he inquired by telephone. With unusual solicitude a "consular employee" came to meet Ketenichev and told him that he could earn his visa by collecting information on certain military installations. When Ketenichev brought some, he signed him up to work for the CIA. Ketenichev was quickly "uncovered," of course, but it was no victory of KGB over CIA; CIA had never heard of him, and he had been in KGB hands from the beginning. Presumably alerted by phone taps or by one of those Soviet nationals who are employed by foreign consulates, perhaps using its switchover phone system that can reroute calls from any given telephone number, the KGB set out to entrap Ketenichev—and its success was crowned when he was sentenced to ten years in strict-regime camps. [11]

Such use of the "false flag" of Western intelligence services is a time-honored technique of Soviet provocation. KGB operatives sometimes dress as Westerners and loiter in the tourist sections of Moscow near their Western-made cars with Western license plates, waiting like spiders in a web for an approach by Soviet citizens infatuated with Western things and manners. By leading them into criminal action the KGB can demonstrate that Western "ideological subversion" is at work, drawing "weaklings"—people described by Andropov as "morally drained and politically spineless persons, avid for sensation," and "inexperienced and inadequately conditioned, confused youth"—onto the road to treason.

If a Soviet citizen, no matter how loyal, travels abroad or is to get access to secrets, he may encounter provocation as part of his screening process. He actually expects it. When the ship's captain Vladil Lysenko, after many months ashore, was about to go to sea again in the 1970s, an acquaintance wrote from a prison camp asking him, while in a foreign

---

title of "distinguished medical worker"—apparently for "playing a major part in revealing an international espionage agent" (*London Daily Telegraph*, 14 November 1977, cited by Shindler, p. 229).

The smell of provocation also surrounds other incidents that occurred just before and after Shcharansky's arrest in March 1977. An explosion in the Moscow subway in January was quickly ascribed, by regime-sponsored rumor-spreaders like Viktor Louis, to "dissidents" and "Zionists." A fire, rumored to be sabotage, broke out in February in the Rossiya Hotel where Shcharansky and his friends had met in mid-1975 with visiting American senators. This was the background against which the KGB staged the provocation against Robert Toth in June 1977.

port, to mail letters for him to the Czechoslovakian and Yugoslav party chiefs asking them to help establish his innocence. But Lysenko, aware of the practice of provocation and knowing that the mailing would violate Soviet law, simply handed the letter over to his office security man, whose reaction was a tacit admission that he had launched it. [12] The international tournament chess player Lev Alburt, after trips to the West, would be asked by his friends why he had come back. "I thought maybe they were KGB," he said later, "so I always said I liked it at home." [13]

So widespread is such provocation, in fact, that a friend has hardly to do more than make an unusual or suggestive remark before a Soviet citizen asks himself, "Has he been sent to say this? Is he testing my loyalty?" He is likely to recall that he was recently warned against spies in his trade union, party, or Komsomol meeting—where campaigns on "vigilance" never end—and report the incident to the authorities.

Manipulation of Groups

A new target for provocation was created by Gorbachev's reforms: those "informal" associations that sprang up in thousands and, by the late 1980s, were posing a threat to the party's monopoly of power. Politburo member Chebrikov warned that "independent, so-called informal organizations pose a great danger" and that some of them, "influenced by extremists," were doing "great harm." Ominously, he linked them with foreign subversion. Foreign spy centers are trying, he said, "to stimulate the organization in our country of illegal, semilegal, and even legal formations which would operate at their bidding. To do this they look for individuals hostile to our society, promote their organizational cohesion, and provide them with moral and material support, pushing them toward direct struggle against the Soviet state and social system." [14]

"We shall allow no one to undermine or weaken the foundations of our socialist system," warned a republic KGB chief about informal organizations in the Baltic states. [15] The Chekists would not fail to use provocation to discredit separatist movements and to prepare the justification for a crackdown when these organizations become too dangerous.

One could detect signs of this in the late 1980s. In Armenia a "Karabakh Committee" had risen to represent the interests of Armenians in recovering the territory of Nagorno-Karabakh from the neighboring Soviet republic of Azerbaijan. The authorities felt threatened and amid the disturbances of late 1988 arrested the committee's leaders. Thereupon an anonymous letter was received by the KGB in Armenia ostensibly from the Karabakh Committee, threatening "mass terror"—using US-made

Stinger missiles—if the detained men were not released. [16] Here the heavy hand of the KGB was visible, laying the groundwork for violent reprisals.

A blatant example was the work of the far-right anti-Semitic organization called *Pamyat* (Memory), whose members, wearing black shirts and favoring fascist-style symbols, were stirring up hatred against Jews in published articles and public meetings—somehow immune from punishment under the constitution and other laws forbidding incitement on racial grounds. No doubt Nathan Sharansky was right to say that *Pamyat* was being "allowed to assault Jews, doing the KGB's dirty work without its reflecting on the regime."[17] In November 1988 a court gave only a suspended sentence to a man discovered to have been the writer of anonymous letters, purportedly from *Pamyat,* threatening violent attacks on party and government bodies in Leningrad.[18]

But much more can be forecast by looking back at the regime's manipulation of such supposedly "oppositional" groups in the past.

As soon as they won power the Bolsheviks began secretly manipulating rival revolutionary parties and groups of anti-Bolshevik army officers through Chekist agents in their midst. They insidiously encouraged them to merge with others and form larger, more influential organizations, while their real aim was to extend the range of the VCheka's eyes and ears inside such organizations. Already by early 1918—i.e., within weeks after taking power—"the Cheka organs were regularly undertaking such dangerous operations."[19]

Lacking such hostile groups, the KGB creates them. In the spring of 1918, within days after the British landed troops in Murmansk to protect their interests in northern Russia, the VCheka sent two provocateurs to draw the British diplomatic agent Robert Bruce Lockhart into contact with "anti-Bolshevik" elements. Today the Soviets admit this, taking pride in their own skill.[20] But at the same time, blithely overlooking their admission that they themselves had instigated it, they point to this so-called "Ambassadors' Plot" as a prime example of capitalist-imperialist efforts to destroy the Bolshevik regime.

By at least as early as December 5, 1920, this kind of provocation had become official policy: Dzerzhinsky issued a secret order to his Chekists on that date: "in order to detect foreign agencies on our territory, organize pretended White Guard associations."[21] That policy has been reaffirmed again and again since then. In the 1970s my old friend KGB Maj. Gen. Sergey Bannikov, as deputy chairman of the KGB, issued a formal training manual instructing KGB officers in this traditional practice. Secret and for KGB eyes only, his manual instructed his younger colleagues to "ideologically destroy" and "disintegrate" their opponents by "preparing material for publicly disarming [them], by measures to split and destroy groups and to isolate individual activists." Bannikov did not need to use the taboo word "provocation"; his readers knew what he meant. In the best traditions of the past he recommended that KGB-controlled penetration agents stir up disagreements within these groups of enemies; that they seize control of the groups (by getting these penetration agents into the top positions); that they compromise prominent members in the eyes of their colleagues (one way would be to suggest that they were working secretly for the KGB)—and so forth for several pages.[22]

In every group of potential enemies the Chekists recruited or inserted their agents. Out of eight delegates to a conference of the Neo-populist Party in 1921, at least five were Cheka agents.[23] This sort of coverage continued through the decades that followed. To neutralize Trotsky's influence in the Soviet Communist Party after he was exiled to the West in the late 1920s, Stalin's Chekists infiltrated and manipulated the organized Trotskyite movement in the West. Mark Zborowski insinuated himself into the "International Secretariat" that Trotsky's son, Leon Sedov, ran for him in Paris, became Sedov's deputy, arranged the theft of the secretariat's archives, and probably set up Sedov's murder.†† Provocateurs practically paralyzed the Trotskyite movement. "By skillful maneuvers and ingenious tricks, they were able to transform the inevitable political differences into sterile quarrels and personal struggles, while morally and physically liquidating both the revolutionary leaders and, once their mission had been accomplished, their own agents."[24]

In response to Dzerzhinsky's order, dozens of mythical organizations came into being. One of these, the "Trust," has become well known in both Western and Soviet writings. For many years the Soviet leaders claimed to have cunningly infiltrated a monarchist resistance organization, but in the 1970s they admitted that they themselves had created it.[25] This shadow organization sent out to the West an ostensible Soviet trade official named Yakushev to establish contact with emigre leaders and Western intelligence services (notably the British, French, Polish, and Estonian, but also the Finnish and others). He succeeded in enlisting their support for this "anti-Bolshevik resistance movement" and for six years couriers (some unaware of the OGPU's control of their organization) moved in and out of the USSR, meeting Western contacts in Finland, Poland, and Paris.

---

††Sedov died unexpectedly while being treated in a Paris hospital in 1938; and although murder was never proved, I heard inside the KGB that our operatives had indeed liquidated him.

It would be a mistake to think, because Trust has become celebrated, that it had some unique quality. It was one provocation among others, the one that enmeshed and exploited monarchists (and not the only one, at that). Similar ones attacked political parties like the Mensheviks, Socialist Revolutionaries, and Constitutional Democrats; groups of intellectuals and philosophers who kept in touch with friends in emigration; the church hierarchy of every denomination; and "nationalists" inside and outside the country, with a "line" of provocation covering each political tendency within each major ethnic subdivision—Ukrainians, Cossacks, Armenians, Georgians, Central Asians. Fragmentary information on at least two dozen "lines" has become known in the West through the years.‡‡

The Chekists successfully repeated the pattern again and again through the years. Take as examples one case that ran into the 1950s and another that ended in about 1980.

From a remnant of the wartime Home Army in Poland, Soviet State Security (helped by its Polish satellite service) created in 1947 an ostensibly anti-Communist resistance movement calling itself Freedom and Independence (its Polish language acronym was WiN). A veritable carbon copy of Trust, WiN sent a trusted member westward across the border to contact Polish exile organizations in London and through them the British and American intelligence organizations. Inside Poland, WiN attracted to its ranks—and thus exposed and incriminated—Poles with the courage and convictions to stand up to their new masters. For five years couriers passed in and out of Poland, among them some unwitting dupes thinking they were really fighting communism and some provocateurs with orders to stay out and implant themselves in the Western organizations. Western services parachuted in arms, money, radios, and codes in preparation for the eventuality of an East-West war, while WiN passed innocuous or misleading information out to the West. At the end of 1952 the entire secret organization was exposed in a blast of publicity in Warsaw and Moscow—to the dismay of its Polish state security managers who ill understood Moscow's peremptory orders to explode it.[26] What they couldn't know was that at this moment Stalin was planning a blood purge of his Kremlin rivals and needed this public evidence of Western intelligence activity that might be amalgamated with his charges against them. (He was simultaneously closing out a similar provocation in the

‡‡A source from inside the OGPU in 1927 reported that he had heard that at least forty or fifty lines of provocation were active in addition to Trust. This source was the provocateur Opperput, when "revealing" (for OGPU purposes) that the OGPU controlled Trust—but his report is credible.

Ukraine for the same purpose.) Thus, when two weeks later Stalin's press announced the "Doctors' Plot," it said that evidence was in hand showing the plotters' connections with Western intelligence.

Thus the KGB was following well-grooved tracks when in the 1970s it hit once again at the prominent emigre organization *Nationalno-trudovoy Soyuz* (National Labor Alliance, or NTS) that for decades had been the target of its infiltrations, defamations, murders, and kidnapings. This time, too, just as in the earlier Trust and WiN provocations, the Chekists sent out a Soviet official who professed discontent. He agreed to help NTS smuggle its literature into the USSR and later, when he came out to the West again, reported that he was now united with other disaffected Soviet citizens in Moscow, led by middle-level Soviet government functionaries. Happily they, like he, had the opportunity to make official trips to the West, and so over the following years they brought out telephone books and other useful (but not secret) information, while claiming to be distributing antiregime tracts in Moscow. They asked NTS to send a leader into Moscow for meetings, to arrange regular courier runs, to send them guns, and to unite them with its other cells inside the USSR. Although wary, of course, the NTS pursued these contacts for more than ten years, until about 1980. [27]

So versatile is the technique of provocation that the Kremlin rulers are likely to put it to work when and if they need to reverse Gorbachev's tolerant policies. To those Westerners who doubt that the Soviet people could ever be made to accept or rationalize a return to the harsh repressions of the past, an ominous precedent lies in a grandiose provocation of the 1920s: the so-called "war scare."

In the first half of 1927 Stalin was getting ready to wrench Soviet history into a new direction—by bringing to an abrupt end the *perestroika*-like New Economic Policy, by forcing all farmers into collectives, by accelerating the buildup of heavy industry, and by eliminating his rivals Trotsky, Zinoviev, and Bukharin. These drastic measures were sure to raise opposition not only within the leadership but also from the population. So Stalin whipped up a near-panic fear of imminent aggression from the West—and succeeded in doing this in a period when nothing really threatened the world's peace. To this end he amalgamated coincidental events with Chekist provocations. The real happenings (in no sense threatening war, of course) included a British police raid on the Soviet trade mission in London in May 1927 (which had caused a break in diplomatic relations) and similar raids a few days later by the Chinese authorities in Shanghai and by the Germans in Berlin. Then someone assassinated the Soviet envoy in Warsaw. The French expelled the Soviet ambassador from Paris. Into the bubbling pot were thrown train accidents (in one of which a senior Chekist was killed and two others injured), fires, and an explosion in an artillery storehouse in the Leningrad Military District. Stalin presented these unconnected events as evidence of accelerated "imperialist sabotage." To heighten this impression he instigated or fabricated others with the aid of Chekist operatives inside anti-Soviet organizations in the West. Within the space of a few weeks in the spring and early summer of 1927, a sabotage team from Poland was "captured" just before it could blow up a factory in Tula; a "plot" to plant explosives in the Business Club in Leningrad was discovered; would-be bombers under foreign orders "surrendered" just before they were to blow up military storehouses in the Kiev area; State Security "uncovered just in time" a scheme supposedly hatched by a British official to blow up the Bolshoy Theater during the celebration of the tenth anniversary of the October Revolution; at least three British spy rings were (simultaneously) "discovered"; other spies, infiltrated over the border from Latvia and Finland by Russian emigre organizations, were "caught" before they could carry out their instructions to blow up power plants and to poison workers' food in Leningrad; and similar would-be infiltrators were cut off in Central Asia. And into this brew the Chekists threw the Trust itself.

By this time Trust's end was at hand anyway; several Western intelligence services had finally tumbled to it. Now the "war scare" offered an opportunity to get some mileage out of its inevitable termination. So the OGPU staged the "defection" to Finland of one of its principal agents, Opperput, "confessing" OGPU control of Trust and of himself. The OGPU's aim, he told the West, had been to prevent sabotage; now he urged Trust's Western supporters to make up for lost time. Just now the Soviet regime would be particularly vulnerable to violent action, he claimed, and to expiate his past sins he volunteered himself for a sabotage mission. The emigre organizations fell into the trap and sent in some parties of saboteurs. All failed in their missions and all were captured by the OGPU—and all fed the fires of Stalin's "war scare."§§

By July Stalin was able to assert publicly that "the threat of a new imperialist war against the USSR" was nothing less than "the main question of the time." He cited some of the above events to show that the

§§Opperput and others were reported killed but only after being separated from their companions; no one could confirm it. One group "succeeded" in getting into the headquarters building of the OGPU itself to bomb it—and Soviet histories (and some Western ones) have duly reported this as an event of the time. The bomb (according to which report one reads) either killed one or two Chekists, or caused little damage, or (as a recent Soviet historian stated) did not go off at all—or there were two separate attempts. Much more likely, the incident was pure fiction.

danger was so real and immediate that the country must immediately "strengthen its defensive capacity, raise its national economy, improve industry." Anyone opposing these policies must be practically a traitor, he suggested, referring to "our wretched opposition and its new attacks on the party in the face of the threat of a new war."[28]

Provocations have also justified the Kremlin's military aggressions and its absorptions of neighboring countries. In the 1980s the world watching Afghanistan became familiar with Soviet charges of meddling by "imperialists" and "foreign centers"—the same charges Lenin had used to justify his invasion and absorption of Armenia, Georgia, Azerbaijan, the Ukraine, and Byelorussia (and attempts to do the same in Poland, Estonia, Latvia, Lithuania, and Finland). With similar accusations, supported by provocation, Stalin justified the Soviet occupations in 1939–40 of Poland, Bessarabia, and the Baltic states. After their military forces rolled over Eastern Europe in 1944 and 1945, the Soviet leaders mounted provocations to discredit and weaken political opposition to their rule. (WiN, the copy of Turst, was one of scores of these.) To consolidate the power of their Communist puppets they provoked or fabricated criminal conspiracies by non-Communist politicians. And then, using evidence invented or staged, they removed from power "nationalist" Communist leaders such as Kostov in Bulgaria, Rajk in Hungary, and Slansky in Czechoslovakia.

To justify the invasion of Czechoslovakia in 1968, the Kremlin sought to demonstrate that NATO countries were planning hostile action. On July 12, two days before a Warsaw Pact meeting was to discuss the Czechoslovak situation, a secret cache of American-made weapons was "discovered" by anonymous denunciation.*** The same day, *Pravda* announced that Soviet authorities had obtained a copy of an American "secret plan" for overthrowing the regime in Prague. A Soviet Politburo member, the Ukrainian Pyotr Shelest, accused the Czechoslovaks of printing and distributing leaflets in the border areas of the Transcarpathian Ukraine demanding its separation from the USSR.[29]

Provocation operations abroad are today directed against the organiza-

---

***A Czechoslovak team during those months of relative independence investigated the discovery and found that the provocation had been clumsily executed: these were World War II weapons packed in Soviet-made bags. This was an old trick even in Czechoslovakia; it had been used to justify the 1948 coup d'etat. As Communist-led special troops moved into Prague in February 1948 and the Communist-led police seized the non-Communist newspapers, the Communist-led Interior Ministry announced the "discovery" of secret documentary plans for a "reactionary coup." Local action committees took over authority (as a "defensive reaction"), and President Benes capitulated.

tions that oppose Soviet objectives: NATO politicians and intelligence services, Soviet Bloc emigre activists, and political-action groups and publicists. In the 1970s the KGB leadership instructed its field agencies anew "to penetrate the state, political, scientific and technical, and espionage centers of imperialist states [and . . .] the headquarters of international capitalist organizations with the aim of aggravating contradictions and difficulties occurring in their activities . . . to implant agents in emigre organizations abroad and to work towards their disintegration and ideological destructions, to give the enemy misinformation for political and operational purposes."[30]

The KGB has long been giving the West such "misinformation for political purposes." One of its favorite aims, pursued successfully for nearly seventy years, is to create illusions about factional struggles within the Soviet leadership. Already in 1921 the Chekist-controlled emissaries of the Trust were telling stories of growing anti-Bolshevism in the country and the rise of reformers in the hierarchy and conveying the impression that Western governments could help them by taking certain positions or refraining from active opposition or disruption inside the country. Modifying the line to fit changing times, the KGB has continued to hoodwink many Westerners, with a success that can be measured today by their unending analyses of conflicts between reformers and conservatives, hawks and doves, hard-liners and soft-liners, new generation and old, technocrats and party bureaucrats, and even between the military (or KGB) and the party. From such analyses often flow recommendations: to avoid rocking the boat, to make concessions to promote the Kremlin reforms, to avoid firm actions that might prove the hard-liners right. It is true, of course, that Soviet leaders disagree among themselves about how to cope with individual problems, but they have not been able to form stable groupings based on permanent attitudes or convictions, nor have they disagreed about objectives.

The West has been vulnerable to this misinformation largely because it lacked—and still lacks—information on the inside workings of Soviet rule. And this is a tribute to the Soviet success in controlling information, even in the era of "openness."

CHAPTER 20

Control of Information—and *Glasnost*

Renouncing Lenin's Legacy?

BY RELAXING CONTROLS OVER INFORMATION GORBACHEV OPENED A breach in the barrier of Leninist defenses. By the late 1980s things were being said and done which would have been unthinkable even in the first years of *glasnost*. Spokesmen for nationalities were openly calling for independence from Moscow, crowds were massing to demand changes, scholars were exposing crimes of the past, leaders were contradicting one another, private newssheets were spreading information unpalatable to the rulers, and individuals were criticizing the leaders and the system to foreign journalists. And all this was being tolerated, if sometimes deplored and threatened. The new Supreme Soviet even passed a law allowing any citizen to publish a newspaper or books, and forbidding prepublication censorship of the mass media. As a result, the pall of fear was lifting and the Kremlin rulers were exposing to criticism and discredit the very foundations of Communist rule: the ideology, the party's monopoly of power, and even the founder Lenin himself.

Gorbachev called up Lenin—who had promoted *"glasnost"* in his time—as a sort of godfather to these reforms; but to anyone who knew much about Lenin this sounded hollow and contrived, for Lenin saw free information as a threat to his power. Earlier, as a plotter against authority, he had himself assigned a central revolutionary role to newspapers and called them "more dangerous than bombs or machine guns." A small clandestine core of professional revolutionaries would pull the strings while using newspapers to inflame the masses with ideas and to organize them with practical advice on tactics and weapons. "The police will soon come to realize," Lenin wrote, "the folly and impossibility of applying judicial and administrative red-tape procedure over every copy of a publication that is being distributed by the thousands."[1] So, as soon as he had taken power, determined to establish "a government no one would overthrow," Lenin made sure that no one could do that to him. He started early; two nights before his coup his men confiscated and burned an issue of a liberal newspaper for its "libelous concoctions," and on the eve of the coup they seized the government's newspaper. The next day they took over all radio transmitters and printing presses and a day later abolished "bourgeois" newspapers, which Lenin called "slanderous" and "disobedient."*

Past tyrants had tried to deny the press to their opponents, but Lenin went further and made free expression a crime.† Within two months he had set up a Revolutionary Tribunal for the Press and had given it power to punish as "enemies of the people" anyone who might dare write or print words he disapproved of. It could impose fines on them, confiscate their property, imprison them, or throw them out of their country. Among Lenin's thousands of victims were the leading poets of the time, Nikolay Gumilyov (shot as a "conspirator") and Alexander Blok, who was deprived of food and heating rations and, like many another creative spirit, died of cold and hunger. It was Lenin who began the long series of beatings and jailings, subtle tortures and killings of writers and thinkers that Stalin carried on so bloodily, Khrushchev so capriciously, and Brezhnev so systematically.

Lenin defended his policy with a sophism that served his successors for generations. "Of course," he wrote, "political freedoms could not be allowed to the enemies of socialism." Now that the "people" had taken control of the press and institutions of culture and education, it would be

---

*Decree of the Council of People's Commissars on the Press, 27 October (9 November, new style): "To be closed are only the following organs of the press: —press calling for open resistance or disobedience; —press which spreads discord by slanderous distortion of the facts, —press which calls for criminal acts, i.e., criminally punishable in nature. . . . This decree has a temporary character and will be abolished by special decree when normal conditions of social life have been established. As soon as the new order has been strengthened, all administrative influence on the press will be abolished and full freedom of the press will be established within the limits of the responsibilities under the widest and most progressive law." Signed, Lenin (Lenin i VCheka).

†Lenin was likely to see criminal conspiracy in even innocent-appearing printed material. His mindset could be seen when, for example, he interpreted a collection of philosophical commentaries on Spengler as "a literary coverup of a White Guard organization"—and referred the matter to State Security (Lenin i VCheka, no. 520, p. 557).

"against democracy" to allow others to have newsprint or freedom to publish. "To tolerate the existence of others' newspapers," Lenin flatly declared, "means to stop being socialist."[2]

This was no mere revolutionary egg-breaking. Although Lenin's decree on the second day of his power promised to remove all "administrative influences on the press" as soon as the new system was firmly established, he soon made them a permanent weapon of his internal warfare. By mid-1922 the civil war had been won, organized resistance had been crushed, non-Bolshevik newspapers eliminated, potential resisters terrorized, and the leading writers and philosophers of the old regime killed, jailed, deported, or cowed; no unauthorized person could get his hands on paper or presses to print opinions contrary to those of the ruling party. It was then that—far from removing his controls—Lenin tightened them. He already had an extensive system of censorship in operation, but to his taste it was insufficiently firm and comprehensive.‡ So on June 6, 1922, he caused the creation of an organization that would "bring together all types of censorship of printed works." This was Glavlit, which survives to the present day.

It is true, as Gorbachev says, that Lenin called for *glasnost*—but he did so while eliminating the possibility of being contradicted, and he had a special meaning for that word so often translated today as "openness." *Glasnost,* Lenin explained, would convert the press from reporting to educating; it would help "acquaint the masses with the need to work in a new way."§ This is true Leninism. "Information does not exist by itself," a

---

‡In 1919, Lenin had organized "the people's" monopoly over press and paper in the form of a "State Publishing House" (Gosizdat, or GIZ; later OGIZ) under his People's Commissar for "Enlightenment." Gosizdat would supervise all publishing, would decide which publishing houses and newspapers should exist (a power the tsar had renounced by 1906), and would tell them what they could and could not print. Gosizdat, through a "political department" in its Moscow head office, supervised branches in the provinces (all dominated by State Security). Publishers had to submit manuscripts, and none would be printed "if the manuscript is not authorized by the Political Department." Only a few small magazines or publishing houses were still not under full control, although of course they had to clear whatever they published (Lenin note of 6 Febraury 1922, in Tsvigun, p. 554). But this organization was diffused through provincial executives and failed to cover every kind of information.

§Lenin said in March 1918, "We must transform—and we shall transform—the press . . . from being a simple apparatus for the reporting of political news . . . into an instrument of economic reeducation of the masses, into an instrument for acquainting the masses with the need to work in a new way. The introduction of *glasnost* in this sphere will of itself be an enormous reform and will facilitate the enlistment of the broad masses in self-dependent participation in the resolution of the problems that concern primarily the masses."—Lenin, *Polnoye sobraniye sochinenyy,* vol. 36, 1962, p. 129, quoted in Radio Liberty Research, RL 14/87, 8 January 1987.

leading party ideologist later explained, "but is part of the system of ideological influence on the conscience of men." It is "an instrument of leadership, a means of education and control."[3]

Using that "instrument" relentlessly, the Kremlin rulers have required everyone to propagate the Leninist truth. According to the 1977 Constitution parents were supposed to rear their children "as worthy members of socialist society"[4]—and if they failed to do so, the state (by law) could take the children away from them.[5] Schools were, by decree, to "develop in students and youth a class approach to the phenomena and events of social life" and "a Marxist-Leninist world view." Textbooks and lectures from kindergarten to the highest technical level carried the single viewpoint. It was pounded in by newspapers, radio and television broadcasts, meetings at work or club, exhortations on billboards and banners. The leaders were trying to harness the creative talent of the country to this effort and regarded the writer as what Stalin called an "engineer of the soul."

To stop all this was surely not Gorbachev's intent when he first broke the intellectual shackles on journalists and creative artists; he was evidently hoping to make them work better. In 1986, for instance, he assembled some writers and pleaded with them to help, as patriots—but stressed that the party would keep the lead. He was not asking them what should be done but asking them to fight the things he said had ruined the economy: alcoholism, the loss of the will to work, mismanagement, resistance to change by bureaucrats.[6] His view was that the mass media should be "used" more fully, striving "for greater responsibility, for stronger discipline at work, for observance of socialist law and order, and against violations of the socialist principles and ethical standards of the Soviet way of life."[7]

He tried to keep a cap on the flow of information, hoping to let out just enough to serve the regime's purposes but not enough to threaten party rule. This was impossible, of course, and one could sense the leaders' bafflement as they attacked overeager editors and writers. The Politburo's chief ideologist criticized the "hysteria, sensationalism, the destructive direction of some statements, the inciting of passions, lack of regard for the facts, a deficit of professionalism."[8] Charges of "slander" and "distortions" became common, as did warnings that repression might become necessary.

Gorbachev may not have foreseen just how quickly and how far writers and journalists would go beyond the bounds, but he surely recognized the danger. Only a few years earlier the Kremlin leaders had seen, in the breakdown in Poland of Leninist controls of information, "clear confirmation of the incontrovertible truth that any relaxation of ideological and political education of the masses boomerangs with the inevitable onslaughts of bourgeois ideology." Such onslaughts, they asserted, come from "counterrevolutionary forces, supported morally and materially from outside," who aim "to disorient the masses, ideologically disarm and disorganize the Communist Party and remove it from the leadership of society, with the aim of seizing power in the country and creating conditions for the restoration of capitalism."[9] These same words, expressing these same worries, could be heard in the late 1980s as the leaders' concern grew over the "excesses" of press freedom. In late 1988 the party's top ideologist said that to publish the works of Aleksandr Solzhenitsyn "would undermine the foundations on which our present life rests."[10]

As *glasnost* approaches the outer limits of the masters' tolerance it is useful to recall just how wide and thick a blanket they had thrown—and could again throw—over contrary information. Their people were not to learn things "that can damage their interests,"[11] and the state must be protected—under *glasnost* just as before—against information that "contradicts its interests."[12] Things that were not "useful" to the people (the masters deciding what is useful, of course) were not to be published, nor things that contradicted "party principle" or might "serve the aims of bourgeois ideology." No information should be printed that contradicted "correct" scientific doctrine.[13] History could be presented from one angle only: "It is essential to oppose vigorously any attempts to reconsider from nonclass, nonhistorical positions any phenomenon, personality, or concept of the past."[14] Anything that is "based on lies" or not "truthful" (again, the masters deciding what is "true") was banned, along with information from "alien" or "enemy" sources.[15]

From such vague and sweeping principles sprang the guidelines for the censors, but what muzzled writers and editors was not so much the censors' detailed strictures as the make-believe world—supported by fear of violent repression—in which they were forced to operate. Who but a "tool of imperialism" would become "reconciled with bourgeois ideology" or "alien morality" and thus give comfort to a mortal enemy? Who in this warlike ambience would want to write "incorrect" or "useless" or "harmful" things, much less to leak a secret to the enemy at the gate? In this framework the vast horde of Soviet censors was practically redundant, serving only to offer a helping hand in the common defense. As the chief censor said of his men, "We do not invent these restrictions. . . . We are press workers and have common aims with the mass media."[16] Gorbachev or another Kremlin leader might tighten or loosen the censors' guidelines; but the doctrine, as long as it survives, cannot be reconciled with "openness."

How effectively did the regime suppress information prior to *glasnost?*

Well enough, even in an era of instant communications. You could measure its success in the halting, stumbling first years of a freer press. Few writers or intellectuals seemed able to articulate any attractive alternative to their repressive and inefficient system. They had long been taught not to question what they were told and had been denied the data and the experience to evaluate the information they got. Even if they discerned the hypocrisy in the official viewpoint (and it is safe to say that almost everyone did), it had hit them from so many angles and was so much a part of their daily lives that it could not fail to shape their thinking. This ideological saturation shaped the society itself, creating bizarre, unspoken conspiracies between writer and reader, teacher and pupil, boss and subordinate, friend and friend, parent and child, ruler and ruled—and made writers themselves the most effective of censors over their own work.

Mechanisms of Control: (1) Self-censorship

The writers, journalists, and editors who in the growing confidence of the late 1980s openly questioned the need for prior censorship—or indeed, any formal censorship organization at all—had a good point. In Hungary or East Germany no one could accuse the pre-*glasnost* press of indiscipline, yet these Soviet Bloc regimes had done without such an organization. In the USSR formal censorship seemed redundant; the writers were their own best censors.

They knew—had practically absorbed with their mothers' milk—what the regime would not permit. They were perfectly aware, too, what the regime could do to them if it came to suspect them of harboring dissident thoughts. In Stalin's day they could lose their life; after Stalin's death they still risked their livelihood, their children's future, their liberty, and their health by displeasing the rulers. Almost every writer and journalist of the pre-*glasnost* period admits to having carefully chosen his words. Censorship ran on fear: the writers' and the editors' fear of the rulers, the censors' fear of their bosses, and the rulers' fear of the writers and editors.

Mechanisms of Control: (2) The Unions

It was not enough that the party leadership controlled the paper and the presses, not enough that it cowed the writers; it still dared not leave writers to their own devices. It corralled them into collectives where it could control and guide them. The purpose—set out in their charters—of the Writers Union, the Literary Union, the Union of Journalists, and similar ones like the Union of Filmmakers was that of any other trade unions in the USSR: to make their members produce more and better, according to standards set by the leadership. Those standards were political, not aesthetic: the union (as its statutes specify) is designed to bring together "like-minded persons who are building communism" and to help them build communism usefully, militantly, and correctly.

The permanent secretaries of these unions were selected for their political conformity and obedience. They would arrange visits to the clubhouse by leading party and government officials, including Chekists, to exhort the writers. If a writer erred, the union would lead him back to the path: "The exacting demands of a spiritually healthy collective have helped those whose blunders and errors were not committed maliciously to mend their ways."[17]

This amounted to licencing writers and journalists. No one could get his work legally published unless he was a member, or had the approval, of the appropriate union. To be expelled from it (as were Solzhenitsyn, Pasternak, and scores of others) was to be cut off from any legal outlet. Until the advent of *glasnost* and the explosive creation of independent associations, writers were not even allowed to suggest breaking out of this enclosure.** From the mid-1960s onward, so many writers were expelled, forced to emigrate, or imprisoned that the survivors were mostly hacks and paid pens who needed no help from censors.

Mechanisms of Control: (3) The Editor

The party leaders have exercised a formidable control through editors, who have been their emissaries and watchdogs. The Central Committee (and regional party committees) have reserved the right to appoint the chief editors and managers of every newspaper, magazine, publishing house, radio and television station, and movie-making studio.[18] The committee would select the editor less for his skill or experience than for his disciplined loyalty, as attested by his party service and by a lifelong KGB dossier, and would assign him like a colonel to command a regi-

---

**When twenty-three of them asked permission in 1979 to publish their works in an uncensored anthology, to be called *Almanak Metropol,* all were blacklisted and two were expelled from the Writers Union. In 1980 seven more (including one of the expellees from the Almanak group) tried to organize an independent club to publish experimental work. The very day they delivered their request to the cultural department of the Moscow City Soviet, some were picked up on the street by plainclothesmen ostensibly "investigating a burglary," their apartments searched, and manuscripts confiscated (*International Herald Tribune,* 27 November 1980).

ment. The media are weapons, and the editor's job was to see that these weapons remain dangerous only to the leaders' enemies.

The editor's purpose has been not to inform or amuse but to exhort and explain. Before *glasnost* took hold in the late 1980s, he could not raise circulation, either; that was arbitrarily imposed by the party leaders. Their propaganda organs dished out ready-made material that the editor was not to cut or change, often telling him on which page it should appear and with what size pictures. The editor got guidance from handbooks, too, general ones for all editors and specific ones for his organization. That of the Tass Publishing House (confidential and published in only 350 copies) was exposed to the West in early 1986. Its twenty-five pages told its editors to print only what supports the aims of the party and to shape their articles to reinforce the decisions of the most recent Party Congress. Even human-interest stories aimed less to entertain than to promote the Soviet way of life. Articles describing the life of the land were to encourage laborers to work better and show how culture contributes to the national effort, and how the armed forces build character. The unity and friendship of different Soviet nationalities must be stressed. [19]

The editor's guidance was kept up to the minute. He was called to biweekly instructional (or ideological) conferences where officials (accurately entitled "instructors") from the party's propaganda department would tell him what is important and how to handle it and inform him of forthcoming decrees, campaigns, appointments, and visits. When something unexpected turned up, such as the Chernobyl disaster or riots in Armenia, the party would call editors together to instruct them on how to deal with it. (If not, they would wait to see how *Pravda* handled it.) These conferences played a disciplinary role, too, for the party instructor would tell about mistakes other editors had made—and each editor would remember predecessors and colleagues who had been fired, made destitute, or imprisoned. Thus the editor would keep his eyes directed not outward toward his readership but upward to the handful of people who held his personal fate in their hands; these were the only readers that counted.

Therefore it was surprising (and for the regime, troublesome) that there were still some independent and courageous editors in place when Gorbachev came along and encouraged editors to use their own initiatives. By the late 1980s some papers were taking on a distinctive flavor (even arguing with one another), livening up their pages with taboo subjects, and seeing their circulation double and redouble as the years went on, particularly after the regime removed its limitations on public subscriptions in the fall of 1988.

And the Kremlin tolerated their daring. In early 1989 some authoritative conservatives published in *Pravda* a denunciation of the magazine *Ogonyok*—calling it "a dirty foam on the new wave" of *glasnost*—for "distortions of history" and "falsification of culture and values." "It was a shock," said *Ogonyok*'s editor Vitaliy Korotich. "In the old days such a letter meant that the next day I would have to retire." Instead, ten liberal intellectuals publicly defended Korotich in a letter which, after *Pravda* refused it, was printed in *Ogonyok*, And Korotich continued his daring policies as his subscribership soared. [20]

Evidently the regime's censor at Korotich's elbow in the *Ogonyok* offices was working under new, more lenient directives. There is such a censor. With all those other restraints on the writer's pen and the editor's blue pencil, a Westerner might suppose that the Soviet regime needed no further censorship. But it relied (and relies) on redundancy, so Glavlit remains at its watchful post.

Mechanisms of Control: (4) Formal Censorship—Glavlit

The censorship institution that Lenin established in 1922 survives intact, despite *glasnost*. It is "just wishful thinking," said its chief in late 1988—when it was "under quite intensive fire from authors"—to suggest that its restrictions are no longer needed. [21]

But why not at least do away with prior censorship, Glavlit's chief was asked, and simply hold the press (and holders of secrets) responsible for any breach of security? (In fact, the tsar himself had done away with prepublication, preventive censorship as early as 1906.) The censorship chief's answer was categoric: "We have drawn a clear conclusion. Prior control is a more effective and less painful method of safeguarding state secrets." [22]

So the censors remained busily at work. Their organization is still called by its original, now outdated, acronym Glavlit†† but its official title is "Main Administration for the Preservation of State Secrets in the Press Under the Council of Ministers of the USSR." This title is misleading in at least four ways. First, protecting state secrets has been only a minor part of Glavlit's mission. Second, although it is "under" the Council of Ministers in a budgetary sense, it is primarily responsive to the direction of party leadership and of the KGB, which is not under the Council of Ministers. Third, its work is by no means limited to the press. It also screens "manuscripts, drawings, paintings, broadcasts, lectures,

††For its earlier designation as the Main *(Glavnoye)* Administration for the Affairs of Literature and Publishing.

and exhibits" plus films and video, both before and after they are made public.[23] Fourth, it does not censor the entire press: the official party press (including *Pravda*) is screened by elements of the CC CPSU's Propaganda Department.

Glavlit's central office is located in the heart of central Moscow close to the Kremlin, the CC CPSU building, and the KGB headquarters. Throughout the country it employed into the 1980s between 50,000 and 100,000 censors although its numbers were reduced in the mid-1980s.[24]

Some of these censors work in sections divided according to the subject matter they review, such as sociopolitical, politico-cultural, or economic, inside Glavlit's buildings in Moscow or the provinces. Other censors are scattered in newspaper offices, radio stations, film studios, and publishing houses, performing what is known as "local censorship" *(mestnaya tsenzura)* but reporting not to the institutions that house them but only to Glavlit directly. Glavlit has several other sections, of which the most important are departments for "evaluation" and "operations."[25]

The Evaluation Department reports periodically to the party apparatus, the Ministry of Culture, and the KGB, giving statistics and samples of the censors' interventions (excisions, revisions, rejections) and calling attention to individuals whose work has had to be censored. The Operational Department—which maintains routine liaision with the KGB and is staffed to a large degree by KGB active and retired officers—gets these reports and helps to identify (and to document cases against) writers who seem to be stepping out of line. In conjunction with the Evaluation Department it compiles the list of topics that are to be banned from publication.

Some of Glavlit's work was reduced under *glasnost,* but its cumbersome processes reflect the regime's deep concern. Take Radio Moscow, for example. Although much of the information it broadcasts has already been selected from prescreened Tass material, censors check it at least four and as many as seven times before it is broadcast. Nothing is transmitted live. Scripts are submitted for approval,‡‡ and later, during recording sessions, the speaker is monitored by an associate who vouches for the correctness of what has been said. After that, the tapes are submitted to a "recording service" for another review before being broadcast. Depending on the importance of the subject, several other "visas" may be required, perhaps even from KGB headquarters.[26]

Until *glasnost* lifted this heavy hand off some phases of movie-making and theater, the censor had to approve every screenplay before an inch of

‡‡After scripts and translations written by employees have been checked (and signed for) by an associate acting as editor, a copy is slipped into a slot in an unmarked fourth-floor door for approval before being recorded. Behind that door sit Glavlit's men.

film could be shot and took several more looks along the way before finally approving a film for release. (He often exercised his right to change plot or characters to make sure that heroes represented positive virtues and said nothing that might even imply criticism of the Soviet system.)§§

Glavlit does its censorship of books twice, before and after publication. Prior approval is called the "lit" and consists of a round or hexagonal stamp bearing the censor's personal number. Without this no printer in the USSR would dare run off even the first "signal copies." And that censor's number remains as part of the colophon in every Soviet book. With the lit, ten "signal copies" of the printing are run off and sent to the agencies whose permission is needed for publication, or whose postpublication review is required—including the KGB.***

Mechanisms of Control: (5) "Special Collections"

A long-standing instrument of information control came under fire from academics as their confidence grew under *glasnost*. In "special collections" in libraries, or "special storage facilities" run by Glavlit and the KGB, were kept vast numbers of foreign publications, archive copies of the Soviet press (history having been changed so often, past versions had to be hidden), writings by authors who had offended the rulers, and other nonsecret writings that they considered—for any capricious reason whatever—to be unsuitable for the eyes of their subjects. Only people with special authorization could refer to them and then only under conditions devised by the KGB.

The regime had in fact performed prodigious feats in consigning people and events to Orwellian memory holes. It was able to expunge—from library bookshelves, book indexes, encyclopedias, textbooks, and public records—references to Stalin, who for longer than a quarter of a century had been the sole leader, exalted in the pages of every work on science and economics as well as history. Later the KGB similarly succeeded in erasing the works of, and references to, Khrushchev, whose speeches and doings

§§The same cumbersome processes have deadened the processes of magazine and newspaper publishing. Articles involving military or space subjects require authorization not only from Glavlit but also from Glavpu, the Political Administration of the Army and Navy—and the censors were more likely to disapprove articles for what they deem "ideological" errors than for revealing any secrets.

***Of these copies, one goes to the censor who gave the earlier authority (so he can double check), two to the Lenin Library, one to the CC Propaganda Department, one (if appropriate) to the Culture Department of the CC CPSU, and another, depending on the subject, to the Ministry of Culture—and one to the KGB.

had filled the pages of ten thousand newspapers and magazines for a decade.

At the end of 1988 the chief censor reported that more than 7,500 book titles had been returned from "special storage" to general library stocks, leaving some 400 others—"mainly publications that stir up national discord, and also pornography." He thought it might be a "good idea" to catalogue all publications, including special collections, to let readers know what is available. Most foreign literature, previously restricted, would now be opened up, too. He admitted that the process was dragging and attributed that to technical difficulties. In fact, his statistics suggested that whole vast realms of knowledge were still being hidden.

Mechanisms of Control: (6) Keeping Information Out

In late 1988 the regime promised to let more information into the country—and confessed that until then it had systematically kept it out. Responding to the demands of scientific and technological establishments (and, to a lesser degree, of the public) for freer access to foreign publications, the censorship chief said that more foreign newspapers and magazines would be sold at regular kiosks not only in Moscow but in many other cities. "In addition to this, all scientific and technical, artistic and reference literature, arts publications, and many other types of books and periodicals will reach the addressee without impediment." Even "religious literature sent to private addresses" would be handled with less onerous procedures. Until 1985, he admitted, "the restriction of foreign literature for general use was the usual rule, but now it is a very rare exemption."[27] Such promises had been made before, however, and just how easily Soviet citizens could get their hands on foreign newspapers (and subscriptions) remained to be seen.

The regime has systematically repelled information at its borders. Just before *glasnost* it was confiscating every year—from travelers' suitcases and freight shipments at the borders—"tens of thousands of publications directed against Communist ideology and morality" and "great quantities of products of a hostile propaganda character."[28]

The regime systematically jammed foreign radio broadcasts until the fall of 1986 and continued to jam selectively until the end of 1988, when even the transmissions of Radio Liberty (the Russian-language emigre station based in West Germany) were allowed to pass unhampered. There were over two thousand jamming devices; every Soviet city of over

200,000 population had its own, while skywave jamming stations covered rural areas. In the years just before Gorbachev took power, the Soviet regime was spending more in jamming than the entire budget of the Voice of America.[29] In 1989 the American government urged the Soviets to dismantle the jamming stations "so that you can't start up again,"[30] and the Soviets claimed to have shifted the facilities to other uses. But some of them surely stand intact, ready to cut off foreign news again in times of crisis. The leaders recognize the danger of outside voices and for decades campaigned against Radio Liberty and Radio Free Europe, calling them "ideological tools" and "remnants of the Cold War" that employ "traitors to their homeland" who make "incendiary" broadcasts. They "deserve to be jammed," said Soviet spokesmen who for a time asserted that neither *glasnost* nor Soviet pledges at Helsinki would apply to them.[31]

During periods of crisis in the 1980s the Kremlin stopped automatic direct dialing to or from the USSR for months and funneled calls through old-fashioned telephone operators who could delay communications long enough to hook in the KGB.

To keep foreigners from learning about conditions in remote parts of the USSR the rulers have shut off areas to foreign travel and harassed foreigners during trips. They try to influence foreign journalists' and scholars' reporting on Soviet affairs by withholding (or granting) visas and travel permissions.

Abroad, too, the regime has worked to suppress information inside the country. KGB provocateurs have smuggled out manuscripts stolen from authors inside the country to sell them to foreign publishers in order to expose the author to prosecution—under laws introduced by the KGB itself. The KGB operative Viktor Louis, for example, sold Solzhenitsyn's *Cancer Ward* to the emigre press.[32] In 1974 the USSR signed the International Copyright Convention partly in order to earn hard currency by selling Soviet books abroad but also to prevent foreign publication of Soviet authors—and the Soviet Copyright Agency formed at that time has been headed by KGB officers. Its deputy director, KGB Col. Vasily Romanovich Sitnikov, earlier worked with me in KGB operations in Vienna.

The Soviet regime pays special attention to former Soviet writers who now enjoy, in emigration, the freedom of writing what they please and broadcasting into the USSR. It tries to intimidate them by threats and pressures against family members left behind and tries to infiltrate their circles to uncover and gain control of the channels through which literary works are smuggled into or out of the Soviet Union. KGB spies infiltrate the staffs of the radios; scores have been uncovered (or have gone home) after working in Radio Liberty or Radio Free Europe, for example. By sowing rumors and planting stories in the press and in books, the regime seeks to create dissension and to blacken the reputation of writers like Aleksandr Solzhenitsyn who are considered dangerous to the regime. In this as in so many other ways, the Kremlin depends on its KGB.

Mechanisms of Control: (7) Control of Printing Materials

The Leninist state has reserved for itself a total monopoly of printing presses and paper supplies. Thus party-disciplined bureaucrats are given the potent political weapon of choosing not only which books shall be printed but also the number of copies and the circulation of each periodical regardless of popular demand. The result has been tremendous printings of boring propaganda and severe shortages of worthwhile literature.

Any equipment that might mechanically reproduce words or pictures is controlled. Every typewriter is registered, and samples of its distinctive type are filed by the town MVD or in the case of institutions and enterprises by the KGB-run First Department. Periodically the staff goes around to each machine to type new samples, keeping up to date with any idiosyncracies the machine develops with the passing of time. These controls work. Iosif Chornobilsky, a citizen of Kiev, typed an anonymous appeal to the Soviet government protesting Soviet anti-Semitism. Someone took it to the West, where—fatally—it was reproduced in an obscure Detroit newspaper. Few Detroiters may have noticed, but the KGB did. The newspaper photo was enlarged, the typescript analyzed and investigated, and the typewriter located in the office of Chornobilsky's wife.[33] Chornobilsky's fate was not reported, but the law on anti-Soviet agitation would have sent him to prison for years.

Photocopiers flood the West—ever smaller, faster, simpler to operate, cheaper—but they are hardly known in the USSR. In the early 1980s it was estimated that were only about 20,000 photocopiers in the whole USSR, every one registered and most of them directly controlled and operated by KGB people in first (security) departments. In 1988 the regime issued a new law outlawing private possession of "duplication facilities" such as copiers and personal computers—and then in early 1989 began opening public photocopying centers. Clearly its fears had not diminished; when representatives of legitimate "informal" groupings asked to have their authorized literature photocopied, they were turned down.

The Hand of the KGB

This whole huge system of repressing information is dominated by the KGB.

Censorship was the Chekists' job for years before Glavlit was set up to help them. On the VCheka's very first day of existence, Dzerzhinsky took note of Lenin's desire that it "first and foremost pay attention to the press."[34] By the spring of 1918 the VCheka had taken over much of the power over the press that had orginally been exercised by the soviets; in March it required all newspapers to submit three copies to it, under penalty of closure,[35] and in May Dzerzhinsky ordered the Moscow City Soviet "to transfer all authority to the VCheka, the organ which knows most about all press matters and printing."[36]

Today the "safeguarding of state secrets" is one of the overt missions of the KGB, [37] and Glavlit, as always, is squarely within its domain. Glavlit's founding decree placed State Security officers in its leadership both at the center and in provincial offices.[38] For many years State Security directly footed Glavlit's expenses, and Glavlit censors reportedly worked in OGPU uniforms until the early 1930s.[39] The KGB grants clearances for Glavlit censors and often transfers its own personnel there. A large number of active and former KGB officers, of almost any rank, serve within Glavit—some occupying its key positions. As a KGB personnel officer I handled reassignments of KGB operational officers and would routinely consider assigning them to Glavlit, which, like any section of the KGB, would have no choice but to accept them.

Indeed, Glavlit functions practically as a part of the KGB. Their functions dovetail; as Glavlit's charter specifies, the KGB prevents any printing or sale or importation into the country of works banned by Glavlit.[40]

The KGB itself decides much of what shall be censored. In each ministry, institute, and industrial establishment, the KGB-run First Department makes a list of matters it wants to be hidden from the public eye. It forwards these proposals upward through regional KGB offices that tack on their own suggestions: local incidents they don't want known, names of authors or artists to be suppressed or discredited, books or music that the public should be made to forget. The KGB center in Moscow assembles these recommendations and passes them to Glavlit, where the operational department—controlled by KGB officers—makes up the final "list" that guides censors throughout the country.

But formal censorship is only one of the ways by which the KGB, as the party's "combat organization," impedes the flow of unwanted information.

From the KGB, in fact, spring the very laws that repress information.

Whenever it feels the need for better legal safeguards, the KGB proposes new laws and helps draft them, as it did in 1966 to cope with *samizdat* by inserting Article 190 into the RSFSR Criminal Code.

Its heavy hand lies on writers, editors, and journalists. It was only natural that a KGB directorate chief should participate in an instruction course for newspaper editors in Moscow in December 1987.[41] In the secretariats of writers unions, KGB officers and agents occupy key posts (controlling membership and funds, for example).††† In the 1960s and 1970s the Moscow Writers Union was headed by KGB Lt. Gen. Viktor Ilyin, who had earlier headed the KGB's Investigations Directorate. Chekists visit the union's clubhouses, too, to lecture and exhort writers. It was the KGB chairman himself (Vladimir Semichastniy at the time) who personally led the members of the Writers Union in their vilification of Boris Pasternak. The KGB keeps permanent ties with the writers unions in Moscow, Leningrad, Kiev, and other centers through liaison committees. So too does the MVD. Through the "Council for Creative Liaison" (*Sovet po tvorcheskim svyazyam*) the MVD organized an all-Union conference on "ethical and legal problems in fiction" in which writers and police talked about ways to improve their cooperation (such as ways to make sure that detective stories don't give useful ideas to criminals).[42]

Intercepting the mail, the KGB's "PK" departments cut off many exchanges of manuscripts and printed material inside the country as well as with the outside. We have already seen the KGB controlling "special collections" and part of its work in keeping foreign information out of the country. KGB-controlled Border Guards are responsible for confiscating foreign literature entering in travelers' baggage or freight shipments.

The KGB also hampers spoken exchange of information. It taps internal phone lines and cuts off conversations or disconnects the telephone of dissidents. As we have seen, it suspends direct dialing to and from abroad. In radio jamming the KGB played a central role, too. Local KGB offices tested the quality of reception in their areas, made recommendations for jamming, and oversaw local jamming stations. The section of the Ministry of Communications operating the jamming stations was directly responsive to KGB direction and like other parts of the ministry had KGB personnel on its staff.

The KGB has not only rid the landscape of unwanted writers by imprisonment or exile but has also disposed of their works and their

---

†††It was characteristic that in 1987 the head of the Russian Writers Union, Vladimir Karpov (a Chekist in the Second World War and a former labor camp inmate, too), issued a warning to writers against overindulging the freedoms of *glasnost* and that he took part in the KGB's celebration of its seventieth anniversary later that year (*London Daily Telegraph*, 24 December 1987).

reputations. KGB officials, directly or within Glavlit, burned proscribed books or relegated them to secret archives or to those special collections in libraries—managed by KGB-cleared attendants.

The KGB masterminded the obliteration not only of an author's writings or a singer's recordings but also of the very name of the author or singer himself. When theater director Yuri Lyubimov was disgraced in 1983 for criticizing Soviet repression, his name was deleted from all programs of his Moscow theater even though some of his productions remained in its repertory. And in 1979 the fame of the rising concert pianist Vladimir Feltsman was speedily wiped out as soon as he made known his decision to apply to emigrate to Israel. Two and a half hours later a friend called him from the State Television and Radio studios, asking, "What's up? I've just been ordered to remove all your tape recordings from the racks and never play them again." Feltsman's concert with the Moscow Philharmonic two weeks later had been advertised all over Moscow—but on the day of the concert his name on the posters was blotted out and two hours before the concert he was told that his appearance was cancelled. All tapes and video recordings were removed from stores, and, with one accidental exception, Feltsman was not heard in public again.‡‡‡

Hardly an independent-minded writer since the 1960s has been spared a threatening "chat" with party or KGB officials as soon as his nonconformism or indiscipline is spotted. Unless he is unusually brave or determined, the KGB calculates that these threats should be enough to cool his pen. If not, the KGB muscles into his private life—harassing him by obvious surveillance or conspicuous searches of his home, planting microphones, recruiting his friends as informers, beating or imprisoning him, or expelling him from his homeland and separating him from his sources of inspiration and his readership.

The KGB has prevented group discussions of writings it disapproves of, cancelled concerts, and broken up poetry readings by force—its men posing (or having obedient *druzhinniki* pose) as hooligans or "outraged citizens." It has had hundreds of students thrown out of universities for as little reason as participating in scholarly discussions of writers proscribed by the regime.[43]

While cutting off unwanted information, the KGB floats its own. It has commissioned thousands of books, articles, and films to stimulate

‡‡‡Seven years later, still being refused a visa, he was still being hounded. When the American ambassador invited him to perform in the embassy in Moscow in 1986, some KGB-controlled employee of the embassy destroyed the low E string of the embassy's piano just before he was to play (*New York Times,* 20 March 1981). In 1987, after ten years of applying, he was finally allowed to emigrate.

"vigilance" and to polish the image of the security organs. I know directly, from my own KGB service, that several writers of spy books did secret operational work for the KGB abroad. One reward was the assurance that their books would be published; spy stories are given bigger printings than are Russian classics; and it is the size of the edition, not actual sales, that determines the author's income.

All these functions were neatly, if euphemistically, summarized by a republic KGB chief at the end of 1981. The KGB, he wrote, "participates actively in the ideological education of members of our society" and combines this with "various preventive means."[44]

The Secrets the Regime Hides

Glavlit's chief said in late 1988 that any information could be printed in the future—except for two kinds. The first is state secrets. The second is anything "that could be detrimental to our country's interests"—a category so wonderfully vague and subjective that it could encompass anything the leadership considered detrimental to its own interests. In fact, before *glasnost,* only one-fifth of all the censors' cuts, corrections, improvements, or rejections had anything to do with state secrets.[45]

And that after giving a very broad interpretation to the term "state secrets." These are listed and updated every five years in a "List of Information Constituting State Secrets."[46] Divided into "military" and "economic" categories, the short (two-page) list bans publication of anything whatever to do with military forces, weapons, budgets, or procurement except for items that have been specifically released. Things that are publicly debated in the West are here made into state secrets: "the state of currency reserves," for example, and "information about the balance of payments" and production of nonferrous, precious, and rare metals. All discoveries and inventions are automatically secret if the leaders consider them to have "major military importance"; and even if deemed only of "major scientific and economic importance," they cannot be published without ministerial approval. The list of state secrets contains a final, catch-all category: "Other data determined by the Council of Ministers of the USSR to represent state secrets."

The list is being reduced under Gorbachev but can as easily be increased. Whole new categories of information outside "state secrets" can be brought under control at the leaders' whim. In the 1970s, for instance, they became worried that foreign intelligence and propaganda services might profit from various kinds of overt information. Their specialists proposed to hide whole new categories of information: "political, economic, cultural, transportation, scientific matters" including "prices of consumer goods, information on the labor force, regulations on issuance of Soviet personal documents, residence registration procedures in hotels, border districts, and big cities, and for checking baggage through customs."[47] And sure enough, the barriers did go up. A law of February 1, 1984, made it a "state crime" (punishable by three years in jail) to divulge a so-called "work-related" or "professional" secret *(sluzhebnaya tayna)* to foreigners or even to collect such information with the intent to do so— and in late 1988, the height of Gorbachev's *glasnost,* a man was convicted under this law.[48]

Thus the Soviet citizen was enjoined to hide anything having to do with his line of work ("economic, scientific-technical, or other").[49] In theory it would open to prosecution a meteorologist who tells foreigners about the weather, a clockmaker who discloses the time.

But this is only the beginning. Glavlit's protective hand stretches far beyond state or even official secrets. Its tasks were once described as "control of politico-ideological, military, and economic information,"[50] whereas the official list of "state secrets" contains only the latter two categories. It has been in that first category, "politico-ideological," that most of Glavlit's work has been done. And that, as we shall see, may include anything.

To cover these other matters the censors have their own list, and there the Kremlin bosses have their chance to specify what they consider "incorrect" or "untrue" or "useless"—or, as today's censorship chief put it, things "that could be detrimental to our country's interests."

It is an impressive document. Subject by subject, name by name, event by event, place by place, over hundreds of pages, the censor is told what he must be alert to. His guide is formally entitled "List of Materials and Information Forbidden for Open Publication in the Press." It is known for short as "the list" *(perechen),* but some editors have facetiously called it "the Talmud." It is a hard-cover, loose-leaf book holding permanent orders, regularly updated, plus special instructions issued whenever events or the changing needs of the leaders require new advice.

Its contents are themselves secret. Indeed, its very existence was unmentionable until *glasnost;* and among its strictures it prohibited, with unabashed hypocrisy, any public use of the word "censorship" or of "the character, organization, and methods" of the Soviet censors' work. So terrible is the punishment for losing it that some censors working on the premises of publishing houses do not dare store it there, not even in a locked safe, but prefer instead to travel to the better-protected offices of Gravlit every time they need to consult it.

The party bosses have good reason to hide this document, because it exposes their fear of and contempt for their own people as well as their arrogance, narrow-mindedness, and cynicism. The Polish version of the Soviet *perechen,* similar to the Soviet model, was leaked to the West in the 1970s and was hailed, with no exaggeration, as "one of the great revelations of the postwar period." A committee of Poles in emigration recognized how it confirmed "the dominant role of lies and noninformation, of falsification of our historical tradition, our national culture . . . an extraordinary policy to annihilate the national conscience. . . . a managing of the news by lies, half-truths, and other insidious means to deprive society of its ability to defend itself."[51]

Through these hundreds of pages[52] the leaders have sought to hide their failures, the emptiness of their ideology and the injustices they have wrought upon society. The censors' list has denied the people the raw data they need to fairly judge their regime's performance or compare it against outside systems or past promises. It has prevented them from learning about resistance to Communist rule in the USSR or its satellite states. And it has eliminated the memory or example of people who have dissented, opposed, or fled Soviet rule.

Its loose-leaf format makes it adaptable to shifts in policies. The leaders have only to remove restrictions—as the Gorbachev regime has done—or add new ones if, for example, *glasnost* gets out of hand or an internal crisis arises. By the end of 1988, according to the unprecedented revelations of Glavlit's chief, the list had been cut by almost one-third. "We are purging the list," he said, "of sectorial and departmental restrictions on material whose publication is not detrimental to our country's defense and economic interests and of material that is easily obtained by foreign intelligence with the aid of highly sophisticated equipment."[53]

Many of the restrictions—and their removal under *glasnost*—were obvious even to the outsider. Even a casual reader of the press could, as Glavlit's chief said, "name dozens of previously closed subjects that are now given extensive coverage in the press. I am thinking of industrial and transport accidents, crime and illness, ecological problems, and so forth."[54] Indeed, until the mid-1980s the censors had been told to cut out "any information about work accidents, natural or other disasters—earthquakes, floods, tidal waves," and "reports about food poisonings" or "illness in the population from cholera, the plague, tuberculosis, typhus, and diphtheria," and any countrywide data (as contrasted to generalities and individual cases) about neglected children, illiteracy, food shortages, and drug addiction. Then under *glasnost* the Soviet population as well as the outside world learned—as it had long suspected—that in the USSR like everywhere else dams do collapse, airliners crash, ships collide, trains jump the tracks, brutal crimes occur, mafia-like crime organizations flourish, and politicians take bribes.

But the leaders kept the lid on information that might discredit them. When the nuclear power plant exploded at Chernobyl in 1986, the people were allowed to learn only what the leaders' communiques told them. The disasters that had occurred throughout the previous decades had not been exposed, not even those that have left dangerous and lasting pollution.‡‡‡

In the economic field, especially, the *perechen* has changed to meet the needs of *perestroika*. Previously there was to be no public mention of the relation between wages and prices, of wage policies, of food shortages or the nonavailability of consumer products. But other bans persist, such as information on foreign credits received or grain purchased—information detrimental to the interests of the leaders.

Whole categories of restrictions survive. No one who has vainly looked to the Soviet press for information about the private life, personality, or health of the leaders, or their relationships with one another, will be surprised to learn that the *perechen* prohibits any mention (other than official communiques) of the "activities, whereabouts, or future movements" of Politburo members. Raisa and Mikhail Gorbachev may seem, especially to Western readers, quite adequately reported—but they are alone. It was not even known whether Yegor Ligachev—number two in the hierarchy—had a wife, for example, until Tass revealed it in 1988 by a brief allusion to her attendance with him at a gala concert (but Tass did not divulge her first name).[55] As for the wife of earlier General Secretary Andropov, the public (and the West) did not know whether she was alive until she materialized at his funeral. This state of ignorance made the West vulnerable to planted lies and fabrications about Andropov's personality, language ability, drinking habits, and reading and music preferences. Gorbachev himself dropped out of sight for months in 1986 with no explanation to the Soviet or Western public, pursuing a tradition that had become notorious and absurd even before his time. Chairman Andropov disappeared for the last six months of his life while spokesmen

‡‡‡In the 1970s an industrial plant exploded and leaked radioactive material in the Volga River; even the cleanup crew, it was reported unofficially, had to work without protective clothing to avoid panicking the population of the town. In late 1957, buried wastes from nuclear weapon production in the southern Urals leaked or exploded and killed hundreds, laying waste to an area of about 200 square miles around Kyshtym that still remains uninhabitable. (See Zhores Medvedev, *Nuclear Disaster in the Urals* (New York: Vintage Press, 1980). A report by the Los Alamos National Laboratory gave further details in 1982; see *Newsweek,* 19 April 1982. Tass finally revealed the accident in June 1989. See *International Herald Tribune,* 11 July 1989.

were telling Western questioners that he "had a cold." Brezhnev, too, disappeared for weeks at a time without warning or explanation. Chairman of the Presidium of the Supreme Soviet Nikolay Podgorniy dropped from sight without explanation; and when the Supreme Soviet routinely met several weeks later, it simply announced that Party Secretary Brezhnev had become its new chairman, without mentioning Podgorniy then or ever again.

The *perechen* is full of names and events that must not be mentioned (or instructions on how they are to be treated). The outsider could almost watch the week-by-week alterations in the censor's list in the late 1980s during the hesitant emergence of names long ago committed to this Orwellian "memory hole" like Khrushhev, Trotsky, Bukharin. The *perechen* accomplished an astounding feat: by suppressing the written memory of Stalin and later of Khrushchev, Soviet history was made to leap a forty-year gap directly from Lenin to Brezhnev—or as the Soviet witticism put it, "from Ilyich to Ilyich." In 1988 the head of Historial Archives Yuri Afanasyev told a conference of historians and writers that "there is no country in the world with such a falsified history as ours." At that same conference a leading writer, Viktor Astafyev, said, "We have been tormented by half-truths to a point of nervous exhaustion," and noted that not only Stalin was to blame but historians also performed just as ignobly under Brezhnev.[56] The phrase "cult of personality" still hides mass murder, imprisoning, torture, and destitution of scores of millions of people; and the pressures of "informal" associations of historians (like the one calling itself "Memorial"), fighting the *perechen,* are pulling those facts out only bit by bit. By 1988 Gorbachev has still admitted only that "many thousands" had been "subjected to wholesale repressive measures" whereas he knew well that, as Soviet scholars were revealing, the number was tens of millions. He confessed his fears: "If we start trying to deal with the past," he said, "we'll lose all our energy. It would be hitting the people over the head."[57] Here the word "people" again stands for the party leadership.

The censor's list has always given concrete form to the leaders' fear of creative artists. But Gorbachev showed a willingness to let old and exiled voices be heard. First the official veil was lifted from some dead writers like Pasternak and Akhmatova, and then in 1989 the regime lifted all restrictions on importing the works of banned authors (except those calling for the overthrow of the Soviet system). Even Solzhenitsyn's *The Gulag Archipelago* was allowed to be serialized in the Soviet magazine *Novy Mir.*

The *perechen* still seeks to hide alternatives to Soviet rule, controlling references to freedoms, living standards, and purchasing power of people outside the socialist camp. The censors' instructions are shaped so as to hide the good things about the West and to emphasize (and exaggerate) the slums, poverty, unemployment, inequalities, crime, racial tensions, and drug abuse.

How Far Can *Glasnost* Go?

Before the era of Gorbachev some observers of the Soviet scene expressed the quite reasonable opinion that if controls over information were completely lifted, the Soviet system would be engulfed within weeks.

The Kremlin leaders have not yet opened all the flood gates—only a third of the *perechen* has been cut—but they have allowed the dam to crack. Why did they do it? The answer was clear: they had no choice. Only with the people's confidence could they rebuild their ruined economy. "If we don't involve the people," Gorbachev said, "nothing will come of it." "If we lose *glasnost,* we lose *perestroika,*" said Boris Yeltsin.[58]

At the beginning there was much confusion. The people were confused and hesitant as to how to use the new freedom of information; the leaders, as to how to keep it in check. One editor remarked in 1987, "Before, I asked and was told what to print. Now they say 'you decide'—so I print it and come to work next morning wondering who's going to call."[59] Some of the most daring proposals appeared in newspapers aimed more at foreign than domestic readers and difficult to obtain in the USSR.[60] The leaders invited President Reagan to address the Soviet people—then jammed the broadcast and printed only selected portions of it; they promised the visiting West German president that he could communicate freely to the people—then deleted what he said about religious freedom and the right to emigrate.

But activists gained confidence and grouped in informal associations to press their claims; journalists and editors gained experience and began to lose their fear. After two or three years of *glasnost,* the press was airing sensitive topics like the regime's abuse of psychiatry and of the penal system, its violations of religious rights, Stalin's crimes, Soviet responsibility for the Cold War, conditions in the army, and restrictions on travel. Then they began to bring into question such fundaments of the regime as central planning and collectivized agriculture. By 1989 the media was carrying *glasnost* far beyond the limits imaginable only a year or two earlier. Some pointed to Lenin's role in creating the "command state" and questioned his wisdom. Others like Boris Yeltsin attacked the leaders' abusive privileges, suggested making the party responsible to the new congress, and proposed discussing the pros and cons of a multiparty system. In several republics huge public demonstrations became common, and nationalist fronts—almost openly acting as political parties—contested political power with the Communist Party and called for independence from Moscow. A few voices began to question even the sacrosanct powers of the KGB.

If Gorbachev had really expected *glasnost* to produce only fresh ideas for repairing industry and agriculture, renewed enthusiasm at the workplace, and wider cooperation in the fight against alcoholism, corruption, bureaucracy, and mismanagement, he was unpleasantly surprised—and confessed it in March 1989. He and his KGB chief uttered repeated warnings and veiled threats against irresponsible excesses.

By 1989 *glasnost* was reaching the extreme limits. Soon the leaders would have to face the question: could press freedom and Leninism be reconciled? The emerging answer was no—and the regime, with its KGB, still had the power to retighten its controls of information. In early 1989, perhaps foreshadowing things to come, the leaders put new legal restrictions on press reporting of demonstations, and in April of that year made it a punishable offence to "discredit" the state's authority or officials. The censors were being especially strict about anything relating to the KGB, and forced editors to make substantial cuts in a letter demanding closer judicial control of it. (*International Herald Tribune,* 21 April 1989.)

The same sort of question arises in another field; the regime's restriction of travel and emigration. Again, how much liberty can be granted without eating away the foundations of the system itself? Can Soviet power survive a friendly, open contact with Western democracy?

CHAPTER 21

Keeping People In

A Border Like No Other

IN MARCH 1988 ELEVEN SOVIET CITIZENS TRIED TO HIJACK AN INTERNAL Soviet airliner. An assault team stormed the plane, shot down at least five of them, and thwarted the crime. A Westerner might wonder at the number of these hijackers and the fact that all of them were members of a single family, a musical group known as the Ovechkins. The Westerner might then recall a similar incident of November 1983 when a dozen Georgians, reportedly members of a wedding party, had tried to force an internal flight to take them to nearby Turkey. (An assault squad killed several of them, too.)[1] The similarity is easy to explain. Lacking any legal way, these otherwise peaceable people were ready to commit a desperate crime in order to escape Soviet rule. They had joined the long list of daring escape attempts across the Iron Curtain.

"Everyone has the right to leave any country, including his own, and to return to his country," says the Universal Declaration of Human Rights of 1948. The Soviet government signed that declaration and twenty-five years later in Helsinki pledged again to honor the principle and "to simplify and administer flexibly the procedures for exit and entry" from the USSR.* By the end of the 1980s it had done nothing of the kind. The Soviet rulers were still doing all they could to prevent their people from leaving. "Escape abroad, unlawful departure from the territory of the Soviet Union," constitutes treason under the Criminal Code.[2] Would-be

---

*"The participating states will act in conformity with the purposes and principles of . . . the Universal Declaration of Human Rights. . . . [They] intend to facilitate wider travel by their citizens for personal or professional reasons and to this end they intend in particular: —gradually to simplify and to administer flexibly the procedures for exit and entry . . ." —Helsinki Agreement, 1975.

escapers—like Boydan Klimchak in the late 1980s—will get the fifteen-year sentence it provides or they might, like Anatoliy Butko who tried to swim to Turkey and Aleksandr Shatravka who tried to cross over to Finland, be committed to insane asylums.[3]

Although these reckless efforts show that the Soviet citizens already regard their land border as impenetrable, the Soviet authorities continued to bolster its defenses.

Look at this frontier; it is unlike any other. For one thing, where else would you find so much praise showered upon border guards? Year after year, books, magazines, and films recount their heroic exploits and make them role models for schoolchildren; their anniversary is the occasion for meetings, speeches, exhortations, and inspiring news stories.

Yet more unusual is the level of technology dedicated to the border obstacles and the fact that they are designed not merely to hinder a crossing but if necessary to kill the crosser. Their defenders get daily orders to destroy (if they cannot capture) any man, woman, or child who dares pass without permission.

Most extraordinary of all is the fact that these obstacles face inward. They are designed primarily not to keep people out but to keep them in—exactly like the walls of a prison.

Already the length of this border is impressive: it runs for sixty thousand kilometers along seacoasts and lakes, along high mountains and arctic wildernesses, across vast plains and deserts. But more extraordinary than its length is its depth. This is no thin line drawn on a map. The innermost obstacles lie in the very center of the country, at the workplace of the Soviet citizen; the outermost, as far out as Paris or New York.

The First Barriers

Even to go out of the Soviet Union on legitimate business, the would-be traveler faces a thicket of formalities full of pitfalls. In 1988 these formalities were suddenly simplified, and in 1989 a new law on "Procedures for Exit from and Entry to the USSR" clarified some of the regulations. But departure still remained a daunting proposition.

The spirit of the Soviet border is reflected in the exit procedures that faced official travelers from the USSR through 1987. Some of their barriers remain, and others can be reimposed whenever the leaders feel threatened. So let's observe them through the experiences of Dr. Izyaslav Lapin, a distinguished Leningrad pharmacologist invited in the mid-1970s to a three-week symposium in Milan.[4] The first obstacle—one that still faces would-be travelers today—was his boss, the director of his institute who, fearful of being accused of lack of vigilance, was reluctant to let any of his subordinates go abroad. He had already refused to let Lapin accept five earlier invitations to conferences in the West and would later refuse yet another. This time, however, he felt daring; "Let's give it a try," he said.

So now Lapin had to send a photocopy of the Italian invitation, along with a Russian translation and a covering letter from his institute, to the Ministry of Health in Moscow. There its Foreign Relations Department (controlled by the KGB) passes on such requests; sometimes this takes so long that the answer arrives too late for the scheduled trip. This time, however, the ministry approved and told Lapin to submit his application for exit from the USSR.

This application—an especially probing version of the omnipresent *anketa*—was still being required of travelers under Gorbachev's rule. First, of course, it provides space for affixing a photograph and giving one's name and address, the names of any accompanying children under sixteen, the country of destination, and the duration of the trip. (A new *anketa* is required for every trip.) Then begin its questions, which we reproduce here in full, for they betray the leaders' distrust of anyone who might want to get out from under their dominion, even if only temporarily and even if on the leader's own business.[5]

1–4: Full name. (If you have ever changed your name, tell how the formalities were accomplished and the reasons for the change.) Date and place of birth. Nationality. [By Soviet definition a "Jew" is a nationality, like ethnic origins of the diverse nationalities under Soviet rule.] Family situation (married, divorced, single).

5 and 6: Party status: year of entry, card number of member or candidate. Komsomol membership: give dates and card number.

7. Were you a CPSU member in the past? When, and why separated from the party.

8. Education and specialized training, when and in what institutions.

9. Were you ever tried before a court? When, where.

10. Have you ever been abroad? Where, when, and why. Where did you obtain exit permit. If you were ever refused permission to go abroad, tell when and why.

11. Military responsibility and rank.

12. Amount of salary or pension.

13. List all your close relatives, alive or dead, who live in the USSR and abroad. [A full page is provided for the answer, with room for 34 entries, including name, birthdate, work place, and current address of each.]

14. List all jobs you have held during your active working life, including periods of study in educational establishments and military service. [Place is provided for duties performed and the name of each organization.]

15. Membership in party, soviet, or other authorities of the center, re-public, kray, oblast, okrug, city, or district, up to the moment of the present application.

16. List all state honors and decorations.

17. Purpose of travel abroad. If you are visiting relatives or friends, give their names and their addresses abroad.

18. When do you intend to go abroad, and by what border crossing point?

19. What members of your family will be abroad at the same time?

20. Passport: number, date, and place of issue.

21. List all documents you are submitting with this application.

22. What else do you want to add about yourself or your close relatives, or other information pertinent to the present application?

The accompanying documents alluded to in Question 21 might have numbered as many as twelve. One had to submit, for example, a health certificate signed by several doctors, a certificate of good conduct (*kharak-teristika*) with three signatures, and the stamp of the party's regional committee. Signatures and a rubber stamp may sound like mere for-malities to a Westerner, but in the USSR they involve grave risks, for they assume a degree of responsibility for the traveler's return. The party secretary of the applicant's own institute would interview him with a skeptical attitude; and even if he approved (and if the applicant had no enemies who out of spite would withhold their signatures), the district, city, or oblast party organization would submit the applicant to a critical, and humiliating, interview before granting him that stamp.†

---

†Since the mid-1970s, each district Party Committee (*raikom*) in Moscow, as well as each republic Central Committee, has its "Commission" (*Komissiya po Vyezdam Zagranitsu*), which can decide without involving the Moscow City Committee (*Mosgorkom*) which in the

A half-dozen party functionaries plied Lapin, for example, with questions like these: "'Why did the United States embark on a political rapprochement with the Soviet Union?' The correct answer is: 'Under the pressure of the Soviet government's peace-loving policy.' If you don't know this formula, you are told that you are not mature enough to be sent abroad. The professor of pharmacology also has to answer questions like: 'What does dialectical materialism understand by "chance"? 'Who is Alvaro Cunhal?' 'What is the peculiarity of the present stage of peaceful coexistence?'" The questions themselves are less important than the applicant's behavior. "If he is hesitant or gloomy or appears vexed by the interrogation, it counts heavily against him. The most dangerous thing is to show the slightest trace of irony or sarcasm—this will be neither forgiven nor forgotten. . . . The party officials have the function of reminding the professor that he is not his own master and must not step out of line."[6]

The examiners were not satisfied with Lapin—so he was not allowed to go. But had he made it past the local party interviewers, he would still have faced other formidable obstacles. His application with all its accompanying file would have passed through the Central Committee apparatus of the CPSU where Lapin would undergo another interview and through the KGB, whose approval is essential.

The regime pared away some of this rigamarole but only for travel within the Soviet Bloc and for officials being sent out. A Moscow photographer who had gone through it all in 1987 for a trip to Spain reported that in September 1988 he submitted only the basic documents (invitation from abroad plus questionnaire) and within two weeks ("fantastic!"), without any interviews (except of course to get his boss's permission) had his permission to travel to the United States.[7] Officials of the level of director who were making short business trips to Soviet Bloc countries would henceforth need only oral permission from their boss unless a set quota had been exceeded, in which case they would still need the approval of their central ministry. Tourists traveling to other Soviet Bloc countries would no longer have to put up with what the Soviet press itself called "the previous tiresome procedure," but even for this relatively safe travel, they still have to apply (in a "short form") and submit references from their doctors and employers.[8]

The leaders would prefer, in principle, that no one go abroad, not even scientists and commercial functionaries whose trips serve the regime's purposes. That being impractical, the leaders make the best of it by

---

1950s gave exit permissions for the whole USSR. Now as then, these commissions are staffed mainly with former KGB officers.

manipulating travel permission as an instrument of rule. They hold down the numbers of travelers; according to a member of the Presidium of the Academy of Sciences, 90 percent of all scientists' applications for travel abroad are refused or acted upon too late for the purpose of the trip.[9] And they ensure that only the most compliant (and their personal favorites) shall be granted this high privilege.

The regime must, of course, send some people abroad: diplomats to South America, KGB officers to Paris, commercial representatives to Japan, engineers to Algeria. But even they are subjected to rigorous procedures, and these procedues are handled so capriciously that even senior officials may be refused permission for one trip or another. Through its exit commissions, dominated by the KGB, the party bosses let everyone understand that if he is permitted out, it is for this time only and thanks to a gracious dispensation that may be withdrawn at any moment.

Everyone is afraid that the KGB might get the impression that he wants to leave. When he is first invited or hears of his assignment abroad, he goes into a compulsory act, protesting that he is too busy, that he really doesn't want to go outside his great and beloved homeland, etc. His act ends, of course, with his "reluctant" acceptance just before the offer is withdrawn. If he misjudges the timing or overdoes it, as many have, he may lose the opportunity.

If this is how the regime treats those who have to travel, what of private citizens who simply want to see a foreign country? The Kremlin's guiding principle is clear and known to everyone, although nowhere stated openly: no such travel shall be allowed.

The Kremlin rulers evidently think that their subjects will betray them at the first opportunity. They have made laws accordingly, like that under Gorbachev in 1986: "Soviet citizens shall not be permitted to leave the USSR on private business . . . if they are privy to state secrets or if there are other reasons of state security."[10] On countless citizens, those who have shown an independence of mind or otherwise run afoul of the KGB, the rulers have imposed a lifelong ban on foreign travel—authorized by no law whatsoever—in the form of a simple stamp in their file: *"Nevyezdnyy"* (not permitted exit).‡ This label is easy to come by. As many as half the students of the Institute of International Relations—people handpicked for service abroad, whose admission to the institute shows that they had the right background, preparation, and connections—come to the end of their five-year course with their personal files stamped *Nevyezdnyy.*[11]

To ask to go abroad is dangerous. At the applicant's place of work the

---

‡They are called *otkaznik* (the term usually rendered in English as "refusenik") and *otstoynik* (the sediment that stays behind as the stream runs on).

First Department delves into his motives and makes a notation in his file that will guarantee, if nothing else, that he will never be allowed out of the Soviet Union—and it may hinder his advancement and deny him privileges controlled by his trade union, such as priorities in getting an apartment.

Tourists do not just go traveling on their own. As spelled out by written rules,[12] they are selected and "sent" out. The trade union organization "will send abroad, above all, picked workers, the best representatives of the scientific and technological intelligentsia, and [those] who have distinguished themselves positively in their social as well as professional activities." Tourist trips are not for fun; they are "an integral part of the cultural and economic relations of the USSR with foreign countries" and have solemn aims: "to give Soviet citizens the possibility of knowing about the life of foreign peoples, of familiarizing themselves with the successes of socialist construction in socialist countries and the achievements of industry and agriculture, the successes of science and technology abroad, enlarging and consolidating friendly relations with the people of the visited countries, and propagandizing the success of the Soviet people in building communism."

Soviet tourists travel mainly to Communist countries and in groups under supervision. They are not left to make their own arrangements either: "It is the trade union committees which take care of all formalities necessary for a trip abroad." To handle applications for travel, these committees "must have itineraries, programs, and the necessary application forms, questionnaires, and medical certificates." It is a long, complicated process: "For tourism to capitalist and developing countries, as well as Yugoslavia and Cuba, these documents must be submitted four months before the trip is to take place."

Even under such controlled conditions the regime remains wary: "Permission to travel to a capitalist country is valid only for that one country. Trips to capitalist countries may be authorized no more than once every three years. Married couples should not be sent in one and the same group traveling to a capitalist country."

To leave for longer, the only possibility is emigration. Although the Soviet regime agreed by treaty to permit emigration, it did all it could to hinder it. After agreeing in the 1960s to let Jews emigrate to Israel, the Soviet leaders imposed conditions: no one could leave who had had "recent" access to state secrets (or who had relatives who had) or whose parents disapproved, or who had no relatives in Israel. They interpreted these conditions so as to prevent escape from their rule.§ They pressured

§To take but a few illustrative examples among thousands, they turned down a man who

parents to withhold their consent or simply refused exit visas on the vague grounds that the applicant's departure would be "inexpedient." When Gorbachev was asked in late 1987 why Soviet citizens were not allowed to emigrate freely, he used a newly minted pretext: that the Soviet Union was defending itself against a "brain drain" plotted by the United States.[13] In 1987 the regime decreed that only those with first-degree blood relatives abroad would get permission, thereby excluding perhaps 90 percent of the Jews who have expressed a desire to leave. So great was the foreign reaction to this rule that it was rescinded in 1989.

The regime evidently hoped to hide from the West the number of "refuseniks." In December 1987 a regime spokesman claimed that only 200 Jewish applications remained not yet acted upon—but by a year later (the barriers having been lowered to improve relations with the West) no fewer than 17,000 had been granted visas and had left the USSR. Jewish organizations in the West had been told by leading refuseniks that 100,000 more had applied in 1988.[14] Others estimate that between 200,000 and 400,000 more Jews, tens of thousands of ethnic Germans, and hundreds of thousands of Russians and others would apply to emigrate—if they dared.

It takes courage. By exposing a desire to leave the country, applicants expose themselves to the wrath not only of the regime but also of a fear-ridden and jealous society. They and their children become pariahs, ostracized by neighbors, deprived of honors and titles, fired from jobs, their telephones cut off, ousted from their apartment, sometimes forced to leave their city, denied any but menial ways to earn their livelihood, and harassed and beaten by thugs. If they do not quickly take some other employment (and employers are often pressured not to hire them), they risk imprisonment as "parasites" (although the law on parasitism was to be rescinded in 1989). Young men are dropped from the universities and called to military service (which would expose them to a long ban on travel abroad) and imprisoned if they refuse.

The KGB controls every stage of this exit process—and the fear that underlies it. Responsible under law for the "regime of state security," its statute endows it with the power "to decide whether to issue permits or not for entry into or exit from the USSR."[15] No application would be sent

---

served as a private in the army twenty years earlier, another whose uncle had been a high air force officer (although he had been shot in Stalin's purges nearly forty years earlier), another who had studied (in a different faculty) in an institute which had a military faculty, and yet another who had worked in the medical clinic of a radio factory where he might conceivably have heard about production figures. Such refusals were reported by the refuseniks themselves and through *samizdat;* those cited here and many others are detailed in Shindler, especially pp. 121–53.

forward by the trade union or party secretary of a workplace without the approval of its Personnel Department, where the KGB reigns. When an application reaches the ministry or other superior institution, it is passed upon by its Foreign Relations Department—a KGB outpost. At every level of the party the exit commissions that review applicants' files and interview them are largely composed of former KGB officers. If the traveler is going to a capitalist country, his application will routinely be checked with the KGB. The MVD office granting exit visas (OVIR) is directed and largely staffed by the KGB. And the promise of permission to emigrate or to make a trip abroad is often the bait by which the KGB recruits would-be travelers for service as informants at home or abroad.

Having thus seen to the administrative obstacles against escape from the country, the KGB runs the physical obstacles as well. By law, it controls the border and the regions adjoining it. [16]

The Border Regions

The closer one approaches the borders of the USSR the more dense become the controls. On the Black Sea or Baltic, although the traveler may be hundreds of miles by road or rail from any land border, the edge of the USSR lies just over the watery horizon and he can sense it. Dropping into a modest restaurant in a port city like Odessa or Tallinn, he may feel suspicious eyes upon him; KGB and MVD informants keep watch within these places that are frequented by foreign sailors and their smuggler contacts. If he wants to paddle around in a little boat he will find rentals more complicated than on his inland river or lake; here any boat can be a vehicle of escape. He must identify himself, sign his name, register the time and purpose of his outing, and observe rules that tell him how far he can go from shore and when he must return. The renter works under strict rules, too: he must report anything unusual to the militia and "is forbidden to maintain boats [of any kind] outside the established wharfs, moorings, and base ports . . . or to leave the shore or to moor outside [these places]." Special border regulations cover the "registration, mainte-nance, and movements" of all boats. [17]

Closer to the land frontier the traveler may have to stop. "Entry to a border zone is forbidden to people who are not permanently resident in it without the authorization of the internal affairs organs." It is not enough just to drop in at the local militia office and ask permision to stay; the traveler must bring with him an authorization from his own militia at home to travel there in the first place. [18] His presence is likely to be noticed. Every resident has been cleared and issued an identity document certifying his right to be in the area; family members living outside the zone must get special permission each time they want to drop in to visit their relatives; even military troops have special passes to return to their posts within the border zone.

This "border zone" is only vaguely delimited; the law says that it includes the territory of districts *(raiony)* and towns along the coast and borders, but in practice it may extend as far into the interior as the KGB Border Guards choose to operate.[19] It may be two kilometers deep or six hundred, depending on the density of population, the topography, what country lies across the border, and other factors.

The last bit of Soviet territory before the formal international demarcation line is called the "border strip."** It too varies in depth from place to place and has been variously defined over the years. By the law of 1927 it might vary from four meters to twenty-two kilometers; the law of 1960 set the depth at two kilometers; and the 1983 law removed all limits simply by not mentioning any. On vast open deserts or in uninhabited swampland, the strip—where any unidentified person may be shot on sight—can be many miles deep; and in the uninhabited far north, scores or even hundreds of miles. In towns that touch the border, the population is removed from a strip perhaps five hundred meters wide (as in East Germany) and houses razed and hillocks leveled to improve visibility and to clear fields of fire.

This is KGB country. The borders have been the KGB's responsibility since the earliest weeks of Soviet rule. Today as then, the "main tasks of the organs of state security" include "organizing and maintaining the protection of the state borders of the USSR and preventing their violation."[20] For this purpose the KGB maintains a powerful army of its own.

**The foreigner motorist gets a look at the zone and strip as he drives out of the USSR. He will have had to get several special documents for the purpose before leaving and to have notified the Soviet Foreign Ministry of exactly where he is going and who will be in the car. The ministry alerts the MVD, which, in turn, alerts its highway watch points— small houses or high towers every fifteen or twenty miles along highways on which foreigners are permitted to drive—each of whom notifies the next of the car's passing. Any of them may stop and check the car and the passengers if it wishes or send out a car to find it if it does not appear within the normal time. The motorist experiences the border zone as a series of checkpoints. Traveling from Leningrad to Finland, for example, the first such point occurs as soon as he leaves the last town, Vyborg, although he is still forty-five minutes' drive from the border. Just outside Vyborg the car is stopped and passports checked. Then, twenty-five miles farther along, the car is stopped until that checkpoint receives clearance to let it go the last five hundred yards to the principal border post. Here the car may be searched—even dismantled—as well as its baggage. This post is still not on the borderline itself; the car now passes through the border strip before it reaches the border line itself, where it encounters yet another checkpoint where again it must wait until the guard gets a phone call authorizing him to raise the barrier.

Border Troops and Their Work

The border guards have always been part of State Security and are today administered by the KGB's Main Directorate of Border Troops (*Glavnoye Upravleniye Pogranichnikh Voysk*, or GUPVO). They complement the Internal Troops (VV), and in the past both have been administered by a single Chief Directorate of Internal and Border Troops.[21]

They number more than 300,000, a major military force not only by their numbers but also by the sophistication of their weapons and equipment. As their commander, Gen. Matrosov, put it, they share the "military-technical revolution" with the armed forces and are equipped with the latest "aircraft and helicopters, cross-country vehicles and aerosleds, fast ships, radar stations and searchlight installations, modern communications and surveillance equipment, and much more."[22] The surveillance equipment includes electronic and infrared detection and warning devices, as well as some other special equipment we discuss later. Their ships, including modern destroyer-type vessels and fast patrol boats, surpass many navies and all the coast guards of the world. On the ground they operate tanks and armored personnel carriers, light artillery, and armored vehicles. They fly their own light aircraft and helicopters and have their own communications.

This battle equipment has been in action. It was the Border Guard Troops who bore the brunt of the fighting with the Chinese along the Amur River in the 1960s, including the well-publicized fracas on Damanskiy Island in 1969. They have frequently shared the task of the Internal Troops in pacifying areas occupied by Soviet troops, such as Central Asia, Transcaucasia, and Sinkiang. Politburo member Geidar Aliyev recalled, during the 1982 celebration of the anniversary of the Transcaucasus Border District, their "great contribution to the consolidation of Soviet power in Azerbaijan" in 1918–20 and "their courageous fight against the remnants of counterrevolutionary forces that had entrenched themselves in contiguous countries."[23]

Their arm extends beyond the Soviet borders, not only by agent operations, but also by control over the border guards of the countries of Eastern Europe. As Soviet troops occupied them in 1944 and 1945, Border Guard Troops set up in each country a model of themselves and took over their command positions for years, often wearing foreign uniforms. Today they continue to guide them through liaison and "advisory" officers who have an unwritten power of command. (No satellite border guard officer will rise high in his service without attending training schools of the KGB Border Guard Troops and without the favor of the

KGB.)[24] Yet the Soviets maintain border defenses against these neighbor countries, too—sometimes very strictly, as during the Polish crisis of 1980–1981.

The Border Troops are divided into ten border districts, each controlling a stretch of border that varies from a few hundred to several thousand miles. Each district *(okrug)* controls a number of detachments *(otryady)*, their number and size varying with the strategic importance of the area (and what country is on the other side), whether it is mountainous or flat or seacoast, and how wide and deep is the district's responsibility.

Each *otryad* has a headquarters staff and controls a reserve group (equivalent to a motorized rifle company) ready to reinforce any point in trouble, and a varying number of commands *(komendatury)* which control sectors of the border zone and major airports or seaports, as well as the border outposts. Each *komendatura* is broken down into outposts *(zastava)* responsible for a designated length of the frontier or for a designated border-crossing point (road crossing or railway station) or minor airport. Here again their size can vary according to the sector, from three or four men up to almost ten; each *zastava* has its posts of three to ten men watching or patrolling a narrow stretch of border.

Not content with mere patrolling, the troops have intelligence units that systematically assess their area, keep an eye on the mood of its people, and try to detect individuals whose loyalty might be shaky. To this end they recruit secret informants to keep an eye on suspect individuals as well as on railway stations, post offices, restaurants, and hotels. They use provocation as a tool to test the loyalty of the local citizens and to keep them on their toes. And as we shall see later, they send spies across the border into neighboring countries.

The Soviet regime has made its border areas resemble enemy-occupied territories. The Border Troops, never local boys, are usually detailed from faraway areas of the USSR. They are fired up by intense "vigilance" briefings that transform almost anyone into a potential enemy. As the Border Troops' commander, Army General Matrosov, said, "Ideological and political education of the border guard's spirit and Communist convictions are just as important as the border guard's equipment and professional skill."[25] There is good reason: it is a dirty job he does, against his own countrymen, and he must be made to see them as traitors and enemies. Also he is close to the border: he must be discouraged from slipping across himself, as so many East German border guards do.

The primary aim is to keep people in, although the regime understandably tries to hide this reality. When the press commends the border guards for their heroic captures of criminal "border violators," one has to read between the lines (and sometimes in vain) to learn what direction the violators were taking. Nowhere do they admit that these were simply men and women trying to flee Soviet rule and "criminals" only because they were going without permission.

Even Soviet law has tried to fudge this reality. "Border violators" are defined as "persons who cross or try to cross the border outside the control points, or at the control points in violation of the regulations." More recent laws give the game away. To deal with people who are caught before they reach the border (stowed away, for instance, in ships, planes, trains, or automobiles) the border law of 1983 adds to that definition "persons who have penetrated or who are trying to penetrate foreign or Soviet transportation facilities with foreign destinations for the purpose of illegally leaving the USSR."[26]

Few indeed are the people who want to sneak into the USSR. *Izvestiya* in 1977 could find no better example of border guards' capture of infiltrating "enemy spies" than the arrest of two American tourists with an intelligence mission—not mentioning that this incident had happened twenty-two years earlier.[27] Of course, if border barriers were less daunting, the guards would face greater numbers of one kind of infiltrator: the smuggler. Any Western tourist who has seen the empty stores in the USSR and had Soviet people try to buy the clothes off his back or the shoes off his feet, knows how welcome are smuggled goods. So lucrative is this business that some smugglers even try to get through these formidable border obstacles. According to a press report in 1983, a border guard was killed in an "unequal battle" against a "group of bandits trying to infiltrate into USSR territory."[28]

The border repels another kind of intruder, too: information. Here the Soviet regime combats the insidious "ideological sabotage" that takes the form of jeans and rock records, books, manuscripts, films, or anything else that contains information the Soviet leaders deem threatening††

The guards patrol in pairs or groups, often with dogs, and check the papers of any motorist, bicyclist, or pedestrian who attracts their suspicion. Like alien occupiers, too, they contrive all sorts of public relations gimmicks to win public approval. They help bring in the harvest, they sponsor games and patronize schools, they stage entertainments for the local population, and they participate in local festivities.

All the while, a huge propaganda campaign tries to excite admiration

††The 1983 USSR Border Law in article 28.6 lists among the "basic duties" of Border Troops "to prevent the shipment across the USSR state border of printed or duplicated works, manuscripts, documents, video and audio recordings, films or other printed or representational matter containing information which could damage the country's political or economic interests, state security, public order, or the population's health or morals."

and support for them. On May 28, Border Guards Day (the anniversary of their formation), high party functionaries and Chekist leaders gather to extol them and burble about their warm relations with the people. A hundred books, articles, and films endow every Soviet child with the mental picture of the border guard and his dog, on a hilltop or "baking deserts" or "harsh barren lands" or along "stormy coasts." The party chief of the border republic of Armenia was not embarrassed to say in the 1980s, "The border guard is a living wall between the motherland and the enemy. He senses with his body and heart the approach of anything alien, mortally dangerous."[29]

The reason for such hype, of course, is that the border guards need the help of the local citizenry. "The border is protected by the entire Soviet people!" runs the slogan. In offices and schools, on farms and construction projects, the citizen gets fresh exhortations to "strengthen his ties" with the border guards[30] and is reminded again and again of his duty to call them whenever he spots a stranger. Every resident is authorized to stop a suspect and demand to see his papers. If he spots a "border violator" he may get a medal—and, conversely, if in a sparsely populated area he encounters a stranger and fails to report, he can be deported or jailed.

He will usually not fail to report, because he knows that provocateurs are afoot. The Border Guards intelligence unit and the local KGB office bring in strangers to drop into shops or farms and ask directions—to test the "vigilance" of the population. In 1983 a Soviet journalist, to pump up a routine eulogy of the border guards, went through the motions (with authorization, of course) of trying to get through a border zone. He reported, with evident satisfaction, how quickly he was detected and how much contempt passers-by showed for him as he was led away.[31] What he failed to mention was that he had, in effect, participated in a KGB provocation: what if some kind soul had helped him?

The citizen's cooperation is not left to chance: in every village and economic enterprise and school in the zone, the Komsomol organizes volunteer squads (*druzhiny*) with a border guard officer as supervisor. They are given training and exhortations, and each member is assigned a certain field or bridge or mountain track or stretch of river or coast or part of town to watch, according to his possibilities.‡‡ The press of the border republics extols these "heroes" in nearly identical (and sometimes invented) stories designed to arouse vigilance. They may be in their teens like Saidali Musabekov or in their sixties like Nurbed-Aga Ashirov, each of whom was

‡‡These "volunteers" continue a tradition begun in the early years of Bolshevik rule; they should not be confused with the secret informants recruited by both the local KGB office and the Border Guards, which are discussed later. They are specifically mentioned in the USSR Border Law of 1983, article 38.

the subject of such an article in the 1980s. Young Saidali saw a stranger and thought, "Who can this be? I must check; it is evening and the border is close. . . ." The stranger tried to bluff but couldn't fool Saidali, who cunningly spotted an error in his documents—forged!—and took him to a police station, where (as in all these cases) he turned out to be a "dangerous criminal." Ashirov, a railway switchman, had been a member of the voluntary auxiliary brigade of his village for twenty-five years (" 'How could it be otherwise?' Ashirov says. 'After all, the station workers know every inhabitant of this village and the nearby settlements by sight. They see everything.' ") Making the rounds "one dark and quiet night" he heard a cough and, like young Saidali, asked himself "Who might that be?" He found a young man who claimed to be a geologist who had lost his way. "Ashirov pointed the way and stood watching the figure disappear into the darkness. But after twenty paces he turned off—his feet crunching on gravel. The gravel road led toward the border! . . . . Ashirov had to inform the border guards as quickly as possible!" This was not the first capture for Ashirov (or his family, several of whom were also members of the volunteer brigade). "He had received the Outstanding Border Guard insignia, 1st and 2nd degree, and a Certificate of Honor, and had received valuable gifts and monetary bonuses many times from the chief of district border troops."[32]

The "Fence"

A sample of the Soviet border fence is visible on the line between East and West Germany. You can climb a raised platform in West Berlin to inspect its most famous part, the Wall. Although nominally East German, these defenses were first set up by Soviet border guards, who also created the East German border guard service, occupied its commanding positions for many years, imposed its regulations, and until the border openings of late 1989, its techniques. The East Germans have, of course, made contributions of their own, including some superior technology that has doubtless been adopted along USSR borders.

What one sees in the countryside of Germany is an example of Soviet border defenses in relatively densely populated farmland facing a capitalist country. In other regions and other terrain they will differ but will always have this in common: that they are more than adequate for their purpose. If one reads from time to time that one or another device has been removed from the border defenses—mines dug up, self-triggering devices dismantled—one should not conclude that the border has become easier to pierce. Rather, it means that the KGB deems the remaining (or substitute) devices to be enough.

Few can ever hope to escape overland through such borders, and that is why people try to swim the Black Sea or hijack airplanes or do other desperate things to get out—like defecting when officially abroad. Much of the border fence is simply impregnable; from East Germany not a single person got through some stretches in five years, while only border guards (knowing its secrets and enjoying opportunities that ordinary East Germans could only dream of) managed to flee through other parts. For each successful escape, there were several failures—would-be escapees blown up by mines, shot down by the guards' machine pistols, shattered by self-triggering devices, dragged down by pursuing men and dogs, or detected before they even reached the border.

Until the Eastern European countries began opening their borders in 1989, the Soviet rulers were continually tightening the defences. As late as April 1985 new and probably impassable barriers were being added to fences already heightened in 1983. The Berlin Wall has been improved every year since it was built in the summer of 1961; in 1983–84 it was doubled by a second wall, heightened, and given a wider glacis, improved watchtowers, and new obstacles. In 1987 yet a third wall was being built in places.

You can get an idea of the forbidding obstacles of the Soviet "fence" (a modest word for such a defense in depth) from those they erected in East Germany. Not every detail is identical, but the general aspect is the same. We describe these obstacles from the inside toward the outside (the only direction anyone was likely to try to go). Having got through the border zone (which follows the Soviet model),§§ one comes, about 400–600 meters before the border line, to a barrier installed as recently as 1985. It uses new electronic technology that warns the guards and employs new metallurgic technology to prevent crossing. Past that, one crosses a paved road that parallels the border and makes it easier for the guards to patrol and to speed reinforcements to trouble spots. After crossing the road, one steps onto a 100-meter-wide strip of plowed, barren earth where a "violator" can be easily spotted from the watchtowers and by electronic beams. Then one comes to a 3-meter-deep concrete ditch designed to stop any vehicle. Next come 60 meters more of plowed, raked earth where, until the fall of 1985, antipersonnel mines were planted. (They were removed by agreement between East and West German leaders, but the East Germans made compensating improvements by adding new trip wires.)

§§In East Germany it is called the "forbidden zone" and is about 5 kilometers deep, stretching all along the 836 miles of the border from the Baltic coast to the Czech border—including about 6,500 sq. km. or about 6 percent of the surface of East Germany. "Unreliable" people in their thousands have been moved away, houses torn down, trees cut, and regulations imposed concerning residence and visits.

Only after all this does one reach the fence or, in some areas, the first fence. In 1983–85 a second one was built inside and parallel to the existing one, with improved razor-sharp mesh too narrow to poke fingers through.[33] Between the two fences is a modern version of barbed wire that, when touched, unleashes flares and alarms. In other stretches, vicious dogs run free between fences set a few meters apart.[34]

The "old" fence—itself a third generation product—is 3 meters tall and extends at least a meter under the earth. On each of its concrete posts 5 or 10 meters apart were installed (and presumably still are along some USSR borders) three so-called "SM-70s," each at a different height. The SM-70 is a sort of shotgun which, if a wire is tripped, blows out 90 pieces of sharp-edged shrapnel quite impartially into the body of any man or woman trying to get through.[35] First installed in 1976 the SM-70s evoked a horrified reaction from the West and by mid-1985 were reported to have been dismantled. But no real concession had been made; other border defenses made up for their removal. And there is no public pressure to get them removed from the borders of the USSR itself.

Along the fence, within sight and machine-gun range of one another, are watchtowers with armed guards behind special new glass that prevents anyone outside from watching them.

But beware, he who has struggled this far may still be on Eastern territory: the exact demarcation line is unmarked. A strip of land perhaps fifty meters wide in places is kept clear of shrubbery so that guards in the watchtowers can still shoot the escaper. This outer strip is patrolled by armed "scouts" of the Border Guard Troops. In some spots tunnels have been built under the fence so the guards can race out and grab the escaper without leaving the country's legal limits.[36] In the Soviet Union, on parts of the border than run through swamps or desert or high mountain ridges, the fence may be two or more kilometers back from the actual line.

Beyond the Fence

Even after he has escaped from Soviet Bloc territory, the refugee has not escaped what the Soviet Union considers its jurisdiction. It claims the right to decide whether a refugee from its territory is still to be considered a Soviet citizen, even if he has subsequently taken foreign nationality. Further, the Soviet government has pressured cross-border neighbors— notably Finland and Iran—into treaty obligations to return any would-be escapers who reach their territory. To India, for example, the Kremlin made it plain that letting a Soviet defector reach the West from there would be considered "an unfriendly act" with implied consequences for Soviet trade and other relations. The Indian government has imposed procedures that make defection more difficult, such as forcing defectors to confront Soviet Embassy officials who invariably arrive with messages from loved ones left behind, promises of forgiveness, and appeals to patriotism, often with implied threats. One defector in India "underwent a full-scale open-court interrogation."[37]

But defenses do not stop at this "legal" extension of the borders. The KGB Border Guards' Intelligence Departments recruit secret agents not only inside their own border zones *(prikordon)* but also beyond *(zakordon)*. They have been doing this for many decades. On 22 August 1927 the Chief of the Pskov Provincial OGPU issued a secret circular to commanders of the 9th, 10th, and 11th OGPU Frontier Detachments on the border with Latvia, drawing their attention to "the need for systematically acquiring information among the enemy's border defense forces and border population on enemy territory within a radius of 12.5 km [with a cross-border espionage system and] a strong network of agents in those places where it can be anticipated that the border will be crossed."[38]

Such agent networks, systematically built up over sixty years by hundreds of case officers at a time, extend as deep as fifty or a hundred kilometers into neighboring territory in Finland, West Germany, Austria, Turkey, Iran, and China. The Intelligence Departments have recruited not just the occasional villager but members of the foreign border police and counterintelligence services, town officials, innkeepers, railway and bus personnel, and even anti-Communist activists. From these agents they get information on the fate of escapees from Soviet Bloc territory, on neighboring border defenses and security routines, on smugglers, on spies the enemy may be infiltrating into Communist countries, and on military installations, industry, and transport. They spot and recruit foreigners through their relatives in the border zone of the USSR or those who come from the neighboring country to do business in the zone.***

The Soviet "border" extends yet further. The KGB maintains records on everyone who has succeeded in leaving the USSR illegally; many, including myself, have been sentenced to death in absentia. Our names are on watchlists of mail and telegraph censors, and KGB penetration agents within Western governments and the Soviet emigration abroad seek information on us. Wherever possible, pressure is brought to bear through

***Sometimes these operations yield important intelligence as well as counterintelligence. A Czechoslovakian border guard intelligence unit, for example, spotted as a potential recruit a Sudeten German, Alfred Frenzel, who later became a member of the Defense Committee of the West German Bundestag and betrayed important NATO secrets to the East (F. August testimony before U.S. Senate).

relatives left behind—either to return or to work secretly for the KGB abroad.

Murder enforces the border law. The KGB residencies abroad continue the pursuit on the streets of New York, London, or Paris. The kidnapping of White Russian activists from Paris in the 1930s, the murder of Trotsky's son in Paris in 1938 and then of Trotsky himself in Mexico in 1940, the mass kidnappings from West Germany and Austria after the Second World War, the murders of Russian and Ukrainian emigrants by KGB assassins through the 1950s, 1960s, and 1970s—all represented, in a sense, an extension of the Soviet border.

In a sense it is strung around Soviet installations in the West, too—to make sure that someone who has legally passed the barriers will not use that privilege as a route to escape. One sees newspaper items from time to time about strange doings in Soviet Bloc embassies and trade missions: killings, suicides, officials returning home under heavy escort, some apparently drugged. In 1983 a Soviet official's wife fell to her death from an apartment window in London; in 1985 another did the same in Canada; when diplomat Arkady Shevchenko defected in New York, Soviet officials bundled his son, on post in Geneva, into an airplane for Moscow before he could learn about (and be inspired by) his father's act.

The KGB, with its experience and its special sources within Western governments, stands ready to help its satellites extend their borders in the same way. In 1962 Karel Zizka, a Czechoslovakian official in New York, led the police on a wild high-speed car chase and, when finally caught in Pennsylvania, shot himself. The Czechoslovakian authorities said Zizka had murdered his wife and then, in wild desperation, made this suicidal dash. Six years later, a Czechoslovakian state security officer defected and told the real story: the Zizkas had planned to stay in the West, the KGB found out about it; and while Zizka was at work in the Czechoslovakian UN mission, a Soviet KGB and a Czechoslovakian state security officer tortured his wife, disfigured her face in a meat tenderizer, and shot her. When Zizka returned and saw the terrible scene, he rushed off—to his death.[39]

When the Bulgarian emigre Georgi Markov—a thorn in the Soviet Bloc rulers' side—was murdered in London in 1978, KGB weapons and perhaps KGB sources helped the assassin. Markov had successfully fled Bulgaria in 1969 and broadcast to his countrymen the truth about the corrupt leaders of his former country. On September 7, 1978, on Waterloo Bridge in London, he felt a sharp pain on his thigh, and turned to see a man pick up an umbrella, mumble an apology, and step into a cab. Markov died four days later of the poison that a tiny, specially tooled pellet had injected into his bloodstream.[40] That weapon and its poison could only have been conceived and developed in the KGB's "Chamber."

Bela Lapusnyik knew this danger; he knew how little protection he was really offered by a "protective cell" in a Vienna jail in 1962. He had successfully fled from Hungary, but—as an officer of Hungarian State Security—he knew he was not really over the border, not this close to his homeland. He knew himself to be one of those "important escapees" who were targeted for killing. He urged the authorities to fly him westward, but the day before he was to leave, he died in agony: a Soviet Bloc agent in the Austrian police had been able to get poison into his food.[41]

Some successful escapees have made the mistake of coming back too close to the border area. A prominent Czech Social Democrat in emigration in Italy, Bohumil Lausmann, traveled to Salzburg in what seemed to him the relative safety of the American Zone of occupied Austria. Czechoslovakian agents learned about the trip, and their state security chief in Vienna, Bohumil Molnar, asked the KGB (via me) to help them kidnap him. I checked with my colleague who commanded the large OO unit in Austria; when he readily agreed to send his strongmen and trucks into the American Zone, I put him in touch with Molnar. Together they made their arrangements, snatched Lausmann off a Salzburg street, and drove him into nearby Czechoslovakia where he died in jail. Molnar later became chief of all foreign operations of Czechoslovakian state security; my KGB colleague who did the job became in 1982 chairman of the KGB and subsequently Minister of Internal Affairs of the USSR: Vitaliy V. Fedorchuk.

CHAPTER 22

Dealing with Foreigners

Quarantine

MISTRUST OF CONTACT WITH WESTERNERS IS OLDER THAN THE SOVIET rule in Russia, of course, but the Communist regime has sharpened it and forced other nations without this tradition—Balts and Moldavians, Armenians and Georgians, for instance—to adopt it. To the Kremlin leaders the outsider carries deadly germs in the form of contradictions of official lies, standards of comparison, fresh ideas—the very things they have taken such pain to eradicate inside the country by censorship and propaganda.

If they had had a choice, the Soviet rulers would never have let a foreigner into their domain or let their own people venture out into "enemy territory," as they describe the West in briefings to their official travelers. But of course they must. Even the early Bolsheviks had to admit "diplomatic agents" and engineers to build factories for them. Today, in the maturity of their power and urgently needing vital Western supplies and technology, they admit foreign bankers and businessmen, scientists and students, Olympic athletes, and tourists by the millions. They send many more Soviet citizens abroad, too: in the twenty years between the mid-1960s and the mid-1980s the numbers abroad on permanent postings rose by a factor of four, those on temporary assignment by a factor of ten.*

They would not accept this risk unless they were confident of their ability to contain it within acceptable limits. That confidence rests on the

---

*In Africa alone the number of military advisers increased from 545 to 6,500, economic advisers from 2,400 to 22,000. Of military personnel there are appropriately 8,000 in Latin America, 4,000 in Sub-Saharan Africa, 9,000 in the Middle East and North Africa, 3,5000 in Asia (including Vietnam), and in Afghanistan during their ten years there, over and above their troop strength, 10,000–20,000 civilian advisers. The number of permanent postings rose from about 4,000 to more than 16,000 by the end of the 1980s.

KGB. As soon as the Bolshevik leaders decided to open trade relations with the West, they set their Chekas the task of warding off the danger this would entail. Through the years, devoting huge resources to the task, the leaders have devised ways to reduce and control contacts with foreigners. In effect, they have put foreign relations into quarantine.

First they warn the people about the disease itself—spreading fear and loathing of "alien" influences. When Gorbachev wrote that "in our country you won't find [any disrespectful mention of America or Americans], neither in politics nor in education,"[1] he was counting on Westerners not reading the Soviet press or textbooks. In reality they incessantly refer to evil plots of "imperialists" to destroy the fruits of Soviet socialism and almost never mention NATO without the adjective "aggressive." The CPSU Party Program of 1986 talked of "imperialism's aggressive aspirations," "the forces of aggression and militarism," "the NATO imperialist military bloc," and the like. Gorbachev himself was using old hate- and fear-inspiring formulas when he wrote of the "strong positions of the aggressive and militarist part of the ruling classes in the capitalist countries," when he recalled darkly that the Second World War fell upon the USSR "from the West," when he said the U.S. planned an atomic attack on his country and had the "immoral intention to bleed the Soviet Union white economically," and when he implied that the United States government does not honor its obligations and seeks "to impose its way of life on others."[2] At the same time as Western journalists were deploring President Reagan's "dangerous rhetoric" in calling the Soviet regime an "evil empire," Gorbachev's spokesmen were repeatedly likening Reagan to Hitler and the American government to fascism. In early 1989, long after Gorbachev's pious statements, the U.S. government vehemently protested to Moscow against its continued spread of lies. Just-published books had again charged the U.S. government with developing the AIDS virus and "ethnic" weapons that would kill only nonwhites, as well as murdering Martin Luther King, the political leaders of Grenada and Panama, the American ambassador to Afghanistan, and the Pope.[3] Soviet schoolteachers and textbooks tell schoolchildren that the danger of war is acute; and in that "splendid school" the armed forces, they tell young conscripts that the United States is actively preparing to launch a nuclear attack against the USSR. The Soviet rulers have created among their people a state of mind that even a Soviet official described as "a sense of crisis, an intensified feeling of terror."[4] Military units organize "hate" exhibits; and it is standard doctrine, taught in the schools, youth organizations, and military units, that "hatred for the enemy is the guardian of love for the motherland. . . . In the modern world, love for the socialist homeland is impossible without class hatred."[5]

You can sense the Kremlin leaders' fear in the very term they employ for Western ideas: "ideological subversion" (or "sabotage"). Since it began appearing in the 1960s this term has become part of the ideology of foreign relations. The current Foreign Minister Eduard Shevardnadze, speaking in 1981 as a Politburo member, said the KGB was "taking the most decisive steps against people who try to bring into our environment ideas and views that are alien to us."[6] These "steps" are being taken on a wide front. "Ideological subversion," said KGB Chairman Chebrikov in June 1985, "extends its activities to every form of social awareness— politics and sense of justice, philosophy, morals, science, art, and re- ligion"[7] "Immature" people "avid for sensation" play into the hands of foreign operatives who sneakily "introduce alien morality to undermine Soviet society." Some such "human rights supporters" (as they are de- risively called) accept money or other support from abroad and cooperate with "various leagues, committees, and other subversive centers abroad that illegally bring anti-Soviet literature into our country and establish conspiratorial links with hostile elements for the purpose of inciting people to antistate activities."[8]

The media constantly remind the people that these foreign "traders in souls" are everywhere. I have counted an average of 1,500 such articles or books every year for the past twenty years, recounting stories of Western tourist-spies, businessmen-spies, diplomat-spies, and journalist-spies vio- lating the hospitality of the Soviet Union or waiting outside the Soviet borders to snare Soviet travelers in their nets.

The Soviet citizen got the message: his masters, on whom he depended for everything in life, viewed foreign ideas, manners, clothing, books, and music—and, worst of all, foreign contacts—as a step down the road to treason.

And while warning about the disease, the Kremlin leaders have set up prophylactic measures to prevent infection in the form of laws and regula- tions. As more foreigners arrive to look into "the real Soviet Union" or to pursue that "dialogue between people" which Gorbachev was promoting,[9] Gorbachev's regime has raised new barriers against it. A law of May 28, 1987, for instance, provided punishments for citizens "pestering or both- ering foreigners for the purpose of buying, trading, or acquiring things from them."[10] This law continued a trend of the 1980s set by at least four other new laws. On May 30, 1984, for example, it became a crime to take a foreigner into one's home, to give him a ride in one's car, or to render "other services" (left vague to inhibit any contact) "if such activity con- travenes the rules governing foreigners in the Soviet Union."[11] (Those are the rules that enable the KGB to know where every foreigner is at any given moment.) Another law made it a crime to tell a foreigner about one's work (so-called "work-related secret"—*sluzhebnaya tayna*); including "economic, technical, scientific, or other information."[12] Its intent was clear: to cut off conversations with foreign diplomats, journalists, scholars, and businessmen inside (or outside) the USSR.†

Laws cut off contacts from the foreigners' side, too. According to one of 1981, for example, the authorities can throw out of the country any foreigners who transgress "rules of the socialist community [or] the traditions and customs of the Soviet people or who endanger state security."[13] Since those "rules" and "traditions and customs" may include just about anything—from flirting to wearing blue jeans—the foreigner's presence in the Soviet Union came to depend more than ever on the whim of the leaders and their KGB.

If the new laws are not enough, an old one of 1947 can be applied, although it rarely is: no foreigner is allowed to have any contact with any Soviet citizen (except emergency services, firemen, hotels, taxis, and other public services) for the purposes of acquiring information of any kind, be it the weather, traveling directions, folklore, or news of recent events— unless he has advance authorization from the Soviet government. The law provides punishments for the Soviet citizen involved in unauthorized contacts.

To meet a foreigner, any employee of an organization or enterprise must have advance clearance from his place of employment.‡ Like everyone else there he has signed an oath, as a condition of employment, that he will never make the acquaintance of any foreigner, invite one to his home, travel abroad, or write any letters to foreign countries (and that he will report any foreign letters he receives). If he violates this oath he will not only be fired (and as a result, barred from responsible employment in the

---

†Another law of 1984 sought to prevent dissidents inside the country from getting help from outside. It states that if a citizen accused of "anti-Soviet agitation and propaganda" has received "money or other objects of material value from foreign organizations or persons acting in the interests of those organizations," the rulers can now put him in jail for ten years instead of five. Material help could be a token gift from a foreign visitor to a Soviet acquaintance; a parcel from abroad—if the regime, for its own reasons, chooses to prosecute—can now cost its recipient years in jail or camp (decree of the Presidium of the USSR Supreme Soviet of 11 January 1984). Though the authorities were aiming particularly at the Russian Social Fund to Aid Political Prisoners and their Families (the Solzhenitsyn Fund), in a deeper sense they are trying to smother hope of help from abroad among those who might dare to disagree with them.

‡This permission is given by the people responsible for its foreign relations, who work under KGB domination. In practice, the enterprise's officials who meet foreigners are usually members of its Foreign Relations Department, put there for that purpose.

future) but may face prosecution under the penal code. This pledge is still required and still enforced in the period of *glasnost*. §

The KGB's shield of front men is there to prevent real contact. Western scholars and other visitors to the USSR get their "Soviet government viewpoints" only from a small number of Soviet officials who have been selected by the KGB and briefed on what to say and not say. Many an American Sovietologist has met Georgiy Arbatov or Radomir Bogdanov or Valentin Berezhkov of the USA Institute, but few indeed have ever met, more than once, their opposite numbers (scholars, scientists, or experts of any kind) from the real Soviet society. In 1988 a perceptive Western journalist spotted the pattern. For his visit to a state farm (for which he had to wait a year until the authorities selected a showpiece example), the farming bureaucracy Gosagroprom lent him a car, driver, and guide, "a charming fellow called Viktor Litvinyenko from the 'central economics department.' Viktor, it transpired, is a hydro-geologist who has worked in Ethiopia and at a United Nations agency in Kenya. When Mrs. Thatcher was here last April she visited a Moscow suburb and ended up in the flat of a 'typical worker.' He was called Viktor Litvinyenko. Yes, the same. What a splendid Soviet coincidence."[14]

While taking these precautions to block off their own citizens from "dangerous" contacts, the Soviet rulers have also set up elaborate barriers around the foreigners inside the Soviet Union, both visitors and residents.

Target: The Visitor

Controlling foreigners may seem an awesome task. More than eight million tourists visit the USSR annually and at any given time in the tourist season there are more than a million within the country; add business travelers and technicians and the numbers boggle the imagination. Surely, suggests the skeptic, no security service could cover them all. Well, for the KGB it is not as daunting a task as it seems.

In the first place, the KGB has a head start in covering foreign tourists, a first general idea of who might be troublesome or, conversely, interesting. It screens foreign visitors before they ever reach Soviet soil, perhaps several times: first at the Soviet consulate, perhaps even at the tourist

§The regime keeps this secret from outsiders. In the 1987 publication for foreigners, *USSR: 100 Questions and Answers* (Moscow: Novosti Press Agency), appears this entry: "Can foreign tourists freely contact Soviet citizens? —Of course. These contacts are the personal affair of each individual. Moreover, meetings with specialists, militants of friendship societies, personalities of science and culture, representatives of Soviet public opinion, are organized by Intourist."

agency that arranged the trip, and then again on the way to the USSR. With this advance notice the KGB can keep out the potentially troublesome and focus its assets on the interesting ones—those who look like potential targets for recruitment by Soviet Intelligence.

The KGB controls and staffs all consulates and decides whether to grant a visa.** All Soviet tourist offices abroad are outposts of Intourist, the official Soviet travel agency, which is a subsidiary of the KGB's department, within its Second Chief Directorate, that is responsible for foreign tourists. The KGB expends some effort recruiting agents in Western tourist agencies too (it can pressure them by granting or denying them Soviet business). From such sources they get advance reports on Westerners who are planning to travel to the USSR, trying to spot those who seem especially sympathetic (or hostile) to the USSR or might be traveling with some ulterior purpose. For similar purposes the KGB also recruits Western guides, bus drivers, and train or airplane personnel who go regularly to the USSR.

Now look again at those masses of tourists. Almost all of them travel in groups with guides, sleep in a very few designated hotels, and eat in designated restaurants. The small minority who travel alone are, with few exceptions, escorted from point to point by guides. If driving a car, they are forbidden to deviate from prescribed itineraries along a few authorized highways where no turnoffs are permitted and where their progress is clocked at militia checkpoints.

The tour guide helps keep an eye on these travelers. None is allowed to accompany foreigners without KGB approval. If the foreigner is of no interest (yet) to the KGB and if linguists are in short supply, the KGB may grant this clearance lightly. But if it has taken an interest in the foreigner, the KGB itself assigns the guide. In any case all guides must report on their clients.

In hotels and restaurants that cater to foreigners, KGB men are in charge. A friend of mine, a KGB lieutenant colonel, managed one popular restaurant. The KGB's methods were accurately reported by former Romanian intelligence chief Ion Mihai Pacepa, who told how the KGB imported them into Bucharest in the late 1970s:

> The Athenee Palace was nationalized, and in the early 1950s a KGB
> adviser spent three years transforming it into a special hotel for Western
> visitors. Over the years [. . . it became] a masterful, Soviet-style intel-

**Under its secret statute, the KGB is "endowed with general powers: . . . 3. To sanction the movement of foreigners into and out of USSR territory. . . . 5. To carry out preliminary checks and decide whether or not to issue permits for entry into or exit from the USSR" (Myagkov, p. 32).

ligence operation. Every one of its over 300 employees, from the top manager to the lowliest scrubwoman, was either an intelligence officer or a recruited agent. The hotel's general director [. . . and deputy director were both undercover colonels]. The receptionists were technical officers responsible for photographing the passports and informing [the Intelligence or Counterespionage Service] about the guests' every important move. The doormen were surveillance officers. The housekeeping personnel belonged to [an Intelligence] unit responsible for surreptitiously photographing every scrap of paper in the guests' rooms and in their luggage. The telephone operators and most of the restaurant and nightclub personnel were officers of the electronic monitoring directorate . . . Some of the "foreigners" staying at the hotel were actually [Intelligence] officers documented as Western visitors. . . . Electronic monitoring devices were concealed in every room, as well as in the lobbies, at every table in the two restaurants and nightclub and in all the private salons and conference rooms. All inside telephones were tapped, as well as the public ones within a half-mile radius. Still and television cameras were either permanently installed or disguised in portable concealment devices ready to be deployed elsewhere . . . [The Surveillance Directorate] also ran the more than 30 cabs assigned to the three taxi stands located near the hotel."[15]

So it goes in the few sites on the whole map of the USSR that are accessible to foreigners. Each of them has been prepared for its dangerous role of hosting foreigners. Townspeople who will have contact with foreigners in the course of their business have been cleared by local police and KGB. Police and *druzhinniki* on the streets and in public places are alert to identify anyone seen talking to a foreigner. Tourist attractions all over the country are under permanent watch by full-time sections of the local KGB offices.

Remember, too, that a huge, complex system is already in place to control Soviet citizens; it works against foreigners, too. For instance mail, telephone calls, and other communications with foreign countries are controlled whether made by Soviets or foreigners. And the *agentura* is alerted to take special note of foreigners; no *seksot* would dare meet one (or see someone else meeting one) without reporting to his KGB controller. Robert Kaiser heard, for instance, of a Leningrad musician who applied in 1972 to emigrate to Israel. The KGB called him in and asked, "Why did you befriend the French spy Lafarge in 1963?" The musician truthfully denied knowledge of any such person—until it emerged that in an old bookstore a foreigner had asked him where to find books in foreign languages. "They could not have been together for more than five minutes, but the KGB had a detailed report on the encounter."[16]

Taxi drivers must report on foreign clients, and in the main tourist centers only certain ones are authorized to pick up foreigners. Others do so at the risk of losing their licences. Foreigners who rent cars are immediately identified to the KGB, and automobile surveillance teams can be quickly brought to the scene by radio.

Although the Soviet citizen cannot know how fully the regime covers foreigners, he knows enough to suppress his curiosity or his sense of hospitality and to protect his own livelihood by shunning them (and potential KGB provocateurs).

So the foreign tourist observes the USSR as from a raised moving platform (built and maintained by the KGB) that prevents him from touching or contaminating the population. Many tourists return from their trip saying that they were never watched or bothered. They sometimes think this a sign of relaxation of controls in the USSR, but it is more likely a sign that they stayed on their moving platform as they were enjoined to do.

But look from the KGB's viewpoint at that adventuresome visitor who chooses to step out on his own after the day's festivities are over or who fails to show up for the outing that Intourist has prepared for his group. Perhaps he wants to meet "the real Soviet citizen" or to see for himself "the real Soviet Union." That, to the KGB, is suspicious. Hotel personnel must tell KGB superiors about any unscheduled departures; the guide will note his absence; people he meets, fearing KGB provocation, may report him. When he returns, his guide will chide him gently and recommend that he not miss any of the wonderful things the tour group will see and do. The KGB itself will probably do nothing about it the first time. But if this adventurer steps repeatedly off the moving platform he will be marked as "different" and will get special attention. KGB provocateurs may be sent to make friends with him, to find out what he is up to. If the KGB does not like the results, it may try to discourage his forays—perhaps having him mugged by "hooligans." Or it may conclude that he is a spy, worth an investigation.

One look at the Soviet Union will normally be enough for a foreigner; tourists quickly run out of fresh itineraries anyway. He who returns raises the KGB's eyebrow, and if he returns yet again the KGB wants to know why. As a KGB officer revealed to a foreign businessman suspected of espionage, "A foreigner like you may come here once without being checked. Maybe twice. But never three times."[17] Such a repeat visitor may be granted a visa, but he will be unlikely afterward to think, as those one-time tourers do, that no one paid any attention.

John E. Thune, a YMCA director from Oakdale, California, conducted groups of young people to the USSR three times—and that was enough for the KGB. When his group arrived at a youth camp near Yalta, Thune noticed that his baggage was being searched every day, and his wallet whenever he went swimming. One night four men knocked at his door, forced their way in, and took him off for interrogation. In threatening tones, they told him, "We know everything about you—and you'd better confess. You could be killed, Mr. Thune. Aren't you worried?" They released him the same night but later accused him and his wife of working for the army, CIA, and FBI, as well as for Russian "traitors" in the San Francisco area. [18]

One Thursday afternoon in 1984, an English radiation specialist on his fourth visit to Moscow as a United Nations lecturer heard a quiet knock and a voice asking, in impeccable English, "Dr. Richard Mould?" He opened his hotel door, and in a sudden rush an assailant pinned him to the wall. The English-speaking attacker asked if he knew Valeriy Kryukov. Of course he did: this had been his official contact on earlier visits. "He is under arrest—and you have been named as his collaborator in the West for breaking currency laws. . . . He took you to wild parties. There will be a big public trial. . . ." The charges were false, except for technical violations of the currency laws, and Mould had done nothing more dangerous than bring Kryukov a book on mushrooms. KGB men asked for a written statement—and the promise that he speak no evil about the USSR. Getting this, they insisted on his being their guest at a lavish dinner, and there said, "We want you to help us." They insisted that he get them information about a (nonexistent) antiradiation pill in England and pass it to a certain Soviet professor at a conference in Germany six weeks later. Mould was allowed to leave the USSR, but doubted he would go back to Russia again. [19]

The defensive barriers thrown up for the Moscow Olympics of 1980 offered a glimpse of how far the regime will go to prevent foreign contamination. The operation was, necessarily, under KGB supervision. (The secretary general of the Olympic Preparatory Committee and chief public spokesman—to name only one example—was Aleksandr Gresko, who had been expelled from England as a KGB officer in 1971.) Bits and pieces of the operation surfaced in the Soviet press and before the eyes of Western observers.

By early spring the authorities were sharpening their permanent lists of "suspicious" and "disorderly" people—including human-rights campaigners, Jews who had applied for emigration, Pentecostalists and other religious fundamentalists, and active nationalists. Weeks before the games, they ordered these people out of the cities of the games to outlying rest homes, vacation places, hospitals, jails, or wherever they could be housed. All schoolchildren in those cities were urged to plan vacations away during the time of the games.

Internal Troops and the militia came to the Olympic cities in tens of thousands from all over the country. A Soviet source reported that "practically all the organs of internal affairs of the whole country took part in this complicated task of security and public order."[20] Westerners estimated that, counting the KGB and the Moscow Militia, there might be a policeman to every one of the 300,000 foreign visitors. Although most of them wore plainclothes, one reporter counted 57 uniformed police along a single mile of downtown street.

Moscow was blocked off from the rest of the country: train tickets to the city could be bought only with special permission. Transport Militia checked passengers on the trains and planes and at checkpoints along all the highways; militiamen turned back cars that did not have Moscow registration. Inside the city, checkpoints were set up to thin out traffic; people were urged not to use their cars; and license plates were confiscated for the slightest infraction. One hundred sixty-five streets were closed to all but Olympics traffic.

Meanwhile, the Soviet press accused the West of preparing to sabotage the games, smuggle in anti-Soviet propaganda, and slip in spy groups including emigres under Zionist and CIA sponsorship. At every workplace and school, lecturers called for vigilance. Avoid contact with foreigners! These villains, they told the populace, would pass out chewing gum poisoned with bacteria, including those of veneral diseases. An hour-long television program a week before the games warned the people of the danger under the appropriate title "Lies and Hatred."

A sort of isolation ward was created, not only for the athletes, but also for visitors and journalists. Masses of police, some in uniform and some in plainclothes, milled around outside the Hotels Rossiya and Kosmos where journalists were housed. Visitors were moved in special buses in which armed policemen saw to it that no Soviet citizen "bothered" them. The specially authorized taxi drivers allowed to carry foreigners wore brown berets to help the watching eyes spot any unauthorized fraternization. Behind the fences of the Olympic Village—where no Soviet citizen could enter without KGB approval—pleasant diversions had been prepared: concert hall, disco, chapels, sports fields.

Thus the KGB isolated Moscow's 8 million residents, and another several million in other cities, from contacts with 300,000 visitors. The regime attributed these precautions, of course, to foreign plotting. Referring to the "massive subversive activity of imperialist special services and subversive centers during the Moscow Olympics [. . . enlisting] 50 anti Communist organizations [. . . and] over 300 extremist terrorist groups," KGB First Deputy Chairman Semyon Tsvigun boasted that "all these designs were thwarted . . . by a system of measures that totally paralyzed and ruled out hostile activities. There were no subversive actions of any note on the USSR's territory during the period of the Olympics."[21]

Target: The Resident Foreigner

The KGB's attention to visitors almost looks like indifference when compared with its watch over foreign residents in the USSR: the French Embassy attache, the Reuters correspondent, the Italian engineer, the Bank of America representative, the Belgian trader, the American exchange student, the African trainee. All are closely surveilled and isolated from the population by a screen of KGB informants.

Some Western residents affect a disdain for the KGB's coverage. "Sometimes the KGB follows you," I heard one of them say, "or taps your phone or plants a microphone in your office. And of course their bureaucracy makes things hard for you—as it does for their own citizens. But you can get around that foolishness." To a degree such skeptics are right: no system is perfect, and with luck one can evade parts of this one. But he who scorns it is probably not aware of its redundancies: if one part fails, others will provide the control the KGB requires. He may not understand the system's hidden purpose, either: more than merely "making things hard" for the foreigner, the system seeks to lure or compromise him into secret collaboration. To scorn it one must be ignorant of its successes.

By barriers both visible and invisible, the Soviet leaders keep the resident foreigner as distant from the populace as it can. He is made to live where the Soviet government tells him to live, and that is in apartment buildings reserved for his sort, some within walled compounds, where his telephone can be tapped conveniently and the microphones in all the apartments can be centrally monitored. There his comings and goings (and those of his guests) can be watched efficiently by guards placed outside, ostensibly to protect him from any inconvenience. These guards are KGB men wearing militia uniforms. They stop unknown visitors and identify them and, if they choose, prevent them from entering, beat them up, and drag them away. When a group of men jumped out of a taxicab in the fall of 1980 and tried to run into a foreign compound, ignoring the command to stop, the guards gunned them all down before they could reach the door.[22] Hardly a diplomat who has served in Moscow has not seen people being bundled off after trying to enter an embassy; L. Pribytkov, a dissident, tells it from the other viewpoint: every time he tried to enter a foreign embassy he was confined to a psychiatric hospital.[23]

Even inside the fortress of their office or compound, foreigners are hard put to escape the KGB's eyes and ears. Every one of their Soviet-national helpers—every office assistant, translator, housecleaner, plumber, or electrician—is assigned to them by the KGB. (The KGB's Second Chief Directorate manages both UPDK and Burobin, the central offices that dispense service personnel to diplomatic and private foreigners.) Embassies are studded with microphones and other electronic listing devices; about 500 had been found in American premises in the USSR by 1980[24] and bugging of the new American Embassy being constructed in the late 1980s became an international scandal. So thoroughly had the KGB infested it with state-of-the-art listening devices that even before it was to be occupied, the American government faced the need to tear it down and rebuild it with American materials under American supervision. For thirty years microwaves were beamed against the offices of the American Embassy (perhaps to activate devices inside or to jam some equipment) and after a respite were resumed in 1987. Not only the walls had ears but equipment too: in 1985, tiny electronic sensors were discovered on a dozen American Embassy typewriters to pick up what was typed.[25] Similar mini-microphones were found in clothing and automobiles. In August 1985 Western newspapers headlined the discovery by Western embassies in Moscow of "spy dust" (nitrophenyl pentadienal aldehyde) sprinkled by the KGB on doorknobs, car steering wheels, and other common articles to help track Western residents and identify things and people they touched. In fact, this was an old KGB practice, known for more than twenty years.[26] Beepers on car bumpers tell the KGB where their moving targets are.

KGB men surreptitiously enter offices and residences of foreigners. KGB safecrackers are trained to photograph secret materials (and code books) and replace them so as to avoid detection. The KGB taps resident foreigners' telephones systematically and permanently through a central exchange with hundreds of recorders.

The KGB does more than merely watch. If a foreigner's presence becomes bothersome (like those tourists who return too often) or potentially harmful to the leaders' interests, the KGB makes life more difficult for him and takes steps to get him out of the country.

The Soviet regime has a hundred ways to do so. For one thing, they can invoke rules that they usually overlook. Under a law a foreign journalist must, in principle, get advance clearance from the Foreign Ministry's Press Department (a KGB outpost) before asking any Soviet citizen for any kind of information. Every successful correspondent overlooks this rule—but the KGB can expel him for violating it. The Leningrad KGB slashes the tires of consular officers and newsmen and even loosened a wheel on the automobile of American correspondent Emil Sveilis to make it fall off at the first turn. A journalist may be compromised by provocation, as was

Robert Toth, or poisoned, as was the correspondent of US News and World Report, Robin Knight.

Knight had irritated the Soviet leaders with his perceptive dispatches from Moscow. First the Soviet press criticized him and then, when he and his wife visited Tashkent, the KGB prepared a nightmare for them. After they had toured the city, their Intourist guide, Zair, took them to a teahouse where, he said, other Intourist guides were celebrating a birthday. There in a private room with three other men and two women, Knight was given a drink that made him feel "most peculiar." He left the room and fainted. One of the guides grabbed Knight's wife, tried to force a cup of vodka to her mouth, and when she fought him off, asked her to sleep with him and dragged her out of the teahouse by the wrist. She broke away and found her husband on the ground, "trembling uncontrollably and vomiting." She got him back to their hotel, but there two uniformed policemen were waiting. They grabbed Knight and tried to drag him away. Though she was able to struggle and get him into the hotel, there two plainclothesmen stepped up and assisted the uniformed policemen to make her sign a statement that her husband was "drunk and disorderly." She tried to call the American Embassy in Moscow but was told that the office telephone was not working. By the time she got him onto his bed, Knight was trembling so violently that his wife put a balled-up handkerchief in his mouth to keep him from accidentally biting his tongue. She finally reached the embassy by phone and the two flew back to Moscow immediately.[27]

KGB men vandalize apartments, make their targets sick during trips to areas the regime would rather not have them visit, drug them and photograph them in gutters seemingly drunk, in bedrooms seemingly cavorting. KGB "hooligans" mug them; KGB-directed traffic policemen stop them for imagined or trivial offenses; KGB agents draw them into illegal transactions for art objects or foreign currency. And some foreigners are threatened with death or injury to themselves or their families.

Foreign students pose special problems—and offer special opportunities to the regime. Unlike the diplomat, confined by Soviet restrictions in a ghetto with his diplomatic brethren and protected by his own guards and security precautions, the student may be in regular contact with young Soviet citizens, even housed with a Soviet roommate. Prudent Soviet citizens are, of course, as likely to fear contact with students as with any other kind of foreigners, but the student can move around with relative freedom.†† Also, he stays longer in the country and learns the language.

††The difference is only relative, and the foreign student is subjected to travel and other

The KGB has a special department operating solely against foreign students, which keeps each student under individual watch. His Soviet-national roommates and classmates are required, as a condition for continuing their own studies, to report on him to the KGB. The roommate, in fact, is invariably selected and assigned there with the specific task of watching and assessing the foreigner. It could not be otherwise: a Soviet student having on his record such long and intimate exposure to dangerous foreign germs would otherwise be ruined before his career even started. Ruined, too, would be the career of the KGB case officer responsible for covering the Western student should he fail to exploit this close contact.

Students sometimes return from the USSR confident that they had enjoyed freedoms denied to other foreigners residing in the USSR, had gotten around more, and had met people outside the circles that foreigners are usually permitted to frequent. Some found their new friends relaxed and willing to discuss politics and other subjects "as freely as in America," as one of them put it (adding naively that "these conversations were made possible by an exceptionally able interpreter, a man who had spent three years of his childhood in New York"). These and other contacts of foreign students do not escape the attention of the KGB. Some of those relaxed, free-talking Russians are admirably bold, but many of them are relaxed because they are doing and saying what KGB case officers have told them to do and say.

Foreign students offer glowing opportunities for recruitment as KGB agents. Unlike tourists, they stay in the country long enough for the KGB to find their weaknesses and play on them. Unlike diplomats, they are out in the cold of Soviet life where the KGB has unlimited access to them; unprotected by diplomatic immunity, they are particularly vulnerable to KGB pressures. Most attractive of all to the KGB is their future: today's student in the USSR—learning the language and becoming an "expert" on the country—is tomorrow's specialist on Soviet affairs in the government, university faculties, research institutes, or newspapers of his own country. Under KGB control he can later influence Western policies and attitudes in directions desired by the Soviet leaders or learn the secrets of Western foreign ministries, intelligence agencies, or high-technology industries. On this task of recruitment, therefore, the KGB concentrates special effort.

---

restrictions. For example, each time he wants to visit another town—even one that is open to foreigners—he must get special permission. He is supposed to arrange any recreational travel through Intourist (U.S. Congress, *Helsinki Report* [1980], p. 289). Many foreigners studying and training in the USSR live and study apart from Soviet student life, either in special groups or in institutions set aside for them.

Recruitment is the ultimate goal of these KGB operations against foreigners. Perhaps the student is more vulnerable and more accessible, but the KGB works hard, too, at recruiting diplomats, businessmen, and journalists.

Each resident foreigner falls into one or another sector of KGB responsibility. Just as there is a group of KGB officers watching students, so too is there one, for instance, with the full-time task of watching and recruiting American journalists. Each such journalist becomes the personal target of a member of that group.‡‡ That KGB case officer's career depends not only on preventing "his" journalist from spying or otherwise harming the security of the state but also on fulfilling his own quota of recruitments.

The KGB provides this case officer immense powers and widespread facilities. He is enabled to offer his target both carrot and stick: making a journalist's time in Moscow a success or a failure, for example. He can arrange behind the scenes to get him a scoop—the first Western look at an otherwise inaccessible area or an unusual interview with a leader—or, contrariwise, can deny him the interviews he requests or the travel permits he needs. The case officer can call on militia or surveillance team, street thugs or money changers, attractive women or homosexuals to pressure or compromise his target or to test his character. (Western Embassy code clerks, a prime KGB target, have noticed the unusual beauty of the women assigned to clean their apartments.)

The case officer collects in a file all the KGB knows: personal information received from the foreigner's home country and tidbits from Soviet-national employees in his target's office or from Intourist guides, supplemented by insights derived from microphones in bedrooms, secretly opened mail, hour-by-hour street surveillance, provocations, and harassments. As the journalist Emil Sveilis rightly observed after two years in Leningrad, "They know when you have quarrels, they know when you have sex and with whom, and they know how much you drink and smoke. Over a period of time, the Russians have a pretty clear character picture of every foreigner stationed in the Soviet Union."[28]

With this information, if it is promising, the case officer goes ahead with an approach to the target, using whatever means seem most promising: sexual or homosexual entrapment, illegal transactions, offer of money or advantage—and whatever manner: sympathy, persuasion, brutality, or menace.

To this activity the KGB has devoted scores of case officers at a time

---

‡‡The case officer may be responsible for as few as one or two targets—if they are as important as, say, cipher clerks or as vulnerable as students—or as many as ten or more.

over many decades. I got intimations of some successes from colleagues who were working in this line while I was serving in KGB headquarters, and so many have been publicly exposed since then that there can be no doubt that this massive effort has paid dividends for Soviet security and intelligence—such recruitments as those of the lonesome secretary in the American Embassy, Annabelle Bucar; the homosexual code clerk in the British Embassy, William Marshall; the girl-hungry American sergeant, Roy Rhodes; the British naval attache's homosexual clerk, William Vassall; the French Ambassador Maurice Dejean; and others exposed as recently as the late 1980s.

While preventing or exploiting its citizens' contacts with foreigners inside the USSR, the KGB works just as vigorously to prevent foreign infection of Soviet citizens abroad.

The Soviet Citizen Abroad

Faced with the need to send some of their citizens out into the temptations of foreign lands, the Soviet leaders hand them over, as they do foreigners in the USSR, to the care of the KGB. Soviet citizens have been in KGB hands all their life, of course, but the grip tightens when they go abroad. There they are more exposed to alien influences and, having got beyond the border defenses, need only slip out the door to escape Soviet rule. So, far from escaping the tensions of Soviet life, the traveler leaving the country finds himself carrying the burden of three relationships with the KGB.

First, the KGB now makes him its active collaborator, whether he likes it or not and whether or not he was already one in the past. As a condition attached to this coveted privilege of travel abroad, he must submit reports and collect information as instructed and snitch to the security officer on the doings and sayings of his colleagues. Second, the KGB brings him even closer under its protective wing; the new world he is entering being full of pitfalls and lurking villains, the KGB carefully instructs him on how to behave and sees that he stays on the prescribed path. Third, because he is now more exposed to enemy wiles—indeed, because he wanted or was willing to leave the home country—the KGB treats him as a potential traitor. Members of his family are held hostage at home, and fellow voyagers and informants abroad are instructed to watch him. If they report that he has broken or bent the rules or shown independence of mind or been friendly with foreigners or adopted Western ways, the KGB, unwilling to take a risk, will send him home posthaste—and never allow him out again. Even if he completes his time abroad with spotless record, he is put on the KGB's list for "PK" (interception and reading of mail) for two years, as are all who have been abroad and exposed to the virus of Western ideas and contacts.

The regime leaves no doubt in the mind of the would-be traveler about the rules of conduct abroad. They are spelled out precisely, and he must read and sign that he understands them. They require him to report to his group chief or the local embassy all contacts with foreigners and if possible to get advance permission to meet with them.

A Soviet delegation is a curious assemblage. Whether it goes abroad to conduct arms control negotiations or to visit farms or scientific institutions, as sport team or ballet company or circus troupe, it has its KGB and GRU staff officers riding along—using it for cover to meet a spy abroad, or to cultivate a personality who might be made a spy some day, or perhaps to do some spying themselves. Each delegation has its informants, spying on or provoking one another. Larger delegations contain at least one KGB officer with the sole purpose of coordinating all this mutual spying and making sure the delegates follow their instructions.§§

How many spies are there in a delegation? Impossible to say, since so many official travelers have won this privilege by long and faithful secret collaboration with the KGB. Certainly the KGB would not allow the proportion to drop below one formally recruited secret KGB informant for every six or eight delegates. That does not count KGB staffers who are simply using the cover of the delegation for convenience. If one were to include all those required to serve as informants during the delegation's work, it would become obvious that the delegation consists of nothing but spies and counterspies. This is no secret to those who go abroad or who seek to go. The satirist Alexander Zinoviev put these words into the mouths of fictional characters:

> The scientific section of the Central Committee confirmed the membership of the delegation to an international conference. Theirs is the ultimate decision, if you do not count the KGB who at the last moment always hold several people back and slip a few of their own people in in their place (even though almost all the members of the delegation or of the tourist group are essentially in their pocket anyway) . . . the process between the drawing up of the lists for a delegation or a tourist group at source and the confirmation of the final list by the Central Committee [is curious]. At source (in the sections and faculties) they included in the lists everyone who had done productive work over the last few years and who had

§§A distinct KGB department—for "Delegatsiya" or delegations work—watches over temporary travelers abroad. Of course it cannot supply watchdogs for every delegation; there are too many delegations now. But this department sees to it that no delegation is without its watchdogs, from whatever part of the KGB.

acquired a decent reputation. . . . Then the list moved up to the level of the administrators and the deans, where a number of the decent people were deleted and replaced by rogues and second-raters. Next, at the level of rectors and academic departments, a few more of the decent people still left were removed and new names added of even more mediocrity. At ministerial level, and in the governing bodies of the academies, almost all the surviving people of any worth . . . were struck off and their place taken by scum of a kind which in the past would never even have been admitted to local meetings. Finally the department of science of the Central Committee took the process to its logical conclusion.[29]

Vladimir Solovyov tells about his own tourist group traveling in Western Europe in the 1970s:

> When a group of Soviet tourists travels abroad, they are enveloped by an especially dense atmosphere of "Sovietism": suspicion, tailing, denunciations, threats, blackmail, secret searches, provocations. Of course, one is surrounded by the same things in Russia itself. But there they exist in a more diluted state, whereas the Soviet tourist experiences them in their quintessence, in sharp focus, in their highest degree. During one such trip to the Benelux countries, I approached a writer whom I shall call X and told him that before our departure the KGB people had warned me that he was especially suspect and had suggested that I keep an eye on him. At this, he broke out laughing and said they had told him the same thing about me and had suggested that he keep an eye on me.[30]

Soviet merchant ships must carry cargoes to and from the West, and fishing boats must trawl in faraway waters. The KGB must therefore ensure that they do not bring back contamination from foreign ports. Sea Captain Vladil Lysenko has told how this is done.[31] The regime always starts from the position that no one should be allowed to go ashore at all. When Lysenko argued that sailors need a change of scene and feet on solid ground once in a while and should at least be able to go ashore in Communist countries like Cuba, his directors found the proposal "shocking" and "absurd": "They will go around in evil spots." And in fact that remains the guiding principle.

Even if the sailor's ship will not touch land but merely fish in nearby waters, the sailor must—to leave Soviet territorial waters—have a form of exit visa called "Visa Number Three." If his ship is going to a foreign port but he is not to be allowed to go ashore, he needs a "Visa Number Two" (and he will be closely watched, all the same, by political officers and KGB informants). With a "Visa Number One" sailors can go ashore abroad, but to get their "seamen's passports" (valid for one year only) they must have the recommendation of three party members and pass a KGB check of background, family, and friends.

They go ashore under restraints that Westerners might find hard to believe. Before arriving at a foreign port a list of those authorized to go ashore is handed to the ship's political officer who makes up groups of three to five men, one of whom must be a party member and representative of the ship's command. Passports are distributed only after the shore-goers have signed a register certifying the exact hour of debarkation and their scheduled return. They are filled with tales of ports teeming with people waiting to kidnap or lead them astray. (Bound for Tito's Yugoslavia, they were told that it is a fascist state.) Trembling with fear and looking over their shoulders to spot the enemy surrounding them, the shore party sticks close together. No one can separate from his group even for a minute; if one breaks regulations, all are held responsible. (Anyone who jumps ship is considered a traitor, and his family back home is punished.) The actual "shore leave," usually limited to two or three hours, is not a matter of tourism or relaxation, but a frenetic shopping trip for cheap articles that can be resold for a profit in the USSR to supplement the starvation wages paid by the Soviet merchant marine. Such transactions are illegal, of course, but the KGB looks aside—until it wants to pressure or punish a sailor.

The watch over Soviets permanently stationed abroad (the so-called "Soviet colony" in a host country) is assigned to a section of the local KGB *rezidentura* (residency) known as Line K (for *Kontrrazvedka,* or counterintelligence).*** Within that section, each case officer watches over one category of Soviet citizens in the area: diplomats, trade representatives, journalists, or military attache personnel, for instance. He keeps security files on "his" people, to which he adds the information he gets from his secret informants.

The Soviet colony is organized so as to simplify this KGB shepherding. With few exceptions (and those for the regime's convenience, not the individual's) the employees and their families live on the premises of the embassy or trade mission or together in nearby apartment houses rented for them. Their leisure time is filled with trade union meetings and group projects and festivities. Wives are expected to keep visible company with

***Its designation distinguishes it from other lines of activity such as collecting intelligence on scientific and technological matters (Line X), collecting intelligence on political, economic, and social matters (Line PR), or supporting KGB operatives abroad under false, Western nationality ("illegals"—Line N). In my time there were separate lines for counterintelligence and internal security work (SK, for *Sovetskaya Koloniya*).

other wives; unexplained absences, however innocent, are usually noticed and reported. ††† Thrown thus as closely together as in crowded Moscow, tensions heightened by everyone's awareness that he is being watched and that he may be sent home for the most minor infraction of the rules, the Soviet colony is especially vulnerable to rivalry, jealousy, friction, intrigue, and denunciation.

Unwritten rules make it delicate, even dangerous in this atmosphere, for denizens to go out alone into the city; they might draw upon them the jealousy of colleagues and the quizzical eye of Line K. During a stay in a Western country in the 1970s, a Soviet trade delegate took the risk of dropping into a Western embassy to talk about eventual emigration. Though he returned to the communal Soviet residence only three or four hours after leaving it, he felt so uneasy about having exposed himself by that one short absence that, in panic, he defected, although that had not been his intention.[32]

If Line K learns that a Soviet official abroad has failed to report any contact with a foreigner (or if his report was not full or frank) or if it has the slightest hint that a member of the Soviet colony is becoming enamored of Western living conditions, it will open an investigation. In Vienna, for example, an untrustworthy informant told the KGB that he had heard indirectly that Okreshidze, the director of a Soviet firm, had told a friend that it would be easy to transfer money to a Swiss account and escape to the West. On this thin lead I had to throw in every asset at my disposal. Microphones were planted in Okreshidze's apartment, new informants were recruited among Okreshidze's friends (this is easy, for everyone cooperates—or is sent home), and a neighbor's apartment was used as a listening post. Nothing concrete was turned up to justify the charge or the KGB effort, but Okreshidze's file thenceforth contained a blemish that would harm his future.

For absurd reasons Moscow reopened an old case against one of the top Soviet diplomats in Vienna, Andrey Timoshchenko, and so I had to set out to surround him with secret eyes and ears. I enlisted the cooperation of KGB men working, for cover purposes, in Timoshchenko's section— among them KGB Col. Vasily Sitnikov, today deputy head of the Soviet Copyright Agency. I recruited a diplomatic underling of Timoshchenko's and the latter's chauffeurs to report on his doings and was planning to have his safe rifled, his office bugged, and his telephone tapped, when I myself escaped to the West. This idiotic investigation seems to have led nowhere:

†††Military technicians in Africa, Latin America, and the Middle East live in barracks, often far from local population centers. Some 15,000 were stationed in Egypt in the 1960s, but the man in the street rarely saw them.

a year later, after the occupation ended, Timoshchenko was made counselor of the Soviet Embassy.

Line K uses all the obvious sources to watch over Soviets. Working for me in Vienna were the chief telephone operator of the Soviet representation, the chief duty officer at the Soviet residence building, the chief of the Communications Section, the head of the motor pool, and the man in charge of the embassy garage. In addition, we also used local citizens as agents, including Russian emigres who could report on Soviet officials' unauthorized contacts with other emigres.

We were frequently asked to shadow visiting Soviet officials, such as Berezin, deputy chairman of the All-Union Central Council of Trade Unions, who was leading the Soviet delegation to an international congress. We put a three-man KGB team on his heels—and although we detected no disloyalty, he was never again allowed out of the USSR.

In the 1970s Soviet diplomat Arkadiy Shevchenko decided to stay in the United States; one can imagine the panic that grabbed Vitaly A. Pochamkin, Line K chief in Geneva, where Shevchenko's son was stationed. Alerted by a telegram, he ordered his men to hustle the young Shevchenko into a plane to Moscow before word of his father's defection spread.[33]

Why is this work given such high priority? The answer is much clearer from the Soviet viewpoint than from the Western one. Better than anyone else the Soviet leaders sense danger to their power. They can distinguish between their own propaganda (which portrays a people solidly behind them) and the threatening reality. If they were to expose their people to the truth about the West or allow them to deal freely with Westerners, their people would have bitten of the apple of knowledge. Russian and Ukrainian and Lithuanian churchmen would really—as propaganda falsely claims they do now—form links with Western church groups; scientists would put their heads together with Western counterparts to work out joint solutions to chemical and medical problems; managers would try to adopt the methods that work in the free world. And all of this would expose the Soviet leaders as barriers to "the radiant future," not as guides to it.

PART V

FOREIGN DIMENSIONS OF INTERNAL WARFARE

"The capitalist states constitute a base and the rear for the internal enemies of our revolution."—Iosif Stalin, 1927.

CHAPTER 23

Internal War and External Policy

The Goals of Foreign Policy

WHEN HE CALLED ATTENTION TO "THE ORGANIC TIE BETWEEN EACH state's foreign and domestic policies" and pointed to "the uniformity of our activities at home and in the international arena,"[1] Mikhail Gorbachev was saying nothing startlingly original, but he was offering the outside world the only reliable guide to Soviet conduct abroad. The foreign policies of the Kremlin are, indeed, the external dimension of its internal policy.

However, Gorbachev was leading his Western readers astray when he suggested that they could better understand the motives of Soviet policies by getting into the shoes of the Soviet "people." No doubt it is true that, as he wrote, "each people and each country have a life of their own, their own laws, their own hopes and misconceptions, and their own ideals,"[2] but it is irrelevant. The hopes or ideals of people under Soviet rule have even less to do with the Kremlin's foreign policy than with its domestic policy. Inside the country, far from representing its subjects, the Kremlin wages against them the struggle that we have described; and there is no reason on earth to suppose that this struggle ends at the Soviet frontiers. Abroad as much as at home the leaders are fighting to hold on to their power; and this, more than anything else, determines how they will act and react.

Other factors also influence them, of course. Some observers think, for instance, that the global mission assigned to "the motherland of socialism" by Marxist-Leninist ideology not only justifies and rationalizes their conduct abroad but actually motivates it. Others emphasize the

337

influence of the Russian historical experience, causing the Soviet leadership, which is overwhelmingly of Russian nationality, to distrust the outside world or to fear foreign invasions. When the Soviet hand stretches out toward distant regions, some historians recall a long tradition of Russian expansionism, while some geopoliticians see the normal drives of a still-youthful world power seeking warm-water ports or raw materials. But whatever the validity of such theories, they offer little help in anticipating Soviet conduct. Again and again Western statesmen are caught unprepared. When Soviet troops invaded Afghanistan, the American president was both surprised and "disappointed."

One way to avoid such surprises is to distinguish between the interests of the Kremlin leaders and the apparent interests of the "Soviet Union." The party bosses have demonstrated their tendency to reject a course of action that favors the nation's economic or political interests if it would weaken their monopoly of power. On the other hand, they have proved likely to adopt a course of action they think essential to preserve that monopoly, even if it damages what outsiders might think of as "national interests." This is precisely what they did when they invaded Hungary, Czechoslovakia, and Afghanistan, and when they built the Berlin Wall— to the astonishment of many a Western observer who assumed that the Kremlin would not sacrifice its growing influence abroad or risk losing the Western sources of technology so desperately needed for its industry and armed forces.

Why do Western analyses of Soviet foreign policy so often overlook the impact of this internal struggle? For one thing, much of Western opinion has been misled about the relations between ruler and ruled in the USSR. For another, perilously little is known in the West about Soviet decision-making. Even with the added facts and insights that *glasnost* has opened, whole institutions remain hidden or barely known. Neither we nor the Soviet people are allowed to know how policy is made nor exactly by whom, and the policymakers we do know remain shadowy figures. Western scholars and statesmen have had to rely on what they are told by people who are screened, selected, and sometimes briefed to mislead them.

This enforced ignorance has left the West vulnerable to illusions. Soviet spokesmen adeptly project the idea that East and West, guided by similar priorities and goals, grapple with similar problems. Conflict, they suggest, arises simply from the different ways that "people" under socialism and capitalism perceive their own interests—while ultimately all people seek the same goal of peace and welfare. So persuasively do Kremlin leaders propose "cooperation in order to reduce tensions" and to find "mutually acceptable solutions" that some politicians of NATO countries routinely refer to the Soviet government as a "security partner." Soviet spokesmen share our horror at the prospect of nuclear war, talk of a common danger in the form of an "arms race," and deplore the "rhetoric" of "hard liners" on one side or the other.

Their constitution claims respect for the "sovereign equality" of states, the "inviolability of frontiers" and "territorial integrity," and the "equal rights of peoples and their right to decide their own destiny." It forbids intervention in the internal affairs of other countries and promises "fulfill-ment in good faith of obligations." These, said the 1986 Party Program, are the "aims and avenues of Soviet foreign policy." Gorbachev says people want a world in which everyone would preserve his own philosophic, political, and ideological views and way of life. He promotes stability and pleads with Westerners to believe in his government's "genuinely good intentions in foreign policy."[3]

Such pieties have little to do with decision-making, however. The Soviet leaders admit that their treaty obligations are not to be interpreted "in a narrow, formal way," for they "are subordinated to the laws of class struggle and social development. . . . The class approach cannot be discarded in the name of legalistic considerations."[4] So saying, they ordered their tanks and half a million troops into a military invasion of "fraternal" Czechoslovakia in 1968, violating written and oral commit-ments and at least four principles of their own constitution. (And, incidentally, causing surprise in the West where "inside information" to the contrary had been "leaked" by Soviet sources to Western diplomats and journalists.) When Gorbachev later called into question the doctrine of international class struggle, he asked rhetorically, "Does this imply that we have given up the class analysis of . . . global problems?" He answered his own question: No. "A class-motivated approach to all phenomena of social life is the ABC of Marxism."[5]

Elsewhere the Kremlin rulers have spoken more frankly. Even in their constitution, alongside the pieties, you can find this more useful listing of their foreign goals: "ensuring international conditions favorable for build-ing communism in the USSR, safeguarding the state interests of the Soviet Union, consolidating the positions of world socialism, supporting the struggle of peoples for national liberation and social progress, prevent-ing wars of aggression, achieving universal disarmament, and consistently implementing the principle of the peaceful coexistence of states with different social systems."[6] Gorbachev's predecessors usefully distilled these aims into three "main tasks" which reveal the Kremlin's true priorities— once you have translated the jargon. "The main tasks of Soviet foreign policy," said Brezhnev and Andropov, are:

- "to defend the achievements of the October Revolution" (which means holding on to the power they seized and have extended since then);
- "to thwart imperialist plots against the homeland of socialism" (which means neutralizing the foreign menace to that power); and
- "to ensure the necessary external conditions for building a Communist society."[7]

These priorities help explain the Kremlin's decision to invade Afghanistan. They help explain why it has sacrificed international goodwill and credibility by apparently unnecessary actions in the West against Soviet emigres and foreign radios and why it has kept its people away from foreigners and penned up inside the country.

Since the advent of Gorbachev the Soviet rulers have been going about these tasks in new ways that may foreshadow a basic change. Therefore they deserve a closer look.

Defending the Revolution

Two events of 1989 starkly exposed the changes wrought by the desperate crisis of the Soviet system. One was the withdrawal of Soviet forces from Afghanistan. The other was the tolerant way the Kremlin dealt with Poland's and Hungary's moves toward a multiparty system and freedom from Moscow's controlling hand.

Never before Afghanistan had the Soviets withdrawn from a position won.* Only a few years earlier they had demonstrated in that same country how determined they were to hold on. In 1978 they had thought Afghanistan was finally in their hands when, after a quarter-century of preparation, Moscow's men had taken power there. In faithful imitation of their masters, they had named their bloody coup d'etat the "Glorious April Revolution" and had followed the best Soviet traditions by jailing, executing, purging, or exiling its political "enemies" and terrorizing the population. Soviet-style institutions were established, and Soviet advisers dominated the government and economy; Afghanistan had joined the Soviet Bloc. So, when a year and a half later this client regime was endangered by growing resistance, the Soviet Army moved in not as invaders but as defenders of a victorious revolution. Now, nine years later, there they were leaving their Afghan puppets to fight on alone.

---

*Their 1955 withdrawal from occupation of a small segment of Austria is not counted. They had never won power over the country as a whole, and Austria had little strategic significance.

Neither had the masters of the Soviet empire previously tolerated the kind of changes the Hungarians and Poles were making in 1989. On the contrary, they had demonstrated again and again how high a price they would pay to prevent such changes. In November 1956, when a rebellious people in that same Hungary dismantled its Soviet-style institutions—the Communist party's monopoly of power, information controls, and travel restrictions—Moscow sent in Soviet tanks, killed and imprisoned thousands, executed the new rulers, and turned back command to local puppets. When in East Germany in 1961 another satellite regime was threatened—this time by the outpouring of its population by hundreds of thousands, to the West through Berlin—the Soviet rulers did not hesitate to violate their international agreements and risk military confrontation with the Western occupiers of Germany: they built a wall and made the country a prison. Then, seven years later when their client regime in Czechoslovakia began to give socialism "a human face"—abolishing censorship, guaranteeing freedom of association and assembly, making passports freely available, allowing greater democracy within the Communist Party, and separating state institutions from party control—the Kremlin sent in a half-million Warsaw Pact troops to "normalize" the situation. In Poland in 1980–81 the people formed in a giant Solidarity workers' movement independent of the Communist Party, censorship was eroding, people were freely traveling abroad, and power was slipping from the hands of the Kremlin's surrogate rulers. So again the Moscow chiefs struck and restored the authority of their loyal minions, this time using (as in earlier Polish uprisings) special Polish troops they had created and trained.

Thus before Gorbachev's reforms the Kremlin had reacted violently to five different situations within the Soviet Bloc: disarray and growing weakness of local rule (Afghanistan), general rebellion (Hungary), mass exodus (East Germany), genuine reform of institutions (Czechoslovakia), and the emergence of social structures independent of the ruling party (Poland). These crises shared one characteristic: each of them menaced the party's monopoly of power.† As Gorbachev later wrote with satisfaction, "Some socialist countries went through serious crises in their development. Such was the case, for instance, in Hungary in 1956, in Czechoslovakia in 1968, and in Poland in 1956 and then again in the early 1980s. Each of these crises had its own specific features. They were dealt with

---

†In Romania where, during this same period, the Bucharest regime was shaking off some of the ties binding it to Moscow, this menace did not exist: the ruling party never loosened its tight, repressive grip over society. Therefore the regime's leaders posed no menace to the Soviet system either in Romania or Moscow—and therefore the Soviets did not invade. (Moreover, the degree of Romania's independence from Moscow was greatly exaggerated; see, for instance, Pacepa, pp. 8–9).

differently. But the fact is that a return to the old order did not occur in any of the socialist nations."[8]

The stakes—in the Kremlin's eyes—are nothing less than self-preservation. The leaders have always feared that the slightest crack in their system, even at an outlying fringe of a satellite society, might spread and shake the whole edifice of Soviet power. Enormities like the Czechoslovak Action Program of 1968 and the creation of Polish Solidarity in 1980 had sprung from small concessions like easing censorship and letting people travel freely or form independent organizations. "The events in Poland graphically testify to what a departure from firm positions, liberalism, and a lack of the proper reaction to antisocial sentiments and manifestations could lead to." From the Kremlin's point of view, little concessions create "a platform for counterrevolution" which is exploited by "forces supported morally and materially from the outside . . . with the aim of seizing power in the country and creating conditions for the restoration of capitalism."[9]

Thus these violent reactions stemmed from the Communist leaders' fear of losing power via their outlying regions. Just before invading Czechoslovakia they embodied these attitudes in what has become known as the "Brezhnev Doctrine." It was not new‡ it was not Brezhnev's invention, and it was much more than a transient justification for the forthcoming invasion.

Briefly, this doctrine asserts that "a threat to the cause of socialism in any socialist country poses a threat to the security of the socialist community as a whole," and "the sovereignty of an individual socialist country cannot be counterpoised to the interests of world socialism." Thus it gathers under the Soviet protective wing any state—and, conceivably, even breakaway parts of a state—that the Soviet leaders deem to be "socialist." "Consolidation and protection of the gains of one socialist country is a common international duty of all socialist countries." And it proclaims defiance: "We will never let imperialism, by peaceful or nonpeaceful means, from within or without, make a breach in the socialist system."§

---

‡The CPSU Party Program of 1961, for example, had stated that "the combined forces of the socialist camp guarantee each socialist country against encroachments by imperialist reaction" and stressed the need for the "closest unity." "Their fraternal unity and cooperation conform to the supreme national interests of each country."

§"There are common laws governing socialist construction, a deviation from which might lead to a deviation from socialism as such. . . . A threat to the cause of socialism in [any socialist country] poses a threat to the security of the socialist community as a whole, which is no longer only a problem of the people of that country, but also a common

It did not really matter whether a socialist state wanted this protection; the decision rested with the leadership of the socialist camp, i.e., the Kremlin. No matter, either, internal laws or treaty obligations or international law: "laws and their principles are subordinated to the laws of the class struggle."

Had Gorbachev now wiped all this out? Did the Kremlin's tolerance of Hungary's and Poland's slip toward multiparty democracy in 1988–89 and its withdrawal of troops from Afghanistan signal a loss of the instinct for self-preservation? There are reasons to think not.

Gorbachev himself has uttered words that echo the Brezhnev Doctrine. While paying lip service to the independence of each socialist country,** he has repeatedly asserted the unshakable principle of the socialist community's "cohesion,"†† which is moreover still written into the CPSU

---

problem, a concern for all socialist states" (Brezhnev speech to the 5th Polish Communist Party Congress on 12 November 1968).

"The sovereignty of individual socialist countries cannot be counterposed to the interests of world socialism and the world revolutionary movement. . . . A socialist country . . . retains its national independence thanks precisely to the power of the socialist community and primarily to its chief force, the Soviet Union and the might of its armed forces. The weakening of any link in the world socialist system has a direct effect on all the socialist countries" (*Pravda,* 26 September 1968, article by Sergey Kovalev).

"Support, consolidation and protection of [a socialist country's] gains . . . is a common international duty of all socialist countries" (communique of the meeting of party leaders in Bratislava on 3 August 1968).

"Never will we consent to allow imperialism, by peaceful or nonpeaceful means, from within or without, to make a breach in the socialist system . . ." (Warsaw letter of 15 July 1968 to the Czechoslovak Communist Party Central Committee, printed in *Pravda* on 18 July 1968). In addition to the above-cited documents, Andrey Gromyko formulated an early version of the doctrine in his speech to the CC CPSU Plenum of 27 June 1968 (*Pravda,* 28 June 1968).

**The entire framework of political relations between the socialist countries must be strictly based on absolute independence. . . . The independence of each party, its sovereign right to decide the issues facing its country and its responsibility to its nation are the unquestioned principles" (*Perestroika,* p. 165). Every Communist country has the right "to develop in its own way" and none has the right to intervene in the internal affairs of another "under any pretext whatsoever" (joint statement with Yugoslavia, 18 March 1988; also in statement in Prague in April, 1987).

††"We are firmly convinced," Gorbachev wrote in *Perestroika* (pp. 165, 166), "that the socialist community will be successful only if every party and state cares for both its own and common interests, if it respects its friends and allies, heeds their interests and pays attention to the experience of others. Awareness of this relationship between domestic issues and the interests of world socialism is typical of the countries of the socialist community. We are united, in unity resides our strength. . . . No fraternal country . . . can resolve its tasks on the international scene if it is isolated from the general course."

In Poland in July 1986 he praised the local leadership for having "used its own

Party Program.‡‡ Therefore it would be foolhardy to consider the Brezhnev Doctrine "dead," as some Soviet Bloc sources—and Western spokesmen—were doing in 1989.

In mid-1989 Gorbachev in France said that his notion of a "common European house from the Atlantic to the Urals 'ruled out' the use or threat of force . . . inside alliances or anywhere else." He labeled as "inadmissible" any attempts to limit the sovereignty of states—friends or allies or anybody else," and admitted that the "social and political order" could change in Eastern European countries if their people so wished.[10] The Western press thus reported that he had "solemnly renounced the use of force within the Warsaw Pact" and to have "unequivocally repudiated the Brezhnev doctrine."[11]

But because this doctrine is rooted in the survival instinct of the Kremlin rulership, it will not so easily go away. The Kremlin feels compelled to take the risk of "democratizing" Eastern European countries, with their traditions of Western democracy, but no one could predict with certainty how it would react if these countries actually break away from the "socialism" that has destroyed their economies. In fact, while "renouncing the Brezhnev doctrine" in France in mid-1989, Gorbachev was leaving no doubt that he foresaw the Eastern European states remaining squarely "within the socialist system." He specifically warned the West against "illusions" such as expecting them to "return to the capitalist fold."

Ensuring the Necessary Conditions

"To build a Communist society" the Kremlin rulers have required very favorable conditions indeed: nothing less than the elimination of all opposition to their power inside the country (which they achieved) and everywhere else in the world. As long as capitalist-imperialist exploiters and plotters exist in the world, "Communism" cannot be built (although

---

resources" in "repelling the onslaught of the enemies of socialism" (i.e., the Solidarity movement) in 1981—clearly suggesting that had they not, the Soviet Army would have intervened (as indeed a Polish officer knew they were planning to do: see R. Kuklinski, "The Crushing of 'Solidarity'" in *Orbis,* vol. 32, no. 1 [Winter 1988]).

Gorbachev also warned in Poland that Moscow understands its responsibility as "leader of the socialist community," and that any attempt "to wrench a country away from the socialist community means to encroach . . . on the entire postwar arrangement and, in the last analysis, on peace" (*International Herald Tribune,* 7 July 1986).

‡‡The Party Program of 1986 says that the CPSU "proceeds on the basis that the socialist countries' cohesion accords with the interests of each one of them and with their common interests and serves the cause of peace and the triumph of socialist ideals."

they claim to have achieved "socialism"). Communism is to arrive with what Marxism promises as the "inevitable" collapse of capitalism. Because that collapse was taking too long, Lenin and his successors took upon themselves the sacred task of hastening it.

Does this mean that the Kremlin has what some Westerners call a "blueprint for world conquest"? Mikhail Gorbachev scoffed at the idea. "Again and again we are accused of wanting to implant communism all over the world. What nonsense!" he wrote. "Nobody has ever heard any statements from us about 'implanting Communist domination.' " Indeed, he added, "No such doctrine was ever entertained by Marx, Lenin, or any of the Soviet leaders." [12]

True, no Soviet leaders used those words. But what all of them did make clear was their view that—as Lenin put it—"socialism and capitalism could not live indefinitely side by side. Either the Soviet system triumphs everywhere or it disappears." Until that final issue is decided, the leaders described the true relations between the two systems (depending who was describing it and when) as a "state of awful war" (Lenin) or "a fierce struggle [in which] there can be no neutrals" (Khrushchev), or communism's effort "to inflict on imperialism such a defeat that it will be felt everywhere throughout the world" (Brezhnev). [13] Gorbachev is right: that is not the same thing as "implanting communism all over the world."

What these Soviet leaders were describing was simply the real state of East-West relations as they see it. They must, to defend their own revolution, eliminate not only active resistance abroad—by "thwarting imperialist plots against the homeland of socialism"—but also the very possibility of resistance. As Brezhnev put it in the 1970s, they "seek to paralyze the forces of imperialism" and "to contract its radius of activity." (The term "imperialism" is loose enough to include any foreign opposition to Soviet rule—and that is what Brezhnev meant.)

Today the Soviet rulers are grappling at home with an economic disaster. They can no longer commit the same resources to contracting the Western powers' radius of activity, and they depend more than ever on Western technology, food, and financing. Thus they have had to tone down their rhetoric and scale down their sponsorship of foreign insurrections and support for poverty-stricken client regimes. Conceivably the Soviet system may so evolve under Gorbachev's reforms that the Kremlin's long-term foreign goals will change. But that has not yet happened and is, moreover, incompatible with the ideology and the survival of Leninist power. The advance has paused but cannot stop.

The advance has been huge, as you can see by a glance at today's political map. When Lenin took power, anti-Bolshevik forces opposed him not only in most of Russia but from other parts of the former Tsarist empire. By the early 1920s they no longer did. By the late 1940s no further opposition could come from Eastern Europe, and by the 1960s the same could be said for parts of Southeast Asia, Africa, the Middle East, Central America, and the Caribbean. In all these areas defeats had been inflicted on "imperialism" and (to continue with Brezhnev's words) the impact of these defeats had indeed been "felt everywhere throughout the world"—reducing still further the terrain available for opposition. Scores of governments (most of them former colonies of European powers) judged it safer to call themselves "nonaligned" than to ally themselves with those who actively resist Sovietization. The Kremlin has also made progress toward its goal (still in Brezhnev's words) of "paralyzing" Western power. Public opinion even in NATO countries came to find ever less moral difference between the two superpowers while some political parties, denying the existence of a "Soviet threat," proposed to disarm rather than risk Soviet wrath or retaliation.

Such progress has been sporadic and has met reverses. But the goal remains constant because the Soviet leaders believe, perhaps rightly, that their survival in power depends on it.

They employ whatever means are available, choosing their course of action according to what they call "the correlation of forces." Going beyond the military balance of power, they assess the capacity and will of foreign governments to resist various pressures,§§ the unity of those governments' alliances, the firmness or weakness of the political leaders, and things that might inhibit their actions and reactions: recent history, public opinion, internal political and economic pressures, and social dissensions such as labor and race relations. However, the Soviet leaders do more than passively ponder these things: they actively try to shift the correlation of forces to Soviet advantage. This makes for a foreign policy that has little in common—either in its objectives or its methods—with that of the West.

The global correlation of forces has turned dramatically against the Kremlin with the near-collapse of its economy and that of its client states, and with the discrediting of its ideological message. Fewer opportunities beckon, and fewer means are available to exploit them. As a result Gorbachev and his lieutenants in the late 1980s were disclaiming any policy of "exporting revolution" and were promoting negotiations in Third World problems rather than violence.

But the long process of the past remains and could be resumed as the correlation of forces shifts. It is useful to recall that, as circumstances have

§§On at least two occasions, for example—in Korea in 1950 and Afghanistan in 1978—Soviet Bloc military intervention followed close on the heels of statements by high American officials suggesting that the United States had no strategic interest there.

permitted, the Soviet leaders have sent invading armies (or those of surrogates) into foreign countries, they have exploited the opportunities offered by rebellions and civil wars, and where such opportunities do not yet exist, they have set out to create them—as we recall in the next chapter. Through it all—at least since the death of Stalin—they have preserved a relationship with their Western opponents that they have called "peaceful coexistence."

Peaceful Coexistence

Since the mid-1950s Kremlin doctrine has labeled its competition with the capitalist world as "peaceful coexistence" (and sometimes as "detente").*** Mikhail Gorbachev subscribed to this doctrine and expanded it in what he called a "new philosophy of peace."†††

The words "peaceful coexistence" seem devoid of meaning for many Westerners; after all, the only alternative to coexisting in peace is for one side to stop existing or to coexist at war. And this coexistence has not been very peaceful: it did not prevent Khrushchev from invading Hungary in 1956, issuing saber-rattling ultimatums on Berlin between 1957 and 1961, implanting offensive missiles in Cuba in 1962, or threatening European countries with nuclear missile attacks. It did not inhibit his successor from invading Czechoslovakia and Afghanistan or repeatedly inciting peoples to insurrection.

Nor has peaceful coexistence restrained the Soviet regime from misrepresenting Western intentions. While calling for "good neighborliness," the 1986 CPSU Party Program again and again called up hostile images, speaking of the need to "curb the forces of aggression and militarism . . . to defend against imperialism's aggressive aspirations [. . . and its efforts] to weaken socialism's position and to disrupt ties between socialist states [. . . and its utilization] of nationalist sentiments for subversive ends,"

***"Detente" was consecrated in the 1972 declaration of "Basic Principles of Relations between the US and the USSR" and signified an improvement of relations rather than a permanent state of affairs, but both terms are used in the same context.

†††Gorbachev's "new philosophy of peace" was described in *Perestroika,* pp. 147–8. This bit of Soviet doctrine changes little except to dismiss even the theoretical possibility of a world war (whereas earlier Soviet doctrine envisaged the possibility that the West might cause one). As always, Kremlin doctrine leaves the choice of peace or war up to the West. Lenin was against violence in theory; it was others who made it unavoidable, by opposing the course of history (Marxist version). Only to the degree that "reactionary forces" choose to resist the tide of "socialism" will war and violence be necessary. The favorite Soviet example of "peaceful coexistence" is their wartime alliance with capitalist states—when Western powers helped the Soviet regime to survive and later acquiesced in its annexation of vast areas and populations of Eastern Europe.

and so forth. The Kremlin justified its invasion of Afghanistan by "American attempts to seize control of Afghanistan and turn it against the Soviet Union" as "a base for imperialist aggression."[14] It is an old theme. In 1953 when East German workers took to the streets to protest cuts in their living standards and in 1956 when Polish workers did the same, the Kremlin blamed "provocation by agents of U.S. subversion" and "emigre reactionaries, Radio Free Europe leaflets, and the West German intelligence service." For more than thirty years they labeled the Hungarian Revolution of 1956 a "long-prepared counterrevolution" designed "to restore the fascist regime in Hungary" with the "connivance of foreign reactionary circles."[15] The 1968 "Prague Spring," they said, was brought about by "right-wing opportunists closely coordinating their activities with reactionaries abroad." "Imperialism" was trying to "push Czechoslovakia off its socialist road."[16] After military force crushed Solidarity in Poland in December 1981, *Pravda* blamed the whole movement on scenarios worked out by the American CIA: the plan was to restore capitalism in Poland and tear Poland from the socialist community and the Warsaw Pact.[17] And Gorbachev pursued this old line. In 1987 he wrote, for instance, that "the West can also be 'credited' with helping [the crises in socialist states] through its constant and stubborn attempts to undermine [their] development, to trip them up."[18] In May 1988 his Tass accused the West of fomenting the labor unrest in Poland with money and radio broadcasts.

"Peaceful coexistence of states with different social systems" has a specific meaning which, as the Soviets themselves point out, has little to do with propaganda fancies about happy competition between East and West in manufacturing, races in trade instead of arms, improved understanding between "peoples," and stabilizing the world by new treaties.‡‡‡ Its real meaning "has nothing in common with Utopian petty-bourgeois pacifism or with the rejection of the revolutionary class struggle."

"To Soviet communists, peaceful coexistence means establishing favorable conditions for the further success of the worldwide revolutionary-liberation struggle."[19] It "facilitates the takeover of power by the working class [and makes it easier] to oppose foreign military bases and to promote

---

‡‡‡Khrushchev enjoyed spreading this propaganda. He said, for example, "We live on one planet and therefore we want peaceful competition. . . . We favor both bilateral agreements to consolidate peace and collective agreements on security in Europe and Asia. . . . You [in the West] are not being threatened with intercontinental ballistic missiles. You are threatened with a peaceful offensive, peaceful competition in the manufacture of consumer goods and things that improve the culture and life of people," and so forth. He repeated such thoughts many times; these quotes are from *Pravda*, 28 November 1955; a broadcast from Prague, 12 July 1957; and Tass, 22 July 1959.

national liberation movements," explained Soviet ideologists.[20] It does not "leave things the way they are." Andropov pointed out that it is a mistake to regard detente as "some kind of agreement to freeze and conserve outmoded social relations and reactionary political practices." In reality, it "implies bitter and stubborn struggle on all fronts—economic, political, and ideological."[21] And it will last only as long as it is needed: "The rules of peaceful coexistence are intended solely for the contemporary era and are transitory inasmuch as the existing situation cannot last forever."[22]

So "peaceful coexistence" is designed to favor Kremlin purposes during this phase of history. The party program points out that in this climate "a broad exchange of the achievements of science and technology and of cultural values for the benefit of all peoples takes place." Put aside those highly abstract "cultural values" and you are left with the transfer of high technology from the West, which—along with financial credits—is what the Kremlin seeks.

In addition, peaceful coexistence has boosted Soviet political influence abroad. Since the mid-1950s when it materialized as "a major concept of Soviet foreign policy" (their words), the Soviets have stretched their political influence over the whole globe, have seen their European military conquests confirmed by international treaties, have overcome their military disadvantage and deployed a huge range of threatening weapons, have received Western goods to compensate for the stagnation of their industry and for the shortfalls in their agricultural production, have directly or via surrogates invaded countries without incurring serious sanctions, and have "contracted the radius of imperialism" by gaining hegemony over more than a dozen states and driving most of the rest into neutrality. "We are achieving with detente," Brezhnev reportedly said, "what our predecessors have been unable to achieve using the mailed fist."[23]

Therefore, peaceful coexistence is no mere ruse. In their state of economic crisis the Soviet rulers desperately need the climate of peace and its benefits.

CHAPTER 24

The Soviet Record Abroad

TO ASSESS THE CHANGES THAT GORBACHEV HAS WROUGHT, IT IS USEFUL to keep in mind the record he inherited not only in domestic policy but also in foreign affairs. All his predecessors regarded the outside world as a source of danger to their own power, preached hatred, propagated fear, and did whatever "the correlation of forces" permitted (and a bit more) to reduce or destroy the influence and power of major Western governments, while exploiting foreign trade and diplomacy not only to build their own military power but also to gain open and secret leverage over foreign governments.

Military Invasion and Occupation

The first Communist military conquest was of Russia, in the civil war that followed the Bolshevik coup. In two years it consumed more Russian lives than nearly four years of the murderous war with Germany that the Bolsheviks had brought to an end.

In those same first years the beleaguered Bolshevik leaders learned that they would get no succor from world revolution and that to save themselves (and to make Marx's predictions come true) they would have to use their own military and subversive forces. As soon as the Red Army had won Russia, Lenin moved it westward, southward, and eastward over the lands of the former tsarist empire. By violent force—and in flagrant disregard for the new independence that he had offered and they had gratefully accepted—Lenin integrated their peoples far more tightly than ever before under Moscow rule. Soviet forces invaded and absorbed the Ukraine and Byelorussia, "normalizing" them in a bloody process that was

351

only completed decades later. On into Poland marched the Red Army, on the pretext of aiding a Polish "revolutionary committee" (nucleus of a puppet government) that the Bolsheviks themselves had installed in Bialystok, the first city they captured. But here they failed; the new Polish army defeated them, the Bialystok committee evaporated, and Soviet conquest was delayed for two decades. (When the Red Army marched back in 1944 the Soviets again formed a "committee" to organize puppet rule, this time in Lublin instead of Bialystok.) Invading Central Asia (as they did a half-century later in Afghanistan) the Red Army and Chekist troops laid waste the country and regrouped the once loosely controlled polities of Turkestan into five Soviet Socialist Republics. In the Transcaucasian states of Azerbaijan, Armenia, and Georgia, the Soviets followed a pattern: first recognizing the independence of the government, then accusing it of dangerous anti-Soviet actions and attitudes, and then sending in the Red Army and Chekists (bringing puppet governments with them) on the pretext that "the people" had called for help. In each country they faced fierce resistance for years and suffered setbacks but by 1924 had "normalized" them and added three more Soviet Socialist Republics.

Still in that eventful year 1920, Soviet forces (following an old tsarist precedent) marched into Iran's in the Gilan province bordering the Caspian Sea and proclaimed a "Persian People's Soviet Republic." Finding it expedient, under British pressure, to withdraw in 1921, Moscow forced a treaty granting itself the right to intervene—i.e., an excuse to try again—whenever it felt "threatened" by circumstances in Iran. Another opportunity arose with the Second World War, and so in August 1941 Soviet forces occupied the northern part of the country, ostensibly temporarily and defensively. Actually they vigorously prepared for Communist takeover, murdering actual and potential opponents. When the war ended and the agreed time came for the Soviets to evacuate Iran, two new Soviet-style regimes suddenly materialized in their occupation area (an "Autonomous Republic of Azerbaijan" and a "Kurdish People's Republic"), announced their independence (both on the same day in mid-December 1945), rose in arms against Teheran's central rule, and called on the Soviet occupiers to protect them. This Soviet ploy failed because of Western pressure. Reluctantly, the Soviet forces withdrew, taking the puppet rulers back with them to the USSR (as they had in 1921) and these shadowy new "republics" crumbled. But the Soviet leaders did not give up: through the 1970s they were smuggling arms to Kurdish rebels and in the 1980s were preparing to exploit any opportunity to return, this time unhindered by the Western allies who had blocked them in 1921 and 1946.

In Mongolia, Moscow's agents went to work soon after the Bolshevik coup in Russia, bringing Mongols to Soviet Russia for training (and clandestine recruiting of the most trustworthy). In 1920 the Kremlin sponsored a Communist Party (the "Mongol People's Revolutionary Party") which seized power in 1924 and proclaimed a "Mongolian People's Republic." Soviet troops moved in at its request, and the puppet state adopted a constitution that abolished the theocracy and substituted a fair copy of Soviet rule. Since then Mongolians have rebelled several times, notably in 1932, when the population was joined by army units in a mass revolt that was beaten down only by overwhelming Soviet forces.

The Soviets established hegemony over Sinkiang in the 1930s and moved in Internal Troops units. In 1943 Soviets organized a revolt against a ruler who had become too independent minded, and proclaimed an independent East Turkestan Republic under one of their agents. They only released their grip in 1950 in deference to the newly victorious Communist government of China.

In August 1939 Stalin allied himself with Hitler; with the latter's acquiescence, Soviet forces invaded six countries in the year and a half until June 1941—Poland, Finland, Estonia, Latvia, Lithuania, and part of Romania—and annexed nearly half a million square kilometers with populations totaling 21 million. Eastern Poland became "Western Byelorussia" and the "Western Ukraine." Independent Estonia, Latvia, and Lithuania became Soviet Socialist Republics. Part of Finland was broken off and made into the Karelian Soviet Socialist Republic. Bessarabia and Northern Bukovina were taken from Romania and are known today as the Soviet Socialist Republic of Moldavia.

Finland proved more difficult. In late 1939 the Soviets demanded partial occupation; but the Finns, recognizing that the Soviets intended to take the whole of the country, refused. On November 30 the Red Army attacked and one day later in Teryoki, the first border town captured, set up a puppet Finnish regime. The Finns exposed this fraud by fighting and humiliating the Soviet Army before the whole world, killing more than a million of them. Chastened even in victory, the Soviets signed a peace treaty in March 1940 that left Finland sovereign, although depriving it of some territory. (The Teryoki regime vanished as if it had never existed.) In 1944 the Soviets made further demands, were again refused, again attacked, again took land in the peace treaty, and—facing powerful Western opposition to occupation—again left Finland its sovereignty.

Victory over German armies opened the heart of central Europe to Soviet power. The leaders annexed East Prussia from Germany and Ruthenia from Czechoslovakia. Within a few years they had set up Soviet-style governments, with only superficial trappings of independence, in the countries their armies had occupied: Bulgaria, Romania, Hungary, Czech-oslovakia, Poland, and East Germany.*

On the day after the German surrender in May 1945, the Soviet regime sensed a lack of resistance in northern Europe and quickly occupied the Danish island of Bornholm in the Baltic Sea. They said they were "protecting" it, made claims on the gratitude of the Danish people for defeating the Germans, built up their garrison over seven months to some 6,000 men, and showed signs of intending to stay. They had underestimated the political impact, however, and, under public and diplomatic pressure from a still-resolute West, withdrew.

Entering the war against Japan in its last week—after the atomic bombs had been dropped—the Soviets annexed southern Sakhalin and occupied a string of other islands off the northern tip of Japan. (Forty-four years later Moscow was still refusing to discuss sovereignty with Japan.) They occupied Manchuria, too (but turned it over in 1948 to the new Communist regime in China), and marched into North Korea and established a Soviet-style regime.

In late December 1979, after a quarter century of preparations, the Soviet Army invaded Afghanistan.

In the meantime, the Kremlin encouraged and directed its client regimes toward further military takeovers in their own areas. One opportunity arose in 1950 when the United States government appeared to renounce the use of force to defend South Vietnam. Pushed by their Soviet sponsors, the North Koreans invaded, only to be pushed back by American forces and finally saved only by Chinese military intervention. Soviet-supported North Vietnamese forces, after conquering South Vietnam, invaded and occupied Laos and Cambodia and made tentative moves at the borders of Thailand and Malaysia. Soviet client South Yemen fought a long war against North Yemen. With Soviet help, Ethiopia fought Somalia.

Such direct invasion was only the most blatant form of "contracting imperialism's radius of activity." More opportunities have been offered by other peoples' internal and external conflicts.

Foreign Interventions

The 1977 USSR Constitution squarely commits the regime to "support the struggle of peoples for national liberation and social progress." With

---

*In Yugoslavia and Albania, native Communists seized power before the Soviet troops arrived; though their communization by bloodletting followed the Soviet pattern, they were able to fend off Soviet control.

his 1986 CPSU Party Program reiterating this theme, Gorbachev had grasped the torch handed down by Marx's 1848 Communist Manifesto: "Communists everywhere support every revolutionary movement against established power."

Gorbachev played down this fundamental principle of Soviet foreign policy, however, in his public statements. He chose to emphasize, instead of "support" for liberation movements, his regime's "sympathy" (both words are in the 1986 Party Program). He denied any intent to "export revolution," asserted that Marx and Lenin were against that sort of thing,[1] and even denied having interfered in other countries' internal affairs in the past. "If the masses rise to struggle," he wrote in 1987, "it means that their vital rights are suppressed. And someone else's ambitions or a 'hand of Moscow' have nothing to do with this."[2]

In reality, however, "the hand of Moscow" had been exposed again and again in other people's wars, rebellions, and discord. The Soviet press itself admitted in 1989 that Soviet "technical advisors" had taken direct part in combat in Vietnam; one Soviet officer was twice decorated for shooting down 24 American aircraft with his anti-aircraft missile battery; a Soviet colonel reported that his regiment fired 43 missiles and downed 23 planes (*Krasnaya Zvezda*, 13 April 1989, cited in *New York Times*, 14 April 1989.) Even in foreign wars that pitted "bourgeois" states against one another, as in 1980s Gulf War of Iraq against Iran and that of Syria against Israel, the USSR has given help to one side or another. It triggered Communist uprisings that led to civil war (as in Greece in 1944–48) and thrust its hand into other civil wars, as in Angola in the 1970s and 1980s and in Spain in the 1930s.† Sometimes it has shifted its support from one side over to its enemy.‡

†The Spanish War illustrated patterns of Soviet intervention that were followed long afterward. Red Army officers using Spanish names commanded Republican armies. Soviet NKVD officers took control of the Spanish Republican security service (Seguridad) through its chief and their collaborator, Antonio Ortega, and of the Military Counterintelligence (Seccion de Investigaciones Militares), structured along Soviet OO lines and commanded by Communists under the control of NKVD officers. This gave the Soviets a parallel control over the Spanish Republican armies alongside the Soviet officers commanding them. The NKVD-controlled Comintern played a central role in recruiting the International Brigades and subordinated them to the political oversight of NKVD agent Andre Marty, who presided over a mad terrorism that killed hundreds of brave and innocent men.

‡This opportunism occasionally led to complications. Ethiopians, armed and trained by the Soviets, fight against Eritreans, also armed and trained by the Soviets. The Soviets were forced to abandon one client (Somalia) to another, more promising client (Ethiopia) that was waging war against it. The Soviets support both sides in the conflict between North and South Yemen and hardliners against other Communists in South Yemen. These shifting priorities have made it necessary to abandon loyal servants—local Communist parties—to the ax of anti-Communist regimes that the Soviets are wooing: in Hitler's Germany in 1939, in Egypt in the 1950s, in Iran, Iraq, and Syria from the 1960s on.

Elsewhere the Kremlin helped rebels with goals as widely different as those of El Salvador, Northern Ireland, Palestine, and South Africa. It helped governments to fight against rebels, as in Angola, Mozambique, and Nicaragua. To carry the brunt of battle and training it enlisted the active assistance of its satellites and surrogates. Through the Ethiopian government in 1987, Soviet arms were sent to the rebels in the southern Sudan. It was East Germans who led Angolan troops when they invaded the neighboring mineral-rich province of Shaba in Zaire in 1977 and 1978. Cuban units battled in Angola, Mozambique, Ethiopia, and South Yemen and helped the Sandinista regime in Nicaragua arm and train Salvadorean rebels—while behind them in Cuba, Soviet armed forces protected the regime and the Kremlin subsidized the Cuban economy. Eastern European pilots (in addition to Cubans) flew combat air missions in at least three wars, in Angola, Ethiopia, and Yemen.

By the late 1980s these interventions—direct or through surrogates— had successfully contracted the radius of "imperialism" by establishing Soviet-style regimes in Cuba, Nicaragua, Ethiopia, South Yemen, Vietnam, Laos, and Cambodia and friendly client regimes in other countries. They had failed, however, in Ghana, Chile, Portugal, and Grenada and under Gorbachev's economic strictures were reducing their support for the Leninist regimes in Angola and Mozambique.

Subversion

Gorbachev cited Lenin to make the point that the master, too, had disapproved of exporting revolution. Revolutions take their own course, Lenin wrote. They "ripen in the process of historical development and break out when a certain combination of internal and external conditions arises."[3] What Gorbachev neglected to mention was that all his predecessors in the Kremlin—including Lenin—had not just watched those conditions ripen but tried in every possible way to ripen them.

The Kremlin has thus pursued foreign aims very different from the normal Western goals of promoting stability, cooperation, and economic growth. Instability is often likely to serve Soviet purposes better than stability, conflict better than cooperation, economic damage and disarray better than construction. The Moscow rulers have pitted Western governments and societies against one another, tried to eliminate political opponents, and recruited secret support for Soviet policies among Western governments, media, and scholars. Kremlin messengers have delivered invitations to dissatisfied political factions: send us your men and we will train and equip them, and when you take power we will support and protect you.

Just in the twenty years preceding Gorbachev's dismissal of "the hand of Moscow" as "a malicious lie," Soviet officials were caught in at least a dozen countries encouraging, secretly paying, and sometimes guiding the plotters of coups d'etat. For this they were expelled from Iran, Egypt, Sudan, North Yemen, Zaire, Liberia, and Bangladesh and publicly exposed in Pakistan, Syria, Saudi Arabia, Oman, and Jamaica. In Sri Lanka, stores of explosives were discovered on the premises of the Soviet-Ceylon Friendship League, and the ringleaders of a coup plot were found to have studied in the USSR. Separatist uprisings by Kurds and Azerbaijanis in Iran and by Baluchis in Pakistan were sponsored by Soviet diplomats who were expelled for it. Others were caught and expelled for fomenting strikes in Mexico, Costa Rica, Ecuador, Finland, and Spain and for planning riots or demonstrations in Denmark, Switzerland, Zaire, and Colombia.

Every regime that comes under Soviet control is enlisted in the spread of rebellion and unrest. In the Ghana government of the mid-1960s, officers of the KGB and its satellite services established, under the benevolent eye of the ruler Kwame Nkrumah, a deceptively named "Bureau for Technical Assistance." Its geographic departments covered some twenty-five African countries and within two years had trained more than three hundred citizens of those countries as terrorists and spies. (The organization plotted to kill, among others, the president of Togo.)[4] In this lies the reality in the "domino theory" that is so often derided in the West.

Take a few examples from the 1980s. After a Soviet-style government had been established in Ethiopia, Soviet-trained Ethiopians supplied weapons and other support to a movement trying to overthrow the central government in neighboring Sudan. The KGB-created Afghan state security organization, the Khad, not only helped the Soviets to "normalize" Afghanistan but also helped them recruit and train Baluchis for an eventual uprising in Pakistan. After Marxist-Leninists took power in Nicaragua, the Soviets supplied and assisted them to support revolutionaries in El Salvador. The Kremlin evidently conveyed this principle to the new pro-Soviet Marxist-Leninist regime in Grenada, for its ambassador in Moscow wrote back to his bosses in 1983 that they should "sponsor revolutionary activity" in their region[5]—which is surely why such vast stores of weapons were delivered to this little island whose neighbors had no standing army at all.

The Kremlin's use of East Germany typifies this process. There the KGB created a local version of itself called the Ministry of State Security (*Ministerium fuer Staatssicherheit,* or MFS), which helped to "normalize" the Soviet half of occupied Germany and to extend the secret Soviet hand into West Germany. Later promoted to proxies, the East Germans trained foreign terrorists in East German camps and went abroad—as far as Ghana and South Yemen—to do in other countries what the Soviets had done in East Germany. Having in its time been created as a model of the KGB, the MFS now set up similar institutions in South Yemen and in Angola.§ The South Yemen service, according to press reports, went on to train the rebels who attacked the Great Mosque in Mecca in 1979 in an effort to destabilize neighboring Saudi Arabia. These are but two examples; in at least eight different countries of Africa, East Germans have trained men brought in from surrounding countries to learn the techniques of security, subversion, and destabilization.

Terrorism

Gorbachev asserted that "the Soviet Union rejects terrorism in principle,"[6] but that has not stopped it from supporting terrorism in practice. Support for terrorism cannot truly be distinguished from support for national liberation movements that depend on terrorist methods. The KGB and GRU and their satellites and surrogates train terrorists in several Soviet Bloc countries and South Yemen.** In any given year students from more than a hundred countries study in Soviet institutions, some of them learning subversive tactics. (The very symbol of terrorism in the 1970s, the Venezuelan known as "Carlos," had studied in Moscow at the Patrice Lumumba Friendship University, the administration of which is under permanent KGB control.)

Thousands of Kremlin surrogates—North Koreans, Bulgarians, Czechoslavaks, East Germans, Cubans, Nicaraguans, and others—train

§One of its tasks was to protect the power of the Angolan leader Jose Eduard Dos Santos, who had been trained in a Soviet university and was married to a Soviet woman.

**Romania offers an illustration. The Romanian intelligence service (DIE)—dependent upon and responsive to the KGB, despite misinformation to the contrary—formed a close liaison with the Palestine Liberation Organization (PLO) in 1972, providing it "enormous quantities of technical intelligence paraphernalia, from electronic eavesdropping equipment for the secret monitoring of government institutions in Israel, Jordan, and elsewhere, to burst transmitters, secret writing materials, and other spy gear." The DIE revealed to the PLO secrets of Jordanian antiterrorist capabilities that it had gotten from King Hussein of Jordan, while the PLO prepared deceptive reports on its own activity to be passed by the Romanians to King Hussein. The PLO assigned two teams of its terrorists for kidnaping and assassination on DIE orders. The DIE sent deception experts to teach the PLO how to create an image of "moderation" in the West and supplied the PLO with a hundred forged Western passports (including American ones) for the use of Abu Nidal's organization (and to Kadhafi for his Libyan terrorists). The DIE trained Western European Communists in sabotage and guerrilla operations and supplied them money and passports for their subversive groups, and received from the PLO captured Western military equipment captured in Lebanon (Pacepa, pp. 16–7, 19, 33, 80, 84–5, 90, 239–40, 254).

guerrillas and terrorists from the Middle East, Asia, and Latin America. Seventeen young Mexicans, for example, were studying in Moscow in the 1960s on a "cultural grant" from the Soviet Embassy in Mexico City when they were secretly sent, on false passports, for training by North Koreans in how to use explosives and weapons against Mexican government leaders and installations.

Klaus Reiner Roehl, the husband of Ulrike Meinhof, exposed the KGB's funding of the Baader-Meinhof terrorist gang through East Germany. The Italian government had received by 1983 "incontrovertible evidence" of KGB efforts to guide Red Brigade operations. Similar evidence links the Irish Republican Army and the Palestine Liberation Organization to the KGB as well as to the Romanians. (The principal KGB contact of Yassir Arafat in the 1970s was my former KGB subordinate, Vasily F. Samoilenko.)

And murder, so closely allied to terrorism, has been a calculated part of Soviet foreign policy, planned and executed since the earliest days of Bolshevik rule by a special organization that I knew within the KGB.

Murder as an Instrument of Foreign Policy

The Soviet regime has committed murder routinely to advance its interests abroad, as I know from my service in the KGB.[7] With each drastic change in a foreign country's political situation the KGB was called upon to suggest how the Politburo could exploit an opportunity or mitigate a loss. Which politicians might be secretly assisted? Should someone be eliminated? (Not necessarily physically, of course; compromise or blackmail might do the job.)

In the West some credence was given in the 1980s to the notion that since the 1950s the Soviets had stopped committing political assassinations abroad. (The notion was advanced to discredit evidence that suggested Soviet sponsorship—through Bulgarian surrogates—of the attempt to assassinate Pope John Paul II in May 1981.) But why, in turning their attention to foreign affairs, would the Soviet leaders reject a practice they used so freely at home? Why after Stalin's death would they stop using this particular one of his techniques[8] while continuing with the others?

The murder on August 17, 1988, of Pakistan's Prime Minister Zia ul-Haq, by sabotage of his airplane, raised anew the spectre of Soviet political assassination. The most likely culprit was the Afghan Communist government—controlled by the Soviets—and specifically by its state security service, the Khad, a tributary of the KGB. The Soviet government had been darkly threatening the "consequences" for Zia if he continued supporting Afghan resistance to the Soviet-satellite regime in Kabul.

Look back, then, at the known record of Soviet assassinations abroad since the 1950s when they supposedly ended. Keep in mind that this record would be a blank page were it not for the revelations of former staff operatives of the Soviet Bloc state security services; no one else could know about these super-secret operations because the KGB hides not only its own hand but also the very fact that a murder has been committed. Anyone can plan a murder, as they say within the KGB, but it takes real skill to organize a natural or accidental death. (Until years later, when the assassin Stashinsky confessed and the bodies were exhumed and reexamined, the German authorities believed that two KGB victims, Stepan Bandera and Lev Rebet, had died of natural causes.) Keep in mind, too, that this rather substantial history was derived from a few fortuitous exposures, within tightly compartmented services to a tiny proportion of all Soviet Bloc staff officers. (Few have defected to the West.) If we few could reveal so many assassinations, the practice must be quite common.

To accelerate what they perceived in 1964 as a shifting correlation of forces in Great Britain, the Soviets were contemplating the murder of political leaders. They drew up a list of prominent British personalities and discussed it with officials in Czechoslovakia, whose help they needed. "The Soviets believed that around the end of the 1970s, economic and social conditions in Britain would have become so desperate that it might be possible to precipitate both a crisis of leadership and a collapse of national morale by assassinating selected British personalities. . . . They made a list of about fifty anti-progressives and sought Czech collaboration on the operational planning and staff work. The Soviet idea was to carry out the murders in Third World countries, preferably former colonies, with the help of extreme nationalist groups."[9]

Charles de Gaulle was to be killed during a visit to Beirut in 1968. On KGB initiative and with KGB participation, the Czechoslovakians planned to kill him to embarrass the United States (on whom they would pin the crime) and to sow chaos in French politics. We know of this operation from two officers of the Czechoslovakian state security service, one of whom was in Beirut and the other in Prague where the KGB gave the orders and the planning was begun. The KGB, in its best tradition, wanted to use third- and fourth-country nationals to cover their tracks (in this case, Czechoslovakians and Palestinians) and sought to plant evidence (through the chief of the Beirut police, who was a KGB agent) that the Americans had done it. De Gaulle, lucky on this occasion as on so many others, did not make the trip.[10]

Another French political figure was the target of the KGB (also through the Czechoslovakians) a few years earlier. For no grander purpose than to cause friction between France and West Germany, they mailed a letter bomb to the French prefect of Strasbourg, Andre-Marie Trémeaud, in May 1957. His wife opened it in his absence and died.[11]

In late 1967 or early 1968 the KGB planned to kill Hafiz Assad (currently president of Syria) because, as minister of defense, he was effectively opposing Soviet efforts to establish hegemony over Syria.[12]

The former head of the Iranian security service, General Bakhtiar, who had made himself bothersome by helping crush the pro-Soviet "republics" created in 1945–46 on Iranian territory, was murdered in Iraq in 1970. The act was attributed to Iranian agents, but two years earlier KGB officials had already been making "no secret of the fact that they would help insure [Bakhtiar's] physical liquidation."[13]

Anwar el-Sadat was the target of Soviet murder plotting in 1971, according to former Soviet diplomat Arkady Shevchenko. "The Egyptians were stalling Moscow on concluding a long-sought treaty of friendship designed to bind Cairo firmly into an alliance," he wrote. "A friend told me, 'Opinions are beginning to solidify in the leadership that we have to be rid of Sadat. . . . I don't know all the details myself . . . but I have my own contacts with the KGB. . . . they have a general plan to take care of Sadat—to liquidate him. Of course, not by their own hands. They have people, though, who are getting ready to act.' "[14]

Hardly anyone in the West doubts the KGB's readiness to seal the mouths of defectors—yet these, too, are political murders and reflections of a policy. At the beginning of 1973, Sergey Kourdakov died of a gunshot wound in a California motel after twice being warned by KGB operatives in Canada, after his defection, that he would be silenced if he continued to inform the world about the brutal persecutions of religious believers in the USSR, in which he had personally participated for the KGB.[15] Kourdakov had warned friends that if he was killed it would appear to be an accident—and so it was judged by the local police. Murders and kidnappings of emigre activists (like those of the Ukrainians Stepan Bandera and Lev Rebet in Munich in the 1960s) are standard Soviet Bloc practice.

I have testified to the U.S. Congress about the special "kamera" of the KGB, the laboratory that developed (and tested on prisoners condemned to death) weapons, poisons, and bacteria to induce death in ways that would defy detection. Its more recent work has been exposed in several operations of the 1970s. The tiny, sophisticated pellet and the umbrella device that injected it and its poison into the bodies of at least two Bulgarian emigres could only have been conceived and developed by the

KGB, as we have already noted. The KGB supplied the Romanian intelligence service with a device it had developed for its own use to induce, by radiation, deadly illnesses into prisoners.[16]

It is not incongruous for a Soviet ambassador to supervise a murder. One who did was Aleksandr Panyushkin. Within weeks after taking global command of the KGB's foreign operations, this high functionary of the Central Committee apparatus and two-time ambassador directed the attempt against Georgiy Okolovich, the head of the Russian emigre organization NTS in West Germany. Here were Panyushkin's words to the hit man, Nikolay Khokhlov: "Yes, yes, by all means, [the murder weapons must be] noiseless. Let the agents feel that they have a chance to retreat. We have no need for suicides. . . . It must be a combat weapon and not an amusing toy. Let them determine the range and figure the efficacy exactly. . . . Should there be any need for currency, we'll give you any kind you want. Take . . . false documents. If you need submachine guns, we'll get them. . . . But remember all the time that the work must be neat, the authors of this mission must not be revealed. . . . Bring this mission to a successful conclusion and the homeland will not forget you."[17] This Soviet-style diplomat also supervised the planning of at least three other murders: during his tenure Lev Rebet and Stepan Bandera were killed and a plot was laid (but not executed) against the Ukrainian prime minister in exile, Jaroslaw Stetsko.[18]

After Panyushkin had briefed Khokhlov and departed, the head of the assassination section, Colonel Okun, said with awe, "What a man, eh? Why, he'll soon be a candidate for the Central Committee. He has a great future."[19] This rings true. It is no maverick "secret police" that commits such murders; these are political matters approved and often sponsored by Politburo members. Not only is the Politburo informed[20], but Politburo members have been personally involved. Aleksandr Shelepin, while serving as KGB chairman between an earlier assignment as Komsomol first secretary and a later one as head of the trade unions (and Politburo member), personally dispatched Bogdan Stashinsky to kill Bandera. After Stashinsky succeeded, Shelepin personally decorated him and read the citation, which was signed by Politburo member Klementiy Voroshilov in his capacity as chairman of the Presidium of the Supreme Soviet—the person Western writers called "president of the USSR."[21]

Political Disruption and Secret Influence

"Divide the bourgeois states," Lenin instructed the very first Soviet participants in any international conference,[22] and these instructions remained valid. In the 1970s the KGB was formally instructing its Czech satellite "to cause conflict and exploit tension between individual countries, even countries that recently gained their independence."[23]

One way the Soviets have sown hatred, fear, and distrust is by forgery. Large staffs of KGB and satellite experts concoct false documents, letters, leaflets, and publications and distribute them surreptitiously to the press or to political leaders in selected countries. In the twenty years from the early 1960s to the early 1980s, at least two hundred "American" or West European "official papers" were publicized to discredit the United States alone, and many more were directed against West Germany and other NATO countries. Each year the Czechs, on the KGB's behalf, were carrying out some 300–400 "active measures" (most of which were forgeries) against Western countries.[24] A bogus Ku Klux Klan leaflet that was circulated in black Africa, for example, warned that black "apes" would be lynched if they attended the 1984 Olympic Games in Los Angeles. Forged American war plans were floated in Europe to heighten fears of nuclear war at times when parliaments were debating the deployment of American "neutron bombs" and, later, cruise missiles.

Every major power has, throughout history, tried to promote its own interests through unofficial channels of influence, but none has ever developed such elaborate and varied channels as the Soviet regime or coordinated them so purposefully. As a U.S. study (based on testimony from many former Soviet Bloc sources, including me) put it, Soviet "political influence operations range from the utilization of what the Soviets call 'agents of influence' to the manipulation of private channels of communication, to the exploitation of unwitting contracts. These operations have a common aim: to insinuate the official voice of the Soviet Union into foreign governmental, political, journalistic, business, labor, artistic, and academic circles in a nonattributable or at least seemingly unofficial manner."[25] The KGB has purchased, through front men, Western newspapers and magazines. It uses the Western prestige and pretended objectivity of secret collaborators to promote the Soviet line on a wide variety of international issues; two who have been convicted (and widely publicized) for such activity were the French journalist Pierre-Charles Pathe and the Danish journalist Arne Peterson (who also passed KGB money to antinuclear groups in Denmark). By blackmail and inducements in the USSR, the KGB has recruited Western students of Soviet affairs and has helped them establish themselves as experts on the USSR (especially as scholars or journalists), with the goal of projecting false images of Soviet priorities and intentions. The KGB passes secret funds not only to such individuals but also to political parties. KGB men have been expelled for this and other meddling in the internal politics of India, Japan, Burma,

Zimbabwe, West Germany, Kenya, Brazil, Uruguay, and Argentina. KGB Maj. Stanislav Levchenko was secretly paying a prominent member of the Japanese Socialist Party to enhance the political fortunes of pro-Soviet party members. Within international organizations like the United Nations or UNESCO or the World Council of Churches, the KGB similarly uses Western and Third World citizens to influence innocent colleagues, who would be outraged at the idea that they were manipulated by or supporting the Soviet regime.

Today, when time has exposed the hollowness of Soviet promises of a "radiant future," the Kremlin needs more than ever the help of Western individuals and groups that do not seem to be agitating directly for Soviet interests. This is the role of front organizations that bring together various categories of people (women, lawyers, students, youth, peace lovers, trade unionists) to fight abstract evils like "neocolonialism" and "imperialism" and "capitalism" by attacking specific targets selected for them: "multinational corporations" or nuclear weapons or American involvement in Vietnam (or, later, Nicaragua) or authoritarian governments in South Africa or Chile (but not the Soviet Union or its friends). Stanislav Levchenko has described, from his own work in the KGB and in the Afro-Asian People's Solidarity Organization (AAPSO), how the International Department of the CPSU, in conjunction with the KGB, directs the AAPSO and other international front organizations. [26]

Some are infamous Soviet creations: the World Peace Council (WPC), World Federation of Trade Unions (WFTU), World Federation of Democratic Youth (WFDY), International Union of Students (IUS), Women's International Democratic Federation (WIDF), and International Association of Democratic Lawyers (IADL). [27] But they and their leading members also sponsor subsidiary organizations, ad hoc "committees," action groups, and conferences that manage to whip up fear and hatred without seeming to act for the Soviets. They assemble the young, the naive, and the idealistic to take sides in quarrels of which they know little or to thwart their own countries' defense against Soviet military force.

These organizations sow their seeds in fertile fields. Everywhere there are haves and have-nots; resentments, envy, and ambitions; frustration of unrealistic expectations raised by television and by the demagoguery of cynical politicians. Everywhere people disagree about how to improve social conditions. And always there are "victims"—from Sacco and Vanzetti through the Rosenbergs, Angela Davis, Salvador Allende, and Nelson Mandela—who can be made symbols and objects of discord. Thus the Soviets have no trouble, even in the late 1980s, finding people to join their "Clubs of Innocents." ††

††The phrase was coined by Willy Muenzenberg, a Comintern and OGPU/NKVD

Uses of Trade and Aid

Failing to provision their own people adequately, the Soviet rulers have come to rely on imports of grain and other food products, in addition to the computers and other high-technology products they are unable to produce. They also rely on the West in building up the military might that alone defines them as a superpower. But perhaps the most important role of foreign trade has been political.

Symbolizing the deeper motives of Soviet foreign trade was the presence of a Chekist at the head of the Soviet Chamber of Commerce and Industry, the regime's principal face to foreign businessmen and industrialists, under Gorbachev as earlier under Brezhnev and Andropov. He was not just any Chekist, but Yevgeniy Petrovich Pitovranov, former deputy chairman of the KGB and one of the few who had ever commanded each of the KGB's two most important directorates, those for internal repression and for foreign operations.‡‡

Pitovranov was surely chosen for this post because of his special Chekist qualifications. He was put there to assess and manipulate Western businessmen and industrialists (and, where possible, recruit them as clan-

---

operative, the founder of this practice. (See, for example, Arthur Koestler's autobiography, *Arrow in the Blue*, vol. 2, *The Invisible Writing* [New York: Macmillan, 1954]; Ruth Fischer, *Stalin and German Communism* [Cambridge: Harvard University Press, 1948], pp. 221, 610–4; Poretsky, pp. 63–4) Recognizing early how international organizations ostensibly dedicated to idealistic goals could help achieve a worldwide Soviet state, he probably discussed his idea with his friend Lenin in exile in Switzerland. Soon after the Bolshevik takeover, Muenzenberg began forming such "Clubs of Innocents." Some survive to this day under other names, whereas others he pasted together only temporarily (and sometimes only on paper) to promote momentary purposes. Thus were formed the Communist Youth International, which was the ancestor of today's World Federation of Democratic Youth; the International Workers' Aid (IWA), to draw for Communist purposes from the well of international sympathy for downtrodden workers; the Council for Russian Relief, to send money and food to alleviate the 1921 famine; the "Committee for Struggle Against War," forerunner of today's World Peace Council, through which he organized an international congress of pacifists; the League Against War and Fascism and the World Committee for the Relief of Victims of Fascism, which helped bring many honest anti-Nazis into secret and sometimes unwitting support for the Soviet regime. The Soviets even succeed in using churches as front organizations—a testimony to the gullibility upon which such fronts feed. Churchmen continue to cooperate in international organizations such as the Christian Peace Conference that have been repeatedly and convincingly exposed as tools of the atheistic Soviet leadership.

‡‡Between these two high posts, Pitovranov's career dipped sharply: he spent fifteen months in a cell in Lubyanka, arrested as a deputy to MGB Minister Viktor Abakumov. He was released and escaped Abakumov's fate because Georgiy Malenkov and he were married to sisters. I worked under him in the foreign directorate (in the former Comintern headquarters at Rostkino) and remember his return from prison, pale and thin.

destine agents) to supply the scientific-technological intelligence so
urgently needed for the regime's survival. Chekism had given him unusual
experience in dealing with Westerners and exploiting their vulnerabilities.
He knew Germans, for example, having headed the KGB's massive
operation from East Berlin and handled several famous "moles" including
Heinz Felfe in the West German Intelligence.[28] He was well equipped to
mislead Westerners, too, about Soviet scientific and technological progress
and aims: he had helped his assistant, Ivan Ivanovich Agayants, plan
operations to deceive the West. In this high foreign trade position
Pitovranov remained a Chekist despite his denials; as he himself once said
in my presence, "Once you are in State Security you are always in it. The
exit door is very narrow and hard to get through. You stay, like it or not,
unless you are fired—in which case you become an enemy of the people."[29]
He brought with him into key chamber positions KGB veterans in
recruiting Americans, like Khristofor ("Khachik") Oganesyan, Pavel
Gevorkyan, and Ilya Demshin. Demshin supervised Soviet contacts with
Westerners at the "Center of International Trade and Scientific-Technological Relations with Foreign Countries," a huge exhibition complex
built in the mid-1970s with the financial participation of Armand Ham-
mer of Occidental Petroleum and under Pitovranov's supervision.

The exploitation of trade is a massive operation. The Soviet regime has
received many thousands of Western businessmen in the USSR and has
sent many thousands of its own citizens to the West to accept machinery
purchases, to find markets for the few products the West might be
interested in buying,[30] to contact clients, and to attend international
trade fairs and conferences.

The regime uses trade to pressure foreign governments. It cut off
promised supplies of oil to Yugoslavia when Tito left the Bloc, to Israel at
the time of the 1956 war, and to China in the early 1960s; and it stopped
supplying spare parts to Egypt for Soviet-built aircraft, tanks, and guns
and threatened to do the same to other Arab purchasers. By means of
natural-gas exports through the new pipeline to Western Europe the
Soviets have increased their political leverage over West Germany and
other NATO partners. This became felt in the 1970s when some Western
manufacturers and traders, fearful of losing profits, were adding their
voices to protests against NATO weapon deployments that might "disturb
detente", as the Soviet leaders repeatedly threaten they will.

Through economic and military assistance to less-developed countries,
the Kremlin started a long-term process aimed at drawing them into the
Soviet sphere of influence or control. Blatantly aiming their aid at their
prime targets for political influence, the Soviets first focused on Egypt and
Indonesia (where, at the time, the Communist Party was on the verge of

winning power). They began in 1955 with a quarter-billion-dollar loan to Egypt and then supported high-visibility projects such as the Aswan Dam and Helwan iron and steel plant in Egypt, the Bokaro Steel Mill in India, and the Euphrates dam and hydroelectric complex in Syria. By the 1960s they were granting smaller loans somewhat wider, to build channels of contact and influence in countries where they had had few, if any, in the past ($18 billion to 67 countries by the mid-1980s); but still they concentrated on countries that they were courting politically. In the years 1974–80, 85 percent went to only 6 out of the total of 67 developing countries: four Arab states, Ethiopia, and India. Subsidies to Communist Cuba, not counted in these statistics, amount to about $4 billion annually, more than one quarter of Cuba's GNP.

The political influence was more important than the aid; in the mid-1980s the Soviets were contributing less to developing countries than were, for instance, Argentina, Colombia, or Indonesia, and less than a third as much as India was.§§. West Germany alone was giving two and a half times as much economic aid to developing countries as were all the members of the Warsaw Pact together. In fact, Soviet Bloc countries in 1983 took four times as much development aid from the United Nations as they contributed. But they attached strings to even this small economic aid. The Kremlin gave no outright grants, only loans, which it encouraged by offering easy credit terms (deferred payments, 2 percent interest) and free training and maintenance for equipment. These conditions were shaped by Soviet political designs. By insisting on repayment the Soviets could reduce the number of applicants for their aid, could stay in contact with (and influence) the officials of the borrowing government, and, by seeking repayment in export products, could reduce that country's foreign exchange earnings and increase its dependence on the Soviet market.

The real priorities of Soviet aid were dramatically illustrated in 1985 in an Ethiopian port: the Soviets and their Ethiopian clients kept long lines of ships waiting to unload food urgently needed by millions of starving Ethiopians while they first unloaded shiploads of weapons.

Military aid affords the Soviets a chance to get closer to and eventually manipulate the most potent force in the politics of many Third World countries, the armed forces. Therefore the regime has given such aid on a grander scale and, as with economic aid, has concentrated on countries targeted for takeover. Of the more than $50 billion worth of military aid that the Soviets had supplied to fifty-four non-Communist countries by

§§Even within its narrow limits Soviet aid was half-hearted. Many foreign governments were repelled by the poor choice and quality of the products and the technical aid the Soviets chose to supply: equipment that didn't work or was of no practical use, advisers who were incompetent or busy doing other things.

the mid-1980s, 85 percent had gone to only nine countries—all in the Middle East or along the Indian Ocean littoral. (One recalls Stalin's secret protocol of 1940 with Hitler, which specified that "Soviet interests lie to the south of our borders, toward the Indian Ocean.")

First hundreds, then thousands of Soviets went abroad on temporary assignments to give technical assistance; in the last six months of 1959, their numbers leapt from 4,000 to 6,500 and then in the next decade multiplied tenfold. By 1987 more than 60,000 Soviet advisers were abroad (not counting those in Afghanistan): about 35,000 economic and technical and 25,000 military.[31]

At the same time the Soviets were bringing soldiers and civilians of Third World countries to the USSR for training: in 1979 alone more than 30,000 from over a hundred countries—Ethiopia, Tanzania, Cuba, Nicaragua, El Salvador, Peru, Angola, Mozambique, Vietnam, India, Bangladesh, and others. Thousands have been assessed by the KGB and GRU and the most promising individuals recruited clandestinely to carry on the fight for Soviet hegemony over their own countries in the name of "proletarian internationalism."

By supplying its client states with arms they could never buy for themselves, the Kremlin has militarized their policies and incited conflict—to the point that "With the exception of the Indo-Pakistani wars in 1965 and 1971, every major local war between Third World protagonists during the past twenty-five years was started by a Soviet-armed state."[32]

The Uses of Culture

Hoping to improve relations through "people-to-people contacts," Western governments have signed agreements with the USSR to exchange information (in the form of books, movies, television programs, magazines, and newspapers), to ease travel and promote tourism, to exchange dance companies, musicians, and art exhibits, to let their students study in each other's institutions, and to allow scientists to exchange their knowledge. We have seen, however, what barriers the Soviet leaders erected precisely to prevent this. Here Gorbachev's impact remains to be seen.

An example of subordination of culture to higher-priority aims is the "University of the Friendship of Peoples named for Patrice Lumumba." It opened in 1960 to help the peoples of the developing countries of Africa, Asia, and Latin America to train their cadres. It has faculties of economics and law, history and philology, agriculture, medicine, and science, with programs of five and six years. By 1979 the Friendship University was handling more than 5,000 students at a time, and by the late 1980s more than 200,000 students had been trained there.

This university—housed, appropriately, in a building vacated by the KGB—is a successor to earlier Soviet institutions that trained people from underdeveloped regions. A University of the Workers of the East was run by the Comintern from 1921 until the early 1940s to train revolutionaries and propagandists, especially for areas like Central Asia and the Caucasus which were still being "normalized" after Soviet conquest. (This foreshadowed the training during the 1980s of thousands of young Afghans in the USSR; it is a permanent technique of Soviet rule.) The stated goal was "sending into the struggle new warriors armed with the powerful weapon of Leninism."[33] To train Mongolians to take over the administration of Sovietized Outer Mongolia, a "Yenukidze Institute of Living Eastern Languages" was formed in Leningrad, while in Moscow the "Sun Yat Sen University" trained revolutionaries for China. A political school in Tashkent during the Second World War trained Koreans, including the future head of North Korea, Kim Il Sung. Thus the training at the Friendship University of the later terrorist "Carlos" followed a long tradition, as did the schooling of the young Mexicans who were taken from the university to more intense training in insurgency and terrorism. The KGB occupies whatever positions in the staff it needs to screen and control these foreign students; the vice-rector in the 1960s, for example, was KGB Col. Pavel Yerzin.

Each student at the Friendship University, like those at other Soviet institutions, becomes the subject of a KGB dossier and is assigned to a KGB staff officer for assessment and development for clandestine recruitment. An Ethiopian medical student, in a typical case, was offered top grades in his examination if, after returning to his country, he would help overthrow the Emperor Haile Selassie.[34] Those the KGB recruits in Moscow are sometimes trained in KGB safe houses in outlying regions of the country (telling their fellow students that they have been shifted to "a special academy"). Those not yet ripe for recruitment are further cultivated after their return home by KGB residencies, directly or through the local USSR Friendship Society. As the university's rector Vladimir Starin said in 1977, "When they get back home, many of our graduates keep in touch with their alma mater through correspondence and consulations with former teachers." The result of all this was summed up by an earlier rector who said, during celebrations of its tenth anniversary in 1970, that the university "is rendering great support to the national liberation movement."

Other cultural flowers grew from the fertile soil of peaceful coexistence. Through Communist front organizations, regime-sponsored (and KGB-directed) Soviet youth, lawyers, historians, war veterans, and writers made contacts with their foreign opposite numbers. The Soviets also plunged enthusiastically into the work of international cultural organizations. A former Soviet official who worked in UNESCO in the early 1980s listed his regime's objectives within that organization: to get as many Soviet experts as possible on its staff; to exert pressure against Israel through Arab representations and those of other developing countries; to promote state control of information in Third World countries (on the pretext that a "world monopoly of international information organisms" misrepresents the situation in those countries); and to try to prevent debate on Soviet Bloc violations of human rights.[35] Another goal is to multiply contacts with Western intellectuals who sympathize with the Soviet point of view, with a view to KGB recruitment.

Soviet radio programs beamed to the outside world in more than eighty-five languages (nearly half of them, including South American Indian tongues and obscure languages of India, not represented on Western radios) had the stated purpose of "serving humanitarian goals and the cause of peace and friendship between nations." These stations were issuing calls to overthrow leaders and accusing Western governments of warmongering and plotting against the receiving country.

"Cultural Relations with Compatriots Abroad" is the misleading title of committees established in each Soviet republic. Their real purpose has been described by a member of the Latvian one: "Its task is to tone down and if possible block entirely the anti-Soviet activities of more than 120,000 exiled Latvians in the free world, bring about conflicts and unfriendliness among various exile factions, and at the same time scout out 'useful elements' for propaganda purposes among Latvian exiles and other immigrants in their new homelands. We were also supposed to find suitable candidates for KGB activity in the West among tourists."[36]

In almost every country of the world there is an "Association for Friendship with the USSR" sponsoring lectures on Soviet and Russian affairs, offering free Russian-language lessons, helping to arrange travel to the USSR, and (working with a cultural staff at the Soviet Embassy) coordinating visits by Soviet performers and lecturers, and picking suitable candidates for study in Moscow. It was one of these associations that picked those young Mexicans who were trained as saboteurs against their own government.

Such was Gorbachev's inheritance in foreign relations. To assess whether he is truly changing the Soviet system in a less hostile direction, one should keep an eye on the strange institutions that these foreign policies have spawned. We describe some of them in Chapter 26, after briefly reviewing a vital objective abroad of the Soviet rulers: getting the technological know-how and materials to support their military power.

CHAPTER 25

The Military Buildup

"AS SOON AS WE ARE STRONG ENOUGH TO DEFEAT CAPITALISM AS A whole, we shall immediately take it by the scruff of the neck," Lenin said,[1] and for seventy years his successors have been working toward that day.

Just how hard they have been working was revealed indirectly in February 1988, when Mikhail Gorbachev told the Central Committee that "basically, for four five-year periods there was no increase in the absolute growth of the national income and at the beginning of the 1980s it had even begun to fall. That is the real picture, comrades!"[2] This meant that the Soviet economy was much smaller—and military expenditures were eating up a far higher proportion of it—than the West had supposed. In contrast to the United States military expenditures of 7 percent of GNP, the Soviets must have been spending between 20 and 30 percent.

The best engineering talents of the country have been enlisted in the task of building a military force far exceeding any conceivable defensive need. Soviet spokesmen admitted in 1988 that the Warsaw Pact—while not necessarily superior to NATO in all conventional arms—has a superiority of 20,000 tanks. In addition, the armies on the European front are well supplied with bridge-crossing and other equipment designed for offensive operations.[3] The Soviets have built a large navy designed for ocean operations far from their shores. So fast were they putting out new types of missiles that by the time the "new" SS-20s were raising NATO's fears in the 1970s, their replacement was already being tested. Between 1970 and 1982 they developed "more than 20 new types of aircraft, 10 types of ballistic missiles, 25 types of aerodynamic missiles, over 50 new classes of naval ships, one third of which have been submarines, and at least 50 new ground force weapons. Equally large numbers of modifications have reached operational status."[4] In addition to developing chemical and biological weapons, they researched "Star Wars" space weapons a full decade before the Americans began.

To this effort is geared not only the Soviet economy but foreign policy too. Paradoxically, this eminently hostile military buildup has produced decades of "peaceful coexistence"—for it depends on foreign technology that can best be bought or stolen in the climate of detente.

To accomplish such prodigies of military construction the Soviet leaders have organized a system unparalleled in world history. They have clamped like a giant leech onto Western science and technology, sucking the blood and channeling it back to give life to Soviet military industry. The immensity of this system testifies not only to the incurable weakness of their own economy but to the urgency of their purpose.

Under the defense-industrial ministries more than a thousand research and development institutions develop new weapons and equipment ordered by the armed forces. When one of them needs information, material, or solution to problems, it has only to ask. Foreseeing the need for heat shields for warheads, for instance, the institute developing an ICBM asks for the carbon-weaving technology it needs; another, developing a new class of submarines, asks for the technology to produce larger titanium plates.

Their requests go via their ministries to a central organization that controls military-related research, development, and production called the Military Industrial Commission (VPK) under the Council of Ministers. The VPK transforms the wish-lists of all the military-industrial ministries (e.g. Aviation, Defense Industry, various Machine Building ministries, Shipbuilding, Electronics, Communications Equipment) into intelligence requirements for agencies that can collect the information abroad. Looking ahead at scientific advances, the State Committee on Science and Technology (GKNT) and the Academy of Sciences (*Akademiya Nauk,* or AN, covering dozens of institutes representing each of the physical and social sciences) estimate which are most applicable to military purposes—advances in computer science, for example, lasers, or cryogenics—and set priority intelligence requirements in those fields, too.

To each of the collection agencies is assigned that part of the task which it can do best. The KGB and GRU may be instructed to steal material or processes or documents through spies—their own or those of their East European satellite services—or to buy them openly through secretly controlled Western companies that send them eastward through intermediaries in neutral countries (also clandestinely set up by the KGB and GRU). The State Committee for Foreign Economic Relations (GKES) is told to try to purchase material legally through the trading monopolies under the Ministry of Foreign Trade. The USSR Chamber of Commerce gets the task of cultivating at international trade fairs (or inviting to Moscow) the representatives of Western companies that produce the goods that Soviet military industry needs. The Academy of Sciences is directed by the VPK or KGB to activate contacts with Western scientists in specified fields.

As the coordinator of Soviet participation in international scientific exchanges, the Academy of Sciences locates the leading Western universities, industries, and research institutes in each priority scientific field. Through the academy the GKNT, KGB, and GRU decide which Soviet scientists, in which disciplines, shall be sent abroad or shall be allowed to meet foreign scientists in the USSR.* It is thus according to the priorities of espionage that members are selected for delegations going abroad to conferences or seminars.

Students for exchange programs are selected in the same way. What the West thinks of as "exchanges" have always been one-sided. Whereas most Western students in Soviet universities study history, social sciences, or linguistics, Soviet candidates "have nearly always proposed research activities involving technologies in areas that have direct military applications and in which the Soviets are technologically deficient."[5]

Much of the information needed by Soviet industry is openly available in the West, and all these agencies collect it: technical books, academic publications, patent and license information and public bids for government contracts, company sales pamphlets and brochures, training materials, library holdings, data in computer banks. "The majority of Soviet acquisitions of Western technology," the U.S. government has noted, "have been achieved through legal means."[6] Soviet mining institutes acquired the civilian application of the principle of the shaped-charge warhead. A Hungarian who studied on a U.S.-funded grant learned about, and gave to the Soviets, magnetic bubble memory technology that advanced their computer research by ten years or more. The little submarines leaving furrows in Swedish and Norwegian inlets in the 1980s were American civilian innovations and not even secret. The United States stores all government research reports in the Defense Technical Information Center (DTIC), where the information is available to people with the proper clearances and the need to know (including government con-

---

*The editor-in-chief of the publishing house *Znaniye* (Knowledge) confided to one of his writers, "The Central Committee . . . told us straight out: the whole purpose of scientific contacts with the West is to get as much from them and give them as little as we can. Of course we need some Western discoveries and technology, but we have no intention of cooperating fair and square with them. Do you understand? No rose-colored spectacles, they told us; don't let the wool be pulled over your eyes" (Popovsky, p. 95).

tractors); DTIC forwards unclassified reports—some 80,000 per year—to the National Technical Information Services (NTIS), which gives them to anyone who asks. Until their subscription was canceled in February 1980, the Soviets bought every last one of the 80,000.[7] Since then, the Soviets have had to acquire them through their East European satellites.

They get Western firms not only to build high-technology factories for them but also to send them experts to give them the know-how. They set up companies in the West—some openly connected with the Soviet Bloc, others secretly established for them by Westerners in their pay—to buy finished products and materials.

What they cannot get in these ways, they go after by recruiting spies in Western companies and governments. At least 1,000 of the 2,800 Soviet and East European diplomats in the United States in the early 1980s were known intelligence officers, many of them in Line X—scientific and technological collection.[8] At the same time about 2,400 Soviet citizens were living in Paris, 700 with diplomatic status; French security services estimated that 600 Soviet Bloc case officers were manipulating some 10,000 spies in France—the majority collecting scientific and technological secrets.[9] A high proportion of the 10,000–20,000 Soviet Bloc spies in West German territory are seeking technical secrets.† So routine have the arrests of such spies become that Western newspapers usually give them only scant coverage.

As the collecting agencies get results, they submit them to the VPK or GKNT, where they are processed and passed along to the research or design institutes that need the information or material. As a specialist on Soviet science reports, "The main task of secret laboratories is to copy models manufactured in the United States," and young scientists jokingly called supposedly complicated laboratory projects "translations from the American."[10]

Sometimes these customers receive the answers only weeks after they put in their original request.

The KGB not only collects but also helps to coordinate the requirements and to distribute the product. As Yuri Andropov put it, "If our Chekist emblem were being designed today, one would boldly add a symbol of modern electronics alongside the sword and shield."[11] The huge Directorate T of its First Chief Directorate (working abroad as Line X) numbers some 400 officers (up from 42 in 1953) collecting scientific and

---

†The annual estimate by the West German security service of the numbers of Soviet Bloc spies on its terrain has never dropped below 4,000; the figure cited is from the early 1980s.

technological intelligence and controlling similar services in East Germany, Czechoslovakia, Hungary, Poland, and Bulgaria. The KGB also has at least one research institution of its own, where more than a thousand scientifically qualified KGB officials sort out and translate the scientific secrets sent in by KGB residencies abroad, test them, and pass them directly to concerned agencies or to the GKNT for distribution.

The KGB dominates the whole effort. It controls all the foreign contacts of each of the coordinating bodies and their subordinate institutes and industries, as well as their internal security. The Foreign Relations Directorates of both GKNT and AN are KGB outposts. Dzhermen Gvishiani, the KGB-connected son of a KGB general, headed the GKNT's Directorate for Foreign Relations for twenty years, until about 1982; his two deputies were senior officers of the KGB and GRU and under them stood three departments: the Foreign Relations Department (headed by a KGB officer with a GRU colonel as his deputy), the Foreign Department (similarly headed by a KGB officer with a GRU deputy— Col. Oleg Penkovskiy in his time—and staffed by nearly a hundred KGB and GRU officers),[12] and a Department for Foreign Science and Technology" headed in the early 1980s by KGB Col. Lev B. Burdyukov. "Scientific and industrial cooperation" within the GKNT was directed in the 1980s by KGB officer Fedor K. Mortin.[13] At the head of the AN's Foreign Relations Directorate, KGB Gen. Vladimir A. Vinogradov succeeded KGB Gen. Stepan G. Korneyev in the 1970s; high KGB officers continue to hold the key positions today. Lower echelons of that directorate with foreign contacts are similarly dominated by the KGB, as for example its Department of International Organizations, which coordinates work with the International Atomic Energy Agency and the Pugwash conferences. The qualifications of its leaders are exemplified by its chief in the 1970s, my old acquaintance Yelizaveta D. Lebedkina, whom the KGB had been preparing for an "illegal" assignment (falsely documented as a Western citizen) along with her scientist-Chekist husband, Vladimir A. Fedorovich, who worked with me in Naval SMERSH. Although their undercover assignment was aborted, they continued to do the KGB's work against foreigners; Fedorovich has been attending international scientific meetings for more than twenty-five years.

The results are breathtaking. Across the whole range of military technology, the Soviet regime has stripped secrets from Western Europe, Japan, and the United States and quickly applied them to its own missiles, aircraft, submarines and submarine-detection systems, tank armor, lasers, radar, air navigation and range finders, and on and on.[14]

"Virtually every Soviet long- and short-term research project for military systems—well over 5,000 in the early 1980s—is benefiting from the documents and hardware of at least a dozen Western countries."[15]

The Soviet space shuttle is an example—"we have seen their model—and it is ours," said a Western specialist. A new fighter plane revealed in the mid-1980s, the Sukhoi-27, was an obvious adaptation of the American F-15 design with antimissile radar technology stolen from the U.S. that alone saved the Soviets five years and $55 million in development costs. A new helicopter in 1984 matched the Americans' Apache. These and other copies recall the Tupolev 144 supersonic passenger plane that so closely resembled the Franco-British Concorde that Westerners nicknamed it "Concordski."‡ When the American cruiser USS *Ticonderoga* put to sea in 1983, she carried the new "Aegis" system, a high point of air defense technology that had cost twenty years of research and development and a billion dollars. Although the Soviets had trailed far behind in this technology, two years before the *Ticonderoga* rolled on her first ocean swell much of the system had already gone to sea aboard the new Soviet cruiser *Kirov*. "The *Kirov's* phased array computerized air defense system is based on technology stolen from us and our Aegis program," reported the American secretary of the navy. The Soviets had managed to leap over twenty years, several billion dollars, and technological expertise they didn't have, and to get their version to sea first.[16]

Although still far behind in computers, the Soviets were able to compete in ultramodern computer-directed weapons in the 1980s thanks to their thefts and purchases from the West. Of 800 Soviet acquisitions from the United States during one period, more than half were electronics, computers, or the equipment to produce them. In the mid-1980s "virtually all major Soviet computer systems, such as the entire RYAD-series and the Soviet SM-series of minicomputers, are based on and reverse-engineered from Western computers acquired both legally and illegally. . . . More than one-third of all known Soviet integrated circuits have been copied from US designs."[17] Most of the rest comes from Japan and Western Europe, not from Soviet researchers.

A minor employee of the CIA gave the KGB details of the most highly developed and strategically important photographic space satellite, the KH-11 "Early Bird," after which the Soviets immediately took precautions to thwart its capabilities—which they had not known. One spy alone—William Holden Bell, an employee of the Hughes Aircraft Corpo-

‡Copying is not always successful: a "Concordski" prototype crashed at the Paris Air Show in 1973; and the plane's commercial service, beginning with great fanfare in 1977, lasted only weeks before the authorities found it "uneconomical" and stopped flying it permanently.

ration in Los Angeles—gave them (through Polish state security) "the F-15 look-down, shoot-down radar system, the quiet radar system for the B-1 and Stealth bombers, an all-weather radar system for tanks, an experimental radar system for the US Navy, the Phoenix air-to-air missile, a shipborne surveillance radar, the Patriot surface-to-air missile, a towed array submarine sonar system, a new air-to-air missile" and more. "The information in these documents put in jeopardy existing weapons and advanced future weapons systems of the United States and its allies. The acquisition of this information will save the Polish and Soviet governments hundreds of millions of dollars in R & D efforts. . . ."[18]

Savings to the Soviet system—aside from the time gained and technological capabilities acquired—have been astronomical. In the one year 1980 more than half a billion dollars were saved by only a part of the year's acquisitions, plus tens of thousands of Soviet man-years of scientific research effort. The KGB alone was collecting data worth more than the annual cost of the entire KGB, according to KGB estimates in the late 1970s.[19] The satellite services of the KGB registered similar results. Josef Houska, head of Czech intelligence, told his officers as early as the 1960s that "the value of innovations gleaned by the Czech S&T intelligence department in capitalist countries annually exceeded the one-year budget of the whole Czechoslovak intelligence service."[20] And it cost the United States government hundreds of millions more to try to change the exposed systems and minimize the damage.

This gigantic collection effort, along with the concentration of Soviet industry on military production, has brought the Soviet Union to military parity with the developed Western countries. Whereas in the 1960s Soviet military technology had lagged ten years behind American, by the late 1970s the gap in most fields had narrowed to five years and by the mid-1980s to only two. Only the steadfast and often painful expenses on the part of NATO countries had prevented the Soviet armed forces from achieving the strategic superiority that would permit the Kremlin to intimidate the West and inhibit resistance.

Western technology has also extended the Soviet reach. In 1966 Moscow had had to stand helplessly by and watch as a Soviet-friendly regime in faraway Ghana was toppled. Its strategists asked for the kinds of ships and planes they would need to move their soldiers and tanks wherever pro-Soviet forces come to power or might come to power. The massive S&T collection effort, combined with Soviet military industry, gave them that capability. By the 1980s they had produced an equivalent to the huge American C-5 Galaxy transport plane and a near twin of the American C-141 Starlifter jet transport, called the Il-76. To airlift troops into back country where only short landing strips are available, they had the An-72—to the specialist an obvious development of the Boeing YC-14 design. Applying Western technology to their own needs, they developed air-cushion landing craft far bigger than comparable Western craft, and small ones able to land their troops quickly on foreign beaches. Already by the early 1970s Soviet military strategists were calling for intervention even in "distant regions of our planet" wherever "national liberation struggles" beckoned. No longer, wrote a top military chief, are the Soviet armed forces restricted to defending the Soviet Bloc; they also have the mission to "oppose oppression [. . . and] the export of counter-revolution" and to "support the national liberation struggle" anywhere.[21] Ten years later Soviet naval bases or repair facilities had been established in the Red Sea, Vietnam, and Cuba, and Soviet military units were stationed within a hundred miles of the American mainland (in Cuba), in the Middle East (Iraq and Syria), and in North Africa (Algeria and Libya).

"Detente" was the essential condition for this progress. The year 1972 was crucial. It is ironic that the former British Prime Minister Edward Heath pointed back to that year as the model for dealing correctly with the Soviets in contrast to the Reagan administration's confrontational "rhetoric" of 1984, which he deplored. It was the Soviet-American agreements of 1972, more than any others, that opened the way for the breakthroughs in Soviet military technology. They led to the creation of 250 working groups and subgroups exchanging scientists, information, and documentation, doing joint research and, sharing the results of their own research and experience.

The Soviet purpose behind these agreements is visible in their exploitation of the consular agreement that permitting each country—in the interest of detente and closer contacts—to add one consulate in the other's country. With a clear eye to their own priorities the Soviets chose, not a bigger city like Chicago or Los Angeles, but San Francisco. Nearby were the highest peaks of American technology—and in the city were convenient peaks for spying. The Soviets moved in a large staff (mostly intelligence officers), chose for their consular offices a tall building on Pacific Heights, crammed its top floor with sensitive electronics, covered its roof with antennas, and set out to spy on the people and microwave transmissions of Silicon Valley.

In the late 1980s despite all these efforts, the Soviet armed forces had failed to gain a decisive advantage over the West, while their military industry was being pressured to keep up with ever-higher technological developments in the West, such as improved reconnaissance systems, "smart" antitank guided munitions, advanced antiradiation missiles, and Assault Breaker weapons.[22] Despite its ability to siphon off much of

Western technology, the Soviet economy was cracking under the strain and Soviet propaganda decried more stridently than ever the "arms race" in which its military industry had run so hard and so fast.

To relieve these pressures while Gorbachev's reformers tried to restructure and reanimate the economy, the Kremlin had no choice but to cut back military expenditures. The time had come to withdraw from the costly war in Afghanistan and to make concessions on arms control. Detente and peaceful coexistence occupied stage front in Soviet foreign policy.

CHAPTER 26

Institutions of Foreign Policy

Institutions to Suit the Purpose

OUTSIDE THE COUNTRY AS AT HOME, THE COMMUNIST PARTY LEADERS, concerned above all to hold on to their power, have given top priority to the tasks described in the foregoing chapters. The skills of diplomacy and trade are less in demand than those of warding off foreign contamination of Soviet citizens abroad, countering Western opponents, and weakening Western regimes. Whereas clandestine political action and espionage are merely distasteful adjuncts to the foreign policies of Western governments, they are the central thrust of the Kremlin's, leaving genuine diplomacy, trade, and cultural relations as the adjuncts. And this reality is reflected in the institutions of Soviet foreign affairs.

The leaders' prime executor of such policies is, naturally, the same as at home: the KGB. They never admit this publicly, of course. Soviet textbooks teach, on the contrary, that "no international relations of the state or its social organizations and institutions can be carried out independent of the Ministry of Foreign Affairs."[1] In reality, the CPSU's Central Committee apparatus carries out foreign relations—directly and through intermediaries—quite independently of the ministry, and so does the KGB. In fact it would be more accurate to paraphrase those administrative law textbooks and say that no foreign relations of priority importance can be carried out independent of the KGB.

The Ministry of Foreign Affairs (*Ministerstvo Innostrannykh Del,* or MID) has played third fiddle in Soviet foreign relations since its earliest days, when it was run by a former tsarist foreign-office official, Georgiy Chicherin. His know-how and diplomatic manners helped create a facade behind which the party leaders' true missions could be carried out. To his foreign ministry was left the difficult and thankless task of trying to keep up the appearances of normal civilized relations with foreign governments while more important Soviet institutions—State Security and the Comintern—went secretly about the primary business of undermining those governments. When Western governments would discover and protest against this hostile activity, the Kremlin would pretend that it could not control the "independent" Comintern.[2] To deny publicly "the hand of Moscow" in subversive activity abroad, Gorbachev must have been confident that he could keep the KGB's work secret or plausibly deny it.

Although the Minister of Foreign Affairs is a Politburo member and although the MID's building looms high on the Moscow skyline and its functionaries, trained in special institutes, impress the Western world by their heightened sophistication and language skills, the MID plays only a marginally more important role today than it did in Chicherin's time—and even that under the shadow of the KGB. The KGB passes on the selection, promotion, clearance for access to secrets, and assignment abroad of MID's employees. It reserves for its own staffers MID positions in Moscow, especially those requiring frequent contact with foreigners, as well as a high proportion of embassy positions abroad. The KGB supervises the custody of MID files, handles MID communications, guards its buildings, decides who will be allowed to enter, and infiltrates its ranks with informants.

And contrary to those textbooks, the KGB directly carries on international dealings independent of MID. In the Kremlin's relations with the so-called Warsaw Pact countries, for example, the KGB plays a key role.

The KGB as Colonial Office

Most of the highest officials of satellite regimes have owed their careers to their secret cooperation with the KGB. The invading Soviet armies of the Second World War brought along the Kremlin's own ready-made puppet rulers for the conquered lands—Boleslaw Bierut and Jakub Berman for Poland, Walter Ulbricht for Germany, Matyas Rakosi for Hungary, Kim Il-Sung for North Korea, Georgi Dimitrov for Bulgaria, along with others destined for leading posts in party and government—KGB agents one and all (and, for that matter, Soviet citizens). After installing them in power the KGB kept its grip on them and as they aged (or fell from Moscow's favor) helped the Soviet Politburo select their replacements. In Afghanistan four KGB agents in succession replaced one another at the top: Taraki, Amin, Babrak Karmal, and Nadjibullah. It is thanks to the KGB that several recent leaders of Eastern Europe (Erich Honecker in East Germany, Gustav Husak in Czechoslovakia, Janos Kadar in Hungary, and others) moved to the top; they had been chief of their party's department responsible for overseeing "administrative organs," a post reserved for KGB agents.

When I worked in the KGB department responsible for operations in Germany, the top East German rulers—Wilhelm Pieck, Walter Ulbricht, Anton Ackermann, and Franz Dahlem—had worked secretly for the KGB. Although they were no longer under day to day KGB control, we still kept their agent-operational files and they would always bow if their KGB masters exerted pressure.

Decisions to remove or appoint East German leaders were made in Moscow, not in East Berlin. A name would be proposed to the CC CPSU, which would routinely refer to the KGB and act on its advice. Moreover, we in the KGB were the first to learn of problems as they arose in East Germany and (working with the Politburo and CC CPSU apparatus) shared the last word on the solutions. When the East German leadership wanted to take an initiative or draft a new law, we in the KGB learned of it from secret agents within that leadership even before the leaders proposed the measure officially to Soviet representatives in Germany or Moscow. The KGB would examine the proposal and the people who made it, add its own information, pass it on to the CC CPSU, and advise in the decision. Ackermann, for example, once suggested establishing contacts with certain Social Democrats in West Germany (foreshadowing the relations that were successfully established in the 1970s). We checked our files and found that the Westerners were relatives of Ackermann's with anti-Soviet connections—and far from approving this foreign policy initiative, the KGB began to probe Ackermann's motives.

The Kremlin does not trust its own puppets but ties them closely with party relationships (which are coordinated since 1988 in the CC CPSU's International Affairs Department and before then in a separate Department of Relations with Communist and Workers Parties of Socialist Countries) and with invisible strings manipulated by the KGB.

The KGB has several channels of control over satellite regimes. First, it invariably has secret collaborators among Soviet Bloc Communist Party leaderships who do the Kremlin's bidding as transmitted through the KGB. Second, it keeps its agents atop the department of their central committee apparatus (modeled on the CC CPSU's Administrative Organs Department) that oversees the country's military, state security, judicial, and police apparatus. Third, the KGB keeps a hand on the ruling parties through the state security services of each country. These the KGB created and, at their beginnings, directly commanded with Soviet KGB officers.

Since then it has kept secret collaborators among satellite state security staff members and has manipulated the services through all-powerful KGB "advisers" in or near their headquarters buildings. Thus the KGB can watch these services watching the doings of their own national leaders.

This "liaison" is facilitated by the organization of satellite state security services, which follows, for the most part, the KGB's table of organization. Thus Moscow departments that collect scientific and technological (or other) intelligence abroad, spy on local embassies of Western countries, or conduct "active measures" such as disinformation, sabotage, and murder are able to exploit and direct the work of parallel departments in the satellites and to coordinate their annual and five-year plans with Moscow's.

Those are some of those ties that Gorbachev was referring to when he wrote in 1987, "The solid network of contacts along party, state, and public lines plays an important and even decisive part in the cooperation among the fraternal countries."[3] It does indeed.

The Soviet leaders indulge satellite leaders publicly as sovereign rulers; they visit back and forth, meet in solemn conferences of Comecon and the Warsaw Pact, and even disagree at times. Certainly each of these countries presents its own problems for the Soviet rulership. But the relations of the Kremlin with their satellite rulers has not been "diplomacy" but plotting among coconspirators and manipulation of levers of control. In this, the CC CPSU and the KGB play the central roles, not the MID.

Controlling Client Regimes

Even outside the Warsaw Pact, the Kremlin encourages client regimes to defend their revolutions with Soviet-style institutions—not only to keep them in power (against "international imperialism and domestic reaction"[4]) but to facilitate Moscow control. Relations with such regimes stretch far beyond traditional diplomacy.

First of all they should have a "vanguard" party, unified by a single ideology: "scientific socialism." It may be kept small and should form a united front with other "progressive" parties, but it must remain the nucleus of all power. Their state machinery should be structured above all in a way that permits the party "to cut short the subversive activity of reactionaries and to rebuff imperialist encroachments"—i.e., put a model of the KGB at the center of the system. And the ruling party should form mass organizations through which it can mobilize the entire society in support of the regime.

It is thus no coincidence that the ruling parties of countries as distant in geography and history as Cuba and Mongolia have central committees closely resembling—down to the details of their internal structure—that of the CPSU. Look, too, at the remarkable resemblance to the Soviet Komsomol of the "Democratic Organization of Afghan Youth" and the "Democratic Youth of Angola" and the Cuban youth organization. "Committees for the Defense of the Revolution" in Afghanistan and Cuba, "neighborhood associations" (Kabeles) in Ethiopia, and "Sandinista Defense Committees" in Nicaragua resemble the Soviet *druzhiny*. When a Polish censor escaped to the West, his "list of materials to be kept from the press" was simply a Polish version of the *perechen* of Soviet Glavlit, of which his organization was a copy.

But it is not enough to pattern their institutions on the Soviet model. In addition, each of these institutions must take up "internationalist ties" with its Soviet parent—i.e., submit to the CPSU's "authority among fraternal parties," which has been earned by its "immense historical experience in the revolutionary struggle."[5] The ruling party and state must act jointly "with socialist countries and forces of national liberation struggles," for this "gives a small, militarily and economically weak state the possibility of retaining its sovereignty and upholding its revolutionary gains irrespective of its geographic location." The mass organizations must be tied in to the (Soviet-centered) international networks. "To ignore the activities of international progressive public movements . . . like the World Peace Council, the Movement of Afro-Asian Solidarity, trade unions [i.e. World Federation of Trade Unions], youth, etc.," may "isolate" and "weaken" national revolutionary forces—and this is "fraught with the danger of defeat."[6]

This unity with Moscow—joining the "socialist camp" and coming under the Kremlin's protective wing—goes under the well-known name of "socialist (or proletarian) internationalism." Up to a point in time, "nationalism" is a good thing: Soviets help "revolutionary nationalists" to win freedom from "imperialism." But after "socialist" power is established, nationalism becomes a bad thing (indeed, a subversive force that, in the USSR, has been suppressed by the KGB's Fifth Chief Directorate). Everyone should then be an "internationalist"—a person defined by Stalin in 1927 as one "who is unreservedly and unconditionally ready to protect the USSR, the base of the revolutionary movement of the whole world."[7]

"Internationalist" Armies

The institutions that control Soviet Bloc armies are projected abroad— for in client revolutionary states the army poses the same threat as the

Soviet Army does to Communist power in the USSR. Local models of the Political Administration of the Soviet Army (indoctrinating and watching over the soldiers), of the OO/KGB (planting spies and informers throughout the ranks), and of Internal Troops (as the party's private defenders) have been set up under Soviet tutelage not only in occupied Eastern Europe but also in Cuba, Ethiopia, Nicaragua, and Afghanistan (and were being established in Ghana during the abortive attempt to consolidate Soviet power there in the 1960s).

And the USSR arms and supports those foreign armies, which according to its teachings must be strong in order to fight off "counterrevolutionary" resistance (like the "contras" in Nicaragua) and to support other revolutions beyond the borders. Therefore one invariably finds astonishingly large armies in countries that have joined the socialist camp. In the 1980s Cuba maintained 225,000 regulars and nearly 200,000 trained reserves and an armed militia that was being doubled in the mid-1980s to one million—putting 15 percent of all Cubans under arms. In Ethiopia before the emperor was overthrown in 1974, his opponents ridiculed the pathological fear of overthrow that impelled him to keep 40,000 men under arms, wasting money (they said) that would be better used for hospital and schools—but the emperor's Leninist successors, despite the country's terrible poverty, maintain 200,000 regulars and 100,000 militia. While Nicaragua's unpopular dictator Somoza was able to defend himself for a generation with an army of 7,000 men, the Sandinistas have over 100,000, plus modern equipment for which Somoza would have had no use. (If this army were not enough, about 3,000 Cuban soldiers and 9,000 military advisory personnel from the Soviet Bloc were there on Nicaraguan soil to help.) Vietnam's post-victory army of more than a million is among the largest in the world. The little island republic of Grenada (total population 110,000), which had gotten along happily without an army before the leftist takeover, was building up to a military force of between 7,000 and 10,000, organized in eighteen active and reserve battalions. The tiny client state of Guinea-Bissau was endowed with an army of some 6,000 men.

Each of these armies has Soviet military advisers, technicians, and trainers, and some have Soviet officers in command positions. In the 1980s Soviet officers were commanding units of the Ethiopian and Afghan armies, while Cubans commanded Angolan units and East Germans led South Yemeni forces. Soviet, Cuban, East German, North Korean, and other pilots commanded air squadrons in Third World client states.

The Warsaw Pact is a facade for a deep integration of East European armies—under Moscow's command. To reach-the top in satellite armed forces, officers must have training in the USSR—where many are recruited as secret collaborators of GRU or KGB—and they must stay in the good graces of their Soviet seniors. Each Warsaw Pact army has its equivalent of the KGB's Third (military security) Directorate, which is closely tied to its KGB parent, ensuring that only friends of Moscow reach key command and security positions in these "internationalist" forces.

Soviet Installations Abroad

As a logical outgrowth of the Kremlin's priorities, the KGB occupies a central position in all Soviet embassies and in many of them, an overwhelming one. This position is enhanced by the KGB's control of communications,* by its responsibility for the internal security of installations abroad (as at home), and by its independence. (The ambassador, like party bosses in the USSR, is forbidden to see KGB communications.) The KGB is, moreover, assured of a dominant voice in local decision-making by its control of instrumentalities that are denied to the MID—such as its spies within the host governments and political parties, sometimes so highly placed—like Guenther Guillaume in the immediate entourage of West German Chancellor Willy Brandt and Norwegian foreign office official Arne Treholt in the 1970s and 1980s—that they can secretly manipulate national policy.

The ambassador—sometimes a senior CPSU official in his own right and sometimes a Chekist—has paramount authority. Much goes on without the KGB's participation; genuine MID personnel, some of them with relatively loose KGB connections, carry on routine embassy activities. In some embassies, too (not only in the Soviet Bloc but also in the West), there are stationed CC CPSU representatives with their own separate responsibilities and powers.

But the KGB—responsible for the essential tasks—occupies the positions it needs. Even the top one: I have counted more than fifty KGB officers who have served as ambassadors. In the mid-1980s the Soviet ambassador to the Democratic Republic of the Congo, in Brazzaville—base for subversive operations in Zaire, that coveted prize across the river—was Vladimir C. Lobachev, who had previously had intelligence assignments in Washington, Hanoi (during the Vietnam War), and India. Vadim Tikunov, KGB deputy chairman, later held African ambassadorships until his death in 1978; so did the MVD Minister Vadim S. Lunov. Alkesandr Panyushkin moved as ambassador to Washington di-

---

*The KGB operates its own (and the embassy's) links to Moscow. The communications of the Ministry of Foreign Affairs—radio, ciphers, diplomatic couriers—are handled by the KGB.

rectly from command of Soviet Intelligence—and, as we have seen, returned to head the KGB's foreign operations. Vladimir Dekanozov, after heading KGB (then NKVD) foreign operations and "normalizing" occupied Lithuania in 1940, went as ambassador to Hitler's Germany, with another top Chekist as his deputy. KGB Maj. Gen. Aleksandr I. Shitov (using the false name Alekseyev) went to Castro's Cuba as the second Soviet ambassador there, replacing the intelligence officer Sergey Kudryavtsev (code-named "Leon" in the atomic spy ring in Canada that was blown in 1945), who went on to serve as ambassador to Cambodia during the Vietnam war and to UNESCO in Paris. And many more.

The positions within Soviet representations abroad are assigned from Moscow according to the Kremlin's priorities under arrangements coordinated by the CC CPSU. As a result, slots normally reserved for diplomats, commercial delegates, or journalists are filled by people sent to do quite different work. But this causes no special problem, so small is the volume of genuine political or cultural work required in most countries. Consuls have relatively few visas to issue and almost no Soviet travelers in the West to look after. Trade with the West is arranged more by visits to and from Moscow than by local trade delegations, as any Western businessman has found out if he has tried to do business through them; they are likely to simply pass on queries to Moscow and often seem detached from, and ignorant of, the details of their business.

Despite this lack of visible work, Soviet installations have swollen ever larger since peaceful coexistence began to bear fruit. Before the late 1950s hardly 4,000 Soviets were stationed permanently in the West at any one time. By the late 1980s this figure had jumped beyond 20,000 even without counting the advisers to client states (more than 30,000 economic and 25,000 military). But even in earlier days these installations were oversized. When Uruguay took up relations with the USSR after World War II, it sent three Uruguayan diplomats to Moscow and later added a fourth; Moscow immediately sent 47 to Montevideo and soon raised that to more than a hundred. In 1968 Mexico had five representatives in Moscow, plenty to handle Mexico's tiny trade and tourism (only 200 Mexicans had traveled the previous year to the USSR)—yet there were 57 Soviets in Mexico. In Columbia there were 29 Soviet diplomats and in Moscow three Colombians. Sovfilm representatives were permanently stationed in countries that wanted no Soviet films, Soviet auto salesmen where few Soviet-made cars were sold.

The reason for these bloated staffs did not remain secret. Western counterintelligence services identified thousands of these officials as KGB and GRU officers. Of those 57 Soviet officials in Mexico, for example, 49 were identified intelligence officers. Of the 72 Soviet citizens in the secretariat and permanent Soviet delegation at UNESCO's headquarters in Paris, nearly half had been identified by French security services as professional intelligence officers. About a third of all the hundreds of Soviet officials in the United States and France (and a much higher percentage of those with diplomatic status) were known to be professional KGB and GRU officers.[8]

And they were busy. Between 1970 and 1989 more than 700 of them were expelled from Western countries for trying to subvert or spy on their host countries.[9]

Sometimes these clandestine operatives use their overt positions not only to explain their presence abroad but also to promote their secret work. Consular officials and Intourist representatives help the KGB to control—and recruit among—foreign visitors to the USSR.‡ "Cultural attaches" are well placed to manipulate contacts with Communist front organizations, with local USSR friendship societies and (like consuls) with emigres from the Soviet Union. In their work for committees of "Cultural Relations with Compatriots Abroad," they pursue the real task of neutralizing the anti-Soviet impact of emigres.§

Journalists, because they are free to roam about and interview parliamentarians or scholars or government officials or businessmen or anyone else, naturally work for Soviet intelligence. Therefore, large numbers of Soviet correspondents could be found abroad representing newspapers that did not even report Western events, and as many as five or ten journalists were stationed in a foreign country where one genuine one could provide all the information likely to interest all the newspapers in the Soviet Union put together. *New Times* had twelve correspondents out in the Western world—and ten of these positions were reserved for the KGB. Of Novosti's correspondents in any capital abroad, only one would be a real journalist. "The rest of the crowd doesn't bother to do anything for poor Novosti; all of them are working in the intelligence field," reported a former Soviet correspondent—and KGB officer.[10] The same is true of Tass, *Komsomolskaya Pravda,* and *Izvestiya,* though the ratio of KGB officers to

‡To attract American tourists, as chief of Intourist's American Department in Moscow, the Soviet system found no more appropriate candidate than Ivan P. Zavorin, who had been twice expelled from foreign countries—Argentina in 1950 and Great Britain in 1970—for spying.

§These committees have been run, since their formation, by the Emigre Department of the KGB's Foreign Operations Directorate in cooperation with the Fifth Chief Directorate (that watches over "bourgeois nationalist" tendencies in the republics). The committees' all-Union first deputy chairman, Georgiy N. Gorshkov, was a KGB emigre operations officer who worked earlier under cover of the Press Agency Novosti. After the Soviet cultural attache in Sweden, Alberts Liepa, was expelled for spying in 1982, he was named chairman of the Latvian Committee for Cultural Relations with Compatriots Abroad.

real journalists may vary. In Moscow, the deputy editor-in-chief of *New Times* in the mid-1970s was my old colleague, Vitaliy Chernyasky, who at one time headed the KGB's Scandinavia desk. [11]

How many intelligence and security personnel occupy these foreign posts? Former Soviet intelligence officers estimate that between a third and half of the embassy staffs are KGB and GRU officers (including three-quarters of the accredited diplomats) and about a third of the entire Soviet presence, for a total of about 6,000–7,000 of the 20,000 people stationed in official installations abroad (not counting the 60,000 technical and military advisers). This sounds about right to me—but needs refinement.

Universal statistics can be misleading. The proportion varies with the job function, the location, and the time. Consular work, for example, contributes so directly to KGB tasks that consulates are often wholly occupied by KGB officers and clerks, only in certain countries accompanied by MID employees and a very rare GRU officer. We have already seen the KGB and GRU taking more than three-quarters of the foreign correspondent slots, which give unusual mobility. And proportions vary according to the situation in any given country. For instance in Grenada in the 1980s, while a Soviet-friendly regime was consolidating its power, it would be absurd to suppose that only half of the staff of the inflated Soviet "embassy" were intelligence or subversion specialists. More likely all of them, from the ambassador down to the cooks and gardeners were emissaries of the KGB, GRU, Soviet armed forces, and CC CPSU.

Finally, such estimates would be meaningful only if the Soviet regime's subversive effort were conducted solely by professional KGB and GRU career officers. Such is not the case. In the first place, some personnel of MID and other agencies and many real journalists have been secretly contracted and trained in the USSR to help KGB or GRU representatives abroad. More important, everyone abroad must help the KGB. No one—with exceptions too rare to discuss here—is allowed out of the USSR for his own convenience; and until Gorbachev permitted cooperatives and joint ventures with Western firms, no one had any private business interests. Every one who is allowed out is cleared by the KGB, given a careful briefing which instills fear of this "enemy territory" and its malevolent people, and made to understand that, be he only the janitor, he is a warrior selected to take part in a struggle. Whatever his ostensible reasons for going abroad, his party or Komsomol charter specifies that he is a *yedinomyshlennik,* a like-minded coconspirator. He has read and signed a paper spelling out his responsibilities and is perfectly aware that if he is to go abroad, or stay there, he must do what the KGB tells him. He must report each contact with any foreigner; and if that foreigner is interesting to the KGB, he will get instructions on how to proceed. Day by day he must also (as part of "revolutionary vigilance") keep an eye on his fellow Soviets. In fact, like many of his fellows, he may have been a KGB *seksot* long before his departure, which might explain why he, not his fellows back home, got this lucky assignment.

Therefore the true proportion of KGB and GRU officers or helpers among Soviets abroad on official assignment is 100 percent. Some are simply less carefully trained and briefed and given less demanding responsibilities than others.

This then has been the face abroad of a regime devoted above all to its own survival. With Gorbachev's reforms a different, more open face was promised, reflecting international goodwill, easier travel, and freer relations between peoples. You can measure the reality of these promises by the evolution—or not—of these institutions, which are dedicated to the very opposite.

Afterword: Is the Cold War Over?

GORBACHEV RELEASED A TEEMING HOST OF SUPPRESSED PROBLEMS. Obscure quarrels between people of different nationalities—Abkhazians and Georgians, Uzbeks and Meskhetian Turks, Armenians and Azerbaijanis, Kirghizi and Tadzhiks—became bloody riots; striking miners stopped the coal production of huge areas to force the government to act fast on its promises; demonstrations for better living conditions turned into shouted demands for greater freedom and changes in the political system; from several republics came demands for independence from the USSR; intellectuals called into question some of the very bases of the Leninist system.

These demands were far outstripping the Kremlin's poor power to respond. The party had "lost its influence and power and ability to act," admitted Chairman of the Council of Ministers in July 1989, while Gorbachev warned that the party was losing its guiding role. The miners' strikes were "threatening the fabric of society"; ethnic conflicts were creating an "enormous danger" to "the destiny and integrity of our state" and threatened "catastrophe."

And so the steely hand under the glove of *glasnost* began to show. In the spring of 1989 Internal Troops killed many Georgians demonstrating for more autonomy, and tanks occupied the streets of a dozen Soviet towns. In just one week in July 1989 Gorbachev issued no fewer than three warnings and threats; he spoke of "special measures" that might be needed to prevent the strikes "from running out of control"; he called for "the most decisive measures" against people promoting separatism, territorial disputes, or ethnic conflict; he categorically rejected the separation of any region from the Soviet Union.

So was the Soviet Union's progress toward democracy really irrevocable, as Gorbachev—and some Western scholars and statesmen—said? Had the Cold War—and the Soviet threat to the West—really ended, as some of them proclaimed?

Neither the opinions of outsiders nor the assertions of Soviet leaders, nor even their conciliatory policies, are enough to answer this question. The winds of Soviet history have shifted many policies and blown away many hopes. Only in the system itself—that system with which the Soviet rulers have fought their internal war to hold power—can the answer be found. The struggle abroad known as the Cold War will end only when that internal war is over.

What then is the state today of the institution and methods that typify the internal struggle? Have the reformers dismantled them, or shown any inclination to do so?

By 1990 none had been dismantled, although a weakening had begun. Above all, fear had begun to dissipate. No result of Gorbachev's reforms was potentially more fateful for the regime, for fear had upheld the lies and greased the functioning of this essentially repressive system. Now people were doing things that they would not have dared only two or three years earlier: talking to one another (and to Westerners) with less inhibition, assembling to promote their interests and claim their rights, striking, demanding more freedom from Moscow's rule, and openly criticizing the leaders and the institutions (a few beginning to defy even the KGB).

Deprived of the binding force of fear, some of the foundations of the system were slowly eroding. The independent organizations, growing bolder, were contesting the party's monopoly of power; people were beginning to point to the ideology and Lenin himself as the causes of the country's failure, and the regime's own crimes were beginning to be aired publicly. (To speak of crimes is to begin to point the finger at criminals— eventually, perhaps, at those still living and active Chekists who, on Politburo assignment, have been guilty of murder, torture, assault, and unlawful persecution.)

But the basic institutions and methods survived intact. Claiming to introduce "the rule of law," the reformers had done little more than slap a new label on "socialist legality" (the "law-governed state") while leaving the party in its leading role over justice. While granting churches new rights to organize some of their own activities, the reformers had maintained their controls over them. They proposed to return some land to private farming but it would take decades before any significant number of farmers would enjoy freedom from collective control. The reforms of industry had created turmoil while leaving the most difficult changes for the future. Private business had been authorized and was thriving (despite envy and opposition) but was as vulnerable to crackdown as the New Economic Party in the 1920s.

The KGB, ultimate embodiment and enforcer of party rule, stood intact and powerful. True, some voices were raised under *glasnost* to attack its secrecy and recommend the curtailment of its powers, but a more reliable guide to the leaders' thinking lay in the new statute on state security that they were to promulgate in 1990 or 1991. They seemed about to enhance rather than diminish the KGB's legal status and powers. Soviet leaders were pointing to a "growing" threat from "foreign centers" seeking to subvert the system through "extremists" in the independent groups. The forthcoming statute was urgently needed, as one jurist wrote, to quell this "rising tide" by strengthening the KGB's legal status, increasing its independence and responsibility, and drawing more help from public organizations and labor collectives. [1]

In the meantime the KGB was maintaining its secret agent networks as before, watching and listening and keeping files open as the more daring elements of the population exposed their hostility to Communist rule. Going the rounds in Moscow in 1989 was a parody of some lines of Pushkin: "We are living through the epoch of *glasnost;*/Comrades, you may be sure that it will pass away/ But the KGB will not forget our names." [*]

The leaders' special troops, far from being disbanded, were engaged more widely than ever in controlling mass demonstrations. Their brutal treatment of demonstrating Georgians in 1989 showed the leaders' determination to keep "democratization" within acceptable limits.

While voices like that of Andrey Sakharov were raised against the internal passport system, the regime had not removed these documentary shackles. Nor had it lowered the barriers against contact with foreigners or stopped issuing hate propaganda against the West. Its inward-facing borders remained as murderous as ever. While it had allowed more emigration and simplified some procedures for travel abroad, the regime was still not letting its citizens travel freely. While many political prisoners were released, others remained in prisons and psychiatric hospitals.

Censorship, was being applied more permissively and was under attack in the new Supreme Soviet, but Glavlit remained intact as an institution. The independent organizations were granted neither paper nor reproducing facilities to spread their word. The rulers had shortened the censors' list of forbidden matters, but that *perechen* is a loose-leaf book designed for

---

[*]Pushkin's lines had been addressed to the Decembrist rebels being deported to Siberia: "We are all living through the epoch of suppression;/Comrades, you may be sure that it will pass away,/And we will not forget your names."

quick additions or deletions. One could sense the enduring grip of
censorship when the elections of April 1989 jolted the party leaders; until
then so seemingly unrestrained, the press remained obediently silent until
Gorbachev got around to telling them what line to propagate—and even
then suppressed much of the bad news.

The ruling party retained its power to hire and fire and promote in
offices, industries, and farms, to admit people to higher education, to
assign apartments and vacation spots, to distribute food, and to punish
according to laws it could shape to its needs—and outside the law if
necessary.

The party leaders were determined to keep these institutions intact and
to hold the reforms within limits. Gorbachev did not want the reforms to
"lower standards of discipline, order, and responsibility" or to entail "any
absence of control." *Perestroika* was designed to heal a sick economy, not to
introduce capitalism; *glasnost,* to build confidence and improve communications, not to throw open all the gates and windows; democratization, to
improve the working of "socialist" democracy, not to introduce the "bourgeois democracy" of a multiparty system, which Gorbachev labeled as
"rubbish." Nor did "restructuring ethnic relations" imply "the breakdown
of the national-state structure of the country," he said when Georgians
massed to demand freedom in 1989. "We are resolutely against this."[2] He
vowed "not to change Soviet power to abandon its fundamental principles"
and wanted none of his reforms to raise the spectre of "any breakup of our
political system." He insisted that the Communist Party's leadership was
more necessary than ever, that its dominance remained "unshakable."

But of course there is a gap between intentions and results, and some
results of their reforms had already surprised the leaders, as they themselves admitted. They had not anticipated the full impact of the "informals" nor foreseen how boldly an unshackled press would use its new
freedoms. And a long and perilous road lay ahead. Looming up beyond the
whole mountain of tasks—building a new infrastructure of research,
marketing, and services, creating new systems of financing and credit—
rose the most daunting task of all: reducing government subsidies for
food, housing, fuel, and raw materials.† For this they would have to raise
prices more than wages, a step that in other Communist countries had
provoked riot and rebellion. They had prudently postponed for years this
trickiest and most dangerous of their reforms.

Moreover, the road ahead was dark. However radical Gorbachev's re-

---

†In 1988 the Soviet citizen was paying for his housing only about 3 percent of his
earnings; for every ruble he was spending on milk or bread, the government was paying
about two. More than 15 percent of the national budget was being consumed by subsidies
on food, housing, fuel, and raw materials.

forms might seem in the Soviet context, they are really only half-measures and more likely to produce chaos than social peace. For decades, Communist Yugoslavia has had the things Gorbachev hopes to bring to the USSR—decentralized administration, looser planning, workers' councils, autonomous factory management, private small-scale business and crafts. Yugoslavia also has things that Gorbachev has no intention of offering: the peasants own four-fifths of the farmlands, the national regions enjoy a large degree of autonomy, and the people have easy access to the Western press and can freely travel and work abroad. Yet these reforms had not prevented Yugoslavia's slide into economic disarray, poverty, a huge public debt, galloping inflation, worker dissatisfaction and strikes, and an accelerating tendency of regions to break away from the center.

This is the Kremlin's dilemma: only truly revolutionary reforms can save the Leninist system—but these reforms would transform it into something other than Leninism. The reformers would have to loosen their grip and let the market begin to work its own laws. They would have to drop the pretense that they are the country's "brains" and let the better qualified, the more talented, and the independent-minded rise to positions of command authority. They would have to offer free access to Western information and Western associations in science, banking, industry, and agriculture. They would have to offer truly attractive incentives to get the workers to pitch in: better housing, consumer goods, the right to travel. They would have to win confidence from the people too, which they had hardly begun to do by the end of the 1980s. For this they would have to install a genuine rule of law that bound the party as well as the people, and to tell the truth about their own past crimes. And they would have to reduce the functions and powers of the KGB.

But they cannot do that, for the KGB is their insurance that *perestroika* will not go too far, that *glasnost* will not get out of hand. "This revolutionary process will be reliably protected against any subversive intrigues," promised KGB Chairman Viktor Chebrikov; and he and other Soviet leaders continued to remind the world that the regime "cannot survive" without the KGB.[3] By preserving their power inside the country‡ the leaders let it be known that their internal struggle and the Cold War abroad continue.

---

‡There were hints in the late 1980s of a possible separation of the KGB's foreign intelligence functions to another agency. This would not reduce the KGB's powers any more than had the separate "Intelligence Committee" *(Komitet Informatsiya)* that in 1947 united the foreign operational units of KGB (then MGB) and GRU (and which began to come unstuck within a year although it survived formally until 1951). The KGB would continue to oversee any foreign activity that in any way touched on its internal responsibilities (just as it oversees and manipulates the MVD inside the country).

If the regime should choose to reverse certain reforms that seemed to be getting out of hand, it could do so.§ The population, still cowed by their residue of fear, would acquiesce when faced with the power the regime could bring to bear—including, should it come to that, military power. As the bloody events in Georgia in 1989 demonstrated yet again, the party leaders command loyal forces of their own,** the will to use them, and the ability to confine disturbances to restricted areas where these forces can handle them piecemeal.

The internal fight is not over. On the contrary, as the people's demands grow and spread ever more fierce battles could be expected. The blood spilled by the Internal Troops in Armenia and Azerbaijan and Georgia at the eve of the 1990s might be little more than a foretaste of things to come. As the confrontation became more acute, the regime would again blame foreigners and "prove" their incitement by secret provocation. The party leaders would feel compelled to brake the reforms, turn a more hostile face to the West, and loose their KGB.

Upon the KGB hangs the fate of the Soviet system. In the long run the system is doomed by its own failure. But if it preserves and uses the powers embodied in the KGB the regime can survive for many years until its final slide into ruin and discredit. If it lets those powers be whittled away in the course of *perestroika* and *glasnost,* its doom will arrive even sooner.

Here then are some points to watch as this process continues in the 1990s:

- How is the regime responding to dissidents' calls for the disbanding or hobbling of the KGB?
- Have the KGB's illegal techniques, such as provocation, murder and beatings, and harrassment and threats been subjected to open discus-

§Reforms that seemed irrevocable at the time have proven, in other Communist countries, such as China in 1989, quite revocable. The exulting population of Poland in 1981, united behind the huge independent Solidarity movement in a wholehearted rejection of Communist rule, had lost their fear of their hapless rulers and shared a conventional wisdom that "now, nothing can turn the clock back any more." In December of that year it took the party—using its own loyal military force—only a few days to turn that clock back and restore a state of sullen fear that lasted for years. The difference, of course, is that in Poland the rulers' protective forces were backed by overwhelming force from outside—Soviet military power. In the Soviet Union that outside force would be the regime's special troops.

**The VV and KGB forces are necessarily more loyal to the rulers than to the people. Compromised and hated, they have no choice but to fight to the last barrier in the defense of their masters—as did the Hungarian equivalent of the KGB when the people rose en masse against the Communist regime in 1956.

sion in the press? Do KGB operatives remain immune from punishment for these crimes?

- Can a body independent of the party take and act on complaints about KGB actions?
- Have the crimes of the Soviet past been openly exposed, including the names of those guilty of them? Not only the massacres of Poles at Katyn but especially of Soviet citizens in Bykovniya and the forest of Kuropaty and hundreds of other places?
- Has the true history of Internal Troops been told?
- Are "informal" groups, including political ones, being legalized and given access to printing presses and paper?
- Has prior censorship been stopped? Has Glavlit been dismantled? Have Western periodicals and books become easily available to common Soviet citizens, as promised in 1988?
- Are nonparty people—including jurists, economists, journalists, scientists, technicians, writers, historians, or others—getting positions of real authority in the state and judicial organs, in public organizations and research institutions, and in the media? If so, does their authority include the right to hire and fire without party approval?
- Has the regime opened to public view its decision-making processes?
- Have the press and textbooks stopped disseminating fear- and hate-provoking distortions of the West?
- Has the ideology been lowered from its pedestal of omniscience?
- Is leaving the country without the government's permission still "treason"—or a crime of any kind? Can people ask to emigrate without being punished? Have the inward-facing, murderous border defenses been dismantled?
- Has the regime removed—and not just renumbered or reworded— the provisions in the Criminal Code that criminalize dissent? Has it admitted and corrected its jailing of dissidents for alleged common crimes?
- Has a way been found to free judges and procurators of party discipline and government supervision?
- Has the press been allowed to inspect and report on conditions in the prisons and camps? Have the authorities eliminated the conditions that induce disease or death there? Have they really eliminated the use of psychiatric confinement to punish dissent?
- Has the regime authorized trade unions independent of the official ones to represent workers' rights and interests instead of those of political leaders and managers?
- Are people allowed to talk with Westerners without fear of sanction?

To invite them to their homes? Have the laws and regulations barring Western contacts been lifted?

Such a list is far from complete, but the answers will tell much about the true state of the Soviet system. As long as the answers to these questions remain negative, the seeming peace is but a truce and the Kremlin is still combatting its own people—and the capitalist West.

Notes

Preface

1. Testimony to Senate Foreign Relations Committee, 4 April 1989. Reported in *International Herald Tribune,* 11 April 1989.
2. Gorbachev, *Perestroika,* p. 202.

Chapter 1. The Origins

1. Cited by Souvarine, p. 192.
2. The first citation is from *Pravda,* June 1917, the second from Lenin, "Can the Bolsheviks Retain State Power?" September 1917, and the third from Lenin, "The State and Revolution," August–October 1917.
3. These quotes are all from Lenin, "Immediate Tasks of the Soviet Government."
4. Both citations are from September 1917, the first from a letter to the Central Committee, the second from "Can the Bolsheviks Retain State Power?"
5. The fourteen issues of the daily newspaper published by the Kronstadt rebels were collected by the Socialist Revolutionaries in Prague in 1921 under the title *Pravda o Kronshstadte.*

Chapter 2. Special Troops: The Beating Heart of the Party"

1. According to the commander of the Moscow Militia, cited by Tass, 2 November 1988. In the first eight months over six hundred such disturbances had occurred in the USSR, according to the Minister of Internal Affairs (cited in *New York Times,* 29 August 1988).
2. The source was cited as "officials familiar with Western intelligence reports" (*International Herald Tribune,* 1 April 1989).
3. Press dispatches, including *Le Figaro,* Paris, 7, 8, and 12 June 1989.

4. Solzhenitsyn, *The Gulag Archipelago,* vol. 3, p. 507.

5. *Izvestiya,* 13 February 1989, reporting an interview with a USSR MVD spokesman, who pretended that the measure was designed to protect the journalists.

6. See, for example, the compilation by Ludmilla Alexeeva and Valery Chalidze, *Mass Rioting in the USSR* (The Foundation for Soviet Studies, Report no. 19, January 1985).

7. For the incident near Kiev see *Possev,* November 1982, citing U.S. Information Bulletin, Foreign Reports, 23 September 1982; for Ordzhonikdze see *Baltimore Sun,* 12 November 1981, *London Financial Times,* 24 November 1981, and *Agence France Presse,* 26 November 1981. The uprising in Chimkent was reported by *The Guardian,* 24 October 1976; that in Barnaul in *Shifrin,* p. 298.

8. A Russian soldier named Yevgeniy Yelin, coming over to the West in Berlin, brought the first news of Novocherkassk four years later. His account was first published in the emigre paper *Nashi Dni* in 1966 and reprinted in *Possev,* No. 8, 1982, on the twentieth anniversary of the events. Aleksandr Solzhenitsyn heard more about the incident from other eyewitnesses returning from the prison camps. He published his account in *The Gulag Archipelago,* vol. 3, pp. 507–10. Information is so sketchy that the details given here may still not be exact.

9. The first quote is from Lenin, *Immediate Tasks of the Soviet Government;* the second from Yakolev, *VV 1917–22,* p. 4.

10. *New York Times,* 29 August 1988; *Vechernaya Moskva,* 22 August 1988; *Pravda,* 24 August 1988.

11. *Pravda,* 18 October 1988; *Cahiers du Samizdat,* no. 136, October 1988, p. 12.

12. Kalachnikov, p. 109.

13. Moscow Television Service, 2300 GMT, 6 December 1987, reported in FBIS-SOV-87-235, 8 December 1987. Col.-Gen. Yuri V. Shatalin's "pain" was reported in *Pravda,* 18 October 1988.

14. Such publicity has tended to concentrate on the most visible VV unit, the Dzerzhinsky Division. See, for example, Belikov et al.; Padzhev; and A. P. Kozlov. (Both the latter had commanded the division; Kozlov later headed the MVD of Moscow City and Oblast.) See also *Prikazano zastupit'* (Moscow: Molodaya Gvardiya, 1974) and "Dzerzhintsy," in *Smena,* June 1974.

15. Belikov et al., pp. 137ff., is but one text among many that uses these standard terms.

16. The most expansive text of all allots them only a single paragraph of generalities about their service regulations (Yu. M. Kozlov, 1979, p. 472). Four others give nothing more than the two words "internal troops" on their lists of MVD components (Sorokin; Kozlov, 1968 and 1973; Yeropkin and Klyushnichenko). The most recent, returning to the pre-1966 practice, does not mention them at all (Vasilenkova, 1981; compare Yeropkin, 1965, and earlier works which omit any reference to them). The *Soviet Military Encyclopedia,* in a volume published in 1976, has only a short paragraph under "Internal Troops" (volume 2, 1976, pp. 164–5) giving only the same information as Kozlov (1979) on administrative matters.

The only scholarly work devoted specifically to the troops is a collection, published in a small edition in the 1970s, of historical documents that end in 1945 and skirt the troops' large-scale repressions of the populace (see Yakovlev; at the time its three volumes were compiled, he was in command of the VV).

17. The authoritative *Encyclopedia of Russia and the USSR* (Cambridge, 1982), for example, does not even mention them, although it does include the words "internal security troops" in a list of the VCheka in the period 1918–22, and refers elsewhere to "KGB Security Troops," which are different. Some specialized works, based largely on reliable defector information, have given them their due, notably Wolin and Slusser in 1957, Reitz in 1982, and Fuller in 1983. But even the authoritative survey of the Soviet police edited by R. Conquest could say in 1968, "Little is known for certain of their tasks" (*The Soviet Police System*, p. 34).

18. Krotov, pp. 14, 24, 39, 46, 51, 80, 102. Yakovlev, *VV 1917–1922* mentions ChON's work with the Petrograd Cheka.

19. Krotov.

20. Sergey P. Melgounov, a former professor and well-known democratic political figure, opposed the Red Terror and was expelled from Soviet Russia in 1922; he assembled the testimonies of the time in a book, *The Red Terror in Russia*.

21. S. Singleton, "The Tambov Revolt 1920–21," *Slavic Review*, September 1966.

22. All these are regime statistics. Those for 1924 and Bryansk come from Ostryakov; those for Smolensk through Leggett, p. 465.

23. Petrov, p. 64. He was a communications officer with NKVD Troops in Sinkiang in 1937.

24. Conquest, *The Great Terror*, pp. 528–9; Solzhenitsyn, *The Gulag Archipelago*, vol. 3, p. 14; information also in the German and international-commission reports.

25. *Cahiers du Samizdat*, October 1988, pp. 14, 16. Also *Daily Telegraph*, London, 26 September 1988 and 6 March 1989; Tass, 24 January 1989. See especially N. Matusovskiy, "The Truth about the Kuropaty" in *Izvestiya*, 27 November 1988. It is reproduced in English translation in *Orbis*, vol. 33 no. 2 of Spring 1989, with comments by Robert Conquest entitled "Unearthing the Great Terror."

26. Between October 1939 and June 1941, 1,692,000 people were deported: 900,000 because of their "nationalistic bourgeois background," 250,000 "class enemies," and 230,000 officers and soldiers of the Polish Army. Of these hardly more than 100,000 returned. These figures come from sworn testimony before the U.S. Congress by exiles and eyewitnesses (*Communist Takeover and Occupation of Poland*, Report of House of Representatives Select Committee on Communist Aggression [1954], Report 2684, pt. 3, p. 11). The official history of the troops touches lightly upon this phase as "struggling with hostile classes" (Yakovlev, *VV 1922–1941*, pp. 29, 491).

27. *Sovetskaya voyennaya entsiklopediya*, pp. 164–5.

28. See Conquest, *The Soviet Deportation of Nationalities*, and G. S. Burlutskiy, who participated in the operation against the Chechen-Ingush people, in Wolin and Slusser, p. 325.

29. *Sovetskaya voyernnaya entsiklopediya,* vol. 2, p. 164.

30. Kalachnikov, p. 107.

31. The Soviet Military Encyclopedia describes the mission of Internal Troops in the reverse order: "guarding state installations and performing other urgent military tasks imposed on the USSR MVD" (*Sovetskaya voyennaya entsiklopediya,* vol. 2, p. 164; *Voyennyy entsiklopedicheskiy slovar,* 1986 ed., p. 134).

32. *Pravda,* 18 October 1988.

33. *International Herald Tribune,* 1 April 1989.

Chapter 3. The Roots of Coercion

1. Lenin, "Immediate Tasks of the Soviet Government," April 1918.

2. *Perestroika,* p. 111.

3. Trotsky, *Stalin: An Appraisal of the Man and His Influence* (New York: Stein and Day, 1967), p. 345.

4. *Perestroika,* p. 110.

5. Statements like these can be found throughout Soviet articles and books. These were taken from, respectively, *A Dictionary of Scientific Socialism* (Moscow: Progress Publishers, 1984), p. 224; A. A. Askerov et al, *Sovetskoye gosudarstvennoye pravo* (Moscow: Institute of Law of the Academy of Sciences of the USSR, 1948), p. 332; and G. I. Fedkin, *"O rukovodyashchey roli VKP(b) v razvitii sovetskogo sotsialisticheskogo prava,"* in *Sovetskoye gosudarstvo i pravo* (June 1950), no. 6, p. 19, the latter two cited in Kulski, p. 86.

6. Leonid Ionin, in *Moscow News,* 4 May 1988, as reported by *London Daily Telegraph,* 5 May 1988.

7. See for example *Soviet Union: Political and Economic Reference Book* (Moscow: Progress Publishers, 1979), pp. 65, 148, 150 (hereafter called *SURB*), and *Fundamentals of Marxism-Leninism,* 1963 ed., p. 526 (hereafter called *Fundamentals*).

8. *Pravda,* no. 86 of 20 April 1923 and no. 104 of 12 May 1923; resolution of the 12th Party Congress.

9. *Fundamentals,* pp. 524–5.

10. Vadim A. Medvedev, in speech to an international scientific conference in Moscow, as reported in *Pravda,* 5 October 1988.

11. Party program of 1986, issued under Gorbachev's leadership.

12. Interview reported in *Sovetskaya Estoniya,* 16 November 1988, translated in FBIS-SOV-88-227, 25 November 1988, p. 61.

13. K. U. Chernenko, *Voprosy raboty partiynogo i gosudarstvennogo apparata* (Moscow: Novosti, 1980), p. 7.

14. *Partiynoye stroitelstvo,* 5th ed. (Moscow, 1978), p. 201; also Article 1 of the Law on People's Control of 30 November 1979.

16. The "rubbish" remark was made in a speech to industrial workers on 14 February 1989, broadcast in the USSR on 16 February, and reported in *Washington Post,* 17 February 1989.

17. These citations, which can be found in any Soviet description of the

"public" or "mass" organizations, come from *SURB*, p. 191, and *A Dictionary of Scientific Socialism*, p. 226.

18. *Perestroika*, p. 56.

19. *International Herald Tribune*, 9 May 1988.

20. Sergei Andreyev, in *Neva*, February 1989. The writer was identified as a 35-year-old oil geologist from Tyumen in western Siberia.

21. *Pravda*, 11 September 1987, 16 November 1987, 27 December 1987, 1 February 1988, 4 April 1988, 12 February 1989. See also *Russkaya Mysl*, Paris, 13 November 1987 and 15 January 1988; *Washington Post*, 23 and 28 December 1987 and 14 April 1988; *New York Times*, 27 September and 28 December 1987, 2 February 1988; *London Daily Telegraph*, 2 February 1988; *International Herald Tribune*, 31 July 1987.

22. *Fundamentals*, p. 337.

23. Souvarine, p. 191. They were Lenin, Trotsky, Stalin, Dzerzhinsky, Bukharin, and Sverdlov (who soon died). Four of these were among the five in the first Politburo (out of a total of nineteen Central Committee members); another, Dzerzhinsky, directed the fight against internal opposition and supervised local administrations, public order, transport of goods and people, and finally the entire economy.

This inner group—in varying combinations—did the essential work of preserving the regime. Dzerzhinsky and Bukharin traveled about helping arrange the peace; Dzerzhinsky and Trotsky stage-managed the first post-coup party congress in March 1918. Trotsky organized the armed forces and directed the conduct of the civil war. Stalin administered the party internally, establishing with Dzerzhinsky a special relationship which was to help shape the evolving Soviet state. While this worried Lenin toward the end of his life (two of his last three notes concerned "Stalin and Dzerzhinsky"—their "persecutions" and their "little indulgences"), he never opposed the principle of the inner ruling circle nor its tight control of the organs of coercion.

24. Souvarine, p. 191; Schapiro, *The Origin of the Communist Autocracy*, p. 77.

25. The quotes are from Lenin's speeches to, respectively, the 8th All-Russian Congress of Soviets and the 11th Party Congress, as cited in *SURB*, p. 172.

26. *Partiynoye Stroitelstvo*, 5th ed. (1978), p. 281.

27. Ibid. Such lists have a long history; already in the 1920s, Stalin's Orgburo (which was responsible, among other things, for assignments of party functionaries) was keeping card files on "active party members" who were not to be transferred, dismissed or arrested without the knowledge and approval of the Central Committee (Avtorkhanov, *Stalin and the Soviet Communist Party*, p. 21).

28. Plenary meeting of party committee of Krasnodar, December 1987; reported in FBIS-SOV-87-238, p. 69.

29. *Partiynoye Stroitelstvo*, 5th ed. (1978), p. 362.

30. Ibid., p. 281.

31. *Pravda*, 16 November 1987.

32. *Fundamentals*, pp. 336, 337.

33. *Ustav*, 1961, Article 19.

34. See, for example, Veremeyenko, p. 373.

35. *SURB*, p. 47.

36. *Pravda*, 30 May 1988, reported by Reuters in *International Herald Tribune*, 31 May 1988.

37. *Fundamentals*, pp. 570–4.

38. *Perestroika*, pp. 89–91, 111; Gorbachev's speech to automobile workers, May 1987, cited in *International Herald Tribune*, 9 April 1987; resolution of Supreme Soviet published in Tass, 1 December 1988, as reported in Radio Liberty Research, RL 520/88, pp. 11–2; Politburo member V. A. Medvedev, in *Pravda*, 5 October 1988.

39. *Perestroika*, p. 79.

40. *Pravda*, 14 December 1987, as translated in FBIS-SOV-87-239, p. 60. In November 1988 Politburo member V. M. Chebrikov reiterated this theme. We will not curtail the openness and frankness of *glasnost*, he said, "but here we must strengthen discipline and strengthen order" (*Pravda*, 15 November 1988).

41. "When the Communist parties come to power, the danger arises of an influx of careerist elements who join the party in the hope of security advantages for themselves. [The CPSU has] periodical purges to rid itself of alien elements" (*Fundamentals*, p. 527).

42. Ibid., p. 528.

43. Ibid., pp. 337, 339.

44. Cited in *Fundamentals*, p. 336; also see his well-known essays of 1918 and 1919, "How to Organize Competition," "Immediate Tasks of the Soviet Government," and "A Great Beginning."

45. Cited in Kulski, p. 249.

46. Andropov, *Izbrannyye rechi i stati*, p. 296 (hereafter called *Izbrannyye*).

47. *Pravda*, 12 February 1980.

48. *Fundamentals*, p. 335.

49. *Perestroika*, pp. 145, 66.

50. Fedor Burlatskiy, *Literaturnaya Gazeta*, mid-April 1988.

51. Aleksandr Tsipko, in the monthly *Nauka i Zhizn*, cited in *International Herald Tribune*, 6 March 1989.

52. *Pravda*, 5 October 1988.

53. Gorbachev's explanation was that the revolution, although victorious, must continue "through several revolutionary stages in order to reveal its full potential" (*Perestroika*, pp. 145–46, 50).

54. *Perestroika*, p. 29. "The fundamental feature . . ." is from *SURB*, p. 160.

55. *Izbrannyye*, p. 266.

56. *Perestroika*, p. 149. Ironically, Gorbachev in the same book accused the United States of needing and creating an imaginary "Soviet menace," to justify its own policies (pp. 148–9, 216–17, etc.).

57. Ibid., p. 219.

58. Kizilov, p. 17.

59. *Perestroika*, p. 41.

60. This is a standard ingredient of Soviet publications concerning the KGB. For recent examples see speeches of Politburo member V. M. Chebrikov and *USSR: 100 Questions and Answers* (Moscow: Novosti Press Agency, 1987). Yuri Andropov used this Lenin citation to support his statement in the late 1970s:

"Inasmuch as imperialism is continuing to engage in subversion, our society cannot survive without special security organs" (*Izbrannyye*, p. 275).

61. Vadim A. Medvedev, in *Pravda*, 5 October 1988.

Chapter 4. Socialist Legality

1. *Perestroika*, pp. 105, 107.
2. Party Conference of June 1988.
3. *Perestroika*, pp. 105–6.
4. *Pravda*, 9 December 1987.
5. *Perestroika*, p. 106.
6. *Sovetskaya Estoniya*, 16 November 1988, as reported in FBIS-SOV-88-277, p. 61.
7. Romashkin, p. 19.
8. *Izvestiya*, 19 February 1987, describing a meeting the day before of the collegium of the USSR Procurator's Office with procurators from the provinces and the military. They were setting themselves tasks to fulfil Gorbachev's decree "On Further Strengthening Socialist Legality and Law and Order and Enhancing the Protection of Citizens' Rights and Legitimate Interests," passed by the CC CPSU Plenum of January 1987.
9. A. Sukharev, first deputy Minister of Justice, in *Pravda*, 15 June 1982.
10. Solzhenitsyn, *The Gulag Archipelago*, vol. 1, p. 87.
11. Neznanskiy, pp. 35–6.
12. This case was cited in the Soviet press and reported in the *London Daily Telegraph*, 6 June 1987.
13. *Perestroika*, p. 109.
14. D. S. Karev, *Organizatsiya Suda i Prokuratury v SSSR* (Moscow, 1954), cited by Conquest in *Justice and the Legal System in the USSR*, London: The Bodley Head, 1968, p. 110.
15. Arkady Vaksberg, a Soviet journalist for *Literaturnaya Gazeta* and specialist on legal matters, as reported by Gary Lee in *Washington Post*, 26 February 1987. Vaksberg added, with some understatement, "Major reforms will be achieved gradually, at best."
16. *Pravda*, 5 December 1987. He similarly admitted that courts had an "accusatory bias" and simply decreed what the preliminary investigation (i.e., the government accusers) recommended. To improve this situation, lawyers who handled defendants and civil suits met in 1989 (exploiting the Gorbachev-era tolerance of independent organizations) to form a bar association which could promote their efforts to improve procedures for defendants—and (as one of them put it) "for the advocate to be able to concentrate during trial on his client's fate, not on his own" (Andrey M. Makarov, cited in *International Herald Tribune*, 27 February 1989).
17. In the 1960s Bannikov wrote a textbook for KGB officers entitled *Fundamentals of Counterintelligence Activities of the Organs of State Security*, top-secret KGB manual. See Myagkov, p. 32.

18. Resolution of the Special Party Conference, July 1988. The last phrase had already found frequent use, as in Gorbachev's book *Perestroika*, p. 108.

19. Solzhenitsyn, *The Gulag Archipelago*, vol. 1, p. 60.

20. *Izvestiya* interview with Soviet legal expert Sofiya Kelina, reported in *London Times*, 30 December 1988.

21. Recent examples include two citizens, one of whom had refused to sign a request to emigrate, who were expelled from Estonia on 5 March 1988 after being accused of nationalist activities (*International Herald Tribune*, 7 March 1988).

22. Letter of 17 May 1922 to the Minister of Justice. Cited by Leggett, p. 347.

23. Interview with Koryagin, *London Daily Telegraph*, 28 February 1987. After an extended Western press campaign, Koryagin was released in 1987 and expelled with his family to the West.

24. Radio Liberty Research, RL 408/84.

25. *Literaturnaya Gazeta*, 15 April 1987, quoting an inmate of a labor camp.

26. Pacepa, pp. 145–46.

27. Their names were Konchakovskiy, Snegirev, and Osipov. See *Cahiers du Samizdat*, no. 62 (August–September 1972), p. 22.

28. Van Voren, p. 82.

29. *London Daily Telegraph*, 25 January 1988; *International Herald Tribune*, 20 January 1988 (article by A. M. Rosenthal).

30. Marchenko exposed post-Stalin prison conditions in his book *My Testimony* and spent more than twenty years of the forty-eight years of his life in prison.

31. Pastor Herman Hartfeld, imprisoned for his Baptist religious activity, survived eighteen months forced labor in two uranium installations in the 1970s and told of his experiences in *The Nuclear Gulag*, a television film screened on British Channel Four, 12 July 1986.

32. These are the cases of Vladimir S. Ivanov, in Kramatorsk; Rustam Faizatuli, in Leningrad; and Sergey Dedyukayev, in Moscow, in February 1986; reported by *samizdat* in June 1987; *Cahiers du Samizdat*. No. 131 (January–February 1988), p. 46.

33. Vyacheslav Talalayev tried to enter the West German consulate in Leningrad in June 1986 and Andrey Odintsov the American consulate there on 29 August 1986; both were held in Psychiatric Hospital No. 4 in Leningrad. Odintsov got three months of injections. Ibid.

34. Pankratova's case was reported in *Soviet Analyst*, 5 February 1985; Kovalenko's and Lokhmachev's in *Cahiers du Samizdat*, No. 131 (January–February 1988); Pristavka's in *Komsomolskaya Pravda*, reported in *Newsweek*, 18 January 1988.

35. *Cahiers du Samizdat*, No. 80 (October–November 1981), p. 4.

36. See Klose, pp. 29–91, and Radio Liberty Researh, RL 166/84, 25 April 1984.

37. Ubozhko's case was reported in the unofficial journal *Glasnost*, cited in *Newsweek*, 18 January 1988. Shteyn's and Rafalski's cases were reported in communications from the USSR published in *Cahiers du Samizdat*, No. 131 (January–February 1988), pp. 33–4 and 43–4. On 20 October 1987 Vladimir Titov, a

just-discharged inmate of a psychiatric hospital, described conditions there to a group of Western journalists in Moscow. In the years 1982–87 eleven patients had committed suicide in his mental institution, he said.

38. *Izvestiya,* reported by Michael Dobbs in *International Herald Tribune,* 1 July 1989.

Chapter 5. The Summit of Power

1. Meeting with members of the Union of Soviet Writers in Moscow, 19 June 1986, *Chaiers du Samizdat,* No. 125 (February–March 1987).

2. *Newsweek,* 4 April 1988.

3. Yu. M. Kozlov, 1980, p. 5.

4. Yu. M. Kozlov, 1979, pp. 5, 7. The author notes that these agencies are there "to carry out the functions of national defense, to protect state security, to protect socialist law and order, and to struggle for peace and peaceful coexistence with states with different social systems."

5. Ibid.

6. Ibid., pp. 9, 6.

7. Top secret regulation issued by the First All-Russian Conference of Extraordinary Commissions, 11 June 1918. Cited by Gerson, p. 41.

8. The 1940 edition of the *Politicheskiy Slovar* (Political Dictionary) defined them as "punitive"; and the responsible CC CPSU department, to my personal knowledge, was called *Otdel karatelnykh organov* until at least 1948. A history of state security organs in Uzbekistan (Aripov and Milshteyn, p. 5) called them "punitive organs" as recently as 1967.

9. Gerson, p. 28.

10. Kizilov, p. 53.

11. Yu. M. Kozlov, 1979, pp. 78, 82.

12. *Izbrannyye,* p. 303.

13. Yu. M. Kozlov, 1979, p. 5: "Administrative-political organs . . . form part of a unified system of organs of state management *(gosudarstvennogo upravleniya).* . . . Each of them has its own specifics [but] at the same time they form a relatively independent subsystem in the field of state management. . . . The subsystem has a center that gives it internal organization and independence of other subsystems. From the outside the subsystem appears as a single mechanism of administration *(yedinogo mekhanizma upravleniya)* with specific activities distinctive to it."

14. *Perestroika,* p. 149.

15. In the early 1960s Marshal V. D. Sokolovskiy wrote that, in wartime, "the whole country and the armed forces will be led by the Central Committee of the Communist Party of the Soviet Union, possibly with the organization of a higher agency of command for the country and armed forces [to which . . .] may be delegated the same powers that the GKO held during [the Second World War]; its presiding officer may be the first secretary of the Central Committee of the Communist Party of the Soviet Union . . ." *(Soviet Military Strategy* [Englewood

Cliffs, N.J.: Prentice-Hall, 1963], p. 494). Perhaps Sokolovskiy already knew that the leaders had no intention of waiting for wartime. The decision to activate it—and perhaps the activation itself—surely predates the 1976 revelation. H. F. Scott and W. F. Scott have called attention, for example, to a series of articles that appeared in the military newspaper *Krasnaya Zvezda* from February 1973 to May 1975, describing the work of the GKO, and rightly noted that such articles always have a purpose (*The Armed Forces of the USSR* [Boulder: Westview Press, 1981], 2d ed., p. 98). They interpret the newspaper articles as preparing the way for its reestablishment the following year, but it is not impossible that what was being preparing was the revelation, in the new constitution, of something already accomplished.

16. Both Gorbachev's Defense Council and Stalin's GKO are officially said to have been modeled on Lenin's civil war "Council on Labor and Defense" (*Sovet Truda i Oborony*). See *Voyennyy entsiklopedicheskiy slovar,* 1986 ed., pp. 206, 684.

17. Sokolovsky, pp. 487–88.

18. Foreign Minister Shevardnadze confirmed this and said that had there been public debate of such decisions, the invasion would not have taken place (BBC, 22 March 1989). Other Soviet officials told American scholars "that no more than five or six officials were involved" in the decision, all Politburo members: Brezhnev, Defense Minister Ustinov, KGB Chairman Andropov, chief party ideologist Mikhail Suslov, Andrey Kirilenko (then responsible for industry), "and possibly" Foreign Minister Andrey Gromyko (*International Herald Tribune,* 31 March 18 June 1988). Leonid Zamyatin, who at the time had been chief of the International Information Department of the CC CPSU, later said he only heard of the invasion five days after it had taken place (*London Daily Telegraph* ["Peterborough" column], 25 February 1989). In March 1989 Gen. Valentin Varennikov, a member of the General Staff at the time of the Afghanistan decision, told the magazine *Ogonyok* that the advice of General Staff chief Nikolay Ogarkov and his deputy, Sergey Akhromeyev, was ignored by Defense Minister Dmitriy Ustinov (*International Herald Tribune,* 20 March 1989).

19. The source was Leonid Zamyatin, at the time chief of the International Information Department of the CC CPSU, and his report was no doubt accurate. Although the regime has delayed or avoided announcing the appointment, this supreme power could not be left in a void for months or years until the Supreme Soviet gets around to appointing the party boss to the job.

20. Yu. M. Kozlov, 1979, pp. 5, 78, 84, 88.

21. *Perestroika,* p. 128.

22. Yu. M. Kozlov, 1979, p. 83: "The USSR KGB according to law (per Article 26 of the Law on the Council of Ministers) is a Union-Republic State Committee."

23. Yu. M. Kozlov, 1968, p. 113.

24. Ibid., p. 282. This supervision by state committees covers "execution of regulations, laws, decrees, administrative instructions of agencies, and instructions of supervisory inspections."

25. "The legal orders issued by the state committees are obligatory for all ministries, departments, offices, and organizations, and the committees see to it

that they are executed." (Yeropkin and Klyushnichenko, pp. 51–52.) "This power to enforce measures of administration coercion [*vozdeystviye*] differs from that of the procurator or control organs. After establishing the fact of a violation of law, the procurator [can merely] start legal proceedings to punish it" (Kozlov, 1968, p. 290).

26. Ibid., p. 58.

27. Yu. M. Kozlov, 1979, p. 77.

28. *Sobraniye postanovleniy pravitelstva SSSR* [Collection of Decrees of the USSR Government], Pt. 1, no. 31, 1986, p. 562, para. 35.

29. Myagkov, pp. 31–3.

Chapter 6.   The KGB: Controlled or Controlling?

1. This story and these citations can be found in scores of articles and books including the official *History of the Communist Party of the Soviet Union,"* 2d ed., 1962 (in its description of the CC CPSU Plenum of July 1953) and several of Yuri Andropov's speeches (e.g., *Izbrannyye,* p. 112). Other examples are a *Pravda* book review by M. Stepichev on 9 December 1987 and a speech by Politburo member and KGB Chairman V. Chebrikov, reported in *Pravda,* 11 September 1987. As Khrushchev put it, "The Central Committee has done much to liquidate the consequences of the cult of the personality of J. V. Stalin, and to maintain in all fields of state administration, without exception, strict observance of socialist legality [and in this context] established the necessary control by party and government over the organs of state security. . . . We have fully restored the rights and strengthened the control by the Procurator's Office." Cited in *40 let sovetskogo prava,* 2 vols. (Leningrad University, 1957), vol. 2, p. 121.

2. We owe this reminder to Michael Voslensky in *Nomenklatura,* pp. 283–4. He was citing Hermann Poerzgen, *Ein Land ohne Gott* (Frankfurt, 1936), p. 70.

3. Both expressions are common in the speeches of party leaders. Andropov among others used the first expression; "The KGB has in practice become the party's combat detachment in defending October's gains."—KGB Chairman Vitality Fedorchuk, in *Izvestiya,* 25 November 1982, p. 4.

4. Sovnarkom resolution of 21 December 1917. See Leggett, pp. 48–49, and Gerson, pp. 26–28. As Soviet sources note, Lenin "personally drafted most of the key directives and resolutions of the VCheka" (*Pravda,* 9 September 1987).

5. People's Commissar of Internal Affairs G. I. Petrovskiy, in *Izvestiya,* no. 230, 22 October 1918. See Gerson, p. 306.

6. VCheka orders of 29 August and late September 1918, cited by Gerson, pp. 191–2. As *Pravda* reminded people on 9 December 1987, when the VCheka was seventy years old (and called KGB), "Lenin kept constant watch to make sure that VCheka activity conformed to the line of the Central Committee."

7. Cited by Gerson, p. 26.

8. Leggett, pp. 132–6.

9. Lenin said this at the 9th Congress of Soviets on 22 December 1921,

explaining why the "temporary" VCheka would become permanent. Viktor Chebrikov cited it in October 1987 (*Pravda,* 11 September 1987) as did Yuri Andropov several times (e.g., *Pravda,* 19 December 1977). It appears, too, in Yu. M. Kozlov, 1979, p. 78.

10. See, for instance, Fainsod, *Smolensk Under Soviet Rule,* p. 73. As recently as 1978, Soviet writers were approvingly reminding readers that in the early 1920s party organizations could not interfere in the Chekas' work.

11. The 1970s information is from Barron, *KGB,* p. 87 (evidently from recent defector sources). The Romanian source is Pacepa, p. 172.

12. Trotsky, *Stalin,* p. 367.

13. See, for instance, the interviews with USSR KGB Chairman Viktor Chebrikov (*Pravda,* 2 September 1988) and Latvian KGB Chairman S. V. Zukul (*Sovetskaya Latviya,* 26 October 1988, translated in FBIS-SOV-88-234, 6 December 1988). Andropov's statement is from *Izbrannyye,* pp. 112, 118.

14. *Partiynoye Stroitelstvo,* 5th ed. (Moscow, 1978), p. 201.

15. Article 1 of the law on People's Control of 30 November 1979.

16. On the early role of the RKI see, Trotsky, *Stalin,* p. 346.

17. For example, KGB Chairman Viktor Chebrikov in *Pravda,* 2 September 1988, and *Kommunist,* no. 9, 1985, p. 52; and Latvian KGB Chairman S. V. Zukul, in *Sovetskaya Latviya,* 26 October 1988.

18. Decision of the Supreme Soviet of 24 May 1955; decree of the Presidium of the Supreme Soviet of 7 April 1956. The KGB's overseer is the "Department of the USSR Procuracy for oversight of investigations by the KGB organs" (*Otdel prokuratury SSSR po nadzoru za sledstviyem v organakh KGB*). Among the authors who called this a step in restoring "socialist legality" was Roy Medvedev, in his biography *Khrushchev* (Garden City: Anchor/Doubleday, 1983), p. 69.

19. Documents in the Smolensk archives from the early years of the Procuracy (Fainsod, *Smolensk,* p. 174) refer to "strength" or "weakness" of the work of certain OGPU departments. This meant their work in preparing cases for prosecution and did not refer to their operational performance.

20. Bukovsky, pp. 68–9. The author also describes how he and other dissidents exploited the legal right to complain and petition; see especially pp. 35–41.

Chapter 7.   The Two-Way Flow of "Good Communists"

1. *Kommunist,* no. 9 (June 1985), p. 51.

2. "*Khoroshiy kommunist v to zhe vremya Khoroshiy chekist.*" He said this at the 9th Party Congress on 3 April 1920. Quoted in Lenin, *Complete Works,* vol. 40, p. 279.

3. Cited in Leggett, p. 161.

4. Khokhlov, p. 204. Under Stalin, Panyushkin had worked in the intelligence service after CC CPSU service, then served as ambassador to Washington and Peking. After Stalin's death and Beria's fall, he returned to run the KGB's

First Chief Directorate. He eventually returned to the CC CPSU apparatus where, overseeing permissions for travel abroad, he remained until retirement in the 1970s.

5. As KGB Chairman Chebrikov confirmed in 1988, when asked how people become Chekists: "People come into the KGB organs on the recommendation of party and Komsomal organizations . . ." (*Pravda,* 2 September 1988).

6. Radio Liberty Research, RL 220/85, 5 July 1985, citing *samizdat* from 1975.

7. *La Corruption en Union Sovietique,* pp. 149–52.

8. Information from former KGB officer Stanislav Levchenko, who served with the officer in Japan.

Chapter 8. Controlling the Armed Forces

1. Pyotr Shastitko in *Asia and Africa Today,* No. 3, May–June 1983, using the appropriate title "The Revolution Must Be Able to Defend Itself." This article is the source of the citations in the following paragraph as well.

2. Trotsky's decree of 6 April 1918, establishing the commissars; also quoted in other contemporary sources cited by Tyushkevich, pp. 38–40.

3. Ostryakov.

4. When the crew of a destroyer mutinied in the Baltic in November 1975, the captain was shot and his family punished, the officers jailed, the crew dispersed, and the ship's name changed. This mutiny aboard the *Storozhevoy* is described in *Chronicle of Current Events,* nos. 43 and 48, and in *Possev* (1976), nos. 7 and 9. See also *International Herald Tribune,* 8 February 1985.

5. Gen. Aleksey Lizichev, head of the Main Political Administration of the Army and Navy, speaking in Taman. *London Times,* 10 February 1989.

6. See, for example, D. Castoriades, *Devant la Guerre* (Paris: Fayard, 1981), pp. 28–9, 256–7, 276–7. Castoriades, dismissing party-political work as insignificant and the party workers as castoffs, goes so far as to assert that the army dominates society in a "stratocracy," using the party as a "sub-contractor" to administer the nonmilitary (and marginal) parts of society. He calls the party a sort of "propaganda staff" of the army and devotes hardly a paragraph to Glavpu. Significantly, his single line of text about the KGB within the army appears only in a footnote on page 277.

7. Speech to secretaries of primary party organizations of the Moscow Military District, August 1959, quoted by Kiryaev, p. 429.

8. The recollections of the top OO officer of the 18th Army, V. Ye. Zarelua, were cited by Ostryakov, pp. 229–30.

9. Malyarov, p. 300.

10. Information as of the late 1970s, from former KGB Maj. Stanislav Levchenko.

11. See, for example, Belikov et al., p. 181.

Chapter 9. Power Struggles and the KGB

1. Deriabin, Peter, *Watchdogs of Terror* (Second Revised and Updated Edition), University Publications of America, 1984, Frederic, MD.

2. See chap. 6. The earlier components responsible for this work, "Operod" of the Guards Directorate and "SPU," are discussed later in this book. The Polish and Czech state security services, whose organization reflects the current organization of their parent KGB, continue to investigate party officials, as confirmed by defectors from both of these services during the 1970s and 1980s.

3. Fedor Burlatskiy, who had reportedly been a speechwriter for Khrushchev, was an intimate associate of Gorbachev when he told this story in 1988. (*Literaturnaya Gazeta*, 14 September 1988. See also *International Herald Tribune*, 16 September 1988).

4. *Wall Street Journal*, 13 October 1987.

5. Simis, pp. 47, 51–5.

6. *Pravda*, 25 March 1987.

7. Simis, p. 48.

8. Parts of the files reached the West, and excerpts of seventy-odd pages were published in *Der Spiegel* in April 1983.

Chapter 10. What the KGB Does

1. An example of treating the KGB as one "secret police" among others is T. Plate and A. Darvi, *Secret Police* (New York: Doubleday, 1981). The second version is to be found in several Western works. This example of the third formulation appears in *International Herald Tribune*, 28 December 1982.

2. That chairman was Yuri Andropov (*Izbrannyye*, p. 273), but his formulation is a standard one that can be found in almost any speech or writing by Chekist leaders. "The Chekists' main mission . . ." is from an article stemming from the KGB (which takes pride in its sponsorship of public writings about itself) but signed by V. Mikhaylov ("*Nasledniki slavnykh traditsiy*" [Heirs of Glorious Traditons], *Neva*, no. 12 [December 1977]. As Brezhnev said while bestowing the Order of Lenin on KGB Chairman Andropov, "You play a direct and active part in working out and carrying through the domestic and foreign policies of our party and of the Soviet state."

3. Lenin said this as he proposed to eternalize the "temporary" VCheka in a speech at the 9th Party Congress, 23 December 1921 (*Collected Works* [Russian]), vol. 44, p. 328). It is a staple of KGB speeches and articles, among them some by KGB Chairman Chebrikov in 1987, Eduard Shevardnadze in 1981, Andropov several times, and Soviet texts like Kozlov, 1979.

4. "The State Security organs' concrete tasks, their responsibilities, and their rights change at different stages of the development of Soviet society and depend upon the specific objectives set for them by the Communist Party and the Soviet

government" (Yu. M. Kozlov, 1979, p. 82). On this point Kozlov cites the Soviet constitution, the CPSU Program, and basic works of Brezhnev, Andropov, and Lenin.

5. Chebrikov speeches at 27th Party Congres, 28 February 1986 (*Pravda*, 1 March 1986) and on the 110th anniversary of birth of Felix Dzerzhinsky, 10 September 1987 (*Pravda*, 11 September 1987).

6. Jurist N. V. Raldugin, "Developing Legislation for USSR State Security," in *Sovetskoye gosudarstvo i pravo*, May 1988, p. 24.

7. Opening speech to the 4th All-Russian Conference of Extraordinary Commissions.

8. Eduard Shevardnadze, in *Zarya Vostoka*, Tbilisi, 26 December 1981.

9. A. N. Inauri, KGB chairman of the Georgian Republic, Zarya Vostoka, in October 1980.

10. Yu. M. Kozlov, 1979, p. 84.

11. Raldugin, op. cit., p. 26.

12. *Izbrannyye*, pp. 153, 251. Andropov continued, "Its task is to elevate the personality and cultivate an active attitude toward one's public duty . . . elevate the working people's ideological-moral and cultural level. Otherwise there could be relapses into a mercantile, petty-bourgeois mentality: money-grubbing, private-ownership trends, and other phenomena contrary to the very essence of our system."

13. The precise wording cited here comes from Yuri Andropov, *Izbrannyye*, p. 297, but this formulation, varying only in minor detail, is a standard one and is repeated in speeches by Chairman Chebrikov and other Chekist leaders. Discussing the law on state security to be published in 1990 or 1991, a Soviet jurist repeated this theme in 1988 (Raldugin, op. cit., pp. 27–8). That same year Chebrikov said that foreign intelligence services are not only "seeking out in our society individuals with hostile attitude" but also "promoting their organizational cohesion, providing them with moral and material support, and nudging them onto the path of direct struggle against the Soviet state" (*Pravda*, 2 September 1988).

14. Yu. M. Kozlov, 1979, p. 77. The KGB is wherever the ideology needs it: "The Communists of the KGB organs—the loyal forward detachment of the CPSU—must always be at the leading edge of the party's ideological activity" (Politburo member Eduard Shevardnadze, in *Zarya Vostoka*, Tbilisi, 26 December 1981).

15. Aleksey N. Inauri, chairman of the KGB of the Georgian SSR, in *Zarya Vostoka*, Tbilisi, 25 September 1980.

16. *Izbrannyye*, p. 301.

17. Politburo member Eduard Shevardnadze, in *Zarya Vostoka*, Tbilisi, 26 December 1981. He went on to say, among other things, that the KGB "protects our society, especially the younger generation, from the demoralizing, corrupting influence of people whose political ignorance, nihilism, malevolence, and incitement and gossip play into the hands of our class enemies."

18. First All-Russian Conference of Chekas, 11 June 1918, cited in Gerson, pp. 41–2.

19. Until Gorbachev's introduction of *glasnost*, very little sociological research was permitted and the KGB was at the center of it. When in 1969 the regime, late and half-heartedly, allowed the creation of a sociological research organization (the Institute for Concrete Social Research), the KGB passed on some of its own information—practically the only valid data in existence. It was to be handled only by the institute's Department for Classified Research, located in a separate building with restricted admission and no doubt run by KGB agents. On this subject, see V. Shlapentokh, *Sociology and Politics: The Soviet Case* (Falls Church, Va.: Delphic Associates, 1985), p. 63.

20. KGB Maj. Stanislav Levchenko got wind of this tightly held secret in the mid-1970s (see Barron, *KGB Today,* p. 453). A Soviet investigator had stumbled on it from another angle, in the early 1970s. Investigating the theft of construction materials, he was put in contact with the KGB's tunnel diggers. A KGB deputy chairman invited him into his office and warned him, "Stay away from this investigation. We'll do it ourselves" (private communication to the author). See also Seymour Weiss, "Why the Big Labyrinth Under Moscow?" *International Herald Tribune,* 26 May 1988.

Part of this KGB-run project includes a secret tunnel from the KGB headquarters on Dzerzhinsky Square all the way into the Kremlin over a thousand meters away. Another secret tunnel has been reported as giving access from the Kremlin to the Moscow metro line leading to the airport used by the leaders. See Viktor Suvorov, *Inside the Soviet Army* (London: Hamish Hamilton, 1982), pp. 150–53.

21. *Pravda,* 2 September 1988; *Kommunist,* no. 9 (1985), p. 51.

22. Letter to the magazine *Ogonek,* cited in *International Herald Tribune,* 4 January 1989.

23. Solzhenitsyn, *The Oak and the Calf,* p. 213.

Chapter 11.   Inside the House on Dzerzhinskiy Square

1. Nikita Struve, introduction to *Secret Report of the Central Committee on the State of the Church in the USSR,* op. cit.

2. Moscow church trial of 26 April–7 May 1922, reported in Solzhenitsyn, *The Gulag Archipelago,* vol. 1, p. 349.

3. Solzhenitsyn, *The Gulag Archipelago,* vol. 1, p. 149.

4. Open letter from Father Sergey Zheludkov, dated Easter 1972, published in *Cahiers du Samizdat,* no. 1 (September 1972).

5. *Washington Post,* 7 March 1975.

1. Although these rules are sometimes violated and copying machines misused, it is usually by the operator. The employees rarely have the opportunity.

6. Kopelev, *To Be Preserved Forever,* p. 111.

7. Solzhenitsyn, *The Oak and the Calf,* p. 368–369.

8. *Izbrannyye,* p. 268.

9. *Izbrannyye,* p. 261.

10. Koritskiy, B. F., ed., *Slovar sokrashcheniy russkogo yazyka* (Dictionary of Abbreviations of the Russian Language) (Moscow, 1963).

11. *Pravda*, 2 September 1988.

12. *Pravda*, 9 December 1987.

13. In May 1984, for example, a competition was announced with the aim of producing works "of a high ideological and artistic level" in time for the 70th anniversary in 1987 of the VCheka-KGB (*Literaturnaya Gazeta*, 16 May 1984). In 1987 a prize of 3,000 rubles was again offered for the best such work.

14. Grishin, V., *Vstupaya v zhizn* (Entering into Life) (Moscow: Molodaya Gvardiya, 1967).

15. Private communication from former KGB Maj. Stanislav Levchenko.

16. Myagkov, p. 64.

17. Ibid., p. 49.

18. Deriabin, *The Secret World*, pp. 82, 212.

19. *Izbrannyye*, p. 165. This was a speech to Chekists on 26 April 1971, exhorting them to apply the instructions of the 24th Party Congress. In 1985 KGB Chairman Viktor Chebrikov called for "an increase in the responsibility of each individual for fulfilling the task in hand" (*Kommunist*, no. 9 [1985], p. 51).

20. Deriabin, *The Secret World*, pp. 77 and elsewhere, and appendix.

21. Amalrik, p. 123.

Chapter 12. The Innermost Ring: The Bodyguards

1. John Miller in *Daily Telegraph*, London 23 June 1983. Romanov had been appointed a CC CPSU secretary and was bidding farewell to the city he had ruled as first secretary.

2. See chap. 6. The source was Pacepa (p. 172), who describes in detail the secret coverage by Romanian party chief Ceaucescu of all other top Communist Party officials. The organization of this activity followed KGB guidelines and involved microphones in homes and offices, surveillance of movements, and secret agents planted among the targets' office staff, household, chauffeurs, and other contacts.

3. *Time*, 7 December 1981.

4. Described in detail in Deriabin, *Watchdogs of Terror*, pp. 365–76.

5. *Counterpoint*, vol. 2, no. 6 (November 1986), pp. 2–3. The photograph appeared simultaneously in *Vechernaya Moskva* and *Krasnaya Zvezda;* in the former (with the larger circulation) the picture had been doctored.

6. Interview of Otto Latsis, deputy chief editor of *Kommunist*, in *La Stampa*, Turin, 6 October 1988 (FBIS-SOV-88-208).

7. *Daily Telegraph*, London 23 February 1989.

Chapter 13. The KGB's Use of the MVD.

1. Decree of 20 May 1974. See N. Bakanskaya in *Soviet Law and Government*, no. 2, 1975.

2. See Yu. M. Kozlov, 1979, pp. 117–21.

3. A. P. Kozlov (later commander of the Dzerzhinsky Division), pp. 159ff, 207, 228.

4. Yu. M. Kozlov, 1973, p. 532.

5. Yu. M. Kozlov, 1968, p. 524.

6. *Sbornik zakonov SSSR 1938–1975*, vol. 4, pp. 532, 544. Other references can be found on pp. 173–74.

7. A. Cockburn, *The Threat* (New York: Random House, 1983), p. 189, citing an emigrant source. Earlier controls, even stricter, had proved counterproductive: the warheads had been kept separate (under KGB control) from the missiles that would carry them. (This information confirms the trend in my day.)

Chapter 14. Identifying the Enemy: The Deadly Labels of "Social Prophylaxis"

1. This was written in the Cheka's periodical *Krasnyy Terror* dated 1 November 1918 (cited by Melgounov, pp. 39–40; Leggett, p. 114). At that time, party members were still debating the Cheka's role, and a *Pravda* journalist could make fun of him: "I can just imagine Karl Marx or Comrade Lenin in the hands of such a ferocious investigator: 'Your name?' 'Karl Marx.' 'Class origin?' 'Bourgeois.' 'Education?' 'University.' 'Profession?' 'Lawyer and author.' What else is there to discuss or search for? Signs of guilt or evidence of opposition to the Soviets with weapons or words? To the wall with him, and that's that" (*Pravda*, 25 December 1918). Even while claiming that his remarks had been quoted out of their context of civil-war front conditions, Latsis insisted that "the most valuable information for the investigator consists of facts regarding class membership, class origin, . . . education, and profession" (*Pravda*, 29 December 1918). Soon thereafter, no one any longer made public fun of Chekist practices.

2. Orders of KGB chairman, no. 00225 of 1959 and no. 00117 of 1964, documents published by Myagkov, p. 35.

3. *Izbrannyye*, p. 168.

4. Ibid., p. 297. This formulation is a part of standard doctrine and is routinely drawn upon for the speeches of representatives of "administrative organs." It is to be found, for example, in the speeches in 1986 and 1987 of KGB Chairman Viktor Chebrikov.

5. Ibid., pp. 310, 268.

6. Ibid., p. 153.

7. Dzerzhinsky report to first All-Russian Conference of Cheka, June 1918.

8. Grigoriy Zinoviev, speech to 12th Party Congress, cited in U.S. Congress, 1956, p. 88. They would soon identify something they classified as "middle peasants," too.

9. For a powerful account of these successive labels, see Solzhenitsyn, *The Gulag Archipelago*, pt. 1, ch. 2; p. 399 (which is the source of the quote on engineers).

10. Politburo member Viktor Chebrikov, *Pravda*, 11 September 1987 and 15 November 1988; *Sovetskaya Estoniya*, 16 November 1988.

11. *Izbrannyye*, p. 168.

12. As required by a decree signed by Lenin on 23 September 1919 (Kizilov, p. 55).

13. Fainsod, *Smolensk*, p. 304.

14. Ibid., p. 156. Archives of the 1930s contained "long lists of 'former people' and 'socially alien' elements in various *sovkhozes* who were scheduled for elimination. In the *sovkhoz* 'Zlynka'" for example, it was discovered that the director was the son of a trusted stableman "of the great prince Romanov. . . . The zootechnician turned out to be the son of a kulak and the veterinarian an expelled Trotskyite of kulak background. In addition, there were more than a dozen brigade leaders, tractor drivers, swineherds, guards, carpenters, and other workers who were either former kulaks, children of kulaks, 'large-scale exploiters' or church elders." Ibid., p. 304.

15. Bazhanov, p. 118.

16. The documents from Lithuania were later circulated by exiles in Switzerland. They are reproduced and translated in Kalme, *Total Terror*. Another list from Lithuania is cited in U.S. Congress, 1955, p. 19.

17. Myagkov, pp. 33–5.

18. Sejna, p. 121. The report rings true. The "undesirable civilians" had been listed, and the number of helpers does not sound excessive: in the early 1950s the KGB already had so many secret Austrian collaborators that one of my tasks was to winnow the excess among the police in Vienna. And it would be the KGB, as Yakubovsky said, that would take over executive power as soon as the country was occupied. Chekists did so in the past: in 1920 in Bashkiria, Turkestan, and Azerbaijan, for example (see Leggett, pp. 225–6, 406.); and in 1940 in Lithuania (where the chief of occupation, Vladimir Dekanozov, came directly from his post as head of all foreign operations of State Security) and in 1945 in Soviet-occupied Germany, where Beria's deputy NKVD commissar (and later KGB Chairman) Ivan Serov headed the civilian side of the occupation.

19. Ibid., p. 144.

20. United Press International, in *International Herald Tribune* of 12 October 1981.

21. *SURB*, p. 50.

22. M. Checinski in Adelman, p. 31.

23. Sejna, pp. 34–35.

24. *Time* 7 December 1981. *Time* went on to say that the West German police had forced these people (on threat of a year in prison) to report twice a day to the police during Brezhnev's visit.

Chapter 15. Violence and Fear

1. *Perestroika*, p. 73.

2. Article by Soviet journalist Vladimir Yavoriskiy in *New Times*, 24 September 1987, reporting the first meeting of the Communist Party organization of the Chernobyl plant after the disaster. See *London Times*, 25 September 1987.

3. *London Daily Telegraph* 29 June 1983, citing *Soviet Labor Review*.

4. Lysenko, pp. 180–81; see also pp. 164ff.

5. Popovsky, pp. 198–9.

6. Chekist leader Ivan K. Ksenofontov, in Alidin, p. 238.

7. Testimony of Mohammed Ayyub Assil at press conference of Afghan resistants in Oslo, reported in *Morgenbladet*, 18 March 1983. And these were the second wave; for more than a year before the invasion the Afghan Communist rulers, under the direction of KGB "advisers," had imprisoned, shot, or expelled most of those who fitted into their categories of potential enemies of Communist rule.

8. In 1988 the Soviet sociologist Igor Bestuzhev-Lada reckoned the figure of "up to 25 million" (*London Daily Telegraph*, 7 May 1988). Even the lowest estimates total 10 million for the period 1928–36; in March 1988 a member of the Academy of Agricultural Sciences, Vladimir Tikhonov, wrote in *Argumenty i Fakty* that 10 million had been "repressed" in the collectivization (*London Daily Telegraph*, 5 April 1988). Stalin himself told Churchill that "10 million kulaks had had to be dealt with" (Conquest, *The Great Terror*, p. 23, citing I. Stadyuk in *Neva*, no. 12, 1962). It little matters that hardly one dispossessed family in three met even the Kremlin's own definition of kulak.) Antonov-Ovseyenko (p. 213) estimates 22 million; the Soviet author Anatoliy Rybakov said 13 million (television interview 14 March 1989).

9. Dyadkin.

10. Letter to Minister of Justice Kurskiy, in Lenin, *Collected Works*, 5th ed., vol. 54, pp. 196, 324; cited by Solzhenitsyn, *The Gulag Archipelago*, vol. 1, pp. 353–4. Two days earlier Lenin had written to Kurskiy, "In my opinion we ought to extend the use of execution by shooting . . . to all activities of the Mensheviks, SRs, etc. We ought to find a formulation that would connect these activities with the international bourgeoisie."

11. Lenin explained this in December 1921 while preparing the shift from VCheka to GPU and further repressions of his revolutionary rivals, the SRs. (He is quoted in Yu. M. Kozlov, 1979, p. 78 and in articles and speeches by State Security leaders and others in the 1970s and 1980s.)

12. Trotsky, *Terrorism and Communism*, 1922.

13. Yuri Andropov in *Pravda*, 19 December 1977; Viktor Chebikov in *Pravda*, 2 September 1988—and many others.

14. Yakov Peters, in *Izvestiya*, 17 October 1918, cited by Gerson, p. 193.

15. Theses adopted by the Second Congress of the Comintern 17 July–7 August 1920, trans. in *The Communist Conspiracy: Strategy and Tactics of World*

Communism, pt. 1, sect. C: *The World Congresses of the Communist International* (Washington, D.C.: U.S. Government Printing Office, 1956), p. 76.

16. Ibid., pp. 76–7.

17. As reported by Henri Barbusse in *A New World Seen Through One Man* (NY and London, 1935), cited by Antonov-Ovseyenko, p. 213.

18. *Report of the Central Committee to the 18th Party Congress* (Moscow: Foreign Languages Publishing House, 1951), cited in U.S. Congress document, 1956, Sect. B, p. 395.

19. U.S. Congress, *Communist Takeover and Occupation of Latvia* (Washington, D.C.: U.S. Government Printing Office, 1954), p. 23.

20. Speech of 25 February 1956, trans. in *The Anti-Stalin Campaign and International Communism,* p. 29.

21. *Kontinent,* no. 5 (1975).

22. Nora Beloff, *No Travel Like Russian Travel* (London: George Allen & Unwin, 1979), p. 114.

23. Dimov, p. 97.

24. *Cahiers du Samizdat,* no. 86 (June 1982), pp. 16–7.

25. *Cahiers du Samizdat,* no. 66 (February 1980), pp. 10–1.

26. M. Latsis, cited by Melgounov, p. 156.

27. Kourdakov, *passim.*

28. Shindler, p. 138, reported the cases of Zhvigun, Panov, and Rubinshtein, Robinson, pp. 220–1, gives details of the attacks on Levin, Kharkev, and Rubinshtein.

Chapter 16. Controlling the Population

1. M. Meirans, deputy head of the Latvian SSR MVD, on Riga radio, 11 September 1981 (FBIS report of 7 October 1981).

2. This definition and those quoted in the paragraphs above can be found, for example, in the *Bolshaya Sovetskaya Entsiklopediya,* 3d ed. (1975), col. 786; Decree of Central Council of Trade Unions (VTsSPS) and State Committee on Wages and Labor under Council of Ministers, 6 September 1973 (printed in *Sotsialisticheskaya Zakonnost,* no. 1 (1974), pp. 81–3; and *Trud,* 22 September 1972.

3. *Bolshaya Sovetskaya Entsiklopediya,* 3rd ed. (1975), vol. 19, pp. 262–3.

4. Shumilin. When he wrote this, he was a deputy minister of the USSR MVD.

5. Sorokin. Also, "it permits the better calculation of the population and a deeper understanding of the processes of migration, which are directly related to the development and planning of the national economy and the rational distribution of production forces" (M. Raylyan, deputy minister of Internal Affairs of the Moldavian SSR, in *Sovetskaya Moldavia,* 2 November 1978).

6. Zinoviev, *The Radiant Future,* Random House, New York, 1980. p. 156.

7. N. Ya. Anosov, chief of the passport department of the MVD Main Administration of Militia, in *Izvestiya,* 26 December 1974.

8. V. Itkin in *Selskaya Zhizn,* 26 December 1974, p. 4. The article, under-standably, mentioned neither Mayakovsky nor the fact that shortly after publishing these lines in *Verses on the Soviet Passport* in 1930, the poet committed suicide.

9. Semyonov; also Anosov; also Raylyan; also MVD Minister Shchelokov in *Pravda,* 26 December 1974, etc.

10. *Sobraniye postanovleniy pravitelstva SSSR,* decrees of the Council of Ministers of the USSR of 28 August and 25 December 1974, hereafter referred to as "1974 Passport Regulations." The paragraphs given in full or in part in the passport itself are nos. 1, 5, 6, 12, 13, 23, 26, and 34. *Sotsialisticheskaya zakonnost,* issue #12, December 1974, Moscow, Yurizdat.

11. Militia Col. P. Semyonov, chief of the Passport Division, Lativian SSR MVD, "Attention Drawn to Passport System," *Sovetskaya Latviya,* Riga, 29 October 1983.

12. Meirans, op cit.

13. *Pravda,* 22 December 1938, cited by Skorodumov. For a good summary of these developments see Vsevolod Skorodumov, "Labor Documentation in the USSR," Radio Liberty Research RL20/75, 24 January 1975.

14. *Trud,* 22 September 1972.

15. Anosov, in "Pravda", 26 Dec. 1974.

16. Article 2 of Decree no. 109 of the USSR Council of Ministers, 28 August 1974.

17. Decree of USSR Council of Ministers, 21 April 1975. See A. Denisov, "Trudovaya knizhka kolkhoznika" in *Sotsialisticheskaya Zakonnost,* no. 1 (January 1976), pp. 45–6.

18. Unpublished section of the passport regulations of August 1974, cited by L. Lipson and V. Chalidze, eds., *Papers on Soviet Law* (New York, 1977), p. 185.

19. The Moscow list was dated 10 February 1975 and was reported in *Arkhiv Samizdata,* no. 4855, 2 October 1975, cited in Radio Liberty Research, RL 240/83, 21 June 1983.

20. U.S. Congress, *Helsinki Report* (1980), p. 171.

21. V. Babkin, in *Izvestiya,* 13 April 1973, cited by Skorodumov, op. cit.

22. Article 34, decree no. 110 of 28 August 1974.

23. Resolution of the 9th Congress of the RKP(b), cited by Skorodumov, op. cit., p. 8.

24. Solzhenitsyn, *The Gulag Archipelago,* vol. 1, p. 54.

25. Skorodumov, op. cit., p. 8.

26. Meirans.

27. Raylyan.

28. *International Herald Tribune,* 21 December 1984.

29. U.S. Congress, *Helsinki Report* (1980), p. 78. Scores of such cases are reported in Shindler, *Exit Visa.*

30. Amnesty International, *Prisoners of Conscience in the USSR: Their Treatment and Conditions,* April 1980, p. 50.

31. The pertinent articles are in the passport decrees of 28 August 1974: article 31 of decree no. 109 and article 1.i of decree no. 110.

32. Information from recent emigrants from the USSR.

Chapter 17. Denunciation

1. Zinoviev, *The Yawning Heights,* p. 501.
2. *Arkhiv Samizdata,* no. 4495, provided a copy of the card.
3. These demands have occurred often in the press—an early example being *Izvestiya* of 15 (28, new style) December 1917, cited by Leggett, p. 30—and in meetings of collectives, throughout my time and on to the present date.
4. Articles 59, 60, 65.
5. *Pravda,* 13 August 1982.
6. Sakharov and Tosi, p. 22.
7. Konstantin Chernenko, *KPSS i prava cheloveka* (CPSU and Human Rights) (Moscow: Agenstvo Pechati Novosti, 1981), pt. 5.
8. Vladimir Amlinskiy in the monthly, *Yunost,* March 1988, as reported by Reuters, 19 March 1988.
9. Ibid.
10. *Molodoy Kommunist,* April 1981, pp. 34–8. Chebrikov was simply repeating a theme often invoked by Andropov, Brezhnev, and others before them.
11. Ibid. Brezhnev was addressing the 26th Party Congress in 1976.
12. Decree of Supreme Soviet, October 1985, published in May 1986. Officially this law was designed to eliminate some of the unnecessary police work caused by spiteful individuals.
13. *Pravda,* 2 September 1988. Soon thereafter the Armenian press, reporting a meeting of the republic KGB's party organization, used precisely the same words, showing them to be yet another part of the standard kit for preparing Chekist speeches (*Yerevan Kommunist,* 18 November 1988). Some of the results could be glimpsed even in the letters themselves; one to the magazine *Ogonek* published in October 1988 told of a citizen who suspected that an anonymous denunciation to the KGB lay behind the authorities refusal to let him travel abroad—but that he had no way to find out or to refute it (Radio Liberty Research, RL 461/88, 21 October 1988).
14. *Perestroika,* pp. 68–72, 77.
15. *London Daily Telegraph,* 30 April 1984.
16. *Pravda,* 13 January 1950. In 1985 KGB Chairman Chebrikov spoke of the "numerous letters and telegrams sent to the KGB warmly supporting the KGB's measures to suppress anti-Soviet manifestations on the part of renegades still encountered in our society" (*Kommunist,* no. 9 [June 1985]).
17. A double meaning lay behind the remarks of KGB Chairman Chebrikov when in June 1985 he said that the KGB "is adopting measures for the strict observance of the established system of examining citizens' oral and written appeals" (*Kommunist,* no. 9 [June 1985], pp. 51–2).
18. *Pravda,* 1 December 1987.
19. "Paskvilyant," *Leningradskaya Pravda,* 29 June 1980.
20. *Cahiers du Samizdat,* no. 41 (January 1977), p. 12.
21. Shipler, pp. 204–6. The literature of dissidence is full of others.

Chapter 18. Secret Collaborators: The *Agentura*

1. The fate of those who try to slip out of the KGB's grip is exemplified by that of Boris Kovhar in the 1970s. Ths Ukrainian party member and journalist, after spying on Ukrainian nationalists for five years, had a change of heart and circulated an open letter to expose the KGB work he and so many others were doing. He was put in a psychiatric hospital and held there for more than four years (Block and Reddaway, pp.265, 368).

2. *Izvestiya,* 10 March 1989.

3. *Izbrannyye,* p. 273.

4. As reported in Tel Aviv by emigrants from the Soviet Union (*International Herald Tribune,* 13 December 1979). Many brave men, trying to persuade the government to observe its formal commitments to human rights, have preferred to go to jail rather than betray their fellow activists to the KGB. *Samizdat* reports have named dozens of them, like Ivars Grabans, Boris Kovgar, and Mikhaylo Kovtuenko in the 1970s.

5. Kopelev, *To Be Preserved Forever,* pp. 92, 111.

6. The son of General Ivan Nikishov, head of the Far Eastern concentration camps, recounted this incident to his KGB colleague, Yuri Rastvorov, who wrote of it in *Life* magazine, 13 December 1954. Wallace later confirmed the accuracy of the account.

Chapter 19. Provokatsiya

1. Melgounov, pp. 253–54.

2. *Webster's New International Dictionary,* 2d ed.

3. Ushakov, *Tolkovyy Slovar Russkogo Yazyka* (Moscow, 1939). The same words are used in a dictionary of the 1980s.

4. A. T. Vassiliev, *The Okhrana, the Russian Secret Police* (Philadelphia: J. B. Lippincott, 1930), p. 53. Vassiliev had been chief of the Okhrana and wrote its history from exile.

5. The reasons to believe that Stalin was an Okhrana informant from 1906–12 are set out by E. E. Smith in *The Young Stalin* (New York: Farrar, Strauss and Giroux, 1967).

6. *History of the Bolsheviks,* cited by Wolfe, *Three Who Made a Revolution,* pp. 535–57. Wolfe gives one of the best descriptions of this infiltration and betrayal.

7. *Izvestiya,* 22 October 1918, cited in Gerson, p. 306, n. 9.

8. Myagkov, pp. 73–5, 76–9.

9. *Newsweek,* 27 June 1977.

10. Gilbert, *passim,* mentions the provocative roles of Lipavsky, Tsipin, Raslin, Ryabsky, Adamsky, Zaplyaeva, and Popova.

11. Ketenichev was still imprisoned in 1989. Evidently Gorbachev's regime did not consider this "traitor" to be a political prisoner (*Washington Post,* 13

December 1988). The Ketenichev incident was reported in *Arkhiv Samizdata*, no. 5218; see Radio Liberty Research, RL 493/84, 28 December 1984, pp. 3–4.

A similar case was reported about the same time. The Soviet citizen Roman Gudovskiy, a Byelorussian who (presumably outraged by Soviet violation of international agreements) collected information on Soviet chemical-weapons development. His attempts to contact the Americans with these data, however, was short-circuited by the KGB, who under the false "CIA" flag recruited him—and set him up for his sentence of eleven years of strict-regime confinement (*Arkhiv Samizdata*, no. 5219).

12. Lysenko, pp. 252–4. Lysenko later defected to Sweden.

13. *Insight*, 11 January 1988. Alburt later defected and lives in the United States.

14. *Pravda*, 2 September 1988 and 12 February 1989.

15. S. V. Zukul, chairman of the Latvian SSR KGB, interviewed in *Sovetskaya Latviya*, 26 October 1988.

16. *Washington Post*, 2 January 1989.

17. *Washington Post*, 13 September 1987.

18. *Pravda*, 18 November 1988.

19. As admitted by the historian Ostryakov, p. 11.

20. See, for example, *Nedelya*, March 1966, cited in R. B. Lockhart, *Ace of Spies* (New York: Stein & Day, 1967), pp. 76, 159–65; Ostryakov also refers to it.

21. Melgounov, p. 253.

22. Myagkov, p. 37. The specific targets here were "nationalists" and "foreign anti-Soviet nationalist centers," but the principles are identical for whatever type of group is targeted.

23. Leggett, p. 318.

24. G. Vereeken, *The GPU in the Trotskyist Movement* (Clapham, England: New Park Publications, 1976), p. 355. Vereeken was a Belgian Trotskyite and a victim of these intrigues.

25. "In late 1921 the Special Section of the VCheka began yet another operation under the code-name 'Trust.' It was intended to reduce anti-Soviet activity and demoralize the White emigrants who had rallied around the Paris 'Supreme Monarchist Council.' Its instrument was to be a mythical underground organization in Moscow called the Monarchist Union of Central Russia" (Ostryakov, p. 114).

26. The Soviet side of the WiN operation has been told by Josef Swiatlo and other defectors from Polish State Security. For Western sources, see H. Rositzke, *CIA's Secret Operations* (New York: Readers Digest/Crowell, 1977), pp. 170–1; E.J. Epstein, *Deception* (New York: Simon & Schuster, 1989) pp. 34–42.

27. *London Times*, 22 April 1983.

28. As late as 1979 Soviet historians (e.g., Ostryakov) were still condemning the misdeeds of the "Trotskyite-Zinovievite Bloc" in the context of these events. For Stalin's 27 July 1927 article and the provocative nature of the "war scare," see Ulam, *Expansion and Coexistence*, pp. 165–6. As another scholar put it, "The deterioration of Trotsky's and Zinoviev's positions in 1927 can be understood only in terms of the war scare . . . which Stalin cynically employed to create a

controlled panic for the purpose of provoking the opposition" (John S. Reshatar, Jr., *A Concise History of the Communist Party of the Soviet Union* [New York: Praeger, 1960], p. 211).

29. Two defectors from Czechoslovakian State Security have reported their inside knowledge of these provocations. See Bittman, pp. 194–5, and Frolik, pp. 172–3.

30. Myagkov, pp. 51–52.

Chapter 20.   Control of Information— and *Glanost*

1. Lenin, "What Is to Be Done."

2. Speech on the press, 17 November 1917. When his old socialist partners, the Mensheviks, complained that their newspapers were also being suppressed, just like those of the former exploiters, Lenin replied, "Of course they are, but unfortunately not the whole lot as yet! Soon they will all be closed down" (Trotsky, *Lenin,* cited by Leggett, p. 306).

3. Ivan Zubkov, in *Zhurnalist,* no. 8 (1972), p. 9. Zubkov was at the time head of the Newspaper Section of the Propaganda Department of the CC CPSU.

4. USSR Constitution of 1977, article 66.

5. Fundamental Principles of Legislation on Marriage and the Family, cited by Chaldize, *To Defend These Rights,* p. 89. This in spite of the legal principle that parents have the right and obligation of educating their own children, which was invoked in January 1980 when the KGB threatened to take away the children of Olga Zaitseva unless she stopped working in the Initiative Group to Defend the Rights of Invalids in the USSR (*Helsinki Report,* 1980, pp. 103–4).

6. Meeting with members of the Union of Soviet Writers, 19 June 1986. Cited in *Cahiers du Samizdat,* no. 125 (February–March 1987). Gorbachev had similarly exhorted filmmakers.

7. *Perestroika,* p. 79.

8. Vadim A. Medvedev in *Pravda,* 26 December 1988.

9. This formulation, doubtless stemming from the propaganda of the CC CPSU, was taken up in the speeches and articles of other leaders, among them Politburo member Eduard Shevardnadze. The version cited here is from an article by Vitaliy Fedorchuk, at the time Ukrainian KGB chief but shortly afterward to replace Yuri Andropov at the head of the USSR KGB (*Pid praporom leninizmu,* Kiev, no. 19 [October 1981], pp. 10–7).

10. Vadim A. Medvedev's news conference on 29 November 1988, *International Herald Tribune,* 30 November 1988.

11. *Bolshaya Sovetskaya Entsiklopediya,* 2d ed. (1957), vol. 46, pp. 518–19; and 3rd ed., vol. 28, p. 490, on "Censorship."

12. At the height of *glasnost* the chief censor cited as the "only basic principle" that in the future nothing would be forbidden except "information that reveals a state secret or that could be deterimental to our country's interests." Interview

with V. A. Boldyrev, chief of Glavlit, *Izvestiya,* 3 November 1988. This, the first public interview ever granted by a Glavlit official, is hereafter referred to as "Boldyrev interview."

13. Order of the Committee for the Press under the Council of Ministers of the USSR, no. 495, 31 August 1967. Cited by Chalidze, *Literaturnaya dela KGB.* Only "scientifically based" information would be permitted.

14. Suslov, 1979.

15. This principle fell victim to the collapse of the Soviet economy. By the late 1980s the top party ideologist was admitting that "we cannot overlook the experience of mankind as a whole, including that of the nonsocialist world, . . . not only scientific and technological achievements but also many forms of social life and economic processes" (V. A. Medvedev, *Pravda,* 5 October 1988). The chief censor promised a change in "the political assessment of [foreign publications] imported from abroad" and freer sales of Western periodicals, while jamming of Western radios was stopped.

Earlier, Gorbachev himself and other leaders had warned against importing alien ideas. As recently as the end of the 1970s the party's top ideologist Mikhail Suslov was still saying that "we must combat every alien influence. . . . Soviet man uncompromisingly opposes any manifestations of any alien ideology and morality." It did not matter whether such foreign information was true or not: "Bourgeois propagandists may in certain cases libelously utilize actual facts and reliable statistical data" (cited in Chalidze, *To Defend These Rights,* p. 69). In 1981 the Soviets accused the BBC of "factological propaganda" and criticized "the abundance of genuine facts in BBC broadcasts." (As reported by Douglas Muggeridge, managing director of the BBC External Services, on 14 April 1983. *London Daily Telegraph,* 15 April 1983.)

16. Boldyrev interview.

17. Vitaliy Ozerov, a secretary of the Writers Union, in *Znaniye,* April 1973, translated in Radio Liberty Research, RL 306/73, 28 September 1973.

18. The CPSU statute specifically assigns "the leadership of the local press, radio, and television" to the regional Party Committee (art. 42b) along with the right to "confirm" newspaper and magazine editors (arts. 45 and 49). Many editors are selected from the ranks of the Party Committee itself. As the CC CPSU (and former Politburo) member Boris Yeltsin pointed out in March 1989, even the newspaper of the building industry (of which he was then a deputy minister) was technically an organ of the CC CPSU (*London Daily Telegraph,* 21 March 1989). Even Glavlit, the censorship organ, had a voice in approving appointments and shifts of editorial staffs (M. Fedotov, in *Moscow News,* 23 October 1988).

19. *London Sunday Times,* 5 January 1986. A general handbook (unclassified) is by V. A. Markus, *Spravochnik normativnykh materialov dlya izdatelskikh rabotnikov* (Reference Book for Editing [or Publishing] Workers) (Moscow: Kniga Publishing House, 1977).

20. *Pravda,* 18 January 1989; *Ogonyok,* 5 February 1989; *International Herald Tribune,* 7 February 1989.

21. Boldyrev interview. An example of that "intensive fire" was the article a

week earlier in *Moscow News* (23 October 1988) by Mikhail Fedotov, entitled "The More Freedom, the Greater the Responsibility. Will Censorship and *Glasnost* Get Along?"

22. Boldyrev interview.

23. 1931 decree on the responsibilities of Glavlit.

24. *London Daily Telegraph*, 1 July 1986; *Newsweek*, 14 July 1986.

25. One Glavlit department, designated as the Second Department, reportedly has the task of destroying books, magazines, and other materials confiscated from travelers at the border crossing points. It was identified in October 1975 when one of its deputy chiefs was put on trial for selling confiscated books on the black market. See Radio Liberty Research, RL 494/76, 8 December 1976.

26. Lesnik, pp. 89–90, 96–7. (The author was an announcer at Radio Moscow until 1981.) In May 1983, in an incident that was well publicized in the West, a Radio Moscow broadcaster named Vladimir Danchev managed to refer to Soviet "bandits" and "invaders" in Afghanistan; he was fired and reportedly confined in a mental hospital. Lesnik could not explain how this could happen except through carelessness and perhaps the absence of the two supervisors who would normally have caught the "error" before it could be recorded or transmitted (*Le Point*, Paris, 6 June 1983).

27. Boldyrev interview. As he put it euphemistically, "Measures are being taken to ensure the fuller, more efficient conveyance of foreign publications to organizations and individuals."

28. Report of Ye. Ye. Sokolov, party secretary at Brest (on the border with Poland), to the USSR Supreme Soviet. *Izvestiya*, 26 November 1982.

29. Radio address by President Reagan, reported in *Washington Times*, 12 September 1983.

30. Secretary of State George Shultz, in *International Herald Tribune*, 17 January 1989.

31. Gennadiy Gerassimov and Yuri Gemistkikh of the USSR Foreign Ministry, reported respectively by Reuters and Agence France Presse in *International Herald Tribune*, 16 October 1986 and 27 May 1987. Gorbachev attacked Radio Liberty and Radio Free Europe frequently, as in *Perestroika*, p. 217.

32. Solzhenitsyn, *The Oak and the Calf*, pp. 208–9.

33. *Washington Post*, 9 January 1967.

34. Protocol of the founding meeting of the VCheka, Protocol no. 21, Meeting of the Council of People's Commissars of 7(20) December 1917 under the chairmanship of V. I. Lenin. Tsvigun, p. 36.

35. Leggett, p. 307.

36. Alidin.

37. Kozlov, 1979, p. 72. Also Chebrikov, in *Pravda*, 2 September 1988.

38. The text reads, "Glavlit is headed by a chief and two assistants, one approved by the RVSR [Revolutionary-Military Council of the Republic] and the other by the GPU." Senior Chekists have always been assigned to this position.

39. Anthony Adamovich in Dewhirst and Farrell, p. 69. I cannot confirm this report but find it plausible.

40. Chalidze, *Literaturnyye dela KGB*, pp. 143–45. The control over importa-

tions of banned works was reconfirmed as recently as 1982 by the law on the USSR borders.

41. The group examined "various aspects of mass media and propaganda activity." *Pravda,* 5 December 1987.

42. *Nedelya,* 22 August 1976.

43. See, for instance, Solzhenitsyn's Letter to the Soviet Writers Union, 1 December 1967. Reprinted in *The Oak and the Calf,* p. 481.

44. A. Inauri, chairman of the Georgian SSR KGB, in *Zarya Vostoka,* 25 December 1981.

45. As estimated by a former Soviet censor who emigrated to the West in the late 1970s. This proportion is confirmed by similar work in Poland, as revealed by documents brought to the West by a Polish censor.

46. This list is approved by the Council of Ministers. The first one was dated 27 April 1926 and was replaced in 1947, 1956, 1966, and probably in 1973–74 and twice since then. A translation of the 1956 list can be found in Conquest, *The Politics of Ideas in the USSR,* pp. 61–63.

47. Klyagin, pp. 81–82.

48. Article 76.1 of the RSFSR Criminal Code. The conviction was reported in *Argumenty i Fakty,* 25 June 1988, and *Trud,* 21 June 1988. See Amy Knight, "Conviction for Passing Economic Secrets Reported," in Radio Liberty Research, RL 359/88, 8 August 1988.

49. Such information had always been protected by each organization's internal security regulations. The absurd extent of secrecy in Soviet institutions, and, specifically, how it hampers Soviet science and technology, is described by the former Soviet science writer Mark Popovsky in *Manipulated Science* (especially pp. 69–91, 97, 105, 113). In 1988 a KGB officer complained, in the highest party journal, that this "cult of secrecy" was forcing Soviet scientists to use foreign sources to find out what was happening inside the USSR and that state institutions, in their zeal to hide their knowledge, "forget about the knowledge itself and only the protection remains" (V. A. Rubanov, in *Kommunist,* no. 13 [September 1988]).

50. *Bolshaya Sovetskaya Entsiklopediya,* 3d ed.

51. *International Herald Tribune,* 5 June 1978. The Polish list was smuggled out in its entirety in 1977 by a defecting censor, Tomasz Strzyzewski, and was translated and edited by Jane Leftwich Curry as *The Black Book of Censorship.*

52. Some of its contents became known to the West in the 1970s. Dissidents copied out extracts to show to Western correspondents in Moscow (see Kaiser, pp. 224–6 and H. Smith, Sphere ed., pp. 455–6) and emigrating Soviet editors, writers, and even censors carried out their knowledge of it. Parts of earlier versions could be deduced from the Communist Party archives of Smolensk Oblast in the 1930s, seized by the invading Germans in World War II (see Fainsod, *Smolensk,* pp. 364ff.). The Polish version offered other insights.

53. Boldyrev interview.

54. Ibid.

55. Reuters dispatch reported in *London Daily Telegraph,* 9 January 1988.

56. Cited by Xan Smiley in *London Daily Telegraph,* 7 May 1988.

57. Gorbachev used the "many thousands" phrase in his speech on the 70th anniversary of the Bolshevik coup. "Hitting people over the head" is from his meeting with Soviet writers on 19 June 1986, reported in Radio Liberty Research, RL 399/86, from *Archiv Samizdata* (AS 5785).

58. Gorbachev's meeting with Soviet writers, 19 June 1986, *Cahiers du Samizdat*, no. 125 (February–March 1987). Yeltsin electoral speech, 20 March 1989, cited in *London Daily Telegraph*, 21 March 1989.

59. *New York Times*, 6 April 1987.

60. The most far-reaching proposals and revelations of those first years appeared in *Moscow News*, a weekly that was printed in five languages with only a small printing of 250,000 for its Russian-language edition. It could hardly be found by Soviet citizens even in Moscow (and not at all in the provinces). A Soviet editor remarked, "I think it's really for foreigners" (Boris Kuchmayev, editor of *Stavropol Pravda*, cited in *International Herald Tribune*, 18 August 1987).

Chapter 21. Keeping People In

1. *International Herald Tribune*, 10 and 11 March 1988, 23 and 24 November 1983; *Newsweek*, 5 December 1983. Some of the captured Georgians were later executed by personal order of Politburo member Eduward Shevardnadze, according to protesters in Georgia in 1989.

2. Article 64, paragraph 16, of the RSFSR Criminal Code. Article 83 of the same code allows, in theory, a lesser charge against "those leaving only because they want to better their way of life." The penalty for this relatively minor offense is "deprivation of freedom for one in three years" (Yu. D. Severin, ed., *Kommentariy k Ugovnomu kodeksu RSFSR* [Commentary on the Criminal Code of the RSFSR] [Moscow: Yuridicheskaya literatura, 1980], pp. 139–42, 161–3). In practice, however, article 83 is little more than propaganda because anyone who, while abroad, answers questions put to him by foreign authorities will have violated other articles of the Criminal Code and will surely get fifteen years.

3. Each of them was committed for four years. Shatravka's syndrome was diagnosed as "overevaluation of living in the West" (Van Voren, p. 38).

4. Lapin recounted his experience to the writer Mark Popovsky. See Popovsky, pp. 103–12.

5. The exit application quoted here is the 1976 version issued by the OVIR of the Moscow MVD, five pages long in the original plus a sixth page with spaces for an official to certify receipt of the application and its attached documents.

6. Popovsky, p. 108.

7. At that point he encountered a new difficulty: he could not get an air flight. No foreign airline would take his rubles, and Aeroflot was sold out for months. *International Herald Tribune*, 22 November 1988.

8. The CC CPSU order was reported by Tass on 2 March 1988. The relaxation of tourist travel to Eastern European countries was reported by *Moskovskiy Komsomolets* (Reuters, 2 January 1988). Director-level travel was reported in *Insight*, 9 November 1987.

9. Popovsky, p. 110.

10. Resolution of the USSR Council of Ministers of 28 August 1986, *Sobraniye Postanovleniy Pravitelstva SSSR*, no. 31, p. 163 addenda to the Regulations on Entering and Leaving the USSR of 22 September 1970.

11. Information from an emigrant who graduated from the institute in the 1970s. The reasons may be what the authorities consider misbehavior or character weaknesses (drink, divorce, etc.) or ideas or attitudes.

12. The document cited here and in the next two paragraphs is a "service document" of trade union authorities (in this case, a city committee of the trade union for secondary and higher educational institutions and scientific institutions) which was based on a decree of the Presidium of the Central Council of Trade Unions "Concerning the Sending of Soviet Citizens on Tourist Trips Abroad." The document is entitled "Recommendations on Formalities to be Fulfilled by Workers Going on Tourist Trips Abroad," and reached the West through *samizdat* channels (*Cahiers du Samizdat*, no. 95 [June–July 1983], pp. 9–11).

13. Interview with Tom Brokaw of NBC Television, 30 November 1987.

14. *International Herald Tribune*, 9 December 1987 and 7 December 1988; *London Times*, 2 December 1988.

15. Yu. M. Kozlov, 1979, pp. 83–5, etc.; Myagkov, pp. 21 and 32.

16. Articles 28–30 of the 1983 Border Law.

17. Article 23, USSR Law on the USSR State Border. This law was introduced in November 1982, but because it only came into effect in early 1983 it is sometimes called the Border Law of 1983.

18. Decree no. 110 of USSR Council of Ministers, 28 August 1974, pt. 25.

19. Border Law of 1983, article 29.

20. Yu. M. Kozlov, 1979, pp. 83–4.

21. The Border Guard Troops celebrate 28 May 1918 as their birthday. At the All-Russian Conference of Extraordinary Commissions on 11 June 1918, the Chekas assigned the responsibility to VCheka Troops, which were separated into "internal" and "border" troops.

22. *Pravda*, 28 May 1974.

23. *Zarya Vostoka*, 24 July 1982.

24. "The organs of state security of foreign socialist states base their activities on the same principles as those of the USSR" (*Bolshaya Sovetskaya Entsiklopediya*, 3d ed. (1972), vol. 7, p. 151).

25. *Zarya Vostoka*, Tbilisi, 24 July 1982.

26. Article 20.1 and 20.2 of the 1983 Border Law.

27. *Izvestiya*, 25 August 1977.

28. *Izvestiya*, 26 November 1982.

29. K. S. Demirchyan, in *Yerevan Kommunist* and *Zarya Vostoka* of 24 July 1982.

30. *Izvestiya*, 26 November 1982: "Each year Komsomol organizations hold Border Guard Week . . . to strengthen ties of collectives in offices, farms, and construction projects with border detachments and ships."

31. *Komsomolskaya Pravda,* 8 December 1983, cited in *Novoye Russkoye Slovo,* 4 January 1984.

32. Saidali's story is taken from *Kazakhstanskaya Pravda,* Ashirov's from *Turkmenskaya Iskra,* Ashkabad, 11 September 1982.

33. *Frankfurter Allgemeine Zeitung,* 30 March 1983.

34. Photographs of these dog runs and other elements of the border are to be found in *Menschenrechte in der DDR und Ost-Berlin,* Document of the Internationale Gesellschaft fuer Menschenrechte (Frankfurt am Main, 1986), pp. 20–62.

35. These and other details of the SM-70 came first from a bold West German citizen named Michael Gartenschlaeger who actually went up to the fence and stole one from under the nose of the border guards in March 1976. His escapade, and the weapon, were described in the West German press—as was his death a month later, when he went back for more (Bailey, pp. 44–6). This weapon was reportedly designed originally for use in the Hitlerian concentration camps but taken and adapted by the victorious Soviets to their own needs.

36. Four such tunnels had been discovered by the fall of 1983 (*London Daily Telegraph,* 7 October 1983).

37. *London Daily Telegraph,* 19 March 1985.

38. Gerson, pp. 240–1. See also the description by Burlutsky and Artemiyev in Wolin and Slusser, and the testimony of F. August before U.S. Senate.

39. Frolik testimony 1975, p. 45.

40. This incident has been much publicized. See Markov's own biography, *The Truth That Killed* (New York: Ticknor & Fields, 1984), with the editor's account of Markov's death.

41. See testimonies of Szabo and Frolik.

Chapter 22. Dealing with Foreigners

1. *Perestroika,* p. 217.

2. Ibid., pp. 148, 149, 215, 219.

3. *Washington Times,* 27 February and 10 March 1989.

4. See, for example, Elizabeth Teague, "Soviet War Propaganda Generates Fear Among the Population," Radio Liberty Research, RL 61/84, 6 February 1984.

5. Boris Pastukhov, First Secretary of the All-Union Komsomol, in *Komsomolsaya Pravda,* 19 May 1982. The Black Sea Fleet set up a book exhibit in 1981 on the theme "Why I Hate Imperialism" (*Kommunist Vooruzhennykh Sil,* January 1982).

6. *Zarya Vostoka,* 26 December 1981.

7. *Kommunist,* no. 9, June 1985, p. 55. His predecessor, Yuri Andropov, used the same words in 1979; see *Izbrannyye,* p. 297.

8. *Izbrannyye,* pp. 251, 310, etc.; Chebrikov, speech from *Kommunist* no. 9, 1985, p. 54.

9. *Perestroika,* p. 152.

10. *Vedomosti Verkhovnogo Soveta SSSR,* 1987, no. 22, st. 312. Published in *Sotsialisticheskaya Zakonnost,* no. 9, September 1987.

11. Decree of the Presidium of the USSR Supreme Soviet, in effect on 1 July 1984. It is a rare Soviet citizen who has the opportunity or the living space to house a foreigner—or the daring: by law he must register any visitor, and a foreigner seen in his room would arouse the suspicion of other denizens of his apartment house.

12. Article 13.1 added on 1 February 1984 to the USSR law of 25 December 1958 on "Criminal Liability for Crimes Against the State."

13. Law "On the Legal Status of Foreign Citizens in the USSR," 24 July 1981.

14. Xan Smiley, in *London Daily Telegraph,* 14 March 1988.

15. Pacepa, pp. 230–1. He added, "So successful was the hotel that its model was copied, although never perfectly, in other luxury tourist hotels throughout Romania, especially in the Black Sea resort area."

16. Kaiser, pp. 13–4.

17. G. Wynne, *The Man from Moscow* (London: Hutchinson, 1967), p. 100.

18. *Los Angeles Times,* 25 August 1970.

19. *Manchester Guardian Weekly,* 27 May 1984.

20. Zhuravlev, p. 61.

21. *Kommunist,* no. 14 (1981).

22. Kevin Klose, American correspondent in Moscow at the time, in *Washington Post,* 7 September 1986.

23. Van Voren, p. 47

24. *Newsweek,* 4 February 1980, citing State Department sources.

25. *Washington Post,* 26 March 1985.

26. *London Daily Telegraph,* 22 August 1985.

27. Los Angeles Times Service; *International Herald Tribune,* 23 April 1980.

28. Emil Sveilis, "A U.S. Newsman in Russia: Tracked, Harassed," in *International Herald Tribune,* 24 July 1978.

29. Zinoviev, *The Radiant Future,* pp. 103–4.

30. "Knowing the KGB," *Partisan Review,* vol. 44, no. 2 (1982), pp. 180–1.

37. Lysenko, pp. 156, 170, 193–9, 223–4.

32. Private communication from an emigre.

33. *London Daily Telegraph,* 3 July 1978.

Chapter 23. Internal War and External Policy

1. *Perestroika,* p. 132.

2. Ibid., pp. 130–2, 149, etc.

3. *Perestroika,* pp. 158, 202. Soviet spokesmen have also claimed that "the main aim of Soviet foreign policy is creating stability in the world." Such declarations leave the words "stability" and "good intentions" to be interpreted according to the listener's own definitions, hopes, and illusions.

4. Letter to the Central Committee of the Czechoslovak Communist Party from the Warsaw Pact leaders, in *Pravda*, 18 July 1968.

5. *Perestroika*, pp. 146–8.

6. The Party Program of 1986 lists the following aims of Soviet foreign policy (with "peaceful coexistence" listed among them): "to ensure favorable external conditions for . . . the advance toward communism in the USSR, to deepen cooperation with socialist countries and to promote in every way the strengthening and progress of the world system of socialism, to develop friendly relations with countries which have won liberation, international solidarity with Communist and revolutionary democratic parties, the international workers movement, and the people's national liberation struggle" (Part III, introduction).

7. Leonid Brezhnev's speech on the 50th anniversary of the October coup (reprinted in *Leninskim Kursom: Rechi i stat'i*, vol. 2, p. 120), endorsed by Yuri Andropov (*Izbrannyye*, p. 114).

8. *Perestroika*, p. 163.

9. The formulation stemmed from the CC CPSU and was used by, among others, future Foreign Minister Eduard Shevardnadze (the first citation here, *Zarya Vostoka*, 26 December 1981) and future KGB Chairman Vitaliy Fedorchuk in October 1981.

10. Just after his visit to Moscow in March 1989 the Hungarian Foreign Minister, in reply to the question of a BBC interviewer, said the Brezhnev Doctrine is dead. Oleg Bogomolov, a specialist in Eastern European affairs close to Gorbachev, said publicly in February 1989 that a multi-party, neutral Hungary "along Austrian lines" would offer no strategic threat to the Soviet Union. And the following month the Hungarian party chief Karoly Grosz returned from Moscow announcing that the Kremlin wholeheartedly endorsed the changes underway in Hungary—including its move towards a multi-party system.

11. *International Herald Tribune*, 6 and 7 July 1989.

12. *Perestroika*, pp.; 130–1, 150. Gorbachev added, "Lenin said that we, the socialist state, would chiefly influence world development through our economic achievements."

13. Lenin several times (including November 1918 and March 1919) called it "unthinkable" that socialism and capitalism could long exist side by side (*Collected Works*, vol. 29, pp. 138–9) and made the "awful war" statement in his Report to the Third Congress of the Communist International, 5 July 1921. Stalin, even while formulating "Socialism in One Country," stressed repeatedly that only on an international scale was it possible to prevent the restoration of bourgeois relations in that one socialist country. Khrushchev's remarks appeared in *Kommunist*, 12 November 1957, p. 12; Brezhnev's in *Leninskim kursom*, vol. 2, cited in A. Weeks and W. Bodie, eds., *War and Peace: Soviet Russia Speaks* (New York: National Strategy Information Center, Inc., 1983), p. 22.

14. This standard formulation appeared hundreds of times in Soviet publications, among them *Pravda*, 16 December 1982, and *Izvestiya*, 20 January 1980. Gorbachev has used it frequently.

15. A useful and recent presentation of this theme can be found in Janos Berecz, *1956. Counterrevolution in Hungary: Words and Weapons* (Budapest:

Akademai Kiado, 1986). Berecz was a member of the Hungarian Politburo and a longtime friend of the Soviet Union. The book was originally published in 1981 as an expansion of his doctoral dissertation at Moscow State University.

16. *Pravda,* 16 July 1968, etc.

17. Reuters dispatch in *International Herald Tribune,* 26 December 1981; Tass and *Krasnaya Zvezda* reported similarly on 18 December 1981.

18. *Perestroika,* p. 163.

19. *Izbrannyye,* p. 161.

20. *Pravda,* 17 January 1960. "Making it easier to promote national liberation movements" is evidently still a goal of peaceful coexistence, for the 1986 CPSU Party Program listed as one of its benefits that "states that have embarked on the path of independent development would be protected from outside encroachments."

21. *Izbrannyye,* pp. 312, 113.

22. G. Shakhnazarov in *Seriya Obschestvennykh nauk* [Social Sciences], January 1981. No one repudiates Lenin (who is credited with originating peaceful coexistence) who said many times that "the Soviet and capitalist systems or states cannot indefinitely coexist; one side or the other must perish."

23. Brezhnev made this statement in Prague in 1973, according to the *Boston Globe,* 11 February 1977. Other Soviet leaders have similarly summarized Soviet progress, as have the party programs of the CPSU.

Chapter 24. The Soviet Record Abroad

1. "It is an imperative of the nuclear century that the export of revolution is excluded," wrote foreign affairs specialist Yevgeniy Primakov in *Pravda,* 10 July 1987. Gorbachev found the following quotation from Marx: "The victorious proletariat cannot impose on any other nation its own ideal of a happy life without doing damage to its own victory" (*Perestroika,* p. 151).

2. See, for example, *Perestroika,* pp. 188,1 76.

3. *Perestroika,* p. 151.

4. The entire organization was exposed and documented in a White Paper after Nkrumah was overthrown by a coup in early 1966.

5. Letter of 11 July 1983 from Ambassador W. Richard Jacobs, in *Grenada Documents: An Overview and Selection* (Washington, D.C.: Department of State, September 1984), Document no. 26, pp. 2, 6.

6. *Perestroika,* p. 173.

7. I testified before the United States Congress on Soviet murder operations. See, for example, U.S. Congress, *Murder International, Inc.: Murder and Kidnaping as an Instrument of Soviet Policy.*

8. Some of Stalin's murder operations abroad, not only against political exiles like Trotsky, but also against leaders of foreign political parties—wiping out the Polish socialists, for example, and foreign Communist leaders—have become relatively well known. He tried repeatedly to have Tito assassinated. (See Antonov-Ovseyenko, p. 286.)

9. Sejna, p. 144. The leader of an opposition party in Scandinavia or Great Britain was to be murdered in the early 1960s, as KGB officer Anatoly Golitsyn heard in late 1961 directly from the chief of the KGB's section responsible for operations in those countries. (See Chapman Pincher, *Too Secret Too Long* [New York: St. Martin's Press, 1984], p. 474.) Without knowing about Golitsyn's report, British counterintelligence became curious about the death of the deputy head of the British Labour Party, Hugh Gaitskell—who was so strongly anti-Soviet that Khrushchev was heard to say with disgust in May 1958, "If communism were to triumph in Britain tomorrow, Gaitskell would be the first to be shot outside the Houses of Parliament as a traitor to the working class" (Sejna, p. 73). Gaitskell had died in January 1963 of systemic lupus erythematosus, a relatively rare disease that (as was later discovered) Soviet scientists had succeeded in inducing by chemicals in animals. The diagnosis was delayed for a long time by unusual clinical features and the absence from his blood of an antinuclear factor, present in almost all true cases of this disease. (See W. R. Heeler, letter to the editor of *The American Spectator,* October 1985. Heeler had been a postgraduate in London at the time and heard much talk among doctors in the hospital common room.) Shortly before he died, Gaitskell himself was suspicious enough to call his doctors' attention to the fact that a few days earlier he had gone to the Soviet Consulate in London for a visa and had been kept waiting for half an hour and had been given coffee and biscuits.

10. Frantisek August testimony, p. 73; Frolik, *The Frolik Defection,* pp. 153–54. August was deputy Czechoslovakian state security resident in Beirut; Josef Frolik learned of it in that service's Prague headquarters.

11. Bittman, *The Deception Game,* pp. 1ff; Frolik, pp. 160–61.

12. Ibid., p. 75.

13. August, p. 73.

14. Shevchenko, *Breaking with Moscow,* extracted in *Time,* 11 February 1985, p. 26. This passage did not appear in the book itself.

15. Kourdakov, p. 254 (publisher's note).

16. Pacepa, pp. 145–6.

17. Khokhlov, pp. 206–7. See also pp. 221, 231, 234–6.

18. U.S. Congress, *Murder International, Inc.,* pp. 164–8.

19. Khokhlov.

20. As mentioned earlier, I can testify personally to the fact that the KGB informs the Politburo of all operations bearing such political implications. I prepared the report to the Politburo on the abduction from West Berlin of a German lawyer who was never seen again in the West.

21. Khokhlov, p. 90.

22. Lenin told his delegation to the Genoa conference of 1922, when his new regime was breaking out of its isolation, not only to win trade agreements and political recognition but to split the Western countries that were now recognizing his rule (Popov, pp. 407–8).

23. August testimony, p. 72.

24. Bittman, *The Deception Game,* p. 16.

25. U.S. Congress, *Soviet Active Measures,* p. 42.

26. Ibid.

27. For a review of the size and spread of these organizations, see W. Spaulding, "Communist International Fronts in 1983," *Problems of Communism*, March–April 1984.

28. Others included George Blake in the British intelligence office in Berlin. Pitovranov also handled the kidnaping or defection of West German security chief Otto John, as described in John's book, *Twice Through the Lines* (New York: Harper & Row, 1972), pp. 247–63.

29. Confronted in 1974 about his KGB background by an Australian journalist, Pitovranov claimed that he had retired from the KGB nine years earlier (*The Australian*, 28 February 1974). However, Pitovranov was 50 years old in 1965 and I know from my days as KGB personnel officer that this was not the KGB's retirement age.

30. The main exportable products include oil, natural gas, metal ores—and weapons, of which the Soviets were selling some $10 billion worth per year to oil-rich countries like Algeria, Libya, and Iraq, able to pay in hard currencies. Machinery and technology were the main imports, of course, but also raw materials (perhaps 10 percent of raw materials used in Soviet industrial production came from abroad). Soviet firms were marketing oil and raw materials, selling automobiles, and banking, in numbers small by comparison to Western business, but increasing.

31. *Soviet Military Power*, 1987.

32. Rubinstein, A. Z., "Soviet Success Story: The Third World," *Orbis*, vol. 32, no. 4, Fall 1988, p. 561.

33. Stalin, *Sochineniya* (1953), vol. 9, p. 313.

34. The student recounted his experiences to a friend in Moscow, a Canadian journalist. See Peter Worthington, "Russia's Vast, Ruthless Spy Empire," in *Boston Globe*, 17 March 1967.

35. Polianski, pp. 329–30.

36. Former KGB Maj. Imants Lesinkis, who went over to the West in 1978, in foreword to A. Lejins, *Guest of the KGB*.

Chapter 25. The Military Buildup

1. *Sochineniya*, 4th ed., vol. 23, p. 413.

2. Reported by William Safire in *International Herald Tribune*, 26 February, 29 March, and 22 April 1988. A year before Gorbachev's own revelation, a Soviet academician, Grigoriy Khanin, had exposed in *Novy Mir* "figure-padding and price manipulation" that, if taken into account, would drastically reduce the official estimate of Soviet GNP.

3. In 1986 the Soviet armed forces counted more than 210 divisions equipped with more than 50,000 tanks, 50,000 armored troop carriers, and 30,000 pieces of artillery plus 6,000 multiple rocket launchers, with 10,000 fixed-wing aircraft and more than 5,000 helicopters (*The Soviet Weapons Industry:*

An Overview. Central Intelligence Agency, report DI 86-100016, September 1986, p. 4).

4. U.S. Department of Defense, *Soviet Military Power,* 1984, p. 111.

5. U.S. Department of Defense, *Soviet Acquisition of Militarily Significant Western Technology,* April 1982 (hereafter referred to as *Acquisition*), p. 4. See also its *Update,* September 1985 (hereafter referred to as *Update*), figs. 9 and 10. Much of this information came from a KGB officer who gave many documents to French Intelligence. See Wolton; also Radio Liberty Research, RL 36/86, "New Light on Soviet Industrial Espionage," 20 January 1986.

6. Ibid.

7. *Soviet Military Power,* 1982, p. 81.

8. FBI director William Webster, cited in *International Herald Tribune,* 7 April 1981.

9. Minister of the Interior Michel Poniatówski, cited in an AP story in *Washington Times,* 11 April 1983.

10. Popovsky, pp. 73, 77.

11. *Izbrannyye,* p. 124. Andropov was referring to defense against enemy technology, but he was unquestionably referring as well to KGB scientific and technological collection efforts that save not only time and money but preserve the regime itself.

12. Penkovskiy, chap. 4 and appendices I and II.

13. H. Regnard, "The USSR and Scientific and Technological Intelligence," in *Defense Nationale,* Paris (December 1983), pp. 107–21.

14. "Soviet military projects using Western technology and hardware design concepts span all areas: strategic offensive missiles, aircraft, conventional ground and naval forces, air defense, and reconnaissance" (*Soviet Weapons Industry,* p. 23).

15. *Acquisition; Update,* p. 11.

16. *London Daily Telegraph,* 20 March 1984.

17. *Soviet Military Power,* 1984, p. 108.

18. *Acquisition; Update;* see also Barron, *KGB Today: The Hidden Hand,* chap. 5.

19. Stanislav Levchenko was told this within the KGB. See Barron, *KGB Today: The Hidden Hand,* p. 196.

20. Bittmann, *The Deception Game,* p. 125. Similar calculations were made by the Romanian Intelligence Service (Pacepa, pp. 396–7).

21. Marshal A. A. Grechko, in *Voprosi istorii KP SSSR,* May 1974.

22. *Soviet Weapons Industry,* pp. 4–5.

Chapter 26. The Institutions of Foreign Affairs

1. Yu. M. Kozlov, 1979, pp. 270–1, 289.

2. The KGB (then called OGPU) had wholly taken over the Comintern's subversive activities, along with its best operatives, by the late 1920s. When in 1943 the shell of the Comintern was formally dissolved, its coordination of

foreign Communist Party activity was taken over by a new "international department" established within the CC CPSU, while the bulk of its files were transferred to the KGB (then NKGB). Symbolizing the whole process, the Comintern headquarters building in the Rostkino area of Moscow was taken over by the Foreign Directorate of the KGB. (A few years later I worked there.)

3. *Perestroika,* p. 169.

4. Pyotr Shastiko, in *Asia and Africa Today,* No. 3 (May–June 1983), using the appropriate title "The Revolution Must Be Able to Defend Itself." This article is the source of the citations in the following paragraph as well.

5. *USSR—100 Questions and Answers* (Moscow: Progress Publishing, 1975), p. 27.

6. Pyotr Shastitko in *Asia and Africa Today,* No. 3, May–June 1983, using the appropriate title "The Revolution Must be Able to Defend Itself." This article is the source of the citations in the following paragraph as well.

7. Lenin, *Collected Works* (in Russian), vol. 10, p. 51. Lenin's definition— "There is only one kind of real internationalism—working wholeheartedly for the development of the revolutionary struggle in one's own country and supporting . . . this struggle, this and only this line, in every country without exception"— is still widely used as a definition. See, for example, *USSR: 100 Questions and Answers.*

8. The exact figures for UNESCO were 8 intelligence officers out of 15 members of the permanent delegation, more than 20 out of 57 in the secretariat (*London Daily Telegraph,* 19 December 1971). The U.S. estimates were contained in public statements of congressional and administration spokesmen.

9. U.S. State Department report cited by Associated Press, 21 April 1987.

10. Stanislav Levchenko (himself a *New Times* representative in Japan in the late 1970s) reported the *New Times* and Novosti statistics in testimony before the U.S. Congress on 14 July 1982 (*Soviet Active Measures,* p. 162).

11. Several countries have ordered Soviet press offices closed, as Switzerland did with Novosti in 1983 and Pakistan with Tass in 1980, but have left behind all the other Soviet correspondents representing, in some countries, as many as fifteen different newspapers or magazines—and the KGB and GRU.

Afterword: Is the Cold War Over?

1. Raldugin, op. cit., pp. 23–24.

2. *London Times,* 13 April 1989; *Perestroika,* pp. 42, 54, 79; address of 25 February 1987 to the Congress of Trade Unions.

3. For example, in *Pravda,* 9 December 1987, by referring yet again to Lenin's oft-quoted warning that "as long as exploiters exist in the world" the regime "cannot survive" without the Chekist organization.

Bibliography

Here are some of the books and other publications that we have used and others that, in my view, offer valuable insights into the institutions and methods that I have described. I list first of all the works by former insiders because they are all too often slighted by Western scholars. Scholars understandably rely on official documentation, suspecting that personal memoirs may be exaggerated for self-serving reasons. But this is a secret system, and the things known to us from inside its secret core will never be documented until KGB archives are fully opened—and they will not be opened as long as Communist power survives. The information in these books, although written by dozens of Soviet Bloc security, intelligence, and party officials with varying experience in different periods of Soviet history, is surprisingly consistent. And they are confirmed—from a quite different viewpoint—by the writings of the victims of the system, of which we list a few here.

I have cited a number of Soviet sources which, although they naturally hide or distort reality behind the regime's deceptive jargon, usefully document some earlier periods of Soviet rule, describe laws and formal procedures, and present the rulers' own justifications of their system of repression.

I. *Works by, or based on the testimony of, former Soviet Bloc intelligence or party officials:*

Agabekov, George. *OGPU: The Russian Secret Terror.* New York: Brentano's, 1931.

Akhmedov, Ismail. *In and Out of Stalin's GRU.* London: Arms and Armour Press, 1984.

Anders, Karl. *Murder to Order.* (The case of Bogdan Stashinsky.) London: Ampersand, 1965.

August, Frantisek. Testimony before the U.S. Senate Committee on the Judicary, Internal Security Subcommittee, 12 April 1976. Washington, D.C.: U.S. Government Printing Office, 1976.

Barmine, Alexandre. *Memoirs of a Soviet Diplomat: Twenty Years in the Service of the USSR.* London: L. Dickson, 1938.

Barron, John. *KGB Today: The Hidden Hand.* New York: Reader's Digest Press, 1983.

————. *KGB: The Secret Work of Soviet Secret Agents.* New York: Reader's Digest Press, 1974.

Bazhanov, Boris, *Vospominaniya byvshego pomoshnika Stalina* (Memoirs of Stalin's Former Secretary). Paris: Tretya volna, 1980. (French translation: Bazhanov, Boris, *Bajanov révèle Staline.* [Souvenirs d'un ancien secretaire de Staline.] Paris: Gallimard, 1979.)

Bittman, Ladislav. *The Deception Game: Czechoslovak Intelligence in Soviet Political Warfare.* Syracuse, N.Y.: Syracuse University Research Corporation, 1972.

————. *The KGB and Soviet Disinformation: An Insider's View.* McLean, Va.: Pergamon-Brassey's, 1985.

Checinski, Michael. *Poland: Communism, Nationalism, Anti-Semitism.* New York: Karz-Cohl Publishing, 1982.

Deriabin, Peter. *Watchdogs of Terror.* Frederick, Md.: University Publications of America, 1984.

Deriabin, Peter, and Frank Gibney. *The Secret World.* New York: Ballantine, 1982.

Dzhirkvelov, Ilya. *Secret Servant: My Life with the KGB and the Soviet Elite.* London: Collins, 1987.

Frolik, Josef. *The Frolik Defection.* London: Corgi, 1976.

————. Testimony before the U.S. Senate Committee on the Judiciary, Internal Security Subcommittee, 18 November 1975. Washington, D.C.: U.S. Government Printing Office, 1975.

Golitsyn, Anatoly. *New Lies for Old.* New York: Dodd, Mead & Co., 1984.

Haiducu, Matei Pavel. *J'ai Refusé de Tuer.* Paris: Plon, 1984.

Ivanov-Razumnik, R.V. *The Memoirs of Ivanov-Razumnik.* London: Oxford University Press, 1965.

Kaznacheyev, Alexander. *Inside a Soviet Embassy.* Philadelphia and New York: J.B. Lippincott Company, 1962.

Khokhlov, Nikolay. *In the Name of Conscience.* New York: David McKay, 1959.

Kostov, Vladimir. *Le parapluie bulgare.* Paris: Stock, 1986.

Kourdakov, Sergey. *The Persecutor.* Old Tappan, New Jersey: Fleming H. Revell, 1973.

Kravchenko, Viktor. *I Chose Freedom.* New York: Scribners, 1947.

Krivitsky, Walter G. *In Stalin's Secret Service: An Exposé of Russia's Secret Policies by the Former Chief of Soviet Intelligence in Western Europe.* Westport, Conn.: Hyperion Press, 1979.

Levchenko, Stanislav. *On the Wrong Side (My Life in the KGB).* Washington, New York, London: Pergamon-Brassey, 1988.

Markov, Georgi. *The Truth That Killed.* New York: Ticknor and Fields, 1984.

Monat, Pavel, with John Dille. *Spy in the U.S.* New York: Berkeley Medallion Books, 1961.

Mondich, Mikhail. *Smersh: God v strane vraga* (SMERSH: Years in the Enemy's Country). Frankfurt am Main: Possev, 1984.

Myagkov, Aleksei. *Inside the KGB.* Richmond, Eng.: Foreign Affairs Publishing Co., 1976; New York: Ballantine, 1983.

Orlov, Alexander. *The Secret History of Stalin's Crimes.* New York: Random House, 1953.

————. Testimony before U.S. Senate, Committee on the Judiciary, Subcommittee to Investigate the Administration of the Internal Security Act and Other Internal Security Laws, 14 and 15 February 1957. Washington, D.C.: U.S. Government Printing Office, 1957.

Pacepa, Ion Mihai. *Red Horizons: Chronicles of a Communist Spy Chief.* Washington, D.C.: Regnery Gateway, 1987.

Penkovskiy, Oleg. *The Penkovskiy Papers.* New York: Doubleday, 1965; Ballantine, 1982.

Petrov, Vladimir and Evdokia. *Empire of Fear.* London: Andre Deutsch, 1956.

Polianski, Nicolas. *M.I.D. Douze ans dans les services diplomatiques du Kremlin.* Paris: Belfond, 1984.

Poretsky, Elisabeth K. *Our Own People.* Ann Arbor: University of Michigan Press, 1969.

Rastvorov, Yuri A. "How Red Titans Fought for Supreme Power" and "Red Fraud and Intrigue in Far East." *Life* Magazine, 29 November and 13 December 1954.

Romanov, A.I. [Baklanov]. *Nights Are Longest There,* Boston: Little, Brown and Co., 1972.

Sakharov, Vladimir, with Tosi Umberto. *High Treason.* New York: G.P. Putnam's Sons, 1980.

Sejna, Jan. *We Will Bury You.* London: Sidgwick & Jackson, 1982.

Shevchenko, Arkady. *Breaking with Moscow.* New York: Knopf, 1985.

Sinevirsky, Nicola [Mikhail Mondich]. *SMERSH.* New York: Henry Holt and Co., 1950.

Suvorov, Viktor [Vladimir Rezun]. *Inside the Soviet Army,* London: Hamish Hamilton, 1982.

————. *Soviet Military Intelligence.* London: Hamish Hamilton, 1984.

————. *Aquarium: The Career and Defection of a Soviet Military Spy.* London: Hamish Hamilton, 1985.

————. *Spetsnaz: The Story Behind the Soviet SAS.* London: Hamish Hamilton, 1987.

Szabo, Laszlo. Statement in Hearings before the CIA Subcommittee of the Committee on Armed Services of the House of Representatives, 17 March 1966. Washington, D.C.: U.S. Government Printing Office, 1966.

"X" with Bruce E. Henderson and C.C. Cyr. *Double Eagle: The Autobiography of a Polish Spy Who Defected to the West.* Indianapolis/New York: The Bobbs-Merrill Co., 1979.

Zemtsov, Ilya. *The Corrupt Society: The Secret World of Soviet Capitalism.* New York: Simon and Shuster, 1982.

————. *The Private Life of the Soviet Elite.* New York: Crane Russak, 1985. (Russian-language original: *Partiya ili mafiya?.* Paris: Les editeurs reunis, 1976.)

II. *Writings by, and testimonies of other actual or former Soviet Bloc citizens:*

Amalrik, Andrey. *Notes of a Revolutionary.* New York: Knopf, 1982.

Antonov-Ovseyenko, Anton. *The Time of Stalin.* New York: Harper Colophon Books, 1980

Avtorkhanov, Abdurakhman. *The Communist Party Apparatus.* Cleveland: Meridian Books, 1968.

————. *Stalin and the Soviet Communist Party.* New York: Praeger, 1957.

Bukovsky, Vladimir. *To Build a Castle.* London: Andre Deutsch, 1978.

Chalidze, Valery. *To Defend These Rights.* New York: Random House, 1974.

————. *Literaturnyye dela KGB* (The Literary Business of the KGB). New York: Khronika, 1976.

Curry, Jane Leftwich, ed. and trans. *The Black Book of Polish Censorship.* New York: Vintage Books, 1984.

Czechoslovak Academy of Sciences, Institute of History. *The Czech Black Book.* New York: Praeger, 1969.

Dimov, Alexandre. *Les hommes doubles: La vie quotidienne en Union Sovietique.* Paris: J.-C. Lattes, 1980.

Dyadkin, Iosif G. *Unnatural Deaths in the USSR 1928–1954.* New Brunswick and London: Transaction Books, 1983.

Djilas, Milovan. *Rise and Fall.* New York: Harcourt Brace Jovanovich, 1985.

———. *The New Class.* New York: Praeger, 1957.

Gilbert, Martin. *Shcharansky: Hero of Our Time.* London: Macmillan, 1986.

Grigorenko, Petr Grigorevich. *Memoirs.* New York: W.W. Norton, 1982.

Heller, Michel. *La machine et les rouages: La formation de l'homme sovietique.* Paris: Calmann-Levy, 1985.

Heller, Michel, and Alexander Nekrich. *Utopia in Power: History of the Soviet Union from 1917 to Our Times.* New York: Summit Books, 1986

Kaminskaya, Dina. *Final Judgment: My Life as a Soviet Defense Attorney.* New York: Simon and Schuster, 1982.

Kopelev, Lev. *To Be Preserved Forever.* Philadelphia and New York: J.B. Lippincott Co., 1977.

———. *Ease My Sorrows.* New York: Random House, 1983.

Lesnik, Renata. *Ici Moscou.* Paris: Hachette, 1982.

Lipson, L., and V. Chalidze, eds. *Papers on Soviet Law.* New York, 1977.

Lysenko, Vladil. *A Crime Against the World: Memoirs of a Russian Sea Captain.* London: Victor Gollancz, Ltd., 1983.

Marchenko, Anatoly. *My Testimony.* New York: E. P. Dutton, 1969.

Medvedev, Roy A., *Let History Judge.* New York: Alfred A. Knopf, 1971.

———. *On Stalin and Stalinism.* New York: Oxford University Press, 1979.

Medvedev, Zhores. *Andropov.* New York: W. W. Norton, 1983.

Melgounov, Sergey P. *The Red Terror in Russia.* London: J. M. Dent & Sons, 1925. (Russian original: *Krasnyy Terror v Rossii.* Berlin, 1924.)

Milyukov, Paul. *Religion and the Church.* Part I of *Outlines of Russian Culture.* Philadelphia: University of Pennsylvania Press, 1942.

Nekrich, Aleksandr M. *The Punished Peoples.* New York: W. W. Norton, 1978.

Neznanskiy, Fridrikh, "KPSS i mekhanizm prinuzhdeniya." *Possev,* no. 6 (1980).

Popovsky, Mark. *Manipulated Science.* New York: Doubleday, 1979.

Sharansky, Natan [Anatoliy Shcharanskiy] *Fear No Evil.* New York, 1988.

Shifrin, Avraham. *The First Guidebook to Prisons and Concentration Camps of the Soviet Union*. New York: Bantam Books, 1982.

Simis, Konstantin. *USSR: The Corrupt Society*. New York: Simon and Schuster, 1982.

Solzhenitsyn, Aleksandr I. *The Gulag Archipelago*. New York: Harper & Row, 1973–78.

————. *The Oak and the Calf.* New York: Harper & Row, 1979.

————. *The Mortal Danger: How Misconceptions About Russia Imperil America*. New York: Harper Colophon Books, 1980.

Souvarine, Boris. *Stalin: A Critical Survey of Bolshevism*. New York: Longmans, Green & Co., 1939.

Vestnik R. Kh. D. (Herald of the Russian Christian Movement) with introduction by Nikita Struve. *Rapport Secret au Comite Central sur l'Eglise en URSS*. (Secret report to the Central Committee concerning the Church in the USSR), Paris: Seuil, 1980.

Vladimirov, Leonid. *The Russians*. New York: Praeger, 1968.

Voinovich, Vladimir. *The Ivankiad*. London: Penguin Books, 1979.

Voslensky, Michael. *Nomenklatura*. New York: Doubleday, 1984.

Zinoviev, Alexander. *The Yawning Heights*. New York: Random House, 1979.

————. *Homo Sovieticus*. London: Viktor Gollancz, 1985.

————. *The Radiant Future*. New York: Random House, 1980.

III. *Works by Western Authors:*

Adelman, Jonathan R. *Terror and Communist Politics*. Boulder and London: Westview Press, 1984.

Ammende, Ewald. *Human Life in Russia*. Cleveland: John T. Zubal, Inc., 1984.

Andics, Hellmut. *Rule of Terror: Russia under Lenin and Stalin*. New York: Holt, Rinehart and Winston, 1969.

Azrael, Jeremy R. *The KGB in Kremlin Politics*. Los Angeles: Rand/UCLA, 1989.

Bailey, Anthony. *Along the Edge of the Forest*. New York: Random House, 1983.

Becker, Jillian. *The Soviet Connection: State Sponsorship of Terrorism*. London: Institute for European Defense and Strategic Studies, 1985.

Beichman, Arnold, and Mikhail S. Bernstam. *Andropov: New Challenge to the West*. New York: Stein and Day, 1983.

Bloch, Sidney, and Peter Reddaway. *Soviet Psychiatric Abuse*. London: Victor Gollancz, 1984.

———. *Russia's Political Hospitals*. London: Victor Gollancz, 1977.

Butler, William E. *The Soviet Legal System: Legislation and Documentation*. New York: Oceana Publications, Inc., 1978.

Byrnes, Robert F., ed. *After Brezhnev*. Bloomington: Indiana University Press, 1983.

Cline, Ray S., and Yonah Alexander. *Terrorism: The Soviet Connection*. New York: Crane Russak, 1984.

Conquest, Robert. *The Harvest of Sorrow: Soviet Collectivization and the Terror-Famine*. London: Hutchinson, 1986.

———. *The Great Terror*. London: Macmillan, 1968.

———. *Justice and the Legal System in the USSR*. London, 1968.

———, ed. *The Soviet Police System*. New York: Praeger, 1968.

———. *The Politics of Ideas in the USSR*. New York: Praeger, 1967.

———. *The Soviet Deportation of Nationalities*. London: Macmillan, 1960.

Conquest, Robert, and Jon M. White. *What to Do When the Russians Come*. New York: Stein and Day, 1984.

Corson, William R., and Robert T. Crowley. *The New KGB: Engine of Soviet Power*. New York: William Morrow and Co., 1985.

Dallin, David J. *Soviet Espionage*. New Haven: Yale University Press, 1955.

Dewhirst, Martin, and Robert Farrell, eds. *The Soviet Censorship: Studies on the Soviet Union* (new series), vol. 11, no. 2. Munich: Institute for the Study of the USSR, 1971.

Dziak, John, J., *Chekisty,* Massachusetts & Toronto: Lexington Books, 1988.

Fainsod, Merle. *How Russia Is Ruled*. Cambridge: Harvard University Press, 1963.

———. *Smolensk Under Soviet Rule*. New York: Vintage Books, 1963.

Fuller, William C., Jr. *The Internal Troops of the MVD SSSR*. College Station, Tex: The College Station Papers, no. 6, 1983.

Gerson, Lennard D. *The Secret Police in Lenin's Russia*. Philadelphia: Temple University Press, 1976.

Goren, Roberta. *The Soviet Union and Terrorism*. London: George Allen & Unwin, 1984.

Hingley, Ronald. *The Russian Secret Police*. New York: Simon and Schuster, 1970.

Jones, William M. *Maintaining Public Order in the Soviet Union: The Militia and the MVD in the Post-Khrushchev Era.* Ann Arbor: Xerox University Microfilms, 1976.

Kaiser, Robert. *Russia: The People and the Power.* New York: Atheneum, 1976.

Kalme, F. *Total Terror.* New York: Appleton-Century-Crofts, 1951.

Klose, Kevin. *Russia and the Russians: Inside the Closed Society.* New York: W. W. Norton, 1984.

Knight, Amy, W., *The KGB (Police and Politics in the Soviet Union).* Boston: Unwin Hyman Ltd., 1988.

Kulski, W. W. *The Soviet Regime.* 2d ed. Syracuse: Syracuse University Press, 1963.

Labedz, Leopold, ed. *Solzhenitsyn: A Documentary Record,* New York: Harper & Row, 1970; Penguin Books, 1972.

Laqueur, Walter. *Terrorism.* London: Sphere Books, 1978.

Lasky, Melvin J., ed. *The Hungarian Revolution: The Story of the October Uprising as Recorded in Documents, Dispatches, Eye-Witness Accounts, and World-wide Reactions.* New York: Praeger, 1957.

Leggett, George. *The Cheka: Lenin's Political Police.* New York: Oxford University Press, 1981.

Lendvai, Paul. *The Bureaucracy of Truth.* Boulder: Westview Press, 1980.

Levytsky, Boris. *The Uses of Terror: The Soviet Secret Police 1917–1970.* New York: Coward, McCann and Geogheghan, 1972.

Linden, Carl A. *The Soviet Party-State: The Politics of Ideocratic Despotism.* New York: Praeger, 1983.

Marshal, R. H., Jr., ed. *Aspects of Religion in the Soviet Union 1917–1967.* Chicago: University of Chicago Press, 1971.

Moore, Barrington, Jr. *Terror and Progress USSR.* Cambridge: Harvard University Press, 1954.

Morand, Bernadette. *L'Urss des profondeurs.* Brussels: Editions Arts et Voyages, 1978.

Nicolaevsky, Boris. *Power and the Soviet Elite.* New York: Praeger, 1965.

Pincher, Chapman. *The Secret Offensive.* London: Sidgwick & Jackson, 1985.

Pipes, Richard. *Survival Is Not Enough.* New York: Simon and Schuster, 1984.

Plate, T., and A. Darvi. *Secret Police.* New York: Doubleday, 1981.

Ra'anan, Uri, and R. L. Pfaltzgraff, Jr., et al. *Hydra of Carnage: International Linkages of Terrorism.* Lexington, Mass: Lexington Books, 1985.

Raid, Robert. *When the Soviets Come. . . .* New York: Boreas Publishing House, 1985.

Reitz, James, "The Soviet Security Troops—The Kremlin's Other Armies." *Soviet Armed Forces Review Annual,* vol. 6 (1982), pp. 279–327.

Robinson, Logan. *An American in Leningrad.* New York: W. W. Norton, 1982.

Romerstein, Herbert. *Soviet Support for International Terrorism.* Washington, D.C.: The Foundation for Democratic Education, 1981.

Rosenfeldt, Niels Erik. *Knowledge and Power: The Role of Stalin's Secret Chancellery in the Soviet System of Government.* Copenhagen: Rosenkilde and Bagger, 1978.

Roxburgh, A. *Pravda: Inside the Soviet News Machine.* New York: Braziller, 1987.

Schapiro, Leonard. *The Communist Party of the Soviet Union.* New York: Random House, 1959.

————. *The Origin of the Communist Autocracy: Political Opposition in the Soviet State, First Phase 1917–1922.* Cambridge: Harvard University Press, 1977.

————. *The Government and Politics of the Soviet Union.* Rev. ed. New York: Vintage Books, 1978.

————. *The Russian Revolution of 1917: The Origins of Modern Communism.* New York: Basic Books, 1984.

Schmid, Alex P. *Soviet Military Interventions Since 1945.* New Brunswick, N.J.: Transaction Books, 1985.

Shanor, Donald R. *Behind the Lines: The Private War Against Soviet Censorship.* New York: St. Martin's Press, 1985.

Shindler, Colin. *Exit Visa.* London: Bachman and Turner, 1978.

Shipler, David K. *Russia: Broken Idols, Solemn Dreams.* New York: Penguin Books, 1984.

Shultz, Richard H., and Roy Godson. *Dezinformatsia.* Washington, D.C.: Pergamon-Brassey's, 1984.

Sleeper, Raymond S., ed. *Mesmerized by the Bear: The Soviet Strategy of Deception.* New York: Dodd, Mead & Co., 1987.

Smith, Hedrick. *The Russians.* New York: Quadrangle/The New York Times Book Co., 1976; London: Sphere Books, 1976.

Smith, Thomas B. *The Other Establishment.* Chicago: Regnery Gateway, 1984.

Sterling, Claire. *The Terror Network.* New York: Holt, Rinehart and Winston, 1981.

————. *The Time of the Assassins: Anatomy of an Investigation.* New York: Holt, Rinehart and Winston, 1983.

Strausz-Hupé, Robert, et al. *Protracted Conflict*. New York: Harper & Row, 1963.

Tokes, Rudolf L. *Dissent in the USSR*. Baltimore: Johns Hopkins University Press, 1975.

Tumarkin, Nina. *Lenin Lives! The Lenin Cult in Soviet Russia*. Cambridge: Harvard University Press, 1983.

Ulam, Adam. *Expansion and Coexistence: The History of Soviet Foreign Policy 1917–1967*. New York: Praeger, 1968.

————. *Stalin: The Man and His Era*. New York: Viking Press, 1973.

U.S. Congress. Report of House of Representatives Select Committee on Communist Aggression. Summary Report and Special Reports nos. 1 through 14. *Communist Takeover and Occupation* of Poland, Estonia, Ukraine, Armenia, Georgia, Bulgaria, Czechoslovakia, Byelorussia, Hungary, Romania, Latvia, Albania, Lithuania. Treatment of the Jews. Washington, D.C.: U.S. Government Printing Office, 1955.

————. *Murder International, Inc.: Murder and Kidnapping as an Instrument of Soviet Policy*. Hearings of the Subcommittee to Investigate the Administration of the Internal Security Act. . . . U.S. Senate, 26 March 1965.

————. Implementation of the Final Act of the Conference on Security and Cooperation in Europe. *Findings and Recommendations: Five Years After Helsinki*. Report submitted to the U.S. Congress by the Commission on Security and Cooperation in Europe, August 1980.

————. House of Representatives, Permanent Select Committee on Intelligence. *Soviet Active Measures*. Washington, D.C.: U.S. Government Printing Office, 1982.

U.S. Government, Department of Defense. *Soviet Military Power*. Editions of 1981–88.

————. *Soviet Acquisition of Militarily Significant Western Technology*. April 1982; updated September 1985.

Valenta, Jiri. *Soviet Intervention in Czechoslovakia 1968*. Baltimore: Johns Hopkins University Press, 1979.

Van Voren, Robert. *Koryagin: A Man Struggling for Human Dignity*. Amsterdam: Vladimir Bukovsky Foundation, 1987.

Waxmonsky, Gary R. "Police and Politics in Soviet Society 1921–1929." Ph.D. dissertation, Princeton University, 1982.

Wolfe, Bertram D. *Three Who Made a Revolution*. New York: Dial Press, 1948.

————. *Krushchev and Stalin's Ghost*. New York: Praeger, 1957.

————. *Communist Totalitarianism: Keys to the Soviet System*. Rev. ed. Boston: Beacon Press, 1961.

Wolin, Simon, and Robert M. Slusser. *The Soviet Secret Police.* New York: Praeger, 1957.

Wolton, Thierry. *Le KGB en France.* Paris: Grasset, 1985.

IV. *Soviet Sources:*

Alidin, V. I., et al, ed. *MChK 1918–1921* (Moscow Cheka 1918–1921) Moscow: Moskovskiy Rabochiy, 1978.

Anaskhin, G. Z. *Otvetstvennost za izmenu rodine i shpionazh* (Punishment for Treason and Espionage). Moscow: Gosyurizdat, 1964.

Andropov, Yuri V. *Izbrannyye rechi i stati* (Selected Speeches and Articles). Moscow: Politizdat, 1979.

Antonyuk, D. I. *KPSS, Spravochnik* (Communist Party of the Soviet Union, Reference Book).

Aripov, P., and N. Milshteyn. *Iz istorii organov gosbezopasnosti Uzbekistana* (From the History of Organs of State Security of Uzbekistan). Tashkent, 1967.

Bazhanov, A. T., and V. P. Malkov, eds. *Sud i pravosudiye v SSSR* (Court and Justice in the USSR), Kazan: Kazanskiy Universitet, 1980.

Belikov, I. G.: I. K. Boyko; and M. S. Logunov. *Imeni Dzerzhinskogo. Boyevoy put ordena Lenina Krasnaznamennoy divizii imeni F. E. Dzerzhinskogo* (Fighting Path of Dzerzhinsky's Division). Moscow: Voyenizdat, 1976.

Belov, G. A., et al., eds. *IZ istorii VCHeka 1917–1921* (From the History of the All-Russian Extraordinary Commission). Moscow: Politizdat, 1958.

Bondarenko, G. P., and I. V. Vartyanov. *Sovetskoye administrativnoye pravo* (Soviet Administrative Law). Lvov: Vyshchaya Shkola, 1977.

Columbia University Russian Institute, ed. *The Anti-Stalin Campaign and International Communism.* New York: Columbia University Press, 1956.

Doroshenko, I. A., et al., eds. *Feliks Edmundovich Dzerzhinskiy (Biografiya).* Moscow: Politizdat, 1983.

Fedosov, A. D., et al., eds. *Obrazovaniye i razvitiye organov sotsialisticheskogo kontrolya v SSSR 1917–1975* (Creation and Development of Organs of Socialist Control in the USSR 1917–1975). Moscow: Politizdat, 1975.

Fundamentals of Marxism-Leninism. 2d rev. ed. Moscow: Foreign Languages Publishing House, 1963.

Galkin, B. A. *Prokurorskiy nadzor v SSSR* (The Procurator's Supervision in the USSR). Moscow: Yuridicheskaya literatura, 1982.

Gladkov, T., and M. Smirnov. *Menzhinskiy.* Moscow: Molodaya Gvardiya, 1969.

Gorbachev, Mikhail S. *Perestroika: New Thinking for Our Country and the World.* New York: Harper & Row, 1987.

Gureyev, P. P., and P. I. Sedegun. *Legislation in the USSR.* Moscow: Progress Publishers, 1977.

Ivanchishin, Maj. Gen. P. A., ed. *Chasovyye Sovetskikh granits: Kratkiy ocherk istorii pogranichnykh voysk SSSR* (A Short History of USSR Border Troops). Moscow: Politizdat, 1979.

Kalachnikov, A. V. *Vospitaniye bditelnosti u sovetskikh voinov* (Vigilance Education of Soviet Servicemen). Moscow: Voyenizdat, 1980.

Khrushchev, Nikita. *Khrushchev Remembers.* Translated and edited by Strobe Talbott. Boston: Little, Brown & Co., 1970.

———. *Khrushchev Remembers: The Last Testament.* Translated and edited by Strobe Talbott. Boston: Little, Brown & Co., 1974.

Khvichiya, Prokofiy. *Ocherki istorii Gruzinskoy Sovetskoy militsii 1921–1937* (History of the Georgian Soviet Militia 1921–1937). Tbilisi: Sabchota Sakartvelo, 1977.

Kiryaev, N. M., ed. *KPSS i stroitelstvo Sovetskikh Voorozhennykh Sil, 1917–1964* (The CPSU and the Development of the Soviet Armed Forces). Moscow: Voyenizdat, 1965.

Kizilov, I. M. *NKVD RSFSR (1917–1930)* (Peoples Commissariat for Internal Affairs 1917–1930). Moscow: Vysshaya Shkola MVD SSSR, 1969.

Klyagin, V. S. *Otvetstvennost za osobo opasnyye gosudarstvennyye prestupleniya* (Punishment for Specially Dangerous State Crimes). Minsk: Vysshaya shkola, 1973.

Kozlov, A. P. *Trevozhnaya sluzhba* (Uneasy Service). Moscow: Voyenizdat, 1973.

Kozlov, Yu. M., ed. *Sovetskoye administrativnoye pravo.* Moscow: Yuridicheskaya literatura, 1973.

———. *Administrativnoye pravo* (Administrative Law). Moscow: Moscow State University, 1968.

———. *Upravleniye sotsialno-kulturnym stroitelstvom* (Management of Social-Cultural Development). Moscow: Yurizdat, 1980.

———. *Sovetskoye administrativnoye pravo: Gosudarstvennoye upravleniye i administrativnoye pravo* (Soviet Administrative Law: State Administration and Administrative Law). Moscow: Yuridicheskaya literatura, 1978.

———. *Sovetskoye administrativnoye pravo: Metody i formy gosudarstvennogo upravleniya* (Soviet Administrative Law: Methods and Forms of State Administration). Moscow: Yuridicheskaya literatura, 1977.

———. *Sovetskoye administrativnoye pravo: Upravleniye v oblasti Administativno-*

politicheskoy deyatelnosti (Soviet Administrative Law. Management in the Field of Administative-Political Activities). Moscow: Yuridicheskaya literatura, 1979.

—————. *Upravleniye v oblasti administrativno-politicheskoy deyatelnosti* (Management in the Field of Administrative-Political Activities). Moscow: Institute State and Law, Academy of Sciences of the USSR, Yuridicheskaya literatura, 1979.

Krotov, V. L. *Chonovtsy* (Soldiers of Special-Purpose Units). Moscow, 1974.

Kudryavtsev, P. I., ed. *Yuridicheskiy slovar* (Dictionary of Law), Tom 1–2. Moscow, 1956.

Kuzmin, A. V., and I. I. Krasnov. *Kantemirovtsy* (Kantemirov Tank Division). Moscow: Voyenizdat, 1971.

Malkov, V. P., ed. *Obraztsy ugolovno-protsessualnykh dokumentov* (Samples of Criminal Investigative Documents). Kazan: Kazanskiy Universitet, 1980.

Malyarov, V. P., ed. *Prokurorskiy nadzor v SSSR* (The Procurator's Supervision in the USSR). Moscow: Yuridicheskaya literatura, 1966.

Mironov, N. P. *Ukrepleniye zakonnosti i pravoporyadka v obshchenarodnom gosudarstve—programnaya zadacha partii* (Strengthening Legality and Law and Order in the All-Peoples State—Program Task of the Party). Moscow: Yuridicheskaya literatura, 1964 and 1968 (2d ed.).

Ostryakov, S. *Voyennyye chekisty* (Military Chekists). Moscow: Voyenizdat, 1979.

Padzhev, M. *Cherez vsyu voynu* (Through the Whole War). Moscow: Politizdat, 1972.

Popov, V. I. *Leninskaya diplomatiya mira i sotrudnichestva* (Lenin's Diplomacy of Peace and Cooperation), Moscow: Nauka, 1965.

Romashkin, P., ed. *Osnovy Sovetskogo prava* (Principles of Soviet Law). Moscow: Yurizdat, 1962.

Rudenko, R. A., ed. *Sovetskaya prokuratura* (The Soviet Procurator's Office). Moscow: Yuridicheskaya literatura, 1977.

Safonov, G. N. *Spravochnik po zakonodatelstvu dlya sudebno-prokurorskikh rabotnikov* (Law-Reference Book for Workers of the Courts and Procurator's Office). Moscow: Yuridicheskaya literatura, 1949.

Shumilin, V. N. *Molotkastyy serpastyy. . . .* (on Soviet passport). Moscow: Yurizdat, 1979.

Skilyagin, A. T., and V. M. Lesov, et al. Dela i lyudi Leningradskoy militsii (Leningrad Militia, Its People and Activities). Leningrad, 1967.

Sofinov, P. G. *Ocherki istorii VChK* (Sketches from the History of the VCheka). Moscow: Gospolizdat, 1960.

Sorokin, V. D., ed. *Sovetskoye administrativnoye pravo, chast osobennaya* (Soviet Administrative Law, Special Part). Leningrad: Leningradskiy Universitet, 1966.

Sovetskaya voyennaya entsiklopediya (Soviet Military Encyclopedia). 8 vols. N. Ogarkov, chairman of editorial collegium. Moscow: Institute of Military History, USSR Ministry of Defense, Voyenizdat, 1976–1980.

Sukharev, A., and P. Pashkevich. *Nash narodnyy sud* (Our Peoples Court). Moscow: Molodaya Gvardiya, 1981.

Sulzhenko, I. G. *Chonovtsy* (Soldiers of Special-Purpose Units). Frunze: Kyrgyzstan, 1975.

Suslov, Mikhail. *Improvement of the Ideological and Educational Work Is a Task of the Entire Party.* Moscow: Politizdat, 1979.

Terekhov, A. F.; M. P. Skirdo; and A. K. Mironov. *Gvardeyskaya Tamanskaya* (The Taman Guards Division). Moscow: Voyenizdat, 1981.

Tleuliyev, Maj. Gen. A. *My iz Cheka* (We Are from the Cheka). Alma Ata. Kazakstan Publishing House, 1974.

Tsvigun, S. K. et al., eds. *V. I. Lenin i VChKa* (Lenin and the VCheka). Moscow: Politizdat, 1975.

Tumanov, G. A. *Organizatsiya upravleniya v sfere obshchestvennogo poryadka* (Administration in the Field of Public Order). Moscow: Yuridicheskaya literatura, 1972.

Tyushkevich, S. A., et al. *Sovetskiye Vooruzhennyye sily* (The Soviet Armed Forces). Moscow: Voyenizdat, 1978.

U.S. Congress. Committee on Un-American Activities. *The Communist Conspiracy: Strategy and Tactics of World Communism. Part I. Communism Outside the United States* (collection of Soviet documents). Washington, D.C.: U.S. Government Printing Office, 1956.

Ustav Kommunisticheskoy partii Sovietskogo soyuza (Party Rules of the CPSU). Moscow: Politizdat, 1977.

Vasilenkova, P. T., ed. *Sovetskoye administrativnoye pravo* (Soviet Administrative Law). Moscow: Yuridicheskaya literatura, 1981.

Veremeyenko, I. I. *Sovetskoye administrativnoye pravo* (Soviet Administrative Law). Moscow: Yuridicheskaya literatura, 1981.

Viktorov, B. A.; K. I. Nikitin; and A. M. Zuzulin, eds. *Deystvitelno narodnaya . . .* (concerning the Soviet Militia). Moscow: Yuridicheskaya literatura, 1977.

Yakovlev, I. R., et al., eds. *Vnutrenniye voyska* (Internal Troops). 3 vols. Moscow. Yuridicheskaya literatura, 1972–77:

—Vol. I: *Vnutrenniye Voyska Sovetskoy Respubliki, 1917–1922* (Internal Troops of the Soviet Republic 1917–1922). 1972.

—Vol. II; *Vnutrenniye voyska v gody mirnogo sotsialisticheskogo stroitelstva, 1922–1941* (Internal Troops in the Years of Peaceful Socialist Construction, 1922–1941). 1977.

—Vol. III: *Vnutrenniye voyska v Velikoy Otechestvennoy Voyne, 1941–1945* (Internal Troops in the Great Patriotic War 1941–1945). 1975.

Yeremenko, I. I. *Upravleniye Administrativno-Politicheskim stroitelstvom* (Administrative-Political Management). Moscow: Yurizdat, 1981.

Yeropkin, M. I. *Upravleniye v oblasti okhrany obshchestvennogo poryadka* (Administration in the Field of Preservation of Public Order). Moscow: Yuridicheskaya literatura, 1965.

Yeropkin, M. I., and A. P. Ylyushnichenko. Sovetskoye administrativnoye provo (Soviet Administrative Law). Moscow: Yuridicheskaya literatura, 1979.

Zagladin, V. V. *The International Communist Movement.* Moscow: Progress Publishers, 1972.

Zhogin, N. V., and F. N. Fatkullin. *Predvaritelnoye sledstviye* (Preliminary investigation). Moscow: Yuridicheskaya literatura, 1965.

Zhuravlev, N. F., et al. *Narodnyy kontrol na sovremennom etape* (People's Control in the Contemporary Period). Moscow: Politizdat, 1982.

Zyryanov, P. I., et al., eds. *Pogranichnyye voyska SSR* (Border Troops of the USSR) 5 vols. Moscow: Nauka, 1968–1975. (Vol. 1—1918–28; vol. 2—1929–38; vol. 3—1939–41; vol. 4—1941–45; vol. 5—1945–50.)

Index